PENGUIN BOOKS

AND THE LAND LAY ST

And the Land Lay Still

JAMES ROBERTSON

PENGUIN BOOKS

PENGUIN BOOKS

Published by the Penguin Group
Penguin Books Ltd, 80 Strand, London WC2R ORL, England
Penguin Group (USA) Inc., 375 Hudson Street, New York, New York 10014, USA
Penguin Group (Canada), 90 Eglinton Avenue East, Suite 700, Toronto, Ontario, Canada M4P 2Y3
(a division of Pearson Penguin Canada Inc.)
Penguin Ireland, 25 St Stephen's Green, Dublin 2, Ireland (a division of Penguin Books Ltd)
Penguin Group (Australia), 250 Camberwell Road, Camberwell, Victoria 3124, Australia
(a division of Pearson Australia Group Pty Ltd)
Penguin Books India Pvt Ltd, 11 Community Centre, Panchsheel Park, New Delhi – 110 017, India
Penguin Group (NZ), 67 Apollo Drive, Rosedale, Auckland 0632, New Zealand
(a division of Pearson New Zealand Ltd)
Penguin Books (South Africa) (Pty) Ltd, 24 Sturdee Avenue, Rosebank, Johannesburg 2196,
South Africa

Penguin Books Ltd, Registered Offices: 80 Strand, London WC2R ORL, England

www.penguin.com

First published by Hamish Hamilton 2010
Published in Penguin Books 2011

4

Copyright © James Robertson, 2010
All rights reserved

The moral right of the author has been asserted

Printed in England by Clays Ltd, St Ives plc

ISBN: 978-0-141-02854-5

www.greenpenguin.co.uk

This book is dedicated to the memory of two other
Anguses and one other Jean. All three were, and
continue to be, influences in subtle and special ways.

Angus Matheson 1926–2007
Angus Calder 1942–2008
Jean Bonnar 1923–2008

The Summons

The year was ending, and the land lay still.
Despite our countdown, we were loath to go,
kept padding along the ridge, the broad glow
of the city beneath us, and the hill
swirling with a little mist. Stars were right,
plans, power; only now this unforeseen
reluctance, like a slate we could not clean
of characters, yet could not read, or write
our answers on, or smash, or take with us.
Not a hedgehog stirred. We sighed, climbed in, locked.
If it was love we felt, would it not keep,
and travel where we travelled? Without fuss
we lifted off, but as we checked and talked
a far horn grew to break that people's sleep.

– Edwin Morgan (from *Sonnets from Scotland*)

Sometimes it felt like walking, sometimes it felt like flying. Or it felt like floating, or drifting, or like nothing at all. No motion. Just, there you were – in, on – and there it was – below, around – a splash of land on the ocean, a splatter of stone soil grass forest road town city, and broken-off bits scattered across the great wet belly of the world. And over it splashed lochs and rivers and burns, so much cold, clear water you'd think the land would drown in it, but it didn't, it lay there still, breathing – sodden and bogged down in some parts, rock-hard and ragged in others, but still breathing. And the sea breathing its endless breaths around it, in out in out in out, great white waves crashing on black rocks, exhausted waves flopping flatly on deserted beaches, weed washing back and forth in bays and inlets, and fish eels lobsters seals ebbing and flowing in the tidal inhalations, exhalations, and sometimes a seal watching you, ten twenty thirty minutes an hour, submerging then resurfacing, always watching you, coming closer, keeping a distance, and you watching the seal, pacing it along the shore, connected but never connected, always apart. The source of stories and legends was in those long mutual observations, those reachings for the unreachable, yearnings for the unobtainable. But that was what they were, unobtainable, and so you turned and came away from the edge, and there was the land again, the earth – rich poor red black brown – and grass flowers trees crops grew from the earth and were nourished by it. And farmers broke the earth and turned it, and that was humankind's relationship with the land, to need it and love it and break it into giving. When you first set out there were still heavy horses pulling the ploughs but before long they were all but gone, and chugging tractors slogged their way across the patterned fields, between drystane dykes and hedgerows and fences and stands of trees, and white plumes of gulls followed the tractors by day, and black parliaments of crows convened in the trees as night fell. And in the days of early summer you might walk on through the empty hours if there was enough light and you weren't tired. So you walked and you were alone, and later you'd lie down to rest, to sleep in the sun you'd once toiled and starved below. At other seasons, or if it was cold or wet, you found a barn or a byre or a shed or some other shelter and you bielded there and you were alone; but if the night was dry and looked like staying that way you wrapped yourself in your many layers and your big coat above them all and found a place to lie among trees, or in the lee of a wall or a hedge, you could make your bed anywhere if you were away from people, if you were in the country, and even in the wettest weather you could find shelter in caves and crannies, in empty structures made and left by men, or deep in under the thickest, lowest trees. You could lie for days if days of lying were required, measuring out what food you had, closing down your energy. Nothing was more comfortable to you than the hard roughness of the ground beneath you, nothing more comforting than darkness and utter silence or the cry of owls hunting in the moonlight and the sudden scuffling of their prey among leaves, the strange and familiar signals of night creatures going about their business. Small living things that crept near you, around you, sometimes over you. They did not frighten you, they reassured you. You could sleep like a bairn in such circumstances, hours and hours of dreamless sleep, then waking in the early light, grass heavy with dew and your breath white in the air. You'd stretch and get to your feet, stamp them, warm yourself with violent self-embraces of the arms, you'd reach into your pocket for a bit of bread or something else you had there, or if there was nothing there was nothing, you'd be off anyway, walking again. You were safe then, you were alone, you could breathe easy, and you did.

PART ONE

The Mouth in the Box

Mike is at the bedroom window, taking in the view of the water, the road and the scattering of cottages along it, when he sees Murdo's red van come round the end of the kyle. The van disappears for a few seconds, then begins to climb the hill. It slows, and pulls in at the gate. After a minute, as if he's been plucking up courage or maybe just thinking something over, Murdo gets out and starts up the track. By the time he arrives at the back door Mike is there waiting for him. With a shy, almost sly grin Murdo proffers a plastic bag. Mike unwraps the newspaper bundle it contains and there are two rainbow trout shining in the morning sun.

'They're beautiful,' Mike says.

'Fresh from the loch last night,' Murdo says. 'Can you make use of them?'

'Of course. I'll cook them tonight. Will you come for your tea?'

'Och, they'll just do yourself nicely.'

'Nonsense. There's one each.'

'They're not that big.'

'They're fine. I'll make plenty of tatties. Will you come?'

'I might at that. I have a few things to do first.'

'Well, it's only ten o'clock. You have all day. But come any time you like. I'm not going anywhere.'

'I will then.'

The necessary negotiations over, they stand enjoying the sun, of which there has not been too much lately. Mike says, 'Do you have a moment just now?'

Murdo looks down at the van and shrugs. 'There's nothing that won't keep.'

'I want to show you something.'

'Aye, do you?'

Inside, Mike puts the fish in the kitchen sink. They go into the hallway, past the front door that's never used, through the sitting

5

room and into the sun lounge that Murdo's uncle built at the side of the house thirty-five years ago for Mike's father.

'I was at my father's archive again yesterday,' Mike says, 'trying to impose a bit more order on it. And going through the photographs for this exhibition, yet again.'

'The one in . . . Edinburgh?' Murdo makes it sound not just two hundred and fifty miles away but as if it's on another continent.

'Yes. I keep thinking I've made the final selection, and then I find I haven't.'

'And there's to be a book as well?'

'To go with the exhibition, yes. I'm trying to write the introduction, but it's not going too well. Anyway, I was sorting through some boxes and I came across this photograph.'

He hands over the print. Murdo holds it by the edges with his calloused fingers and looks at it thoughtfully, as he might at a diagram of how to assemble a new tool.

'I'd never seen it before last night,' Mike says, 'but as soon as I did I remembered everything about it. You're looking at probably the only photograph in existence of the three of us together. My father, my mother and myself, I mean. Maybe my mother has some others secreted away, but I doubt it.'

'It's your father right enough,' Murdo says. 'A good-looking man. And is that your mother? She's a bonnie woman. She doesn't look very pleased though.'

'She wasn't very pleased,' Mike says, thinking that being pleased hasn't ever been one of Isobel's strong points, not that he can remember. 'That was the first time I was ever in these parts. July, 1964. We were on holiday. That's Dounreay, of course, in the background.'

'Aye. Awful-looking place, isn't it?'

'At the time we didn't think so. It seemed clean and bright and modern.'

'I never liked it, right from the start. They only put it there in case it blew up. Who'd care if it blew up there? It employed a lot of people over the years, I suppose, but what are they all meant to do now?' He reins himself in. 'But you surely didn't spend your holiday at Dounreay?'

'No, it was just a stop on the way. We had a week and we drove over to the west, then round the north coast, down to Inverness and home again.'

'That's a fair distance in a week.'

'It certainly was then. There were no bridges. It was all ferries and some of them only took a couple of cars at a time.'

'There wouldn't have been so many cars though.'

'No, not many. Anyway, I just wanted to show you. My family, such as it was. My father moved out later that year and they got divorced not long after that.'

'And this is yourself. How old are you?'

'I was nine.'

'You have very thin legs,' Murdo says. 'In the picture, I mean.'

'I look a bit delicate, don't I?'

'If you'd lived here we'd have toughened you up.'

'Oh?'

'We'd have been at the school together. I'd have beaten you up regularly.'

'There's three years between us. You wouldn't even have noticed me.'

'Believe me, boy, there was no way you could not be noticed. Everybody noticed everything about everybody.'

'And do they still?'

'Not so much. You incomers guard your privacy well. But people around here have always been pretty discreet, you know, whatever they notice.'

He hands back the photograph, and they go outside again, round to the front of the house, and there they pause before Murdo takes his leave, standing beside the rowan tree Mike planted for his father. Angus's rowan. It is naked but looking resilient. It's too early yet for there to be new growth.

'I wonder how long this will last,' Mike says, meaning the weather.

'Ach, just until it's over.'

The air is cold, but there's hardly a cloud in the sky and the sunlight is catching every ripple in the water. Maybe Mike will go out for an hour with the camera after all. On the other hand, he has to get on with preparing for the exhibition and the book.

'I'll see you tonight then?'

7

'Aye, I'll look forward to it,' Murdo says, without a trace of antici-pation in his tone. Mike is still not quite sure when Murdo is having a gentle joke at his expense.

'We'll have a dram or two after we've eaten.'

'If you insist. Before, too, if you insist. Will you leave the gate open?'

'I will.'

So Murdo can drive straight in and park at the back of the house. Mike puts out a hand and touches him lightly on the shoulder, and Murdo gives him a look that barely acknowledges the contact, as if it were accidental. But it is anything but that.

§

There is something else unique about the photograph. It is, almost certainly, the only image in the entire Angus Pendreich archive not actually taken by Angus Pendreich.

It shows the Pendreichs – Angus, Isobel and Michael – picnicking in the lee of what was then the future. That was how it felt and how Angus talked about it. He'd brought them there for that very pur-pose, to demonstrate his faith in better things to come. On that patch of thin grass above the beach they could be witnesses to a new era. Thirty yards one way the blue-black sea filled the view as it always had done; in the other direction cows grazed green fields bounded by stone slabs embedded in the earth; beyond these was another strip of water, and then the giant golf ball of the Dounreay atomic power plant. The future. The triumph of science. The har-nessing of unimaginable might for the eternal benefit of mankind. Electricity so cheap you wouldn't be able to meter it. Angus wanted to believe all that and he wanted Isobel and Michael – it was always Michael then – to believe it with him. It should have been exciting and heartening, on the second-last day of a trip where almost every-thing had been new, at least in the sense that Michael had not previ-ously experienced it: the wee car ferries, the twisting narrow roads with passing places, palm trees nurtured by the Gulf Stream. Fur-ther west they'd found hairy cows sunbathing on beaches next to children chattering away in Gaelic, but now this was Caithness and the weather had turned cloudy and cold, and, regardless of what-ever bounty the future might hold for mankind, as a family unit the Pendreichs were heading for destruction.

8

A nuclear family indeed, was Mike's first thought when he came across the picture. But where did we think we were going to store our poisonous waste? They didn't, of course, think about it at all. The future wasn't going to be about waste.

The only other pictures Mike has of Angus are ones he took himself, and none of these are from before 1970, the year he got his first real camera and made up his mind to be a photographer, like his father. Since Angus was always the one behind the camera, he was always absent from the image. Here he is, though, just as Mike remembers him from that summer holiday – tall, handsome, with thick, dishevelled dark hair and a caddish smile, standing defiantly against the world and the weather. He's wearing light-coloured, summery trousers and an open-necked, short-sleeved shirt, and he seems to find the wind bracing. His wife and son, on the other hand, crouched on a tartan rug on the grass in front of him, are obviously feeling frozen. The photograph is black and white – of course, since Angus never used colour film in his life – but somehow he looks ruddy and healthy, whereas Isobel and Michael are as grey as the sky. Isobel is in a stylish raincoat with the collar turned up, while Michael sports an unstylish green anorak with a fake-fur-lined hood, although as a concession to the moment he has pushed the hood back from his face. Also, he is wearing shorts. And sandals. Mike knows it's himself – it looks like him, the way he was – but it doesn't feel like him. There's a basket on the rug beside Isobel, elements of a picnic scattered around it. All three of them are raising plastic mugs to the photographer, in a kind of grim toast to holiday fun.

The photographer? A man who happened to be walking along the road at the time. Angus had already taken a couple of shots of his wife and child, and then the man came by. There was the road, then a rough bit of ground where the car was parked, then the grass, the beach and the sea. Angus called out to the man, would he mind taking their picture? He seemed not to hear at first, maybe it was the wind, but Angus bounded over and asked again. If the man said anything back Michael didn't catch it. He was whip-thin and yet somehow bulky, very upright, and he had a khaki pack slung over his shoulder. The face was brown and hard-looking. A scrape of beard on the cheeks, that was all. He was wearing a beret so you couldn't see the colour of his hair or indeed if he had any, but Michael thought that he looked quite old, and then that perhaps he wasn't much older than his father. The man listened patiently while Angus showed him how to work the camera. All he had to do was look through the viewfinder and press the button. But he did this before Angus was in position, and then it seemed he might have pressed something else by accident and Angus had to go back and check it and then return, and all the time Isobel and Michael were holding their pose in the cold, Isobel with her legs folded beneath her, one hand clutching her mug and the other holding her hair off her face, and Michael on his hunkers a couple of feet away, feeling the pins and needles in the backs of his knees, and he heard Isobel say through clenched teeth, 'For God's sake,' and somehow knew from the way she said it that it was over between his parents and that whatever this photograph was recording it wasn't family happiness, and he wondered why on earth his father was going to all the trouble.

For posterity, perhaps, is what he thinks now. Maybe Angus already knew he would shortly be leaving them.

Mike studies his nine-year-old self. The white, hairless legs, poking out beneath the anorak and shorts, do seem pathetically fragile. He studies his mother. She's thirty-one, still a beautiful young woman if only she'd smile a bit. But Isobel was never going to smile for this photograph, just as the stranger holding the camera – Michael knew this instinctively – was not a man who was ever going to say, 'Say "Cheese!"' And then it was done, and Angus thanked him and took the camera back, and that should have been the end of it, but it wasn't.

The man lingered, as if he expected something more than Angus's thanks. A tip, perhaps? Michael sensed his mother's rage simmering again. But it was the man who put his hand in his own pocket and drew something out. He stepped towards Michael with his clenched fist extended, and the boy automatically stood up and went towards him. 'Michael,' Isobel said, but whatever the mystery was in that fist he wanted it. He held out his hand and the man dropped something in and with a quick, fierce movement closed Michael's fingers over it. The man's hand was rough and dry. Michael glanced up at him. His stare was intense and distant, as if he were looking both at and right through him, and then he let go and walked away without a word. He was separate again, he seemed separate from everything, a lonely figure hunched into the wind, and then he stopped and turned and stared at Michael again, and Angus must have seen the potential of *that* picture, the man in the road staring like a prophet, the cows, the light bouncing between the clouds and the sea, the looming Dounreay dome, and he took it. The decisive moment, Cartier-Bresson called it. And what a great photograph it is.

When Mike first came upon it, he immediately decided that it would have to be a late addition to the exhibition. But it's the other one, the not very good one of the family, that he keeps going back to. As if somewhere in it there is a clue, advance notice of how everything was going to be. That was why he wanted to show it to Murdo: to say, look, this is where I come from, do you think that wee boy ever imagined life turning out like this?

When the man was twenty yards down the road Michael opened his hand, and there in the palm was a pebble. That was all. A small, smooth, disappointing pebble about the size of a broad bean. It could have come from a beach or a field or a garden path – anywhere. Isobel demanded to know what it was, and Michael showed her and she told him to throw it away. But he would not, and when she failed to appeal to his father for support Michael slipped it into his pocket, where he kept it for days, feeling its inconsequential smoothness with his fingers and thinking about the man. Eventually he lost it. It was nothing, but the man had given it to him, and even now when he thinks of the pebble he remembers the intensity of the man's stare.

They carried on with their picnic. In the basket was a Thermos flask of Heinz tomato soup, heated up by their landlady of the previous night, and a bread-wrapper full of cheese-and-ham sandwiches she'd also made for them. They drank the soup, dredged their way through the sandwiches. The wind gusting in off the sea made sitting still an endurance. Isobel and Michael stayed on the tartan rug only because it held a suggestion of warmth. He didn't want to be too close to her because of the mood she was in but he felt a kind of loyalty to her because he suspected that Angus was a bad husband. He wasn't that great a father either. He spent too much time away, working, or – as Mike now knows – not working. Even at nine years old he had a dim understanding that he was the only reason, if it was a reason, that his parents were still together. And so he felt a childish responsibility towards his mother and her misery, because his father was showing none.

Angus paced around like an eccentric lecturer, firing information at them between bites and swallows. He was trying to explain how a fast reactor worked: how it produced more fuel than it consumed, converting uranium into plutonium, so in effect could go on making electricity for ever. There wasn't much uranium in the world but the fast-breeder process meant once you had enough to start a chain reaction you were away. Energy in perpetuity. He wanted to convince them of the significance of where they were, how their lives were linked to the power of the atom. But he was wasting his breath, because Isobel and Michael were hardly listening, they were eating and drinking as fast as they could so they could pack up and move on, so he could take them to John o'Groats, where they'd get out and do whatever you were supposed to do at one end of the British Isles and after that drive on to the God-awful hotel or bed and breakfast he'd earmarked for them for the night, where hopefully there'd be a hot bath and maybe even a fire. That was all. They didn't care a docken about nuclear fission, and he probably didn't understand half of what he was trying to explain. They were all out of their respective depths. And so they packed up the picnic things and drove away from the wondrous white-domed building perched on the edge of Scotland, and as they were going Isobel said, 'That man was a tramp.'

'What man?' Angus said.

'The man who took the picture.'

'No!' Angus said, dismissive but quite jovial at first. 'Surely not? Tramps have long straggly beards and ten overcoats. And they smell. He didn't smell too bad.'

She sighed at his childishness. 'There was something about him.'

'What?' Michael could tell her sigh irritated his father. There was a tone to it, and a tone to his short response. Two noises full of impatience and disrespect.

'I didn't like him. Giving that stupid stone to Michael.'

'Och, well, that's him then, condemned and transported if *you* don't like him. Bloody vagrant, handing out stones to kids. Anyway, what if he was a tramp?' He scowled in the mirror. 'Michael, do you think he was a tramp?'

Michael said, 'His clothes weren't that dirty, but they were old-looking.'

'You see?' Isobel said.

'His face looked like it was made of leather,' Michael said. 'Like he spent a lot of time out of doors. And I think he had quite a lot of clothes on, but he was very thin.'

'You see?' Isobel said again, so that Michael, who hated being on her side, had to add, 'But I don't think he was a tramp.'

'Well, what was he then?' Isobel snapped.

'I don't know. Maybe he was mad.'

'Don't be ridiculous,' Isobel said. The idea of insanity scared her more than vagrancy.

'Tramps don't go around handing out stones,' Angus said. 'But *I* don't give a damn who or what he is. I asked him to do me a favour and he was kind enough to oblige.'

'You're lucky he didn't drop your camera,' Isobel said. 'Or steal it.'

Angus muttered something Michael couldn't hear.

'If we pass him, *don't* offer him a lift.'

'I might just do that,' Angus said. 'One good turn deserves another.'

'If he gets into this car, I'm getting out.'

Michael prayed fervently for them to pass the man, just to see what happened, but they didn't. A heavy, hateful emptiness gathered under the roof of the car. Michael slumped back, pulling the anorak hood up over his head, preferring the seashell effect of the fake fur against his ears to the dead silence that he was learning to recognise as the soundtrack of a marriage beyond repair. And in his pocket he felt for the pebble and wondered why the man had given it to him, and what it might mean.

Looking at the photograph brings it all back. It's like a still from a film of other people's lives. Michael and Mum and Dad. And they became Mike and Isobel and Angus. Shifting, uncertain identities. When he thinks about those shared lives, about human existence in general, he finds there is not much to put faith in. But this he knows for sure: our ability to look back on the past, our need or desire to make sense of it, is both a blessing and a curse; and our inability to see into the future with any degree of accuracy is, simultaneously, the thing that saves us and the thing that condemns us.

§

Holiday over, they got home to Doune, their Perthshire village, and the next morning Angus took Michael into Stirling and bought him the new Beatles single, 'A Hard Day's Night', six shillings and eight-pence from Hay's Music Shop, and when they came back Michael went into the sitting room and played it on the gramophone, first the A side then the B side, 'Things We Said Today', and wondered what he would do, apart from that, for the rest of the holidays. And then Angus came in and waited till the record finished for the sixth time and said he quite liked it and how would you fancy a couple of weeks' extra holiday? Because your mother and I have been talking things over and we think it would be better if you don't go to the local school any more but go away to a boarding school, they have the English holidays so you wouldn't start there till September. So where is this school, in England? No, it's not far up the road, near Aberfeldy. So why do they have English holidays? They just do, it's a different system, you'll get longer holidays at Christmas and Easter too. And if it's at Aberfeldy would I have to stay there? Yes, you'd board, it's a boarding school, it's too far to drive there every day. But you said it wasn't far up the road. Well, it's not, but that's not what I meant. Anyway, these schools, you get the most out of these schools if you board. But why can't I just stay where I am? Because I'm away so much. What's that got to do with it? Well, it would be helpful to your mother. Your mother thinks – we both think – you'll get a better education at this other school, and from there you can go on to another boarding school, it's a great opportunity, it's not cheap but we can manage it.

They talked about it some more but Angus had already sold the idea with the bit about longer holidays. Also, there were two other boys who lived in a bigger house in the village who went away to school, and Michael had always kind of envied them although he didn't know them, he only knew *of* them, and maybe that was why he envied them, they were remote, almost anonymous. That was one of the things that would happen if he went away, he would become anonymous. He'd be distinct from the other kids in the village, and this appealed to him because he suspected that in some deep way he already was. And then Isobel came in and reinforced everything Angus had said, which was strange because they so seldom backed each other up. Michael was only nine so he didn't fully see that they were conspiring against him; that Isobel, being a snob, had always wanted him to have a private education, and Angus, who was vaguely opposed to it in principle, was willing to concede the principle because that would offer a solution to his own problems. For Michael was indeed the reason why he was still with Isobel and if that reason were removed then he could go off and have the life he wanted with the women he wanted to be with. Michael didn't understand all this, not then, but he knew his father was in some way at fault. He still loved and admired him, though. He still thought he wanted to be like him.

So that afternoon they drove the forty miles to the school near Aberfeldy, an establishment called Bellcroft House, where it turned out an appointment had been made to see the headmaster before they'd even gone on holiday. The headmaster had doubtless seen it all before, middle-class people looking for a safe place to dump their inconvenient offspring, and treated Michael with a rough kindness that was intended not only to put him at ease but also to allay any parental fears or suspicions. They were given a tour of the empty buildings, and Michael was given an inquisition, because it seemed *he* was on trial not the school, even though Angus was going to be forking out hundreds of pounds to send him there. But to no one's great surprise he was acceptable and therefore accepted, and the three Pendreichs came away smiling, all for their different reasons. And in September, kitted out with a new school uniform, Michael entered a new phase of his life.

§

And now Dounreay is being decommissioned at a cost of God knows how many millions, possibly billions, of pounds, and they still haven't worked out what to do with the waste: the stuff, that is, they can account for, the stuff they haven't chucked down shafts or allowed to piss out into the Pentland Firth and wash up on the beaches in tiny ticking wee cancer-bombs. No doubt there's more they've not told anyone about, because one thing Mike believes about governments and government agencies is that they won't tell you anything bad if they can possibly avoid doing so. Even an outright denial – for example, that depleted uranium shells have ever been used on the Cape Wrath firing range – only inclines him to believe the opposite. Perhaps, however, that says more about him than about the Ministry of Defence.

From the bedroom window he looks out on the Atlantic every morning, sixty miles from Dounreay, and there is something ironic about the fact that he's chosen to be here for the tranquillity, to inherit the peace and quiet that Angus found when he bought the place, when for half a century the whole area's been used as a kind of open laboratory and he suspects he's looking out not on wild, unspoiled beauty but on a silent, pernicious sickness. And yet it doesn't make him afraid or want to leave, it just makes him want to record it, endlessly: the ocean, the land, the light, the weather. There's no doubt in his mind: there, in his father's house, sorting out Angus's work and engaging in his own, is where he wants to be.

§

They've eaten the trout, and the dishes are piled in the sink and Mike will do them later, after Murdo has gone. They're in the sun lounge with an electric fire on, whiskies in their hands, looking out at the dark sea loch and the shoulders of the hills, and clouds building around the moon. They are reminiscing – or, rather, Mike is – about 1964: the year he went away to school, the Forth Road Bridge opened, and he saw *Mary Poppins* with his mother and *Goldfinger* with his father.

'I managed to miss *Mary Poppins*,' Murdo says, 'I am pleased to report.'

'*Goldfinger* was great,' Mike says. 'My dad took me to see it on my first half-term break. He fetched me from school but instead of going straight home we went to the pictures in Perth. I think he just wanted to stay out of the house because he and my mother were fighting about everything by that stage. Politics included. There'd been a General Election the day before and when we finally got home that was what they fought about. Mum in the blue corner, Dad in the red. Labour had won the election but only by four seats. My mother took it personally because the outgoing Tory Prime Minister was our own MP, Sir Alec Douglas-Home.'

'You are a font of knowledge,' Murdo says. 'Or should that be a mine of information? I couldn't have told you about the four seats, but I'm guessing the Labour leader was Harold Wilson?'

'It was.'

'Now there was a slippery customer.'

'Aye, but my dad kept saying how wonderful he was, just to infuriate my mum. He wasn't a very profound socialist – my dad, I mean – he'd just enrolled me at a prep school, after all – but he believed in the Welfare State and the general idea of redistributing other people's wealth. And he despised Sir Alec Douglas-Home, whom my mother admired. But something else happened at that election: right there, in our very own constituency, Hugh MacDiarmid stood for the Communist Party.'

'The wild-haired poet,' Murdo says.

'Yes. It was sheer provocation. He made inflammatory speeches against capitalism and rude remarks about the person of the Prime Minister, and although –'

'Rude remarks?'

'He said he was a zombie.'

'Good.'

'And a yes-man of the Pentagon –'

'Very good.'

'– and although MacDiarmid didn't have an earthly chance of winning, neither did the Labour candidate, so my dad, who'd met MacDiarmid in Edinburgh and taken pictures of him, not only decided to vote for him but went around telling everybody that's what he was going to do. My mother was horrified.'

'I imagine it didn't do much for her social standing,' Murdo says.

'Not a thing. MacDiarmid came bottom of the poll with a hundred and twenty-seven votes,' Mike says, 'and apparently demanded a recount because he said there couldn't possibly be that many good socialists in Kinross and West Perthshire. My dad spent the weekend telling this story to anyone we met, the man in the paper shop, the neighbours, anyone. "I was one of them!" he said. Shouted, in fact. It was quite embarrassing, even for me. I think if my mother could have cited political incompatibility as grounds for divorce, she'd have done so. But she didn't have to, because by then he was having an affair with a woman in the BBC in Glasgow and was about to move out. I knew something was afoot, because he spent part of that weekend packing things into boxes in the garage. And when he took me back to school on the Monday the car was laden with his stuff, whereas I just had my toothbrush. He must have gone straight back to Glasgow. I don't think he ever slept another night in our house.'

'It must have been upsetting for you,' Murdo says. 'Divorce wasn't exactly common in those days. Even in the fleshpots of Doune, I would guess. It was practically unheard of here.'

'No, I don't remember being that upset. I just got on with it. But that was the first Christmas I had without my father.'

'Christmas was practically unheard of here too,' Murdo says.

§

On the journey back to Aberfeldy, Angus asked Michael if he was happy at Bellcroft House. Mike still believes that if he had said that he was miserable, that he was being bullied, that he hated it with all his heart, Angus would have done something about it. But he didn't tell him any of those things, because they weren't true. He'd adjusted without any great difficulty to his new situation. A place away from the parental fighting had something to recommend it. In just a few weeks he'd made it his own. He'd lost touch with the children he'd grown up with and transferred his affections, such as they were, to a couple of the Bellcroft masters, the brusque but motherly matron, and a boy in his year called Freddy Eddelstane.

§

Mike's father was left-leaning politically, at least partly because of his experience during the war. He'd joined up at eighteen and at twenty was doing his bit in the invasion of Europe. The comics Michael read as a boy, which poured in vast quantities from the presses of D. C. Thomson in Dundee, were stuffed with Second World War adventures, and he liked to imagine his dad in one of them, revolver in one hand and a camera round his neck, leading his troops on to a Normandy beach under enemy fire. The reality was less heroic. Angus was a second lieutenant who hardly ever got near the front line, and whose war consisted mainly of organising convoys and fuel supplies. The twenty or thirty photos that survive from his war years are small, creased snaps of groups of men in front of lorries, and some hazy images of ruined Berlin. No sign of the unorthodox 'Angus angle' that would later make his name. Once Michael asked him if he'd killed anybody. No, Angus said, there were plenty of other people doing that. Michael must have looked disappointed. Angus said, 'I saw people who'd *been* killed.' 'Germans?' 'Yes. And French and British and Americans. And you know what, they all looked pretty much the same when they were dead.' Then he went on to speak of the camaraderie of the army, the way the younger, non-regular officers like himself would mix with their men, exchanging jokes and ideas and opinions, and how he shared the general view that when it was over and they went home things were going to change. 'We were all for Labour. It was our war, and it was going to be our peace. Some of the senior officers hated us. Thought we were fraternising with the enemy, politically speaking. But there wasn't much they could do about it.'

Apart from a commitment to Labour, Angus brought something else back from the war – a Leica IIIc, a hefty camera of impeccable German design, bought for next to nothing in occupied Berlin. It was the camera with which he made his name, and he used it for twenty years until the mid-1960s when he replaced it with a Nikon F, a virtually indestructible beast much favoured by photographers in war zones. Both cameras still sit in their hard, burnished-leather cases on a shelf in the sitting room at Cnoc nan Gobhar. They are antiques now, or soon will be; as redundant as darkrooms or Kodachrome film. But Mike keeps them, because of their intrinsic beauty, and because – who knows? – one day they may come into their own again.

§

There were eighty boys at Bellcroft House, aged between seven and thirteen, doing time in deepest Perthshire because their fathers had before them, or because – as in Michael's case – one or both parents believed such an incarceration a necessary prelude to a successful social and professional career, or because the parents were overseas with the Hong Kong and Shanghai Bank or the British Council or the Foreign Office, or because they hadn't managed to secure a place for their offspring in one of a dozen better prep schools, out-posts of an alien education system, dotted about the Scottish coun-tryside. Of those eighty boys, some were bright and others stupid, some fat and others tall, some athletic and others athletically incom-petent, some musical and others growlers, and all of them were white. Perhaps because neither of them quite 'fitted' with the crowd, Freddy Eddelstane and Michael began to go about together. If they were not close friends, they were at least mutually tolerant companions.

Back from that half-term break, Michael told Freddy about the election battle – the one between his parents – and how it had come about. Freddy had actually met Sir Alec Douglas-Home, because his father was a Tory MP too, or had been until the election, in the next-door constituency of Glenallan and Somewhere Else, Freddy forgot where. Had he been beaten? Michael wanted to know. It seemed to him that if your father went around in public asking people to vote for him, the overwhelming likelihood was that they wouldn't, and he would lose. 'Of course he wasn't beaten,' Freddy said, 'he retired.' 'Is he very old then?' 'I don't know,' said Freddy. 'I suppose he is, he's fifty-something. How old is yours?' 'Forty.' 'That's not so young.' 'It's younger than fifty.' But even though fifty was a great age, Michael knew people didn't retire until they were in their sixties, practically dead. 'But what'll he do?' Fathers earned money. Freddy and his family might starve. Freddy was not in the least concerned. 'There's always something,' he said.

Gradually, by such exchanges, they learned about each other: how both sets of parents fought incessantly but only Michael's were splitting up; that Michael was an only child whereas Freddy had an older brother called David and an older sister called Lucy. What was it like, having a sister? Terrible, because she was insane. Freddy's brother was weird and his sister was insane. In fact, Freddy said with pride, his whole family was insane: his father was barking, his mother was bonkers, and even the gardener was a bad-tempered old lunatic. The gardener! If Michael hadn't been laughing so much already he would have been astonished at the idea of a gardener. Freddy could make him laugh very easily. He had a plummy voice, the face of an ugly old man, and a clumsy, carefree attitude to life, and almost everything he said seemed funny to Michael. In his Sunday letters home, which for the rest of that term began 'Dear Mum and Dad' because his mother didn't tell him till Christmas that his father was no longer there, Michael wrote about how Eddelstane and he had done this or that, and that Eddelstane told good jokes and said Michael could go and stay with him in the holidays.

Isobel, having worked out that this Eddelstane was the son of Sir Malcolm and Lady Patricia Eddelstane of Ochiltree House, Glenallan, would have been delighted if this had happened, but it never did, because Freddy never got around to organising it. It meant nothing to him, throwing out such an invitation, except that he liked Michael well enough to say it.

The teachers at Bellcroft were a collection of unworldly oddities, most of whom looked as if they had awoken from one strange dream only to find themselves in another. Michael felt he had something in common with them, from the impossibly shy, tongue-tied Mr Veitch, who taught Geography and, after a fashion, Science, to the French master, Monsieur Lucas. M. Lucas was a dishevelled, shambling, straggle-haired man of uncertain vintage, with a tendency to conclude his sentences with a shout. He and his wife lived in Aberfeldy with their three sons, who attended the local school. He was Belgian, or half-Belgian, and proud of it. 'Je suis belge, Monsieur Michel,' he said, 'et je ne l'oublie *jamais*.' He called all the boys 'monsieur', except when he called them 'mon ami', which was equally pleasing. There was an air of mystery about him, enhanced both by his penchant for recounting tales of the supernatural and the fact that he had a life outwith the bounds and hours of the school. He often arrived looking as if he hadn't gone to bed the previous night, or had slept in the clothes he was wearing if he had. Maybe he was a poacher? Maybe he had been in the Resistance during the war? 'Peut-être,' he said, when the boys asked him. 'I resist *everything*.' He corrected their vocabulary tests with flamboyant ticks, crosses and exclamation marks, and read their feeble efforts at composition with his nose an inch from the jotter, being severely short-sighted although he resisted wearing *les lunettes*. They loved it when he bellowed at their stupidity, for, loud though he barked, his bite was non-existent, and he was easily distracted from the task in hand by a well-timed question about the war, or ghosts – or politics. For M. Lucas was so unbalanced as to be a member of the Scottish National Party, and went to political meetings and conferences and rallies, and wrote letters to the papers on the subject of independence for small nations, and saw it as his duty to tell his pupils stories of Wallace and Bruce and the Black Douglas so that they would have a true understanding of the history of their country. Once, when Winnie Ewing won her famous victory at the Hamilton by-election in 1967, he was so carried away that the entire lesson was given over to an analysis of the campaign and its implications. But another time, during a particularly long, loud and gory session on William Wallace, the headmaster opened the door suddenly and asked if he could speak with M. Lucas for a moment, outside, and when M. Lucas came back he was glum and roarless, and for a fortnight thereafter would not be diverted. But then he forgot, or remembered that he resisted *everything*, and life returned to abnormal. All this endeared M. Lucas greatly to Michael.

But if schools like Bellcroft House were outposts of an alien system, sometimes infiltrated by men like M. Lucas, then the places you went on to from them were veritable fortresses of the occupation. And this network of garrisons had its own complex pecking order. If you went to a certain prep school – one, say, in the vicinity of Edinburgh – then you would probably go on to one of three or four 'public schools' in or around the capital. If you were at a certain 'public school' then you had probably come from one of half a dozen prep schools which supplied that school with its annual intake. In this pecking order Bellcroft House came close to the bottom. It was one of the reasons why Angus Pendreich could afford it. It did not, generally speaking, turn out high-academic performers and even when it did there was no guarantee of admission to one of the 'top' schools. There existed, however, a ready-made receptacle for the products of Bellcroft House: located a dozen miles deeper into the wilds of Perthshire, it was called Kilsmeddum Castle. At Bellcroft, the underlying ethos was benign. Kilsmeddum was a crumbling, damp, cultureless hellhole infested with mice, where greed, selfishness, snobbery and bullying were the order of the day. The Oxbridge third-raters who posed as teachers, far from feeling thankful for having found sanctuary from the world, as Mr Veitch did at Bellcroft, resented being there and took their resentment out on their charges. In every respect, Kilsmeddum Castle was the last place a loving parent would deposit a loved child.

Within a few days of arriving there Michael detested the place and never wavered from this antipathy. He put up with it because by then there seemed little point in objecting – and because Angus did, albeit sporadically, come to rescue him.

Freddy Eddelstane was there too, as his brother had been. Michael didn't get this. Why, with their background, weren't they sent to a more prestigious school, possibly one south of the Border? Freddy said his father was a cheapskate, but even if he weren't it wouldn't make any difference. 'We've got loads of house,' he said, 'rooms and rooms and rooms of it, but no money.' But, Michael wondered, what did 'no money' mean when your father was a 'Sir'?

They stayed friends, kind of, but more and more Michael learned to rely on his own resources, distancing himself from the crass obscenities and boorishness of the mob. Whatever it was he wanted, he knew it wasn't that. Some of the mob grew suspicious and cornered him. 'Are you a poof, Pendreich?' He realised that how he responded would determine how, or whether, he continued to survive. For the first and only time in his life he punched someone in the face. A bright red stream spurted from the boy's nose and he started to cry. Michael was as surprised as any of them at what he had done but managed to conceal it. They left him alone.

Later, Freddy caught up with him. All the slight exaggeration of features that had made the child Freddy ugly had burst forth at adolescence into loose-fleshed, ogre-like coarseness. He was a kind of human toad. As such he was regularly set upon by the mob, but had learned to deflect the aggression by becoming a self-mocking court jester to the ringleaders. So he had to be careful about displaying any loyalty to Michael.

'I heard what happened,' he said. 'Are you all right?'

'Nothing happened.'

'Yes it did.'

They were in a corridor, with other boys coming and going. Freddy dragged him to the changing rooms, where they were alone among the rows of pegs, each loaded with its boy-shaped, sweat-and-mud-streaked collection of tracksuits and rugby shirts. The place was rank with boy smell.

'Are you all right?' he asked again.

'I'm fine.'

'What happened?'

Freddy was impressed by Michael's hitherto unrevealed capacity for violence, but what interested him more was the psychological element of the confrontation.

'Well, are you a poof?'

'What?'

'Something made you hit him.'

'Well, I'm not a poof. Are you?' Michael really didn't want to have to punch Freddy too.

'No.'

'Fine. That's that settled then.'

Michael wanted to get away, and started walking towards the door. Suddenly Freddy said, 'But I think my brother is.'

This was astonishing news. It seemed to reveal to Michael something not about Freddy's brother, not even about Freddy, but about himself.

'Really?'

'Maybe.'

'You always said he was weird, but weird's not the same as queer, is it?'

'No.' He smiled, or scowled, it was hard to tell which because he was so ugly. 'Maybe he's just weird.'

The door opened and somebody came in, a prefect. 'What are you two doing here?'

'Nothing,' Freddy said.

'Well go and do it somewhere else.'

They went, and nothing more was said.

§

'Did you make any progress with that introduction?' Murdo asks.

'I read over what I'd already written and then tinkered with it,' Mike says. 'Not at all productive.'

'I wouldn't know where to start,' Murdo says. 'I've not tried to write anything since I was at school.'

He picks at the window ledge beside his chair, and looks round at the rest of the sun lounge.

'This place needs a coat of paint.'

'I know. Outside and in.'

'More than paint. You've let the woodwork go.'

'Do you want to do it?'

'I will if you want me to.'

'I'll pay you for it.'

'Aye, you will. Used notes only.'

Murdo can turn his hand to just about anything. His cousin took over the uncle's building business and Murdo sometimes works for him. He also does painting jobs and other repair and maintenance work for people who either can't or don't want to do it themselves. He services his own van and will do other people's vehicles if they're not too fussy about them. He does Mike's car although he says it would be kinder to roll it over the edge of a cliff. His customers pay him in cash and if he doesn't declare more to the taxman than what he earns from the cousin nobody is blaming him for it. God knows it's hard enough making an income around here, they say, and one thing about Murdo, he's no scrounger, you'll not catch him sitting on his backside claiming benefit like some. Sometimes folk are short of money and they owe him it, or they pay him in kind – a lamb for the freezer, a fill of red diesel from the farm tank. 'It's how a real economy works,' Murdo says. 'Not that you'd expect economists to understand.'

'How long would it take you?' Michael asks.

'Two days. Maybe three. It depends on the weather. Also on how much of the wood needs to be replaced.'

'Well, I'm going to have to go to Edinburgh some time soon. To do with the exhibition. You could do it then.'

'Aye.'

'I'll let you know when I've arranged the dates.'

'I'm sure we'll sort something out.'

They have run out of things to say. This is fine. They sit in companionable silence and the night grows around them. This is absolutely fine.

§

By morning the weather has changed back. It's warmer, but the cloud is low on the hills and there's a steady downpour. Mike has another look at the introduction, essay, memoir, whatever it is he's trying to write. That's the problem, he doesn't know. But a deadline is looming: it's March and he has until 1 May to deliver the final text. He should be writing about Angus – the photographer, the father – and has made several stabs at it but it just isn't happening, he doesn't seem to be touching him at all. Faced with the blank computer screen and that deadline, and the memories provoked by those photographs at Dounreay, he is also confronted, and not for the first time, by the possibility that he didn't really know his father at all. He looks again at the family in the photograph: the tall man, the cold woman, the fragile boy on the tartan rug. Angus is dead, but physically Mike has grown to replace him. Isobel, though so much older, still looks like Isobel. It is the boy who has completely gone. How did we get from there to here, Mike wonders. How did *I* get to here? His fifty-three years, and all that they contain, seem suddenly elusive and intangible.

Still, it's Angus he's supposed to be making some sense of. Everything else is in place. He has the title – 'The Angus Angle' – easy and obvious, for exhibition and book, and Duncan Roxburgh at the National Gallery of Photography agrees. He's selected the images down to the last three or four. The original prints are being used where possible and if they're not good enough new ones are being made and will be mounted and framed by the gallery. He's written notes to go with the pictures in the book. He has a set of the picture proofs. All that's left is the introductory essay, and he can't get a fix on it. The more he worries over it the worse it becomes.

Duncan has been no help. 'How long should this essay be?' Mike asked, and Duncan said, 'As long as it needs to be. Three thousand words, five thousand, ten thousand. Whatever you feel comfortable with.' So far he has about four hundred and sixty, and he doesn't feel comfortable with them at all:

THE ANGUS ANGLE:
FIFTY YEARS OF SCOTTISH LIFE,
1947–1997 BY ANGUS PENDREICH
National Gallery of Photography 2 August–2 November 2008

INTRODUCTION
by Michael Pendreich

When Duncan Roxburgh, Director of the National Gallery of Photography, first proposed an exhibition of my father's work, more than two years ago, my initial reaction was enthusiasm, rapidly succeeded by a certain panic. This was because I knew full well that to agree would oblige me to address a matter I had been avoiding for some time: namely, the chaotic state of my father's archive. He had made a start on cataloguing his work in the late 1990s, but a preference for almost any other activity, and then declining health, meant that he had achieved very little before his death in September 2005. It therefore fell to me to review and catalogue some 30,000 negatives and 20,000 prints, many of them unidentified by subject, location or date. Despite the collection being in far better shape now than it was in 2005, this process is still ongoing.

From this astonishing record of life – mostly Scottish life – in the second half of the twentieth century, I selected just 200 photographs to form the exhibition. All of these images are reproduced in this book, in chronological order. Some of them have accompanying notes. These notes are mine, and contain information that I gathered from my father in general conversation over the years. Angus Pendreich was sociable and opinionated, but he was extraordinarily reluctant to talk about his art, let alone write anything down about it. Consequently, where I quote a comment or observation by him I am almost always doing so from memory. I cannot, therefore, claim that such quotations are one hundred per cent accurate, although I do not believe they misrepresent what he said or thought.

Generally, my father steadfastly refused to call what he did 'art'. 'Craft' he would allow, but he consistently downplayed the idea of photography as anything special. It was not, he insisted, on a par with literature, painting, architecture or music. He believed a photograph to be the outcome of a mechanical operation undertaken by someone who happened to be in the right place at the right time. Nothing was imagined, nothing original was expressed. We argued about this, but I could never detect the slightest disingenuousness or false modesty in these views, which were all the more remarkable given his creative expertise and the respect accorded to him by his peers.

My own view is that film, whether moving or still, was the medium for *the* art form of the twentieth century, and that there is no reason to doubt its continued significance in the twenty-first. My father's contribution to that art form was not inconsiderable. I am biased, of course, but for me he ranks with some of the other great names of Scottish and world photography . . .

At this point he ground to a halt, wondering whether he really believed that last sentence and if so what names he would insert. David Octavius Hill, Harry Benson, Oscar Marzaroli, Albert Watson? Ansel Adams, André Kertész, Henri Cartier-Bresson? *Would oblige me to address a matter . . . My father's contribution to that art form was not inconsiderable . . .* Such a pompous tone! It's not how he thinks, he hopes it's not how he speaks, so why does it come out like that? The prospect of continuing in the same vein for another ten or twenty pages makes him want to go out and take some photographs of his own, in spite of the weather, or open a bottle of wine and forget the whole exercise. How can he be writing about his own father and yet seem to be writing about a stranger? How, after a mere four paragraphs, can he have run out of things to say?

He doesn't need an analyst to work out the answers. Not really. Nevertheless he picks up the phone and calls Jean Barbour.

'Mike,' she says. 'Well, well. And how is the frozen north?'

'Wet,' he says.

'Not frozen then?'

'No, just wet.'

'And yourself?'

'Keeping under cover.'

'Are you still being a hermit?'

'Pretty much.'

'What do you *do* up there? Apart from take pictures?'

'That's what I do. All the time. The beach, the sea, the sky, the hills.'

'Is there a limit to how many you can take?'

'If there is, I've not reached it.'

'Then I assume the chances of seeing you are slim.'

Her voice sounds terrible: faded, weak. 'Are you all right?' he asks.

'A dose of the flu,' she says, 'but I'm through the worst of it.'

He's not convinced by this, but lets it go, for the time being.

'Well,' she says, '*am* I going to see you, or have you just phoned up to tantalise me?'

'Actually, there's stuff I have to do in Edinburgh. Any chance of a bed for a couple of nights?'

'Only if you promise to stay in and talk to me on one of them.'

'That's fine with me. I don't go out on the town these days.'

'Did you ever? What are you coming down for?'

'A couple of appointments, to do with this exhibition of my dad's work. Did I tell you about that?'

'Months ago. Christmas, New Year, whenever we last spoke. I can't remember.'

She sounds drunk. It isn't even eleven. 'Are you sure you're all right?'

'I'm fine,' she says testily. So he knows for certain that something is wrong.

'Anyway,' he says, 'apart from all that, I'd like to see you. There's going to be a book to go with the exhibition, and I've to write something for it, and I'm stuck.'

'Stuck about what?'

'I'm trying to write about Angus. His career, his character, his significance.'

'Oh Christ,' Jean says. 'Everybody has to have significance these days. Once it was just fame, now it's significance.'

He knows her well enough to recognise a diversion when she starts one. 'It's tough,' he says. 'I don't do words, I take pictures. I thought you could help.'

'Write it for you? I don't do words either. Not written-down ones.'

'No. But I thought you could tell me about him.'

He hears her sigh, imagines her in her big, shabby, cluttered room, Arthur's Seat visible through the window, through the rain. She says, 'Mike, it was a long time ago. Him and me, I mean.'

'I don't mean that. But you knew him before I was around. Before he married my mother. I can't talk to *her* about him. Anyway, it's time you and I caught up properly, face to face.'

'Aye, well,' she says, 'I would like that. How *is* your mother?'

'Same as ever, as far as I know.'

'So you've not seen her lately either?'

'We speak on the phone. She's frighteningly healthy. Still gardening, still going to church, still driving.'

'Still driving you mad, you mean?'

'She would if I spent any time with her.'

'Maybe you should. There can't be a lot left.'

Again, that slur in her voice. It makes him uneasy.

'My mother will go on and on,' he says. 'Like Margaret Thatcher, her role model.'

'No she won't. Anyway, Thatcher didn't go on. She lost her job, remember? That wasn't all she lost, in my opinion.'

'Mother is in prime physical and mental condition, believe me. She thrives on outlasting everyone she knows.'

'Good for her.' Very abrupt. 'Well, when are you coming?'

They make the arrangements. He'll arrive on the Thursday, see Duncan and anybody else he needs to on the Friday, come home on the Saturday.

'Will that give you enough time to do everything you have to?'

'More than. It'll be good to see you.'

'I wouldn't be so sure,' she says. 'I'm not looking that great.'

'Why? What's wrong?'

'Old age, that's all. Anyway, you'll have had enough of me by Saturday, I'm sure, but you can stay as long as you like. Are you driving down?'

'God, no,' he says. 'My car can limp around the roads here, but a trip down the A9 would finish it off. I'll get the train.'

'Very wise,' she says. 'Parking here is impossible unless you're prepared to pay a fortune for it. Not that I disapprove of *that*, you understand. We're being killed by cars.'

'I'll bring a bottle of whisky to take your mind off it.'

'Good idea. Better bring two. That'll help us sort your father out.'

§

Murdo gives him a lift down the strath to Lairg – 'I need to be going down there anyway for a couple of things' – for the mid-morning train to Inverness. All the way south it pours incessantly. There are delays caused by engineering works, resulting in a missed connection at Perth, but eventually the train pulls into Waverley in the early evening. The rain appears to be easing off so Mike chances the five-minute walk from the station to the High Street, and gets soaked.

Jean lets him in by means of an entryphone, a new installation. In the old days somebody had to come to the door. By the time he reaches the front room she's back in her armchair by the fireplace, wrapped in a blanket, a thin roll-up between her lips and a full ashtray at her side. There's a new gas fire, one of those glass-fronted, energy-efficient ones, another addition since his last visit. The old radiators under the big windows, which used to wheeze and rattle as they heated the room, are cold and silent. The room is as dusty as ever, but perhaps the contents have been thinned out. Everything is still a mess, but there isn't so much of it.

'I'm not getting up,' Jean says. 'I'm rid of the flu, but it's left me like a rag. I'm sore all over.'

She has the grace to take the fag out of her mouth to return his kiss. His hand on her shoulder feels how thin she is. Paper and bone. But it's she who chides him.

'You're wet. You should have got a taxi.'

'I know that now. I didn't think it was raining that hard.'

'It's been raining all winter. We used to get snow, even here, but not any longer. We've knackered the climate.' It's one of her pet topics. She's been on about it for decades, long before it became common-place. 'How can we pump all these noxious fumes into the atmosphere and not harm it?' she would say, lighting another cigarette.

'You'll have had your tea?' she says now, trotting out the old standard about Edinburgh stinginess, and he almost laughs, but she means it. 'If you haven't, Mike, you'll need to get a carry-out. I'm not hungry.'

He had sandwiches on the train and isn't hungry either. She's made a bed up for him and he dumps his bags in the room, changes out of his wet clothes and goes back through. She brightens considerably when he puts the malt whisky on the oak table. A Highland Park and a Clynelish.

'You did bring two,' she says, sucking the last millimetre from her cigarette and pinching it out. 'How lovely. I'll look forward to discussing *them*.'

That voice: once, long ago, Mike told her how sexy it was and she laughed and said he needed his head examined, she was old enough to be his mother, but he was serious. A voice thick with years of storytelling, hoarse from the speaking and the smoking but not harsh; knowing and kind, mostly, though the cutting remark and the quick putdown are not absent from her repertoire. There is still something that stirs Mike down in the depths when he hears her speak. In the days when she still entertained multitudes, she could hold the attention of the entire room packed tight with people – bodies sardined on to sofas, two to a chair, folk crouched and crammed on the rugs, backed up against the radiators and even a couple squeezed under the round oak table that was always covered with newspapers, bottles and scum-bummed mugs and glasses. Jean could keep that crowd entranced, and not just because the stories she told were good, but because of the voice she told them in. It worked for women as well as men, it didn't matter if you were gay or straight or didn't know what you were, as plenty didn't back then. Maybe it wasn't just the sound of sex that folk heard, maybe it was also the sound of natural, non-bookish wisdom, that special female quality which, in times past, made some men fear some women and cast them as witches. Whatever it was, Jean had it, and Mike reckons she still does.

She doesn't want to drink alcohol tonight. He makes a pot of tea instead, pulls a chair across to the other side of the gas fire, and they sit like two old crones and chat away about not very much. Life in the north, life in the city. People who've died, people who've moved away, people they've lost track of completely. Politics, wars, collapsed banks, fallen bankers, dying planet. But they've been through all this before, down the phone at least. There is another, more pressing issue. Mike hasn't seen her since Angus's funeral, two and a half years before. She was fit and rose-cheeked then. Now she is a grey skeleton.

'You may as well tell me.'

'Tell you what?'

'What the hell's wrong with you. Other than the flu.'

She looks at him angrily through her smoke. 'I don't want to talk about it.'

'Why not?'

'Because there's no point.'

'You look awful. You've no colour.'

'Not enough fresh air. I've given up the daily run round the park.'

'Don't be facetious. You're clearly not well. Have you seen a doctor?'

'No.'

'Why the hell not?'

'I've never seen a doctor in my life. I don't believe in doctors.'

'That's ridiculous, Jean.'

'No it's not. Some folk need doctors, some dinnae. I'm one of the dinnaes.'

'You look like you've got cancer.'

'Thanks a lot,' she says. Then, 'Aye, that's what I think too when I look in the mirror.'

'This is absurd. Why don't you go and find out?'

'Find out what? That I'm going to die? We're all going to die, Mike.'

'That's childish.' And then, childishly, he adds, 'And you're still smoking like a lum.'

'Don't start.'

'Well, it can't exactly help.'

'It helps a lot. What's the alternative? My life is taken over by doctors who cut me open, fill me with drugs, blast me with radio-therapy, or all three of the above, my hair falls out, I can't manage living on my own here at home, I feel like crap and *then* I die. Delaying tactics, that's all. Thank you, but no.'

'So what *are* you going to do?'

'Let things take their course. It's time. Look at this place. You might not believe it, but I'm shedding things. Honestly.'

'That seems a bit premature.'

'I'm nearly seventy-nine, Michael. That's late enough. I've not had a bad run.'

'You sound defeated. It's not like you.'

'I'm not defeated. I'm actually winning. Don't tell me I'm defeated.'

'Are you in pain?'

'Sometimes. I've got lots of different painkillers, though. Amazing what you can get over the counter these days. Drink's the best, although it doesn't go very well with some of the other stuff. That's one reason why I'm a bit down today. I've not taken any pills because I want to have a good drink with you tomorrow.'

'I appreciate that.'

'It's for my benefit, not yours, you arrogant wee shite.'

She's always had a quick temper, although often in the past she would turn it on simply in order to play devil's advocate more effectively. If you didn't know her it was disconcerting, watching her switch from revolutionary socialist to diehard reactionary in a moment. The Demon Barbour, someone nicknamed her.

Mike remembers a phone conversation with her from a couple of years earlier, just before the ban on smoking in public places became law. He made some remark about how devolution was going to reduce her rights but she would have to thole it for the good of the nation, and she rounded on him.

'Don't knock it. It *is* for the good of the nation. It'll save thousands of lives.'

'So you're giving up?'

'Of course not.' There was a shuffling sound at the other end of the line as she lit up. 'I'll just carry on in the privacy of my own smelly hoose. But I approve of the ban. It's not for the likes of me. It's for the coming generations.'

'I thought you'd be furious about it.'

'Why? Because they're taking away my civil liberties? Rubbish! People like me have had it our own way far too long when it comes to blowing smoke in other folk's faces. I tell you what, if Scottish human rights come down to being able to light up cancer-sticks and get blootered whenever and wherever you like, we're in a sorry state. It's time we stood up for freedoms that really matter. It's time we grew up.'

'Anyway,' she says now, 'what about yourself? How are you?'

'I'm fine.'

'You look well. Still on your own, I take it?'

'Aye.'

'Really?'

'Aye.'

'That's a shame. I thought you might have found yourself a strapping young fisherman by now.'

This is so close to the truth that Mike is tempted to tell her about Murdo. But he's not ready. He shakes his head, not exactly lying.

'Ironic, isn't it,' Jean says, 'that we ranted on about solidarity and community and standing together against the Tories, and what some of us wanted more than anything was to be alone.'

'Is that what *you* wanted? Surely not. All those years of folk piling in here night after night, and you holding court – that was meat and drink to you, wasn't it?'

'Aye, it was. I loved it, and I like to think it was important, that all those people passing through here took something away with them that made a difference in the way they thought and acted. It was my contribution to the cause, providing this space. But it was nice to stop. I don't miss clearing up the mess, I'll say that. And I've grown attached to the peace and quiet.'

'I think we're still in a minority,' Mike says. 'Most people are disturbed by solitude. They think silence is odd. Open country disconcerts them. They panic when they run out of pavement.'

'Maybe,' Jean says, 'but you don't have to live in the back of beyond like you do to be alone.'

Again, he lets that one go. She says, 'Do you ever hear from Adam?'

'Occasionally. We exchange Christmas cards. He's in Barcelona.'

'I know. He comes back now and again. He came to see me last year.'

'With the new boyfriend,' Mike says. 'You told me.'

'So I did. Well, anyway. So you're fine and you're settled in Angus's old hideaway. But what do you *do*? You don't produce books or cards or have shows of your own. Or do you?'

'No, nothing like that. I'm busy enough. I get obsessed with things and can't stop taking pictures of them. Last week it was seaweed, next week it might be driftwood or drystane dykes. It's not just taking the pictures, it's manipulating them later. But I suppose I have been marking time a bit, ever since I moved up there.'

'Ever since Angus died, you mean. That was nearly three years ago, Mike.'

'I know. But the archive, and now this exhibition, they've been taking up a lot of time too. And with him leaving me the house and some money, and the odd local job now and then, I'm not really in any hurry. I lead a pretty frugal life.'

'Why do I always think there's a mismatch between being gay and frugality?'

'We're not all Elton Johns, you know.'

'Well, all I can say is *you're* far too young to be winding down,' Jean says. 'And far too young to be celibate.'

'I'm not winding down,' he says. 'I'm consolidating.'

'What you're doing,' she says, 'is talking shite.'

§

My contribution to the cause: Jean's words. But what was the cause? It's easy to remember what they stood *against*: Thatcherism, London rule, the destruction of old industries, the assault on the Welfare State, the poll tax. But what were they *for*? A Scottish parliament, of course. But now they have it, what is *it* for? Forget smoking bans and other worthwhile legislation, what is its primary function? Maybe it's for saying, *Look, listen, this is who we are*. And maybe that is no insignificant thing, and the purpose of a parliament is to say it again, over and over. What can be more important, politically, than to know who you are, and to say it?

Mike likes to consider these things. It's only with the passing of time that the picture comes fully into focus, as the present slides and settles into history. Who are we? One of the unintended effects of Margaret Thatcher's revolution, he sees now – and let's face it, that's what it was, a revolution – was to destroy Scottish loyalty to the British state. If it didn't provide you with a job, if it didn't give you a decent pension or adequate health care or proper support when you were out of work, what was *it* for? It wasn't for anything – except maybe things you didn't want or believe in, like nuclear weapons on the Clyde, or the poll tax. In the Thatcher years the great presumption of the left – that the industrial working class would eventually tame capitalism – came crashing down. The class war may not be over but it's certainly not what it used to be. In its stead there are many creeds, ancient and new, ethnic and national and religious and green, all jostling for position; and though Mike has escaped from the din, he still likes to ask what the din is all about.

Is his kind of solitude – call it independence if you like – different from Jean's? Does it diminish the whole, or does the whole diminish it? And is Highland privacy different from Lowland, or Scottish privacy different from English? By becoming more private do we become less of a community? Probably. Less Scottish? He doubts it. We just become different versions of ourselves.

§

Jean is still in her bed when he goes out in the morning. He has a meeting with the publicity and marketing manager at the National Gallery of Photography, followed by another with Duncan Roxburgh, looking at the space and a plan of how the photographs will be arranged. Duncan is very proud of the fact that there is no

'Scottish' in the title of his gallery. 'I'm sick of the word,' he says. 'Why do we always have to be qualifying ourselves like that? The English don't do it. They just *assume*.' The NGP is located in the former High School on Calton Hill, a building that in the 1970s was earmarked as the future home of a Scottish assembly; then, when that came to nothing, it was mothballed during the eighteen years of Conservative government. For the last five of those a vigil was kept outside the gates, from a ramshackle caravan, by an organisation called Democracy for Scotland. Appropriately, one of the last photographs in Angus's exhibition will be from that period: it shows a couple of bearded Democracy for Scotland campaigners in big jumpers sharing a flask of tea with two laughing traffic wardens beside a blazing brazier. There's an Angus angle to this image, because the way he's taken it draws the observer's eye away from the people and towards the brazier. The thing that catches the attention is a piece of burning timber stamped with the words THIS SIDE UP.

In the afternoon Mike goes for a walk around the town, wandering in and out of second-hand bookshops, pleased to be back but thankful he'll soon be leaving. Edinburgh is hardly overwhelming, it isn't that kind of city, but already he misses the Highlands – the sense of space, the mountains, the water, the absence of people. What is it, this desire in him for retreat? There's Murdo, of course. Does he miss him? He does, and this makes him fearful.

In a café in the Grassmarket he orders a coffee. The place is quiet, a couple of women in one corner, a guy reading the *Scotsman* in another. He sits in the window and watches people passing by. Edinburgh in March: so long as there isn't a rugby international, it's one of the quietest months, with hardly any tourists. The man reading the paper looks pretty ragged: he's unshaven, keeps sniffing. An old fellow, mid-sixties maybe. Mike has to check himself for thinking that. Old? The guy's probably only ten years older than he is. Bang. One minute you're a student, the next you're a pensioner.

When he gets back in the early evening Jean is up and about, has applied make-up and put on some clean clothes, and looks altogether more like herself. She's hungry too, and recommends an Indian restaurant ten minutes' walk away for a carry-out. 'We'll phone in an order,' she says, scrabbling about for a menu, 'but you'll have to go and collect it. They tried to deliver once but you know what it's like finding this place if you've never been.'

An hour or so later they're pushing the cartons and plates aside and sitting back in their seats at the kitchen table. Jean's at first keen appetite deserted her after a few minutes and Mike has tried to compensate but can eat no more. She tips the remains, curry and rice together, into one carton and sticks it in the fridge. 'I'll have it for breakfast.' Then they retreat to the front room, light the gas fire, and open the first bottle of whisky.

He has brought the picture proofs of the book and they spend some time passing these between them. He is anxious to know what she thinks of his selection.

The first proof is of one of Angus's signature photographs: *Funeral of Sir Harry Lauder, Hamilton, 4 March 1950*. In it, a line of bareheaded men and headscarved women stretches along the street. They're all looking away, following the route of the cortège, except for one small boy among them, who stares directly into the camera. He seems oblivious to the sense of occasion, the fact that he's at the funeral of a 'great man'. A cheeky happiness lights up his face. 'Wonderful,' Jean says.

Then for a while she says nothing as she turns the loose sheets. There are two photos taken at Arbroath Abbey in April 1951. She looks at them both carefully and he watches her doing it. She glances across at him.

'I'm surprised more of these aren't familiar to me,' she says defiantly.

'But those two are.'

She ignores this. 'It's a terrible title, by the way. Was that your idea?'

'It was the only title, realistically. It's the phrase everybody recognises. Angus's unique take.'

She goes through some more images, stopping at *Elvis Presley, Prestwick, 3 March 1960*. This is one of the few pictures Angus liked to talk about. He was in Glasgow when he heard a rumour that somebody special was going to be landing on Scottish soil. Elvis had finished his military service in Germany and was heading home to the USA, and these flights often stopped to refuel at Prestwick. So Angus rushed down there along with a number of other pressmen.

The news had leaked out, and there were dozens of fans waiting when Elvis stepped off the plane. It was the only time he was ever in the British Isles. In Angus's image, Elvis is on one side of a wire fence chatting to a crowd of young women on the other side. He looks spruce and fresh in US Army uniform and cap. Three sergeant's stripes and the word 'Spearhead' are on his sleeve. He is smiling, relaxed, slightly bemused. The women, many holding out pen and paper for his autograph, are probably mostly teenagers. Several are wearing headscarves, all are in heavy, shapeless winter coats. He's twenty-five, but they look older than him, and their expressions range from happy to disbelieving to slightly desperate, as if they know this may be the most exciting moment of their lives. The picture is really more about those women than about Elvis.

Mike says, 'Do you think there's a good-enough spread of his work?'

'Depends what you're trying to do. Are you trying to represent the range of his work or are you telling a story with these pictures?'

'Well, both. I've picked images for their quality, of course. But I do think there's a narrative running through them.'

'A narrative of what?'

'What the subtitle says. Fifty years of Scottish life.'

'Ah, but is that a narrative Angus would have acknowledged, or have you imposed it on his photographs?'

This question has been bothering Mike greatly, sometimes even waking him in the night. Is he adding something to his father's work, or stealing from it?

'I don't think he would have approved,' he says. 'He didn't like structures much. And yet, this is the story I see in his work.'

'So it's about you as much as him,' Jean says.

'It's about us all,' Mike says.

He's also brought what he's written so far of the introductory essay. He hands it over, and she fires up a new roll-up and reads through it while he refills the glasses and sifts, for the thousandth time, through the pile of images.

'It's not exactly impassioned, is it?' he says, when she's finished. 'Not the warm tribute of an admiring, grateful son.'

'Is that what you want it to be?'

'It's what it should be.'

Jean makes a gesture that is half-nod, half-shrug: *I'll come to that later.* ' "Chronological order",' she says. 'Interesting phrase. Arranging things by time. It seems to be the natural way of releasing a narrative, but maybe it isn't. It's not how we remember our own lives, our own stories, after all. Bits of them come at us in any old order. Mixed-up memories. So maybe chronology is just a regime to stop us going insane. Sensible, but not very . . . *imaginative.*'

'Most of us can only take so much chaos,' he says.

'I'll tell you something I've always wanted to do, Mike. I've always wanted to tell a story with no beginning, no middle and no end.'

'How would that work?'

'I'm not sure. That's the point. There's a tyranny about beginnings and endings and the routes between them but we seem to like being tyrannised. And I've been wondering if I could do it differently.'

'But why?'

'Bloody-mindedness, probably. Because stories aren't supposed to be like that.'

'And yet,' he says, 'they almost always are. All the years I came here, listening to you, it was like dipping into this big swirling pot of stories. There was always another bit at the end of this one, or there was a different version to that one, or it was just a wee path off the main track. You know what I mean. One thing leads to another.'

'I suppose that's right enough. Everything's connected. But lately I've been thinking over exactly what a story is.'

She rolls another cigarette. He waits. They respect each other's intervals, and this is one of the things that has kept them friends. Two and a half years is just a longer interval. He watches her shaping the words in her head before she lets them out. There is something hugely civilised about allowing long pauses in a conversation. Very few people can stand that kind of silence.

She lights up, inhales, speaks again. 'A story is a whole mass of details that come together and form a narrative. Without that coming-together they're just a lot of wee pieces. So what happens if you take a story and break it into its wee pieces? When you put it back together again, will it turn out the same way?'

'Like a jigsaw puzzle,' he says.

'Exactly. It's like you're making a jigsaw puzzle. You cowp this thousand-piece jigsaw puzzle on to a table and turn all the pieces right way up and then you stare at them. Where do you start? But what I'm thinking is that this particular puzzle came in a big plastic bag, not in a box, and there's no picture to guide you. You don't know what the hell the picture is you're supposed to be making. You have to start somewhere, so you look for the bits with straight edges. And the four bits with two straight edges that mean they're the corners. But maybe it doesn't have corners and straight edges. Anyway. You find bits that are the same shade of red, the same shade of green, you sort them into separate piles, and occasionally you find two bits, three bits, that actually seem to fit together. And gradually, spread out all over the table, this picture begins to emerge.'

'That's assuming you have all the right pieces,' Mike says. 'Which means you're relying on somebody else. Somebody else already made the jigsaw puzzle, the picture, and cut it up, and put it in the plastic bag.'

'Right,' she says. 'Well, that's okay up to a point. The storyteller has to get her material from elsewhere. But I'm bothered by the idea that somebody else already made the picture. So maybe a story is more like a painting than a jigsaw. *You're* the creator, but you're working from life, putting what you see on the canvas but with your own take on it. And when it's finished, there are all kinds of things going on at once, and you can look at the whole thing or you can look at the detail, but it's all there, all the parts moving in and out of one another. Like a complex piece of machinery – working, but captured, held. Motionless motion.'

'Suspended animation,' Mike says. 'Like a photograph, in other words.'

'Aye,' she says. 'Like a photograph. Okay. Jigsaw puzzle, painting, photograph. Now we're getting somewhere. Or are we? It's complicated, isn't it? Maybe one shouldn't analyse this stuff too much.'

Another silence. Mike thinks about the complexity and the simplicity of taking a photograph. The tens of thousands he's taken over the years, each one part of a narrative, following on from the one before, preceding the next. Could he have taken them in a different order? He thinks about what happens when he selects one image out of, say, every ten or fifty or hundred he takes. How the narrative is reduced, fractured. How the chain is broken. He thinks about Angus, doing it all before him.

'Dad would have said, *don't* analyse. As a photographer you just have to be there, take the shot. He'd have said it was partly skill and mostly chance.'

'I know that's what he thought,' Jean says, 'but I think he was wrong. I envied him, you know. He didn't seem to have to try. Yes, you have to be there at the right moment, but there's something else. That's why I never liked that phrase, "the Angus angle". It always struck me as being lazy journalese. It suggests that all he was doing was bending down and getting the angle right, the exposure, the focus, ticking those technical boxes. Well, you can have all the technical skill in the world, but that's not enough. If you're really good, there's an instinct in there too, an extra layer of knowledge. You learn it by experience, but it's like you always had it deep inside. Do you see?'

'I used to argue with him in just that way,' Mike says. 'There has to be more to it than chance, I'd say. A photographer's an artist, what you do is art. He'd say no, it's about technique, the quality of your camera equipment and how well you operate it and even then there are too many other external factors – light, movement, colour – for you to be fully in control. An artist makes something, he'd say, I just record what already exists. In the end I gave up arguing, and one of the reasons was because in a way he was right. We don't really know what we're creating, we just take the opportunity. In that sense, we're all chancers.'

'Well,' she says, 'I still think being a chancer takes a certain amount of expertise.'

They sit in contemplation while the gas fire hisses at their pretensions. Then Mike says, 'So what is it, this story you want to tell? The one with no beginning, no middle and no end. What's it about?'

'It's what you said earlier,' she says. 'It's about us, all of us. It's the story we're in.' And then, after another silence, she adds, 'But I'm not likely to be in it much longer. Which is maybe why I don't want it to be finite, why I'm rebelling against the tyranny of time.'

'But you're not rebelling,' he says. 'You're not fighting to stay alive. You're letting go.'

'That is rebelling,' she says. 'Challenging the orthodoxy. Anyway, it's different. That's life and death.'

'The simplest chronology of all,' Mike says.

§

The divorce was completed in 1965. Angus rented a flat in Glasgow and bought a run-down house, for virtually nothing, at Cnoc nan Gobhar on the north coast of Sutherland. He must have taken note of the location on the family holiday of the previous year. 'I need a bolt-hole,' he told Michael, the first time he brought him there. 'Somewhere I can escape to every so often. This is perfect.' He paid Isobel whatever she was due, paid the school fees, and then carried on behaving the way he always had.

It's not hard for Mike to see, in retrospect, how his father operated. He was such a handsome, intelligent charmer that he didn't have to try very hard to have women fall in love with him. When he and Isobel got married, perhaps she really believed that he would settle down and be hers alone for ever, but it was never going to be like that. Angus enjoyed the company of women – women other than the one he was with – too much. He couldn't resist making them unable to resist him. He was a wanderer in other ways too. When the Pendreichs still all lived together in the semi-detached villa in Doune that Isobel had inherited from her parents (who were dead before Michael was conscious of them being alive), Angus would go off for a day's hillwalking, even in the foulest weather, rather than stay at home to be tortured by domesticity. And if there was the possibility of a job that would take him away, anywhere in the British Isles or, for preference, abroad, he would grab it.

So Michael was used to not seeing his father for long periods, even before the divorce. After it, the phone would sometimes ring early on a Saturday morning during the school holidays, and Michael would rush to answer it before his mother could, and it would be Angus saying he was in Glasgow and did he fancy a day out? He'd arrive an hour later, honking his horn outside the gate so that none of them had to bear the strain of him and Isobel failing to commu-nicate. They'd go to Edinburgh or Glasgow, to see a film or an exhib-ition and go for a meal. When Michael got home Isobel would ask what they had done, and sniff at what he told her. It was all very well for his father to appear once in a blue moon and spoil him but what about her? How did he think it made her feel, after all she did for him? And she was right and justified and Michael despised her for it, and longed for the next time the phone would ring.

Even better, Angus would turn up at Kilsmeddum Castle, unannounced, during term. He would time it so as to arrive at the end of morning classes on a Saturday, and take Michael to Perth for the rest of the day. The school objected, of course, but Angus overruled the objections: he was paying good money to have his son educated there and he reserved the right to remove him whenever it suited him. The school would subsequently complain to Isobel, who would forbid Michael to go with his father if he tried it again. When he tried it again, Michael would at once go with him. They saw *Where Eagles Dare*, *Butch Cassidy and the Sundance Kid*, *Diamonds are Forever*, *Soldier Blue* (gleefully sneaking Michael in since it carried an X certificate). They ate Chinese, Wimpy and anything else exotic that Perth had to offer. For Michael, the trouble that ensued at school and at home on these occasions was easily worth it.

It was on one of these outings that Angus presented him with his first *real* camera. Up to then he'd played around with a couple of cheap and easy models, but he was ready for something more challenging. He wanted something new but what he got was a second-hand Pentax Spotmatic, a model that had only been around for three or four years. It was the first serious camera to have a built-in light meter that really worked: you focused first, then flicked a switch to activate the metering system, and set the shutter speed and aperture yourself by lining up two needles in the viewfinder. The great virtue of the Spotmatic was its simplicity; Michael learned a huge amount about light exposure and depth of field by the time-tested method of trial and error.

And then there was Sutherland. Every summer, Angus spent a month at Cnoc nan Gobhar, and Michael would go by train to join him for the middle two weeks of his stay. These were the times when he first became 'Mike', and this was another bond between father and son, since Isobel was averse to his being anything or anyone but 'Michael'. They barbecued sausages and burgers in front of the house, went for huge walks into deserted glens, climbed the great hulks of Ben Klibreck and Ben Hope, fished in lochs and rivers and afterwards sat together, Angus drinking pints of beer and Mike half-pints of shandy, in musty, antler-festooned, wood-panelled bars where no one ever questioned Mike's age. Sometimes they drove over to the west, camped by the white beaches of Assynt, swam in the ice-cold Atlantic, and greedily viewed the strange mountains of those parts: Suilven, Stac Pollaidh, Quinag. And they did work on the house, or Angus engaged others to do it, men like Murdo's uncle, while they played. For eight successive years they had these fortnights together, all through Mike's years at boarding school, and he loved them, and loved his father because of them.

Often there was a woman, Angus's latest, at the cottage: always younger than him, always bonnie, smiling and kind to Mike, behaving *almost* as if she were a wife and mother, and treated by Angus with breathtaking casualness. These women were of a certain type – sunny, ambitious, not very clever. They were often English, or spoke as if they were. They were light and airy and entirely lacked the burden of responsibility that Isobel carried like a cross. They had a breathy confidence that suggested nothing would ever go much wrong in their lives. 'Your father's little friends' was how Isobel described them, as if she felt sorry for them because they did not see that their participation in his life would be only temporary. Whether there was heartbreak when it was over, as it always eventually was, or whether they were actually stronger in themselves than Isobel could ever understand, the following summer Sally or Mandy or Katy would be gone and a successor installed. Mike didn't mind in the least: he enjoyed being made a fuss of by the little friends, and having vague crushes on them that didn't quite make sense either to them or to him. There was a Julie who lasted two years, right at the end of the sequence, whom he particularly liked. When he thinks about it now he wonders if it was his fortnight at Cnoc nan Gobhar that precipitated the end of each of these relationships. Angus seemed more or less to abandon the girlfriend as soon as Mike arrived, and by the time he left had probably lost the desire to reconnect with her. And though Mike knew his father was at fault in the way he treated his women, as he had been in the way he treated Isobel, it wasn't until that second fortnight with Julie that he felt his loyalty diminish a little.

§

He finished at Kilsmeddum at Christmas 1972. He'd had enough of the school and the school had had enough of him. He had the Highers he needed to go to art college and had filled in the appropriate forms. He was quite skilled at drawing – he'd produced a set of drooling, ghoulish caricatures of the teaching staff of which even the mob approved – but his real interest lay in photography. What was the point of staying on to sit more exams? Angus agreed, and since he paid the fees Isobel couldn't argue against it. From Christmas until the summer Mike was at home in Doune, taking photographs, drawing, listening to music. To keep Isobel at bay and demonstrate that he had more of a sense of responsibility than his father, he got a part-time job in a local hotel, working in the kitchen. He began to take an interest in food and how to prepare it. Sometimes he'd make the evening meal at home, surprising Isobel with his skills, although she was suspicious of the ingredients he sought out, things that were still almost exotic: garlic, red peppers, pasta that wasn't macaroni. She was suspicious of anything 'creative'. If only he'd been inclined towards teaching, or the law, he might have made her happier. She worked part-time as a typist and receptionist for a firm of solicitors in Dunblane, and made futile attempts to interest him in conveyancing. Photography, being what his father did, was bound to end in tears.

They maintained a truce over those months, in order to keep life tolerable. Sometimes they watched TV together. There was a political thriller, *Scotch on the Rocks*, running that spring. A group called the Scottish Liberation Army was busy blowing up statues of Queen Victoria and the toll-booths at the Forth Road Bridge. They kidnapped some Unionist bigwig called Lord Thorganby and for good measure drowned the Secretary of State for Scotland. It was fanciful stuff but it was on the BBC so Isobel watched it with absolute trust, as if it were a documentary. It fed her fears that the country was about to descend into anarchy and it fed Mike's gut sense that he was some kind of nationalist, even if it wasn't the M. Lucas kind. At the end of the series the SLA's rebellion fizzled out and normality was restored, to Isobel's relief and Mike's disappointment.

§

It was the final evening of Mike's stay at Cnoc nan Gobhar, and Angus, Julie and he were in the sitting room, drinking bottles of beer. They'd been outside, catching the last of the sun, but the midges had driven them in. Angus was explaining how he wanted to make the side window into a door and build a sun lounge on, so that one could go on enjoying the view without being eaten alive. He was going to get Donald MacKay on to it.

'That'll be nice,' Julie said, and Angus said, 'Yes, it will,' and the way he said it made Mike think it unlikely that Julie would get the benefit. In the morning Angus was going to take him to the station at Lairg. He'd go back to his hotel job for a few weeks, then he'd be off to Edinburgh, to art college. Angus was about to go to America for three months, and wouldn't be back until the autumn. Wherever Julie was going, it wasn't to America.

'You should look up Jean Barbour when you get to Edinburgh,' Angus said. 'She'd love to meet you.'

'Who's she?' Mike said.

'Just an old pal.' Angus was on his third beer and was a little drunk. 'Haven't seen her for years, but I can't imagine she's any different. You'll like her.'

'What does she do?' Julie asked. She gave Mike a smile. They both knew better than to ask how Angus and Jean Barbour had met.

'Do? She doesn't have a job, if that's what you mean. She never used to have, anyway.' Never normally reluctant to lambast the idle rich, he sounded slightly repelled by the idea of Jean having to work. He turned away from Julie and said to Mike, 'She was involved in a bookshop but that was ages ago. The thing about her is she gathers people around her. There's always a get-together of some kind at Jean's. Always something going on.'

'Sounds good,' Julie said, sounding doubtful.

Mike was also unconvinced. 'Yes, it does,' he said – to Julie, because he wanted to counter the way Angus was excluding her – and then, to Angus, 'So have you got an address or something?'

'That's the thing. She's just off the Royal Mile. I could take you there, but I couldn't tell you the name of the close or the house number. It's not that easy to find.'

'Great,' Mike said. 'This is going to be simple, isn't it? Do you even have a phone number?'

'It's been more than twenty years,' Angus said. 'She didn't have a phone then.'

'Maybe she's not there any more,' Julie said, trying to stay in the conversation.

'*She* won't have gone anywhere,' he said. There was an unpleasant edge to his voice now. 'Jean's steadfast, a fixture.' Outside, the loch and the land lay still, but in the room the atmosphere was suddenly bristling. 'Look,' Angus said, 'sooner or later you're bound to come across her. Edinburgh's a village. Just remember her name, Jean Barbour.'

He'd known her in the late 1940s, early 1950s, he said. He wasn't long out of the army, and was working freelance for magazines, mostly, although he had a brief spell at the *Scotsman*. He always tried to look for the pictures nobody else was taking. Often he simply turned the camera away from the obvious subject and photographed something in its shadow, or somebody looking at it. The ridiculous next to the sublime, the commonplace made special by association. That was all there was to it. It was then that someone came up with the 'Angus angle' tag. He didn't like it much but it opened a few doors. There was plenty to photograph in Edinburgh – it was the early days of the Festival and there were all kinds of characters on the streets and in the pubs. And Jean Barbour, whom he met in this bookshop, had also recently arrived but somehow she had a lot of contacts. She moved between two Edinburghs, the semi-bohemian festival city and the poker-faced Presbyterian one, and she was useful.

'Useful?' Julie said.

'She made herself useful, yes,' Angus said. 'She knew a lot of people.'

It was obvious to Mike that Jean and Angus had been lovers. Julie saw it too. The word 'useful' seemed to goad her into action. She stood up, said she was going to make some food, and went through to the kitchen. Mike thought she was stifling tears. Angus made a face and Mike thought, aye, if it was me I'd cry, you bastard.

'I'll go and give her a hand,' he said, getting out of his chair.

'If you see her, tell her I'm asking for her. Jean, I mean,' Angus said.

§

Edinburgh in the early 1970s had a special, dowdy kind of magic, especially in streaming, wind-chilled winter: the marvellous and the mundane inhabiting the same stairs, worlds of night and day rubbing shoulders both begrudgingly and with relish, often without acknowledgement and sometimes without realising it. Shoppers at a bus stop might breathe in a hint of marijuana drifting from some shaded window and, not knowing what it was, find this exotic invasion of their senses oddly, dreamily pleasant. Tourists perambulating the cobbled streets of the New Town could remark on the quiet, sober appearance of a particular Georgian terrace, unaware of the brothel operating behind one solid, firmly shut door. In lanes behind the noble, upright department stores of Princes Street drunk men swayed and vomited, while a few yards away, in Rose Street pubs, staff from Jenners and R. W. Forsyth jostled to get served alongside rugby players, actors, bankers and Lallans-spouting poets. In Marchmont and Stockbridge young women yawned and poured themselves more vodka while their boyfriends did the cheese-shop sketch from Monty Python yet again. In the Old Town, nationalistic students at all-night parties roared, over and over, the chorus of a new song they'd recently, imperfectly, learned: 'Flower of Scotland'. They said 'Kiss my arse' in Gaelic and discussed the proposition 'It's Scotland's Oil' until the sun came up and they could no longer sing or speak. Up the Dalry Road folk put Billy Connolly on the hi-fi, cracking up as he went on about jobbies and willies, and recognising themselves in his outrageous jokes. Jakies in coats that smelled like hill sheep slipped into oblivion in the Grassmarket. Book-laden, bespectacled academics trailed between the university and the National Library. Beacon-nosed advocates in High Street bars patronised hippyish, long-limbed feminists whose politics they dismissed as infantile, and the feminists were mildly flattered by the attentions of middle-aged men they in theory, and when sober, despised. Businessmen going home to their families in the suburbs diverted of an evening to Calton Hill, searching among the trees or gravestones for some nameless stranger and a brief release from their hypocrisy. All over the city there was hypocrisy, and irony, and heroism: fabulous views from despoiled viewpoints, squalor and refinement propping each other up, dissolution in progress behind impregnable façades, and dreams of glory in crumbling tenements.

Into all this, at the age of eighteen, Mike Pendreich wandered, an innocent. He came with a purpose – to be a photographer. He was enrolled at the art college to do drawing and painting. There wasn't a degree course in photography then, but he could do it as an elective. He was inspired by Angus and wanted to emulate him. And, like all sons following on the trail of their fathers, he wanted in time to surpass him.

Edinburgh to him was like a place out of legend or a fantastic novel. It had seven hills, a castle on one of them, neo-Athenian ruins on another, and on a third, Arthur's Seat – which was not far short of being a mountain – a flock of sheep. The great area of the city that stretched from there westward, from Holyrood to Tollcross, was soiled and seedy and vibrant. In the old streets of the Southside, he found plenty to intrigue him: a mysterious bookshop that sold titles no other shop stocked; pubs stained and rich with the smoke of pipe tobacco and the smell of sweet black sixty-shilling ale, places so narrow men had to shuffle themselves like cards in order to get served; steamy, dripping cafés patronised by noisy crowds of upper-class students, who adored the chipped cups, the tarnished cutlery, the chewable tea and especially the abuse heaped on them by the coarse-tongued women who served them; sweaty markets and small, incense-hazy shops selling records, posters, Afghan coats, Navajo jewellery, tie-dyed T-shirts, cheesecloth smocks, denim jackets and cowboy boots. In all this there was a sense of something about to happen, of things already happening in rooms just out of sight and reach.

And there was Sandy Bell's – the pub where Angus had taken pictures fifteen, twenty years before: of Hamish Henderson, the folklorist; of Stuart MacGregor, the wild medical student who'd sung of the men building the hydro schemes in the Highlands; and of numerous other singers, musicians and neglected geniuses. It was still going strong: any night of the week you could reckon on some decent music to go with your pint, and there was always a chance that Hamish – or one or more of his cronies – would drop in. Mike found his way there early on. Apart from anything else it was en route from the college to his digs in Newington.

And it was in Sandy Bell's one November night that, as Angus had predicted, Jean's name came up in conversation. Mike was standing on his own but – the way it sometimes happens in a crowded pub – not in isolation. In the back of the bar a guy with a guitar was alternating between Jacobite laments and protest songs. To one side of Mike a heated political discussion was in progress.

There were three men involved: a long-haired, long-bearded student in an army-surplus greatcoat; a bald man in a biker's leather jacket; and a middle-aged-looking guy in a brown duffelcoat. The argument had started about Chile, where two months before the elected socialist government had been ousted by a military coup led by General Pinochet. The question was whether Allende, the deposed president, had shot himself or been killed by soldiers. The student in the greatcoat was emphatic that Allende had been murdered. This was an article of faith to him: it was inconceivable that the fascists were not responsible. The biker, on the other hand, didn't think it mattered either way: his understanding was that the Allende regime had been corrupt and on the point of collapse anyway. The man in the duffelcoat seemed to float between them, saying 'Aye' and 'Maybe' but not much else. When they ran out of things to say about Chile, Greatcoat wanted to know what the biker thought about what was going on closer to home. The National Union of Mineworkers had announced an overtime ban; the electricity engineers and train drivers had done the same; and now Ted Heath, the Prime Minister, had countered by declaring a state of emergency. Where did he stand on *that*, then? Duffelcoat nodded fervently and waited for the biker's answer.

On Mike's other side, listening to the singer and throwing occasional, irritated glances at this trio, stood a heavy, hard-faced man who looked like he could deck the lot of them with a single punch and might be about to do so.

The biker said he'd noticed there was a stock of candles behind the bar and if Ted Heath was calling it an emergency *he* called *that* pretty smart planning by the Sandy Bell's staff.

'Call it what you like,' Greatcoat said. 'It's not a state of emergency, it's state repression. You can't impose a pay freeze on the workers while prices are going up. It's totally unjust.'

'Well, there's a freeze on prices too,' the biker said.

'Yeah, but there's still inflation, isn't there?' Greatcoat said. 'Why is it always the workers who have to make all the sacrifices? The bosses are still lining their own nests.'

'There won't be any nests left soon,' the biker said. 'Everything's falling to bits. If you ask me, the whole fucking country's fucked.'

'Aye, but who's responsible?' Greatcoat insisted. 'You can't blame

51

the NUM for defending their members' interests. You've got to blame Heath and his cronies.'

'Moscow's interests, more like,' the biker said.

'You think the NUM's been infiltrated?' Duffelcoat said, suddenly enlivened.

'Aye, I do,' the biker said.

'No way, man,' Greatcoat said. 'That's bullshit. Capitalist propaganda. The system's crumbling so they need to find an external enemy. Typical diversionary tactic.'

'Everybody's been infiltrated,' the biker said. He was looking across at Mike, as if for support, even though he wasn't part of the discussion. 'The unions, the universities, the boardrooms. They're all riddled, one way or the other.'

'The political parties,' Duffelcoat said.

'Aye, sure,' the biker said. 'Them too. Commies in the Labour Party, fascists in the Tories, all kinds of weird sects in the Liberals.'

'And in the SNP,' Duffelcoat said.

'What's wrong with being a communist?' Greatcoat said. '*I'm* a communist. I'm a Trotskyist actually – a *true* communist.'

'Nobody's what they seem,' the biker said. And he glanced over at Mike again.

'Plenty of nutters in the SNP, eh?' Duffelcoat said. He'd clocked the biker's glance and followed it. Mike felt he was being assessed in two different ways. There was something about the way Duffelcoat watched everybody.

'Oh, don't let me get started on them,' Greatcoat said.

'No, don't,' the big man next to Mike said under his breath.

'The Scottish Nutter Party,' the biker said.

'Tartan Tories,' Greatcoat said. 'What's the difference between a London capitalist and a Scottish capitalist? Four hundred miles and a kilt. The SNP are a bunch of wankers.'

'That's not what they seem to think in Govan,' Mike said, surprising himself as much as the others. The previous week the SNP had triumphed over Labour in a by-election in Glasgow Govan. It was a depressed, deprived, overwhelmingly working-class constituency and it should have been rock-solid for Labour. But a feisty young woman called Margo MacDonald had snatched the seat for the SNP with a 26 per cent swing.

Greatcoat seemed to welcome somebody new to argue with. 'A one-off,' he said. 'If you ask me, they were voting with their dicks. They were mesmerised by the blonde bombshell.'

'Even the women?' Mike said.

'Very funny,' Greatcoat said. 'Listen, it was a by-election, a flash in the pan. They'll come to their senses. The last thing the Scottish worker needs is to be diverted from the class struggle by pipe dreams about independence.'

'What about Vietnam?' Mike said. 'Or Ireland? I take it you're not opposed to them being independent countries?'

Greatcoat rolled his eyes at the biker. 'Listen to Robert the Bruce,' he said. 'That's totally fucking different. I mean, come *on*, man!'

The biker seemed in two minds about whose view to favour. Duffelcoat was staring at the smoke-yellowed ceiling.

'It's just that I've noticed,' Mike said, 'that there's always one rule for Scotland when it comes to independence, and another rule for everyone else.'

He was aware that the big man had turned slightly and was listening to what he was saying. It made him nervous.

'In Vietnam,' Greatcoat said, with the patience he might show a small child, 'the class struggle and the anti-imperialist struggle are the same thing. The SNP isn't a working-class movement, it's a bourgeois pressure group.'

'Oh,' Mike said. 'My mistake then. I hadn't realised.' He was trying to be ironic, but Greatcoat seemed to take it as an admission of ideological backsliding and gave him a patronising smile. Greatcoat and the biker moved on to some new subject. Mike stepped away.

The big man had ordered himself another pint. As the barman was pouring it the man nudged Mike and nodded towards the singer, who was retuning his guitar between songs.

'This guy, he's aw right, ye ken, he's got a no bad voice and he kens some good songs, but they're no really inside him, he disna sing them frae his guts.'

The man's eyes, which had seemed narrow with menace, widened now as if he had merely been half-asleep. Altogether friendlier.

'I wouldn't know,' Mike said.

'He's had to learn them aw and it shows in the way he sings them.'

As if he was saying, Don't you worry about that tosser.

'But surely everybody has to do that?' Mike said. 'Learn them?'

'Aye, that's right,' the man said. 'But wi some folk a song gets right deep doon inside and then when it comes back oot ye can tell that's where it's been. And wi other folk it just gets skin-deep and nae mair.'

There was a quiet intensity about the way he spoke, the look in his eyes, which suggested he knew what he was talking about. It didn't sound like snobbery. It sounded like expert analysis.

'I've learned scores o songs,' the man said, 'hundreds o them, but I've done it frae listening tae other folk singing them, and this boy's learned his frae a book or aff a record.'

The barman put the pint in front of him. 'There ye go, Walter. Staying in town the night?'

The man handed over a couple of coins. 'Aye, at my sister's. I've been putting a new sink in her bathroom. Trouble is, I'm on the settee and it's no wide enough for me. I'll need to anaesthetise masel or I'll never sleep. So maybe I'll drap in on Jean Barbour efter this, see what's what. Crash oot there insteid.'

'How's Jean?' the barman said. 'Hivna seen her for ages.'

'Same as ever,' the man called Walter said. 'The world may come to an end, and Jean'll be sitting among the wreckage, telling us how it happened.'

'You're right there,' the barman said.

'Did you say "Jean Barbour"?' Mike said.

Walter looked at him. 'Aye.'

'Does she stay down the Royal Mile somewhere?'

'She does, aye.'

'I'm supposed to look her up. She's an old friend of my dad's.'

Walter said, 'She's an old friend of a lot of folk, Jean. What's your name?'

'Michael Pendreich. Mike. My dad knew her years ago.'

'D'ye ken her yersel?'

'I don't even know where she stays. It's just when I heard her name . . .'

'I'll take ye doon there,' he said, 'when this place shuts.'

It was coming on for ten o'clock, closing time. Walter said they should buy a carry-out and take it to Jean's as a way of extending the evening.

'Will it not be a bit late?' Mike asked.

'Ach away, man. That woman never sleeps. Dinna fash.'

Walter was from Ayrshire originally, but had come east and now stayed in Dalkeith, a few miles to the south of Edinburgh. Mining country, he said, although there were hardly any pits left now, just the big ones, Monktonhall and Bilston Glen, and the Lady Victoria at Newtongrange. He was talking about places just a short bus ride outside the city but the names meant nothing to Mike. Walter was a plumber by day and a singer by night. He'd always had a good voice, he said, could belt out any number of songs, when he was an apprentice in the 1950s he'd sung in a skiffle band but it hadn't come to anything, it had only been a ploy to attract women. 'In thae days, if ye were a working-class boy and ye wanted a better kind o life than the one that was mapped oot for ye, there was just two ways o daein it: ye could become a professional footballer, if ye were skilled enough, or ye could become a professional boxer, if ye were hard enough. And then this third opportunity came along: ye could form a band and sing your way tae glory if ye were bonnie enough. Weel, I wasna skilled or hard or bonnie enough for ony o thae things, sae I became a plumber. But then something amazing happened. I was on a job doon at Lauder, on the road tae England, and I was there for aboot a week wi a couple o other boys, up and doon the road every day, and on the last day, when we'd finished the job, we went for a few pints in a pub afore we came back up the road. And there was this auld man there, and he just started singing. There was a wee lull in the general noise, ye ken, and he started singing intae that space. The haill pub went silent as he sang, he didna hae the best voice, it was auld and quavery and a bit flat but by Christ he had us aw spellbound, we aw listened, even the guys that were wi me, on and on he went, verse efter verse efter verse, a story aboot a sister and her lover, and her brothers killing him because he wasna good enough for her, and her defiance when the faither tried tae mairry her aff tae another man. Weel, I'd never heard anything like it in my life, and when he was done I went over and bought the auld fellow a drink and asked him aboot it. It was a ballad, he said, "The Dowie Dens o Yarrow", and he sang some verses frae a couple mair, just tae gie me a taste o them, he said they were hundreds o years auld but the odd thing was, they were brand new tae me and yet I kent them. How d'ye reckon that, eh? I *kent* them. See, where I grew up ye had tae fight tae survive, and it was aw different faimlies, different clans if ye like, and there were these codes ye had tae ken, and if ye stepped ower the mark you were for it. Weel, I was often ower the mark, and I was often for it. I was a right scrapper, and tae tell ye the truth I enjoyed it. There were things I would fight for and things I wouldna. I would fight ower a woman, I would fight if somebody kicked my dug, I'd fight if my faimly was insulted or if I thought somebody was lying tae me, or if there was a debt that hadna been paid or a score that had tae be settled. But I wouldna fight onybody because of fitbaw or religion or politics, because I didna think they were worth it, and I wouldna fight a man just because he was drunk and wanted tae fight, I would walk away frae that. I was sure o mysel, ken, I didna *hae* tae fight, but I liked tae. And here was this auld man in the pub singing these ancient ballads, and the stuff that was in them, weel, he could hae been singing aboot the places I grew up in. That stuff happened aw the time, just wi nae weapons – or different weapons. So he tellt me aboot fairs and festivals where I could hear mair o these songs, no just in the Borders but all over Scotland and in England tae, and I started tae spend my spare time at these gatherings and learning the auld ballads. And the thing is, the mair I learned, the mair it seemed I already kent them. They were in me, but I just hadna kent they were. And something else, the mair I sang them, the less I wanted tae fight. It was the days of the big CND marches against Polaris, and the singing and the protesting kind o went thegither, there was a big overlap, and I found myself on marches tae the Holy Loch and suchlike, so half the time I was singing all these bloodthirsty songs aboot battles and murder and the other half I was singing anti-war songs but either way it stopped me fighting. I canna mind the last time I was in a fight, but it's years ago. I dinna hae time tae fight noo. There's no enough time tae learn aw the songs.'

They bought half a dozen bottles of beer and clinked down the street. Greatcoat was still at it when they left, arguing about everything. The biker looked over his shoulder at Mike as they went.

So what was Jean Barbour like, Mike wanted to know. 'Ach, she's a fine woman, ye'll get on great wi her,' Walter said. She wasn't from Edinburgh originally, she was from Argyll, somewhere over that way. Well, her ancestors were. Or were they? Now that he thought about it, was there not something about Glasgow too, and the Highlands? The way she went on, you were always picking up information about her and you always swore that this time you weren't going to forget it, but you did somehow. Some folk said she had a bit of tinker in her, quite a bit in fact, and that would explain her ability to tell a tale, but not how she'd come to own this house in the middle of Edinburgh. And not how she spoke either, her voice and her accent seemed to shift all the time depending on what she was saying. Oh, you would hear some bonnie tales if you listened long enough to Jean Barbour, so you would.

'Pay attention now,' Walter said, and lumbered off through a narrow entry. Mike had to negotiate something at his feet that had earlier been somebody's dinner, then followed through the half-dark, trying to run a mental thread from the street to a door where he found Walter working the bell pull as if he were raking out a fire. After a minute the door opened and a pale female face looked out at them.

'Oh, it's yersel, Walter, in ye come.'

'Thanks, Maggie,' Walter said, and Maggie stood aside and shut the door behind them and they were in, down a passage and into a smoky, shadowy room around which a number of bodies were seated and sprawled. There was a general murmur of conversation. A boy was strumming a guitar while a couple of girls sang along to the chords, quietly and not very confidently. Mike and Walter stood in a space in the middle of the room and Walter put the carry-out down on a big table.

'Is that you, Walter Fleming?' said a wee woman in an armchair by the fire.

'Aye, it is.'

'About bloody time. It's weeks since you were here. I'm glad to see you've not come empty-handed. But you've brought more than drink with you.'

'This is Mike. I found him in Sandy Bell's. Mike, this is Jean.'

'Hello, Mike. Make yourself at home. Clear some space, boys and girls. Dinna make him stand there like a stookie.'

People shifted themselves. Conversations restarted. Walter opened two bottles of beer and passed one to Mike. The imperious wee woman summoned him.

'Come and talk to me. How do you have the misfortune to have fallen in with Walter?'

He stepped over people to reach her.

'Sit, sit,' she said, and he squeezed himself down at the side of her chair.

'We just started talking in the pub,' he said.

'Was he not singing?' she asked.

'No.'

'Well, he does. That's a treat in store for you. He's one of the best. If I didn't know otherwise, I'd swear he learned the muckle sangs at his mother's knee in a tent or a caravan. And what about yourself? You look like a boringly sensible young man. Tell me something that'll surprise me.'

'Well,' Mike said, 'I think you used to know my dad. A long time ago.'

'Oh? Who's your dad then?'

'Angus Pendreich.'

There was a lamp on a small table on the other side of her chair, the shade turned to the wall. Jean tilted it the other way so the light shone full on his face.

'Now that *is* a surprise,' she said. 'And then again, it isn't. When you came in the room I thought, I've seen that face before. Angus's son. Good God.'

She studied him a little more. 'I see his name every so often. He's still doing well, it seems. Very successful. Famous, even.'

'I never really think of him like that,' Mike said.

'And how is he, leaving aside the fame and fortune? How is he in himself?'

'He's fine. I shouldn't think he's changed much.'

'I haven't seen him for many a year. Where is he these days?'

'He's always on the move. London, Glasgow. He has a place in the Highlands too.'

'Lucky him. And your mother, how's she?'

'You know her as well?'

'Not really. I only met her once.'

'They're divorced. They split up years ago.'

'Yes, I knew that. They weren't right for each other. Did she find anybody else?'

'No.'

'I bet *he* has.'

'He's good at finding them,' Mike said, 'but he doesn't keep them.'

'That's Angus, right enough,' she said. 'And what about yourself? Do you have somebody?'

He put a hand up to shield his eyes from the glare of the light. 'No.'

She turned the lamp away. 'You will,' she said. 'With those looks you'll be fighting them off. Anyway, that's not for now. We'll have a proper talk some other time. Whenever you speak to your father next, say hello for me, won't you?'

'I will,' Mike said. 'He was asking for you, by the way.'

'I should bloody think so.' She raised her voice. 'Walter!'

Walter had found himself a seat by the table and was chatting to the girl who'd let them in.

'What?'

'You don't get to sit down in here without a song. Leave Maggie alone and give us a song.'

'Tell us a story,' Walter retorted.

'I call the shots around here,' Jean said. 'Wheesht, everybody. Walter's going to sing.'

Walter cleared his throat and sang. He had a slow, gentle voice and he sang two or three slow, gentle songs. One had a chorus that everybody but Mike seemed to know. The room swelled and ebbed with the sound of it. People clapped. Somebody else sang something. Then somebody else, as if an invisible plate of songs were being passed around. Mike leaned against the side of the armchair, part of what was going on and yet not part of it. He said nothing. It was his first time in such company, and he saw that he had much to learn.

§

'There are good listeners and there are those that are not so good at listening,' Jean said. 'If you know what you're doing, if the story you're telling is good enough, you can hook them all, some more securely than others but you can hook each and every one of them. But sometimes you get the awkward buggers, the fykie folk that can't sit still at all, they fidget away and pick their nebs and shift their bums from side to side, they're bored or they want to be the centre of attention – something I deplore, of course –' she said with a sly look, 'or maybe they can't help themselves, they just want to know the end of the story long before you've got to it.' She fixed her eyes on somebody who'd been a bit restless. 'Once a few years back I was telling a story and there was a young lad sitting just where you're sitting, he kept looking at his watch and half-rising to go and then sitting back down but he couldn't settle, I knew he really wanted to be away but he couldn't bear to leave, he was that anxious to know what happened. But he was spoiling it for everybody else.' So Jean broke off from her telling – it was a story about young Jack, who was off on his adventures as usual, seeking good fortune and life-long happiness – and she asked the lad what ailed him. 'Oh,' he says, 'it's just that I've an exam I should be revising for, and I need to get back to my books.' He was a student, you see, and he'd come away from the library for an hour but Jean's story was taking more than an hour to tell and he didn't want to go without hearing the end. So she says to him, 'Look, I'll not be finished here for a while, if you don't have the patience to hear the whole thing you should just leave now while you can.' But he wasn't content with that, he was eager to know the end of it, so she says, 'If you want to know what happens to Jack, go through that door there to the kitchen, my old Aunt Greta's in there making the tea, ask her what happens at the end of the story, and then you can just slip out and not disturb us any more.' Well, nobody knew that Jean had an Aunt Greta but, anyway, away through to the kitchen goes the student, and there's a wee wifie barely four foot tall with a scarf on her head and big jangly earrings, making the tea, and she looks up and says to him, 'Aye, what is it you want?' in a sharp voice. He says, 'I've come to ask you what happens at the end of Jean's story.' 'What story's that?' the wee wifie says. 'The one she's telling just now,' he says. 'Well, what's it about?' He says, 'It's about a fellow called Jack and all his adventures.' 'Och, that story,' she says, 'it goes on for ever that one.' 'Aye,' he says, 'and I can't stay to hear the end of it, I have to go away now to do some studying, but Jean told me to come through and ask you what happens.' 'Och, I never heard the end of that story yet,' says Aunt Greta, 'so I canna help you. But if you go through that door and along the passage, the first room you come to, my auld mither bides in there, and she'll maybe ken what happens.'

There was this other door out of the kitchen, not the one he came in by, so away he goes through it and down the passage, and the first door he comes to he chaps and he goes in. It's a dark room with the curtains pulled, just a chink of light coming in, and in the corner of the room is a big old armchair, with someone sitting in it. So he goes up to her, it's an auld, auld woman, even wee-er than Aunt Greta, all runkled and shrunken, staring at him through a pair of glasses thick as bottles, her eyes are all screwed up but she can see him all right in the darkness. 'Who are you,' she says, 'and what do you want?' So he goes through the same thing, telling her about Jean's story and how Aunt Greta had sent him through because she didn't know the end of the story, and the auld woman gives a frown that ripples her forehead up like a beach when the tide goes out and she says, 'Well, I never heard the end of that story either, but if you go further down the passage there's another room where my auld mither bides, she's an invalid in her bed but she kens all the stories, she'll maybe can help you.' So away he goes to the next room, there's an iron bedstead heaped up with blankets and it's very dark but he can just make out, in the middle of the bed, a tiny body, all grey skin and sticking-out bones, almost like a skeleton and barely three foot long, and with just wee scraps of white hair on the skull. The boy's awfie feart by this stage but he's come this far so he leans over and clears his throat, gives a wee cough, and these vicious wee eyes open in the skull and a voice that seems to come from the depths of the blankets croaks, 'Who are you and what do you want?' He tells this strange, half-dead creature the whole thing and she lies there staring at him hatefully and then she says, 'I never heard the end of *that* story. If you want to ken the end of *that* one you'll need to go next door and ask my auld mither, she's asleep in the kist at the end of the bed.' And he goes to the next room and in there it's just an iron bedstead, no blankets, no pillows, no mattress, just the old bed with the springs, as if somebody used to sleep there but they've died or gone away or something, and the laddie looks in the gloom and right enough there's an old kist at the end of the bed, so he goes to lift up the lid, it's like a coffin, and inside there's this wee cot, with a creature no bigger than a doll lying in it, and if the last one was thin, well, the flesh on this one is stretched so tight you can actually see the bones through it, and under the bones the vital

61

organs working away. And the student is terrified but he can't turn back now so he leans right in and calls out and at once these two piercing eyes are staring out at him. 'Who are you and what do you want?' It's as if the voice is coming from a hole in the floor. He starts to explain but she cuts him off after just a few seconds. 'How would I ken the end of that story? You'll need to ask my auld mither and you'll be lucky if you get an answer at all she's that auld and crabbit.' He asks her where he can find her and she says, 'Lift out the shoebox that's lying at the other end of the kist, she's in there.' So he finds this shoebox, just a simple cardboard shoebox, and he takes it out and slowly, oh so slowly, he removes the lid. At first he thinks there's nothing there, there's just a lot of auld yellowish cotton wool. And then to his horror he sees that there are three things lying on the cotton wool: an ear, an eye and a mouth. That's all, just an ear, an eye and a mouth. And the eye is staring at him with a venomous look, and the mouth says, 'Who are you and what do you want?' so he leans right down and puts his own lips to the lug and tells his story, starting with Jean telling him to go through to her Aunt Greta, but after a sentence or two the mouth interrupts. 'No,' it says, 'begin at the beginning.' So he goes further back, to when he arrived at the house that evening, but the mouth says, 'No, further. Begin at the beginning.' So he goes back to when he first started at the university and what he was studying, but the mouth breaks in again, 'No, before that.' So he goes back to his childhood, and then to his earliest memories, and then to his parents, and how they met, and where they came from, and who *their* parents were, and his great-grandparents, he goes back as far as he can in his family history, and when he's run out of ancestors the mouth says, 'And what happened before *that*?' and he finds he's telling the lug everything he knows about history and prehistory and geology until he finally runs out of words. He's exhausted and close to greeting, and the mouth says, 'And what happened before *that*?' 'I don't know,' he says, 'I don't know.' 'And *I* don't know how the story *ends*!' the mouth shrieks, and it starts to cackle, and the eye never blinks, just stares at him all the while the mouth is cackling, and at that his nerves are in tatters, he can't stand it any more, he shoves the lid back on the shoebox and throws it in the kist and slams the kist shut and rushes out of that room and down the passage with that horrible laugh in his ears and he runs out of the house and back on to the street and, do you know, Jean said, that young laddie has never shown his face in this house again.

§

Mike did. He turned up regularly, sometimes alone, sometimes with other stray seekers after traditions in which they wished to be included. Jean and the Old Town seemed to go together. She was part of the magic of the city, a benevolent spider at its heart, fascinating, witchlike, imperishable.

Even the journey you had to make to visit her was something of an otherworldly experience. It took Mike two or three shots before he felt confident of the way. Her house was hidden, deep in where the tourists didn't penetrate. It was a flat but it had a door all to itself and, though there must have been neighbours above and to either side of her, you never heard or saw them. You reached the door via a close, a courtyard, another close and a stone stair, and you never seemed to arrive there twice by quite the same route. The noise of traffic and people died away as you made your way from the street, and it was as if you were also stepping out of the moment, going a long way back in time or maybe forward. And the door was dark and low and no matter how many times you'd rung the bell before it always seemed, as you waited to be let in, that it could only open on to a cramped, narrow place, two or three rooms at most. But the house was larger somehow on the inside than on the outside, as if over the centuries it had grown tired of being constrained by the stone walls and had shouldered and stretched itself into more comfortable dimensions. There was a big hallway and a passage that led to three bedrooms. There was a kitchen with a range and a dresser filled with plates and dishes, pots and glassware, and a pine table that could seat twelve. There was a bathroom, panelled from floor to ceiling in dark wood, with an enormous bath resting on clawed feet right in the middle, a sink you could have washed a large dog in, and a toilet with an overhead cistern that whistled and spluttered like a toothless man in his sleep. And then there was the 'front room', which actually was at the back, looking out over a jumble of slates, skylights, lum-pots, crow steps and TV aerials to Salisbury Crags, through three windows under each of

63

which sat a cast-iron radiator with ribs like tubas. The house lived under layers of dust and piles of books, papers, clothes, records and anything else Jean couldn't be bothered to put away, but 'If I can look out on that view,' she used to say, 'I know I'm still here. I know I'm still in the world.' It was a weird observation, but in that secret, misshapen house, where time and location seemed habitually distorted, it more or less made sense.

As Angus had promised, there was always something going on at Jean's, always one or two familiar faces, and always one or two new ones. Walter Fleming might be there, or some other performer; and sometimes they would bring others from elsewhere: a Cape Breton fiddler, a Nigerian poet – once, an Egyptian oud player who appeared unannounced, played and smiled without cease for two hours and was never seen by anybody again. And, as well as such entertainment, there was talk: talk of literature, history, art, music, travel and – more than anything – political talk. Mike had never come across such enthusiasm for political debate, especially when it revolved around questions of national identity and self-determination. There was none of Greatcoat's dismissiveness when it came to these matters. Arguments were plentiful – often conducted at maximum volume and with the most outrageous insults traded between otherwise perfectly good friends – and occasionally they degenerated into brief, ridiculous fights, but for most of the people who came to Jean's the 'Scottish question' was as integral to their political thinking as any other issue. They were in the world, they were of the world, that's what they thought and felt.

Mike was in the habit of taking his camera with him wherever he went, and he began to take photographs of the drinking, the smoking, the singing, the arguing, the hugging and the kissing. Nobody seemed to object to him doing this.

One night he was astonished to see Duffelcoat from Sandy Bell's hunched up against one of the radiators, just behind an easygoing pair of students he knew slightly, who'd formed a vaguely nationalistic whisky-drinking club called the Clan Alba Society. Mike didn't recognise him at first because he'd taken the duffelcoat off. The man caught his eye and nodded, with that same calculating look he'd had in the pub, then leaned back into the Clan Alba boys' conversation as if he were part of it. There was something disconcerting about the watchful, sharp eyes, the paunch, the thick but unfashionably short hair, the nervousness that was also somehow cynicism, the grey trousers, collared shirt and V-necked green pullover: he looked too old and too young simultaneously, and he sent out some kind of signal that he didn't want his picture taken, and Mike didn't take it. There were lots of misfits at Jean's, but Duffelcoat didn't even fit among the misfits.

There was a Highland crew, mostly female. They were from various different places – Skye, Inverness, Dingwall, Brora – but they had a camaraderie and a fierce loyalty to one another that impressed Mike. The ones from Sutherland were themselves impressed that Mike had not only heard of places like Kinlochbervie and Tongue but had actually been in them. Some of the girls had sung in school choirs at the Mod; they could still sing the songs even though most of them didn't speak Gaelic. And they were all full of a play that had been touring the village halls earlier that year, which seemed to have entered their collective consciousness: *The Cheviot, the Stag and the Black, Black Oil*. This stirred something in his memory, he recalled posters stuck up on noticeboards that summer, but he and Angus hadn't been to see it. How could you have missed it? they berated him, it was brilliant. Some of them had seen it three times. It was about the destruction of Gaelic culture after the Battle of Culloden, the clearing of people from the glens to make way for sheep, the evil factor Patrick Sellar and the big landowners he worked for like the Duke of Sutherland, the huge estates they had for deer stalking and grouse shooting and salmon fishing, and now the North Sea was full of oil and *that* was going to be exploited too, only by the Americans this time, and would the *real* people of the Highlands reap anything but a fraction of the rewards? Would they buggery! The play had been put on by a theatre company called 7:84. 'What?' '7:84.' 'Why's it called that?' 'Because 7 per cent of the population owns 84 per cent of the country's wealth! Do you not know *any*-thing, Mike?' they screamed, half-angry and half-laughing at his naivety. 'Not much,' he said, and took a photograph of them screaming at him.

There was one girl, as bright and bubbly as he was shy and with-drawn, a real beauty, Catriona MacKay from Inverness. He liked her more than the others. She loved to get drunk, and he didn't mind joining her, although it took a lot less alcohol to put him on the floor than it did her. That autumn they spent more and more time together, at Jean's and elsewhere. Sisterly, brotherly love, or the love of two drinking cronies, but with the promise of something else in it . . .

His digs weren't working out and Jean took pity on him and occasionally let him sleep in one of her spare rooms when he couldn't face going back. Mrs Petrie, his landlady, was well into her seventies and her ability to cope with life was sinking under the weight of her years just as her house – the lower half of a crumbling Victorian villa – seemed to be sinking under the ever-lengthening list of repairs both it and the upper level needed. The rent was cheap but there were reasons: the sheets were damp and the rooms cold, and there was only ever lukewarm water for the bath. Mrs Petrie provided a breakfast of cornflakes, thin blue milk and suspect, cardboardy toast that he got into the habit of scraping with his knife in case of mould. The butter was rancid, the cutlery was greasy and the dining room smelled of mice. There was another lodger, a medical student called Eric Hodge. They had to be out of the place by nine in the morning and weren't supposed to come back before five, and although they each had a Yale key for the front door Mrs Petrie had a security chain that went on at eleven every night. Fortunately, by creeping down next-door's drive, climbing over the wrought-iron fence and through Eric's bedroom window, using a knife they kept in the garden for the purpose of unsnecking the catch, they could come and go as they wished, but it wasn't convenient. Mrs Petrie was deaf, dirty and obstinate, and whatever pity they might have felt for her was erased by hatred of her petty tyrannies.

On the weekend the clocks went back, when they should have had an extra hour in bed, Mrs Petrie put *her* clock forward and roused them for breakfast at six-thirty. She refused to believe them when they protested, and when they made her listen to the seven-o'clock news on the radio she accused them of conspiring to send her mad and have her locked up. Eric the medic said that could easily be arranged. She shut herself in her room and the two of them started to look elsewhere for accommodation. Mike half-hoped that Jean might take them in but she said no, the only permanent resident of her house was herself, that was how it had always been and that was how she preferred it. By the end of November Eric and Mike had found a two-bedroom flat near Tollcross.

At Christmas Mike went back to Doune – 'Doom', Angus had taken to calling it, more or less from the minute he left – to spend a chilly week with his mother. He resented having to go, resented being an only child, resented his father for being back from America but not being at home. He was in Sutherland, or Glasgow, or London, wherever the hell he was it wasn't Doom. Mike missed Catriona but not with passion and he knew this represented a crisis of some sort. He looked at himself in the bathroom mirror, wondering who he was and whether to try to train his desire or let it off the leash entirely. When he went back to Edinburgh, he decided, things were going to be different.

Relations with Isobel were strained, as usual. She was convinced that the country was about to succumb to revolutionary socialism. Her own circumstances encouraged this belief: just on the edge of the really rich county set, she shared their views and opinions but lacked their financial and architectural insulation from real or imagined political troubles. She found crushed lager cans and cigarette packets in her front garden and interpreted these as menacing signals from the Perthshire proletariat. Every flicker and dim of electric light was a portent of class war.

Mike had a war of his own going on inside him and showed her no sympathy; she, quite rightly, thought he was siding with the enemy. Fired up by Catriona's rants against Highland landowners, he managed to upset his mother two days before Christmas by describing Sir Alec Douglas-Home as an antique joke. Home was Ted Heath's Foreign Secretary, and Isobel had a sighing respect for him, tinged with mourning because he was having to deal with the Chinese and the dreadful natives who wanted to take over Rhodesia. 'How can you say he's a joke?' Isobel said. 'He used to be the Prime Minister!' 'Exactly,' Mike said, and they argued about privilege and wealth until Isobel went to bed with a headache.

On Christmas Eve she said, 'You won't want to come to church tomorrow morning, will you.'

It was more a statement than a question. He couldn't work out if she didn't want him to join her or was already disappointed that he wouldn't. 'Wasn't intending to,' he said.

'That's fine,' she said swiftly. It seemed he'd given the right answer. 'I've asked Mr Syme to come back for a drink afterwards,' she hurried on, turning pink. 'You know, Mr Syme, along the road. He's a widower. I feel sorry for him spending Christmas on his own. Do you mind?'

'You've already asked him,' Mike said, 'so what difference does it make if I mind or not?'

'Don't be so ungracious,' Isobel said. 'I'm trying to be neighbourly.'

'So why don't you ask him to share the turkey with us too?'

She looked affronted, as if he'd suggested a post-service orgy. 'If you're not coming to church,' she said, 'perhaps you could get the glasses and things ready before we come back.'

'What does he drink?'

She seemed to consider this for a moment. 'Sherry, perhaps. Or whisky. I think there's some whisky.'

There was a bottle and a half of Famous Grouse in the drinks cupboard. This was odd, as Isobel didn't touch the stuff. Or maybe not so odd: Famous Grouse turned out to be Mr Syme's favourite tipple. He liked it in generous measures – 'Keep going, Michael' – and he didn't want much water in it either. He was manager of a branch of the Clydesdale Bank in Stirling, bald and plump and very genial, and in spite of being childless and having lost his wife to cancer looked like the last person Isobel needed to feel sorry for. In fact it occurred to Mike that Mr Syme might well regard Isobel, sipping her sweet sherry as if it were about to catch fire, as a charity case. Mike had hardly ever spoken to him before but he seemed quite at home in their sitting room, and didn't have to ask where the downstairs toilet was. He also seemed to know quite a lot about Mike.

'I gather you're a bit of a Scottish Nationalist,' he said. 'A bit of a radical too. So your mother tells me anyway.'

Mike was drinking a beer. He looked over the rim of his tumbler at her. 'Am I?'

'You're almost a red,' she said. 'But don't let's talk politics today of all days.'

Mr Syme, however – 'Call me Bob, Michael' – was desperate to talk politics.

'I must be the Antichrist as far as you're concerned,' he said. 'A bank manager! God help us! You probably want to string people like me up on lamp-posts.' He said this with a beaming smile and considerable relish.

'No, not really,' Mike said.

'Aye you do,' Bob insisted. 'You want to string us up.' He took a slug of whisky, as if to buck himself up enough to face his own brutal murder, and resurfaced radiant as a martyr. 'You may not think so but that's what it would come to. Believe you me, Michael, I'm the first to admit the system, as you call it' – Mike hadn't in fact called it anything – 'the system isn't perfect, but it's the best one we have. You can put another system in its place and it won't work, it'll just create misery and mayhem, and you know who'll suffer the most? The people at the bottom of the heap. They always suffer the most. People like me are insulated. We plan. We protect ourselves. Which is why we'll all end up dangling from lamp-posts.'

'Please, Bob, that's quite enough,' Isobel said.

'It's all right, Isobel, we're not going to come to blows, are we, Michael? Anyway, we're not that different underneath. I used to be a bit of a rebel myself when I was your age. I think it's perfectly normal for you to have these ideas, it's probably a good thing. But I guarantee, in twenty years – ten years – you don't believe in socialism any more.'

Mike laughed. 'I don't think I really said –'

But Bob wasn't letting him off the hook. 'Tell you what,' he said. 'I'll bet you. Ten quid. In ten years you'll say to me, "Bob, you were right, I've grown out of it."'

'I don't bet,' Mike said.

'Spoken like a true comrade,' Bob said. 'Surprised you're not teetotal. But it won't last. Ten years I give you, if that.' He twisted in his armchair to fish for his wallet, pulled out two Clydesdale Bank fivers, and slapped them on the table between them. 'There. Just to prove I'm not a heartless bastard. You're an impoverished student, I'm a banker. We'll make it a one-sided wager. You have that ten quid now, for party funds and I'll not ask whether it's the revolutionary party or the all-night party, and if you're still a socialist in ten years, you can pay me back. With inflation the way it is, you can't lose.'

'That's so kind of you, Bob,' Isobel said. 'Isn't it, Michael?'

'Happy Christmas,' Bob said.

'Happy Christmas,' Isobel said, and giggled.

Mike left the money on the table but they all knew he'd take it. 'Happy Christmas,' he said, feeling thoroughly depressed.

There was a silence, and into it Isobel inserted her own bit of festive madness. 'Here's to Iona,' she said. Mike stared at her. Why was she toasting an island? Bob seemed a bit nonplussed too, then recovered. 'Iona,' he said. Isobel turned and mouthed at Mike, *'Bob's wife.'* 'Oh,' Mike said. 'To Iona,' he said.

Bob sat looking appropriately glum for all of ten seconds. They all did. Then Bob had had enough.

'Well,' he said, 'Iona didn't like Christmas much anyway. Thought it was all a bit pointless without kiddies. But *I'm* enjoying myself. Happy Christmas.'

What depressed Mike wasn't that Bob Syme was a windbag. He was, but he was quite an amiable windbag. It was that he stayed three houses along the road and was therefore geographically the most convenient single man his mother could have picked. Mike could tell that she found Bob a wee bit *coorse*, and that this, perversely, gave her a thrill. The way he said he wasn't a heartless bastard: he was like a rotund version of Mike's father, with all the grace and danger removed. Was that what she wanted? And what was in it for Bob? Isobel had been a beauty in her twenties, and was still good-looking, but did Bob see anything else in her? They seemed happy together. Mike couldn't work it out. If he had, he might have suspected himself of envy.

By Hogmanay he'd had enough of Doom. He caught a bus back to Edinburgh. Midnight found him in a hot, beery, sweaty crush at the Tron Kirk on the High Street. The ceilidh at Jean's that followed went on till dawn, 1974.

§

That was the night Walter Fleming sang a song called 'The Wee Magic Stane'. Before he did, he had to explain what it was about, since most people in the room hadn't been born when the event it celebrated happened. It was, Walter said, a true story that became a myth even as it was unfolding. Early on Christmas Day, 1950, somebody broke into Westminster Abbey and removed the great block of sandstone known as the Stone of Destiny or the Stone of Scone from its place under the coronation chair behind the altar. It had been there since 1296, when Edward I of England had carried it south from Scone as a trophy of war and a symbol of his dominion over the kingdom of the Scots. Tradition held that the Scottish kings had been crowned on this stone for centuries before that, so whenever an English sovereign sat over it, he or she was effectively renewing Edward's claims on Scotland. And since the Union of Crowns in 1603, the presence of the stone under the chair at every coronation had reinforced the idea that the two nations were joined in perpetuity under one monarch. But in 1950 somebody challenged that notion by levering it out of its space and making it disappear, and this was what the song was about.

It had a jaunty tune, familiar and easy, but to Mike the humour was quaint and old-fashioned, the words far removed from a land working at 60 per cent capacity and regularly being plunged into darkness. The comic point of the song was that only the Dean of Westminster believed the wee stane had any magic attached to it: the Scots, who were supposed to invest it with all this significance, just thought the whole escapade was a great joke and carry-on. To Mike it seemed an irrelevance. Why make such a fuss about a bit of rock? Yet, from the way Walter described it, an enormous fuss was exactly what had ensued.

Then Jean chipped in. 'Of course there was an aftermath,' she said. 'Removing the thing was all very well, but what did you do with it then? Bury it? Hand it back? Let me tell you what happened. It had broken in two when it was taken, and the two bits were moved around separately for a while, a step or two ahead of the hunt, and eventually they were reunited in a stonemason's yard in Glasgow. The stonemason was a city cooncillor, and he repaired the stone. He knew what he was doing because years before there'd been a scheme to take the Westminster stone and the cooncillor had made a couple of replicas of it in connection with that plot, which had come to nothing. So this meant, if you believe the rumours of the time, that there were two other stones in existence while the police were hunting for the missing one.

'The King, George VI, was not a well man, he had lung cancer and various other ailments and there was a certain anxiety among the high heid yins of the realm that if George died and his daughter Elizabeth succeeded him without being crowned sitting on top of this lump of sandstone it would invalidate the process in some way. So the authorities were keen to get the matter resolved as quickly as possible. It was an open secret by this time that a group of Glasgow students was involved, and they were brought in for questioning by the police. One minute they were warned of the dire consequences of holding out, the next they were promised they'd be let off with a wee slap. In those days the methods of the Glasgow constabulary were infamous. They would use every trick in the book – sectarian chanting, reading the *People's Friend* out loud, Chinese burns, dead legs – there wasn't much they wouldn't do to get what they wanted. One of the students was subjected to hours of interrogation under a bright light until eventually he cracked. "All right," he said, "turn the light off and I'll tell you who stole it." They turned the light off. "Right, who stole it?" He looked at them grimly. "Edward I."

'Well, something had to be done to bring the stand-off to an end. These four students couldn't get on with the rest of their lives until it was. So negotiations were entered into, with sympathetic members of the Scottish establishment acting as brokers, and a plan was hatched that would enable the stone to reappear without anybody being arrested or prosecuted for handling what the government deemed to be stolen goods.

'One morning in April 1951, a car drives up to the entrance of the ruined Arbroath Abbey, and three men get out: two young fellows and an older man, the Glasgow cooncillor. They must be expected, because there are two Arbroath cooncillors already there. And the janny, the keeper of the abbey, is there too, in his peaked cap and uniform, watching proceedings, but maybe he's been pre-warned because he makes no attempt to interfere.

'Why have they come to Arbroath? Because the abbey is associated with the Declaration of Arbroath, a letter sent by the Scottish nobility to the Pope in 1320, asserting not only Scottish independence from England but also the right of the people to overthrow any monarch who tries to surrender that independence.

'The suspension is down at the back of the car. There's a block of sandstone on the back seat. The young men unfurl a flag of St Andrew and drape it over the stone. They lift it out and set it on a wooden litter, the kind masons use. It's a great, heavy thing, this stone, a quarter of a ton it weighs, and one of the Arbroath men goes to help them. With a man at each corner of the litter, they solemnly carry the stone the length of the nave and set it down where the high altar once stood. Remember, this is a ruin, disused since the Reformation, and the folk of the town have carried away a lot of the stonework to build their own houses over the centuries, so it's a strange sight, this formal, silent ceremony being performed by a group of bareheaded men in modern clothes amid these red medieval remains. And then the three men shake hands with the two Arbroath cooncillors, and with the keeper, and they go back to their car and drive away. No names, no pack drill, as the saying goes. And one of the Arbroath cooncillors phones the local paper and tells them to get up to the abbey fast and up comes this young reporter with a camera and gets the biggest scoop in the paper's history. Later the keeper will be asked to give a description of the men. "Well-set-up lads," he'll say, but more of a description than that he is unable to give. The registration number of the car? No, sorry, he failed to note that too. You would almost think that they'd not been there at all, that the wee magic stane had just magically reappeared all by itself.'

Jean paused, looked slowly round the room, and found Mike watching her. Their gazes held.

'But an odd thing happened, something that isn't recorded in any account of the return of the stone I've ever seen. Just before the three men leave, a couple emerge from behind the south transept. A man and a woman. God knows how they got in and how long they've been there but they stroll over towards the group and the man starts whistling a tune – the very same tune that that song Walter's just sung is set to. You see, "The Wee Magic Stane" has been doing the rounds of the pubs and clubs for weeks. And it's as if the man, by whistling those notes, is giving a password or a code. And he and the young woman smile and shake the hands of everybody there and that's odd too, a handshake but nothing said, as if they're all members of some resistance movement or something. Resisting what? Who knows? And then the man and woman walk out of the gate and away, and no doubt the men in the abbey can still hear that tune being whistled in the distance.

'It was funny and yet serious. As if they were being told they'd done something symbolic and special and it was being acknowledged but without making too much fuss about it. Maybe that was what the whistling man wanted them to feel anyway.'

'How do you know about that,' someone asked, 'if you've never seen it written down? How do you know it happened?'

'Maybe it didn't,' Jean said. 'As you say, if it's not written down, where's the evidence? Maybe it didn't happen at all.'

'It was you, wasn't it?' somebody else said. 'That's the only way you could know.'

'That would be one way,' Jean said. 'Or somebody could have told me.' She smiled what Mike supposed was meant to be a disingenuous smile. 'Anyway, that's enough of that,' she said. 'Somebody give us another song.'

§

Maybe Isobel's fears were not so far-fetched. Because of the miners' action coal was in short supply and because of the railway workers' action a lot of the coal on the surface wasn't getting to the power stations. From the first day of the new year the government imposed a three-day working week on industry, to conserve energy. The speed limit on roads was restricted to fifty miles per hour. Television closed down at ten-thirty every night: people had to talk to each other instead, or read books, or go to bed. Shops ran short of bread and sugar. Power cuts were frequent. Negotiations between the TUC and the government dragged on for days, weeks, until the end of February, when Ted Heath called a General Election to decide who was in charge of the country. Mike was nineteen. He'd be able to vote for the first time.

One evening, a week before the election, he was in Sandy Bell's and the biker was there again. He wouldn't leave Mike be. It turned out he wasn't a biker at all, he just wore the leather jacket. His name was Sam and he didn't merely glance at Mike now, he stared at him as they talked, long meaningful stares, and Mike knew what they meant and he didn't want it. He wanted to find Catriona and have a drink that didn't come with complications. He wanted to go to Jean's but not with Sam tagging along. There were two Irish fiddlers and a whistle player going like madmen in the corner and a good crowd encouraging them with rounds of Guinness and applause. Sam said it wasn't really his scene, the folk music, and Mike asked what the fuck was he doing drinking in Sandy Bell's then? Sam said he liked a change and anyway the place was an institution, you had to try everything once or twice, see if you liked it. And now he'd made up his mind: he didn't. His scene was more New Town, he liked things a little more sophisticated. Mike said the Old Town was fine for him. Sam said, as if they'd made a deal, come on, I've tried this, you should try the bars down there. He named some: the Kenilworth, Paddy's, the Marquis. Mike said, no thanks. He finished his pint quickly and went to the toilet, intending to walk straight out when he came back. He did but Sam drained his glass too and caught up with Mike on the street, just before Greyfriars Bobby.

'Come on,' Sam said, crowding in on him. 'Come down the road with me. Live a little.'

'I'm not going your way,' Mike said. Sam had an arm round his shoulder. There was a crowd of students coming towards them, a couple of faces Mike knew. 'Fuck's sake,' he said, and allowed himself to be pushed into the shadows, in through the gate of Greyfriars kirkyard. There was a rough wall and Sam had him pressed up against it, one hand between Mike's legs, kneading his crotch. Mike pushed back. 'Fuck off, will you?'

'It's what you want,' Sam said.

'It fucking is not.'

'I can see it in your eyes. You want it as much as I do, you just don't know it yet, that's all.'

Mike struck down hard on Sam's wrist with one fist, slammed him in the chest with the other, and made a run for it. He reached the gate, astonished at how breathless he'd suddenly become. He wasn't being pursued. Sam was still among the gravestones, leaning on one, waiting for him.

'It's what you want,' Sam called. And Mike knew he could go back, that half the reason he was breathless was because the choice was there. But it *wasn't* what he wanted. Not like that. Not then and not there, and not with Sam.

§

They've just about finished the Highland Park. Mike shares out the last half-inch and indicates the Clynelish on the table. 'Is that wise?'

'Very unwise,' Jean says. 'But we don't have to drink it all, do we?'

Mike fetches it over, feeling the malt waves crash through him. Earlier he brought a big jug of water and a couple more glasses through from the kitchen, and when he remembers to do so he gulps down some water to offset the whisky. Jean doesn't bother. He takes the Clynelish out of its box but doesn't open it.

'If we drink even a quarter of this we will die,' he says.

'Aye we will,' Jean says. 'But we're going to anyway, remember?'

'You are. I'm not ready yet.'

'Good.'

'You've corrupted me. When I first met you I didn't drink this stuff. Made me throw up.'

'You were a bairn. You had a lot of growing up to do.'

'Aye. You're not wrong there.'

'You were still trying out lassies, if I remember correctly.'

'Couldn't make my mind up.'

'It wasn't about your mind, of course. Or it was but only because you needed to chase the fear and ignorance out of it.'

'We all needed to do that,' he says. 'You knew right away, didn't you?'

'Pretty much. Don't ask me how, and I certainly wasn't going to *tell* you. You had to find out for yourself. And you did.'

'Do you remember Catriona MacKay? Who came down from Inverness, and I thought she was the one?'

'You *thought* you thought she was the one. The lovely Catriona. Drank like a fish. Aye, I do remember her. She had a very fine voice.'

'We were almost an item for a few weeks in my first year. We really liked each other and I feel bad about it now because she didn't know what was wrong and I didn't know for certain so I couldn't tell her.'

'You don't need to feel bad about it. She was growing up too.'

'We were both so inexperienced. She was doing Languages. She was going to be a teacher. It was when the power cuts were happening because of the three-day week, and we'd been here one evening and were both a bit drunk and she said I could go back to her flat and we could save electricity by having a shower together. Remember all that stuff? Save hot water, shower with a friend? So that's what we did. She suggested it as a joke and then we both realised we were going to do it and suddenly it wasn't a joke. We hadn't even kissed properly up till then. We kissed on the way to her flat and a bit more in her bedroom and then we got undressed and went through to the bathroom. I remember we held hands crossing the hallway. If there was anybody else in the flat they were asleep. We stood in the bath under the shower in the dark until the hot water ran out and it was lovely but I knew it wasn't right. She had a beautiful body, perfect skin. I remember us kissing and the water running into our mouths and me soaping her breasts and her thighs and her bum and then her doing me, she was soaping me down there and it should have been the start of something but it wasn't. I closed my eyes and it wasn't her I imagined being there with, even though I didn't have anybody in mind it wasn't *a her*. Then we towelled each other dry and went to bed and hugged each other and she said, "Mike, is it you or is it me?" And I said, "It's me." And she said, "Yes, it is, isn't it?" which was when I really knew, for certain, and then we went to sleep and when we woke up it was like we were just friends, like I was one of her girlfriends or something, and I walked out of her flat and I finally knew who I was.'

Jean is smiling. Mike has the vague sense of having woken from a dream.

'Did I just say all that?'

'You did.'

'Jesus, I must be pissed.'

'You are.'

'Sorry.'

'Don't apologise,' Jean says. 'We're way past that.'

He smiles back at her. She even looks quite healthy again.

'The lovely Catriona,' she says. 'She was out for fun, that was clear. I wonder what happened to her.'

'She got serious in the '80s,' he says. 'Very active in Gaelic, environmentalism, land ownership, those issues. I think she gave up teaching to concentrate on all of that. She stays in Glasgow. I haven't seen her for years.' He thinks, I still have an address for her, I'll invite her to the opening.

'Those were called fringe issues back then,' Jean says. 'They're mainstream now.'

'And it's great that they are, but you lose something when you stop being on the edge. Things get sanitised, normalised. Somehow it's disappointing.'

'The realisation of hope always is. That's why the early years of devolution were such a let-down. We expected miracles and we got the mundane.'

After a few moments she goes on. 'I wonder what happened to all those other people who came through my door. Most of them were hopeful, I think. I wonder where they all ended up, and if they're disappointed. God, there were a lot of them over the years.'

And suddenly the memory clicks into place for Mike. 'Jesus, that's who that was!'

'Who what was?'

'I saw this guy today, in a café. He used to come here. I just didn't recognise him because he looked that much older. Out of context. But it was him, definitely. Duffelcoat Dick.'

'Who?'

'Do you not remember him?'

'Remind me.'

'Older than us students. He wasn't one of us, but he wasn't one of the people we came to listen to either. Like yourself, or Walter. He always wore a brown duffelcoat. I think he thought it made him look like a student, but actually it made him look like a prat. Like a middle-aged man pretending to be a schoolboy. That's what we called him, Duffelcoat Dick, but his real name was . . . No, I've forgotten.'

'Oh, him,' Jean says. 'He called himself Peter.'

'Peter, that's it. He was sitting in this café in the Grassmarket reading a paper. No duffelcoat and thirty-five years older, looking pretty rough, but it was him all right. Amazing.'

'Not really. Edinburgh's a wee place. Scotland's a wee place.'

'Aye, but still . . .'

'He was a spook,' Jean says.

'What do you mean?'

'Just that. He was a spook. A spy. He worked for the Intelligence services.'

'You're kidding.'

'I can't prove it, but I know I'm right. We were bound to attract the attention of the Brits, Mike, even though we weren't doing anything wrong. We had all sorts dropping in on us back then. It was a very worrying time for the defenders of the Union, poor dears.'

'I had no idea.'

'I told you, you were a bairn. We had one lad who used to come who'd been mixed up in some of that tartan terrorism business. His pals had bombed an oil pipeline or an electricity substation or something and he'd been on the edge of it, although I think it was mostly wishful thinking on his part.'

'We've all done our share of that,' Mike says.

'Anyway, this boy used to get drunk and talk about blowing up the Duke of Sutherland's statue at Golspie. The Highland lassies loved that idea. Do you not mind him?'

He shakes his head. 'I wasn't here all the time.'

'Well, if you had folk like that calling on you, you were bound to get visits from the Secret Service too. They assumed we were some kind of cell. What kind of cell I've no idea, but that Peter, that Duffelcoat Dick, he came along to investigate.'

'What did he find? Did I miss some bomb-making workshops?'

'He found a lot of people beginning to think themselves into a new place, a new country – some consciously, some unconsciously, but that's what was happening. He dropped in for about six months on and off, between the first General Election in 1974 and the second one. Remember that? Two General Elections in a year. The Nats did well in February but they did even better in October. Anyway, I was fed up with him. He never contributed anything, he just sat around drinking other people's wine and I'd had enough. I cornered him in the kitchen, it was just him and me and I said, "What is it you're looking for?" and he said, "A corkscrew," and I said, "You know what I mean," and I shut the door and stood with my back to it. I said, "You sneak into my home and sit in the shadows with your lugs waggling like antennae and you think I don't know who you are? Don't worry, I'm not going to blow your cover, but what's so special about us?"'

'And what did he say?'

'He said, "There's nothing special about you. Do you think this is the only place I go?" And I said, "I don't care where else you go or who else you like eavesdropping on, but I'm interested to know what you're doing here." He said, "The same as I'm doing everywhere. I'm trying to gauge whether we've reached point critical." And I said, "Meaning what?" He said, "The point of no return. The point where you can't stop it even if you want to." "And have we?" I said. "No," he said. "This will all pass. They're not ready." And I said, "Who? The people through in the other room?" And he said, "The people in general." So I said, "Well, then, you'll not need to come here any more, will you?" And I opened the kitchen door and stepped aside and he went down the passage and let himself out and I never saw him again."

'Just like that.'

'Aye. But you know the funny thing? He was smiling at me as we were talking, quite friendly like, and when he was telling me we weren't ready for independence – because that's what he was saying, we weren't ready so it wasn't going to happen – it wasn't like he was dismissing it, or us. It wasn't like he was chalking up a victory. It was like an objective assessment.'

'If he was a spook that would have been his job, to assess and report back.'

'That's true, he would have had a control. But there was something about him that made me think he was out on his own. Like he'd lost them, or they'd lost him. Lost control, you could say. You know those lines from Yeats? *The falcon cannot hear the falconer; / Things fall apart; the centre cannot hold.* I don't think he was necessarily opposed to the idea of an independent Scotland. I think he quite liked it.'

'And you really think he was a spook?'

'He wasn't the only one. They were getting pretty paranoid about Scotland. We were a hard one for them to get their wee heads around. I mean, Northern Ireland was easier for them to understand – there were bad guys shooting at them. They kept thinking all hell was going to break loose here too and it kept not happening. When I showed your man Duffelcoat Dick the exit, as he went by me I said, "Do you think we'll ever be ready?" and he looked at me – I remember this as clear as anything – and he said, "Couldn't tell you, Jean. We might just drift into it without meaning to." I often think of him saying that. Maybe that is what we're doing, drifting; but we know it's happening and we like the direction of travel. We're on a journey and sooner or later we'll get to wherever we're going.'

§

As soon as Catriona and he had redefined their relationship, Mike was hit by an overwhelming need to make up for lost time. He was nineteen and had no sexual experience. Suddenly he wanted to do for real things he'd hardly allowed himself to imagine. Where did you start, where did you go? There were a few very camp students at the art college, but he felt he had nothing in common with them except his sexuality. He thought of the places Sam had mentioned. He didn't want to run into Sam again but maybe those places would be his way in.

He opted for the Kenilworth in Rose Street. Everybody knew its reputation, so simply pushing through its doors was an act of self-recognition. But he was very nervous. He bought a pint and got talking to an older man sitting at the bar who said his name was John and that he was a lawyer. Maybe it was and maybe he was, it was no less likely than that Mike's name was Mike and he was a student. John was guarded at first. Later he explained that in his professional life he sometimes had to deal with men facing ruin because they had fallen for handsome young policemen in public toilets. When the pub closed, everybody spilled on to the street and headed en masse towards Frederick Street. 'Crawford's Tearooms,' John explained. 'Last chance for a cup of something and a fairy cake. It's fun, but you and I don't need to go there tonight.' His home was in Heriot Row and he invited Mike back. It was a basement flat, stylish and expensive. He made coffee in a cafetière and they went into the sitting room and John closed the shutters and put some Bach on the stereo. All of this – the cafetière, the shutters, the classical music – was new to Mike and so was the kissing and fondling on the settee that followed. Then John said, 'What do you like?' 'This,' Mike said, 'I like this.' 'Do you like to gie it or take it?' There was something wonderfully salacious about the fact that he said *gie*, just the one word like that. 'I'm not sure,' Mike said. 'This your first time, eh?' John said. 'Well, we've got all night.' And they had. John pushed him out of the door at five o'clock in the morning. 'I don't do relationships,' he said, 'but we can do *that* again some time if you want.'

By nightfall that same day Mike wanted very much to do it again. At nine o'clock he walked down Lothian Road past the glassy, bright, scary bars Eric the medic said it was best for students to avoid at the weekend, and crossed over to the New Town. He went down the steps to John's flat and rang the bell. Nothing happened, although a light was on. He rang again. He heard movement, and the door was opened on the chain.

'Hello,' he said. He half-expected John to be fresh from the bath, in his silk dressing gown, but he was fully dressed, in jacket and tie. The door was not unchained.

'What the fuck do you think you're doing?' John whispered. There was no trace of the previous night's kindness in his voice. Then, loudly: 'No thanks, goodnight.' And the whisper again: 'Don't ever, *ever*, come here like this again. Understand?' The door shut in Mike's face. He heard John's voice retreating down the hall. 'Jehovah's bloody Witnesses, can you believe it, at this time of night?'

That was a lesson. A few weeks later he saw John again, in another bar, and he apologised, and so did John. The thing was, John said, there were rules. Some played by one set of rules, some by another. With him, the rule was, you met in a public place. Then maybe you went home, maybe you didn't. But you didn't just turn up. Anybody could just turn up, and that was risky. Anybody could already be there. John wasn't really 'out'. Most of the men he knew, professional men, weren't. 'And another thing,' he said, tapping Mike's camera in its case (he'd been taking pictures earlier in the evening, and still had it with him). 'Leave that at home. That makes me nervous.'

§

He told Isobel. He knew it would upset her, which was why he told her. He'd already told Angus. Telling them in that order was also calculated to upset Isobel.

Angus said he didn't give a damn. Mike was disappointed. He'd hoped for a little more than that.

Isobel said, 'You can't be.'

'Why not?'

'Because . . . because . . .'

'Because you never thought it would happen to you?' Mike said. 'And before you start trying to make excuses, it isn't a phase and I don't need to see a doctor. This is who I am, so you may as well get used to it.'

She kept looking at him as if trying to spot the difference between Michael at Christmas and this new, adulterated Michael. They were in the kitchen, he at the table, she backed up against the worktop where she'd been making a pie. Her hands were covered in flour, and she held them away from her as if they cradled an invisible bomb.

'Nothing's changed,' he said. 'The only thing that's changed is now we both know.'

'Of course something's changed,' she snapped. 'How *could* you?'

'How could I what?' He'd come home to appal her, and she was appalled. Now he could be angry with her. He'd brought an overnight bag but he'd be going straight back to Edinburgh. Perhaps somewhere deep inside he'd hoped for a miracle, an acceptance, a new and better understanding between them. And perhaps he'd just wanted to hurt her.

'Do *those things*,' she said in a shocked whisper. 'I can't bear to think about it.' And she went to the sink to wash her hands.

'Then don't,' he said. 'I'm not asking you to. I'm just not going to go on pretending I'm something I'm not. You must have had an idea, surely?'

'Why would I have suspected *that*? You always seemed perfectly normal to me.'

'Maybe you weren't paying attention,' he said. 'When I was at home, that is.'

She spun round, hands dripping. 'Oh, you're going to blame it on being sent to boarding school, is that it?'

'I'm not *blaming* anything. I don't feel bad about it, not any more. I feel good about it.'

'Well, I'm glad for you, Michael,' she said, 'because I don't.' She dried her hands and stood in the middle of the room with them on her hips. 'And before you accuse me of not paying you attention, when was the last time you gave me any consideration? Well? And how long have you "known"?' He could hear her putting the inverted commas round the word.

'Not long enough,' he said. 'But I do now.' He twisted the knife a little further. 'And so does Dad.'

'For God's sake, you've not told him, have you?'

'On the phone, yes.'

'And he approves?'

'He doesn't disapprove.'

'He wouldn't, would he? He's always indulged you. The only thing I can say is you didn't get *that* from him.'

'It's not a disease.'

'Is it not? It's a sickness, that's what I think.'

'Don't be so ignorant.'

'Don't you dare speak to me like that.'

'Don't speak to *me* like that.'

It was hopeless and horrible and predictable but even then Isobel's sense of propriety began to assert itself. Something closed over her face. Already she was working out how to accommodate the dreadful fact into the other facts of her existence.

'Well, we'll just have to get on with it, won't we? When you said you were coming I invited Bob Syme round for dinner, since you seemed to hit it off at Christmas. So. Can we agree that we won't discuss this in front of him?'

'Don't you think he'll be able to handle it?'

'I don't think,' she said, 'it's something we'll want to talk about while we're eating.'

'I'll tell him before, when he's got a big whisky in his hand. That should help.'

'You really are making this as difficult as possible for me, aren't you?' she cried. 'I'll just have to phone Bob and put him off.'

'Don't,' I said. 'I'm not staying.'

'But I've bought all this food.'

'Well, make up your mind, will you?' he shouted. 'Do you want me as I am or as you'd prefer me to be? Do you want a happy wee party with your boyfriend where no food gets wasted and nobody says anything that might possibly upset anybody else or do you want a bit of honesty in your life? Do you think Bob will even care? He'll probably think it's a huge joke. He'll probably bet me twenty quid I'll have grown out of it by the time I graduate.'

She gave him a wounded, contemptuous look.

'Bob Syme,' she said, 'is not my *boyfriend*.'

He went to his bedroom to collect his bag.

§

Jean says, 'Pour me just a touch more, Mike.' He breaks the seal on the Clynelish and fills her glass. She says, 'I don't suppose this is helping much, is it?'

'Helping what?'

'This thing you're supposed to be writing about Angus. Part of the reason you came was to talk about him, and we've polished off a whole bottle of whisky and hardly mentioned him.'

'He's not been entirely absent from the conversation.'

'No, and it's true we did start with the photographs.'

'Yes. Was he here often?'

She hesitates, but only for a second. 'Quite often. Sometimes in the chair you're in. Does that feel strange to you?'

'Probably not as strange as it feels to you.'

'You do look just like him.' She smiles. 'But you're a lot older now than he was when I knew him.'

'So now you know how he turned out. Like son like father.'

'Well, I have something to say about that.' Again she hesitates. 'And it's going to be difficult, and my question to you is, do you want me to say it now or in the morning?'

'Why not now?'

'Because I want you to remember it.'

'I'm listening.' Finally, he thinks, after all these years, she's going to talk about their relationship. About Angus and Jean.

'I wouldn't say this if I didn't love you, you understand that?'

'It's going to be bad, then.'

'That depends on how you take it.' She has another roll-up ready, and lights it. 'So do you want me to tell you, or do you want to tell me? Because unless I'm very much mistaken, you do know.'

'Stop talking in riddles, Jean.'

'Okay. The reason why you're struggling with it? Why you're not writing it? It's because you can't, not without facing up to something.'

'And what's that?' he says.

'He was better than you. There, I've said it. Would you like me to elaborate?'

'I'd love you to.'

'Don't get defensive, Mike, and don't blame me. It's written all over your face. You know it as well as I do. You've known for years, which is why you hide away up there in the north endlessly photographing the same things in the same places and never showing anyone what you've produced. And it's why you've taken it upon yourself to be the custodian of his archive, why you've spent the last

two years preparing this exhibition. You set out to be better than
Angus at what he did, and it didn't turn out that way. You're a perfectly good photographer, but you haven't got that special thing that
Angus had. You just haven't got it. And you spend your days – I'm
guessing, because I don't know *how* you spend your days – circling
round that big, unavoidable truth, dealing with his photographs
because that way you don't have to deal with *it*, or maybe you take
hundreds of photos of your own, hoping that just one of them will
be better than the photo he would have taken without even thinking about it. Your dad is always going to be better than you. Nothing
you can do can change that. Tell me I'm wrong.'

He feels queasy, not with the whisky, not because she's hurt his feelings, because she hasn't, but with a kind of excitement. He thinks of
his obsessive ordering of digital images, the ranks and ranks of disks
marked by date, the other disks containing his best pictures of boats,
stones, sand, sea, clouds, heather . . . So there are thirty thousand negatives in the Angus Pendreich collection. There are three, five times
that many digital files in the Michael Pendreich collection. And this is
not simply a matter of technological advance. This is not only about
hard-drive capacity. There is no mystery in what she is telling him.

'Of course you're not wrong,' he says.

'So accept it and start engaging with the real world again. Tear up
what you've written. If you're going to write about him, do it honestly. Say what a shit he was. Say what a child he was. Say how much
you loved him. Did you ever actually tell him any of those things?
Or did you just let him get away with it all?

'Or maybe you shouldn't write this essay at all. Get somebody
else to write it – Duncan whatever his name is. Let the pictures
speak for Angus. Cut out the notes unless they're absolutely necessary. Everything else is a distraction.'

He nods. There is nothing he can say that won't sound like
whining. So he keeps his mouth shut.

'And go and talk to Isobel,' she says, 'before she's away too and
you're left with all *that* stuff unsaid. She's your mother, for Christ's
sake.'

He breathes out heavily.

'Sorry,' she says.

'It's all right. Like you said, we're way past that.'

'Do you hate me?'

'Don't be absurd. What are a few home truths between old friends?'

'That's very generous of you.'

He says, 'Now it's my turn.'

§

Stupid. Cutting across the Meadows, not drunk but not sober either, he saw three guys coming in his direction and didn't register that he might be in trouble until they were almost on him. He was heading home from a party he'd managed to gatecrash that same night, after leaving his mother with too much food in Doom. He'd snogged a lonely girl then abandoned her as some way of getting back at Isobel. Stupid. The three guys fanned out to cut off his escape routes. One was roaring, 'There's the cunt that stole ma fucking money!' Another was shouting, 'That's a fucking poof!' The third didn't say anything, just steamed in, boots and fists going like a windmill. Mike tried to jink past off the path and on to the grass but the grass was wet and he slipped, went down on the ground and the three of them were on him and then in some mad silent-movie moment they all slipped and fell too, the four of them scrabbling to see who'd be back on his feet first and it wasn't Mike and the boots came in. 'Ya fucking poof ya fucking cunt try this up your fucking erse take this in your mooth.' He curled up tight as he could trying to save his balls, hands over his head trying to save his head, feeling his fingers and elbows and shoulders and legs getting battered, Jesus they were going to break his fingers. Don't kick my head, he was thinking, just don't kick me in the head, and they were laughing, 'This is what we fucking dae, poof, we fucking kill ye,' and he thought, how do they know I'm a poof, then there was shouting from somewhere and they gave him another couple of kicks like they had horseshoes on and were away jeering into the night. And he lay there thinking, well I'm not dead anyway, and slowly, slowly uncurled himself and a group of students were there, lassies as well as guys, 'Are ye all right, mate? Are ye all right?' and somehow he got to his feet and his legs were jelly and he fell off them and stood up again and the girls said, 'Oh my God!' and he couldn't see for blood and a couple of the guys helped him to the infirmary which handily was just a few minutes' stagger, where they left him, thank you, thank you, to sit

87

with the other walking wounded in A&E, the drunk and bloody battalion of victims of a Saturday night in Edinburgh.

A nurse cleaned him up and bandaged his bruised hands and put a patch over one swollen eye, and a doctor put a few stitches in his head and said he was lucky. 'Lucky?' he said. A policeman who seemed to be on permanent statement-taking duty and who must have been getting cramp in his fingers took one from Mike that wasn't going to lead to anything unless he lost the eye, in which case, the officer said, he could claim criminal-injury compensation, and between times Mike sat in a dwam and thought, well, I had a choice. I could have betrayed myself and had a quiet night in Doom with Isobel and Bob Syme or I could have done what I did. And I did what I did, and that was the right choice, but there's a price, Michael Pendreich, for being gay in this country, and you just paid it. Even if the bastards who did this to you didn't care if you were gay or straight, a Hearts fan or a Hibs fan, a Proddy, a Tim or an art student, they gave you a doing for being available, and in a way they were just putting into actions what your mother couldn't put into words. Then the hospital people gave him some extra dressings and let him go home, and he limped down the road to Tollcross and crawled into his bed.

When he got up late on Sunday afternoon he could hardly move. Eric was watching the telly when he edged into the front room. 'Bloody hell, Mike,' he said, 'what happened to you?' So he told him, and he told him everything, because up until that point, in spite of what he'd said to Isobel, he'd not been up front and honest about his sexuality, it was still only 1974 after all. And Eric said, 'Well, what if you are gay? Who gives a damn except ignorant bigots?' 'You mean you don't?' 'Of course I don't,' Eric said, and then, being a medic, he took charge. He changed the dressing on Mike's eye and checked the cuts and bruises elsewhere and said, 'You'll live,' and although Mike suspected Eric didn't really know what he was talking about, he agreed with him. 'Aye, I will.' Then Eric ran him a bath, and while he lay soaking in it made them their tea, and they sat and watched garbage on the TV till close-down.

§

Mike used to see Sam – 'the biker' as he'll always think of him – from time to time. Sam would come on to him – 'I tellt ye, I tellt ye,

I said this was what ye wanted' – and Mike would tell him to get lost till it became a joke between them. 'I'm invincible,' Sam said. 'I'll persuade ye sooner or later.' Sam wanted as much sex as he could get. Why not? The worst that could happen would be a dose of the clap but he'd have a lot of fun getting it. There was one club, you went in and there were more cocks on display than bottles on the gantry. Not Mike's scene. He wanted intimacy, not excess. Sam said Mike was copping out, if you were gay you had to flaunt it. 'Why?' 'Because if you don't, if *we* don't, we're still not visible. If we slink about in the shadows the way you do then all we're doing is saying thank you for tolerating us, we promise we'll be sweet and discreet and we won't upset you. That's not good enough.' Mike said, 'I don't see it like that, but even if I did I can't *make* myself be like you. It's just not who I am.' 'Suit yourself, dear,' Sam said, and he did. He drifted back to his preferred haunts in the Old Town, to Sandy Bell's, to Jean Barbour's. It was easy enough to get sex when he needed sex. A lot of the time, he didn't need it.

At the end of his first year at college, he decided he couldn't face a summer in Doom. He stayed on in the flat at Tollcross, as did Eric, and got a job in a café on the High Street, serving weak coffee and overpriced cakes to tourists. Money was tight. On his days off he wandered round the city, taking pictures, going to free exhibitions. It was Festival time: there were endless opportunities for photographs. He used the college facilities to develop them, and stuck them up outside the Fringe office and in other locations with his name and phone number written on the back. Somebody might notice. Somebody might want more of the same.

One day, on Princes Street outside Jenners, he bumped into Freddy Eddelstane. He'd had no contact with him since leaving school, but there he was, as antique and ugly and fleshy as ever, accompanied by a taller, thinner, altogether more prepossessing version of himself. This was his older brother, David. It turned out that they knew somebody who knew Eric Hodge and they were all supposed to be meeting for a drink when the pubs opened.

'What are you doing these days?' Mike asked Freddy.

'Not a lot. Didn't want to do any more bloody exams after school, so I've been hanging out at the ancestral pile mostly, but things are getting a bit fraught there. Threat of expulsion if I don't get off my arse. Think I'll go to London and make pots of money. That's what David does.'

'If he's going to London, I'm coming to Edinburgh,' David said. 'Little parasite.'

'It's the way I was brought up,' Freddy said. 'Youngest child and all that. David has a more heightened sense of social responsibility. He's decided to follow the noble Eddelstane tradition and go into politics. He fought a seat in the election in February. Lancashire or somewhere. Didn't do badly, did you?'

'Lanarkshire, Freddy. No, not badly. Better than expected. Safe Labour seat, of course. If they put up a donkey it would win it.'

'He's going to contest it again whenever the next election happens,' Freddy said. 'Glutton for punishment. Meanwhile, we're going shopping. Want to come?'

'No, thanks. I'm going to an exhibition at a gallery down at Canonmills.'

'Well, why don't you join us for that drink later?'

He named a bar at the other end of the New Town. Mike said he'd see them there.

'What's the exhibition?' David Eddelstane asked.

'Photographic. It's called "Love Hurts". The photographer's from Edinburgh originally, makes a lot of her humble roots, but she's been away a long time. More *Guardian* than Granton now, I think. Her stuff's been causing a bit of controversy because it's about sex. The usual Mrs Grundies want to close it down.'

'Sounds better than trailing round the shops with him,' David said. 'Mind if I tag along?'

In those few seconds looks passed between them. Mike remembered what Freddy had said once about his brother. David seemed affable enough. Surely there was no harm in spending an hour or two with him, even if he did have ambitions to be a Tory MP.

'Not at all,' Mike said.

'Great. Let's go and see what the fuss is about.'

Freddy said he'd give it a miss and meet them later at the pub. He headed off, and the others set off to find the gallery.

'Love Hurts' was disappointing, and crowded with the disappointed. The photographs expounded a thesis on relations between men and women that was obvious, possibly even correct, but deeply depressing. There were a few breasts and a flaccid penis or two, and some images with S&M connotations, but most of the pictures were of couples, in various states of dress or undress, failing to communicate with each other. A naked man looking out of a window while a woman sleeps. A man and a woman at opposite ends of a sofa, both for some reason in their underwear, both staring straight ahead at the television. A woman trying to feed a squalling child while a man reads the paper. They gave the impression of documentary but to Mike looked like they'd been posed, and however worthy the thesis he didn't think they were any good as photos. 'They don't do anything for me either,' David agreed. The gallery was hot and oppressive. They left and walked through the Botanic Gardens, busy because of the fine weather, then across Inverleith Park, until they came to the path leading to the Water of Leith. Down there it was shadier and cooler, and there weren't so many people.

'I'm serious about moving back to Scotland,' David said. 'I've been in London six years and it just gets dirtier and noisier and smellier. There's no denying it's where everything happens, politically, I mean, but I intend to stand in a winnable Scottish seat eventually so I should really set myself up here too. Get the best of both worlds.'

'Freddy said you made money,' Mike said. 'What is it you do?'

'Investments, of one kind or another. Property's my thing, really. There's a lot one could do in Edinburgh. It's all just waiting to be exploited. We need a change of government, of course, but then that's why I'm getting into politics.'

'We've just had a change of government.'

'I mean a *real* change of government. Even if Heath got back in, it wouldn't change things. Not *really* change things.'

Mike could have made an argument out of it, but couldn't be bothered. Why spoil the moment? It was August and the sun was shining, and Edinburgh was looking its best, and there was something else in the air, something in the way they caught each other's eye, the way their arms brushed as they walked. They talked about Kilsmeddum Castle and agreed what a dump it was, and after that line of conversation was exhausted Mike thought it quite likely that they didn't have much else in common. But still they walked on together, under Telford's bridge and into Dean Village, and on through Stockbridge. They were killing time, really, before the pub opened. Mike said, 'I think there's a short cut up this way, shall we try it?' They went down a mews and came to a dead end, and were about to turn back when David said, 'What about in there?' pointing to a low wall with a bit of broken fence and a gap where the grass had been worn away by the passage of many feet. They looked as if to dare each other. David said, 'I'm up for it if you are,' and they went through the gap. There was a faint path between bushes and trees, and on either side were quiet streets full of parked cars. The streets seemed abandoned, they could see out on to them but if they didn't move they wouldn't be seen *from* them, but to be sure they went deeper, past broken glass, dropped cigarette ends, bits of paper, a plastic bag or two, with the rich smells of vegetation and cat's pee and something dead and something human mixing and closing around them. The ground was dry mud with occasional scraps of pale grass. They were mere yards from everything but it felt as if they'd entered a magical yet decaying space. And then it happened. They were down on their knees and groping, feeling for each other through their trousers, and then they both unzipped and masturbated each other on to the hard ground. Like a competition, a schoolboy trick. They had to stifle their giggles and then Mike stopped laughing and felt stupid and ashamed, as if he were thirteen, and if only he had been, if only he'd been thirteen, if only he'd got to do this at thirteen, but he hadn't, he was a grown man and he'd just tossed off a prospective parliamentary candidate for the Conservative and Unionist Party.

Afterwards – when they'd brushed themselves down, 'made ourselves respectable' as David put it, and finally extricated themselves from the short cut – David said casually, as if it wasn't *that* important, 'No need to say anything about this, is there?' and Mike said no, there wasn't. 'Wouldn't be wise,' David said. 'No.' And then a smile, relief of the non-hand variety. 'Good man. Freddy said you were all right.' Another pause. 'I'm not really, you know, like that.'

'I am,' Mike said.

David blanched. 'Oh God. I just want to try different things out. I can't imagine why I allowed myself –'

'Oh be quiet,' Mike said angrily. They walked on to the pub, a tiny, plush place with a row of barrels along one wall and a good range of real ales and malt whiskies. It was full of wealthy, well-kept men who lived in the wealthy, well-kept neighbouring streets. In one corner was Freddy, with another couple of friends who sounded just like him, and then Eric Hodge turned up. For a few hours much drink was consumed. And Mike was thinking, what am I doing, these are not the people I want to be with, but I'm with them so I'll make the most of it, and he stayed, but on the sidelines of the jokes and the raucous laughter, feeling strange and out of place. David Eddelstane hardly looked at him, and when he did it was with a blank, bland gaze that did not speak at all of what they had done. It was never to be spoken of, never to be repeated, Mike saw. He understood that it really had been an aberration of some kind for David, but would it always be like that for him – unacknowledged, childish moments in the undergrowth, nights of love in places he must not return to? He longed for something better.

Later, trailing back to Tollcross, Eric expressed the view that the Eddelstanes were toffee-nosed wankers, quite amiable wankers maybe but if he had to be in their company all the time he'd be reaching for his revolver. 'Especially David. I mean, what a wanker.' And Mike wondered if he'd guessed that something had happened, if he'd seen some signal and his overuse of the word was his way of saying that he knew. But no, it was pure coincidence. And then Eric said, 'Mind you, he must have something going for him, he's got the most gorgeous wife.'

'He's *married*?' Mike said. But why was he surprised?

'Oh, aye,' Eric said. 'Hitched to the beautiful Melissa Braco. Her dad's a Tory MP. He got the seat David's father had, what is it, Glenallan and something? It's close to where you're from, isn't it?'

'Glenallan and West Mills,' Mike said. 'It's next door.'

'Well,' Eric said, 'that's who he's married. Keeping it in the family, I guess.'

§

Work did come to Mike from those Festival pictures, sporadically at first, and much of it unpaid, and then more and more through word of mouth. He was competent and cheap. A theatre group doing *Macbeth* set in outer space wanted a record of their production, photos of every scene, and publicity shots too. The show was crap but they paid him a tenner. The man who ran the venue saw the results and liked them. His daughter was getting married. Would Mike take the pictures? They negotiated a price and nothing went wrong and everybody was happy. The new academic year started and he found more work coming his way – another couple of weddings, and some publicity shots for another theatre company about to follow in 7:84's footsteps on a Highland tour. A publisher doing a guide to Edinburgh pubs wanted a mix of exterior and interior shots capturing the character of each establishment. It wasn't art but Mike learned more on these jobs than he was learning at college. He turned up there less and less, doing just enough to keep his supervisor off his back.

The pub guide came out and on the strength of it an advertising agency hired him for a one-off job, a series of portraits for a life-assurance company. People looking relaxed and content in different situations. The message was that they were safe, their loved ones were covered. The campaign ran on buses and he was amazed how often he found himself staring at his own images. The agency paid £50 for two days' work, untold riches. He had business cards printed. People he gave them to sometimes asked, 'Any relation to Angus Pendreich?' and nodded knowingly when he said yes. 'Oh, I *love* his work,' one woman gushed. She didn't hire Mike.

Angus was in London. Mike had a number for him there. When Angus came north he based himself in Glasgow, but he hardly ever seemed to have enough time to fit in a meeting with his son. They saw each other maybe twice a year – about as often as Mike made the trip home to see Isobel, out of a continuing sense of duty he couldn't account for.

When he phoned the London number a woman answered and said her name was Cindy. Surely not, Mike thought. 'I hope we're going to meet some time,' she said, in a sexy, rich, little-friend voice. 'I hope so,' he said. She passed him on to Angus. After a few preliminaries Mike told his father he was beginning to make some cash with his camera, and was thinking of dropping out. The conversation went downhill from there.

Angus said, 'What do you want me to say?'

'I don't know. I thought I'd run it past you.'

'I can't advise you. I didn't go to college. But you're there, the government pays your fees, you get money from me every month, and at the end of it all you'll get a degree – so why would you drop out? Doesn't make sense to me. Can't you carry on as you are, do a bit of both?'

'I could get more work if I didn't have to study. The course isn't right for me. I feel like I'm wasting my time.'

'Have you talked to your mother about it?'

'No. I'm talking to you.'

'Mike, do what you have to do. It's your call.'

'Is that it?'

'What do you want me to say? That I'll put in a word for you at the *Observer*? You can't ride on my coat-tails, you know.'

'I don't want to ride on your fucking coat-tails.'

'Good. Just checking. Look, you're young enough, if it doesn't work out you can do something else, so just do it.'

'I will. I don't intend to do anything else.'

'Are you broke?'

'I'm okay.'

'I'll keep sending you money. As if you were still a student, is that reasonable? Until you tell me I don't have to.'

'You don't have to.'

'Don't be daft. What about equipment? Lenses, a back-up camera. How much are you shelling out for film?'

'I'm fine, honestly.'

'How's the rest of your life?'

'Fine.'

'Do you want to elaborate on that?'

'Not really. How's yours?'

'Very good, actually.'

'Cindy sounds nice.'

'She is.'

'Is that her real name? Like the doll?'

'Aye, but with a C. C-I-N-D-Y.'

'Isn't that how the doll's spelled?'

'No, the doll has an S.'

'Is that right? I didn't know that. Are you sure?'

'Yes.' A note of irritation was in Angus's voice now.

'Oh. Is that her place or yours?'

'Ours. We're renting it. Listen, Mike, I have to go. We were just on our way out. You're okay though, eh?'

'Sure.'

'All right. Let's get together when I'm next up. Have you seen any more of Jean Barbour, by the way?'

'Aye, I saw her just last week.'

'That's good. I'm glad you made contact. She's some woman, isn't she?'

'Aye, she is. You should go and see her yourself.'

'Maybe I should.'

They said goodbye and Mike hung up and swore. He imagined Angus telling Cindy what a waste of space he was. He'd only suggested that he go to see Jean because he knew there wasn't a chance of it happening. Angus didn't revisit the past, not physically anyway. Angus was with Cindy, for as long as that lasted. Jean was Mike's now. He didn't want his father involved with her.

§

'What about you and him?'

Jean shakes her head. 'I told you, it was a long time ago.'

'So?'

'So what's the point in raking over old ashes?'

'Isn't that what we've been doing all night?'

'Aye, but.'

'Well, come on then.'

'I'm tired, Mike. What time is it?'

'It's not even midnight. Jean, how long have I known you? Thirty-five years or thereabouts. And I only know you because you once knew my dad. It's because of him I'm here now. But I don't know anything about what you had, the two of you. You've never talked about it, he never talked about it. Every time I tried to ask, you found a convenient way of not answering. So I stopped asking. It always seemed to me that you were special to him, but maybe that's me being sentimental. Maybe he was as much of a shit to you as he was to Isobel and the others. I'd just like to know. Especially if you're about to peg out.'

'I could quite possibly be gone by morning, the way you've been pouring these drams. At the very least I'll be on my hands and knees for two days.'

'I am absolutely not accepting responsibility for that.'

'You sound just like your father. Sorry, bad joke. I'm not blaming him for who he was. I knew what I was getting into. But when you fall for someone who makes you happy, and you think you make him happy, and then he tells you he likes his own company best, and not long after that he marries somebody else you know he'll never be happy with, it leaves you a wee bit bruised. And you don't always want to relive the experience.' She raises her glass. 'But here's to him anyway. Cheers, Angus.'

Mike picks up his own glass, which still has a dribble of Highland Park in it. 'Angus,' he says. And then, before she can move on, 'What about that time in Arbroath, Jean? Won't you tell me about that?'

She hesitates.

'I really need to know.'

'When the stone was delivered there,' Jean says. Her terminology is bland yet precise.

'Aye. You told that story once, about the man and woman turning up at the abbey just at the crucial moment. I mind when you told it, somebody asked if it was you, and you gave some evasive answer. I didn't need to ask. I knew it was you and my father.'

'How could you have known that?'

'I just did. The way you looked. However many people were in this room, that part of the story was for me.'

'I'm sure I didn't intend it to be. Anyway, in 1951 your father wasn't your father, was he? You were four years away. He hadn't even met your mother then.'

'But it was you, wasn't it? You and him?'

There is a long pause.

'Aye it was. And what you said just now, about me maybe being special to him – well, if I was, then it was then. A special time.'

After another thought-gathering silence, she says, 'You must have realised when you first saw those photographs at the abbey. You must have put two and two together.'

'Long before that. I didn't see them till after he died – till I was preparing this exhibition, in fact. But the moment he first mentioned you I knew you'd been more than just a friend. The more casual he pretended to be about something, the more important it probably was. And then, when I met you, all the things you didn't say made me certain of it. I may have been innocent, Jean, but I wasn't a total idiot.'

'They're not very good, are they?' she says. 'As photographs, I mean.'

'Technically, no. But as historical artefacts, they're pretty special. That's why I've included them. The one of the keeper, standing beside the stone, that's okay. But the gem is the one of the three men through the arch, with the stone at their backs. It's a bit blurred, but it's a moment in history that nobody else captured. It places them at the scene. And yet it doesn't really, because it's taken from behind, and they're in silhouette. Three anonymous men and yet we know who they are. A typical Angus angle. And you were there when he took it.'

'I was there when he took a lot of his pictures back then,' she says. 'For a while we went everywhere together.' Again she pauses. He knows that she is finally going to talk.

'We met here in Edinburgh,' she says, 'the year before. We just fell in love, or at least that's what I thought happened. It turned out that I fell in love, and Angus . . . did whatever Angus did. Imagined he was in love. We used to go off on walking expeditions, long summer weekends in the Cairngorms. He was taking landscapes then but what he really wanted to take were people, so when we weren't wandering about in the hills we'd go on these outings. All over the country we'd go, places neither of us had ever been to. He would pick up some bit of gossip or local news, and off we'd go to photograph a tinker in Hawick or a blind golfer at St Andrews or something. And this particular time we had two days on the east coast between Montrose and Arbroath. There were all these wee communities there, making hard livings from the land or the sea. We drifted in and out of those places for a day and then the next day we went to Arbroath. Angus was determined to get out to the Bell Rock lighthouse. He found the story of how it was built quite awesome. I don't mean "awesome" the way kids use that word these days. I mean he was truly in awe of the achievement. It represented the high point of Scottish industrial heroism to him. So he persuaded a man to take us out in a wee boat with an outboard motor. He had to pay him something, quite a lot I think, but he said we might never get the chance again. The lighthouse is about twelve miles off the coast, a long, cold trip in that boat. It was calm enough when we set out but there was quite a swell by the time we arrived. The sea was smooth and grey and slow and somehow that was more horrible than if the waves had been breaking over the rock. You couldn't see the rock at all, just this tower rising straight out of the water. It was amazing to think of them building it between tides. It was so obviously solid and man-made and real but at the same time it seemed unreal. It made me feel sick just looking at it. Not the sea, the lighthouse.

'Anyway, Angus got his photographs, including the one you've picked for the exhibition. God, there's even a twist in *that* photograph. He's focused on the swell somehow, a lump in the water, that's what your eye is drawn to, and then there's the lighthouse off to the side. How did he manage that?'

'The lighthouse doesn't dominate the sea, it exists in spite of the sea,' Mike says.

'Yes, that's it, isn't it? Och well, anyway, the boatman had had enough, and so had I, so we turned back to Arbroath and got in just before the rain came down. We decided to stay the night because Angus wanted to photograph the abbey in the morning. We booked into a crummy hotel – I had a ring that I kept for such eventualities – and we had fish and chips down by the sea. It was bloody cold but I can still taste that fish. And in the morning we went to the abbey.

'I can't remember what time it was but it must have been early because the gate was locked. Nobody was about so we found a bit of the wall we could scramble over and got in that way. Angus took some pictures and we were just about to leave when we heard someone at the gate, so we hid behind a pillar. It was the keeper, and not long after he arrived a couple of other men turned up. We waited for a convenient moment to slip out, but they just hung about, talking. Then a car pulled up. Two young lads and an older man got out. There was something odd about all this. They started to get something very bulky and heavy out from the back seat and your father whispered, "I know what's going on. I know what that is." And suddenly so did I, because the stone was still in the news and in our minds. So we stayed put and watched the whole procedure as they brought it into the abbey and set it down at the altar.

'Your father said, "I'm not missing this," and we edged our way round so he could get a picture, and he snapped the lads walking away from the stone. But then somebody spotted us. We walked down to where they all were and Angus started whistling the tune. Mr Wishart, the keeper, had a cheerful sort of face but at that moment he wasn't looking best pleased. He wanted to know how we'd got in and how long we'd been there, and one of the cooncillors wanted to know if we were press and how on earth we'd got wind of it. Angus assured them we were sympathetic and not about to cause any trouble but, he says, could we not just get a picture or two? They said no, absolutely not, which told us that they didn't realise he'd already taken one. They wanted to get rid of us, so eventually they agreed to let him take a photo of Wishart and the stone on its wooden litter, and meanwhile the three that had come in the car drove away. Angus promised not to sell or use the picture unless or until the stone was permanently back in Scotland, and he kept his word. By the time it did come back, half a century later, it didn't matter. Or maybe Angus had forgotten about it. Anyway, that picture of the three men and the stone is a real gem for the exhibition.'

'It's a curiosity, certainly,' Mike says. 'Maybe that's all it is. I've never been able to get excited about that whole Stone of Destiny thing. All that stuff about replica stones and who's got the real one. It seemed like a daft student prank when I first learned about it and now it seems even more so.'

'Well, that's what it was,' Jean says. 'But what a prank! You have to remember how totally moribund the national movement was in those days. Sure, it was just a wee stane wi a ring, as the song goes, but the prank made people think a bit. Made them laugh too, which was equally important. Not the government of course, the po-faced bastards. The police came and took the stone into custody, locked it up in Forfar for the night, and the next day it was whisked off south and reinstated at Westminster.'

'No sense of humour,' Mike says, 'is a failing in most governments. But you know, Jean, you've changed your story. When you told it all those years ago, you said the young couple left first, still whistling. And you didn't say anything about pictures being taken.'

'Did I not? Well, it was a different story then. A different story with a different meaning.'

'How convenient.'

'Stories aren't static, Mike. That's what we were talking about earlier. They grow, they shrink, they change with the retelling.'

'What about the rest of *your* story? The one you shared with my dad. How has that changed over the years?'

'What do you mean?'

'Well, it wasn't just 1951 that you and he were together, was it? It went on a lot longer than that.'

She lights another cigarette.

'Didn't it?'

'Aye,' she says. 'Aye, it did.'

§

The decade when the world changed. This is how Mike thinks of the 1970s. Maybe this is because it was in those years that he himself changed, came to know who he was. And maybe that's nonsense, because who ever really knows who they are? And does the world, or anybody, ever stop changing?

Still, this is what he thinks. It was in the 1970s, for example, that people first understood that oil, on which everything else had so recently and completely come to depend, would not last for ever. It had been plentiful and cheap, but no longer. Wherever it was – in the Middle East, the Americas or the North Sea – it became more than just fuel. It became the currency of hope, security, greed, power, threat and counter-threat. In the wake of this realisation, politics shifted and lurched. People took up causes. Other people took up defensive positions. Nothing was safe, nothing was certain. Nowhere was unaffected.

There was oil in Scottish waters. On land there was nationalism. The discovery of the oil did not lead to the nationalism but it certainly focused minds on the constitutional arguments. In response to nationalism's growing appeal various politicians cobbled together a plan intended to ease the political frustrations of the Scots while keeping them, and the oil, within the United Kingdom. The new deal was called devolution. There followed a continuous, mind-numbing stream of debates, conferences, speeches, commissions and reports on constitutional change. How to devolve power? What powers could or should be devolved? How would an assembly in Edinburgh be funded, how elected, how many members would it have, should it even be in Edinburgh? (Similar questions were being asked in and about Wales, but less urgently, because there was no oil off the Welsh coast.) The letters page of the *Scotsman* was crammed daily with opinions for and against. There were people who seemed to do nothing *but* write letters to the *Scotsman*. Mike would see the address at the top or the name at the bottom and know what the letter was going to say before he read it. Occasionally there were letters about the correct pronunciation of 'devolution'. Was it devolution or dee-volution? Some people cared, even about that.

Harold Wilson stood down as Prime Minister, and Jim Callaghan succeeded him. Mike almost felt sorry for him, genial Jim, struggling to keep his own backbenchers on board the devolution slow train while many of them did everything they could to delay it further, and if possible derail it. The Labour Party had a single-figure majority in the House of Commons and hours and hours of parliamentary time was being taken up with the issue because they had to keep the Nationalists at bay. Meanwhile, across the dispatch box from Callaghan, Ted Heath was long gone. The Conservative leader now was Margaret Thatcher, a steel-haired, abrasive Britannia. Consensus, if it had ever really existed, scuttled off stage, exhausted. Within eighteen months of replacing Heath, Mrs Thatcher had undone his commitment to devolution and positioned the Tories in staunch opposition to it. Less government, not more, was the new Conservative cry. It had a certain appeal. People in the Borders, in the North-East, in the islands, were far from happy at the prospect of ranks of grey-faced Labour councillors from Glasgow and Lanarkshire, Dunbartonshire and Ayrshire, dominating the proposed assembly, even though many of *them* detested the very idea of devolution.

Mike wanted devolution – he wanted that at least, since it had never made sense to him, if Scotland really was a nation, that it didn't run its own affairs – but he had a bad feeling about what was likely to be on offer. And when he spoke to others and heard their confusion, their outrage or their lukewarm support, but most of all when he saw their indifference, the bad feeling increased.

Angus's monthly cheques became quarterly, then occasional. Then, about the time Mike would have been graduating, came one – more substantial than usual – accompanied by a note saying that it would be the last. What would he do with this money? Save it for a rainy day? He'd had enough of rainy days in dismal, indecisive Scotland. He applied for a passport, gave some money to Eric to cover his share of the rent, borrowed a rucksack and, with a couple of changes of clothes and his camera, caught the overnight bus to London. The next day he was in Paris.

He spent a week there, wandering the streets, riding the metro, sitting in cafés, visiting museums and galleries. When he was stuck for words he summoned M. Lucas to his assistance. M. Lucas roared broken sentences in Mike's head, and somehow he got by. Every angle revealed a photograph, every moment was an opportunity. He fell in with other travellers, some innocent, some experienced, and mixed with Parisians, some generous, some exploitative. He vowed to himself that nothing he experienced was to be regretted or resented. Nor was it. He slept the first three nights in a dirt-cheap hostel by the Gare du Nord, camera case clutched to his chest and the straps wrapped round his wrist. On the fourth day he found a bar near the Place des Vosges that didn't close till three in the morning and was the haunt of men looking for easy company. He went home with a different one each night for four nights. Then, sated with sex and with Paris, he left, and spent the next few weeks on buses and trains, or thumbing lifts, meandering through France in a generally southern direction. In late August he wound up in a village near Lyon, where he picked grapes till the end of the season and met a lot of brown, lean, happy people doing the same thing. He was brown and lean and happy too, but eventually there was no more fruit to pick. He turned again to the north, and was back in Edinburgh, and the Tollcross flat, in time for the onset of autumn.

Scotland had seemed both smaller and potentially greater from abroad. It seemed simultaneously both to defy and encourage imagination, and returning felt not entirely like the defeat he had feared. Although he'd spent most of Angus's final cheque in France, there was a little left, and together with his meagre grape-picking earnings it tided him over until he began to get photography work again. This was sporadic and the rate of pay unpredictable. Some months he was flush, others he was tapping Eric for a loan. He never starved, but it was no way to prosper.

The jobs that interested him most were the ones that paid least or not at all. Campaigners heard about him through other campaigners.

He took pictures of charity events, community groups fighting corporations or councils, he sneaked on to industrial sites and photographed evidence of pollution, safety lapses, illegal practices. Some of this work was dangerous and very little of it earned him any money. To continue doing it he would have to subsidise it. He sharpened up his culinary skills and got a job in a restaurant kitchen, Thursday and Friday nights, cash in hand and a quick exit out the back door if anybody official came inspecting. And he signed on the dole, which meant he could also claim housing benefit. He remembered Bob Syme saying 'the system, as you call it'. Well, he was playing the system now, biting the hand that fed him crumbs.

'Don't you have a guilty conscience?' Eric asked one Friday when Mike came in from the restaurant. 'I mean, that's the tax from my soon-to-be-hard-earned salary that's paying for the likes of you to be a scrounger.'

Mike took it from the formulation that Eric wasn't entirely serious. He was in his final year of medicine and seemed to spend every waking minute studying. He had a girlfriend called Moira, but they hardly ever saw each other. On this occasion he was slumped in front of the television, watching a vampire movie and drinking a can of lager as a nightcap. A pile of textbooks was on the floor beside him. He looked exhausted.

'I'm performing an essential public service,' Mike said. 'It's not as if I'm being idle, is it?'

'You bloody lefties,' Eric said. 'You think the world owes you a bloody living. When are you going to get a proper job?'

He enjoyed trotting out such clichés, the kind of reactionary tosh he said his father, a GP, spouted. But he was very convincing. Mike reckoned that in twenty years Eric would have become his father, and would be delivering the same lines for real. Mike, of course, was never going to become Angus.

'Do I owe *you* any money?' he said.

'Not at the moment.'

'Well, then. My conscience is clear. The state is simply paying me for work that wouldn't otherwise get done. What are you going to do, shop me?'

'Fuck off. Get yourself a can from the fridge. And get me another while you're there.'

'How's Moira?' Mike asked when he came back. 'Haven't seen her for ages.'

'Nor me,' Eric said. He popped the can without taking his eyes off the screen. There wasn't a lot of dialogue in the vampire movie and it seemed you could keep up with the plot so long as you kept watching the picture. 'She's fine. It's her birthday tomorrow. I'm having the day off. We'll do romantic stuff and then I'll take her out for a meal.'

'Where to?'

'Not your place. The New York Steam Packet.'

'Hamburgers, steak, chips, cheesecake. She'll love it almost as much as you will.'

'Fuck off. What about you?'

'Thanks for asking, but I'd be in the road.'

'No, idiot, what about you and romance? Have you not met the man of your dreams yet?'

'Not yet. Is Moira the woman of your dreams?'

'I think she could be, aye.'

'That's good.'

They sat and watched the vampires for a while. A lady vampire in a red dress that struggled to contain her bosom was clamping on to a younger woman in a white dress with a lesser but also heaving bosom. The first one was after the second one's blood but there was a lesbian subtext.

Mike said, 'It doesn't bother you at all, does it, me being gay?'

'Why would it bother me?'

'It would bother a lot of people.'

'A lot of people are stupid. I'm going to be a doctor. What am I supposed to do, pass moral judgement on my patients before I start treating them?'

'There's plenty of doctors that do, I'm sure.'

'Then they're not good doctors. Watch the film.'

They watched the film until everybody with a personality had been staked through the heart. Then they went to their beds.

§

It was a while since Mike had been at Jean's. The next night he walked up there with a bottle of wine borrowed from the restaurant. It was after midnight when he rang the bell. The door was opened by Catriona MacKay.

'Mike!' She gave him a hug and a kiss.

'What are you doing here?' he asked. She'd graduated the year before and moved to Glasgow, where she was at teacher-training college.

'I'm through for the weekend,' she said. 'Where else would I end up in Edinburgh on a Saturday night but here?'

Walter was there too, and a few other familiar faces. It was May, and the night was warm. In the front room the big windows were open wide but only occasionally did the noises of the city reach through them. Jean was holding sway, as usual.

'Come in and find a space. Over here. There's somebody I want you to meet.' She indicated a man in the chair across the fireplace from her own. 'Mike, Adam Shaw. Adam, Mike Pendreich.'

The man half-rose, put out his hand and said hello. He was wearing a pale blue denim shirt and dark jeans and had a sandy moustache and long hair swept back from his high forehead. He looked a few years older than most of the others. His handsome, serious, almost severe face gave the impression of a man who couldn't stop thinking of all the important things he had to do, but when he smiled his eyes brightened – as if he'd realised nothing was that important after all.

Jean had met Adam through Walter and the folk scene. Walter had been singing at a club in Dunfermline and she had gone along to support him and Adam had also been there. They'd shared a table and had got along well, and she'd told him he was welcome in her house any time – if he could find it. And he had, she concluded, and so here he was.

He was a hospital clerical officer, and also a district councillor for the mining town of Borlanslogie, which was just over the Fife boundary in neighbouring Central Region. He'd grown up in Borlanslogie and still stayed near by, just a mile out in the country.

Jean couldn't hear the words 'Central Region' without bristling. 'Can you believe some bureaucratic imbeciles took it upon themselves to give the historic heart of our country that name?' she demanded.

'It's nae worse a name than "the Highlands" or "Queen Street" when ye think aboot it,' Adam said.

'That's your opinion,' Jean said.

'We're just no used tae it.'

'*I* never will be.'

'Borlanslogie's near Glenallan, isn't it?' Mike asked.

'Geographically, it's just ower the hill,' Adam said. 'In every other sense, they're aboot a million miles apart.'

'I grew up in Doune,' Mike said. 'Just over the next hill.'

'Ye'll ken what I'm on aboot then – but only up tae a point.'

'If you represent Borlanslogie you must be Labour?'

Adam nodded. 'A few years ago I might have been a Communist but the CP's getting thin on the ground even in a place like Borlanslogie. And you?'

'I'm not in any party,' Mike said. 'I've thought about joining the SNP, because I believe in independence, but I prefer being, well, independent.'

'Belief in independence,' Adam said. He cast his eye over the assembled company. 'There's a lot of that aboot. Is it the same sort of state of mind as belief in God?'

'I don't know. I don't believe in God.'

'So what else do ye believe in? Socialism, capitalism, fairies?'

There was an aggressive directness to his questioning but the glint in his eyes charmed Mike. He stammered and gave a foolish response.

'I believe in Scotland,' he said.

'What does *that* mean? Do ye think there's anybody that *disna* believe in Scotland? Or is the Scotland ye believe in like Brigadoon, no really here at all?'

'Well, we're not free and independent, so I suppose in that sense it isn't here, not yet anyway.'

'*I'm* free and independent,' Adam said. 'And I believe in Scotland tae, but my Scotland's real, here and now, whereas yours –'

'Sssh,' said Jean, because Catriona had started to sing.

Mike had heard her sing before in Gaelic, but never alone, and never with such confidence. It was a slow, aching lament and although he didn't know what she was singing about he felt the pathos of it. And at the same time he felt that slight embarrassment of being in a room full of non-Gaels listening to a Gaelic song. How much longer would it last? Were they all being too deferential? Not deferential enough? If they understood the words would the song lose its mystery and be revealed as banal and sentimental? And should they worry about such things?

Catriona finished and there was applause, and then Walter sang and the usual round proceeded. Between songs Adam and Mike talked. Adam knew from Jean who Mike's father was. What was that like, having a famous father? Mike said it was fine, he didn't see much of him anyway. 'And your mother?' 'The less I see of her the better.' Every time he spoke of her he betrayed her. Adam's father had died when Adam was six, in a mining accident; his mother when he was eight, of pneumonia. Mike felt like a spoiled, selfish brat. 'I'm sorry,' he said. 'It was a long time ago,' Adam said. He had a twin brother, Gavin, they'd been very close when they were boys, they'd had to be. They still got on well. 'We're no like we were, but we're no bad.' 'What changed?' 'This and that. Maistly this. We grew up, I guess. What aboot yersel? Dae ye have brothers or sisters?' 'No,' Mike said, and he remembered asking Freddy Eddelstane once what it was like, having a sister, and it struck him with a sudden, unexpected force that he would have liked one. 'I've got a sister,' Adam said. 'Ellen. She's my cousin really, but efter oor mother died Ellen's ma took us in so we grew up thegither and I ayewis think of her as my sister. She's a journalist. Actually she's writing a book just now. She stays oot at Joppa. Maybe ye'll meet her sometime. Ye'd like her.' And Mike wondered why he said that, and what he meant by *maistly this*, and why they were so carefully circling each other.

He excused himself and went to the toilet. He'd hardly spoken to anybody else since he arrived. Adam hadn't made any move to get away. Was something, could there be something, about to happen?

On his way back across the room he spoke to Catriona. 'That's the best I've ever heard you sing,' he said. 'I've been learning Gaelic pretty intensely for two years,' she said. 'Soon I'll be speaking it like a native. That's a joke, Mike. I *am* a native, I just didn't have the language before. But the more I've learned the more I think I must have heard my grandparents speaking it when I was wee. I think I don't know a word and then it just pops up from somewhere. They thought they weren't speaking it in front of us but they were.'

'Why wouldn't they speak it in front of you?'

'They were ashamed of it. Or, at least, they didn't think *we* should have it. The future was English. My granda's dead now, but last year I went to my granny and said to her, in Gaelic, why did you hide it from us? And when she realised how much I could speak she started crying. She said they'd thought it was for the best. Gaelic would handicap us. But now I speak nothing but Gaelic to her and she loves it. I'm learning loads from her. I'm not fluent yet, but I'm getting close.'

Mike felt a sting of jealousy that she had rescued something so deep in herself that it had barely been there. He asked her about her song and she said it was the song of a woman to her former lover. 'She says she'll never stop loving him even though he's deserted her. And she sings of his beauty and her grief, and how she'll not take another lover as long as she lives, and then, in the final verse, she apologises for not being good enough for him and – and this is the bit that breaks the heart – gives him her blessing to go with another. All in three minutes,' she added. 'Olivia Newton John, eat your heart out.'

He could have read much into her explanation but there was nothing to read. It was nothing to do with him. She looked happy and strong and confident. 'It's good to see you, Catriona,' he said. 'You're looking great.'

'And you too,' she said. 'And, you know, you shouldn't be too shy over there. I was speaking to him earlier. He's a very nice man, I think. And he's gay.'

'How do you know?' he said, suddenly hopeful.

'Because I have a track record on this, remember? And anyway, he told me. Go for it, a' bhalaich,' she said. She landed a kiss on his cheek and turned away to speak to someone else.

Adam was supposed to be staying the night with friends in March-mont. They'd given him a key so that he could let himself in whenever he liked, but when Mike said he was thinking of going home Adam said he'd see him along the road. Catriona, noticing them leaving together, called out, 'Oidhche mhath, a' Mhicheil,' and gave Mike a not very discreet thumbs-up. And so they went. They reached the infirmary, where their roads should have parted, and Mike said about the beating he'd received crossing the Meadows, and Adam said he would walk the long way round, and they continued down to Tollcross. They'd got on to politics, and Adam was going on about devolution, which he wholeheartedly supported. The Bill for a Scottish Assembly was making its snail-like way through Parliament, and Adam was vitriolic against those in his own party who were trying to destroy the whole project. 'The assembly'll no be perfect,' he said, 'but it'll be better than nothing.' 'Aye, it will.' 'And better than the shite we put up wi in Westminster.' 'Aye, it will.' 'And once we hae it they'll never be able tae take it away.' 'No, they won't. Are you coming in for a coffee?' 'Aye, and another thing is . . .' 'Adam?' 'What?' 'Shut up, would you?' And they went into the close, and up the stair, and somewhere between the street and the flat their hands clasped and Adam said, 'Actually, forget aboot the coffee.' And in the morning he had to take his borrowed key back to his friends and shamefacedly – or so Mike likes to imagine when he thinks about it – let himself in just as they were sitting down for breakfast.

§

Adam was a busy man, steeped in politics. He'd been an official in the health workers' union before he was elected as district councillor for Borlanslogie, and he was a key figure in his local Labour Party branch. Still, he managed to come through to Edinburgh often after that first night. Most Saturdays he'd arrive in the late afternoon, and they'd eat in or go out for a drink or to a party, and on Sunday buy the papers and spend the morning in bed reading them, with bacon rolls and mug after mug of tea, and make love with sunlight invading the room and Joan Armatrading playing on the cassette player. Or they'd drag themselves out of the flat and go to the National Gallery or an early feature at the Cameo, or just for a walk round the city. Precious times. Mike still thinks of them with fondness.

But there was a problem. Probably it was there from the start, in the way Adam framed his questions in that slightly condescending manner that first night at Jean's. And probably Mike saw it but chose to ignore it, because there was something comforting in the rough paternalism. Adam was eleven years older and never disguised his greater experience of life. He seemed to know about everything – in particular everything concerning the history, music, art and literature of Scotland that Mike's education had entirely omitted. Mike was embarrassed at how little he knew.

'I have some catching up to do,' he said.

'Aye, well, we all hae tae start somewhere.'

'But I'm so ignorant.'

'So was I once. Ellen, she was a demon for finding things oot when we were bairns. Gavin and me, we just wanted tae be ootside, playing football or whatever, but Ellen was aye reading. I thought she was stupid but we were the stupid ones. I was aboot fifteen before I saw that, and from then on it was me and Ellen, baith o us wi oor noses in books, and Gavin was ootside on his ain. It took me years but I eventually caught up wi Ellen. Ye could dae it if ye applied yersel.'

'What, catch up with you?'

'Aye.' And they both laughed, because neither of them believed it.

'That's when Gavin and I began tae go oor ain ways, when we were that age,' Adam said. 'I kent I was gay, though we didna call it that then, and he kent it tae, and for a lang time he couldna reconcile himself tae the fact that we were twins yet there was this fundamental difference between us. But we're fine noo. He's all right, ye ken, he's my brother.'

'What does he do?'

'He's a lecturer in Politics at the university here. Ironic, eh? He ended up studying mair books than I ever did. Disna sound like himsel ony mair but we still get on. Ye'll meet him sometime.'

'You said you knew you were gay?'

'Aye, of course I did. Kent it as soon as I kent onything aboot sex. No that I said anything tae onybody, forbye Gavin, and later Ellen. It wasna easy in a place like Borlanslogie but there were others tae, ye just had tae ken where tae look. How tae look.'

'So when did you first have sex?'

'Aboot then. Aye, I would hae been fifteen. We did it in the moonlight, up on the bings. A man would go oot for a smoke at night, just say tae his wife he was away for a walk, and ye'd meet up there. There was nae hairm in it. It was harder for them, though. They *had* tae be mairrit. And they loved their faimlies, maist o them, same as onybody. But they wanted this other thing, and sae did I.'

'I didn't know about myself,' Mike said. 'Not for ages.'

'Ach.' Adam shook his head. 'What a waste o time. Ye were brought up tae believe ye should like lassies, that's all. Nae wonder ye were confused. They *wanted* tae confuse us. Dae ye think your average straight person wastes a lot o time wondering aboot what way they are? They just get on wi it. And sae did I.'

'Well, I didn't,' Mike said. 'And look. Everything comes to he who waits.'

'Bollocks. Suffer on earth and ye'll get your reward in heaven? To hell wi that! Anyway, how could ye no hae kent, gaun tae that school ye were at? There must have been plenty opportunity.'

'It wasn't like that.'

'I bet it was, if ye'd looked.'

§

Eric had proposed to Moira, and she had accepted, the same night that Mike and Adam got together. For a whole year the Tollcross flat hummed with contentment. Eric and Adam had little in common but they tolerated each other when they met. Two things they did share were self-confidence and a reality-defying faith in Scotland's footballing prowess, but in this they were not alone, especially not then. It was 1978, the summer of the World Cup in Argentina. Whatever differences might have divided them, Eric and Adam were united in their conviction that Scotland was going to win the competition.

It's easy, Mike knows, looking back, to see Argentina 1978 as the surreal rehearsal to the political events of 1979. Even Karl Marx might have struggled to determine which was the tragedy and which the farce. Would the outcome of the devolution referendum of March 1979 have been different if the national team had triumphed, or even performed with reasonable dignity and adequate skill, over those nine humid days of June 1978? Such speculation is purely academic now, and maybe there never was a connection, but both are indelibly stamped with the phrases 'what if?' and 'if only'. And Mike has no interest in football! He regards it as a circus of deception, a mad and useless expenditure of emotion, physical energy and money – yet even he cannot prise the two episodes apart in memory. And even he could not – quite – avoid being caught up in the excitement.

In the end the Scottish team in Argentina exhibited very little dignity, and only occasional flashes of skill, and just one burst of brilliance as the team crashed out of the competition in the first round. First was the fire, fed by all but a sober few in the media, that blazed briefly then turned to ash against Peru; then was the ash that was pissed on by Iran; and last was the fire again, miraculously brought back to life against the Netherlands and as suddenly snuffed out. Mike carries in his head two images of that short campaign, each game of which he watched with Adam, Eric and Moira on the television in the flat in Tollcross. The first is of Archie Gemmill's goal against the Dutch, the only time Mike truly understood the meaning of the phrase 'the beautiful game'. The other is of the hapless manager, Ally MacLeod, with his head in his hands during the game against Iran. And they *are* images, one forever in motion, one forever still. No words could be more articulate.

§

On a Saturday in late June, Mike went by train to Stirling, to witness the annual SNP rally at Bannockburn. This was the day before the World Cup final – which, as if anybody cared by then, the hosts Argentina would win against the Netherlands. (Actually, some people did care, deeply. Because Scotland had beaten the Netherlands, and because the Netherlands were beaten by Argentina, it followed that Scotland, if you contorted your logic enough, were theoretical runners-up in the World Cup. There were folk desperate enough to think like that in 1978.)

For a site of national significance – the battlefield on which Scotland's medieval independence from England was won – Bannockburn is an unspectacular place, hemmed in by housing schemes and roads. Angus had taken Mike there as a boy, but Mike had never been to the Nationalists' rally. In the aftermath of Argentina, he thought it might yield some interesting images. All through the 1970s the event had attracted big numbers as the SNP's popularity grew, but the tide was beginning to turn. The Nationalists' confidence had recently taken a couple of knocks from Labour. In April, a forty-year-old lawyer, Donald Dewar, had beaten them, with relative ease, in a by-election in Glasgow. And on the last day of May they had been defeated again in Hamilton, scene of Winnie Ewing's triumph in

1967, the one M. Lucas had been so ecstatic about. It seemed to Mike that the air at Bannockburn was failing to lift the saltires or make the lions rampant; the pipes and drums sounded thin and plaintive, and the speeches, relayed through a ropy PA system, sounded more anxious than celebratory. And was there not a touch of disdain in the way Robert the Bruce, armour-clad and mounted on his warhorse, looked down from his plinth on the bright yellows, blues and reds of the banners, on the abundance of kilts and plaids of every shade of tartan, and on the pale or sun-blotched faces of the milling crowd? Has it come to this, *here*, Mike imagined Bruce thinking. He took his pictures with discretion. Not everybody was happy to be photographed.

After wandering among the crowd for an hour or so, he'd had enough. He was about to leave when he found himself in front of an extraordinary but familiar figure. Wearing a kilt that hung down below one knee and was hoisted up above the other, sporting an enormous hairy sporran, a tweed jacket and a Glengarry bonnet, and supported by a shooting stick embedded in the ground at one end and in the tartan glen of his substantial rear at the other, was his old French teacher. He had aged greatly in the ten years since Mike had last seen him, but it was, without question, M. Lucas.

'M. Lucas?' he said. The older man looked around wildly. Mike went closer. 'Do you remember me? You taught me at school. I'm Michael Pendreich.'

He was just a yard away, stretching a hand towards him, yet M. Lucas stared in his direction uncomprehendingly. Then his whole face brightened. He leaned forward on his stick, found the hand and grasped it. He did not let go but drew Mike closer to him.

'M. Michel? *Comment ça va?* You are *here*? This is wonderful, *merveilleux*! My life, then, has not been entirely *wasted*.'

M. Lucas, Mike realised, was almost totally blind.

'I'm here to take photos,' Mike said. 'It's what I do for a living. I'm not a party member.'

'Cela n'a pas *d'importance*!' M. Lucas roared. 'Who cares about membership? You are *here*, that's all that matters. It's good to hear your voice! But don't take my photograph, *s'il vous plaît*!'

'I was hoping you'd allow me.'

'I forbid it. I *hate* to have my photograph taken.'

'You resist it,' Mike said, disappointed, but immediately sure that he would not go against a wish so vehemently expressed.

M. Lucas roared again, this time with laughter. '*Oui, oui*, I resist it. *Bien sûr*, what else is there to do but *that!*' And he hooted and wheezed, and released Mike's hand only once he had calmed down.

'Now,' he said, 'my son Bernard is somewhere in the vicinity. He is my guide dog today. You will have noticed, *mon ami*, that my eyesight has not improved. You are, I regret to say, only' – his voice took on the tone he had once used in class to tell spooky stories – 'a shadow, a spectre. Do you see him anywhere?'

'What does he look like?'

'Like me,' he said, 'only less *presentable*.'

Mike could see nobody who might be Bernard. 'I'll wait till he comes back,' he said.

'Yes, I am grateful. He won't be long. He has gone for some *refreshments*.'

'Are you still at Bellcroft?' Mike asked hesitatingly.

'That school? Pfff! They put me out to graze three years ago. But I cannot blame them. I could barely find my way from one classroom to the next. *Alors, je suis retraité*. An O-A-P.' He spelled the letters out with disgust. 'Unfortunately there are some affairs in which resistance is *useless*.'

'Your spirit,' Mike said, 'does not seem diminished.'

'No, thank God. We are poor, but we are happy. The thing is to be happy. Everything is tolerable if you are *happy*.'

Bernard, neat in shirt and trousers and with his long black hair tied back in a ponytail, arrived bearing two ice-cream cones. He handed one to his father and M. Lucas went to work on it. A trickle of ice cream ran down his chin but when Bernard tried to wipe it off M. Lucas waved him away. 'Plus tard, plus tard,' he said. He introduced Mike to Bernard and they shook hands and exchanged a few pleasantries while M. Lucas was engrossed in his ice cream. Then Mike said he would have to go. He had a train to catch back to Edinburgh.

'M. Michel,' M. Lucas said dramatically, 'we shall meet again. Or we shall not meet again. But you fill me with hope because you are here today. There are hard times coming, *mon ami*. But hard times come for a purpose. They are to be *resisted*. Remember that.'

'I will,' Mike said.

'But then' – he flung the last bit of his cone away and grabbed for Mike's hand again, and when he found it clasped it stickily in both of his – 'but then a time will come to *accept*. The time of resistance will be over, *terminé*! The ghosts of history will whisper in our ears, and we will go forward into the future. *Oui, c'est vrai!* You think I speak in strange tongues, but what I say is true. These things will come to pass.'

Mike glanced at Bernard, who nodded his head – to signify, it seemed, not that his father was to be humoured, but that he agreed with him.

'Au revoir, M. Michel, au revoir,' M. Lucas said. 'Remember, until the time comes to accept, resist *everything*!'

The contrast between the glow of his optimism and the decrepitude of his appearance could not have been more stark. Mike retreated in confusion. He'd not gone twenty feet before another familiar voice greeted him.

'Hello, Mike,' Angus said.

'Dad! What are you doing here?'

'The same as you, I expect. Who was that you were speaking to?'

'M. Lucas.'

'A *monsieur*? Well, I have to thank you. While you were busy talking, I got some great shots. Who is he?'

'My old French teacher from Bellcroft,' Mike said. 'If you'd taken more interest in my education you might have recognised him.'

Angus was oblivious to the criticism. 'Really?' he said. 'You must have had interesting lessons with a guy like that in charge.'

'You can't use anything you've taken of him,' Mike said hotly. 'He doesn't like being photographed.'

'I didn't see a sign round his neck saying "No Pictures". Anyway, it'll be down to the magazine editor what he uses. I'm on a commission. Scotland post-World Cup. Are we all about to commit suicide? I thought this would be a place worth coming to and I was right.'

'Don't use M. Lucas,' Mike said.

'Out of my hands,' Angus said.

He had what he'd come for, and was leaving too. He offered Mike a lift back to the station at Stirling. The car he kept in Glasgow was parked a few streets away. They walked over to it. Angus started the engine and they moved off.

'You might have got in touch,' Mike said. 'I never see you.'

'Sorry,' Angus said. 'It was all a bit last minute. And I'm not staying. I was up first thing this morning to catch the start of an Orange march and tonight I intend to see what Sauchiehall Street's like on a Saturday these days. Loch Lomond tomorrow if it's fair, a quick spin through a few towns and villages, then back down on the sleeper. So I just didn't have time.'

'You could have taken an extra day.'

'Look,' Angus said, 'I'm back soon for my annual retreat. A month at Cnoc nan Gobhar. Why don't you come up for a while? You've not been for ages.'

'I just won't have time,' Mike said.

'Don't get smart,' Angus said.

'Who are you bringing with you this year? Cindy?'

'Cindy? I'm not with Cindy any more. That was years ago.'

'Was it?' Mike said. 'I can't keep up.'

Angus swung in to the kerb and pulled up sharp. 'I can take you to the station or you can walk. It's your choice. A bit of respect is what's required.'

'You're right there,' Mike said. He opened the door. 'Don't use M. Lucas.' He got out and slammed the door.

Angus leaned over and wound down the window. He was smiling. 'Mike,' he said, 'grow up a bit.' He drove off, tooting his horn. Mike stood on the pavement, shaking his head as if he were the father and Angus the wayward son. You bastard, he thought. Then, because there was nothing else for it, he headed for the station.

The spread was in one of the colour supplements a couple of weeks later. Angus had certainly captured something – if not the mood of the country, then moods of various kinds. There were drummers, defiant and wary, warming up before the Orange march; there were some kids kicking a ball around on a bald patch of grass in front of grim-looking housing and a notice that read NO BALL GAMES; there was a handsome, tall white man and a short, balding Asian man outside a shop, next to a display of produce and a hand-written sign, BRAW NEW TATTIES, and although it was probably the Asian man's shop you didn't know this, and although they were standing together neither was smiling so you weren't sure what the relationship was; there was a family paddling in a few inches of water, trousers rolled, skirts hitched, and the dad had a Scotland top on and they all looked ridiculous against a background of sublime loch and mountain scenery. And there, taking pride of place and a full page to himself, was M. Lucas, perched on his shooting stick in his absurd kilt with all the trimmings, his hair unkempt and with ice cream running down his chin, and if you didn't know you wouldn't realise he was blind but you'd guess there was something not right with his vision. There was litter scattered around him and hints of flags and tartan at the edges of the picture, and he sat amid this debris like King Lear, mad and proud. Mike was incensed that his father had allowed it to be used: it was all very well saying it was out of his hands but of course it wasn't, he needn't have submitted it. But Mike looked at it and looked at it, and what incensed him most was what a wonderful photograph it was. And he wanted to phone Angus to tell him what he thought, but he couldn't. How could he say how sorry he was that his old teacher made such an eloquent symbol of something so tragicomic, how glad he was that M. Lucas couldn't see it, and how jealous he was that the Angus angle had triumphed once again? He told himself that he was a better person than his father, that he had shown restraint and respect by his actions, but it was small consolation. He looked at his father's photograph and two thoughts reverberated in his head. The first was, *what if I had taken that?* The second was, *if only I had!*

§

What if, what if, what if? If only, if only, if only. Those phrases sit like crows on the passage of the years. They settle on politics, they settle on love, they settle on life. You clap your hands but not all the crows fly away. What if Mike had not ended up with Adam that night at Jean's? If only he had been sure of his sexuality at thirteen, or sixteen. What if he had become a lawyer, not a photographer? If only Scotland had scored two more goals in Argentina. What if Jim Callaghan had called a General Election in the autumn of 1978, before the so-called Winter of Discontent? If only the result of the devolution referendum of March 1979 had been different. He understands, of course, that all such propositions and regrets are now completely pointless, but he finds it hard, almost impossible, *not* to look back and wonder.

The Bill for setting up a Scottish assembly made its way, ground, squeezed and crushed by friend and foe, line by line, clause by clause, through late-night sittings in the House of Commons. In amongst those clauses was provision for the holding of a referendum, so that the Scottish people could decide if they really wanted such a squeezed and crushed assembly as the Bill proposed. On Burns Night in 1978, one of the squeezers and crushers, a Scot called George Cunningham, the Honourable Member for Islington, proposed an amendment to the legislation, requiring 40 per cent of the registered electorate to vote in favour of an assembly before it could be established. George Cunningham was not in favour of an assembly himself. Many of his fellow MPs were not in favour of an assembly. They voted for the amendment. The pro-devolutionists howled in outrage. In no General Election since the war had the victorious party won the votes of 40 per cent of the registered electorate. George Cunningham had not won the votes of 40 per cent of the registered electorate of Islington. The amendment, the pro-devolutionists said, was a wrecking amendment, designed to frustrate the democratic process. The anti-devolutionists taunted them: if their plans were so popular, what were they afraid of? From the Tory benches came further jibes: the sole reason the Labour government was insisting on pushing devolution through in the face of mass indifference was that it felt threatened by the SNP in so many of its Scottish seats. But, the Tories said, creating an assembly in Edinburgh wouldn't halt the Nationalists: it would give them a platform from which to argue for their ultimate goal of complete independence. Encouraged, the grinders and crushers on the Labour benches worked tirelessly on. Their selfless endeavours were reported in stifling detail, day after day, in the newspapers. The longer it continued, the more depressing it became. It looked as if the Scots were genetically and historically conditioned to fall out amongst themselves. Eventually, in July 1978, when the Bill could be ground and crushed no more, it limped into being as the Scotland Act.

The Honourable Member for Edinburgh Central, the constituency in which Mike stayed, was Robin Cook, one of the grinders and crushers. Adam, furious at them all, condemned them as backstabbers, betrayers and deceivers. Mike said it could hardly be claimed that Robin Cook had deceived anybody. He was implacably opposed to an assembly and never missed a public opportunity to say so. His constituents, he said, wrote to him about housing, the health service, schools, unemployment and crime, but he'd never received a single letter about devolution. Adam immediately instructed Mike to write to Cook about it, which he did. The dismissive reply he received riled Mike enough to make him turn up at one of Cook's constituency surgeries to pursue the matter. Cook, wee, wiry and red-bearded, was more prickly in the flesh than he had been on paper. Mike did not take to him. Unless Cook changed his stance, he said, he wouldn't be able to vote for him at the next General Election. Cook shrugged, completely unimpressed: then he would have to survive without Mike's vote; he was pretty sure he would have no difficulty in doing so. He believed that the vast majority of his constituents were profoundly uninterested in a Scottish assembly, and the referendum would prove it because so few would turn out to vote. 'We'll see,' said Mike. 'Yes,' said Cook, glancing at his watch, 'we shall.'

§

In October 1978 the SNP lost another by-election, in East Lothian, this time trailing in behind both Labour and the Conservatives and losing their deposit. It looked as though nationalism might have peaked. Jim Callaghan was personally popular, and Labour were ahead of the Tories in the opinion polls. He still had a year left before he had to call a General Election. He didn't. He missed his chance.

Collective and separate madnesses bloomed. The unions had had enough of pay restraint and they brought their members out on strike with demands for bigger and bigger wage increases. It was a winter of constant drizzle, damp, slush and grey cloud – or so it seems to Mike, thinking back. A winter of discontent. There were closed libraries, closed benefit offices, picket lines outside schools and hospitals, uncollected rubbish and barely functioning public transport. There was a prolonged strike by lorry drivers, which led to food shortages in shops and material shortages in factories. The crows of *what if* and *if only* gathered in the trees.

Mike sympathised with the strikers, but sometimes they displayed incredible naivety in the way they allowed themselves to be portrayed by the media, and sometimes they displayed incredible arrogance. When Adam came through to Edinburgh at weekends, he and Mike argued. Adam was directly involved – both as a union activist and as a district councillor – in the turmoil, whereas Mike was only inconvenienced. Adam would not or could not see that the endless wage disputes and the ideological battles within the Labour movement were driving people in their tens of thousands towards the Conservatives – revitalised by Margaret Thatcher, de-cluttered of compromises and consensus, and gearing up for their own kind of revolution. He still thought society was progressing – slowly and with setbacks, but progressing nonetheless – towards a benevolent, municipal kind of socialism under which most people would be healthier, better educated, better housed and better paid. Mike, supposedly the naive one, thought that Adam was deluding himself. But neither of them saw what was really coming.

The referendum campaign for and against a Scottish assembly ran for the month of February 1979. There was a No camp and a Yes camp, but each camp contained factions, some of which detested their supposed allies more than they did the opposing camp. The Yes for Scotland campaign had the support of the SNP, a renegade Tory or two, and various clerics, trade unionists, writers and actors. There was also a Liberal campaign and another non-party grouping called Alliance for an Assembly. But the SNP ran its own separate Yes campaign and some Nationalists wouldn't appear on platforms with people from other parties. Labour banned its members from any cross-party activity, refused to work within any umbrella group and also ran its own campaign, Labour Movement Yes. Think of a football team lining up before kick-off, each player with a ball at his feet, determined not to pass it to anybody else – except maybe the opposition.

Scotland Says No was the main campaign against devolution. It was composed of an assortment of businessmen, lawyers and Conservative politicians. To the right of this grouping were two hard-line Unionist cadres, Scotland is British and Keep Britain United. To its left was the Labour Vote No committee, populated by members of the grinding-and-crushing tendency. The No team was as much of an unholy alliance as the Yes team, but its members had one great advantage: they had just the one ball, and they were willing to pass it around.

Mike felt an obligation to get involved. Adam urged him on, but he would have acted anyway. He delivered Yes leaflets to hundreds of homes, and handed out many more on the streets. He started off reasonably sure that, in spite of all the divisions, there was a chance of winning and even of surmounting the 40-per-cent barrier. But as the days went by his confidence waned. There was an office on Leith Walk where he went to pick up flyers and leaflets for distribution. It should have been buzzing, but the first time he turned up the solitary man minding the shop raised an eyebrow at him, indicated the piles of paper and said, 'Help yersel, son. Naebody else is wanting them.' On a later visit, one dark afternoon, the place was locked up. Through the window Mike could see the same stacks of material, largely undiminished, piled up in the gloom. He rattled the door but nobody came.

Polling day arrived. Mike went out to vote Yes, but did so more in despair than in hope. Later, Eric came in. By then a houseman at the Royal Infirmary, he had become increasingly exasperated by strikes and bureaucracy. He liked the idea of more political decision-making happening in Scotland but was highly suspicious of the contents of the Scotland Act. He had voted No.

He wasn't alone. When the results were announced, a third of the country, 1.23 million people, had voted Yes. Slightly fewer, 1.15 million, had voted No. Both of these figures were exceeded by the number of people who didn't vote at all. The 40-per-cent hurdle was way beyond the reach of the Yes vote. Robin Cook's prediction proved accurate: the people appeared not to care enough.

The failure of the referendum led directly to the end of the Labour government. In theory Callaghan could have held on till October, but in practice everybody had had enough. What if? If only? It was all over. The SNP tabled a motion of no confidence, the Tories followed up with one of their own, and in the debate that followed the government was brought down by a single vote. Callaghan said the SNP were like turkeys voting for an early Christmas, and in one respect he was right: all but two of its eleven MPs lost their seats in the General Election that followed. Margaret Thatcher swept into power and began the process of rolling back socialism, trade unionism, local government, community, consensus, compromise, Scottish and Welsh nationalism and anything else that stood in her way.

§

'I'm not proud of myself,' Jean says. 'I should have stopped it but I couldn't. First of all he went to London for a year and we only saw each other occasionally – sometimes he'd come north on the train and once I went south. That wasn't very successful. I knew there were probably other women but I didn't have the courage to confront him about them. Then he came back to Scotland with a lot of commissions and we started being together again but it was different somehow. And then he met Isobel and told me it was over between us but it wasn't, he still came to see me and I still let him in.

'I think it was all some long after-effect of the war. He'd joined the army as soon as he left school, and a lot of inhibitions go out of the window when you're that young and there's a fair chance you may die before your next birthday. I was only fifteen when the war ended but that sense of "now or never" rubbed off on me too. There were all these young men in uniform making daft wee lassies like me weak at the knees, and maybe that had an impact. You saw uniforms everywhere – men home on leave, boys doing their National Service, even years after they were demobbed some men still put on their battledress to do the gardening or go for a hike in the hills. They wore it till it wore out. The war didn't suddenly end, it faded away, and some of the attitudes hung on too.

'Anyway, your father was the handsomest man I ever saw, in or out of a uniform. I was smitten when we first met, and I just let it carry on. I liked everything about him – his looks, his intelligence, his sense of humour, his passion for life, the fact that he stuck two fingers up at anything that didn't suit him. And I liked the things we did together – the hillwalking, the journeys to different places, the talking, the drinking, the dancing . . .'

'The sex,' Mike says.

'Thank you for reminding me,' she says, a little acidly. 'Yes, I liked the sex. He was a very good lover. I was careful though, even though I was smitten, and I made him be careful. I didn't want his babies. I point-blank refused to have children. I've never wanted them. I wanted to keep my independence. It was one of the things that kept him coming back to me, because I wouldn't give in. I think your father needed to conquer women by making them beholden to him – emotionally, sexually, domestically, one way or another. As soon as he'd achieved that he got bored. It drove him mad that he wasn't in control, but he liked it too, my independent streak. And maybe I didn't want to be as independent as I claimed, but there we both were, full of contradictions.

'I think that's why he was so reckless when he met your mother. She was – well, let's say she was less liberated than I was. He was certainly the first man she'd been intimate with.'

'How do you know that?'

She looks slightly abashed. 'He told me. But it was pretty obvious. Most young women didn't go to bed with anybody except their sisters or their husbands or *perhaps* their future husbands. Even I'd only had a couple of lovers before Angus.'

'Did you have a job?'

'A sort of job, working for a sort of publisher-cum-bookseller, an old man called Henry Kersland who'd been a friend of my father's. I typed his correspondence, read manuscripts for him and kept his accounts, and generally did everything in the back of his shop on the High Street while he sat in the front pretending he still had a viable business. He was a sweet old boy, but he was about a hundred years out of date. Sometimes I can hardly believe he was a real person. He liked to flirt with me when we had our tea breaks together. It was all quite harmless. He didn't pay me a wage as such, but every Friday he'd ask if I was all right and I'd say no and he'd pull a few banknotes out of his wallet and hand them to me. And then he died, and I discovered he'd left this place to me in his will. He didn't have any family.'

'Did you never have to work?'

'It's a terrible admission to make,' Jean says, 'but no. Between what Henry left me and what came to me when my parents passed on, I've always had enough. I've been lucky, I know. Some people would say I've had a wasted life, achieved nothing. But my good fortune gave me some space to think, and maybe that meant I was able to give other people space to think. Maybe I've been a facilitator. Ghastly word. But anyway, not altogether a wasted life.'

'There was always a bit of mystery about you,' Mike says. 'I remember Walter Fleming telling me that the first time he brought me here. We all thought we knew what the storyteller's story was, but we didn't. It got mixed in with all the other stories.'

'Well, you know now. The shop and the stock that was in it paid for Henry's debts, which were not inconsiderable, and for his funeral, which was attended by me and half a dozen of his customers. And I found myself in possession of this place. It was Henry's home, and it's been mine ever since. That was in 1954, the year your parents got married.

'We'd had an argument and Angus walked out and I didn't see him for a fortnight and in the meantime he met Isobel. It was at some country-house dance and I think she was so *not* his type he saw her as a challenge and had to seduce her. She was, of course, very beautiful. They looked very fine together. I met them for afternoon tea once, in the North British Hotel, so I know. How Edinburgh is *that* for a *ménage à trois*?'

'Did she know about you and him?'

'If he didn't tell her she must have worked it out. Perhaps it was the way the scones passed between us. I mind at his funeral I introduced myself to her, said something about how she probably wouldn't remember me but we'd met once, and she gave me an icy stare, up and down, and said, "Oh yes, I remember *you* very well." You were talking to somebody else at the time. Anyway, that's probably why she finally let him have his wicked way with her, to trump the opposition. He pushed her and pushed her to have sex, and at last she did, and that was that.'

'That was what?'

'Well, think about it. She didn't have the obsession about avoiding pregnancy that I had. Or even the knowledge, maybe. And he would have told her it would be all right. When was their wedding anniversary?'

'I've no idea. They divorced when I was ten. I was never conscious of them ever celebrating their wedding.'

'Because neither of them thought it was anything to celebrate. They got married in the summer, August, I think. You were born in January 1955. Work it out, Mike.'

But he doesn't need to. He worked it out a long time ago. 'I was a mistake,' he says, 'and they had to marry because of me. Even if she persuaded herself that it would be okay, that he'd settle down, it never was and he never did. It's why she resents me so much.'

'You really believe she does, don't you?'

'Of course she does. Seventy-five years old and she still holds it against me.'

'Well, that's for you and her to sort out. Think about it from her point of view. That's what happened back then. People got married because they had to. You couldn't *be* a single mother. Thank God for contraception and the Abortion Act, I say.'

'Thanks a lot, Jean.'

'Sorry. That's not what I meant.'

'My father probably said that to her at the time. "Sorry, that's not what I meant." And he told you all of this, did he?'

'He couldn't help himself. And I'd get angry but I let him tell me. I preferred hearing it to not hearing it. At least it meant he was with me.'

'And you were still having sex with him, *not* getting pregnant, while Isobel was swelling up with me?'

'Yes, I was.'

'You must have been seeing him almost while he was getting married to her?'

'Yes.'

'How could you? How could *he* get married to her in those circumstances?'

'It was what people did. The *right thing*, even if it was the wrong thing. Even if it meant you were going to be miserable for the rest of your life. As I said, I'm not proud of myself. He should have been loyal to Isobel and tried to make it work, and he didn't. And I was complicit in that, in their marriage being a sham from the beginning, and I'm sorry for it. Can you imagine what it felt like when you walked into my house? I'd decided to keep my independence and Angus had decided to have a child by somebody else. He wanted a son, Mike. He wanted you. And then he sent you to me, to show me what he'd achieved.'

A thought occurs to Mike, too suddenly for him to suppress it. 'You're telling me the truth now, aren't you? This isn't a story that's going to have a different ending next week?'

'I could be dead next week. It's the truth, and nothing but. Why?'

'I'm not yours, am I?'

'What?'

'You didn't give birth to me and then, for some reason I can't even begin to imagine, Isobel raised me as her own? That's too ridiculous, isn't it?'

Jean laughs. 'It *is* too ridiculous. This isn't *Little Dorrit*, it's reality. You are Angus and Isobel's child.'

'Such things happen.'

'Good God, look at yourself. You couldn't be anybody else *but* their offspring. Whatever else they saddled you with, they gave you their looks.'

'We know so much now that people didn't know then,' Mike says. 'Kids who grew up with a much-older sister who then turns out to be their mother. Kids shipped off to Australia and brought up to believe they're orphans, who discover their mother's alive in Glasgow forty years later. Apparently happily married men who are blackmailed or driven to suicide because they actually prefer happily unmarried men to whatever pretence they've maintained for decades. It was all kept hidden and secret while politicians went around telling people they'd never had it so good.'

'There's something else I'm sorry for,' she says. 'I'm sorry I was never able to tell you all this while your dad was alive. It's so strange how the past makes you keep its confidences. I didn't even *know* I couldn't tell you, not until after he was dead. Not even then, in fact. I couldn't speak to you at the funeral. It's just now that time is running out . . .'

'Time isn't running out.'

'Aye it is. And it's important – I can't tell you how important it is, Mike – not to leave things unsaid.'

They have come, by some route the details of which are lost in the amount of whisky they have drunk, back to where they started. And Mike understands that whatever he has learned from Jean tonight he has really always known, though perhaps not admitted. None of it really surprises him. And none of it changes anything.

'I said to you yesterday,' Jean says, 'I'm shedding things. So I gave you a hard time about your dad. You've made me shed this. Let's call that a fair exchange.'

'What about after my father?' Mike says. 'You said you didn't have many relationships before him. What about after? Was there nobody else?'

'There have been several,' she says. 'And that's been fine and pleasurable and made us feel better about ourselves, I hope. But none of them matched him.'

'Walter?' Mike says.

'I'm not giving you names,' she says. 'You're not, so why should I?'

'I'm not what?'

'Giving me names.' Her stare is very direct. For a moment he is on the verge of telling her about Murdo. Then the moment passes.

And a little later, just before they stagger off to their beds, 'The truth is,' Jean says – as if, since they can't beat the second bottle, she has to drain the very dregs of her thoughts – 'the truth is, we had great fun together and he didn't want that to end, even when he and Isobel got married. And neither did I. So we kept it going for a while, but after a year or so it stopped being fun. It began to feel sordid. And he was getting too well known, so we couldn't be anonymous. Before he had his fling with Isobel it was much better, much healthier. That's what I remember most, and best.'

'And there was me thinking it was you he had the fling with,' Mike says. 'I know their marriage was crap, but it did last ten years. It always seemed to me that Dad's flings happened away from home. But I suppose it depends where you're looking from.'

'I suppose it does.'

'There's no certainty, is there?' Mike says. 'It's the curse of the age we live in. Having to take everybody's point of view into account. Bigots on radio phone-ins and arseholes adding their online comments to news and blogs full of nothing but ignorance. I mean, what can you trust?'

'Trust the story,' Jean says. 'That's all you can do. Trust the story.'

§

Maybe it's the whisky, maybe it's Jean's voice, but one of her stories is in his head when he drifts off, and it's there when he surfaces hours later. It's about Jack again, the hero of so many of her stories. Sometimes he's cunning, sometimes lucky, but more often than not he's an innocent. So. Jack was wanting to go on a journey, and he told his mother he'd be away in the morning and asked her to make him up a piece to take with him. Well, his mother made up a piece, just a hunk of bread and some cheese, and while she was doing this she said, 'And where are you going on this journey, Jack?' Because he wasn't very bright, Jack, he was daft really, and she wanted to see what he'd say. 'Well, Mother, I thought I would go to the edge of the world and have a bit look over the edge and see what lies beyond it.' Because he thought the world was flat, you see. 'Right,' she says, 'and how are you going to get there?' 'I don't know that,' says Jack. 'Usually when I set off on an adventure my two older brothers have gone before me, and I follow on behind them, but I seem to be on my own this time.' 'That's right,' his mother says, 'you've no brothers in this story so you'll need to make your own way to the edge of the world.' 'Well, I suppose I'll just set off and keep walking till I get there,' he says, 'but there's one thing,' he says, 'do you have something to give me before I go, because in the other stories you ask us if we want a wee piece and a blessing or a big piece and a curse, or some such thing, and my two brothers are greedy and take the big piece and a curse, and they always end up in trouble, and I usually take the wee piece and a blessing, and somehow things work out all right for me.' 'Ach, well, that's just stories, Jack,' his mother says. 'I'm not going to bless you or curse you, and the piece I've made for you is just an average kind of size, but I will give you some advice. If you do reach the edge of the world,' she says, 'have a look over it but don't, whatever you do, step off it, because if you do I doubt you'll ever get back again, and I'd like to see you safe home again after your adventure.' 'Right,' he says, 'I'll mind that.' She says, 'There's your piece wrapped up for you, Jack, and I'll kiss you good-bye now for I think you'll be up and away before I'm out of my bed in the morning.' And she kisses him, she was awful fond of him for all that he was daft, and away they go to their beds.

So in the morning Jack's up early, and off he goes with his piece and his mother's advice, and he walks and walks and walks, miles and miles he goes, further than he's ever gone before, until it's coming on evening and he reaches the very end of the land. There's a long sandy beach and the sea breaking on the beach, and Jack is tired, just worn out, so he sits down and eats his piece, and while he's eating he says to himself, 'Well, I know that's the sea, and there must be a lot of it before you reach the edge of the world, so somehow I'll have to get across it but I don't know how. Anyway, I'm too tired to go any further, so I'll just have a sleep here and when I wake up I'll see what's to be done about it.'

So he stretches out in the lee of the dunes and goes to sleep to the sound of the waves breaking not far away. But hardly has he closed his eyes when he feels a terrible *dunch* on the bottom of his left foot, and then another *dunch* on the bottom of his right foot, so he sits up, and here's a wee man with a long grey beard, just the ugliest wee bodach you ever saw, kicking the soles of Jack's feet as hard as he can. Jack says, 'Here, what do you think you're doing?' and the wee man says, 'What do you think *you're* doing? This is my beach and ye canna sleep here.' 'And who are you?' says Jack. 'I'm the ferry-man that ferries folk across the sea,' says the wee man. 'Who are you?' 'Well,' says Jack, 'I'm Jack and I'm wanting to go to the edge of the world, to have a bit look over it. Is it across this sea?' 'It is,' says the wee man. 'And can you take me there?' 'Aye, I can that,' says he. 'Well, I would like to go there,' Jack says, 'but I'm needing a sleep right now.' 'Well, if you're to be my passenger, you can sleep here after all,' the wee man says, 'and in the morning I'll take you over the sea to the edge of the world. When you wake up, just walk along the beach, round the end of the point there, and that's where I keep my boat. You'll see three boats pulled up on the sand. The first boat has a pair of oars and the second has a set of sails and the third one, that's mine, and it has an outboard motor.' 'Och away,' Jack says, 'in a story like this?' 'Aye,' says the wee man, 'I'm all for modern conveniences. When you get there yourself you'll see if it isn't true.' 'And is there a fare to pay?' Jack asks. 'Well,' the man says, 'if you take the boat with oars there's no fare, and if you take the boat with sails there's no fare, but you'll have to steer them yourself and I can't tell you if that will be easy or no, but if you come with me I'll make sure you get across the sea but there is a fare.' 'And what's the fare?' Jack asks. 'You must give me the most precious thing you have,' says the wee man, 'until you come back.' 'Well, I haven't anything,' Jack says. 'I've no money, and no rings or fancy clothes, I've nothing valuable at all.' 'The most precious thing any-body has,' the wee man says, 'is his soul, and if you want to go across the sea you must leave yours with me.' 'Well,' Jack says, 'I'm not doing that, I'd be mad to hand over my soul to a complete stranger.' 'It's just a loan,' the wee man says, 'you'll get it again when you come back. In fact,' he says, 'it's really for safe keeping because if you're away at the edge of the world you might drop your soul over it, whereas I can keep it safe till you come back.' 'Well, I'll need to think about it,' Jack says. 'Well, you think about it and I'll see you in the morning anyway,' the man says, and off he goes along the beach. And it's very near dark now, so Jack stretches himself out in the lee of the dunes and goes to sleep.

In the morning he wakes up, and it's a fine, sunny morning with just a light breeze blowing, so he says to himself, 'I'll take a stroll along the beach to where these boats are, and see what's what, but I'm not sure if I'll be going anywhere with yon mannie.' So he walks round the point and sure enough here's a boat drawn up on the sand with a pair of oars in it. And Jack thinks, now, if only my older brother had been here before me, no doubt he'd have taken this boat to save himself the fare, and rowed out on the sea, and I'm pretty certain he'd have come to a sticky end of some sort, so I'll just pass on by. And he walks on a wee bit and here's the second boat, all ready to go with its sails flapping against the mast, waiting to be made taut. And Jack thinks, if my second brother had been here before me, surely he'd have saved himself the fare by taking *this* boat, and I think he'd have capsized it or something, so I'll just pass on by. And he walks a bit further and here's a wee boat with an outboard motor at the water's edge, and the bodach with the long grey beard is sitting on an old kist beside it, smoking a pipe.

'Are you ready to go then?' says the ferryman. 'Well, I'm not sure,' says Jack. 'I'm not sure about this fare. How do I know I'll get my soul back if I give it to you?' 'You don't,' says the ferryman, 'that's a chance you'll have to take. But I notice you didn't take the boat with oars and you didn't take the boat with sails, so you must have had a reason to come this far.' 'Well, I'm wanting to go to the edge of the world,' says Jack, 'but I don't want to lose my soul.' 'It's up to you,' the man says. 'The only way across the sea is with me – unless you take one of the other boats, but I don't think you fancy that.' 'No,' Jack says, 'I've got a strange feeling about those boats, I don't want to get in either of them.' 'Well, it's me or nothing then,' says the man. So Jack thinks to himself, he thinks, ach you only live once, I've come all this way and if I go home now I'll always wonder what I missed. 'Right,' he says to the ferryman, 'let's go.'

As soon as he says that the ferryman jumps up and starts getting the boat ready. He says, 'Now, I'll just take your soul and put it in this kist here, and lock it away safely, and you'll get it again when you come back.' 'And will you fetch me when I'm ready to come back?' Jack asks. 'Aye, I'll do that,' he says. 'And how will I let you know I'm ready?' 'All you need to do,' the man says, 'is turn three times widdershins, that's anticlockwise, and I'll be there. Now, get into the boat and sit in the bow, and I'll sit in the stern.' So Jack climbs in and sits in the bow, and the ferryman reaches over and touches his middle and Jack gives a gasp, a wee blast of cold air goes through him, and the ferryman's holding something in his hand, and he goes and opens up the kist and puts the something in it and closes it again and turns a key in the lock and the key is on a string, which hangs round his neck. And all of a sudden Jack feels an emptiness inside him, a wee sadness, and he thinks to himself, so this is how it feels when your soul's been taken from you. He doesn't like the feeling but he thinks, well, I'm in it now, I may as well see this through. And anyway the wee man's already pushed the boat into the water and jumped in and started the motor and they're heading off out through the waves.

It's a pleasant journey at first. The sun is shining down on them, the water's glittering and calm, and the wind on Jack's cheek is warm. Soon enough they've left the coast behind them and they're out in the middle of the sea, and after a while when Jack looks back he can't see the land at all. He's not so keen on that, never having been at sea before, but then he starts looking down into the water, which is clear and clean, and he sees the most beautiful things – fishes of every shape and size and colour, and rocks covered in forests of weeds and flowers, and all kinds of wonderful creatures moving around on the seabed. And there are birds of great beauty flying near by, and seals and porpoises and dolphins in the sea, and everything is a delight. And all the time the sound of the engine is going chug-chug-chug in a friendly kind of way, and whenever Jack looks at the ferryman he's staring out over the water minding his own business, just steering with the tiller, but whenever Jack looks away again he has a feeling that the man's eyes are upon him. And Jack can't make up his mind whether to trust the man or not, but then he thinks, well, it's too late now, he has my soul in a box back on the beach and if he has ill intentions then there's not much I can do about it.

Well, as they journey on with the boat going chug-chug-chug the sky begins to darken and clouds gather, and the sea gets a wee bit rougher. It seems to Jack that they're travelling faster now, and that the boat's engine isn't what's pushing them along, it's like they're being pulled by some great force underneath them, and in fact when he looks down now he can see that the water is rushing in the same direction as them, so fast that it makes him feel sick. And he shouts to the ferryman, 'What's happening?' and the ferryman has a wicked grin on his face and shouts back, 'Well, Jack, what did you expect? We're getting close to the edge of the world and all the water goes over it.' 'What about us?' Jack shouts. 'Oh, we'll be all right,' the man says. 'I've been here many times before, I'll not let the boat go over.' And Jack's shaking with fear and wondering what's going to happen next, but what's strange is you'd expect a terrible noise with all that water going over the edge, you'd expect a roar like a hundred Niagaras, but there's hardly any noise at all. The ferryman says, 'Now, Jack, get yourself on your feet and be ready to jump, for in a minute I'm going to bring the boat round, right on the edge of the world, and there'll be a rock beside the boat, and you must leap on to it. Don't leap too far or you'll go over the edge, and don't leap too short or you'll go in the water and be swept over.' And Jack wants to ask if it's too late to change his mind but suddenly the ferryman says, 'Ready? One, two, three – jump!' and pushes the tiller away from him so the boat suddenly swings round to face the opposite way and Jack, before he knows what he's doing, is half-thrown and half-leaps from the boat and lands on a bare, dry bit of rock sticking out where the water disappears over the edge.

Well, what a place it is! To his left is a waterfall, a straight line stretching off into the distance as far as he can see, and to his right is exactly the same thing, and here's Jack, on a wee bit of rock about three feet above the water, a kind of ledge two feet wide and six feet long, about the size of a bed but very narrow. And the water sweeps round it on either side but it doesn't go over it, the top of the rock is completely dry. And then, when Jack looks carefully over the edge, all he can see is the water dropping away from him, down, down, down, as far as he can see. And there's no roar, no clouds of spray, no foaming and gushing, just an endless sheet of water flowing over the edge and down. It's like it's turning a corner rather than falling. And it's a terrifying place to be, crouched on this stone just where all the water turns, and what with the silence and the speed of the water and the fact that it's not like any waterfall he's ever seen before – well, all Jack really wants to do is get back in the boat as quick as he can. But already the engine is chug-chug-chugging away from him, fighting the current to get clear. Jack shouts at the ferryman, 'Come back! I knew the world was flat, but I didn't think it was so tall!' And the ferryman calls back, 'The world isn't flat, Jack, it's a cube, like a sugar lump. The water flows over the edges of the six faces, from one face to another, it never stops, and this cube is so big that if you're on a bit of land you'd never know it because all the land in the world is so far from any of the edges of the cube. Think about it, Jack!' he says, and the boat gets wee-er and wee-er until at last Jack can't see it any more.

Well, he's crouching there on the rock and he's afraid to stand up and he's afraid to sit down, and every so often a fish or a seal or some other sea creature shoots out of the water as it goes over the edge, and then lands back in it and disappears again. And sometimes a seagull appears above him, and flies over the edge, and then changes direction and continues on its way. And apart from these things, Jack is there at the edge of the world all alone, and he doesn't like it, not one bit.

So he thinks, what I have to do is turn three times widdershins and the ferryman will come back for me, if he was telling the truth. God, I hope he was telling the truth, he thinks. But when Jack tries to turn round he loses his nerve. He's already dizzy on that rock, and he can't bring himself to do it, he's that frightened of falling off. So there he is, stuck on the rock, and it's getting dark, and he's awful hungry and tired, and eventually he's so tired that he just has to sit down, and he manages to do it. And then he begins to fall asleep, and wakes up with a start, and then he lies flat out on the narrow bit of rock, as far away from the edge of the world as he can get, and falls asleep again, dreaming of cheese pieces.

Now as Jack dreams he turns over in his sleep. He turns once – and he rolls into the middle of the rock – twice – and he rolls again – three times – and he's just teetering on the edge where the water falls away when there's a shout from near by, and he wakes up with a start and only just stops himself from falling off. It's morning again and there's the ferryman with the boat alongside the rock shouting, 'Jump, Jack, jump! Quickly now, for I can't come back again!' So Jack jumps, but he jumps too hard and he crashes into the ferryman at the stern of the boat, and knocks him over, and the man loses his grip of the tiller, and the boat spins round and suddenly the boat and Jack and the ferryman are shooting over the edge of the world and Jack's falling out of the boat. He tries to grab hold of the wee man who's grabbed hold of the side of the boat but all he gets a grip of is the string round the wee man's neck, which breaks, and Jack shoots up in the air and lands with an almighty

DUNCH!

Not a splash. A *dunch*. He's not in the sea at all. He shakes himself and sits up and there he is, where he fell asleep in the sand dunes. Och it was all just a dream, he thinks, but then he looks in his hand and there is a length of string and at the end of it a key. How can that be if it was a dream? And oh, how cold he feels. The sun's just coming up and he's cold and stiff and hungry, but the coldest, emptiest bit of him is just in at his chest and he knows what that means: it means his soul is missing. And he remembers that the ferryman took it, so Jack stands up and walks along the beach and round the point. And there are the two boats, the one with the oars and the one with sails, but there's no sign of the third boat, the one with the outboard motor, and there's no sign of the ferryman. But there's the old kist lying on the beach. Jack takes the key and he unlocks it, and opens the lid, and as soon as he does something rushes out and he feels a warm blast of air go through him, and he feels whole again.

So he hurries off home. He can't get away from that shore quick enough. But it's a long, long walk back the way he came, and by the time he gets home it's dark again, it's the middle of the night, so he lets himself into the house very quietly because he doesn't want to wake his mother, and he creeps up the narrow stair to his room and gets into his old familiar bed and in a few seconds he's fast asleep.

In the morning, he's woken by the sun shining through the window, and up he gets and down the stair he goes to the kitchen for his breakfast. There's his mother working away at the fireside. 'Here I am back again, Mother,' says Jack. 'What do you mean?' she says. 'You've only just got up.'

'Have you forgotten?' he says. 'I've been away to the edge of the world.'

'Oh aye,' says his mother. 'Well, there's the piece I made up for you last night for your journey, just a hunk of bread and some cheese, but since you're still here you can have it for your breakfast.' And Jack remembers that she made it up for him, but did he not eat it before? Well, he's puzzling this out, but he's that hungry that he sits down and eats it anyway, and while he's eating he tells her all that happened.

Well, she listens to him and at the end she says, 'Aye, Jack, you tell a good story, but there's one thing I know and it's this. The world isn't flat, as you thought, but it isn't a cube either, it's round like a ball. When you said you were wanting to go to the edge of the world I thought you'd just go to the coast and come back again. But you've not even been away yet.'

'Oh yes I have, Mother,' he says, 'and anyway you're wrong, just as I was wrong. The world *is* a cube. It's like a sugar lump. I know it is because I've been to the edge, or one of the edges, and I've seen it.'

'Jack,' she says, 'dinna be a daft gowk. The world is round. You were dreaming.' So he puts his hand in his pocket and draws out the key. 'So where did I get this from then?' he says. 'Och, Jack,' she says, 'where *did* you get it? We have no need for keys here.'

Just at that moment the door opens and in come Jack's two older brothers. They've been out working in the fields and this is them coming in for their breakfast. But just a minute, did you think Jack didn't have brothers in this story? Aye, well, neither did Jack. So that just shows why you shouldn't believe everything people tell you. And the brothers sit at the table next to Jack and say, 'Aye Jack, what have you been up to now? You're always dreaming about something.' 'But I wasn't dreaming,' Jack says. 'Here's the key I took from the ferryman's kist.' 'What ferryman?' they say, so he tells them. Well, the brothers listen to his story, but they don't believe him, they think he's stolen the key from somewhere, and they decide they'll have to bury it to keep Jack out of trouble. So they take it off him and bury it out in the fields and it's never been seen again. And Jack says, 'Well, at least I left the kist unlocked and the lid open, so that ferryman can't take anybody else's soul and lock it away.' 'Ach Jack,' his brothers say, 'you just think what you like.' And he does. Jack knows what happened. And that's an end to this story.

§

In the morning – the very late morning – Mike wakes and tentatively assesses his physical and mental condition. Astonishingly, he doesn't feel too bad. His mouth is dry, his stomach a little unsettled, but generally he seems to have got away with it. He slides out of bed, washes, gets dressed and goes through to the kitchen. Jean is there, reading a book, smoking away.

'There's tea in the pot,' she says. 'And there's bread in the bread bin if you want toast. I've had something already.'

He can see that she has. The carry-out cartons are empty.

'I don't think you're anywhere close to dying,' he says. 'You're indestructible.'

'No doubt I shall pay for it.'

Despite his escape, he isn't ready to risk food yet. He opts for several mugs of black tea.

Jean puts down her book. 'Are you definitely going back today?'

'Aye. It's a non-transferable ticket. The train's in an hour and a half.'

'You can stay if you want.'

He shakes his head. 'I'll come again soon. For the exhibition, if not before.'

'Well, it's been good,' she says. 'At least, I think it has. I hope it's been useful.'

He remembers Angus describing Jean as having been 'useful' to him.

'You've given me plenty to think about,' he says.

'Don't get too hung up on this essay,' she says. 'The photographs are what matter.'

'I know. I've known it all along really.'

'Get someone else to write the essay.'

She pushes her empty mug towards him and he refills it, and his too, and goes to put the kettle on again.

'Did you ever tell me,' she says, 'what you did with Angus? After the funeral, I mean.'

'I took him back to Cnoc nan Gobhar,' he says. 'We'd talked about what he wanted. For a while he'd said he wanted to be taken out on the water and scattered. But then he went off that idea. First he said he didn't want to be fish food, then that he didn't want to get mixed up with radioactive particles drifting along from Dounreay. Just keep me on dry land, he said. Plant a tree on top of me. So I did. I dug a hole at the front of the house, mixed him up with some compost and packed him in round a rowan sapling. To begin with it didn't look like it would take, it gets such a blasting from the wind in winter, but last year it was healthier. So that's where he is.'

'I'm sure he – it – will do very well,' she says. 'And it will keep the witches away. Not, I suppose, that any of them are likely to visit.'

'None so far,' Mike says. 'So it must be working. I don't suppose you'd like to come?'

'Let's see how things go,' she says.

'We covered a lot of ground last night, didn't we?'

'Aye, we did. It's odd, but the things from thirty or forty years ago still feel like they only happened yesterday, whereas the things that happened yesterday – well, ten years ago, twenty at the outside . . .'

'. . . seem ancient,' he says. 'I know. It's an ageing thing.'

'Is it?' Jean says.

'The detail isn't so clear either,' Mike says. 'I mean, do you really *remember* the '90s? The way you remember the '70s? I don't. Maybe not enough time's gone by, they're not in focus yet.'

'Maybe that's what it is,' Jean says. 'Well, I'll look forward to them when they sharpen up.'

'Another story,' he says. 'But I thought you were going to die soon.'

'Oh aye,' she says. 'So I am.'

§

On the way to Waverley he tries Murdo's mobile, but there's no answer. He leaves a message asking to be collected at Lairg at half past seven. At the station he buys a big bottle of water for the journey and a newspaper, but he can't concentrate on the latter. By the time the train reaches Perth he's beginning to feel unwell. He closes his eyes, trying to induce sleep. His mind travels northwards, ahead of his physical self, towards Murdo. And he remembers.

Once, early on – when they knew each other but were not yet bold enough to act on that knowledge – Murdo told a story that revealed something of his deep mystery, and made Mike want to fall headlong into that deepness. He'd not been more than a few months at Cnoc nan Gobhar, and was finding it difficult to manoeuvre around the remnants of Angus's life. He'd thrown out some things – towels beyond redemption, mugs so discoloured he couldn't bear to drink from them – but other stuff, like rickety old chairs and chipped vases, seemed to offer a kind of connection or continuity between father and son. Perhaps it was just his own squeamishness that made the distinction between what should be saved and what must be discarded. Sometimes he became incapable of making decisions and had to escape the house altogether. All through that autumn and into winter he ran away with his camera for whole days, heading for remote beaches, or at least beaches where he could be remote. An empty beach in summer is a delight, but it is nothing to an empty beach in winter. The brutality with which the meeting of land and sea reminded him of his insignificance was mesmerising. He'd walk for miles, sometimes taking many photographs and sometimes none at all. When he returned, tired and hungry, he found he liked the house more, and that during his absence it had somehow become less Angus's and more his – until the next time he needed to get away.

He'd asked Murdo if he would do some work on the kitchen. A worktop made rotten by water needed to be replaced, and some of the unit cupboards were in disrepair. Murdo had had a look: yes, he could fix everything. When Mike had tried to pin him down to a date, Murdo had been non-committal. 'I'm not always at home, you see,' Mike had said. Murdo had given his slow, shy smile and said, 'Well, just leave the door unlocked if you go out. That way neither of us will be tied to any firm arrangements.' What could Mike do but agree? And it was at the end of one of his days of escape, returning from the west, that he drove up the track and found the red van parked at the back of the house, and Murdo just packing away his tools in the kitchen.

He showed Mike what he'd done. His work was neat, careful and complete. Mike thanked him and asked how much he owed. 'Och, call it fifty pounds.' 'You sure?' 'Aye.' 'Cash?' 'That would be preferable.' 'I'll get it to you in the next day or two. Are you wanting a cup of tea before you go?' 'That would be grand,' Murdo said.

They sat at the table across from each other and talked about what else Mike might do to the house, and sometimes their glances met, and when they did Murdo looked away. Needing something else to say, Mike found himself talking about how he hadn't yet fully adjusted to Angus not being around the place.

'Well, maybe that's because he *is* still around,' Murdo said.

'Aye, quite likely,' Mike said. 'So, anyway, I go away. Today I drove to Oldshoremore and walked to Sandwood Bay. Have you been there?'

'Oh aye,' Murdo said. 'Not for a while, though. A few years.'

'It's a good long walk,' Mike said. 'I'm shattered, actually. But it was well worth it.'

'It's some place.'

'It's magnificent.'

'Yes it is,' Murdo said, and a silence lay between them, and to Mike it was as if they were both remembering it together: the empty, austere beauty of the beach and dunes, the great waves rolling in, the sheer expanse of sand and sea. And then Murdo said, 'The last time I was there I found a dead man.'

The images in Mike's head crashed. 'On the beach?' he asked.

'Aye,' Murdo said. 'How far did you go? Did you go past the outflow of the loch?'

'Just that far. It was running pretty full, and it was getting late, so I turned back.'

'I crossed over,' Murdo said. 'It was about this time of year, a fine day like this but there was a strong wind blowing off the sea. If you cross the outflow the beach goes on at least as far as you went today, but it narrows. At high tide there's not much of it. Then you come to another river running into the sea, and the bay comes to an end there. There are some small dunes, and then rocks and a cliff. It's an unforgiving kind of place. And that's where I found him.'

'Were you on your own?'

'Aye. He had been there a long time. He was half-buried in the sand and in fact I think it was the wind that had uncovered him. Perhaps he had been buried and uncovered several times over, for there wasn't much left of him. But there he was.'

Stuck once more for something to say, Mike said something trite. 'That's terrible. Horrible.'

'No,' Murdo said. 'It was neither. He had been dead so long that all the flesh was away. He was a skeleton and a few rags. You could just about tell what had been his trousers and his coat but that was it. He was more like the remains of a big bird than a man. It was not horrible or terrible at all. It didn't look like a terrible death.'

'Do you think he had drowned?'

Murdo shrugged. 'And been washed up there? Who can know?

Perhaps he had, but I don't think so. If that was the case, I don't think he would have been so high up, in among the dunes and the rocks. No, I think he came to that place the same way I did, by walking.'

'People go that way,' Mike said, 'if they are walking to the lighthouse at Cape Wrath.'

'A few do that. It's very rough walking beyond the bay. You have to be very determined.'

'Maybe that's where he was going.'

'Maybe. Or maybe he just sat down to rest. Who can know?'

'A man, not a woman?'

'From the size of him, I'd say so.' He hesitated a moment. 'You know, I never even considered that it wasn't a man. But somehow I'm sure it was.'

'How long do you think he had been there?'

'Years, certainly. He was almost part of the place, half-buried as he was. There were twigs and seaweed and pebbles and things in among his ribs. Gull feathers.'

'What did you do? Did you tell anybody?'

'I was on my own,' Murdo said, as if it were a stupid question.

'The police, for example,' Mike said, as if Murdo had given a stupid answer.

'Well, I did think about that. But it seemed a little pointless. I didn't think he'd been murdered or anything.'

'But presumably he was a missing person.'

'Presumably. I decided the best thing to do was to sit down beside him and ask him what he wanted.'

Mike, seeing that Murdo was quite serious, remained silent. He was learning.

'I did ask him, you see, if he wanted the police involved. Of course he didn't answer, but it seemed very unlikely. It seemed more likely that he didn't want to be disturbed. He had come there for some reason, and he'd stayed. I could do nothing for him. So we sat for a while, and looked out at the sea with the wind blowing in our faces, and then I said goodbye and came away again.'

'You just left him there?'

'What was I going to do, carry him all the way back to Oldshoremore? Give him a Christian burial? He wouldn't have thanked me for either. Why, what would you have done?'

Mike shook his head. 'I don't know.'

'Anyway,' Murdo said, 'I've never been back, and I expect he has long since disappeared, so it doesn't matter now.'

They sat there, sipping their tea.

'I suppose,' Mike said, after a minute, 'I'd have taken a picture of him.'

'For the police? Or for yourself?'

'For the picture.'

'I suppose you would have,' Murdo said. 'But I don't have a camera. I'll tell you this, though, I have the picture of him in my head. It is stored in here and I can view it any time I choose.' He tapped the side of his head. 'Until the day *I* die,' he said.

Mike, on the train passing through the wastes of Drumochter, remembers the intensity of that moment. He remembers the deep wells of Murdo's eyes. He thinks of Murdo, and what happened at the end of their last evening together, and he wonders if it will happen again when Murdo meets him at Lairg and brings him home to the house at Cnoc nan Gobhar.

§

The glasses are empty. Mike indicates the bottle. 'Another?'

Murdo seems to consider this, then shakes his head. 'No thanks. I should be going.'

They both stand up together. This is how it is. There is nothing awkward about what happens next. They like each other's company and then they want more.

They go up to the bedroom where earlier Mike turned the duvet down, folded it right back off the sheet. They stand at the foot of the bed and Mike unbuckles Murdo's belt and pulls down his jeans and boxers and his cock springs out and waves there like a boat's mast. Mikes drops down on his knees and takes it in his mouth and feels Murdo's hands on his neck and in his hair as he works on him with his tongue. He brings him to a certain pitch and then pushes him away and stands up. They strip off with a silent urgency and lie down on the bed. The condom and lubricant are on the table. Mike slips the condom on and squirts lube into his left palm. Murdo turns away and lifts his knees and Mike reaches over and takes Murdo's cock in his right hand and starts to massage between his buttocks with his left. Murdo is grunting, gasping with the pleasure of it, and slowly, slowly Mike pushes with his own hardness and Murdo gives suddenly and Mike is in, as far as he can go. And then they are into the rhythm, thrusting and jerking, and then suddenly, too quickly, crying out together as they come. Mike's heart is pumping, it feels about to burst, then gradually it eases off. They lie in a sweat of exhaustion, a minute, maybe two minutes, they might almost be about to drift off but no, that isn't going to happen. Murdo pulls himself away, off the bed, gathers up his clothes and goes to the bathroom to wash himself, and when Mike hears the stair creak he gets up and washes and dresses too. When he comes downstairs Murdo is standing in the kitchen, waiting to go.

They look at each other in wonder for a moment, as if perhaps it hasn't happened but they've had the same dream.

'All right?'

'Aye.'

So it has happened. But there is a distance between them again, though it is not unfriendly. It is never unfriendly. So far it has always been like this, and this is for Murdo's sake. Mike would prefer more intimacy. He would like it if Murdo fell asleep, stayed the night. A kiss now would not be unappreciated but it does not come. And to stay would be too difficult for Murdo so this, for now, is how it is.

They talked about it a little, the second or third time. Murdo said he'd always known what he wanted but had never thought to do anything about it. He'd never had girlfriends when he was younger. He had two sisters who were married and away, one in Canada and the other in Inverness, but he'd stayed, living with his parents in the house he was born in, until they died and the house became his alone, and no doubt he'd be there now till *he* died. He'd never made a pretence one way or the other, people could think what they liked and now, if they thought about it at all, they probably thought he was just a confirmed bachelor who wasn't interested in sex, or love, or marriage. But whatever they thought they kept it to themselves, and he did the same. And until Mike had come to live there, and in the course of day-to-day life they'd met and each seen the curiosity and then the desire in the other's eyes, the possibility that he might have sex with another person had never really entered his mind.

'But you could have gone away. You could have gone some place where you could have been yourself.'

Murdo doesn't often get angry but he flared up at that. 'Be myself? Do you think I've not been myself all these years? Do you think I would have to go away from here to be myself? This is my home. I love it. Why would I go away from it?'

'But –'

'There's no buts about it, boy. Wild bloody horses wouldn't drag me away from here, and don't think that you will either. Or change me, not for anything, by God.'

And so, when he comes over in the evening, as he does perhaps twice or three times a week, sometimes for a meal and sometimes for a dram, Mike opens the gate and the red van slides up behind the house, out of sight unless you're really looking for it. And always Murdo will be back in his own house every night, the van parked outside, and in the morning go about his business just the same as ever. And after he's away, Mike will wash the glasses and dishes and ponder the strangeness of it, the normality of it, and he'll go up the stair to his bed and there is the damp patch on the sheet and although he feels the lack of Murdo he also likes the fact that they are independent and alone. He understands why Murdo prefers it that way and in spite of himself he agrees that it is probably better, at least for the time being. Perhaps one day soon there will be a change. Perhaps there will be a different future. He hopes so. But for now, yes, for now this is how it is.

You kept a pocket full of stones. The stones had no purpose, they were just a story. You kept the story going. That was what you had to do. You picked the stones up where you found them and you took them on, and every so often you laid them down again. You were making a pattern but you didn't know what the pattern was. You didn't know where you were in the pattern or where or how or if it would end. Sometimes you took a pebble from a beach, sea-washed and smooth as a pearl, and left it under a tree miles up a glen; sometimes you took a rough, ragged stone from an inland field and weeks later you threw it into the sea. And sometimes you handed the stones on, to small, unknowing hands, and let the pattern take care of itself. It was not your concern. Your only concern was to keep the pocket filled with stones and never let them run out, to gather and to give, to take and to release. You yourself were released. You'd escaped and you weren't going back. That was the sum total of everything you were and did.

You heard another story about stones once, or did you read it? Memory was a confusing place of mist and time. This story was much older than yours, but you liked it, you felt it. It became you. Became in the sense of suited. Or maybe in the sense of became. Maybe it was the same story but on a different scale. Long ago back in the mist there was a giant. He was building a house in the mountains. He went down to the shore with a creel and collected a number of rocks for his house, and placed them in the creel. When it was full he swung it up on to his great back, but the weight was too much and the bottom of the creel broke and the stones fell into the sea as he swung it round, and that was how the Hebrides were formed.

Things fell into place. You might not have anything to eat on you, you might be hungry or wet or cold or tired or all of these things, but they were states of being, they weren't responsibilities. And the states of being passed, one into another, and it amazed you to find that that was what they did. You wore out your boots and a farmer gave you his old ones. You needed a new coat and somebody in a cold, grey village found you one. These were gifts, not debts. Gifts were acceptable. You were hungry and there was a field of potatoes only waiting for a fire to bake them in, or a trout lying under the bank of a burn waiting for your hand, or a squad of pheasants walking down the road, almost into your arms they would come, daft creatures too bonnie to know what the rock in your hand was for, or a hedgerow full of wild white raspberries to gorge yourself on. Redcurrants like gleaming jewels, fat blaeberries staining your fingers with their dark blood. Or you worked for a few days on a farm or some remote place where they needed some extra help, and sometimes there was money but usually there wasn't, but always there was food and a place to wash and a place to sleep, though never a bed even if it was offered, you were far beyond beds by then. And food to take with you when you went on your way. Things fell into place.

You travelled light. Three pairs of socks, a change of underwear, a couple of shirts, a big jumper and a coat. Sometimes a bit more if you picked up some good items, sometimes less. The important thing was keeping your clothes and yourself as clean as you could. Some of the other men on the road were so dirty you got the stench of them even before you saw them. They'd lost all sense of themselves, they'd no dignity left. Washing and drying your clothes was hard in the winter. You offered to work in exchange for a washing and if the offer was rejected you went elsewhere or fell back on your own resources, making use of the shelters you found to hang things for days at a time. You used a particular territory for a few weeks, stashing things away till you needed them. There were endless possibilities of places to rest, places to wait, places to store, if you only took the trouble and time to look.

And you had all the time in the world now you didn't have anything else. If you had nowhere to be you could be anywhere. Soap in a tin. A razor and a whetstone. A billycan. Your needs were pared down to the minimum. You didn't have to ask for much, and your preference was to ask for nothing.

You went out into the world to leave the world behind. You went out into the open to find the places where you could be invisible and silent.

Silence. That was the best thing of all. Words were something else you didn't need, written or spoken or heard. You talked if talk was necessary, letting the words go with care, the way you might release a butterfly or a pebble from your hand; but mostly you listened, picking up news of things that no longer concerned you then forgetting them, offering an opinion if it was sought but more and more you had less and less to offer. You were in retreat, like a monk, not like a soldier. Like a monk. You preferred to listen. You listened to birds, to beasts, to water. You chinked the stones together, listening for their meaning. You learned the meaning of changes in the wind, the meaning of dogs when they barked or did not bark. Dogs loved you. Once, a man in Argyll near the end of a summer – the heat was still in the days but it was beginning to fade – could not believe how his collie, that would go like a mad thing for anybody that trespassed on his turf, rubbed and slumped against your legs and yearned to be clapped, and whined like a bairn when you stopped. I never saw that, the man said. Never saw the like o that wi that dug. That's a strange power ye have on ye. And he didn't like it, it was like a threat to him somehow, and he shook his head and said he had no work for you and so you left, and did the dog not try to follow till its master roared and it slunk back like a beaten thing, to forget your passing and to snarl and snap at the next stranger? And you turned your face to the road and went on.

Things fell into place. Down the road a mile or two you came on a gypsy camp set among trees by a burn, and the same thing happened, the dogs came out to bite you and they ended up licking your hand and competing for your attention. The men observed this and invited you in, the women made you sit and they fed you and gave you tea in a tin mug and offered you tobacco and you took the tea, and you stayed with them, listening to their stories and their songs and watching the dirty-faced barefoot bairns at play and there was no meaning in any of it. It stirred a memory in you but you did not look into that, and after a day or two you went on.

But before you left you counted the bairns, there were seven of them, and you reached into your pocket and brought out seven stones and put one into each outstretched hand. And two of them looked at what you had given and threw them away, and one put the pebble in his mouth and spat it out, and three collected more stones and began a game with them, and one, the smallest, watched you sullenly from under her black brows and clutched the stone in her fist and went away with it to some place on her own. And you were happy at what they had all done, together and separately, and most of all you were happy at the thought of the lassie who hid the stone away, though you didn't know why. But her face came back to you for many days after that, as you walked on into the autumn of the year.

PART TWO

The Persistence of Memory

On a Saturday evening in the summer of 1950 Don Lennie walked into the Blackthorn Inn in Wharryburn at eight o'clock, as usual, and Jack Gordon was there at the bar, as usual: tanned, thin as flex, in light flannels, neatly pressed jacket and clean white shirt, with a pint of light ale in his hand. He nodded curtly and raised the pint to his mouth. Don ordered the same for himself. Their friendship – you could call it that – was based on a set of tacit understandings, one of which was that Jack's need for independence prohibited the buying of rounds. He didn't want to be in debt to anybody else, not ever, not even for twenty minutes. Don accepted this, as he accepted almost everything about Jack, including his dislike of being touched. They never shook hands at the start or end of an evening, for example. How Jack's wife coped – with the touching, or the not touching – was anybody's guess. Maybe he was different with her, but Don doubted it. Still, he'd been through a lot, Jack Gordon. You couldn't blame him for having a few, what was the word, peccadilloes.

Straight up, without even a hello, Jack said, 'Do you know one of the things that kept me going? Imagining this. I'd picture myself in a pub with a beer and I'd drink it inch by inch and lick the foam off my top lip.' He enunciated very clearly, consonants clicking and popping with precision.

Don had heard this story before, or a version of it. He said, 'I bet ye did, Jack.'

'I'd imagine I'd had a weekend in the hills, Glen Coe or some-where, just as I used to in the old days, and this was me with a pint of Scottish beer after, waiting for the bus from Fort William.'

Don lifted his own glass. 'Cheers,' he said. 'The old days,' he said, and drank to them.

'And I usually thought of it being winter,' Jack went on. 'Snow on the tops, but the sky clear, the air dry and fresh. Sunny even. But cold. I tried to imagine feeling cold. Pretty difficult.'

'Aye, it would be,' Don said.

'I've been thinking about this all week. What home meant.'

Don nodded. When Jack said he'd been thinking about something all week he probably meant it. Seven days, every waking moment. They both worked in the town of Drumkirk, three miles down the road. Jack worked in the sales and dispatch department of an engineering firm that made small parts for industrial machinery – some kind of overseeing role that involved checking other men's work and a lot of form-filling – and Don reckoned you could probably go all day doing that and have your mind on something else. Not where he was, in Byres Brothers Haulage. He did what he'd done before the war and during it and what he'd probably do till he stopped working – servicing and repairing trucks and lorries. An office job like Jack's was one thing, but at Byres Brothers you had to concentrate or something would jump up and bite you. Burn you, crush you, slice your fingers off.

'It was home that kept me going really. Scotland. I dreamed about it, and when I woke up I thought about it. I tried to remember everything I could down to the finest detail. Mountains I'd climbed, rivers I'd fished, towns I'd visited. I thought of walks I'd done and I did them again.'

He paused, and Don wondered how Jack had had the time and the money before the war to do all that. That was one difference between them, money. Not that Jack was rich but he came from people who went away on holidays, trips to the Highlands, that kind of thing. It gave you a different perspective. Don had been in Egypt and Italy but he'd never been as far as Dumfries or Aberdeen.

'I imagined a map of the country,' Jack said, 'and I filled it with all the counties, just like on the real map, in the right colours. Yellow for Perthshire, green for Inverness-shire, pink for Argyll. I'd list every major town, every football club, every football ground. Dates of kings and queens, battles. I could do all that while I was working. Clearing the undergrowth, digging, levelling the ground. It was like being in a kind of dream. You could almost dream yourself out of the pain and the heat and the hunger. Almost. We were like machines by that stage, we hardly knew we were real.'

Jack spoke very distinctly, but quietly too. The other customers couldn't hear him. They wouldn't want to. It was Saturday night, the war was five years over, they were trying to move on from it or already had. But Don, standing next to him, could hear every word. Jack might almost have been speaking to himself but he wasn't, he needed a listener. Not just anyone, but Don. For some reason he could say these things in his presence, things otherwise too rotten to be exhumed.

Don had read that other survivors from Japanese camps were bonded together because of the experience; there was a sympathy, an understanding between them that nobody else could share. But Jack was alone. He had a sister over the way at Slaemill, but Don didn't get the impression they were close. Jack wasn't close to anyone, maybe not even his wife – but anyway you couldn't talk to a woman about the war, not the really deep, bad stuff, you couldn't inflict it on her. So if Jack was going to open up to anybody, it would be to Don, over a couple of pints in the Blackthorn Inn on a Saturday night.

They caught the same bus every morning into Drumkirk. From exchanges they'd had at the bus stop, over weeks, months, years, Don had gradually come to know Jack, or some of him, grabbing morsels of information that he built into a kind of shape. Jack didn't really volunteer intelligence about himself, it slid out of him bit by bit, reluctantly, painfully, as if he were boaking up wee sharp slivers of metal. And most of it was about the years between 1941 and 1945, when he'd been in the world but also absent from it. He didn't say much about his life before or since the war: everything turned on what had happened to him in those years. And yet that very period was sometimes out of bounds, a space you trod gingerly round the edges of.

Ach well, everybody had places that were off-limits to others. Don had. Jack didn't venture there, didn't know about them. What he knew was that Don had also been a soldier, and that connected them. Don had had a very different war but he understood what it was like to come close to death, to survive.

They didn't talk on the bus, they sat in separate seats and Don dozed while Jack didn't. If Don opened his eyes Jack would be staring intently out of the window, as if he were trying to spot a rare bird. Don's stop came first. He'd to be at his work for eight o'clock sharp. Jack had further to go but he didn't start till half past the hour. When Don got on in the evening to come home there Jack would be again, with his steady, watchful gaze, as if he'd been travelling all day scanning the countryside instead of writing out dispatch sheets. They'd say a few words then, maybe. Don had the impression that Jack was assessing him. When the bus reached their village of Wharryburn they'd walk in the same direction for a hundred yards before Don turned off into his street and Jack carried on up the brae. 'Goodnight,' Jack would say. 'See ye the morn's morn,' Don would say. That was their routine. It was enough for two men to say that they knew each other.

Then one Saturday morning, as Don was going past Jack's seat to get off, Jack said, 'Fancy a pint in the Blackthorn tonight?' and Don, not really having time to think about it, said, 'Aye, all right,' and Jack said, 'Eight o'clock, then,' as if there were no other time he could envisage being there, and that was how their weekly sessions had started.

Don felt he'd earned a drink or two after five and a half days at his work and an afternoon tending the garden. He'd have a thick slice of bread and jam and a cup of tea when he got home on a Saturday, then he'd be out there, digging or planting or weeding, wet or dry, hot or cold, it didn't matter. At first Liz had been put out that he didn't want his dinner when he came in, surely it was what a man needed, but he said if he ate a full meal he'd just want to sleep all afternoon. She fed wee Billy at the back of five while Don cleaned himself up, then he'd sit down at six for his tea. Liz cooked them a lamb chop each, with potatoes and a vegetable, followed by bread and margarine and plenty of tea. The chops were the highlight of the weekly menu. Afterwards Don would wash the dishes, read the paper while Liz put Billy to bed, then leave her listening to the Light Programme with a detective novel in her lap, and stroll down to the Blackthorn. A pint or two. He reckoned he deserved them.

'There were three of us,' Jack was saying, 'all Jocks – well, four of us before they killed MacLaren – we stuck together like brothers, kept each other going, there was a kind of rivalry about it. Who could think up the most details about Scotland.'

'Who could be the maist Scottish,' Don said helpfully. 'Daft what ye'll do, eh?' He was fascinated by the neatness of Jack's clothes, everything about him. Even the veins in his neck looked like ironed creases. He had hard, smooth skin and very little hair up top and not much growth on his chin either. His head was like a large wooden egg. Don tried to picture him coming out of the jungle barefoot, skeletal, naked except for a loincloth, after twelve hours on the railway.

Jack said, 'It wasn't daft, it made perfect sense. And the closer it got to the end, the more sense it made. There was a radio in the camp, I never knew who had it, you didn't ask, it was too dangerous, but somebody had built this receiver and the news from All India Radio was that the Japs were in retreat and you chaps were winning in Europe, and we were worried about what the Japs would do when the crunch came. More torture, more killing – they were capable of it. Maybe they'd shoot us all. So we were all keeping our heads down, fighting off the disease and the hunger, just trying to stay alive – and imagining Scotland and what it would be like to be back here was one of the ways to do it.' He was speaking very rapidly now, short vowels and clipped consonants as if he had only a few seconds before somebody came, a guard maybe, that was how it seemed to Don. 'There was Sim Mackintosh and myself and a chap called Geordie Spiers, Geordie was from Ayrshire, grew up on a farm but he wanted an adventure so he ran away to Stirling and joined the Argylls and that's how he ended up in Singapore in '41. "Out of the byre and into hell," he used to say.'

Jack paused and drank deeply from his pint. Don thought about what 'hell' meant. He'd been in North Africa and Italy himself, there'd been a few times he could describe as 'hell', one in particular, but not even that matched up to Jack's version because it hadn't lasted three and a half years.

'There were no fences,' Jack said, 'no locked gates, because we were surrounded by thousands of square miles of jungle, so where were we going to run to? MacLaren used to make a joke of it. "Fancy a stroll to India?" he'd say. We all knew it was hopeless, including him, but was it less hopeless than staying where we were? That was the kind of thinking that could drive you mad. And then one night he slipped off by himself.'

'MacLaren?' Don said. He thought, why does Jack only ever refer to him by his surname? There was Geordie and Sim and there was MacLaren. Like he was in a different category. Well, he was.

'MacLaren, aye. A week later they brought him back. He'd been picked up in a village twenty miles away, starving, sick. The whole camp was assembled. They lined us up as three sides of a square and trained machine guns on us from the fourth side. Then they dragged MacLaren into the middle of the square, hands tied behind his back, and made him kneel, and one of their officers took out his sword and beheaded him. One stroke. And we all stood there watching the blood pouring on to the ground and there was nothing, absolutely nothing, we could do.'

Don did not speak. What could he say? Jack wasn't looking for sympathy or anger or grief. He was just telling a story. And in the next breath he'd moved on, as if it were necessary now to consider only the other men he'd been with out there, the ones who were still, at that point, alive.

'I don't suppose Geordie spoke any different from the way Robert Burns himself spoke,' Jack said. 'In fact if Burns had come back from the dead for a day he'd have been able to speak to Geordie as if he was one of his cronies from the Tarbolton Club. And Geordie taught Robert Burns to the rest of us. We all had wee bits and pieces, a few of the songs and a few verses you learn at school, "To a Mouse" and things like that, but Geordie knew them all. I mean, the lot. I don't know where or when he'd learned it but there wasn't a bit of Burns he couldn't give you. We had no books or paper, they were forbidden, but Geordie had the entire collected works of Robert Burns in his head and he taught us from that. He'd recite or sing and we'd listen, and pick it up from him. I mind the first time I had "Tam o' Shanter" off right through, I felt I'd won this tremendous victory. It wasn't that I'd defeated the poem; somehow by learning it I'd beaten the Japs.

'When the news finally came in that they'd surrendered, well, we were all down to our last reserves, and a few of the lads just took their eye off the ball, they stopped concentrating. I just kept at it, thinking of Scotland, reciting Burns and all that, I wasn't going to come that close and not see it again, but Sim and Geordie, they both relaxed too soon, and they went down with yet another bout of dysentery and they were too weak this time and it killed them both. A dirty trick. I mean, the war was actually over. Sim just slipped away one day but Geordie knew he was dying. The last thing he said to me was, "Weel, Jack, looks like I got mair o an adventure than I bargained for."' He paused, and Don could see he was hearing it again, Geordie's last sentence chiselled into his memory like words on a tombstone. 'I thought that was a dreadful waste, all that poetry in his head, getting buried out there.'

'It *was* a dreadful waste,' Don said. 'The haill war was a waste o human life.'

'Except the atom bombs,' Jack said. 'I know you disagree with me but you'll never get me to say dropping the bombs was a waste. I wouldn't be here if they hadn't dropped them, and neither would a lot of other folk. I don't care how many Japanese they killed.'

'I'd say the same in your shoes,' Don said. 'I *dae* say the same. I ken the Japs had orders tae kill all the POWs as soon as the Allies set foot in Japan.'

'Aye, they did,' Jack said.

'It's just . . . what the hell have we produced? What terrible power have we created?'

'Be thankful it was the Americans that created it first,' Jack said. 'Or we'd be dust.' His gaze swept briefly, dismissively, round the room. 'All of us.'

'I just worry aboot what happens when somebody else has these weapons,' Don said.

'The Russians already have,' Jack said. 'Their technology's crude, they've a long way to go, but they'll catch up. They can't afford not to.'

Sometimes Don felt, because of what Jack had been through, that he had special insight into the workings of the world – although, God knows, they'd all been through enough, so what did Jack know that he didn't? But he didn't want to believe the worst about the Russians. He wasn't soft on Communism, but he felt a burden of debt to the Russian people, after what *they'd* been through. Was it really their leaders' ambition to destroy the planet? Was it not just that they wanted to defend themselves?

The present signs weren't good, though. North Korean Communists were rampaging through South Korea and it looked like they'd have the whole country wrapped up before the clocks went back. Certainly before the newly established United Nations could agree how to respond. Russians were in there advising the North Koreans. The Chinese were sitting on the frontier, waiting to move in. The Americans were there already, trying to stem the tide, while the British, Canadians, Australians and others prepared to join them.

The papers were beginning to use a new term, 'cold war'. Jack said it was only a matter of time before things got very hot indeed.

'The Russians can't reach America yet so Britain'll be the target. And that means we'll have to have the Bomb too. If we haven't already got it. Everybody wants it. The Chinese, the French. It's too big not to want.'

'Then we're living in a world where there's a clock ticking,' Don said.

'That's right,' Jack said. 'We are.'

§

Don rubbed Liz's back as she lay turned away from him. She was nearly eight months pregnant and wanting it to be over. 'It's going tae be another boy,' she said. 'I ken it. A footballer or a soldier, the way he's kicking and shoving.'

'No a soldier,' Don said. 'We've had enough o that.'

He put his arm over her and cupped her in his big hand, feeling the life moving inside her. His mind flitted from one thing to another. He was aware of the beer slopping in his own belly. He'd have to watch himself or he'd turn soft and fat, struggle to get himself out from under the lorries. Still, it was the only drink either of them took, apart from New Year when Liz would have a sherry and he'd get in a half-bottle of whisky. The one time of year when there was alcohol in the house. He didn't much like whisky himself, but you felt you had to have it in at New Year for visitors, and you had to join them in drinking it. What kind of a man were you if you didn't take a dram at Hogmanay?

He heard Billy make a small sigh as he turned in his cot next door. He wouldn't wake. Billy would have slept through the Clyde-bank Blitz.

'If only Jack Gordon would just let it all go,' he said. 'It comes oot in wee dribs and drabs, but I ken he's no telling me the half o what happened to him ower there.'

'I dinna ken how ye can stand it,' Liz said, drifting into sleep. 'I ken ye feel sorry for him, but it's hardly a good night out for you.'

'It's no aboot feeling sorry for him,' he said. 'I like my pint on a Saturday.' And, he thought, he liked Jack too. Nobody else did, but he felt an affinity with the man. He respected him, what he'd survived, his present purposefulness. Maybe that was all it was, respect. He couldn't explain it to Liz.

'Ye'll no get oot sae much when this one arrives,' Liz said. 'We'll hae oor hands full. And no sae much money in them.'

'I ken that,' he said. 'But I'll get promotion. Works manager by next year.'

She elbowed him gently. 'Aye, that'll be right. You'll be the one that closes the place.'

He was in the union, cajoling, arguing with other men to get them to join. If a majority of the workforce signed up they'd have real bargaining power. The management didn't like it but they couldn't stop him, couldn't get rid of him either, he was too good at his job, there wasn't a mechanical problem Don Lennie couldn't solve. There'd been two Byres brothers originally, in the 1920s, but one had died without issue and the other had kept the name, Byres Brothers, in case he had more than one son. He hadn't, but the name stayed. Byres Brothers had escaped nationalisation in 1948, they were too small and most of their work was short haul, forty miles or less, but that still enabled them to reach most of central Scotland. Auld Tam, the father, had managed to keep the business intact and out of the hands of the British Transport Commission, and since the railways had been nationalised more and more firms were turning to lorries to shift their goods, and Byres Brothers were experiencing a steady growth in trade. It was a shame, Don thought, they hadn't been bigger: then he might have been working for British Road Services, the new national organisation. The pay and conditions were better. On the other hand, he was beginning to hear stories from men in BRS about petty officials, union and management, enforcing petty rules and making it impossible to get on with your job. Maybe he was safer where he was.

'Better the bastards ye ken than the faceless bastards ye never meet, eh Don?' Wullie Byres, Tam's son, had said, with the big, sleekit grin on his face it was hard not to grin back at. He wasn't as hard as his father, not yet anyway, but he'd inherited the same creed: that work was the chief end of man. Home was all very well – a place where you rested between shifts, tholing the ministrations and demands of your womenfolk – but work, the dirt and noise and machinery of work, was everything. And when it came to the workplace every man was judged equally, measured by the quality and extent of his graft and nothing else – unless he was divorced or a Catholic, but if you were in either of those categories you didn't work for Byres Brothers anyway. 'A man that canna mend his ain marriage has nae business meddling wi an internal combustion engine,' Auld Tam used to say. As for why he didn't take on Catholics, well, if you had to ask the question you wouldn't like the answer.

'Dinna you fash about Byres Brothers,' Don said to Liz. 'Plenty work there. Plenty money in their coffers, tae. We just need tae squeeze a bit mair oot for the workers.'

For a moment he thought she must have drifted off. Then she said, 'Canna be easy for his wife. Dae ye ken what she's like?'

'Jack Gordon's wife? Naw, he hardly mentions her. There's a bairn tae, a lassie.'

'I never see them,' Liz said. 'I see everybody, but I'm no even sure I'd recognise them. What's the wife's name?'

He thought for a moment. Jack must have mentioned it, surely? But then, Don didn't speak much about Liz to Jack either. 'I canna mind,' he said.

'Maybe we should get them here for their tea one night,' Liz said. 'Instead o you pair gaun tae the pub.'

'I'm no sure. He's a bit mair polished than us. We're no really the folk for dinner parties, are we?' *Polished* was right: there was something buffed and burnished about Jack, like some object in a glass cabinet you weren't supposed to touch.

'Nothing fancy,' Liz said. 'Just their tea. Their bairn might get on well wi Billy.'

'We'll see.' He thought of the cost of the extra food. He'd save money not going to the Blackthorn of course. Everything was so tight. You couldn't breathe for thinking about money.

They lay like that for a few minutes. He thought of his own mother and father, Molly and Will, how they would coorie in with one another in bed, not through choice but because they had to, there was that little space. They stayed in Drumkirk, in a single-end in a tenement that was overdue for demolition. They slept in a bed in the recess and as a wee boy he'd often slept there with them. Fortunately there'd been only the three of them: Molly had not been able to have more bairns after him. His own bed was a mattress on wooden slats that folded away during the day. Some of the families in the building had been six or seven to a room. When he'd gone off to the war he could hardly believe the amount of space there was, in barracks and tents and the backs of lorries and out in the open air. It was almost worth having a war for, the men used to joke, having a bit of elbow room. And he'd vowed often, in Tunisia and Egypt and Sicily and all the way up Italy, that he was never going back to the kind of conditions he'd grown up in. Then he met Liz and saw the relative comfort of rural living. Her father was the cattleman at Hackston's Farm, two miles along the road from Wharryburn, and they had a cottage with two bedrooms, a scullery off the living room and a dunny in the garden all to themselves – and a garden! Don determined then and there that if they got married they would find a place out of town, away from the grime and overcrowding. And they had. After just a year cramming in with Liz's parents and her youngest, unmarried sister, and with Liz expecting, the council had offered them a braw house in Wharryburn, with its own kitchen and bathroom and two good-sized bedrooms. The village was not too far from his work and close enough to the farm. It had grown fast – more urban than rural now with its streets of 1930s council houses such as the one they were in, and the private properties, like the Gordons' bungalow – but it still had its core of kirk and shops and pub, not that he went near the kirk. He loved living there. When he thought of Will and Molly and their home it made him embarrassed and angry simultaneously. Liz's mother had never quite forgiven him for coming from where he did, although she tried to hide it. But Don liked Liz's dad fine, a good man, he didn't say much but you could tell from the look in his eyes if he thought you were all right.

Liz was almost away, he could feel her breathing change as she went. He loved that. He was thirty, with a wife and son, and another bairn on the way. This was his second life. No, his third. First there was growing up in Drumkirk, then the war, now this. The war was over but it would always be there, the big mad moment of all their lives. Never again. Tam and Wullie Byres might be dour and tight-fisted but he'd thole them and just about anything for peace. Yet when he thought of being the head of a family it made him tremble, a different fear from what he'd experienced in the war. And it was a different courage he needed to be a good husband and father.

The country had changed and it needed to go on changing. The Labour government was still there, but only just. At the election in February its majority had been cut to single figures, and it had watered down or abandoned its plans for taking more key industries into public ownership. People were tired of austerity and blamed it on the government. Potatoes, bread and jam were no longer rationed but in the run-up to the election there'd still been Chads appearing on the sides of lorries and derelict buildings: 'Wot? No bacon?' 'Wot? No eggs?' And then Tate & Lyle, fighting the threat of nationalisa-tion, had invented Mr Cube, a cartoon sugar lump with legs who ranted against the perils of socialism. Mr Cube was everywhere, on sugar packs, Tate & Lyle-designed ration-book holders, newspaper ads, leaflets, posters. 'TATE not STATE' he girned, striking out the S with relish. One day Liz had come home with a set of five Mr Cube dice they were giving away at Reid's the grocer's. Each die had a picture of Mr Cube on one face and the letters S, T, A, t and E on the others. If you rolled Mr Cube and T-A-t-E you won. Your reward was free enterprise. If you rolled S-T-A-t-E you lost, a victim of gov-ernment controls. Liz thought it was funny, clever even. Don wanted to crush the dice beneath his heel. Aye, and no doubt that was how the sugar barons expected a socialist to behave.

Six months on, things were sliding towards exhaustion. Events in Korea had started an urgent argument within the Labour Party: guns versus butter. It seemed a lot more than five years since the landslide victory of 1945. A lot more than that since the war.

He remembered reading the Beveridge Report in the desert after El Alamein, a copy that was passed from man to man till it was in tatters. It was written in heavy, booming language that gave it ser-iousness and weight. To slay the five giants of Want, Sickness, Squalor, Ignorance and Idleness – it was like a fairy tale but there was something solid and noble and chivalrous about it. The soldiers – even many of the officers – saw it as the natural outcome of the war. What were they fighting for if not for a decent life for every-body, from the cradle to the grave? *Let Us Face the Future* – that was the title of Labour's manifesto in the General Election of 1945, and the future was contained in Beveridge. Churchill had grumbled dire warnings about socialist totalitarianism but what else was he going to say? However much you respected him as a war leader, Churchill was an old reactionary. And Attlee and Morrison and Bevan and Bevin and the rest of them had done a good job, Don reckoned. The things that had been put in place in the last five years – National Insurance, pensions, the Health Service – these were changes for the good, they made ordinary people's lives better, safer, happier and longer. Any government that tried to undo them, Don believed, would risk the wrath of the people. By the time the Tories regained power, as they would, families like his were going to be in a better situation than they'd ever been. Even Churchill wouldn't dare turn the clock back.

The bairn inside Liz kicked again, and Don wondered who they would be bringing into the world, and what the world would be like when the new bairn was the age they were. And if the world would still be around.

§

'It's the age of new nations,' Jack Gordon said. He ran a finger up the side of his glass, leaving a clear line through the condensation, and Don thought of sweat and jungle heat. 'India, Pakistan, Ceylon, Burma. The Africans'll not be far behind. The West Indians. Nobody can stop it. You just have to enable it.'

'Which is what the government's been daein. I agree wi ye, make it as smooth as ye can. The less trouble the better. But dinna hand places ower tae madmen and gangsters.'

Don was thinking of the Middle East. A right mess. Aye, the Jews deserved a home of their own after what had happened to them, but did they have to set off bombs and lynch British soldiers and treat the Palestinians like dog-dirt to achieve it? It made you despair. Partition in India had been the same. The Empire was over, or soon would be, and glad he'd be to see the back of it. But as the British withdrew from the world voids opened up that were being filled with corruption and hatred and violence. No doubt it had always been like that but had folk not had enough? It seemed they hadn't.

'New nations and old ones,' Jack said. 'Scotland would have had Home Rule thirty-five years ago, but the First World War happened. There was a Bill that reached its second reading in the House of Commons in August 1914. Did you know that?'

'No,' Don said. 'Afore my time.'

'August 1914,' Jack said. 'How's that for bad timing? And then in the 1920s there were more Bills, but most of the politicians didn't have the stomach for it by then. And the Irish situation scared people. They were frightened of a bloodbath. But we'll be getting in the queue soon. No thanks to your Labour Party though. Nothing about Home Rule in their manifesto this year. They think it's a dead issue. Well, it is. Full-blown independence is the thing.'

'Canna see there's much appetite for that,' Don said. 'Why would ye go doon that road, after all we've been through thegither? Why are you sae keen on independence?'

'I love my country,' Jack said. 'It's what kept me alive. I've told you that.'

Don felt uneasy. *Love your country*, what did it mean? You could love a woman, your bairns, but a country? Scotland was all right but it was nothing special. The Germans had loved the Fatherland, the Japanese had worshipped their Emperor. He said, 'Nationalism's what's done this tae ye, Jack. You of all people dinna need mair o that.'

'Done what to me?'

'Landed ye in that hellhole for three years. Nearly bloody killed ye.'

'I'm all right, though,' Jack said. 'I came through it. Survived. Thousands didn't, but I did. Scotland saved me. Don't you think I owe the place something? Scottish nationalism's different,' he went on. 'It's not about conquest or oppression. It's about freeing ourselves. We're not going to invade anybody, we just want what's ours. Our own country.'

'A poor country it would be, on its ain,' Don said. 'Kirk ministers running local cooncils and no enough money tae dae it wi. We canna just cut oorsels aff frae England.'

'You've swallowed the propaganda,' Jack said. 'That's what they want us to believe, that we can't stand on our own feet. They tricked us into believing it in 1707, and it's been the same ever since. Bought and sold for English gold. Burns was right about that.'

'He was a poet, no a politician,' Don said. 'There's been a few changes since then, Jack. The Industrial Revolution. One man, one vote. Votes for women. Socialism. The border now is between capital and labour. Ye're living in the past. Ye'll be wearing a kilt next.'

'Nothing wrong with a kilt,' Jack said.

'Och, man! I've never seen *you* in one. Aw that Harry Lauder cairry-on? Made us a laughing stock.'

'That was the intention, I think,' Jack said drily.

'I dinna miss it,' Don said. 'Or him.'

Back in February the old comedian had died, eighty years old, and there had been an outpouring of 'national grief' that had made Don boil with frustration. He'd never seen the appeal of Lauder. Aye, fine, the tunes were good enough if you liked that kind of thing, cheery and light, but all that hirpling about with a knobbly stick, dressed up like a tartan doll and making cracks about his own meanness, Don couldn't thole it. Liz and he had been at the pictures to see *The Blue Lamp* – a rare night out, with a neighbour in to watch Billy – and they'd seen the funeral on Pathé News with the headline 'Sir Harry Comes to the End of the Road' and footage of thousands lining the route from Lauder Ha' to Hamilton, the cortège of black cars moving below a skyline of factory lums and the town gasometer. There was a wreath from Buckingham Palace and another from Mr and Mrs Churchill. If you believed the commentary all of Scotland was awash with tears. Not Don! The thought of Lauder cavorting on stage still aggravated him.

'The only person a kilt looks good on,' Don said, 'is a Scottish soldier.'

'Cannon fodder,' Jack said. 'That's what the Scottish soldier is and always has been. Cannon fodder for English wars.'

'No, no, Jack, I'm no haein that,' Don said. '*We* weren't cannon fodder and it wasna an English war. It was a war against fascism, against brute force and evil. You should ken that better than maist.'

'What I'm saying,' Jack said, 'is that it's time we stood up for ourselves for a change. Or soon there won't be anything Scottish about us.'

'Speak for yersel,' Don said, growing angry. 'I'm as Scottish as the next man. I'm nothing *but* Scottish, but I dinna need tae wrap masel in a kilt or play the bagpipes tae prove it.'

'So you wrap yourself in the red, white and blue of the Union instead,' said Jack.

'No I dinna. I'm against *ony* kind of nationalism. *That's* the propaganda, the nonsense that sends young men aff tae fight other men they've never even heard o, that has them re-fighting battles frae centuries ago. I'm opposed tae that.'

His voice had become raised. The barman went by them. 'Steady on, gents,' he said. Jack nodded at him, then carried on in his quiet, insistent way.

'Yet you support independence for India, Burma, Sudan, Ghana. Every country but your own. Why? What's different about us?'

'We dinna need it,' Don said, dropping the volume. 'Naebody's oppressing us. Naebody's haudin us back, or haudin us doon.'

'No?' said Jack. 'Think about it. Where was the worst unemployment in the '30s? Who sent the most soldiers to the trenches in the First World War and who lost more of them than anybody? Cannon fodder. One in four didn't come home, think about that. Whose young women were commandeered during the last war and forced to work in English factories hundreds of miles from home? Why are the Highlands so destitute? Why does Glasgow have the worst slums in Europe? Why is Scotland the only European country except Portugal where TB's on the increase? Why do more people emigrate from Scotland than any other part of Great Britain? Half a million of our youngest and strongest to other countries between the wars. Looks to me like something's holding us back. But even if you're right and we're not oppressed, what argument is that not to be a country like any other country? Why *not* be independent? Surely that's the question?'

Don shook his head. 'The question's no why *not*. The question's *why*? Why change things? Why build Hadrian's Wall again? What's the point? I'm sick o frontiers and boundaries.'

They drank in silence for a minute. Don remembered Liz's suggestion about asking the Gordons for a meal.

'How d'ye feel aboot coming roond tae oors next Saturday?' he said.

'Coming round?' Jack said.

'You and your wife and lassie. Come for your tea. Liz says I've tae ask ye.' Faced with Jack's stony blankness, he made a joke of it. 'Or the week efter. Ony Saturday that Liz isna in labour.'

'No, I don't think so,' Jack said.

'We'd like tae meet your wife. What's she cried again? Her name's gone oot o my heid.'

'Sarah?' Jack said. He seemed surprised that anybody should want to know.

'And the bairn? It is a lassie, is it no? I'm sure I mind ye saying that.'

'It is. Barbara. Thank you, but no,' Jack said. 'We're not good company.'

'Ye dinna need tae mind us,' Don said. 'We're easy. Nae airs and graces.'

'Thank you,' Jack said again, with a note of finality, 'but no.'

Was it shyness, fear, shame? Don had heard stories of former POWs who couldn't bear eating in other people's company, other people's houses. It was a private thing for them. They had to eat everything quickly, all at once, or they took an age. Or they couldn't abide waste, slid potatoes into their pockets before they left the table. Was that it? Whatever it was, there seemed no sense in pushing it if Jack didn't want to come.

§

Liz was determined, though. If the Gordons wouldn't come to them, they'd go to the Gordons. Something in her reached out to the unknown Sarah Gordon. The following Saturday afternoon, after Don had had his bread and jam and tea, she suggested they all go for a walk. It was the end of August, sunny and still. They set off, Liz braving the world with her bulge, Billy half-silly at being out with his father, Don content to saunter along and pass the time of day with a man clipping his hedge, with another oiling the chain on his bike. They went up the hill and along the road of slightly bigger, detached bungalows where the Gordons stayed. Liz paused in front of a house with a striped, shorn lawn and white paintwork.

'This is it,' she said. 'I asked at the post office, just tae be sure. I'd hae come on my ain, but I thought it would be better if you were here, at least the first time.'

All through the village front doors lay open to the day, but the door of the Gordons' house was shut. Liz saw Don's reluctance.

'Come on,' she said, 'it's no a criminal offence. We're just being friendly.'

She unsnecked the gate and went in. Billy made a dash for the expanse of green grass and started running around in circles on it. Liz went up to the door and rapped the knocker.

'He'll think we're interfering,' Don muttered.

'Well, we are, but there's nae harm in it.'

The door opened. A thin, pale woman with a hank of blonde hair falling over her face stood there. At her side, peering anxiously out at Billy on the lawn, was a little girl.

The woman's brow furrowed up. 'Can I help you?'

'We're the Lennies,' Liz said. 'I'm Liz and this is Don and that's oor wee lad, Billy. Don kens your husband. We were oot for a walk and thought we'd chap your door and say hello.'

The woman looked bewildered, as if nobody had ever called on her before. She stared at Liz and her mouth opened but she didn't say anything.

'You must be Sarah,' Liz said. 'And *you*,' bending her knees, 'must be Barbara. I would get doon and say hello properly, but I'm no very good at getting back up again just noo.'

'Oh,' the woman said, as she took in the expanse of Liz's belly. 'I'm sorry. You must be tired. Would you like a glass of water?' She had a frail, uncertain, English voice.

'If it's nae bother.'

Sarah Gordon seemed not to know whether to leave them on the step or ask them in. Billy had run out of steam and come up to the door, and was eyeballing the girl hiding behind her mother.

'Would your little boy like something too?' Sarah managed.

'That would be grand. Would ye like something, Billy?'

'Some milk perhaps?' Sarah said.

Billy nodded. 'Whit dae ye say?' Liz prompted. 'Yes, please,' he said. Don stood awkwardly behind his family. Sarah moved back as if she felt them pressing against her, and without having been invited they found themselves inside, following her and the girl through a cool, dark hallway into a bright kitchen with pale blue doors on the cupboards. Everything was spotlessly clean and well ordered.

'By, ye keep a trig hoose,' Liz said. 'Ye pit me tae shame, so ye dae.'

'Jack likes things tidy,' Sarah said. 'We both do. We don't like clutter.'

She started opening cupboards, getting out a glass for Liz, mugs for the children. Barbara stayed close to her mother, while Liz tried to restrain Billy's inclination to test the feel of every surface in reach.

'Ye're no frae round here, then?' Liz said. 'I mean, ye don't sound it.'

'No,' Sarah said. 'I'm from the south. Dorset.'

'That's a long way. How do ye find Wharryburn?'

'It's fine. People are kind.'

'It's funny we've never met,' Liz said. 'A wee place like this.'

'No,' Sarah said. 'I don't go out much.'

Don felt he was too big for the room. 'Jack hame, is he?'

'In the garden,' Sarah said. 'You can go out the back door.'

He stepped out. The same precision here. A weedless path, trees that looked like they'd been reprimanded for not standing up straight, a flower bed with perfect edges and in it a company of uniformly shaped rose bushes. Jack, at the far end, was standing on another path, raking a square patch of soil into submission. He was wearing khaki-coloured cotton trousers and a white shirt with the sleeves rolled up above his elbows. His brown, shiny forearms looked as if they were made of wood.

'Jack,' Don called when still some distance away. It was best not to give Jack any surprises.

Jack went on raking for a few seconds, then slowly raised his head, as if his brain had taken that long to register the sound.

'What are you doing here?' It was almost an accusation.

'We were oot for a walk. Liz wanted tae stop by and say hello. She wanted tae meet Sarah.'

He walked over to where Jack stood inspecting the raked patch. Close up, Don could see that it was not entirely flat. There were drills across it, but raised so slightly that the ground looked as if it were undulating, like the surface of a loch on a nearly windless day.

'Why?' Jack said.

'Why what?'

'Why did she want to meet Sarah?'

What kind of question was that? 'Just tae be friendly, Jack,' Don said. He pointed at the ground. 'What's gaun in there, then?' A winter crop of some sort, he presumed.

'Potatoes,' Jack said.

'Bit late, are ye no? I had mine in six weeks syne.'

Jack ignored him. 'A great insurance,' he said. 'If you have a supply of potatoes you'll never starve.'

'I ken, but –' He stopped himself. This was the man's home territory. He could plant his tatties whenever he liked. Don tried to think of something else to say. It was like talking to a wall.

'I'll tell ye something,' he said. 'I've never seen a better-dug bit o ground. There's no a weed on it. No a daud o earth oot o place.'

'You have to prepare the soil properly,' Jack said. 'You have to make the conditions right. Otherwise there's no point. You'd be better not planting at all.'

'I'm no sure aboot that,' Don said. 'But then, I'm no a perfectionist.'

'I realise that,' Jack said.

From the house came the sound of a child's voice protesting at something. It wasn't Billy. Jack didn't appear to have heard it. He was still gripping the rake handle, and now he turned and began raking the soil again.

'I better go and check if everything's all right,' Don said. 'We should be getting along onywey. Liz just needed a drink of water.'

'I thought she wanted to meet Sarah,' Jack said, not looking up.

It was something beyond rudeness. Don felt completely wrong-footed. It was his own fault, Liz's fault. They shouldn't have come, shouldn't have intruded. A man's own house was his own house.

'I'll be away, then,' he said.

'Will I see you at the Blackthorn?' Jack said. There was a different note in his voice, anxious, as if Don might not appear. He stopped his raking.

'Aye, if ye're gaun?'

Jack nodded. He seemed both to want to say something else and unable to do so. Finally he managed, 'Eight o'clock as usual?'

And Don felt like telling him to forget it, but couldn't. 'Aye,' he said.

'See you later, then,' Jack said, and went back to work.

In the kitchen, the two women were sitting at the table, Barbara curled up on her mother's lap while Billy stood beside Liz and she stroked his hand. He was too big for her to pick up in her condition. Don didn't get the sense that he'd interrupted a deep conversation.

'Everything all right?' he asked. 'I heard somebody starting tae greet.'

'Barbara wanted Billy's mug,' Liz said. 'But we're fine now. Aren't we, pet?'

Barbara put her face to her mother's insubstantial bosom.

'She's shy with strangers,' Sarah said.

'We should be on our way,' Don said. He reached for Billy and hoisted him up. 'Will we go hame, wee man?'

He hadn't finished the sentence before Sarah was on her feet, holding her daughter. 'Well,' she said, 'it was kind of you to come.' She sounded regretful and relieved at once.

'I'll come again,' Liz said. 'Another day.'

Out on the street, Don put Billy on his shoulders and they started down the hill.

'Satisfied?' he said to Liz.

'No,' she said. 'That's a sad hoose. There's plenty no right there. A sad hoose and a sad woman, and a poor bairn. How was Jack?'

Don shook his head. 'I wouldna ken how Jack is,' he said.

'I could hardly get a word oot o Sarah,' Liz said. 'Hardly a word.'

'She looks like she's no weel.'

'It would mak ye no weel, living wi a ghost. I saw ye talking tae him through the windae. That's what he's like, a ghost.'

He knew exactly what she meant. He felt haunted by Jack. It wasn't an unpleasant feeling, just strange. He felt there must be a reason for it. There was a reason for everything.

§

Their conversation that night might have been about Korea. The Communists had overrun virtually the whole peninsula apart from the south-east corner around the port of Pusan. A vast American army had been pouring into Pusan throughout August. British and other Commonwealth troops were being dispatched there too. It looked like the start of the next world war, but Jack seemed completely uninterested. What he wanted to talk about was 'the Covenant', a document drawn up by a non-party organisation, the Scottish Convention, established by a Glasgow lawyer called John MacCormick. MacCormick had been leader of the tiny Scottish National Party but, tired of moderating between neo-Jacobites on his right and pan-Celtic revolutionaries on his left, had left the party during the war and set up the Convention instead. The Covenant was his dream of a cross-party, non-party declaration of intent. It was a three-paragraph statement that began 'We, the people of Scotland who subscribe this Engagement' and ended with a 'solemn pledge' to do 'everything in our power to secure for Scotland a parliament with adequate legislative authority in Scottish affairs'. In not much more than a year this document had secured the support of more than a million people across the land, who had added their names to copies of it from Glasgow to Wick, from Stornoway to Dunbar. It had even gone the rounds of Scottish soldiers serving in occupied Germany and bits of the shrinking British Empire. Jack said that all these signatures represented a stirring of the popular will. Don thought they represented a monumental irrelevance.

'Ye've pit your ain name tae it, then?'

'Of course. What Scotsman wouldn't?'

'I've no, and nor will I. The world's aboot tae go up in flames, Jack, and ye're bothered aboot getting a wee talking shop tae sit in Edinburgh and tell us what tae dae. I've nae time for it. Dukes and bank managers strutting aboot like puffed-up doos? No on my account. And that MacCormick, what's he noo he's left the Nationalists? Is he a Liberal? Or a Tory in disguise? He's no Labour onywey. I canna be daein wi him.'

'Forget about MacCormick,' Jack said. 'He's just one man. What matters isn't what *he* wants, it's what the people want. What do they think they're signing up for when they sign the Covenant? They think they're signing up for Home Rule within the United Kingdom because that's what the document says, but the days of wanting Home Rule are already over. The people don't yet know what they want, they can't articulate it, but something is happening deep within them, something instinctive and fierce that isn't about the average weekly wage or the net surplus or deficit of the Scottish economy or whether we would have higher income tax or lower stamp duty if we were free. They're making a pledge, a promise to themselves about who they are. That's what the Covenant means and that's why it's important. It's the first stage of a process.'

A queer kind of distance was in his eyes. For the first time really, Don, who had always made allowances for Jack because of the war, thought he might be slightly insane.

'I ken where that kind of process ends up,' Don said. 'Flag-waving and folk goose-stepping round city squares. I'm a socialist, Jack. I've mair in common wi a bus driver in Manchester or a welder in Wales than I'll ever hae wi the Duke o Montrose. And you too. Why are ye cluttering your heid wi that mystical rubbish? Ye'll be speaking aboot souls next. Ye've nae mair insight intae what the people of Scotland want than I dae. Why are ye mixed up in aw this?'

'I'm not mixed up in anything. I'm just observing. It's too early to get involved. The soil is still being prepared.'

'Ah, right, I'm wi ye noo. This is like your tattie patch, is it? Sae, when are the tatties gaun in, Jack?'

'You can laugh,' Jack said, 'but I know what I'm talking about. This Labour government's done some good things, some principled things, I don't deny it, but it's on its last legs and when it falls the principle that will survive will be that London knows best. Everything must be controlled from London. Folk get a taste for that and they want to hang on to it. The Tories won't let it go. They'll build on it. And if Labour get in again in a few years they'll build on whatever the Tories leave them. It's not about left and right, it's about power. And the people of Scotland are just like people all over the rest of the world. They sense it when somebody is just dictating to them, not listening, and they don't like it. They'll turn against it, sooner or later. They'll want power here. The Covenant is only the beginning.'

'Your wife's English,' Don said. 'What does she think aboot it?'

'She doesn't think about it,' Jack said.

'She must hae an opinion, surely?'

'She's not interested in these things. We don't discuss them.'

'How did ye meet her onywey?' Don found himself quietly belligerent. Jack's attitude, his strangeness that afternoon, had made him so. He wanted Jack to give him something more.

'When we came back in '45,' Jack said, 'we landed at Southampton. They sent me to a place near Bournemouth to convalesce. Not that I needed to go, I was pretty fit by then after the voyage, but you know the army, no point in arguing. Sarah was working there.'

'A nurse?'

'I didn't need nursing,' Jack said sharply. 'No, she was in the office, doing the paperwork. Signing us in, signing us out, all that. The men liked the female company, didn't matter if they were cooks or cleaners or office girls, they just liked talking to them. They'd been starved of it for years. Starved of everything, of course, but the company of women, they really missed that.'

Don noted how Jack managed to exclude himself from his own analysis. Was he a loner even then? Before? Maybe it wasn't the Japs that had done the damage. Maybe he'd always been like this.

'Anyway,' Jack said, 'in the end I got her.'

There was something hard and ungenerous in the way he said it. He might have been talking about catching a cold, or drawing the short straw. Don saw him in the hospital, or commandeered hotel or country house or wherever it was they'd put him, setting himself apart from the others, untouchable. I bet she took pity on you, he thought. Or maybe you pitied her. Either way, Don reckoned it was a poor thing to build a marriage on.

'And when I was passed fully healthy, and demobbed, we were married and came home.'

'No *her* hame, though,' Don said. 'Does she like it?'

'Aye, I think she does,' Jack said, as if he'd never considered it before. 'Apart from the cold, which she's not used to. It's a better life. We could have stayed there, I suppose, but why would you? It's a bloodless kind of place. She's well out of it.'

He said it thin-lipped. He seemed to be talking not about his wife, the mother of his child, but an evacuee that had been foisted on him, someone for whom he felt a vague sympathy but no deep affection. His coolness was beyond Don's comprehension.

'She's gien ye a bonnie wee dochter,' he said, trying to spark some slight glow of appreciation. 'But she looked tired this efternoon. Maybe she misses her faimly.'

'We are her family,' Jack said. 'Barbara and me. I appreciate your concern, Don, but she's fine. We're all fine.'

§

In the first week of September the news reported heavy fighting all around Pusan, with the Americans punching their way out of their corner, beginning to drive the North Koreans back. Don and Liz sat by the wireless night after night, getting used to the strange names of towns and rivers. He thought of how he'd driven lorries full of equipment up through Italy in '43, the dust on the dry roads, the mud and slog when it rained, the constant waiting while mines were cleared, roads repaired, Bailey bridges built across slow, brown rivers, the almost total absence of engagement with the enemy because the Germans had withdrawn to embed themselves in a defensive line south of Rome. He thought of the early months of '44, when that unreal advance against minimal resistance had come to a grinding halt at Monte Cassino. He suspected that what was going on around Pusan bore more resemblance to the carnage there than to the breezy drive north from Sicily.

Liz was due any time. She'd had a long labour with Billy but no complications so they anticipated the birth happening at home, as Billy's had. They had two plans. If she went into labour while he was at work she was to get their neighbour Betty Mair to go for Dr Logan, or leave a message for him if he was out. If there was anything wrong Betty was to go to the telephone box outside the post office and phone Byres Brothers to let Don know. 'But only if necessary,' Liz said. 'Nae point in spending fourpence if we dinna need tae.' Betty would look after Billy till the birth was over. Don didn't like leaving Liz alone when it could happen any time but what else could he do? He was just the man. 'Ye gied her the bairn but ye canna cure her o it,' his mother said. Deep down he knew Liz would be all right. She was sensible, a good woman. Strong and sound physically, too. He couldn't ask for a better wife.

If she started in the evening or at night, Don would go for the doctor himself. If anything seemed untoward Bill Drummond, a few doors away, had made them promise to call round for him, whatever hour it was. Bill had a motor car. He'd been in the Royal Army Service Corps supply branch for the last year of the war, and somehow had persuaded the army to sell him a deep green Austin 10HP, an ex-staff car, for a knockdown price when he was demobbed. He'd stripped it down and built it back up, repainted and polished it, and loved to take people for rides to show off his driving skills. It was all worked out if an emergency arose and they couldn't rouse the doctor or he was on a call: Don would run round to alert Bill while Liz got herself ready; then when Bill arrived they'd all climb in, Liz in the front-passenger seat, Don carrying Billy in the back, and drive back to leave Billy with Bill's wife, Joan, who was five months gone herself. Then it would be down the road to the hospital in Drumkirk. They could call an ambulance from the phone box, but it would take more time. Anyway, Liz would be all right. She might need Bill Drummond's car but she'd not need an ambulance.

Bill was a journalist on one of the local papers, the *Drumkirk Gazette*. He was all right, but he fancied himself like mad. Although his war service had consisted, Don had worked out, mainly of shifting ordnance from one depot to another, from the way he went on you'd think he'd been in the Commandos. He slaistered his hair with Brylcreem and, given his surname and Ronald Colman moustache, he'd gained the mildly mocking nickname 'Bulldog', which he took as a compliment. He appeared in the Blackthorn on an occasional Saturday, dropping hints about something afoot in local politics or business that he was keeping his eye on, a big story about to break. But Don reckoned the biggest story on Bill's horizon was the one he would tell about racing a pregnant woman to hospital beneath the moon and stars. You could tell he secretly hoped it would happen and that it would be the dead of night when Don chapped the door. And if it wasn't Liz you could guarantee his own wife, Joan, was going to need a hurl into town – in the depths of winter that would be, and with luck there'd be snow about and a good chance of a skid or two on the way.

The second weekend in September came but still no sign of the bairn. That Saturday Jack wasn't on the bus into work, and when Don got on the bus to come home at midday Jack's usual seat was empty again. The sky was grey and there was an autumnal chill in the air. It had been raining all day. It had been raining all week, in fact. All the talk at work had been of a mining accident at Borlanslogie, twenty miles the other side of Drumkirk. On Thursday night there'd been a collapse on the surface, due to the ground being saturated. The land had just given way, and thousands of tons of mud now blocked the roadways of the mine workings below. There were men trapped down there, scores of them. Peering through the streaked, dribbling glass at the countryside, summer just beginning to go brown at the edges, Don thought about that. Another kind of hell. He could never have worked down a pit.

Sarah Gordon was waiting at the bus stop. She was holding Barbara high on her chest, hoisting her up as passengers got off so that she could see their faces. It was obvious from Sarah's expression that something was wrong.

'Mr Lennie,' she said as he reached them. 'I'm sorry to bother you. Have you seen my husband?'

'Jack? No. He wasna on the bus this morning. Did he get a different one?'

'I don't think he went to work,' she said. 'He left the house before

I was awake, but I know he wasn't wearing his work clothes. They're hanging in the cupboard. I remembered you'd be on this bus. I thought I'd come down and check, in case.'

He looked blankly at her.

'In case you'd seen him,' she said imploringly. He realised that she was not just worried, she was frightened.

'No, I'm sorry. If he didna go tae his work, dae ye ken where he might have gone insteid?'

She shook her head. Then she said, 'I wondered if you'd see if he was in the pub.'

Don glanced at his watch. 'What for would he be in the pub at this hour?'

'He might have gone for a drink,' she said. It was such an obvious response he nearly laughed, but the fear in her face stopped the laugh coming. Barbara was frowning at him too, as if she dimly remembered him from somewhere.

'Ye've no had a keek in yersel?' he said.

'I don't like to,' she said.

'Right, then,' he said. 'We'll go and hae a look.' He reached out for Barbara. 'Come on, darling, let's gie your mother a rest.' But she squirmed back from him, gripping Sarah's arm and shoulder with sudden ferocity.

'She won't go with anybody else,' Sarah said. 'I'm sorry.'

'Never mind,' Don said. 'It's just ye look a wee bit wabbit. Tired,' he added, seeing she didn't understand. 'Exhausted.'

'I suppose I am a little,' she said.

They walked up the brae together. He thought, we might almost be a family. As if she'd read his mind, she said, 'How's Mrs Lennie?'

'Liz,' he said. 'And please call me Don, no Mr Lennie. Naebody calls me that, no even at my work. She's fine, but she's due ony time noo. Overdue in fact.'

'Then you need to go home,' she said.

But he felt an overwhelming pity for her, a need to help. Liz would be all right about it, he thought. She would understand.

'The bairn'll be born when it's born,' he said. 'Let's see if we canna find Jack first, eh?'

He wasn't in the Blackthorn, nor had he been. Don asked, while Sarah and Barbara waited outside the door. They continued on, past the end of his own street, back to the Gordons' bungalow. She had to put Barbara down while she found her key and unlocked the door. Don glanced away, slightly embarrassed. There was a key for their own house, in a bowl on a table in the lobby, but he couldn't remember the last time they'd used it. He wondered if Jack carried a key too, if he and Sarah came and went, locking their house against the world and each other. What if he'd gone out keyless that morning and come back in the last half-hour to find the door shut against him? The idea of that happening to Don himself was inconceivable.

They went in and through to the kitchen. She filled the kettle and put it on the electric ring. Barbara, back in familiar surroundings, let go of her mother at last, although she still steered a wide path around Don. She left the kitchen but returned a minute later carrying a teddy bear. Sarah helped her up on to a stool and she sat there rocking the bear and watching the two adults talking.

'What now, then?' Don asked. When Sarah turned to face him she looked disappointed, and he realised she'd been hoping he would have a plan.

'Think now,' he said. 'Where else might he be? Has he gone off afore?'

'Oh yes,' she said. 'But not like this.'

He screwed his face up, puzzled but relieved. 'Well, then. Surely he's just gone a bit further than usual? Maybe he's decided tae go climbing hills, like he did afore the war, and he left early and didna want tae wake ye.'

'No,' she said, 'you don't understand. He doesn't *go* anywhere. He's just not *here*. Like that time you all came round. Didn't you find it hard to speak to him out in the garden?'

'Aye,' he said, 'but . . .' He stopped, not sure of his ground. 'But does he never go away? I mean, physically go away, for a lang walk or something. He can be quite solitary, I would think.'

'Oh yes,' she said. The kettle was coming to the boil. 'Do you want some tea?'

He nodded. 'Just milk, thanks,' he said.

She said, 'Sometimes he doesn't speak for days. But he's never disappeared like this.'

'Did ye hae an argument or something?' he said, feeling clumsy and intrusive. 'He can be a wee bit touchy, I've noticed. I tried telling him he was late wi his tatties but he didna want tae hear it.'

'The soil's not good enough,' Sarah said.

'Not at all. It's braw. I never saw soil like it.'

'He doesn't think so. Do you know how long he's been preparing that patch?'

'Since aboot April, frae the look o it,' Don said, trying to lighten her mood.

'Three years,' Sarah said. 'Ever since we moved in. He keeps digging it and weeding it and raking it, but he's never satisfied. I don't believe he's ever going to grow anything in it. He says the soil's too poor.'

Don hardly ever swore. Occasionally at work, if he hit his hand against something or a tool broke. Even in the army, when other men couldn't utter a sentence without cursing, he'd kept his language clean. He prided himself on not using even mild swear words in front of a woman. 'Bloody hell,' he said now. 'Three years? That's crazy.'

He'd said it before he could stop himself. But she looked at him with relief, as if she no longer needed to pretend.

'Yes,' she said, 'it's crazy. That's the word.'

Neither of them spoke for a minute. Barbara stared. Maybe the silence, the child's eerie witness, weren't so unusual for Sarah, but they unnerved Don, forcing him to say something.

'Dae ye think he could hae just jumped on a bus and headed aff for the hills? He sometimes talks aboot Glen Coe and places, miles away, where he went climbing. Maybe that's where he's gone. Mind you, it's no exactly the weather for tramping aboot the hills.'

'Weather wouldn't stop him,' Sarah said, 'if that's what he decided to do. I think he gets hemmed in sometimes. It's like he can't breathe properly in the house, or even in the garden or the street. And he just has to go.'

'So he does go off? Where?'

'Up into the woods behind the village. That's the direction he heads in anyway. Up the hill. It's the nearest place where there's not likely to be anybody about. It's usually only for an hour or so, but sometimes it's much longer. But never in the middle of the night. Oh no, that's not true. A couple of times he's got up and gone there at night. He says he likes to watch the owls hunting. But he doesn't call them owls. He has another word for them.'

'Hoolets,' Don said.

'Yes, that's it. Hoolets.'

'Well,' Don said, 'maybe that's where he's gone this time. All we can dae is wait, I suppose. I mean, ye dinna want tae tell the polis or onything, dae ye?'

'I don't know,' she said. 'I just want him to come back. I want him safe. I want all of us to be safe.'

'I ken,' he said. 'Well, we'll no get the polis yet.' There would be something defeated, shameful almost, about involving them. 'Is there onything that might have set him aff? Onything unusual that's happened? If I had a clue where tae start, I'd go and look for him.'

She shook her head. Don caught a movement out of the corner of his eye and spotted Barbara shaking her head, and making the bear do it too. Bloody hell, he said again, into himself.

'Do you know anybody called MacLaren?' Sarah said suddenly.

'In the village, ye mean?'

'Not sure. In the pub? Somebody that might have upset him.'

She went out of the room. Barbara, twisting on the stool, followed her anxiously with her eyes but Sarah was back in a few seconds, holding a piece of paper, a lined sheet from a notebook. 'Maybe it's nothing,' she said. 'But it doesn't look like nothing, does it?'

Don took the sheet from her: the name MacLaren appeared three times on each line, neatly inscribed in block capitals, the M and L slightly bigger than the other letters: a perfect line-up of – he counted the lines – a hundred and twenty MacLarens on parade. A certain extra pressure had been exerted occasionally, so that the nib had pierced the paper at the apexes of some of the As or the ends of the Cs. Don thought, once he'd written the first one he'd have to match it with another, then he'd have to balance the paper up with a third, then he'd have to balance the line with a second line, then he'd have to fill the page. He could picture Jack working away at it obsessively.

'Has he ever talked tae ye aboot the camps?' he said. 'During the war?'

'No,' she said. 'Never.'

'No even when ye met him, when he was recovering?'

She looked shocked. 'Especially not then. Why?'

'There was a man called MacLaren he tellt me aboot.'

'What happened to him?'

'He died. He was killed by the Japs.'

'Oh God,' she said. She took the paper back, stared at it as if it might speak. 'What does it mean?'

'I dinna ken. Maybe it disna mean onything. Look,' he said, 'I better get hame. I'll come back efter I've seen Liz and maybe take a walk up intae the woods. He'll probably be here by the time I get back, but that's what I'll dae. Will ye be all right?'

She nodded. 'Thank you very much. Don.'

'Aye, right,' he said. 'Try no tae worry.' But he felt like a deserter, even though it was nothing to do with him. And something else: being in the house with her on his own – it made him feel treacherous, as if he were there behind Jack's back, when he was only trying to help.

As he hurried home he thought about what she'd said about Jack and the owls. It didn't surprise him. Jack had a way with animals. Once, coming back from the Blackthorn, they'd come across a hedgehog in the road. Jack had hunkered down and put a hand out to its snout. Don expected it to curl up in a ball, but it didn't, it came towards the outstretched hand, and Jack carefully led it off the tarmac and into the long grass, as if he had it on an invisible leash. And sometimes, at the bus stop, a blackbird would land on the wall a few inches away from his head, just stand and wait with its own head cocked as if it too were waiting for the bus. When Don or anybody else went close, it flew off, but it had no fear of Jack. The same bird. You could tell by a white patch on its wing. Jack didn't speak to it or feed it, he just stood beside it. As if the two of them knew something that nobody else did. And maybe they did.

§

It was after two o'clock when he got in. Billy came running to the door when he heard it open. Don picked him up, roughed his hair, tickled him. 'All right, wee man?' He went into the living room. Liz was sitting, splayed out and hot despite the cool day, in her armchair. She said, 'Where have ye been? There's some soup in the pan on the stove, but it'll need heating up.'

He explained about Sarah waiting for Jack at the bus stop. 'I couldna just leave her there,' he said. 'I looked in the pub for Jack and walked her hame. She's feart for him.'

'Or frae him,' Liz said.

'How are ye?' he asked, putting Billy down.

'Sair,' she said. 'It's started at last.'

He clapped his palm to his head. 'Liz, I'm sorry. Dae ye want the doctor?'

'God no,' she said. 'It's far too soon for that, he'd come and just have to go away again.'

'How often are ye getting the pains?'

'No often enough,' she said. 'Aboot one every hauf-oor. Away and get your soup.'

'Are ye wanting some?'

'Christ, Don, dae I look like I'm wanting soup?'

He went through to the kitchen. He'd not dared to say anything about going back to Sarah Gordon's afterwards. How could he, with Liz maybe about to give birth any minute? He ladled the soup straight from the pan into a bowl, found half a loaf in the bread bin and sliced off a hunk, then sat at the table, gulping and cramming and chewing, trying to think what to do.

'Have ye heated it up?' Liz called.

'Aye!' he shouted between lukewarm mouthfuls. Slow down, he thought, you'll make yourself sick. But he kept going at the same pace, glancing at the paper as he ate.

For once, Korea was relegated from prime position in the news. The front page was taken up with the drama unfolding at Borlanslogie. Forty hours after the original collapse some ninety men were still underground, unable to progress in any direction and with a diminishing supply of air to sustain them. Rescue teams were trying to dig through to them from adjacent old workings, but it was slow going. Firedamp was everywhere: it had to be driven out with fans, and only hand tools could be used to tunnel through the thick wall of coal and rock to where the men were. Machinery couldn't be brought in for fear of igniting the gas: even a spark from a chisel could be enough to blow the tunnel and the rescuers to pieces.

He washed and dried the bowl and put it away, then went back through to the other room and stood, hesitant, at the door.

'Well, what dae ye think?' he said after a minute.

'Aboot what?'

'How long dae ye think ye'll be?' It came out wrong, as if he was asking her to hurry up, and he saw anger flaring in her eyes. Quickly he added, 'The rain's stopped. I could take Billy oot for a walk, get him aff your hands and let ye hae a sleep, if ye think it'll be a while yet?'

Her irritation seemed to pass. She even managed a smile. 'That's no a bad idea. He needs some fresh air. I canna see me being ready for a few oors yet. But I might get intae bed. It's better lying doon.'

'I thought it was supposed tae be better standing up, walking aboot.'

'Well, I'm telling ye, at the moment it's better lying doon.'

'Right,' he said, suddenly certain again. 'That's what we'll dae. Come on, wee man, let's get your shoes on and we'll go for a dauner.'

'Dinna gang far,' Liz said. Her eyes were closing already.

'We'll no,' he said.

§

'I'll hae tae be quick,' he said. 'I'll need tae get back tae Liz.'

Jack had failed to return. Don had jogged round, with Billy on his shoulders. Billy had enjoyed the ride at first but then, finding it too hard, or discerning that his father's urgency was not about entertaining him, had begun to whine. By the time they got to Sarah's a full-scale tantrum was threatening, and Don's plan, which had been to leave him with Sarah and Barbara while he had half an hour up in the woods searching for Jack, was clearly not going to work.

'I really appreciate this,' Sarah said.

'Thing is,' Don said, 'if I canna find him, I'm no sure what else tae dae. I mean, he hasna been away for a day yet. The polis'll no dae onything aboot it till at least the morn's morn.'

'There's something wrong,' she said. 'I know it.'

'Well,' he said, 'nae point in me standing here. Come on, Billy, let's go up in the woods.'

'Wouldn't it be better to leave him with me?'

'He'll no settle,' Don said. 'I can see the signs.' Somehow he'd got himself into a position of being dishonest to both women, and duplicity was not one of his strong points. He was regretting not having told Liz they were coming here, but he'd also decided he didn't want to leave Billy in that house. He felt sorry for Sarah, but he wasn't confident she was capable of looking after two bairns at once. And every time he looked at the silent, watchful Barbara, he felt uneasy.

He let Billy walk and run for a while as they headed past the last of the houses and through a kissing gate, which led into the woods. It took longer with Billy walking but Don couldn't carry him any more. He wondered if Billy's memory was stirred. They'd pushed him up there in his pram once or twice, lifting him over the gate and bumping him along over tree roots and loose stones, but that was half his lifetime ago. The path led to an old wooden bench, camouflaged in bird droppings and flaky green paint, with a view back over the village and all the way down to Drumkirk. As far as he knew, Liz had never been back since. He hadn't himself.

On a good day the view was great, you could see right over towards Fife. Borlanslogie lay in that direction, though it was hidden by hills, and in this kind of weather you couldn't even see the hills. In the other direction, if you kept on through to the other side of the woods, you ended up on the moor. At this time of year there were often parties of shooters out after grouse. They came from the far side of the moor, from the north, Glenallan, a different breed with their tweed breeks, fore-and-afts and whiskery cheeks, rough-hewn ruddy-faced men with thick accents – not the plummy voices of the gentry, but the peatbog tones of their henchmen and farming neighbours. Fierce, some of them could be. And indeed when they reached the bench he heard the faint pop-pop of shotguns, toylike in the distance, and he wondered, not really believing it a possibility, whether Jack might have strayed up on to the moor and got himself mistaken for a grouse and shot.

Billy was happy again, picking up damp twigs and pine cones and collecting them together in a pile beside the bench while Don peered, as if with some definite purpose, into the trees. He called out – 'Jack! Jack Gordon!' – and his voice came back from the hill and Billy heard it and they had to spend a few minutes making their voices echo. Nobody shouted back. Then they went deeper in, along sodden, slippery paths, Don in the vague, hopeless hope of spotting something related to Jack. But what? A dropped handkerchief? Jack hanging from a branch? He put the thought from his mind. He was wasting his time. There was no possibility of him searching properly – not with Billy in tow. They should just go home. He had another bairn on the way, a wife needing attention. What the hell was he thinking of?

What he was thinking of was that if Jack turned up, as he probably would later in the afternoon, he'd no doubt be expecting Don to meet him in the Blackthorn at eight o'clock, same as any other Saturday night. Never mind that he'd worried his wife sick, and obliged Don to engage in this ridiculous half-hearted hunt for him. Well, he'd be in the pub on his own. Don couldn't go, even if he wanted to, because of Liz. But the truth was, he didn't want to. He was tired of Jack's half-baked theories about nationhood and freedom. Jack would have to do without him tonight. But would he find anybody else soft enough to keep him company?

'Come on, son,' he said to Billy. 'Let's get hame and see how your mother's daein.'

They stopped briefly at the Gordons' house and Don reported to Sarah that he'd had no luck and suggested that if Jack still hadn't turned up by early evening she should think about contacting the police. He couldn't help her any more – not, at least, till Liz had had the baby. Everything he said seemed to wound Sarah. She looked like a woman utterly alone – which, he thought as he hurried back home with Billy on his shoulders again, she doubtless was, Jack or no Jack.

They'd been away two hours, more. When he opened the door Liz was coming down the passage towards him from the kitchen, brisker and slimmer than she'd been for months. 'Where have ye been?' she said, just as she had earlier. But it wasn't Liz, it was Joan Drummond. She said, 'Ye've tae get doon tae the hospital quick as ye can. Bill took her in aboot forty minutes ago. Billy'll be fine wi us.'

There was another woman in the house, emerging from the kitchen now. There was a lot of steam behind her, and Don could see what looked like sheets draped over the side of the Belfast sink. It was Betty, the next-door neighbour. 'Don,' Betty said.

'What's gaun on?' Don said. 'Why does she need tae go tae the hospital?'

'She came on a lot quicker than she expected,' Joan said.

'But she said she wouldna be ready for oors,' Don said. 'I would never have gone oot if I'd thought ony different. And why's she at the hospital?'

'She got frightened,' Betty said. 'She started bleeding. She sent me roond for Dr Logan but he's away oot fishing. Mrs Logan said tae get an ambulance but it was quicker tae get Bill. Luckily he and Joan were at hame,' she added reproachfully.

'Liz said tae say sorry tae ye, but she couldna wait,' Joan said. 'Though what she needs tae say sorry for beats me.'

Don didn't know Joan that well. He'd never heard her nippy like that and felt a momentary twinge of sympathy for Bulldog. But none of that was important.

'Right,' he said. 'I'm away.'

'If ye run,' Betty said, 'ye'll catch the bus on the half-oor.'

Don ran.

§

Things get jumbled in your head. Not at the time of their happening perhaps, but afterwards, when you try to tease out the strands, recall the order in which they occurred. When what you are facing is triumph or disaster, one or the other, everything has definition, force, threat. It demands a response. The nearest thing in peacetime to being under enemy fire. It's later that the confusion sets in, the overlapping, the fuzziness of detail. At the time you deal with it, you cope. Later you wonder how you did.

It was raining again. Don was intimidated by the hospital, a blackened pile with turrets and dripping rones. Inside, some of the decor had been modernised, but the whole place still had an air of gloomy Victorian philanthropy. It was part of the National Health Service now, but only at some abstract political level did he think of it as belonging to him in any way. Physically, emotionally, what he felt mostly was that he was an inconvenience to the people who worked there; that his presence somehow detracted from the efficiency or purpose of the building as staff came and went through the entrance hall; that he was taking the shine off the polished linoleum by stepping on it.

He approached the reception desk and asked about Liz. 'She's aboot tae hae a bairn. There was an emergency, she was bleeding. A neighbour brought her in his motor.' The man at the desk frowned when he spoke of the bleeding, as if it were neither necessary nor appropriate to mention it. He asked Don to wait while somebody was contacted. He pointed out a bench near the door where he could sit. An orderly appeared, was given instructions and went away again. There was a big clock on the wall behind the desk. Twenty minutes passed. Half an hour. Don, struggling to contain himself, was on his feet every time a nurse or doctor came by. He went back to the desk.

'I really need tae find oot what's gaun on. If ye tell me which ward she's in I'll go masel.'

'Oh ye canna dae that,' the man said. 'Somebody will be with ye in a minute. Just take a seat.'

A minute. Another. Ten, eleven, twelve of them. More clip-clopping shoes, uniformed nurses. There were three sets of double doors leading off in different directions from the hall, and one set in particular was forever swinging to the passage of nurses, porters, cleaners. A few lost-looking men and women came in and approached the man behind the desk, who seemed to relish the power he exerted over them, either directing them to some other part of the building or sending them away altogether. It was the visiting half-hour, six till half-past. Don should be part of this vague disruption to the hospital's routine, surely? He stood up again, but the man at the desk caught his eye at once and shook his head, sending him back to the bench. He wondered where Bulldog had got to. He'd kept an eye out for the Austin on the way in but hadn't seen it. Bulldog must have gone home.

Don looked at the clock again, then at his watch. It was approaching seven. The last of the visitors scurried out, glancing questioningly at him. He was about to get up again when a doctor in a white coat arrived at the reception desk. The man behind it pointed at Don. The doctor came towards him and Don met him halfway across the space. Close up, the doctor looked tired and grey. He was maybe about fifty although it was hard to tell.

'Mr Lennie?'

'Yes.'

'I'm Dr Lang. I gather you've been here a while.'

'Nearly two hours. Naebody's tellt me onything.'

'Well, we've been very busy, you know.' As if Don had accused him of slacking.

'How's my wife, doctor?'

'Your wife's in labour. She's doing very well.'

'I wasna wi her when she was brought in. My neighbour brought her. She needed tae come in because she'd started bleeding.'

'Yes, we've managed to stop that. We've given her a transfusion.'

Don searched his eyes for news, good or bad, but Lang was giving nothing away.

'Is she gonnae be aw right?'

'She's a strong, healthy woman, Mr Lennie. There's every reason to suppose she'll be perfectly fine. We've stabilised her condition and now it's simply a question of letting nature take its course.'

'The birth, you mean?'

'Yes.'

'And is the baby aw right tae?'

'As I said, your wife's in labour as we speak.'

'Will everything be aw right though?'

'Yes, we think so.'

They stood in silence. Lang, it seemed, had given him all the information he thought he required.

'Can I see her?' Don asked.

'No, not at the moment. Look,' Lang said, 'why don't you go off and get something to eat, a cup of tea or something? There's nothing you can do here.'

'I'd rather wait.'

'Well, suit yourself, but you'll be here some time. Now, if you'll excuse me . . .'

He gave the impression of someone devoid of emotion. Maybe it was because he was tired, and afraid that Don was going to weep, or become violent or hysterical, and that was the last thing he needed. His mouth twitched – a kind of smile – and he said, 'She's in good hands, Mr Lennie. Try not to worry. Everything is under control.' Then he turned and left. Don sat down again.

Another hour passed. Outside the light was all but gone. It was a quiet night in the hospital, apparently. There didn't seem to be anybody but himself waiting. Waiting for what? For his wife to be well, to have given him a second son? Or for some awful, heart-stopping news he couldn't bear to consider?

Despite himself, he suddenly felt ravenous. He thought, Lang's probably right, he's the doctor after all. I may as well nip out and get a bite.

He walked into the town past the Toll Tavern, a bar he had been in twice, once just before the war and once on returning home after it. A rough, comfortless place full of men seeking oblivion, possibly preceded by a few jokes and a fight. A sickly yellow light was cast against the bottle-thick glass of the windows. Further down the street was Rinaldi's Café. Joe Rinaldi had been interned in 1939 on the Isle of Man and his place had had its windows smashed, but his wife, Maria, had repaired the damage and reopened for the rest of the war, supported by some locals but struggling against the aloofness and gossip of others and the constant attention of the police. Joe had got home in the spring of 1944, six months after Italy had surrendered, and seemed to bear no malice towards the town that had treated him and his family so poorly. Maybe he felt lucky: a cousin had been lost when the *Arandora Star*, packed with internees being sent to Canada, was torpedoed by a U-boat. The café did a fair trade these days, in spite of the austerity. Folk seemed determined to demonstrate that they themselves had never held any suspicions about good old Joe, let alone flung bricks through his windows. It was a quarter to nine. The smell of frying was irresistible. Don went in.

There were a few other people inside – mostly young couples, and a group of boys in one corner – but, apart from Joe, nobody he recognised. Was he getting too distant now he stayed up in the village? In the past there would always have been some familiar face in Rinaldi's.

He ate his supper with a mug of tea in one of the booths. The Light Programme was on the wireless but at nine o'clock Joe switched over to the Home Service. The news was all about Borlanslogie. The inrush had left a huge crater on the surface and, to try to stop more moss and water cascading in and blocking up what little air supply the trapped men had, volunteers had been filling the hole with tree trunks, straw bales, pit props, anything that might slow the rate of collapse. But firedamp was still the main problem. There was phone contact with the trapped men but it was sporadic, and the men themselves were growing weak from want of food and water. Various fire brigades had supplied dozens of respirator sets and the idea was, once a passage had been made, to take the kits in, instruct the men in how to use them, and bring them out one at a time along a chain of rescuers, also wearing the apparatus, stretched along the gas-ridden roadway, a journey of more than a mile. That was how things had been several hours earlier – hours that seemed to have swollen into weeks since Don had been reading the paper – and now, the newsreader was saying, the long and difficult liberation process was under way, and would go on for several more hours. There were eighty-nine men to bring out, and a further seven who were missing, presumed dead.

Sitting there with the food filling his belly, the low chat of the others in the background, the radio news, the sounds from the kitchen and the heat and smells of the café combining in a kind of cheap luxury, Don almost dozed off. Bits of news about the miners mingled with images from the war, images of Liz in a room full of nurses and Dr Lang, Liz pushing and straining, the bloody head starting to emerge. He hoped everything was all right. He'd seen animals give birth – a horse in Italy, cows and sheep at Hackston's Farm – but a human birth was women's business – apart from the doctor, if a doctor was needed – and men like him were not encouraged to know about it, nor did he particularly want to. He kept imagining blood, because that was what Betty had told him: she'd started to bleed. He'd seen plenty of blood during the war, blood spilled through violence, and birth could be violent too, though in a different way. He didn't like to think of Liz involved in anything violent. He thought of her in bed with him, hot and eager but not violent, and always under the sheets with the lights out. This was the outcome, what was happening now in the hospital.

And he kept thinking of Jack. He couldn't help it: Jack kept appearing between the newsreader's words about the miners and Dr Lang's words about Liz. *Huge crowds have formed at the pithead as relatives wait anxiously for word of their menfolk. Your wife's in labour. She's doing very well. The presence of highly flammable gas, known as firedamp, means that great care has to be taken in breaking through to the buried men. We've been very busy, you know. A great insurance. If you have a supply of potatoes you'll never starve.* And Sarah Gordon: *Jack likes things tidy. We don't like clutter. Your wife's in labour. She's doing very well. It's one of the greatest rescue operations in the history of Scottish mining. What do they think they're signing up for? The people don't yet know what they want, they can't articulate it, but something is happening deep within them.* They were bringing the men out one by one, after two days in the tomb. The earth giving birth, rebirth, to all these men, but keeping its tribute, the missing seven it had swallowed. And meanwhile his bairn was fighting to be born, and Liz was fighting to let him be, and doctors and nurses were there to assist them in that effort, and yet some other undefined force was preventing it from happening. And Jack was somewhere, struggling with whatever dark thing it was that gripped him inside. And Sarah was at home with her daughter, alone, waiting anxiously for the word that would not come. Don knew something bad was happening, and something good, that a tortured, torturing battle between two forces was going on across all their lives, across the whole world. If he had any faith he'd say it was God versus Satan, but that was fairy-tale stuff. This was about human beings struggling in the vastness of the universe, a much scarier concept.

He paid for his meal and set off back to the hospital. It was now nearly ten o'clock, and he'd miss the last bus home. He'd have to go round to his mother and father's and sleep the night on their floor. He'd go up to the hospital, see what news there was, and then he'd walk back into town and chap their door.

A different man, a night porter, was on the desk, with a newspaper folded open where he could read it discreetly. Don gave his name again and explained what he was doing there. The man seemed friendlier than his predecessor. 'Haud on a minute, Mr Lennie, I'll see what I can find oot for ye.' He picked up the telephone and dialled while Don stood a few paces away. The man called him back. 'A nurse is coming doon tae see ye. Dinna worry, everything's aw right.'

A few minutes later a young woman – younger than him, anyway – appeared through the swinging doors. 'Mr Lennie?' she said. 'Aye, that's me,' he said. 'I've good news for you. Your wife has had a baby boy. They're both fine.'

'See?' said the man at the desk. 'What did I tell ye? That's grand, so it is. Congratulations.'

He put his hand out over the counter and Don, in a kind of dream, took it. He felt himself sink within himself as he did so, hearing again the nurse's words: *they're both fine*. He'd not realised how stiffly he'd been holding his body against the prospect of bad news. When he let the man's grip go he felt weak, unanchored, and without thinking put out a hand to steady himself on the nurse's arm.

'Are you all right?' she asked.

'Aye,' he said. 'Aye, aye, I'm fine.' He laughed. 'Like them! It's just . . . well, it's been a long day, and she wasna awfie weel tae begin wi. I'm glad, that's all. It's a relief. And they're baith fine, really?'

The nurse smiled at him, a genuine, warm smile. 'Your wife's exhausted. She's sleeping. But she's strong, she'll be back to normal in no time. And the baby's very healthy-looking. A good set of lungs in him.'

'That's grand,' said the other man again, beaming at him. 'Dae ye ken what ye're gonnae call him?'

'Charles,' he said without hesitation, but speaking more to the nurse. 'It's my faither-in-law's name. Oor first wee boy, he's called William efter my faither. But he's aye just Billy tae us, so I doot Charles'll be Charlie soon enough.' He stopped, aware he was rambling. The nurse still had the smile on her face, and he saw her bonnie, shining eyes, and, pressed back under her cap, the dark curly hair that looked like it was about to escape at any time. He thought of Liz, strong and solid-framed, a bonnie woman too but plain-built, and here was this wee, lithe, neat-looking nurse in front of him, and he couldn't help comparing them. She's like an angel, he thought.

'Did ye . . . were ye there at the birth?' he asked.

'Yes,' she said, 'I was.'

'Thank you,' he said.

'I didn't do anything really. But after your baby was born, I took him away and washed him.'

He saw how young she was. Seven or eight years at most between the two of them, but what a difference that was. It made him feel ancient. And she'd seen his son come into the world. For all that he'd witnessed during the war, she'd seen more than he ever would.

'Thank you,' he said. 'I canna thank ye enough.'

She blushed. 'Nonsense. That's what we do. Babies are born every day. It's different when it's your own though, isn't it?'

For a moment he thought she was speaking about herself, but of course she couldn't be. She was looking at him, waiting for him to answer.

'Aye, I suppose so,' he said. 'This is oor second, though. Ye get used wi it.'

She harrumphed sceptically. 'That's all very well coming from you. I'm not sure if your wife would agree.'

He was embarrassed and changed the subject. 'Ye're English, aren't ye?'

'Yes,' she said. Her chin lifted defiantly. 'Why, is that a problem?'

'No, of course it isna. I just couldna help noticing your accent.' To him it was just like Sarah Gordon's. 'Where are ye frae, Dorset?'

'Good guess,' she said. 'Hampshire actually. Next door. Southampton. I need to go. I'm off duty now and I'm not supposed to linger. But I was coming off the ward anyway so I said I'd give you the good news.'

'I canna see them, can I?'

He said it to the nurse but the man on the desk, who'd gone back to his newspaper, looked up when he said this and, without turning round, stuck a finger up at the big clock behind him. He made a wee explosive noise with his mouth and shook his head.

'Come on, man,' Don said.

'Ye're no even supposed tae be *here*,' the man said, 'let alane *there*. Ye'll need tae come back the morn's efternoon.'

Don said, 'I havena seen my wife for eight oors. The last I heard she was bleeding tae death. Noo I've got a new son. I mean, come *on*, man!'

The nurse and the porter exchanged glances. The porter shrugged. The nurse said, 'You can't see your wife because she's asleep in a ward full of other women.' She was weighing something up in her mind. 'But – just a peek at your baby. If you come with me, I can maybe arrange that. Turn your head the other way, Frank,' she said, and then, to Don, 'Quickly now. And not a word to a soul or you'll lose me my job.'

She set off at a pace, through the double doors that had seen so much traffic all evening, and on down a long corridor, dim with night-lighting, then left through more doors, up a flight of stairs, briskly, briskly, right along another corridor, Don striding along behind her watching her curly hair giving tiny bounces under the cap as she marched. He didn't have time to thank her, to say anything, only to follow as she led him through the silent hospital. He lost all sense of direction. She held up her hand suddenly and came to a halt, and Don's chest came up against her back and they stood there motionless, he was so close to her his nose was tickled by her hair. Two female voices close by. He could smell the soap on her skin. Receding steps. She signalled him on. Another set of doors and then, suddenly, a wall with a long, thin window in it. The nurse held a finger to her lips and pointed through the glass. There was a room, half-lit like the passages they had hurried down, and spaced out in neat rows were a dozen cribs that looked for all the world like miniature coffins. Don stared harder, and thought he could make out a bald head, possibly a tiny fist, in one of the nearer ones. He turned to the nurse. 'But which is mine?' he whispered urgently. 'Wait,' she said. There was a door further along the wall and she went to it and slipped inside. He saw her moving among the cribs, towards one in the row furthest away. She bent over and then picked a bundle in a blanket out of the crib. She carried it to the other side of the glass, cradling it in her arms, held it up to him. A squashed, wrinkled, dark wee face, eyes squeezed shut, and a slick of black hair on the head. The hands and arms wrapped tight in the blanket. The nurse smiled at him. It might have been her own baby, it might have been theirs between them, but he was separated from them by the glass, and it was Charles, Charlie, it was his and Liz's second son, sleeping his first night in the world. Don had to struggle to stop whatever was coming up in him. A whoop of joy? Tears? Joe Rinaldi's fish and chips? Whatever it was, he had to fight to hold down the lump that threatened to burst from him.

After a few more seconds the nurse returned the baby to the crib, and came back to him. 'Let's get out of here,' she whispered. And they returned the way they'd come, out from the maternity ward, along the corridors and down the stairs, into the entrance hall and past the night porter, who raised his head from his paper just enough to nod and say, under his breath, 'Well done, sir. Congratulations,' as they went, out into the cool September night. And the nurse stopped and breathed out a big sigh of relief.

'I'd be dismissed on the spot if I was caught doing that, but it doesn't seem right, you dads being kept out of it so much.'

He liked the way she said 'you dads'. There was something pleasingly different about some English accents, especially when it was a young woman speaking.

They walked away from the entrance, along a path under horse chestnut trees towards the nurses' quarters.

'I'm really grateful,' he said. 'I mean, what mair can I say?'

'Nothing,' she said. 'I liked doing it. It was an adventure, wasn't it?'

'Aye,' he said.

'You haven't got a cigarette on you, have you?' she asked.

'No, I'm sorry, I dinna smoke.'

'Seriously?'

'Gave it up when I came oot the army. Canna afford it. Couldna afford *no* tae afore, when we got them in oor rations.'

'I love to smoke,' she said. 'We're not allowed to here, of course. Not even when we're off duty in the nurses' home. But we do, leaning out the windows when Matron's gone to bed. It's like a row of factory chimneys sometimes.'

'I'd buy ye a drink,' he said, 'if there was onywhere open. Tae thank ye, like.'

'I'd let you,' she said, 'if there was anywhere open.'

He saw the silhouette of her curls in the moonlight and a shiver went through him. Her mouth pouted up at him, a cigarette-sucking shape. He wanted to kiss it. Mad, he knew. It was Liz he loved. It was just madness because of everything that was churning inside him.

'So,' he said. 'Southampton, eh? How'd ye end up here?'

'I was evacuated to Scotland during the war, when I was thirteen. My little brother and me. You just got a label stuck on you and were sent anywhere. We ended up in a village in Fife. And you know, even though I couldn't understand a word anybody said, I liked it. People were kind. We were there for about a year but I always said I'd come back. And here I am.'

'Here ye are,' he said. 'Dae ye no miss your hame?'

'Southampton?' She laughed. 'Nothing left to miss. The Germans bombed it flat. The docks, the Spitfire factory, everything. It's a mess. I don't think it'll ever be the same again.'

'I really wish I could buy ye that drink,' he said. A ridiculous thing to say: he'd never bought any lassie a drink, not Liz, nobody. Why did he want to buy this English nurse one?

'Well, thanks anyway, but I'd better be going,' she said, 'or I'll be locked out.'

The nurses' home was round the side of the hospital, whereas his road lay directly ahead, through the gates on to the road. 'We wouldna want that,' he said. 'Another time, then.'

She gave him a look. 'Yes, another time.'

Yet he did not move, and nor did she. And then she shivered and said again, 'I'd better be going.'

'Aye,' he said. 'I'll need tae go tae. Well, goodnight.'

'Goodnight, Mr Lennie,' she said with a kind of laugh, and she started to move away, and it was so strange, after what she'd done for him, to hear her address him in that formal way, that he turned and caught her elbow, and she turned back. 'Oh,' she said, a daft response that didn't make any sense. It was as if they were both disturbed by something beyond their reach, something wondrous and fearsome loitering in the dark grounds of the hospital.

'What's your name?' he asked. 'I don't even know your name.'

'Marjory,' she said. 'Marjory Taylor. What's yours?'

'Don.'

'Goodnight, Don,' she said.

'Goodnight, Marjory,' he said. And suddenly their hands clasped, and they were kissing, a hard, hot, mind-spinning kiss, he could taste the sweetness of her but just as suddenly she broke away, and said 'Oh' again, and then turned and hurried off, breaking into a trot, along the front of the hospital and towards the nurses' quarters. And he stood and let her go.

Total bloody madness.

He looked up at the front of the hospital, with its turrets and dirty stonework, wondering where Charles and Liz were within it. Then he strode off through the gates and towards the part of town where his parents lived.

All he could think of was the kiss, her smell and taste, her loveliness.

There was nobody about, but he'd gone only a few yards when a horn honked and the green Austin was pulling up alongside him.

'Don!' Bulldog called. 'I've been sent as a search party. The womenfolk are getting restless upby. What's the news?'

Don opened the passenger door. 'A boy,' he said. 'A healthy young laddie. I couldna see Liz, it was too late, but they've just let me ken. It was a long wait, but everything's fine, so they tell me.'

'That's great,' Bulldog said, and leaned over and shook his hand. 'Here, hop in, and I'll give you a run home.'

Don was on the point of excusing himself – he could do with a walk, to clear the madness – but the thought of his own bed, a good sleep, and time at home in the morning with Billy before coming in to see Liz, was too appealing. Forget the nurse: it hadn't happened. So why hadn't he mentioned her to Bill? The fact that he'd not mentioned her meant that it *had* happened. He climbed in and pulled the door shut. The engine ticking over sent its throbs through Don's legs and for a second he was somewhere else entirely, sitting in a lorry in a stuck convoy in Italy. Bulldog pulled a slim flask from inside his jacket and unscrewed the top. 'A wee something to wet the bairn's head,' he said, passing it over.

'What is it?' Don said, but as he put it to his lips he could smell the whisky smell of it.

'What would it be but a dram?' Bulldog said. 'I know you're not one for the drink, Don, but you missed yourself at the Blackthorn tonight, and it's an occasion for celebration, is it no?'

Mention of the Blackthorn brought Jack suddenly to the front of Don's mind. He took a small mouthful, just to please Bulldog, and swallowed, wishing a life to his new son as he did so. The whisky burning down his throat and into his chest was surprisingly pleasant.

'Were ye there yersel the nicht?' he asked. 'In the pub, I mean?'

'Me?' Bulldog said. 'No me. I've been entertaining your wee Billy and generally keeping the ladies happy.'

'Ye'll no hae seen Jack Gordon, then?'

'The Gay Gordon?' Bulldog said. 'Haven't seen him for a while. Find him a bit much, to be honest. A bit too morose for my liking. Why?'

'No reason.' Don said. 'Is that what ye call him, the Gay Gordon?'

'Aye,' Bulldog said. 'He's aboot as gay as Stornoway on a Sunday. We dinna mean any harm by it, but you know yourself what he's like.'

Don wondered who the 'we' were who called Jack that. He'd never heard the nickname used before, so maybe it was something that Bulldog had just invented. Or maybe this was another example of how he himself was losing touch, not picking up on the Blackthorn banter. What might they call *him* behind *his* back? He took another mouthful of whisky and returned the flask. Bulldog took a swig himself, closed it up and slipped it back inside his jacket.

'Much obliged tae ye, Bill.'

'My pleasure,' Bulldog said, which clearly it was: the drink, the driving, the sense perhaps of being part of something bold and brave and new. He turned the car and they roared off into the night, and Don, had he not been so tired, had he been able to clear Jack Gordon and Marjory Taylor out of his head, could almost have felt the same.

§

He woke at four in the morning, his mind instantly alert, as if some subconscious warning of an intruder had been triggered. But the only sound in the house was the ticking of the alarm clock in its folding leather case on the bedside table, and he knew he was alone. It had been pointless to disturb Billy, tucked up and sound asleep on the Drummonds' sofa, so he'd left him there for the night. When they'd got back to the village, not far short of midnight, he'd sat for half an hour with a cup of tea, talking to Bulldog and Joan. Again he'd said nothing about seeing the bairn, nothing about Marjory Taylor. Then he'd walked home and gone to his bed. He'd closed his eyes thinking of the nurse – a wee smasher but did she kiss every man she met? – and had kind of hoped he would dream of her but he hadn't, he'd fallen instead into dreams of miners in cumbersome breathing-gear stumbling in single file along endless passages, the lamps on their helmets scything the blackness. But now he sat up in the dark, head clear. The name of the intruder was MacLaren.

The man who tried to walk two thousand miles to India. The prisoner who wanted freedom at any price. The starving wreck they brought back and finished off with a sword sweep in a jungle clearing. And Jack had made a paper company of him, ranks of Mac-Larens marching across a page. Why? What was he trying to say? Was he trying to say anything?

Don couldn't sleep any more. He got up and made a pot of tea, drank the lot thinking about the nurse and then putting her aside and concentrating on the people in his life: Liz, Billy, Charles, his parents, Bulldog, the men at Byres Brothers, but mostly about Jack. It was ridiculous: he was a father again, he had two sons and a wife to look after, and yet it was Jack Gordon he couldn't stop worrying about. He thought of Jack setting out at this time of the morning the day before, heading for somewhere. Some promise of release, of a life beyond mere survival, of a life that wasn't destroyed at its core.

At that moment the fear he'd been resisting since Sarah Gordon met him off the bus, that had underlain his fear for Liz and the bairn all those hours he sat waiting for news in the hospital, came through as an unstoppable certainty. He was convinced that Jack had killed himself.

§

They brought the last of the men up in the early hours of Sunday morning. All those lives surfacing, one after another. Hundreds more, gathered at the pithead like a crowd in some medieval painting of the Day of Judgment. Cheering and weeping, and prayers offered silently into the night. And the ones who had not come back, the seven left to haunt the bowels of the earth, remembered and mourned.

Journalists making notes in shorthand, queuing at phone boxes, heading back to Glasgow, Dundee, London. Through the wireless, a kindly, eager Oxbridge voice asking rescued miners about their experience. 'What did it look like, this stuff that was coming towards you?' *It was like porridge, thin porridge, a sort of brown colour, that's when we were at the top of the return airway outlet.* 'And was that where you were trying to get out?' *Aye, but we couldna, so we made doon the hill again tae the main hall, and there it was black, dirty sludge, twelve feet high, just slush, moss.* 'And later, while you were waiting to be rescued, how did you spend your time?' *Well, there were a few songs, and a hymn frae one of the young lads, and we all joined in on that, 'The Old Rugged Cross'. And tae keep the spirits up there was one or two dances.* 'Dances?' *Oh aye.* 'I bet you were glad, when you first saw the rescuers coming through to you?' *Oh, it was like seeing angels coming tae meet you then, when ye seen the lights of the brigade coming. We knew then there was a great hope.* 'And were any of your own people waiting for you at the pithead?' *Oh aye. In mining towns like this everybody's their own people, everybody's alike. We're all Jock Tamson's bairns.* 'Yes, I've heard that said often.' *It's true. There was one there, a brother of mine, he flung his arms round my neck, and I don't mind telling ye the big tear was in my eyes.*

The big tear was in his eyes. This was Scotland in 1950: coast to coast Jock Tamson's bairns stood or sat, lugs cocked to the wireless for news from home and abroad, from Borlanslogie, from Korea, or tuned in for *The McFlannels* on a Saturday night, or *It's All Yours* on a

Monday with young Jimmy Logan doing the daft laddie Sammy Dreep, spluttering, 'Sausages is the boys!' This was Scotland in 1950: land of 250 pits and 80,000 colliers, 100,000 farmworkers and four universities; land of Singer sewing machines in Clydebank, the Saxone Shoe Company in Kilmarnock, Cox Brothers jute mills in Dundee and the North British Locomotive Company in Springburn, every town and city and every part of every city with its own industries and hard-won skills; land of textiles and paper, hydraulic pumps and valves, carpets and linoleum and twenty-eight shipyards employing 60,000 workers on the Clyde. This was the land recovering from war, the land of nationalisation and council-house building, its old grease-thick, reeking, clanging heavy industries reinjected with life and a grim, tired kind of hope, the grinding last surge of steel and shipbuilding before Japan and Germany got up off their knees; this was the land that had change coming to it, like it or not, the closure of factories and the shedding of skills, the land of £10 emigrants dreaming of fresh starts and sunshine in Australia, of letters written to cousins in Toronto and Auckland and Durban giving dates of expected arrival, of new investment from NCR, Honeywell, IBM, Hoover, Goodyear. This was the land of Leyland Tiger buses from Thurso to Dalbeattie, and double-deckers crowding the city trams towards oblivion, of grandiose department stores and miserable slums, tearooms and single-ends, savage sectarianism and gloomy gentility, no-quarter football and stultifying Sundays. This was the land of few cars and no seat belts, no motorways but a railway station in every town of any size, and marshalling yards full of wagons laden with coal and iron and timber and grain, sleek black cattle and black-faced sheep, towns of 20,000 with three or four cinemas; the land of Tom Johnston's Hydro Board building new dams at Loch Sloy, Loch Tummel and Glen Affric; the land of old folk in Harris and Wester Ross and Sutherland with no electricity yet and barely a word of English; the land of tatties and herring, of oatcakes and shortbread, of anthrax on Gruinard and no hedgehogs in the Uists. This was the land of Shetland fishermen who despised the mackerel, of children in Skye who grew bored of too plentiful scallops, and crumbling, condemned, crushed-in Glasgow, desperate to disperse its people and breathe a new breath, raze the slums and raise new towns and peripheral estates; this was the land of blackhouses and prefabs and sandstone tenements, and baronial villas named Woodstock and Ivanhoe in streets named Abbotsford Crescent and Kenilworth Road; the land of railway posters showing golfers and anglers and Highland Games; the land of working men out of Glasgow climbing the Arrochar Alps and women from Aberdeen hiking the Cairngorms from the Linn of Dee, and thousands of thin, pale bodies cramming the beaches at Portobello and Saltcoats and Largs; the land of paddle steamers bound for Tighnabruaich and Rothesay and Millport, weighed to the gunnels with trippers in July; the land of no swings on the Sabbath, no Polaris submarines in Holy Loch, no nuclear reactors at Dounreay, no television, no cassette recorders, no photocopiers, no calculators, no PCs, no mobile phones, no microwave ovens, no supermarkets, no tights, no duvets, no drip-dry shirts, no tracksuits or trainers; the land of semmits and girdles and long, aching-cold Januaries and thirty-foot snowdrifts on Border farms that buried whole flocks, and wet days in March when the air hung with coal dust from Clackmannan to Galston and Kelty to Fallin; the land of TB, of rickets and kinkhoast, measles and buffets, the cartoon land of Desperate Dan and Black Bob, Korky the Cat and Keyhole Kate, Lord Snooty and Pansy Potter, Wuzzy Wiz, Plum McDuff and Biffo the Bear, the Broons and Oor Wullie, Ba-Bru and Sandy. This was Scotland in 1950, when Rangers won the League and the Scottish Cup, and East Fife won the League Cup, and Scotland beat England at rugby but were beaten at football, and the Edinburgh Festival was a three-year-old bairn just learning to talk in a foreign language. A land of rain like thin mist, *smirr*, rain that would not stop, that got into your bones and into your head, that clung to the fabric of Don's old battledress tunic as he stood, collar upturned, sick at heart, staring at the Gordons' house at seven o'clock, and then went through the gate and towards the door. His hand was raised to knock when the door opened and Sarah was there, in a dressing gown wrapped tight up to her neck.

'I saw you from the upstairs window,' she said. 'I knew you'd come. But it's all right. He's back. He's home.'

She opened the door enough for him to step inside the lobby, and whispered an explanation of what had happened. She'd got Barbara off to sleep but couldn't contemplate going to bed herself, and had made up her mind to contact the police first thing in the morning, when she heard the door open and Jack's footsteps. It was half past ten: she'd not long switched off the radio after the news. The light was on in the front room, where she was, but he did not come in. She heard him go upstairs. She called, ran to the stairs, called again. He didn't answer. She followed him upstairs, heard him undress and get into bed. She went into the bedroom. He had folded his clothes and put them away, put on pyjamas, and was lying on his back, arms at his sides, the top of the sheet neatly crossing his chest. She said his name. No response. In the light from the open door she saw his eyes were closed, his breathing deep and regular. He was fast asleep.

'He's not moved for eight hours,' she said. 'I didn't want to disturb him so I slept in Barbara's bed. Not that I've slept much. I've been up every hour to check on him. It's almost like he's in a coma. Do you think I should wake him?'

'I dinna ken,' Don said. 'Maybe ye should get Dr Logan.'

She shuddered. 'He won't have a doctor near him.'

'Weel, let him sleep then.'

'Thank you,' she said. She seemed to need permission for everything. 'Thank you for everything. It'll be all right now. Now that he's back.'

'Ye canna just leave it at that,' Don said. 'Ye'll need to find oot where he's been, what's been going on in his heid.'

'Yes,' she said. 'I'm sure there's an explanation. But he's home, that's the main thing. You'd better go, before he wakes up.' It was clear to Don that she was already preparing herself to ask no questions, that she would cope with this latest manifestation of Jack's strangeness, even though it would mean her own life always being on the edge of some unknowable disaster. She had her husband back, after a fashion, and there was, at least for the moment, some kind of relief in her voice and on her face.

Don thought, I'll have it out with him. It wasn't right for any of them, living like that.

She saw the thought in his face. 'Don't say anything to him. I'm really grateful to you for everything, but please don't say anything.'

'Somebody needs tae,' he said.

'It won't do any good,' she said. 'Please.'

A thin, desperate smile appeared on her lips. There was nothing he could do. Perhaps there never had been. He opened the door and stepped back out into the rain.

'Goodbye,' she said. 'And thank you again.'

Don turned back. He said, 'By the way, I'm a faither again. Liz had a boy.' But the door was closing in his face as he said it.

§

So it went, between the Gordons and the Lennies. They were not close, they were not warm, but something linked them, a shadow of the past lengthening over their future. Jack was back at the bus stop on the Monday. He congratulated Don on the birth of his new son – which meant that Sarah must have heard him speak – and Don half-stretched out his hand for it to be shaken and then stopped, remembering that Jack didn't do physical contact.

'What the blazes happened on Saturday, Jack?' he said. 'Ye had Sarah thinking the worst. Ye had me thinking it.'

Jack shrugged. 'I was tired,' he said. 'I had to escape, clear my head, that's all. No need to be concerned.'

'How could we no be?'

'A man requires space,' Jack said. 'Space to breathe, time to think. You know that.'

'You went *missing*,' Don protested.

'No, I absented myself. *I* knew where I was.'

'Naebody else did. What was on your mind? What were ye thinking?'

'Nothing.' His eyes brightened, an almost evangelical smile played on his lips. 'My mind was gloriously empty.'

Don shook his head and turned for the approaching bus. The man was deranged.

§

He never said to Liz about seeing Charlie on the night of his birth. If he had, he'd have had to mention the nurse. He couldn't mention the nurse, he'd have coloured up. He'd never been any good at dissembling. But wasn't that what he was doing?

What was he supposed to do, confess? Get Liz stirred up about nothing? Because that was what it was, nothing.

He looked for the nurse when he took Billy in the next day to see his new brother, but she didn't seem to be on duty. He thought about asking for her but didn't want to get her into trouble. On other visits, he found himself glancing around nervously every time a nurse approached. It was never Marjory Taylor. He wanted it to be her, was fearful that it might be. What would they say to each other? He hated the furtiveness with which he negotiated these visits. Liz sensed something. 'What's up wi ye?' 'Nothing. I'm just tired.' 'You're tired?' she said. He put it from his mind. It was nothing.

Liz and Charlie came home, and Charlie filled the house with the din of his hunger and general dissatisfaction with his new surroundings. Billy stared at the roaring, red-mouthed addition with curiosity and bewilderment. Don made a fuss of Billy, but the toddler could clearly see that the balance in the household had shifted, that he would never again have the undivided attention of his mother and father.

Ten days after the great rescue at Borlanslogie, news came in of a calamity in Korea. There wasn't much in the papers but what there was stirred evil, sickening memories in Don: *Mistaking the position of British troops, US planes yesterday swooped down on them with firebombs and machine guns. About 150 men all believed to be Argyll and Sutherland Highlanders were killed or wounded.*

The Argylls were almost the only British troops then in Korea. They were on a hill above the Naktong river and the enemy were on another hill near by: the Americans bombed the wrong hill. 'Firebombs', Don knew, meant napalm. He thought, I'd rather be killed outright than hit with that stuff.

He went to the Blackthorn the following Saturday. It might have been an assertion of independence except that Liz told him to go. Charlie's constant crying was getting him down. It was getting them all down, but Liz had an idea that the baby was disturbed by Don's presence. She sent him to the pub for a couple of hours: if she could get Charlie to settle, establish some kind of routine, maybe they'd all have a better night's sleep. 'Are ye sure?' Don said. 'Aye,' she said. 'On ye go.' There was a slight distance between them. It had been there since she got home. Nothing serious, nothing identifiable. He put it down to the stress of the birth, the added burden of a second bairn to look after. He thought of Marjory Taylor, the English nurse. He kept pushing her from his mind but she kept popping back in, brisk and bonnie and nothing to do with the life he was trying to lead.

He and Jack talked about the hill in Korea. Jack had that old, familiar air of superior knowledge: nothing surprised him about the Yanks, the way they went in like idiot cowboys, guns blazing. On this occasion, Don agreed with him. He remembered Italy: the longest half-hour of his life. There was only one thing worse than being under German fire and that was getting support from the Americans. At least you knew the Germans were deliberately trying to kill you. With the Yanks, you were never quite sure.

When he got home the house was quiet. Liz was in bed, dozing over a library book. She loved mysteries, devoured Agatha Christie and Rex Stout and John Dickson Carr. She woke up when he came in, enough to mouth at him, 'It worked,' and point to the peacefully sleeping Charlie in the crib. Don undressed and got into bed as quietly as he could. 'That's it then,' he said. 'I'll need tae go oot for a walk when he's girning. We canna afford for me tae go tae the pub every nicht.' She smiled at him, a warmer look than she'd given him for days. 'Are you all right?' she said. 'Aye,' he said. 'Why?' 'Ye look a bit pale,' she said. 'Clammy. Ye look wiped oot, Don.' She sat up. 'I'm fine,' he said. 'Had a bad pint, I think. Felt a bit sick coming up the road. I'm fine noo.'

A minute later Charlie began to whimper, prelude to a full-blooded howl, and Liz's attention was diverted. Don closed his eyes. He *was* exhausted. In seconds, in spite of Charlie, he was asleep.

So his Saturday nights at the Blackthorn were re-established, and nothing more was said about the cost. Business at Byres Brothers was increasing, and he was earning overtime some evenings and some Saturday afternoons. They were even saving a few shillings every week. They were both practical when it came to finances: neither of them resented the extra hours Don worked if it meant more money coming in; but there were days when he thought she wasn't that pleased to see him home on time, and days when he was surprised at how happy he was to be away from the house – from the demands of the boys, the chores Liz was always asking him to do, the order she imposed, of necessity, on all their lives. The workshops at Byres Brothers offered a kind of Vulcanic refuge from domesticity: the noise of motors being tested; the rattle and clang of tools striking metal or being dropped on concrete; the hot, oily atmosphere – it was all oddly soothing. So too were the passages between work and home, the waiting at bus stops and the bus journeys themselves. Sometimes he'd walk for a mile or two out of town before catching the next bus, for the pleasure of being alone and in silence. He remembered Jack's words – *I absented myself. My mind was gloriously empty* – and thought he could see what he'd been after.

§

Don said, 'Congratulations, Bulldog,' and lifted his pint glass in salute. Jack Gordon did the same, and Bill Drummond, looking as if he'd won on the pools, raised his own glass and took a long drink. His wife, Joan, had delivered him a daughter, precisely on time and with no complications, on Christmas morning, and now, five days later, he'd come down to the Blackthorn to celebrate. There had been no alarms, no mad dash to hospital in the Austin: the bairn had been born at home, hardly even needing the assistance of Dr Logan, and was as healthy as you could wish for. Bulldog had a grin on him he couldn't suppress. Pride shone from his eyes at what he and Joan between them had made. Wait till she starts screaming and won't stop, Don thought, that'll wipe the smile off your face.

Charlie was difficult, a bairn that didn't seem to know how to sleep for more than an hour at a stretch. The strain was showing in Liz, who had to deal with him day and night, as well as manage Billy, increasingly resentful of his wee brother although only rarely did he misbehave as a consequence. Sometimes when Don came in from his work it was obvious Liz had been crying. But she still reckoned Charlie was better when Don wasn't around. 'Does he no like me or something?' Don said. 'How can he no like me when he disna even ken me?' 'I dinna ken,' Liz said. 'But he's easiest when it's just him and me. It's a phase. He'll grow oot o it.' She seemed to like Charlie's cussedness more than Billy's acquiescence. So Don took Billy off her hands whenever he could, put him to bed and read to him, or trailed for hours with him up in the woods behind the village at weekends, and wondered how long Charlie's phase – or was it Liz's? – would last.

'Well, Jack,' Drummond said, 'I'm glad tae see ye've no done a vanishing trick.'

Don looked at him sharply. How did Bulldog know about that,

and what was he thinking of by mentioning it? It was months ago, and Jack had been behaving normally – whatever that meant in his case – ever since. He'd even become more sociable – as demonstrated by the fact that he was prepared to have a drink with Bulldog. But Jack's disappearance back in September wasn't what Bulldog was referring to.

'If ye hadna been here, ye'd have been my prime suspect. I'd have assumed ye'd gone intae hiding. Mind you, ye could be playing a cunning game, have it hidden in your garden shed or something.'

'What are ye on aboot?' Don asked.

'The Stone of Destiny, of course,' Bulldog said. 'I'm thinking Jack might have had a hand in stealing it.'

'It's not been stolen,' Jack said. 'It's been recovered from the thieves that took it in the first place.'

Bulldog thumped the table. 'Ye see,' he said. 'Ye sound just like a member of the gang, justifying your ill deeds. A sympathiser at the very least. No that I'm no sympathetic masel. Nothing better than giving the English a bloody nose.'

The newspapers were in a frenzy: it was the kind of story they loved – mystery and intrigue wrapped up in ancient tribal rivalries and with hints of sacrilege and disloyalty thrown in. *A coarse and vulgar crime*, declared *The Times*; *Is nothing sacred to these criminals?* raged the *Daily Mail*. The Scottish press seemed on the whole to think it was a great adventure – while the *Daily Worker* almost managed to be delighted: *The grim humourless English ruling classes cling more and more to their obsolete ceremonies and symbols because they are fearful the whole monstrous system is going to crash about their ears.* Police were hunting for a young man and woman with Scottish accents seen in the vicinity of Westminster Abbey in the small hours of Christmas morning.

'You're the one wi the car,' Don said. 'Where were you when Joan was in labour? Maybe ye nipped doon the road tae London, stuck it in the boot and stashed it in *your* gairden shed.'

'Aye, that'll be right,' Bulldog said. 'The polis are looking for a Ford Anglia, no an Austin 10. And who was my lovely accomplice, eh? Apparently a polis doon there caught them in a clinch in a wee lane at the back o the abbey. No, it'll be students. Only students would be daft enough. What dae ye reckon, Jack?'

'It doesn't matter,' Jack said. 'It's an irrelevance.'

Bulldog was astonished. 'How can you say that? You, a diehard Nationalist? This is the best thing that's happened for Scotland for decades. I just hope it turns up here and I get the scoop.'

'It's an irrelevance because it's not the real stone,' Jack said. 'Do you think Scottish kings sat on a building block to get crowned? The original Stone of Destiny was shaped like a chair. It was made of basalt or maybe marble, not sandstone. When Edward I was approaching Scone Abbey the monks dug a big slab of red sandstone out of a local quarry and left it in a prominent place, while the real stone was hidden away somewhere. Edward fell for the ploy like the arrogant bully he was, or maybe he knew he was being palmed off with a fake but couldn't afford to lose face. He had to take *a* stone of destiny home with him, so he had the sandstone slab carted off to London. But he also killed all the monks at Scone and the secret of where they'd hidden the original died with them.'

He spoke with such confidence that it was as if he'd witnessed it all himself. Don wondered where he got his information from. The whole escapade put Don neither up nor down. He couldn't be doing with all the medieval claptrap the affair was generating, but he was intrigued by the effect it was having on otherwise sober, sensible people around him. Men at Byres Brothers shouting 'SCOTLAND!' for no apparent reason in the middle of their work; auld Tam Byres, a terrible reactionary and dour pillar of the Drumkirk Unionist Association, chortling, rubbing his palms at the notion of four hundredweight of stone being wheeched out from under the noses of some toffee-nosed English bishop and a glaikit London bobby; even Liz brightening up at the news, saying she hoped whoever the brave wee lassie was she didn't get the jail.

'So what dae ye mean?' Don demanded of Jack. 'Are ye saying it's irrelevant because it's the wrang stane, or it's irrelevant because it disna make ony difference at all tae people's lives, whichever stane it is? Which is my position, in case ye didna realise.'

'Both,' Jack said. 'It's a distraction. Although,' he added, 'there's a certain satisfaction in seeing the authorities so upset about it.'

'Is that all ye've got tae say?' Bulldog said. 'A certain satisfaction? Man, it's the greatest drubbing the English have had since the Wembley Wizards beat them five-one.'

'Ye weren't even alive for that,' Don said.

'I was tae,' Bulldog said defiantly.

'How old were ye?'

'Two. All right, I dinna mind it exactly, but everybody's always going on aboot it. And everybody'll go on aboot *this* as well. It *does* make a difference. The day the Stone of Destiny was taken back frae the English. It'll go down in history.'

Jack began solemnly to intone:

> Forward! my heroes, bold and true!
> And break the archers' ranks through and through!
> And charge them boldly with your swords in hand,
> And chase these vultures from off our land.

'What's that?' Bulldog asked suspiciously.

'An old poem,' Jack said. 'Bruce's address to the troops at Bannockburn.'

'Burns?'

'Much older. Very ancient, in fact. Anonymous.'

'Great stuff,' Bulldog said. 'Ken any more?'

'No,' Jack said, 'that's it. Just that fragment.'

'Shame,' Bulldog said. He drained his glass. 'Same again, Don?'

'Aye, thanks,' Don said.

Jack was maintaining his independence, as usual. 'I'll get mine when I'm ready, Bill,' he said, and Bulldog winked at Don and went up to the bar.

'What on earth was *that*?' Don said.

'William Topaz McGonagall,' Jack said. 'Does it matter?'

'It could be Shakespeare for all Bill kens.'

'Precisely my point,' Jack said.

'I wonder how lang it'll be afore the thing turns up.'

'Do you care?' Jack said. He looked very hard at Don. 'It's all a distraction,' he said. 'It's all irrelevant.'

The odd thing was, in spite of himself Don did care. It was like the English nurse. He wasn't bothered *about* it. But he was bothered *by* it.

§

Liz was in a mood again, and Charlie, as usual, was fractious. It was a Sunday afternoon in March, cold but sunny. Don and Billy escaped up the hill to the woods, where they found clumps of snowdrops past their best and daffodils just ready to open out. As they went higher the ground hardened and a few thin patches of snow showed. Billy was intrigued by the streams of white breath he could send out into the air, so they practised that for a while, and stood watching the chaffinches flitting about and puffing their chests out in song. When they moved on a robin led them along the path, striking poses on tree stumps and rocks and chivvying them in his nippy way before flying off. Billy was full of questions, full of energy. He was so easy. Don wished they could just keep walking, for miles, for days. The more they walked, the more spring asserted itself, the further he felt from the weight of responsibility, the oppression of the house.

At the green bench they stopped and looked for their roof down in the village, and Don pointed out factory lums and kirk spires in distant Drumkirk, gleaming and clean-looking in the sunshine. 'D'ye want tae go on a wee bit?' he asked, and Billy did, so they followed the path deeper into the woods. It was chillier at first out of the sun, then warmer and brighter again as the trees thinned and the incline rose towards the great moor that stretched north to Glenallan. Don was amazed that his four-year-old son could go so far and at such a pace, and wondered when he would tire and if he would have to carry him all the way back, and didn't care if he did.

As they reached the last of the trees two figures appeared in front of them, a man and a boy. It was for a moment as if they had somehow come upon themselves, only the boy was older, twice Billy's age at least, and the man, taller and more gaunt than Don, was Jack Gordon.

'Hello again, Jack,' Don said as they approached. They'd met in the pub the previous evening, the usual routine. They'd talked a bit of politics, had some longish silences, walked up the road together. Now Don said, 'Fine day for it, eh?'

'Aye,' Jack said. He stared at Billy staring curiously back at him. 'This your boy?'

'Aye, this is Billy.' He remembered that Jack hadn't met Billy the day they'd called round. 'This is Mr Gordon, son. And this . . .'

'. . . is my sister's son, Jimmy,' Jack said.

Don held out his hand. 'I'm Don,' he said. 'Pleased tae meet ye.'

The boy, who had been standing slightly behind and apart from Jack, came forward to shake hands. He didn't say a word. There was a physical resemblance, Don thought, but the greater likeness to Jack lay in his watchfulness, his taciturnity. It was Jack in miniature.

'We just came oot tae stretch our legs a bit, did we no, son?' Don said. 'Gets us oot the hoose, oot frae under Liz's feet. How's Sarah and Barbara?'

'They're fine,' Jack said. 'My sister's family are visiting from Slaemill. Jimmy's family. So we came out for some fresh air too. Right, Jimmy?'

'Aye.'

'We've been having a talk,' Jack said. 'Getting to know each other.'

'Very good,' Don said.

'Discussing the state of the nation.'

'Och, that's a hot topic wi your uncle,' Don said to the boy. 'Dae ye feel the same aboot it as he does?'

The boy nodded. Barely a nod. Don felt that he was being assessed, analysed. The boy's gaze was intense yet also somehow offhand, as if he were simultaneously interested and bored.

'He says a lot,' Don said, attempting joviality.

'He says all he needs to say,' Jack said. 'Suits me fine.' A smile flickered. 'As you might expect.'

They stood there, the four of them, all waiting in their own ways for something to happen, or not to happen, until Don could bear it no longer. 'Weel,' he said, 'we're aboot tae head back hame again. Are ye coming?'

'Not just yet,' Jack said. 'We'll follow you down in a minute. We'll catch you up, perhaps.'

'Fair enough,' Don said. 'See ye later.' He nodded at the nephew, and he and Billy set off together back through the woods. At one point he turned round to see what the others were doing. They were standing watching them go, silhouetted among the trees. Don raised a hand to wave, but they didn't respond. He thought, what are they waiting for? Then Billy called on him, and he turned and broke into a trot towards where his son was standing, holding his arms out for a carry. He didn't look back again.

§

Where did ye go, Jack? For years afterwards, Don would silently ask that question. He'd wake in the middle of the night and the question would be there, even though he hadn't thought about Jack Gordon for weeks. Liz was sleeping beside him, real and dependable, but his mind was away chasing shadows. Or he'd be at his work, and a man coming round the front of the lorry he was working on would be Jack for a second, and then not Jack, just his ghost. He'd see a man enter a shop, and some need to be sure would make him follow, and it wasn't him of course, it was never him. That was what it was like: Jack haunted Don, not because he was dead – which he almost surely was – but because he might still be out there somewhere, alive.

There was no trigger, no rational explanation that Sarah or anybody else could think of – but why would there be for such a thing? A man disappears. There is only the fact that he went missing before. A precedent, but not a pattern. How do you make a pattern out of absence?

It was the Tuesday after the meeting in the woods. Jack hadn't been at the bus stop on the Monday morning, nor had he been on the bus home in the evening. When he didn't appear on the Tuesday morning Don began to feel anxious, but he refused to let his mind dwell on it. He wasn't going to get worked up for nothing, not again.

When he got home that evening Liz had his tea ready for him, a shepherd's pie heavily biased in favour of the potatoes. While he ate she stood over by the sink with her arms folded, watching him. 'Are ye no eating?' he asked. 'I'm no hungry,' she said, in a brittle tone. He knew something was coming.

'Sarah Gordon was here this morning.'

'Oh aye?'

'Her man's missing.'

He held the forkful that was on its way to his mouth in mid-air.

'Jack's missing?'

'That's what I said. Since yesterday. He never came hame frae his work. It turns oot he never went *tae* his work. She didna ken what tae dae. I tellt her tae call the polis.'

'Aye, weel,' he said cautiously, 'that's probably the best thing.'

'She was getting hersel in a right state, though she didna want tae break doon in front of me. And she had the wee lassie wi her tae. I'll need tae go up there, see how she is.' A pause. 'Or maybe you should go.'

There was a sting in the way she said it. He put his fork down and looked at her.

'Ye've got the experience, Don, efter all.'

'What dae ye mean?'

'Well, it's no the first time, is it? Sarah was telling me aboot how ye helped her afore. Asked in the pub. Searched in the woods. Like Sir bloody Galahad ye were, apparently.' She was eyeing him steadily. With *suspicion*, for God's sake.

'What are ye looking at me like that for?'

'Are ye denying it?'

'Denying what?'

'That ye were roond at her hoose.'

'Aye. No, I'm no denying it. There's nothing tae deny. I was trying tae help her.'

'Withoot saying a word tae me? What am I supposed tae make o that?'

'I tellt ye, Liz. She met me aff the bus. I tellt ye that. Ye were aboot tae gie birth tae Charlie. It was that same weekend. I went roond tae help her while ye were haein a nap and when I came back ye were away intae the hospital.'

'Ye never said that. Ye said ye were taking Billy for a walk.'

'I was, but –'

'And ye never said a word aboot it efter. Never a word in seven months.'

'It went oot my heid.'

'Aye, and mine buttons up the back. Why would ye keep it a secret? Were ye up tae something wi her?'

'No, for God's sake! It wasna a secret. I forgot, then later it didna seem worth fashin ye wi.'

'So what were ye daein?'

'I was trying tae find oot what had happened tae Jack. But I didna find oot, and then he came hame the next day.'

'Aye, weel, he's away again noo. Maybe he'll no be back this time. Maybe that would be better for everybody. That's what I think onywey.'

'Oh, Liz!' he said, appalled.

'I dae. I said it afore, I feel sorry for her being saddled wi him. Did *you* feel sorry for her?' That nippy note again, making him feel guilty about nothing. But if it was nothing why did he feel guilty?

'No the way you're implying. I was trying tae help, that's all. I've never looked at another woman, Liz, and ye ken that's the truth.'

'Ye'd better bloody no,' Liz said.

He held her stare, fighting back images of the English nurse that night in the hospital. They had come to a crisis but neither of them wanted to face the real root of it: the fact that since Charlie's birth they'd had little to say to each other that wasn't about the mundane details of daily life; that one child had been a blessing, two felt more like a penance; that they lived like drones, sacrificing their own aspirations in order to feed and nurture the boys. But what were their aspirations? It was easier – had less awful implications perhaps – for Liz to imagine that Don might have strayed, and for Don angrily to deny that possibility, than to answer that question.

Then it passed. Neither of them apologised. Liz said, 'You make up a bottle for Charlie, and get Billy tae his bed. I'll go roond and see her.' And Don said, 'Aye, all right.' 'Leave the dishes, I'll dae them later,' she said, but as soon as she was out of the door he did them anyway, then went to see Billy, who'd been playing quietly in the front room all this time. Charlie was asleep in his crib, but on cue woke up and began to cry, so he had to deal with him first. 'Ye've the patience o a saint,' Don said to Billy, who answered with one of his wee, slightly uncertain, totally disarming smiles. 'No like your brother, eh?'

By the time Liz came back he'd fed Charlie and quietened him, and Billy was asleep. The police had been and gone, Liz said. They'd asked questions, made notes, and taken away a wedding photo as Sarah didn't have anything of Jack more recent. By then he'd been gone maybe forty hours. 'He's got a head start,' she said, as if he was a fugitive from justice, a character out of one of her mysteries. Liz had quizzed Sarah much as Don had on the previous occasion. Had Jack said anything, done anything, that might offer a clue as to why or where he'd gone? He hadn't. Had he taken money from the house? Not that she could see. Sarah found the bank book and there were no recent withdrawals. But then Jack was secretive, she said, he could have had money hidden away somewhere. It looked like he'd taken a change of clothes, his good boots, a heavy coat, a haversack.

'He'll no go far withoot money,' Liz said. 'I said tae her, he'll be back soon enough when he runs oot o money.'

Don didn't think so. It sounded planned to him. He reckoned

Jack could survive on almost nothing – he'd had plenty of experience. He'd be back only if he wanted to be. But what *did* he want? Was he trying to get away from Sarah and Barbara in their spotless house with its barren vegetable plot and immaculate flower beds, or was it more that he was trying to reach something? But what? Don thought of the sheet of paper covered in MacLarens. Maybe he was still trying to succeed where MacLaren had failed, still trying to get back to some distant, dreamed-of Scotland.

Two more days passed. Liz walked up to Sarah's in the afternoons with the boys, sat with her for a while, came away with no news. She seemed to have got over the notion that there was or had been anything between Don and Sarah, or at least she never raised it again. The weekend came and Don went to the Blackthorn at eight o'clock, just in case. Jack failed to show. Bill Drummond was there. Because the police were involved, everybody knew. Most people thought Jack was cracked. They didn't hold out much hope for him. The Japs had a lot to answer for.

Don spent an hour with Bill, then headed off. He thought about calling in on Sarah but decided it wasn't worth risking Liz's wrath. He walked round the village, wondering what the English nurse was doing, if she were on a shift or out on the town, smoking and drinking. Somehow he felt justified thinking about her because Liz had been so wrong about him and Sarah. Then he went home, made himself a cup of tea, checked on the boys, took *The House with the Blue Door* by Hulbert Footner from Liz's sleeping fingers and creaked in beside her.

After a week they feared he was dead. After two they wanted his body to be found, at least. After three they thought it unlikely it would be. He'd gone to the coast and drowned himself and his body was at the bottom of the sea; or maybe he'd not actually killed himself but had killed the person he'd been and was starting afresh, in England or Ireland or wherever, a man trying to leave Jack Gordon behind for ever. Could he have got right away, to Canada, say, or Australia? There was no trace of him, no sign, no sighting. The police said this wasn't that unusual. Even in normal times, they said, you'd be amazed how many people just vanish. But these weren't yet quite normal times: the war was still only six years over, there were people on the move all over the British Isles, all over Europe, leaving their old losses and injuries behind. Don understood this. When you saw newsreel of London or Coventry or Berlin at the pictures, what you were watching was destruction already being built over. When you saw films like *Hue and Cry* and *Passport to Pimlico* the high jinks of Alastair Sim and the like might make you laugh but also you saw a ruined landscape through which people were moving in an endless stream. Why would Jack not be part of that? Why not, unless he was dead?

It was still early April when the Stone of Destiny was deposited among the ruins of Arbroath Abbey, then bundled back south under a police escort. For a day or so Don thought it possible that there was some connection, that with the stone's reappearance Jack might also emerge from wherever he'd been hiding. But he didn't, and Don heard Jack's clipped tones dismissing the idea. *Come on, Don, what are you thinking of?* The stone was a sideshow after all, a distraction, and in any case the one taken back to London was a fake, the genuine article was lying in a peatbog or some forgotten vault in a castle or wherever it was supposed to have ended up. Like that original stone he believed in, Jack was gone for good.

Three months, six months, a year passed. Sarah waited. There were financial difficulties. Jack's employers were sympathetic, but they couldn't go on paying for him not being at his work. There were some savings in the bank: Sarah lived on them for a while. As soon as Barbara was old enough for school Sarah got a job in the post office as a counter clerk. Most days Liz collected Barbara from school along with Billy, and Sarah picked her up on her way home. Barbara was clever, industrious, isolated. She and Billy developed a kind of silent mutual affection and tolerance that the adults – and Charlie – were excluded from. Sarah was grateful that her friendless daughter had at least one friend. Liz and Don were less sure it was good for Billy, but what could they do?

Usually by the time Don came home the Gordons would be away, but sometimes Liz, in spite of her determination not to get closer than she had to, would have them stay for their tea. Over the years she became not exactly Sarah's best friend, but her most reliable support. Yet when Liz spoke about her to Don when they were on their own, it was to wonder why she didn't pack up and go back to Dorset where she belonged.

'Maybe she feels she belongs here,' Don said. 'And what if Jack turns up and she's away doon sooth?'

'Jack's never coming back,' Liz said. And though Don knew she was probably right, he himself kept a small hope burning. Even if Sarah goes, he thought, I'll be here if he ever comes home.

He still went to the Blackthorn once a week. It was like keeping a pledge. Eight o' clock every Saturday. A couple of pints, standing at the bar, talking to whoever was there, or not talking. And most Sunday mornings he took Billy for a walk up in the woods. When Charlie was big enough he took him too. A long lie for Liz and time with the boys for him. It wasn't that Liz and he didn't get on, it was that they knew each other too well, had nothing much left to say. It was what happened.

For a while Liz took the boys to church and the walks were shunted to the afternoons. He decided not to make an issue of it and it didn't last. He was glad. He didn't believe in God and didn't want his boys indoctrinated. The church he took them to was the big outdoor one, the cathedral full of trees and flowers, bees and creepie-crawlies, cows and sheep and birds. He tried to teach his sons the names of things, as many as he knew. Billy absorbed, Charlie got bored. Don didn't like to admit it, and tried not to show it, but he had a favourite son: he enjoyed these walks most when it was just himself and Billy. At such times he felt a reason for being a father, a reason for Billy being his son.

Sometimes he'd catch himself searching the trees ahead, as if Jack and his nephew might suddenly be there, as if they'd never been away. Sometimes he thought he glimpsed them.

Time quickened. It wasn't just the speed at which the boys grew, it was the way he felt himself being left behind by change in general. The 1945 General Election had seemed to be the dawn of a bright new day, but it wasn't turning out as he'd hoped. Labour, exhausted, had been put out in October 1951 and Churchill had come back, seventy-six, imperious, ill, but a hero to millions. Liz had voted for him. They'd had a row over that, and from then on hardly discussed politics again. Don missed that as much as anything from his Saturday nights – how Jack had always had an opinion about what was going on in the world. A couple of the men at Byres Brothers were up for political talk, but it wasn't the same.

There was a lot of ignorance about, especially when it came to anything abroad, a place full of dirty wogs, ungrateful niggers and treacherous Russians. He read about the Mau Mau revolt in Kenya and the way it was being repressed and longed to discuss it with Jack. The name of a Scottish colonial police officer, Ian Croick, came up often: described as a no-nonsense chap who knew how to deal with the natives, he sounded cold, hard and brutal to Don. He listened to reports from Malaya praising the way the British were combating the Communists there, and wondered what the real stories were there too. Jack would have had a view.

Then Churchill retired and suave, handsome Sir Anthony Eden took over. Women couldn't see past his looks, his sophisticated manner. Don thought he was incompetent, but that didn't stop the Tories winning another election in 1955. The Labour Party didn't seem to know what it stood for any more. Don voted for Attlee even though he was due to retire. Liz voted for Eden's moustache. The Tories won more than half the Scottish vote. The SNP contested just two seats and lost their deposit in one of them. So much, Don thought, for Jack's age of small nations.

Could a man really just vanish? Don thought of Jack stepping out in sunshine along a country road, a car slowing to offer a lift, Jack waving it on. He wouldn't take assistance but the driver would remember him, surely, give the police something to go on? He thought of him trudging through rain. He'd need to take shelter, dry off. There were byres and barns and, with all the reduction in farm labour, plenty of disused cottages scattered about. Maybe he'd earn his breakfast or a bob or two doing a bit of gardening work at a big house somewhere, for an old dame that couldn't get the staff any more. Make himself a nest in one of the outhouses. No names, no pack drill. It mightn't be a bad way to live over the summer months, but then would come winter. And someone would be bound to say something to somebody. Word would filter back. He must be dead. It was the only explanation.

Where did ye go, Jack? Every time some big thing happened, Don would wonder if Jack knew about it, what his opinion might be. When Nasser nationalised the Suez Canal, he thought of Jack: everybody from Churchill to Wullie Byres, even senior figures in the Labour Party, was badmouthing the Egyptian leader, calling him the new Hitler, but what would Jack think? Then Eden resigned, grey and shattered, the shine off his shoes, and Don wanted to know what Jack thought of Macmillan, of Gaitskell, of Alec Douglas-Home. What about the Bay of Pigs, the Cuban-missile crisis? Did he think Kennedy clever or scheming, lucky or foolhardy? Was Khrushchev a shoe-banging boor or a match for the American upstart? A year later, Kennedy was shot in Dallas. Everybody was supposed to remember where they were when it happened. Don was on the bus coming home from his work, a Friday afternoon: when he got in and switched on the news on the newly rented television, there it was, but where was Jack? When the Buddhist priest set himself on fire in South Vietnam, did Jack see it? When Profumo resigned, when Harold Wilson won the election in 1964, and again in 1966, when England won the World Cup, when Celtic won the European Cup the following year and Winnie Ewing won the Hamilton by-election, was Jack alive to care?

Sarah and Barbara were long gone by then. Through the years Sarah had struggled to keep up the payments on the house, gradually diminishing the savings in the bank. She had some help from social security, but there was the awkward issue of Jack's status. Unless his body or some other convincing evidence could be produced, the law presumed he was alive. But as far as his estate was concerned, and Sarah's marital status, after seven years the law said she could act as if he were dead. He was neither one thing nor the other. When the seven years elapsed Sarah got the court ruling she needed. She had to do it, she explained: otherwise nothing else could happen.

'Have ye gien up hope for him, then?' Liz asked.

'Yes, I have,' she said. 'But' – and a gleam of defiance came into her eyes, lighting up her pallid face – 'I've not given up hope for Barbara. I don't care about myself but Barbara deserves a fresh start. That's why we're leaving.'

She'd been offered a full-time job in another post office. It was forty miles away in Fife, in a place that was hardly on the map as yet: Glenrothes, one of the new towns going up in different parts of the country, so modern and important they were given capital letters, New Towns. The mortgage was too hard for her, she would sell the house and use the money to pay off her debts and start again. They would get a brand-new corporation house, be part of a new community. Barbara was eleven, she'd finish up at the village school and then transfer to a secondary school that was barely a year old. Folk were moving to Glenrothes from all over. There were paper mills there already, but what was really drawing them in was coal. Miners from old, tired coalfields in Lanarkshire and the Lothians were coming with their families, lured by the promise of a lifetime's work in the best of conditions. The Rothes Colliery was going to be a Super Pit. It would need five thousand miners to work it, extracting five thousand tons of coal a day. The coal would go all over the country from great railway yards. There was enough to last a hundred years. The future of Glenrothes would be built on this vast black treasure vault, and the whole economy of Fife would be powered by it. The New Town would be a shining place of clean concrete, broad roads and precincts of neat, comfortable houses in rows and circles and crescents. There would be green parks and gardens, a covered shopping centre. There would be people walking dogs, cycling to work, going to the shops by bus and car. It would be safe. It would feel young. It would be a better place for Barbara to be.

'It's a big decision,' Liz said, 'but ye're right. It's an opportunity for ye baith. I would dae it if it was me.'

'Would you?' Sarah said.

'Definitely,' Liz said, as if the one thing she was determined on was to see Sarah and Barbara on to the bus to Glenrothes. 'Ye'll no regret it.'

'The only thing is,' Sarah said, 'she'll miss your Billy.'

'No, she'll no,' Liz said. 'Maybe for a few days, but once she starts at her new school, she'll be fine. She'll no be the only new face, they'll aw be looking for friends. And Billy'll be fine tae.' She could hardly keep the enthusiasm out of her voice, and Don had to come in at the back of her and say, 'Onywey, it's no like ye're emigrating. Ye can aye come back and see us.'

'She'll no hae the time,' Liz said. 'A fresh start, Sarah, that's what ye said. Ye canna aye be looking ower yer shooder.'

Every time Don threw Sarah a rope, Liz hauled it back. She wanted the Gordons out of their life and maybe she was right. They'd only been connected by two unlikely friendships – the one between Barbara and Billy and the one between Don and Jack. No doubt the children would grow out of theirs, and Don's, well, it was with a man who didn't any longer exist. They would all move on. They would have to. The world wouldn't wait for them if they didn't.

§

There was that one September night, walking back from the Blackthorn, when Jack came into his own. Whenever Don considered it in later years, he understood why he'd tolerated him, why he'd liked him in spite of everything, why he continued to remember him: because of that night. Everybody has a still, sheer place in them where light doesn't penetrate. It had always seemed to be Jack who struggled with bad memories, but on this particular night, it was Don who found himself looking over the edge of the cliff.

It was the earlier talk about the hill in Korea that did it. That and the extra pint maybe. Halfway home, Don's bladder suddenly couldn't wait another five minutes. There were houses on one side of the road and a park on the other. 'Just a minute, Jack,' he said, and hurried across the tarmac and into the shadow of some trees. It was a calm, cloudless night. As he stood relieving himself he closed his eyes, breathing deep, and in a moment was in northern Italy. The same season of the year; the same cool smell coming off the hills.

There was a river, the Germans dug in on the far side. A couple of British infantry divisions supported by tanks were waiting to cross, but they couldn't move till the German defences had been softened up. Don was further back in a column of lorries loaded with ammunition, stuck on the main approach road from the south. It wasn't a comfortable place to be, out in the open with two tons of explosives at your back. He was sitting in the passenger seat, scanning the sky for planes. The driver was a guy from Glasgow, Brian Kelly. The engine throbbed then died as Kelly switched off. All down the line you heard the same noise.

'What's the fucking problem this time?' Kelly said.

Don said, 'Dinna ken, but as long as we're here I'm away tae stretch my legs.'

He opened the door and dropped to the road, into the path of a young lieutenant marching up the line of vehicles. No more than a boy really. Don had maybe three or four years on him, but he didn't think of himself as a boy any more.

'You there,' the boy said. 'Want to make yourself useful? Come with me.'

Don thought about objecting. *Never volunteer for anything* was the golden rule, but he was bored so he followed the purposeful stride of the lieutenant. Half a dozen lorries further on, they stopped.

'There's a bicycle in the back of that,' the boy said. 'Fetch it down, would you?'

Don hauled himself up over the tailboard and made his second mistake in two minutes. 'Which one dae ye want, sir?' he said. 'There's two in here.'

'Jolly good. Can you ride a bicycle?'

'Yes, sir.' Thinking, as the words came out, that he shouldn't have let them.

'Jolly good. Throw them both out.'

Don lifted the bikes in turn and lowered them as far as he could, then dropped them on their tyres.

'What's your name, private?'

'Lennie, sir.'

'Right, Private Lennie, follow me.'

Even then he might have said something about staying with his unit, but he didn't. He got on the second bike. Maybe that was all the reason he needed: the prospect of a bicycle ride. The lieutenant began to weave his way through the jam, and Don followed.

'Let's find out what's causing the hold-up!' the boy shouted over his shoulder.

Don could have told him and saved them both the effort: Field-Marshal Kesselring and the 10th Army. The Germans were falling back to the mountains, their last line of defence before the Lombardy plain and Austria, but they kept stopping and putting up another fight. Pointless really. Everybody knew they were going to lose the war now. It was just a question of when, and how bloodily.

Somebody had at least had the sense to stop the bulk of the column before it was in view of the German positions, but as Don and the lieutenant came over a slight rise in the road they could see that four lorries had driven down towards the river. A belt of trees and scrub screened the British positions a little. The wreckage of a bridge lay in the water. Guns were going off on both sides, and there was occasional light-arms fire. Don could see tanks and field guns manoeuvring into protected positions. There were troops on the ground too, keeping their heads down. He didn't blame them.

'Right, come on then,' the boy lieutenant said, and he was off, freewheeling down the hill towards the group of lorries. What the hell are you going down there for, Don thought, we don't need to go down there yet; but he pushed off after him anyway.

It was surprisingly quiet by the river. It felt safer than being stuck on the open road. The lorries were parked in a kind of paddock, protected on three sides by trees. The lieutenant flung his bicycle on the grass and marched over to another officer. They began to talk earnestly with one another. None of my business, Don thought as he dismounted, and at that moment he heard his name being called from beside the lorries.

He recognised several of the men, good lads, a Cockney, a couple of Geordies, a Cornishman called Paddy Harris. He knew all their faces. They had a brew of tea on, and offered him a mug. 'We thought we'd take the chance while we could,' Paddy said.

'What are you carrying?' Don asked, hoping it wasn't ammunition.

'Compo rations,' Paddy said. 'Sorry, no cucumber sandwiches.'

'Compo rations? Up here?'

'We got ahead of ourselves. Some stupid cunt waved us on and then we couldn't stop or we'd have blocked the road completely. So here we are. Who's that you're with?'

'Dinna ken,' Don said. 'Just a young lad wanting tae be in the thick of it.'

'Well, what the fuck are *you* doing with him then?'

'Good question,' Don said. It felt like a dream. What *was* he doing there? He should have been back with Kelly and the rest of his unit.

The lieutenant came over. 'Any more tea?' he asked. And while somebody found him a mug he said, 'Soon be moving. They've called up air support to knock the Krauts up a bit. Going to put up some smoke so the Americans know the target. Ah, there it goes.'

The twenty-five pounders further down the river fired off a salvo of smoke shells. Through gaps in the trees they could see a line of thick red smoke spreading along the opposite bank, marking the German positions.

The tea went straight through Don. He handed back the mug and headed off across the paddock, forty yards or so, and stood facing the trees while he pissed. A breeze was coming off the river. He sniffed. Traces of red smoke drifted above him. He thought, that's a bit close. As he was buttoning up he heard the planes coming over the hill.

The next thing he knew he was flat on his face, drowning in noise, being shaken like a bottle of sauce. The world seemed to be collapsing in on itself, splitting into chunks. Branches cracked and fell around him. The ground fountained up in the air and showered down again, mud rain. His mouth was pressed into mud and he was shouting, no words, just a repeated, formless roar. He wanted to get up and run somewhere – into the woods, into the river, back up the road. He fought down the urge. Stay where you are, stay flat. There were flashes and bangs going off all around him, shrapnel whizzing through the air, he could feel some of it whipping past his head. He flattened himself further. The stuff was missing him by inches. They were hitting the wrong side of the river, the stupid bastards, how could they possibly have thought the Germans were on the south bank? Another wave of explosions rolled through the air just above him. It was anti-personnel bombs they were dropping, with spikes that hit the ground first and detonated the bombs at chest height. Stay down, stay down. He thought he heard screams amid the incessant roar but couldn't be sure if anybody other than himself was screaming. Something crashed beside him, a yard or two away, he didn't dare look to see what it was. His eyes were screwed tight, his mouth full of earth and smoke. He was struggling to inhale, couldn't go on much longer without a proper breath. Then suddenly, like a demented fairground ride crashing, the madness juddered to a halt.

He opened his eyes. A bicycle, a twisted mess of metal minus one wheel, lay next to him. He tried to work out if it was his or the lieutenant's. Didn't matter. Nobody would be riding it again.

He was standing in the trees at Wharryburn, finishing off his pee. He swayed with faintness. He was out in a sweat. 'Jesus fucking Christ,' he said, putting himself away. He never swore like that. Over on the road, he heard Jack say, 'You all right?'

'Aye,' he said, and started coughing violently. 'Jesus,' he said again, and cleared his throat and spat into the bushes. He stayed in the darkness a moment longer, to wipe his eyes, then staggered back to Jack standing in the moonlight.

'I just had a kind o dream,' he said. 'A memory. Something frae the war. Just oot o naewhere.'

'Aye,' Jack said evenly.

'Shook me up a bit,' Don said, and told Jack about it.

How he got to his feet, tottering as he found his balance. The green paddock was gone. So – completely – were two of the lorries. The other two lay smouldering and smashed, like dead fairground horses. Much further away he could hear men cursing, shouts for help. There were tins and bits of wooden crate and food everywhere. Pudding, concentrated soup, chopped meat. He thought, where are the others? But then he saw that some of the debris was pieces of the men he'd been talking to a few minutes earlier. The lieutenant's cap. Somebody's foot and leg, still booted and trousered. Somebody's hand. Blood everywhere. If you shovelled it all up you'd have approximately twenty men. The other bike. When he saw a blackened football rolled up against a lorry wheel and realised it was Paddy's head he was sick.

Jack stood patiently in the road while Don let it all out. He didn't try to interfere. The best he could do was what he did: stand and wait. Don was a mess. He found his handkerchief, blew his nose and wiped his eyes again. He said, 'There were other times, but that was the worst. And the fact that it was the Yanks . . .'

'It doesn't help,' Jack said.

'I dinna ken tae this day how I came oot o that,' Don said. 'I was the only one, ye ken. Everybody else was deid, and I didna hae a scratch on me. How was that? How did I survive?'

'I don't know,' Jack said, with such gravity and force that nothing else could be said by either of them. *I don't know*. It went through Don like a knife. And then, for the only time in their friendship – you could call it that – Jack reached out and touched Don; rested a hand on his shoulder for a moment, then slipped it under his arm.

'Come on,' he said. 'I'll see you home.'

Just once you came back, you didn't plan it but one day you were close, and drawn closer by the familiarity of landmarks, road signs. You came to the town. You walked past an entrance to a place you recognised. Nobody was around to recognise you. You'd hardly have recognised yourself. You thought of your wife and daughter, and something tugged, you half-remembered what that life had been like. It was gone, over, but for a moment you wondered if some ruins of it might still exist that could be repaired or built on. But while you were still a few miles away from the village something else happened, a coldness came over you that you read as a warning, an urgent message to escape while you could. The impossibility of normality. Because you'd pulled yourself back once before and it had been a mistake. So you cut out of the town, head down, avoiding glances, the curiosity or pity or fear or distaste in some eyes. You were a tramp to them, that was what they saw and what you let them see, and you tramped east, through the mill towns, onwards to coal country. You escaped as you had before. And things fell into place again.

You'd escaped because.

Poor towns and villages gave you more than other, wealthier, places. The people in them saw how near their lives scraped to yours, how a piece of bread and cheese or a few pennies or a kind word might keep your life away from them. That was the difference: you wanted it, they didn't. You were walking along a street of miners' cottages and a lassie who might have been the same age as your own stood watching you go by, and you stared hard to see who was inside her, to see who she might become, and you didn't see it, but then you were blind to the pattern, if there was one, so you stopped and made an offering to her from the pocket of stones, and she was afraid, so you placed it on the road for her and went on, and when you looked back from the end of the street she was gone, and so were you.

You'd escaped because.

You hadn't planned to leave. Or you didn't remember planning it, but at some deep level you must have, because when it happened, when you found yourself away, you found yourself equipped for not coming back. The haversack, the spare socks, underwear, shirt, the knife, the boots in which you'd worked the garden till they felt like your feet, boots you could walk a continent in, or a country of many twists and turns. The heel of a loaf was all the food you took, you kept it in your pocket as an insurance, you wouldn't eat it till you had some other food for later. Never be without something, however small, for later. And it need be only enough to keep hunger at bay, enough to give you strength to go till the next meal. And then there was the money. You must have been laying money aside, squirrelling it away in hidden places, the garden shed, behind the fuse box, in the loft. You must have done this because you knew the places, you saw your hands moving dusty jars and tins, pulling a note from here, from there, and yet you couldn't remember putting the money away, only retrieving it. The money was for eking out, for learning how to do without money, because it wouldn't last for ever. No money would ever last for ever.

You'd escaped because everybody else was hell-bent on wanting every-thing and you saw it wasn't going to work. Didn't matter what your pol-itics were after all. Irrelevant. Didn't matter whether you were free or independent or democratic or oppressed, everybody wanted everything and they couldn't have it. It wasn't the age of small nations as you'd thought, it was the age of money and waste and garbage and pollution and destruc-tion and it was all going to get worse, you could see it coming and you couldn't do it, you couldn't keep your place in such a world, couldn't sup-port a wife in such a world, couldn't bring up a child in such a world. It was time to go. It was time to abandon.

When you left there was some kind of journey in your head, though you didn't know the shape of it. You didn't go on the bus, you weren't risking being seen and brought back, you weren't trusting anybody else. You were going on a journey and if nobody knew you were going or where, if you didn't know yourself, then nobody could betray you, and after that it would be between you and the land. And so you went up the hill, through the woods, on to the moors. North. That much you did know. You were going north. In time you would go in every other direction too as you followed coastlines and paths and tracks and sometimes as you followed no discern-ible route at all, east and west and south you'd go, but always, sooner or later, north again. North, always north.

PART THREE

The Original Mr Bond

All these fucking conversations in your head. Single-sided, a lot of them. One-versations. Nobody talking back, or you to yourself. Years, decades of dialogue, monologue. Thousands, tens of thousands of words. Millions. And who gives a fuck? You don't yourself but that doesn't stop the words battering round the inner wall of your skull.

Aye you do.

It would be good to have someone to talk to.

Croick, maybe. Even Canterbury. Somebody who actually understands where you're coming from. But Croick's dead and Canterbury's God knows where. In some care home for the politically deranged maybe. Or a cottage in rural Britannia pruning his roses. Never knew exactly how old either of them were, but Canterbury must be close to ninety if he's not beyond it. If he isn't dead too.

Ach he'll be dead, surely?

Lots of other people are definitely still alive but you can't speak to lots of other people. You're a ghost. You made yourself a ghost some time ago. You're on the other side of an invisible something. People see you but they don't speak to you, and you can't speak to them.

Maybe they don't even see you.

Aye they do. The guy in the café saw you. You read the signs. The glance. The frown. The second glance. The guy didn't place you, not then, but he will have by now. The memory will have come back. Or not. It doesn't for everybody.

It does for you, Peter Bond. The memory always comes back. You've that kind of brain. Full of filing cabinets. That's what the inside of your head's like. A dome like the old British Library's and round the walls shelves and shelves of reference books, and corridors leading off lined with stacks, the stacks laden with cardboard folders, box files, arch files, and rooms off the corridors crammed with grey steel cabinets. Every document catalogued and retrievable. You can retrieve anything. Could. Not so good now. You're like a computer but you don't imagine your head as a computer because you're from a pre-computer age; you can visualise card indexes not gigabytes – how the fuck do you visualise a gigabyte? – you were born in an age of small libraries in small towns and bigger libraries in bigger towns and huge libraries in cities and that's what you are, a walking library, that's how you grew up, how you were trained, how you were and are and will be till the doors close and the lights go out for the last time.

Which, the way you're feeling, might not be that far off.

All the more reason why it would be good to have someone to talk to.

And maybe that's what Croick thought, away back then. That time he summoned you. Maybe that was all he wanted. He'd run out of time, and he wanted to talk, and you were the only one even vaguely approaching the idea of a friend he had left.

That was in the days when you still had a telephone. Well, you still have a telephone but it's been dead for years. Another reason for the one-versations. No bastard ever calls you because your phone's been cut off by the bastard phone company.

But Croick called you. Because you were the only one he had left. He called you because he wanted to get it all off his chest, out of his system, before the lights went out.

Wait a minute. Who's putting the lights out? Who's closing the doors? And who's this coming at you? Wait a fucking minute. Some kind of uniform. A security guard. What the fuck is a security guard doing in your head? In *your* head? And why doesn't he have a face? STAY BACK, YA CUNT!

All right, all right, calm down. Deep breaths. Nobody there after all. Just yourself. Empty room, empty corridors. Everything as it should be. Apart from one thing. One particular door at the end of one particular corridor. Security-locked. Sign on it saying NO ENTRY, AUTHORISED PERSONNEL ONLY. Stuff in there you should have access to but never did, too late now. In your own fucking head. Somebody put the bodies in and sealed the door and now you're like Bluebeard's wife, you want the key but you don't, you want to know but you don't, you can't face it, you can't face it, you can't face it.

Get a grip, Peter. Behave yourself. Aye, right. Just sit in the corner like a good auld boy and read the papers. That's it, that's it. Deep breaths. Now. Let's try again.

He placed the guy in the café at once. Pendreich, Michael. Photographer. Did some of the covers for *Root & Branch*. Devoporn. Twenty-five issues, 1984 to 1989 or thereabouts. Provided a lot of the photographs. Did some of the cartoons too. All donated freely to the cause. Peter recognised him instantly.

What else does he know about him? Father: Angus, also a photographer, a better one, more successful anyway. Much more. Died two or three years ago, a few more-or-less respectful obits. Aye, Peter still reads the papers and he still reads between the lines. So. Michael Pendreich: soft-left, soft-nationalist, presumably still is but who knows, we're not what we were. *Self-determination*: that was the catch-all term folk like Pendreich used, trying to be as inclusive as they could. Let the people decide how far they want to travel: a worthy and reasonable enough sentiment, if you think the people give a damn. Peter first clocked him years before as a student, in Sandy Bell's, then hanging out at Jean Barbour's place. Then later, in his journalist phase, he saw Pendreich from time to time, this meeting, that march. You take care, Peter wanted to say to him. Maybe he did say it to him and doesn't remember because although he never forgets a face he often forgets an incident. You take care, you're being watched. He didn't know if it was true because by then it wasn't himself doing the watching, but he knew it was more than likely.

In the self-determination wars Pendreich was only ever a foot soldier not a strategist, indian not chief. That was the thing about Scotland back then, nobody wanted to be a chief. Still true today. You can see it as healthy or limiting. The downside of 'A Man's a Man for A' That': if I try to be a chief some other bastard will take the feet from under me. The sliding tackle of the Democratic Intellect.

There's intellect and intelligence and then there's Intelligence. Peter's stock-in-trade, or used to be. God, how Intelligence hates having to deal with indians. It prefers chiefs, ringleaders. It struggles with decent, ordinary human beings who become political radicals not because they're either very political or very radical but simply because they've had enough: it means they can't so easily be victimised, demonised, isolated, framed, entrapped, beaten up, imprisoned or otherwise neutralised. Decent? Does he really mean decent? Aye, he does, certainly in comparison with some of the shites on the other side, his side as was. Decent and thrawn. They just dig in their heels, these people. Doesn't matter what the cause is. Take that Jim Swire whose daughter was killed in the Lockerbie bombing. Jesus, Intelligence loathed him. Like a terrier he was, just got gripped on with his teeth and wouldn't let go, and it was clear as day to everyone that *he* was a decent man with nothing to gain but the truth and what he was getting was evasion and obstruction and downright fucking lies and he was never going to be satisfied with that. No, no. Pick a self-promoting radical any day if you want a victim or a demon. Pick a George Galloway or a Peter Tatchell. Oh aye, something else about Pendreich: he's gay.

Otherwise neutralised. Very good. Like *extraordinary rendition, collateral damage*. One of *those* phrases.

When Peter saw him in the café he thought, now there's somebody I could have a dialogue with. Some shared ground, some mutual acquaintances. We could talk about the old days. But he didn't go over. He went on reading his *Scotsman*, initiating imaginary conversations as his coffee got cold, and ten minutes later Pendreich stood up and left.

He might have followed him but he doesn't maintain much of a pace these days and Pendreich looked fit. Anyway, what would have been the point? It's not as if the guy has anything to hide, or Peter has anything to find out. Those days are over, if they ever existed.

It's not as if he has a job any more. A *role*. Freelance, floating or otherwise. There'll be somebody out there, trying to fuck things up Croick-style, trying to drag the process out, but it isn't Peter.

How far apart people's lives are, and yet how closely they miss each other. How small an adjustment would have left you leading another man's life, and him leading yours.

He paid the waitress at the till. She was glad to see the back of him. He knows he's deteriorating fast, on the edge of being completely unacceptable in public places. He's not yet quite so far gone that he doesn't wash his clothes, there's a launderette where he takes everything, wouldn't mind getting in the big machine himself sometimes, nevertheless he's not the favourite client of Edinburgh teashops, no sir. It's not happened yet, not that he can remember anyway, but the day is coming when he'll be ejected before he's even managed to spot a vacant seat.

On the way back to the flat he had a pint in Maggie Dickson's, and in a shop on Bread Street he bought a bottle of cheap whisky to replace the one he finished the night before.

The flat is a midden. The kitchen trails dirty plates and coffee mugs and biscuit crumbs into the living room which spills newspapers and books and pens and folders into the tiny passage and along it in one direction to the front door where the junk mail lies and in the other to the bathroom and the bedroom. The bathroom is sticky and foul and foreign, he goes in there as seldom as possible, to do the basics, to shit and pee and occasionally puke. Sometimes to clean himself up a bit. Standing room only in the bath, Christ you wouldn't want to sit down in it, there's a shower over it and a shower curtain with a slimy hem and if you're not too fussy about the soles of your feet it's tolerable. Silverfish everywhere. Resilient wee fuckers. Then there's the bedroom: a dark, bio-hazardous hole he ends up in sometimes when he doesn't fall asleep in a chair. If he wakes up in his bed he wonders how the fuck he got there. Welcome to the Hotel Caledonia.

This is the wreckage he lives among: the wreckage of an edifice he tried to construct for more than forty years, but which was crumbling almost from the outset, was mothballed in the late 1970s, suffered a serious structural failure in the mid-1980s and collapsed more or less completely in the spring of 1997. It's a fitting monument to his own wrecked life. In modern-art terms, a kind of un-installation made up of unfound objects. If his name was Tracey Emin he'd be a genius. A rich fucking genius too. He scrabbles around on the debris, vaguely trying to piece it together again even though there's now no point. He could clear it out but he doesn't. That would mean clearing out his entire adult life.

What makes him shudder, what makes him so disappointed in himself, what makes him sit there on the stale settee with the whisky on the table in front of him, him staring at it, it staring at him just sitting there like Alice in fucking Wonderland saying drink me drink me, what makes him pick the bottle up, its lovely cool familiar glassiness, what makes him turn the metal cap, feeling the retaining seal give a little, letting go, turning it again, letting go, testing himself, resisting, testing, ah fuck it turning the cap completely, the click of release, the beautiful fumes, lifting the lovely weight of the full bottle, pouring the first glassful, glug glug glug, what makes him do this night after night isn't the fact that he's been taken for a total ride, that he's been fooled and used and discarded. It's the fact that he conspired to allow it to happen, that he pretty much knew all along, even as it was happening, that he didn't have the guts to call time, walk away, blow the whistle, whatever phrase you want to apply he simply didn't do it. He can hear a voice, from years back, sounds like his father: *Ye've let yersel doon, son.* That's it, he let himself down and this is him not letting himself get back up again because that's how he deals with it. Or doesn't deal with it. He is sixty-eight years old, for fuck's sake. One minute you're listening to 'Telstar' by the Tornados, the next you're a pensioned-off drunk in a stinking flat in a run-down street that you, ya shaky auld cunt, to quote a youth he accidentally nudged when crossing it recently, should be afraid to go out in at night. But that's one thing at least: he isn't afraid of the dark or what might lie in wait outside. The stuff that unnerves him is right there with him in the flat.

Actually, in retrospect maybe he bought two bottles.

So, if he's a ghost. How would that have happened? Ex-spook becomes ghost. One thing he knows from his life in the shadows is how people fade in and out. They matter, they don't matter, they're tailed, they're not tailed, somebody cares, nobody cares. Other people remember them, forget them. Over time this has an effect: their existence starts to break up, like a bad TV picture or a dodgy phone connection. We're not talking here about climbers going missing in a blizzard, fishermen lost at sea. We're not talking about the ones search-and-rescue operations are launched for. We mean the many others who go, eventually, unnoticed and

unlooked for. Sometimes they don't even know they're away
themselves. They just fade and flicker until they disappear
altogether. Ghosts, right enough. Thousands of them every year.
They're here, then they're not. Stories without endings. Like a
book you can't be bothered finishing. So why wouldn't it have
happened to him? He's been half-absent for decades anyway. All it
would take is a few stumbles further into the darkness. And let's
face it, Peter stumbles from time to time. So aye, why not him?
Why wouldn't he already have joined the spectral crowd? And who
else is out there? Lucy Eddelstane? Aye, she'll be wandering the lost
zone somewhere, no map or compass. Must be. He recognised a
kindred spirit when he slept with one. But she's gone, long
gone. They passed like ghost ships in the night.

Who knows though? If he sticks around long enough their
paths might cross again. Oh he would love that. Sweet bitter Lucy!

He might even bump – can ghosts bump? – into Mad Uncle Jack,
a ghost now for more than fifty years.

In retrospect is better than *with hindsight*. *In retrospect* suggests
sustained reflection, coherent analysis. *With hindsight* says you'd
have done things differently, if you'd only fucking known.

One time – years ago this was, and years after he came to
Mr Fodrek's mansions for the falling and fallen – he was in the
launderette, sitting on one of the wee metal chairs with the wobbly
backs, waiting for the drier to finish. Daisy and Linda were slaving
away as usual, unsticking stuck token slides, filling beakers of
powder, hauling bundles of wet clothes from washer to drier,
folding sheets between them, bagging up service washes. They
worked well together: Daisy the bright one, Linda the not so, but
they were friends, he could tell that, they were loyal to each other.
They never stopped for more than two minutes, their mugs of tea
were only ever half-drunk, they had no airs and little grace about
them yet they were always helpful and never impatient with the
students, the businessmen with no wives or washing machines, the
waifs and strays like himself. A friendly word or a smile was never
distant from their lips. They called everybody 'dear' regardless of
age, sex, race or religion: a democracy of endearment. It was one
of the reasons he liked going there, he felt safe in their domain of

churning machines, humidity, tangled clothes and washing-powder scents, safe and comforted.

So anyway. It was the year the minimum wage was introduced, of course it was. Up until then he'd always done his own washing and drying because it was a pound extra for the service wash and he was watching the pounds, kind of, by then. On this occasion there was a lull in the human traffic even though all the machines were going, and for five minutes Peter was the only customer. Then the door banged open and in came a big guy in an expensive wool coat, a quality suit underneath it, polished leather brogues, polished mean face. Peter thought, I know that face, but he couldn't get it, not straightaway. Behind the man was a skinny, psychotic-looking sidekick in synthetics and trainers, carrying a briefcase.

Aye, ladies, the big man said. What's going on? It was nothing, what he said, but he made it sound intimidating, like he'd just caught them at it, whatever 'it' was. They looked at him from under their brows. Aye, Mr Dobie. It was obvious that they were afraid of him even though they were afraid of nobody else that ever came in. They didn't like him but when he smiled his mean smile it said they were pals, weren't they, and dared them to disagree.

Mr Dobie. Peter remembered. It was his old landlord from Leith, when he had the agency. His own business, for fuck's sake. He'd met Dobie only a couple of times, right at the start when he'd taken on the premises. In those days Dobie was wearing jeans and a leather jacket and was on his own. Not so fleshy. Harder, but that didn't mean he was any less dangerous now. He'd just acquired a dangerous sidekick.

Peter had paid the rent in Leith by monthly cheque, made out to some spurious business name and posted to an address out in the sticks. West Lothian: Broxburn or Bathgate or somewhere. He'd never been late with the rent, because he didn't think Dobie was the kind of guy you'd want to piss off even temporarily. So he'd never given him any trouble and he'd never had any back, or any property maintenance for that matter. When he wound up the agency – when it collapsed under the weight of his inability to stop drinking – he'd not bothered to say he was leaving, just locked up and left. Hadn't asked for his deposit back. It wasn't that kind of arrangement.

Daisy carried change in a money belt round her waist. It was usually her job to manage the cash transactions because she was better at adding up than Linda. Notes went in a till at the back of the shop. Nothing was ever rung up on the till, the women just pinged open the drawer and put the cash in it. Now Daisy handed over the money belt to the sidekick, and Dobie went to the till and opened it. He counted and pocketed the paper money and muttered a number at Sidekick that Peter didn't hear over the sound of the driers. Sidekick added up the change, made a note of the totals, bagged some of it and put it in the briefcase. The rest went back in the money belt, which he returned to Daisy. All this took no more than two minutes.

Everything all right? Dobie said. His voice was different. He spoke with a weird drawl, California out of Leith, which seemed to twist the mouth into its thin, cruel smile. Good-looking bastard all the same, if you liked slime. It's Daisy, isn't it? Daisy and Linda, that's it. Plenty of business, I see?

Oh aye, Mr Dobie, we've been busy this week right enough. Never stopped.

All the machines working okay?

Aye. A couple of jams, the tokens get bent sometimes, but we got them free.

Good. He was profoundly uninterested in their trials, so long as the machines were all working. Bryce here looking after you?

Aye, Mr Dobie. Here's the record sheet for ye. She handed him a bit of paper. It's aw doon there, the jams and that.

He didn't look at the paper, but passed it on to Sidekick. Go ahead, Bryce, he said.

Bryce opened the briefcase again and took out a notebook. He went down the washing machines, looking at a meter on each one beside the token slide, and making an entry. Peter had noticed the meters before. They recorded the number of washes each machine did. Bryce went through the same procedure with the driers. When he'd finished he handed the book to Dobie, who glanced at it and handed it back. Bryce put it in the briefcase. Dobie nodded at him again and he pulled out two brown pay packets and handed them to the women.

There you go, Dobie said. One for each of you. As if he was Santa Claus and Bryce one of his elves.

Thanks, Mr Dobie, Daisy and Linda said, and Linda dropped hers into the pocket of her apron and went off to take a load out of one of the driers. Daisy waited, like she was steeling herself to say something.

Dobie didn't notice. Aye well, he said, looking around with a sneer on his face. It was his place, apparently, but he didn't seem to like it much. His gaze fell on Peter, moved on. As if he were a piece of shit Dobie didn't want on his gleaming brogues. No recognition, apparently, but why would there be? Peter thought, okay, I am a piece of shit but I'm not your piece of shit and never was.

See you next week then, ladies.

Daisy said, Mr Dobie?

He'd already started to leave. He stopped, turned round. Yes?

Bryce was gonnae put oor wages up.

What's that?

Wi this new minimum wage that's come in. He was gonnae put them up.

Dobie looked at Bryce. I thought you'd explained that to everybody.

I did, Bryce said.

You explained how we're working to comply with the new legislation? How it's quite a complicated process, making sure everybody's treated fairly?

Aye, I did.

Dobie sighed. It was all a bit beneath him. Next week, he said to Daisy. These things take time. Bryce says he's already explained it to you. Obviously we have to comply, but there's not much point in paying you a higher rate if I put myself out of business, and you out of work. You understand?

Aye, Daisy said.

If everything balances, you'll get the increase next week.

That's two weeks late, Daisy said boldly, but her voice was shaking. We'll need to get it backdated.

Bryce scowled, mouthing at her to shut the fuck up.

Is that so? Dobie said. The drawl ceased and there was no smile left. Do you think you're being hard-done-by, Daisy? Think you're losing out?

She couldn't quite speak, but she managed to stay looking at him.

Dobie turned to Bryce. There were discrepancies last week, isn't that right, Bryce?

Aye, Mr Dobie, and the week before.

And quite a few weeks before that? Going back years even?

Aye, Mr Dobie.

So, Daisy, the reality is I'm the one that's losing out. The reality is I should be docking you both, because I can't run a business if the numbers don't add up. If I'm down at the end of the week, what am I supposed to do, ignore it?

Daisy started to say something. Didn't have a chance.

But Bryce tells me Linda's arithmetic's not that hot. So, I don't ignore it but I'm prepared for a bit of give and take. You sort it out between yourselves. You'll get your minimum wage next week, like I said. Bryce tells me you're both good workers. I'll take his word for it, and I'll turn a blind eye here and there, but – a measured pause – don't push your fucking luck.

He glanced at Peter again, a little longer this time, as if to say, that applies to you too, piece of shit, and then he and Bryce were out of the door, Bryce flinging a murderous look at Daisy as he went.

Peter's load finished drying. He stuffed it all into the black bin bag he'd brought it in. Daisy and Linda were counting their wages and cursing Dobie for a grasping, thieving, cheating, lying, bullying bastard. When Peter came up to them to say goodbye they softened immediately. Aye, cheerio, dear. See ye next time.

You should report him, he said. They laughed at him kindly, as if he'd offered to buy them an ice cream each. I'm serious, you should take him to a wages tribunal.

Aye, that'll be right.

He's got to pay you the minimum wage.

We'd be oot o here afore we could say 'tribunal', never mind turn up at one.

We'd mair likely turn up in the Union Canal.

He teased the details out of them. There were always discrepancies, from one week to the next. The takings never tallied with the number of machine uses, even when Daisy was meticulous in writing down the number of jams, breakdowns and so on. Bryce always underpaid them, so they always scraped a bit of loose change into their pockets to make up for it. Bryce knew they did it, they knew he was underpaying them, they knew he was skimming on his own behalf, Dobie knew Bryce was skimming. Everybody knew what the game was, and so long as it stayed small-scale Dobie was cool about it. But the fact that he'd come in at all, the first time in months, meant he was letting them all know. *Don't push your fucking luck.*

So now he says he's going to up your wages, Peter said. Will you get what you're due? Three-sixty an hour?

They laughed again at his naivety.

Look, he said, it's none of my business but . . .

Aye, we ken, we ken. Daisy said. Three-sixty's aboot right. By his way of adding it up, we'll get three-sixty an hour, all right? An hourly rate of two pound sixty plus what we get for a service wash and that makes it up tae three-sixty.

That's what Bryce tellt us, Linda said.

It's a pound for a service wash, right? Daisy said. We get that. Straight in oor hand. Suits us, suits them. So there ye go.

But not everybody pays for a service wash, Peter said. I don't.

What are you, an inspector or something? Linda said, and they both roared with laughter. Look, dear, the best thing you could dae, if ye're feeling sorry for us, is let us dae your wash for ye. That'll dae us a lot mair good than any tribunal.

He's ripping you off, he said.

Well? We're ripping him off, she said. Anyway, canna stand here chatting aboot it aw day. You mind what I said, dear, aboot us daein your wash for ye.

I will, he said.

And you keep your nose oot of it, won't ye? Ye dinna want tae get on the wrang side of Dobie.

Or Bryce, Linda said.

Don't stir things up for us, Daisy said. We're fine as we are.

What could he do? He was a broken man, no use for getting on the wrong side of anyone. So he'd complied with their request. Complicit, yet again. And ever since, he'd paid the extra for the service wash, and left his black bin bag with them. He'd never seen Dobie in there again. Or Bryce, come to that. Still, it rankled. Frank Dobie, Leith landlord, launderette king of the Lothians. He thought, if I'd been on the ball at the time, maybe I could have made something of the old connection. Maybe I could have done something for the women.

Kidding himself, of course. He was way past doing anything about anything.

There's a TV in one corner of the living room. Most of the time it's dead, a kind of blocked conduit through which the outside world used to come in, but he plugged the gap by unplugging the lead and now the world doesn't come in that way. Occasionally when what's inside gets too oppressive he reverses the procedure, just for some relief, but it doesn't last. The news is too much, the game shows too banal, the reality shows incomprefuckinghensible. Documentaries just rub his face in their so-called revelations. He caught one about an MI5 plot to undermine the Wilson government in the 1970s – a load of rubbish, he ended up roaring at every utterance coming out of the telly, RUBBISH RUBBISH RUBBISH, because he couldn't remember which bits of the story were actually true, and this is a man who's something of an expert when it comes to theorising about conspiracies but he'd taken a fair drink by the time it came on, and eventually a neighbour was hammering at the door threatening to kill him if he didn't can the fucking racket. Another one was a programme about Ian Fleming, footage of Fleming in his Jamaican home explaining how he'd wanted a bland, flat name for his hero, he'd had a book called *Birds of the West Indies* by James Bond and he'd thought, that'll do, and now he was wondering in his toff voice what the original Mr Bond thought about it all, and Peter was shouting *I'M* THE ORIGINAL BOND, YOU BASTARD and then had to unplug the TV to stop himself before the neighbour came again and broke his door down and really did kill him. Aye, the telly's not a good idea these days, it's all crap that's on it anyway and he doesn't need it, he has plenty of cartoons and scary monsters and fuck knows what else to keep him entertained without having to fork out for the TV licence that he doesn't, in any case, possess.

Another time, long before the launderette incident but just how long he cannot say with any certainty, can't even remember where he was living at the time, whether he was a tenant of Mr Dobie or Mr Fodrek, anyway what the fuck, he was on the batter one evening, rolling from bar to bar, a downward trajectory, and eventually he found himself in the New Town needing a place to piss. Staggered down ancient steps into a basement area on George Street, secreted himself in the shadows and let a long, lovely stream of relief flow across the flagstones. Climbing back up he found himself virtually tripping on the heels of two police officers, one male one female, and thinking they'd probably see his condition as an excuse for unwanted discourse he turned sharp left through the doors of a bookshop that happened to be passing at that moment. He wandered blindly among the shelves, and slowly became aware from the drone of a voice towards the back of the shop that he'd gatecrashed a reading. A guy in a cravat posing as a writer was holding forth to an assembly of twenty or so. After a minute Peter understood that the guy really *was* a writer, a novelist. Somebody from the audience asked him why he set his books in Italy, France, America and England, but not in Scotland. The writer stroked his chin. Because nothing happens here. The centres of activity, the places where decisions are made, where politics and personalities and power collide, are elsewhere: London, New York, Paris, Rome. Anywhere but this quiet backwater. Delightful to live in but nothing to write about. That's why. There were hums of agreement, an undermumble of dissent. Peter thought, You're wrong. Things *do* happen here. Political things. People get locked up on dodgy evidence procured by servants of the state. People get murdered for obstructing the wishes of the authorities. Then the murderers get murdered. Keeps it neat and tidy. Hush hush. Believe me, I know. But then on the other hand you're right, nothing happens here. I'm talking crap. Nothing will ever come to light. Nobody need ever find out. You're right, this is a quiet fucking backwater but there are bodies weighed down with stones lying at the bottom. Believe me, I know. He was aware of a voice shouting, not the voice that had previously been droning, he was aware of heads turning, a security guard approaching. I'll have to ask you to leave. You're creating a disturbance. Hand firmly under the elbow, other hand in small of back. Go placidly, Peter told the turned heads, amid the noise and haste, and remember what peace there may be in silence. He heard laughter, the writer saying, Well, *as* I was saying . . . And it was too late, as they got to the door, it was no fucking use protesting to the guard at that stage, Look, I'm a child of the universe, no less than the trees and the stars, I have a right to be here, because with one good shove the guard had propelled him ten yards along the pavement and suggested that an early return would be met with renewed and fiercer hostilities. It was too late and no use, and the rest of the night was a cloud of unknowing, morphing into a slow, remorseless awakening sprawled on the floor of a room nobody ejected him from, which meant it was probably somewhere he then called home.

Mr Fodrek comes for his rent once a month. Sometimes Peter has it, sometimes only part of it. When he's short he makes an effort over the next few weeks, stashing extra tens and twenties away in places he'll forget about until the knock at the door and there's Mr Fodrek again. Mr Fodrek is a reasonable man. He understands the insecure circumstances most of his tenants are in. That's why they are his tenants. He stands just inside the door and waits while Peter scrabbles around collecting the cash. Mr Fodrek prefers cash, in fact he insists on it for accounting purposes, which is why he's prepared to be flexible from one payment to the next. Plus he has two months' worth of deposit from way back whenever, and both of them know that Peter won't be seeing a penny of *that* again. Mr Fodrek stands by the door amid the junk mail and looks around, no doubt taking in the cracks in the ceiling, the stain from when the flat upstairs flooded, the grime along the skirting boards, the lampshade thick with dust. But he never comments, never criticises, never wants to check the rest of the place. Breakages? Not bothered. Repairs? Not interested. That's what the deposit was for. Mr Fodrek is a reasonable man.

This is the arrangement. Tenants may come and tenants may leave, especially the kind of tenants Mr Fodrek caters for, but Peter Bond goes on for ever. Well, he's still there for now anyway. And he finds a kind of reassurance in the fact that his landlord calls round for rent, and wants it cash in hand, month after month. It's old-fashioned. It's not the way things are done any more and Peter likes that. Mr Fodrek doesn't say much – pleasantries not required – and Peter doesn't say much back. It's perfectly, perversely civilised. Is Mr Fodrek contented? Doubt it. Is he wealthy? Shouldn't think so, not from rents like his. Does he mind his own business? Aye, he does, and he keeps his nose out of Peter's, which is one of the benefits of living in a shithole. Even the landlord doesn't give a fuck about you, so long as you keep up, more or less, with the payments. And Peter knows that, if he ever does leave – which it may come to some day because the bank balance is slowly but inexorably shrinking, the pension credits just don't equate to the drink debits – if he ever does leave Mr Fodrek still won't say much. He'll pay someone fifty quid to sort of clean the flat, and the next tenant will move in. Maybe he dreams of the day the building becomes uninhabitable, and everybody moves out, and he sells the site for redevelopment and makes himself a half-millionaire. Maybe, but if he does his dream is buried deep and it doesn't make him smile.

Christmas, 1962. Christmas Day was a Tuesday and for most people in Scotland a working day, but Peter was home for the English holiday.

Prompted by his father calling him Jimmy three times in the space of a minute, he made an announcement.

I'm calling myself Peter nowadays, he said.

Oh aye? his father said. How's that?

I prefer it, he said. But also . . .

His mother said, I can't see what's wrong with the name we christened you with, James.

His father said, We gied him two, Peggy. If Peter was good enough for my faither then it's good enough for the boy, if that's how he wants tae be kent.

The boy! He was twenty-two, a man by any measure except theirs. They were small-time folk, Hugh and Peggy Bond, who thought of him as their small-time wee laddie, a minnow who'd gone off to swim in the big pool that was London. Even if he could get a word in to explain the real reason they'd think he was overreacting. A nine-day wonder, son. Why should *you* change *your* name? And his older sisters, Elspeth and Etta, if they were consulted, would say the same, too wrapped up in their own families to bother thinking it through. But *he* knew. He knew it had to be done.

What it was: he had to distance himself from the *other* James Bond. He was getting sick of people doing double takes whenever he introduced himself. When the other Bond had just been a character in a series of books it hadn't been such an issue, but now there was a film, *Dr No*, and it was clear to Jimmy / Peter that something big was happening, that 'James Bond' was going to be around for a while and he would have to do something about it.

It wasn't Hugh and Peggy's fault. How could they have known in 1940 that some Old Etonian ex-Naval Intelligence officer was going to start writing spy novels and call the hero James Bond? It wasn't their fault and yet somehow he blamed them – their naivety, their small-mindedness – for not seeing it coming. Hugh and Peggy Bond: a case study in being oblivious to the bigger picture.

It wouldn't have mattered so much if he had been on the outside. On the outside he could have made something of it. People would enjoy having a plumber, a car mechanic, a teacher even, called James Bond. But in 1962 he wasn't on the outside, he'd been allowed in, *taken* in, and nobody on the outside – family, friends from school if there'd been some but there weren't, he'd kept up with none of them – knew what he did and therefore why his name was so ironic. But *he* did. He was the butt of a joke he couldn't share with anyone except the very people taking the piss. Literally taking the piss. A couple of guys were developing a routine around the film's theme tune. Standing on either side of him at the urinals one of them would do the guitar riff while the other came in with the brass section. They said, How's it going, 007? They'd enjoyed attempting to imitate his accent before: now they had the Edinburgh tones of Sean Connery to model themselves on. It was pathetic but inevitable. Reinventing himself as Peter gave him a bit of leeway.

He'd taken Christmas Eve as leave too, so he could come up by train on the Saturday, have three days in Slaemill and go back to London on Boxing Day. Some people in London still found it hard to make him out even though he'd toned the accent down a lot.

Now Hugh was looking at him queerly when he spoke. Ye're awfie English gettin, he said, but there was a touch of pride in his resentment. Peggy, who'd spent years rooting out Scotticisms from her own speech and endlessly correcting her children's language, glowed with pleasure, not least because to her the difference between how father and son spoke only underlined how far up in the world Peter had already risen.

First night home, she greedily watched him fight through the mountain of food she'd prepared for him. She'd started setting it on the kitchen table before he'd even got in the door, from the minute, in fact, that the timetable said the bus from Drumkirk was dropping him off in the High Street. She stood with her back against the bunker, arms folded. She and Hugh had already had their tea. From a chair at the other end of the table Hugh watched him, equally intently. Peter felt like he was the sole entrant in an eating competition and they had bets on about how much he'd put away before he burst.

So anyway, Peggy said, deciding to ignore the name change, how's the Big Smoke? You're like a wire. You're not looking after yourself.

In fact he'd begun to get a paunch, from sitting behind a desk all day and swilling too much English beer after work.

I'm fine, Mum.

You're not. Don't look at me like that. I'm your mother. I know about these things. You're not getting fed properly.

This'll make up for it.

Don't be cheeky. So do you still like it, London?

It's great.

Job gaun weel? Hugh said. Keeping your nose clean, are ye?

Spotless, he said, between mouthfuls. I'll be a permanent under-secretary before you can blink.

Hugh frowned. Is that good, is it?

I'm having you on, Peter said. That's the top civil-service job, the highest you can get. I've nae chance.

No chance, Peggy said automatically.

You have to have been to public school and Oxbridge, Peter said, and eventually you get a knighthood for services rendered.

I see, Hugh said cautiously. Ye shouldna joke aboot these things, son.

It's no joke. They beat folk like us back with their brollies.

His irreverence made them nervous. Shades of Mad Uncle Jack maybe? His mother moved the subject on.

A lot of paperwork, I imagine? she said.

What's a lot of paperwork, being a permanent under-secretary? Somebody else does all the graft for you up there. That's why they're all OBEs. Other Buggers' Efforts.

Peggy looked wounded. Hugh tutted. Just for a moment Peter felt he'd overdone it.

I meant *your* job, Peggy said. You must have so much on your desk all the time.

Och, I get through it, he said.

His parents were very literal people. Peggy doubtless had him barely visible behind great piles of paper, while Hugh, who liked the sound of phrases like *oiling the machinery of government* or, a newish one, *the corridors of power*, probably pictured him striding down long passages in a bowler hat with an oil can and a rag. The kind of 'man frae the ministry' you might see calling on the Broons in the *Sunday Post*. In reality he didn't wear a bowler hat and mostly what he did was read information and sort it into files. Routine stuff that had him nodding off at two in the afternoon. The other Bond would have been tearing his hair out, but Peter had the right temperament. There were hunters and gatherers in Intelligence. He was a gatherer.

But it must be so difficult keeping on top of things, Peggy insisted. Especially if your colleagues aren't . . .

If they aren't what? he asked. Keeping on top of things too?

You know, she said. Trustworthy. Like that terrible man in the navy.

What man?

Oh, what's his name, Hugh? Vessel?

Well, that would be the navy right enough, Peter said.

Vassall. John Vassall, that's it, his father said, taking his cue.

They must have been desperate to mention him: a clerk at the Admiralty who'd just been imprisoned for eighteen years for spying for the Russians. Peggy would take it as a personal affront, a threat to her son's good name, that such treachery could lurk at the heart of the British state, a stone's throw from Buckingham

Palace. Worse, the Russians had been blackmailing Vassall with photographs of him in compromising poses with other men. Viewed from the parish of West Mills, Peter reckoned, it must all look unimaginably sordid.

I didn't know him, he reassured them. It's a vast, complex business, government. Thousands of people working in dozens of different departments.

There's aye bound tae be a few bad apples, I suppose, Hugh said.

Always, Peter said, thinking as he said it that there was worse to come – although, from his parents' point of view, could anything be worse than homosexuality mixed with Communism? Rumours were flying around Whitehall about the Secretary of State for War and a showgirl called Christine Keeler. If true, they would make Vassall's compromising poses look like family snapshots.

How come it's always the nancy boys? Hugh said. Ye'd think the powers that be would be wise tae them by noo. Ye dinna get ony o that nonsense here.

Now, Hugh, his mother said. You know nothing about it. It's way over our heads.

I ken mair than you do. All I'm saying is, the lads at the mill would ken how tae sort that kind o thing.

His parents understood that he was an Executive Officer in the War Office and, awestruck by that title, or so he assumed, they never dared probe too far into what it meant or what exactly it was he did. Checks would have been done on them to make sure he hadn't sprung from a Nest of Communists, but even if they suspected they'd been investigated they'd be flattered. They were the best kind of citizens a state could possess, with a simple, unquestioning faith in the goodness and greatness of Britain. They saw his new work as an extension of his National Service, which in a way it was, since he'd been siphoned off from the square-bashing and weapons-training at Redford Barracks after just a fortnight, taken to a room for aptitude tests, an IQ exam, then the next day a two-hour interview, and at the end of all that offered the possibility of 'special duties'. You've been spotted, the man who interviewed him had said. We'll let you know in a few weeks, one way or the other. And they did. He finished his basic training, then went home for three days' leave, then it was off to London. Peggy and

Hugh were goggle-eyed with the effort of suppressing their excitement. His father said, Son, we'll say nae mair aboot it. But we're proud of ye, Jimmy. We canna tell ye how proud we are.

The man had introduced himself as Edgar. My name's Edgar, he'd said. Presumably it was his surname because that was how it was back then. Never saw him or heard anything from him again. There was another man in the room who didn't introduce himself at all, didn't speak during the entire interview. Thick, black-rimmed glasses and a hand over his mouth, sitting off to one side, hard to get a good look at him.

You're a bright young chap, Edgar said. The sort of chap we're looking for.

What did he mean by 'bright'? Intelligent but not intellectual, conscientious but not attached to a cause? Dull, in other words. And lower class, respectful, dependably unambitious. Since the revelations in the 1950s about a Cambridge spy ring and the resulting defections to Russia, the Service had been under pressure to clean up its recruiting procedures. One of the ways to achieve this was to bring in people who were not ex-public school, homosexual dilettantes. If you were Scottish and from a skilled working-class or lower-middle-class background (Hugh Bond was a foreman in one of the local paper mills), not only were you unlikely to be any of these things, there was also a good chance you'd had a solid education unsullied by imagination.

So what have you been doing with yourself since you left school? Edgar asked. Before you got called up, I mean.

He'd managed to get a start on a local paper, the *Drumkirk Gazette*, because his English teacher knew the editor, Mr Gray. That was how it was described, a 'start' not a 'job', with a paltry wage and a clear understanding that he was being done a favour that would last only as long as there was goodwill in Mr Gray's heart. He was a trainee reporter. This meant he made the tea, sharpened pencils and sorted the mail. After two hours he was bored; but he was patient. After a week he was allowed out with one or other of the two full-time reporters, Bob Singleton and Bill Drummond, to cover court cases, football games, fêtes and motor accidents. Bob was a chain-smoking grizzled guy in his mid-fifties whose breath smelled of alcohol first thing in the morning and any time after noon. Bill was twenty years younger and loved himself, he wore sharp, cheap suits and combed his oily hair over a bald patch and was always fingering his moustache and catching his reflection in windows. They made out that they were intense rivals but in fact there was nothing to fight over; the news they gathered was petty and paltry and they growlingly divvied it up between them in such a way as to make their lives as easy as possible. They called Jimmy 'the cub' – Where's the cub, Bill? Tell the cub to get the kettle on – and hardly ever addressed him to his face, but by sticking around them he learned how to listen, or how not to, how to ask the right questions or the wrong ones, how to pick out the essentials of a story or miss them. He knew he could be sharper and better than Bill and Bob without even trying, but he kept this opinion to himself. They were dying on their feet and so was the paper. There was a rival rag, the *Drumkirk Observer*, and the *Gazette* was losing sales and advertising to it week on week.

Every Tuesday he went on a train to Edinburgh and attended classes in shorthand and typing in a seedy private college near Haymarket where all the other students were female and frumpy and suspicious of him. He, for his part, was filled with a total absence of desire for any of them. There seemed to be a financial arrangement between the college and the paper that made his journey worthwhile to both parties: each week a sum was deducted from his wage, a sum he managed to discover was greater than what the college received for taking him in. He swallowed his pride and said nothing, but when, not long after turning eighteen, his call-up papers came, he didn't protest or seek a deferment. Other boys dreaded National Service and did everything they could to avoid it, but Jimmy Bond was off like a whippet.

Sounds like a lot of fun, Edgar said. *Citizen Kane* in, where is it again, Drumkirk? Are you going back?

Not if I can help it, Jimmy said, and the man with the hand over his mouth grunted his approval.

What do you think of all that trouble with Burgess and Maclean? Edgar asked. Not much of a Scotchman, eh, Donald Duart Maclean? He rolled the name out with as much of a burr as his southern tongue could muster. More of an English fop, wouldn't you say?

Jimmy nodded agreement. Here was Edgar doing this pathetic put-on Scottish voice while he was concentrating on squeezing his own words out as flat as he could get them. He could hear his mother's voice – *Don't say* dinna, *say* don't – and for once he was grateful for her efforts. He was in a play, or an audition for a play, and he wanted to set the right tone. He wanted to be a country cousin, not a barbarian.

Actually, he said, I don't think anything much about it. He's got nothing to do with me.

Quite, Edgar said, and the other man nodded. Nothing to do with you, Edgar said. You wouldn't be inclined in that direction, would you?

No fear, he said vehemently, assuming they meant homosexuality, not the USSR. Another right answer, which also happened to be the truth. It was easy, given the cues he was getting. Don't venture an opinion, say what they want to hear. When Edgar asked how he'd feel about a move to London, he hesitated just enough to reinforce the image of a backwater boy they could mould to fit their own purposes: he'd miss home, he said, but it would be a challenge, a chance to see the world. Inwardly he was praying this would be his pass out of Slaemill, West Mills, Drumkirk and Scotland.

If you're selected, Edgar said, you will learn things about the world, and about yourself, that you would never otherwise know.

Four years later, he couldn't believe how tiny home was. Not just Slaemill and its neighbouring communities tucked under the hills, but the whole country. He'd been back at least once every year and each time it shrank a little more, and the bustle and noise of London seemed magnified, and he wanted to be back amongst it. And it wasn't that he'd made new friends there and was missing their company: it was the opposite. He didn't want closeness. That was what he'd wanted to get away from. He realised he'd come home only out of a sense of loyalty that was fast draining away.

Sunday was interminable. He was reduced to reading the *Sunday Post* cover to cover, twice – including the Fun Section, which wasn't fun the first time. In the afternoon, desperate, he walked to the next village, where he had a coffee in the only café: it seemed slightly ashamed to be open, the few customers ashamed to be patronising it. They spoke in low tones, as if in church. On the way back he bumped into a couple of old schoolmates. They exchanged news, but it was an unfond reunion. One of them worked in the paper mill, and talked about being trained to use a new Hyster forklift as if he'd landed the best job in the world. Peter could tell they thought he'd got above himself by leaving: he felt they'd diminished themselves by staying put.

On the Monday everybody was at work. If Uncle Jack had still been around he'd have gone over to Wharryburn to see him, but Uncle Jack was long away and so were Sarah and Barbara, off to a new life in Glenrothes, not that he'd have bothered with them. He took a bus into Drumkirk and wandered the grey streets, the cold of them creeping up through the soles of his shoes. He tried a pub at dinner time, the Toll Tavern – a dark, cheerless retreat which he'd had rare glimpses into as a boy walking by – exchanged a few droll comments with other men propping up the bar, then thought he'd drop in on the *Gazette*.

Neither Bill nor Bob was in. There was a new girl on reception who just about managed to keep the grin off her face when he gave his name as Jimmy Bond and asked to see Mr Gray. After a minute the editor emerged from his office. He seemed to have aged about twenty years since Peter had last seen him.

We're winding down, he said, back behind the firmly shut door of his room. It'll all be over by spring. I'm too old for this game, and the proprietors don't want to replace me. Can't say I blame them. We're losing money hand over fist.

That's too bad, Peter said. How are Bill and Bob?

Bob's gone, Mr Gray said with grave finality.

Gone?

Fired. I felt bad about it, but somebody had to go, there's hardly enough to keep Bill on, if I'm honest. The *Observer* will clean up after us. Well, you can't stand in the way of progress. But what about you? You've done all right. The War Office, eh? Enjoying London?

Aye, it's fine.

Good for you. Glad I was able to put in a word for you.

How do you mean?

You know, give you a recommendation. Eyes and ears of the local community, that's me. Was, I should say. Happy to oblige when they asked.

When who asked?

Mr Gray tapped the side of his nose. Och, Jimmy, he said. What a question! Goodness me!

He wouldn't be drawn any further, just tapped his nose again and winked. Well, thanks for coming in, Jimmy. Just as well you did. Shouldn't think you'll find us here next time you're home.

On the bus back to Slaemill he pondered this revelation. He knew that the Service had a network of people – teachers, professors, doctors – who provided recruitment tips and other information. Nothing was an accident. Yet he was surprised, and disappointed. He liked to think he'd got where he was on his own merits.

His mother's nose wrinkled at the beer on his breath. Her disapproval reassured him a little. He went to his room and slept for a couple of hours before tea.

Christmas Day loomed, a day like any other, and he recognised what a mistake he'd made coming home at this time of year. And vowed never to do so again.

Uncle Jack – Peggy Bond's younger brother – was special. Set apart. Probably the family wouldn't have had much to do with him, but blood's thicker than water, Hugh said. *Special* was one word for him, Jimmy's word, but the ones he heard his parents use were *odd*, *strange*, *cracked*, *damaged*. And *mad*. They didn't say *mad* often but Jimmy liked it best because it was way off the scale of normality, and so he thought of him as Mad Uncle Jack although he was careful never to say it out loud.

He must have been nearly six when he first met him, back from the war, with Sarah, his new English wife. It was the war that made those words fit Uncle Jack. Being captured by the Japs and made to work on their hellish railway for four years. Hugh sucked in his cheeks and shook his head at the rotten shame of it. No, Jack was never going to be right again. Not that he could ever be *completely* right, Peggy said, and Jimmy understood from this that the war wasn't to be held entirely responsible. And there was that other weird, embarrassing thing about Jack: he was a Scottish Nationalist. Hugh and Peggy were Unionists but a number of their friends were Labour and they even knew a couple who voted for the Liberals, but the only Scottish Nationalist in their circle was Uncle Jack, if you could call it a circle and if you could pretend that he was in it. Hugh was only able to say *Scottish Nationalist* out of the side of his mouth, and usually raised his eyebrows in a meaningful way when he did. Jimmy wondered why the two words went so insistently and inseparably together. Uncle Jack wasn't going to be an English or a French Nationalist, was he? Jimmy filed this riddle away for further consideration.

He saw Uncle Jack only once or twice a year at most. So maybe he was in his company eight or nine times before The Disappearance. Feels like it should have been more: Uncle Jack looms larger than that. But just before Jimmy turned eleven, Jack was gone.

Jimmy's grandparents on that side, the Gordon side, both died during the war and never saw Jack come home, but they left him all their money. Jimmy's mother never complained about that, she said she'd nothing to complain about, she was provided for and anyway there wasn't that much. Enough for him to put down the deposit on a bungalow in Wharryburn, though, and he and Sarah settled down there and a while later Barbara was born. A bought hoose, Hugh used to say, weel, weel. There wasn't much communication between the two families, but from time to time a reluctant sense of duty, and sympathy for Sarah, got the better of Jimmy's parents and the Bonds boarded the bus to Wharryburn and descended on the Gordons en masse.

Jimmy would have detested these visits but for the brooding presence of Uncle Jack. The way he managed not to participate in conversations, or the way he dropped in a remark that reduced the other grown-ups to silence, was a marvel to Jimmy. His sisters didn't like Uncle Jack, they found him intimidating, but Jimmy was fascinated. He admitted it once, on the bus home, one of the occasions he learned it was better not to speak at all. I really like Uncle Jack, he said. His mother turned in her seat and gave him a hard stare. Liking him's fine, she said. Just don't grow up to *be* like him. How no? he asked. Why not, she corrected. Because you're enough like him already, that's why not. He started to say something else but his father, sitting next to him, said, That'll do, Jimmy.

How was he like him? He didn't think he looked like him but then he didn't think he looked like his father either, or his mother. He didn't say much, and Uncle Jack didn't say much, maybe that was it. The way you could say a lot by saying very little.

There was this one time they were at Wharryburn, a Sunday in March just a day or two before The Disappearance. Elspeth and Etta were cooing over Barbara in the living room and Barbara was just about tolerating them, Peggy was putting a brave face on being with Sarah in the kitchen, and the men – his father and Uncle Jack and himself – had stepped out of the back door and were standing in manly silence with their coats on. Well, Uncle Jack was standing in silence, staring at the grass that was not yet ready to be cut or at the neat, empty beds or maybe not staring at anything, and Hugh stamped his feet and got out his pipe and lit it and made a comment about the cold and when there was no answer grumbled about family life and wondered when Barbara might be getting a wee brother or sister to keep her company, and still Jack said nothing but Hugh just kept on and on, what it was like having a house full of bairns, Jack would never have a minute's peace if *his* experience was anything to go by, not that he resented his own flesh and blood, he wasn't saying that but that was the truth of the matter, *not a minute's peace*, and Jimmy thought if his Uncle Jack was thinking anything it was exactly that and he just wished his father would shut up. There was something intense and dignified about the way Uncle Jack didn't respond, didn't even look at Hugh. But eventually the insistent prattle must have triggered something inside him.

I think I'll take a stroll up the hill, he said, still staring ahead. Get some fresh air.

Oh, Hugh said. I think it's pretty fresh oot here masel, he said, through a cloud of pipe smoke.

Not for me, Uncle Jack said. And then he said a truly wonderful thing: Are you coming, Jimmy? And in a concession to Hugh that was also a very definite indicator that he wasn't invited, he added,

If that's all right with you, Hugh? It's time Jimmy and I were better acquainted.

Jimmy glanced at his father who, wrong-footed, suddenly seemed to him more childish than he was himself. He didn't think of himself as a child anyway. Weel, I dinna ken, Hugh said, flustered, I mean it's three o'clock noo, how lang dae ye think ye might be? We'll hae tae catch the bus hame soon enough. Jack said, calm as anything, Och, the bus doesn't go till five. We'll just take a walk up to the woods and back, we'll be no more than an hour, and Hugh looked out of breath at the very thought and conceded defeat with a nod. It'll be the five-o'clock bus for us then, Jimmy, mind that, he said, and Jimmy felt a thrill that his uncle, Mad Uncle Jack, had asked him to go with him, alone, but he kept it off his face, held it down inside him, smiled reassuringly at his worried-looking father and then he and Jack set off round the house and away up the street past the last of the bungalows to where the tarmac gave out and the track into the woods began.

The first Jimmy knew about The Disappearance was three or four days later, back in Slaemill. Peter doesn't remember the exact sequence of events but he has a definite memory of his father taking him through into the front room one evening, where they hardly ever went, and in a very serious voice telling him to sit on the sofa. Opposite him, in one of the armchairs, was a big, blue-jawed policeman in a blue uniform, with his hat in his lap and a notebook and pencil resting on top of it.

This is Sergeant Ritchie, Hugh said. Now Jimmy, it's aboot your Uncle Jack so I want ye tae think carefully and tell us everything ye ken.

No need tae be afraid, son, Ritchie said. Just tell us aboot last Sunday.

What aboot last Sunday?

Was there anything your Uncle Jack said that was odd, when you went for that walk wi him? Anything at all.

How, what's happened?

It's all right, son, ye're no in any trouble, Ritchie said.

Your uncle's gone missing, Hugh said, and the police are trying tae find him.

So did he say anything odd, or did anything unusual happen on your walk? Ritchie said.

Jimmy did what he thought was a good impression of weighing up the question.

No, he said.

Think, Jimmy. Ye were away wi him for an oor and a hauf at least, his father said. Whit *did* ye talk aboot? Ye must've talked aboot something?

We just walked, he said. He doesn't say much, Uncle Jack.

That's true enough, Hugh said. A man of few words is my brother-in-law, Sergeant. But did he no say *onything*, son?

Nothing, Peter remembers, that he cared to repeat. Uncle Jack had started to tell him about when he was a prisoner of the Japanese. He'd talked about a man who'd tried to escape into the jungle and what had happened when he was recaptured. Jimmy saw it all, heard the slice of blade through neck, the horror of it. But he said nothing, just strode along beside his uncle, up through the trees, up and up till they came to the edge of the wood and a stone dyke and beyond it the moor and hills in the distance, and they stood there, warm in the cold afternoon, and Uncle Jack put his hand on Jimmy's shoulder and said, I love this country, Jimmy, but there's too much wrong with it. There's too much wrong with the world. Do you know what I'm saying? And the hand squeezed his shoulder and Jimmy felt awkward. The word *love* made him uncomfortable. Uncle Jack turned and crouched down till their faces were level, and his eyes were very blue as they stared into Jimmy's, and he said in a harsh whisper, Of course you don't. But you will. You're the same as me, lad, you don't fit. I can tell. I've had enough. I'm going away. Don't tell anyone I told you that. When you're old enough, you get away too. You'll understand when it's time. And Jimmy didn't know what he was on about, it was a bit scary but exciting too, and then Uncle Jack's hand swept the ground and he put something into Jimmy's hand, a wee stone, and he said, Don't forget this. And he stood up and said, in a different kind of voice, We'd better be heading back or your father will be anxious. And the stone was in Jimmy's pocket and they made their way back to the path and came up over a rise and there was a man and a much wee-er boy coming towards them out of the trees.

We just walked, Jimmy said again. He said about how he liked Scotland. That was all.

Did ye see anybody when ye were oot wi him?

He might have made a mistake, lying about that as well, but he was too smart for them.

Aye. A man called Don.

How d'ye ken his name?

He tellt me it. He had a wee boy with him. His son, I think. Called Billy.

Ritchie consulted his notebook and nodded at Jimmy's father. That's right enough. Very good, son. You should be daein my job.

How long's he been missing? Jimmy asked.

Here, steady on, I was joking, Ritchie said, and he and Hugh laughed, and then Ritchie said, A couple o days, and Hugh said, We're worried aboot him.

So if there's anything ye've no tellt us, Ritchie said, it's important that ye speak up noo. Ye're practically the last person he spoke tae.

Jimmy shook his head and there was silence in the room. Eventually Ritchie spoke again.

I'm going tae ask ye something difficult, he said.

A pause. Peter remembers that Jimmy knew exactly what was coming next. Something in the way he accumulated and filed information, even then, meant that when it came to being questioned he was, almost always, ahead of the game.

Did anything happen that your uncle might have felt ashamed of? Ritchie said. Or that *you* feel ashamed of? Anything that might have made him panic? Anything that might have driven him tae run away?

Jimmy looked at his father. His father looked away. Jimmy thought, you can't deal with this but I can. He shook his head.

Anything bad happen? Ritchie said.

He shook his head again.

Did he touch ye at all? Ritchie said. Did he interfere wi ye?

No, Jimmy said, indignant. He never laid a finger on me. He's no like that.

All right, son, Ritchie said. I guess ye ken what I'm talking aboot. I just had tae ask. We're trying tae establish what makes your Uncle Jack tick.

Hugh's forehead was glistening with sweat.

So are ye gonnae find him? Jimmy asked.

Oh aye, we'll find him, Ritchie said. Dinna you worry aboot that.

Jimmy nodded. He wasn't worried. They wouldn't find Uncle Jack. And they didn't have a clue what made him tick. He felt the stone in his pocket.

Dinna get mixed up wi thae folk that want tae ruin your life.

That was Hugh, his father, on the platform at Waverley Station, shaking his hand, the first time he went south. He said it shyly, almost surreptitiously, as if the mysterious folk he referred to were already hovering in the background, amid the steam and din of the station, ready to pounce on his son and lead him off into temptation. A parade of bad people hurried through Jimmy's mind: card-sharps and gangsters in coloured shirts and flash cars, winking purveyors of mysterious cigarettes, salacious women in dangerous bars. Lead me to them, he thought, releasing his dry hand from his father's sweaty grip and stepping up into the carriage. Peggy had stayed at home: she'd only have made a scene if she'd come through to Edinburgh to see him off. Don't worry, Dad, he said. I can look efter masel. Hugh looked wee and lost on the platform. He'd have to get the train back to Drumkirk alone, then a bus home, and Jimmy experienced a moment's anxiety on his behalf. His father was a child, always would be, whereas he was about to grow up. Up and away.

The train pulled clear of the city and he settled himself to look out of the window at the smeary countryside. He was off! He knew he wasn't heading for anything glamorous, he wasn't going to be the next Sidney Reilly. But London itself was something. London was new, the future. London was different and vast and anonymous. It was going to release him from the tired old certainties of small-town Scotland.

He started in a basement in Curzon Street, buried there with a handful of other young men and subjected to lectures on Marxist-Leninist theory and practice. Object: to get a 'thorough grasp' of the aims and activities of the Communist Party of

Great Britain. Practical training included participating in the ongoing monitoring of the entire membership of the CPGB, and learning intricate, tedious procedures for creating and updating files on them and anybody else suspected of subversion. Every day a class-set of the *Daily Worker* was delivered to the recruits, and they scoured the pages for information on individuals and groups. It was said that if it weren't for the bulk orders from the Service and the Soviet Embassy the paper would have folded.

After six months he was moved to another part of the building, then out of it altogether. These moves happened without discussion or explanation: in his lowly position he did not need to know the reasons for his redeployment. He was just a cog. Better to be that, though, a cog in the secret arm of government, than to be shifting pallets around in a Scottish paper mill.

The Service was full of cogs and wheels. There were wheels within wheels, circles and inner circles. You never quite knew where among them you were, in or out. Sometimes you thought you were in and then you'd request a particular file and access would be denied and you realised you'd inadvertently tried to enter a space that wasn't yours to enter. Maybe in time it would become yours, maybe it wouldn't. You were in an intricate game, a complex dance, but nobody explained the moves to you or how many other dancers there were, and just when you thought you'd mastered one sequence the formation changed.

He thought he was getting on fine. He thought they were preparing him for greater things. One of the Service's roles was to provide Intelligence advice to colonies and former colonies. There were security liaison officers scattered from Delhi to Trinidad. Peter thought he detected hints that he might be suitable material for a foreign posting. He fancied the Caribbean. Anywhere really. So he can still remember the crushing disappointment, three years in, when the Scottish stuff was dumped on his desk.

Why did they do that? At the time he hadn't a clue. Maybe he does now? Aye, maybe. Could it have been, for example, because he was Scottish, therefore he understood the people, the culture, the politics? Don't be ridiculous. That would be far too fucking logical. The Service didn't think like that, certainly not about

Scotland. The Scots were the same as the English, just less civilised, more indecipherable. Their culture was non-existent if you discounted Burns Night, their politics a joke, parish-pump stuff. Once maybe, when Glasgow was second city of the Empire and Clydeside was Red, Scottish politics might have mattered. John Maclean: *We are in the rapids of revolution*. Not in 1963. By then the tanks in George Square were a fading legend.

But there would have been another logic at work, and with hindsight he recognises it. God, he hates hindsight. Anyway. The twisted, doublethink, illogical logic: they probably dumped it on somebody else's desk at the same time, to see if the other bloke came up with a different version of events. They'd be checking up both on them *and* on what was going on in Scotland. Which, as far as Peter could see, was pretty much fuck all.

And then there is the other reason, the one he can barely bring himself to consider. That they *did* give it deliberately, personally, to him. That they started loading him like a mule even way back then. Could they have? When it comes to conspiracies there is no more dedicated theorist than Peter Bond, but could they have set him up that early? A Trojan Mule? Just the thought of it's enough to make his knees give way. Thank God for whisky. How he loves the feel of that Alice in Whiskyland bottle.

Still, what could he do? He buckled down, familiarised himself with the history, the known names, the groups and splinter groups, the almost total absence of any current activity. Periodically his section head, Henry Canterbury, would ask for an update. But there was nothing to update, so they just went over old ground, and then Canterbury went away again. Until the next time.

Bond the gatherer, the explorer. He did his job, in an office at the back of a faceless government building beside the Thames, then in the early evening he slid up to Soho and carried on with his other, unofficial occupation: familiarising himself with the unfamiliar. He believed he had a knack for the double life. Maybe the recruitment officer Edgar and his silent companion had clocked that in him even before he knew it himself – not even taking into account the recommendation of the editor of the *Drumkirk* fucking *Gazette*. Or maybe they'd seen the other potential, the one that ends thirty years on in a pile of debris and a bin full of empty whisky bottles. The self-destruct mechanism built into one in ten Scots. Approximately. According to unsubstantiated reports. According to Croick. Anyway. He walked the grimy streets, through drizzle and wind and the sulky glare of street lamps, till he could have walked them blind. He hung out in bars and cafés, followed strangers for the sake of following them, listened in on arguments and assignations, threats, promises, worked out who was paying for protection, who was taking, who were the men behind the rackets and who were the men behind the men. He watched, watched, watched, identifying the amateurs and the pros, the day trippers and the lifers, the ones who lived in fear and the ones who didn't give a fuck. He read the tarts' cards in doorways and cracked the codes for every straight and weird sexual service they were selling; he lingered at the edges of deals and exchanges; he bypassed the ranks of girlie mags – *Poetic Beauty, Femme, Beautiful Britons, Funfare, Titter* – and insinuated himself into back rooms and behind counters where the real porn was kept. He paced out the long and short distances between the overworld of Westminster and Whitehall and the underworld of Soho and Notting Hill. He spotted MPs, junior ministers and senior civil servants on their furtive journeys to particular addresses, and he worked out what their tastes and proclivities were. Some like Bishopsgate, some like Maida Vale. In the summer of 1962, around the time Macmillan sacked a third of his Cabinet and another nine ministers outside it, Peter noted an increase in the number of politicians taking taxis to addresses that weren't their marital homes. Ach well, they had to work off their frustrations somehow. Dean Acheson, the ex-US Secretary of State, put it neatly in a speech at West Point at the end of the year: *Great Britain has lost an Empire and not yet found a role.* Indeed. Why not have some fun while you're waiting? Peter filed all the fun details away in the mental vaults. Call it professional interest, call it saving for the future. He liked the idea that he knew things about people who didn't even know he existed.

Once or twice he went with a tart himself, a different one each time. It was all right; nothing more or less than that. He kind of stepped outside himself, watched himself doing it. If he got kicks from anything, it was from that: observation, not action. He was a model customer: clean, no fuss, no emotion, no surprises, money up front, thank you, darling, thank you, love. The girls thought he was lonely, a Scotch boy far from home wanting some comfort. Maybe he was, or maybe he was happiest being alone. Maybe he didn't actually want intimacy but liked the pretence of it. They put it down to loneliness, he put it down to experience. He knew there was every chance he himself was being watched, and didn't care. Whoever was watching him it wouldn't be Canterbury. Somebody else, the same cut as himself, a bad fit. Somebody out on the fringe. Somebody who'd expect him to be like that.

Jesus. Was that really his name, his real name? Henry Canterbury? Jesus.

He enjoyed a drink.
    No, correction. He enjoyed drink.
    No, correction. He liked to drink.
    He didn't know he liked to drink until he liked it too much not to. It wasn't that he couldn't handle it. He could handle it all right. It wasn't that there was a bit of him saying, Don't do this, Peter, don't do this, it's bad for you. Like smoking was bad for you. He cut out the fags around 1970. Clearly they *were* bad for you. But the drink? No. The drink was good for him. The drink kept him going. That self-destruct button: he'd have pushed it a lot fucking sooner if it hadn't been for the drink.
    Maybe he should have.

In early 1963 the Profumo revelations were still not out in the open and the collapse of public faith in Macmillan's government was yet to take place, but the Vassall incident had been a warning shot. Kim Philby, the 'third man' despite the pack of lies Macmillan told the Commons back in 1955, had just shipped out of Beirut for Moscow, a nasty reminder of past scandals. You could smell it in the air: the whiff of decay mixed with the scent of spring. Wind of change, right enough. You were waiting for something to happen, something you didn't yet know about but maybe you'd recognise it when it came along.

The February sky outside his window was as drab as the walls of his office. The window was so small and so high that the only thing you could see through it *was* the sky. Canterbury came in, as usual without knocking. Peter hated that: the presumption of senior rank, which was really the presumption of having been to a top public school and Oxford. Christ, you might have just dropped a really poisonous one, or be playing with yourself behind the desk. Not that he would be, but it was the principle. No bastarding way he could ever walk into Canterbury's office without knocking and waiting for an answer.

Bond! Canterbury said, in that irritating manner he had of sounding surprised to find him there. No, don't get up. How are things?

Fine, sir.

Good. Somebody mentioned to me the other day that you've started calling yourself Peter.

Yes, sir.

Why is that?

Too much confusion with the other James Bond, sir.

Canterbury's sceptical gaze swept round the barren room. Do you think so? he said. I haven't seen this film, what's it called –?

Dr No.

– so I couldn't comment. Never read any of the books. Never met Fleming. Before my time. Colourful character, apparently. More fancy than fact. The film certainly sounds a little colourful. Racier than, ah, this. Do you really think people will be confused?

Possibly, sir. Or make unhelpful comparisons. *Like they already do every time I go for a piss.*

Nothing to do with the other *Doctor* films, is it? The ones with Dirk Bogarde?

Nothing at all, sir.

I find them rather amusing. Anyway, about changing your name, is this a permanent decision?

Yes, sir. I'm not really changing my name. It's more of an adjustment.

Redeployment of existing resources, eh? Well, you should run these things by me but I can see your point. Once knew a chap. Scientist. Surname Duck. First name Donald. Absolutely genuine.

One of yours, Aberdonian I think. Brilliant mind, but nobody really took him seriously once the Walt Disney duck came along. Well, I expect you'll survive. This other James Bond business sounds very far-fetched. Shouldn't think it'll last.

I think it's caught the public imagination, sir.

Canterbury was staring at some marks on the wall where there had once been, before Peter's time, a row of pictures. Really? he said.

Like the Beatles, sir. Who were going to be huge too, Peter knew it. 'Please Please Me' was at number one in the pop charts. Outside of his working life, he could feel change everywhere.

The Beatles, Canterbury repeated. Yes, well, we'll see. It wasn't clear which he was dismissing as worthless, Peter's judgement or the Beatles' music. Maybe both. Probably he was trying to remember what the pictures on the wall had been of. Whereas Peter was thinking: Donald Duck, James Bond, the Beatles. These names happen and they change everything. The world shape-shifts in the wake of their arrival. We must be, we have to be, aware of this.

Canterbury had sent him a note a few days earlier asking him to look out what they had on C. M. Grieve, better known as the poet Hugh MacDiarmid. He was a member of the Committee of 100, a group of prominent troublemakers set up by Bertrand Russell a few years before to promote civil disobedience in protest against nuclear weapons. MacDiarmid was always firing off letters to the press, and made frequent trips behind the Iron Curtain to give poetry readings. Peter had summarised the files on Grieve on a single sheet. Canterbury glanced over it.

What do you think? Dangerous? Conspiring to bring down the state?

Was Canterbury just testing him or did he genuinely want to know? And how could he possibly *not* know?

Not much of a conspirator, sir. Whatever his opinions are, he doesn't keep them hidden.

Still a thorn in our flesh, though, would you say?

He makes a lot of noise, sir, but very few people pay him much attention.

That doesn't mean he's not dangerous.

Most of the Scottish people don't even know he's talking, let alone what he's talking about. You could say he's completely out of touch. Or they're out of touch with him.

There's a difference, is there?

Yes, sir. One school of thought says he's ahead of his time, and always has been.

Canterbury looked at him strangely, as if he'd just said something self-incriminating. Which school of thought is that, then?

Among the literati – some of the literati – he's regarded as a prophet. Others just hate his guts.

We've been watching him for thirty years, I see.

Yes, sir. He's an old man now. I can't see the point really.

Canterbury frowned. Can't see the point? Constant vigilance, *that's* the point. Goodness, you've been with us long enough now to know that. What about his connection with the Nationalists?

They threw Grieve out years ago. He's a Communist.

I'm well aware of that, Bond. And I also know there are parts of Scotland that are little less than Soviet fiefdoms. The question is, are there connections between the Nationalists and the Communists? Are Grieve and his associates able to make those connections and cause any serious trouble?

In my view, sir, no. Absolutely not. Yes, there are pockets of support for the CP still, but they're getting fewer by the year. And the Scots aren't about to vote for independence either. There's nothing in it for them in material terms. Anyway, who would they vote for? A few poets and a couple of farmers? They haven't got the imagination. He was surprised at how angry, almost impassioned, he sounded.

Canterbury assumed a grave, headmasterly expression. We're not concerned with voting, though, are we? Not our business. But tell me more about the poets. Poets can be trouble. Look at the Irish. What do we have on Grieve that's recent?

Nothing of any substance. Most of what we do have is pre-war. *This man is a menace. This man and his wife are sworn enemies of the British state.* That's what we were saying then. The British state doesn't need to lose any sleep over Hugh MacDiarmid.

In your opinion.

And the state's presumably, sir. It's been paying him a Civil List pension since 1950.

Attlee, Canterbury said, as if he'd just trodden on a slug.

Grieve's seventy, Peter said. He's been spouting the same claptrap for decades. Have you tried reading his poetry?

That's your job.

Well, it's impenetrable. We should ignore him. Everybody else does.

Not true. The literary world had fêted him on his seventieth birthday even if it was divided about him. A collected edition of his poems had been published to mark the birthday and Peter had stolen a copy from Foyles so he could see what the fuss was about. He could have bought it and put in an expense claim but he preferred to steal. He didn't understand much of what he read, except the obviously polemical stuff, but there was something in the earlier work – the lyrics MacDiarmid had made up, so it was said, by trawling through old Scots dictionaries – that he found disturbingly fascinating. They lured you in, hooked you. It was weird, because if he stood back from them he could see them as mere sterile arrangements of dead words. But they were more than that. He felt, reading them, that they put him in touch with some kind of throbbing undercurrent of life, something simultaneously ancient and modern, tiny and huge, parochial yet soaring into space. They made him feel uneasy. But they were just poems, so how could they possibly have that kind of effect?

When Peter urged Canterbury to ignore MacDiarmid it was almost like he was trying to keep the poet to himself. He didn't know if he believed the old man to be harmless. He kind of hoped he wasn't.

Canterbury said, His wife said she'd like to cut the Queen's throat, if I remember rightly?

Peter pulled himself back. Yes. Again, pre-war. Referring to the Queen Mother, of course. Valda Grieve thinks Cornwall should be independent.

So what do we conclude? That they're powerless?

Powerless and penniless. The more Scottish Nationalism is associated in the minds of the people with Grieve and others like him, the less likely it is that it'll ever have any kind of mass appeal. Let them get on with it.

He supported the extremists who blew up pillar boxes when the present Queen came to the throne.

He was bound to, sir. He's a republican. He doesn't believe in
monarchy and in particular he doesn't believe in the English
monarchy. It was the presence of the numeral in 'EIIR' that people
really objected to. Since there never was an Elizabeth I of Scotland.

People?

Some people, sir. The extremists.

Canterbury said, Do you know, Bond, you almost sound
sympathetic. How old were you when the Coronation Stone was
. . . stolen?

That pause before the last word. Canterbury's idea of a trap, to
see if he'd dispute the terminology.

Ten, sir.

And how did it make you feel?

Feel, sir?

Yes. Did it make you feel good? Did your heart do a wee
Highland fling?

Peter's expression was deadpan but *Fuck off, you patronising
bastard* was what he was thinking.

I don't remember feeling anything very much, sir, he said.
(Delight, elation, euphoria. *Good on you, whoever you are.* The same
when the Edinburgh pillar box blew up.)

One thing leads to another. We don't want bombs going off in
Scotland again.

I think that's a very remote possibility.

One of Grieve's acolytes might try something.

I doubt it, sir. But if by some miracle one of them did gain the
technical ability to make a bomb they'd almost certainly blow
themselves up with it. So we'd gain both ways. There'd be some
good bad publicity about extreme nationalism, and there'd be a
dead extremist as well.

There was a pause. Canterbury looked at the ceiling, around the
room, up at the window. His gaze ran along the row of absent
pictures. As if what Peter had said had never occurred to him
before. Eventually he spoke.

We don't want it to get that far. We want to stop things long
before they happen.

Why?

Why? Because it gets messy, Bond. And there's always the

danger, you know, that one creates martyrs. The last thing one wants is a martyr. Our policy is containment, not persecution. If we ever have to resort to persecution, then we'll have failed. You understand that, don't you?

Yes, sir.

Good. Well, nothing more to be done for now. But constant vigilance, Bond, constant vigilance. We don't want to get caught napping.

When the pillar-box campaign started Jimmy was twelve, a good age to appreciate it. It was half-comedy, half-adventure, like the *Beano* and the *Wizard* simultaneously. But Jimmy Bond read about it avidly in the senior section of the public library in Drumkirk, where they'd allowed him a ticket because he'd read everything in the junior section. He went there on Saturday mornings and sat with the old men in heavy overcoats, turning the pages of the *Glasgow Herald*, the *Weekly Scotsman*, *Punch* and the *Illustrated London News*. The pillar box that received most attention was in a new housing scheme on the south side of Edinburgh. The Corporation had decreed, apparently believing in the power of historical romance to ennoble ordinary lives, that all the streets in the scheme be named after characters from Walter Scott's novels: Redgauntlet Terrace, Ravenswood Avenue, Balderston Gardens, and so forth. In November 1952, nine months after Elizabeth became Queen but seven months before her coronation in Westminster Abbey, a new Royal Mail pillar box bearing the legend 'EIIR' is installed on the corner of Sir Walter Scott Avenue and Gilmerton Road. Three days later its bright red paint is covered with tar. It's cleaned up. A week later the police, acting on a tip-off, retrieve an envelope full of explosive from the box. Shortly after that the numerals in 'EIIR' are obliterated with white paint. It's cleaned again. A week later there's another attempt to blow the thing up, and a month after that the numerals are freshly vandalised and further repairs take place. Finally, the day before St Valentine's Day, somebody puts the pillar box out of its misery with a parcel of gelignite. When it is replaced, only a Scottish crown adorns the new box, without any letters or numerals. The Postmaster General has got the message, and the new monarch remains anonymous on all Scottish post boxes installed thereafter. A victory for common sense, or common hooliganism, depending on your point of view.

Not long afterwards Jimmy was on a bus going to Drumkirk and a couple of young, bearded men in duffelcoats started to sing:

O, Sky-High Joe was on the go, some gelignite tae buy,
Sae he goes tae the Carron Iron Works tae get a good supply,
Ricky doo-dum-day, doo-dum-day,
Ricky-dicky doo-dum-day.

They sang two or three verses and broke into laughter at the end, and the weird thing was the other, older folk on the bus didn't object, they laughed too. And Jimmy thought, how did the police manage not to catch him, this mysterious saboteur with a pantomime sense of humour? Had they not been watching that pillar box day and night? Well, they had but they couldn't go on doing that for ever, and they'd had to leave its mouth open for the general public to stick their legitimate mail in. Sky-High Joe had not been working alone, Jimmy concluded. There'd been folk looking out for him, telling him when the coast was clear. The cops were useless. *He'd* have caught Joe. He knew even then that he had the right temperament, the patience, to be a spy.

But maybe he wouldn't have handed him in. Maybe he'd just have observed, let him get away with it. The way his cheeky demolition job had pissed off the stuffed shirts, people like Canterbury, it would have been worth it.

A voice in his head. Or he hopes that's where it is, anyway. Let's say he'll be happier if that's the case. Voices outside his head but inside the flat he does not need.

Peter, Peter, in 1963 what were you? You were twenty-three, a servant of Her Majesty's Secret State. You should have felt guilty about these seditious musings, but you didn't, did you? You couldn't help it, you were infected with the spirit of the age. You despised the values and attitudes of the people you worked for. But do you think they couldn't see that? Do you think they were really that stupid?

He remembers thinking that they were. He remembers thinking that he was smarter than them, that they didn't know him deep down. He remembers saying to himself, I'm not going to rock their boat but I'm not bailing it out for them either.

He pours another drink, just a splish. Another. Splosh. Another. Splash. More. Fool. Him.

Something in his attitude must have got under Canterbury's skin, though. Not so stupid. He kept coming back with supplementary questions. What do you believe in? God? Doesn't matter. Country? Good, but which country? Scotland, England, the United Kingdom? Not England, Peter said, to get a laugh out of him. It was the wrong thing. Canterbury had no sense of humour when it came to such matters.

Look here, Bond, you're sailing a little close to the wind, you know. It's all very well you saying that kind of thing to me, within these walls, but it could lead you into some very dark places indeed.

It sounded like a warning against the perils of masturbation.

What do you mean, sir?

Separatism, Bond. Nationalism. Fascism, even. Didn't the Scottish Nationalist Party – Canterbury was constitutionally, interesting word, incapable of giving the SNP its correct title – publish a pamphlet a few years ago asking whether we were human? We the English, I mean. My God, that's only a step away from building gas chambers.

I think the title was tongue in cheek, sir. (*The English: Are They Human?* There was a copy in the files.) It was put out by a group within the party. The 55 Group. Formed in 1955. The party expelled them shortly after. You won't find a more cautious, respectable independence movement in the world than the SNP, sir.

I'd rather not find them at all.

Later, Peter ordered up the pamphlet, just to remind himself that it was as harmless as he recalled. Actually it was pretty strong stuff. He was surprised at the vehemence with which it condemned the English: *putrid with sexual perverts and shameless adulterers in high places.* Not pleasant. But the leadership had swiftly ejected the troublemakers. You got the impression that the SNP just wanted a quiet life.

Just shows how wrong you can be. A few years down the road you could hardly hear yourself think for all the noise the Nats started making. As for the adulterers in the English establishment, their day was just around the corner.

He comes to with a start. Must have dropped off. Something on his arm, fuck fuck fuck he brushes it off furiously, okay it's okay, nothing there.

He's out in a sweat. He's wrapped in a sheet of sweat.

There's something in the room with him.

This isn't supposed to happen. It can't be happening. He's not off the booze. Dimly he makes out the bottle of High Commissioner. That proves it. Far from off the booze. But there's something in the room, a scratching sound, he can hear it, maybe whatever was on his arm is now somewhere else in the room.

The problem's not the drink. The problem is he's not drinking enough. Got to keep the fuckers at bay.

Or is this the endgame, the other endgame, not the political one, when the drink can't keep the horrors at bay and the horrors can't keep you off the drink? Is that where he's got to?

The sound was not, definitely not, in his head. It came from a corner of the room, a splashing in the paper swamp of political ideas. A sound like a mouse riffling through the pages of *Scottish Vanguard*, *Scottish Worker*, *Red Weekly*, *Red Rag*, *79 Group News*, *Crann-Tara*, *Radical Scotland*. Too big for a mouse though. More like a rat. Oh fuck, has he got rats? He doesn't think he could handle rats.

He peers through the haze. Hopeless. Realises he's gone to sleep with his reading glasses on. No wonder he's toiling. There's an east coast haar smeared all over the lenses. He takes them off. Can see the High Commissioner better now. Clutches him by the neck and tips him to the glass. Thank you, Your Excellency. Ah yes. Much better.

Or maybe not, because he catches something in his side vision. There's a kind of gremlin thing sitting on top of the piles of magazines. A gremlin? Concentrate. He looks straight at it, it disappears. Looks from the side, there it is again. Like a troglodyte, no not troglodyte. Scandinavian goblin thing. Troll. Could be cave-dwelling right enough. Ugly wee fucker. Grey-brown, pointy lugs, wicked teeth, lizardy skin. Couple of feet tall. Just sitting there, watching him. Concentrate and it'll go away. Does he want it to go away? Yes, please. He's seen its sisters and brothers before. The last time he stopped for a few days they came out of the walls at him, dozens of them, it was all he could do to keep them off, swinging wildly, flinging cushions, papers, pushing them back under the fucking wallpaper with the long-handled brush. So what the fuck is this one doing out on its own? Not a rat, thank fuck, but still.

Thought you wanted somebody to talk to? So talk to me.

Strangulated sort of voice. Sounds like it's got a cold. Like himself. He's got a cold. A permanent dreep at the nose, rasping noise in the throat whenever he speaks.

He's puzzling this one out, trying to establish if he said it or the beastie did, when, from over his shoulder –

Don't listen to that brute. Talk to me.

Nasal tones but no cold this time. He recognises it – the first voice from a while back. He turns round but it's not a gremlin or a troll, it's a butler. Aye, a fucking butler holding a silver salver with a white serviette draped over one arm, and speaking like Michael Jackson. No, not Michael, the other one, that heid Scotch lackey in *Upstairs, Downstairs*. Gordon Jackson, keeper of the keys, holding the downstairs mob back from rushing upstairs and slaughtering their masters and mistresses with their own silver cutlery. Hudson, that's who this butler sounds like. Black trousers and tails, white tie and stuffed shirt, you can just see the glisten of his silvery chest poking through between the buttons. Eh? The what? Oh fuck, it's not a man, it's a fish *posing* as a butler. The black breeks turn into a kind of tapered skirt at the bottom and coming out of it is a fishtail, on which the butler is balancing.

The troll on the other hand is naked.

A kind of merbutler, only all fish. Apart from the clothes. A buttlefish.

What the fuck is going on?

Is it them? Croick and Canterbury come back to freak him into throwing himself through the window? Two storeys down and splat on to the tarmac? But which one's which?

Well, he thinks. I'm no fuckin daein it.

Right, he says, and it is definitely him this time, he knows it because the butler has shuffled round on his fishtail and taken up position alongside the troll but just out of touching range, so he can see them both at once and neither of their mouths is moving, just the malevolent fish-eye of the one and the evil wee glint of the other. Right. Since we're all here.

But of course it isn't Croick and it isn't Canterbury. How could it be? It's a troll, a fish and Peter Bond. Furthermore, and he sees this with something of an uplift in his heart, what does that look like on the silver salver but another bottle of the High Commissioner?

Did he buy two? He thinks maybe he did. But now the Gordon Jackson creature's got it. Here's a test. He reaches out a hand towards the buttlefish and it gives a shimmer, and when he stretches closer it begins to fade. He pulls back, it solidifies again. Okay. Now then. He reaches for the bottle, which is slightly closer, slowly, slowly, don't panic the buttlefucker, almost there, almost, NOW! He lunges, grabs the bottle round the belly, it slides away for a horrible moment he thinks it's going to crash but he holds on jarring his knee against the low table in front of him fuck fuck fuck he's sprawled across the table clutching the bottle it's all right it's all right Your Excellency I've got you. He pulls himself back off the table, which it turns out is where the second bottle was the whole time, not on the silver tray at all, his knee is throbbing but yes yes yes it's real, it's his, numero twa, solid as a fucking rock Your Excellency.

He sits back, rubbing his knee. Looks like it's going to be a long night.

The buttlefish says, in a completely different, English, voice, *So what have you been doing with yourself since we last met?*

It's Edgar! Peter sits up straight, rubs his eyes. The buttlefish has gone, but sitting in the armchair opposite him is the very same guy who interviewed him nearly fifty years ago, and not looking a day older either. This is definitely better. The High Commissioner doing the business. By Christ he doesn't hang about, sorts the natives out good style.

He hunts around for the gremlin. Gone too, *yes!!!* Anybody or anything else taken its place? Doesn't look like it.

I always wanted to know, he says, is Edgar your first name or your surname?

Edgar inclines his head slightly. There's a kind of delayed-reaction shimmer.

Surname of course, he says. Why would I tell you my first name?

Peter does the same trick with Edgar as he did with the buttlefish. Reaches towards him, pulls back. Edgar fades, returns, fades, returns. And now he understands. Edgar's dead. This is his ghost. All right. He can handle ghosts. He is neither unfamiliar with nor disturbed by the concept of ghosts. Plus, major benefit, he doesn't have to offer him a drink.

Where were we? Edgar says. 1963, I think. Would you care to give me your views on the last days of the Macmillan administration?

Peter says, Macmillan's health wasn't good, and the political fallout from the Profumo affair damaged him irreparably. He resigned in October, replaced as Prime Minister by Sir Alec Douglas-Home.

EDGAR: A safe pair of hands.

BOND: That's one interpretation. Or you could say Supermac's last act is to bypass Rab Butler, the Deputy PM but too liberal by half, and land the party leadership in the lap of another toff. No election, no public debate, just a bunch of grandees sorting it out over the port.

EDGAR: May I remind you that Macmillan's grandfather was born on a croft in the Isle of Arran?

BOND: May I remind you that Home was the fourteenth Earl of Home until he renounced his peerage, and that both of them were at Eton?

EDGAR: It's my view that Sir Alec was an honourable and decent man, whatever you may think of his aristocratic background.

BOND: He was a sanctimonious upper-class tosser. What was it he came out with when he was Macmillan's Foreign Secretary? 'The British people are prepared to be blown to atomic dust if necessary.' *If necessary?* To prove whose fucking point? He never asked me about it.

EDGAR: He was standing up to the Russians.

BOND: Oh, like the way he stood up to Hitler when he was Chamberlain's bag-carrier at Munich? Fucking marvellous.

EDGAR: I can tell you, young man, you would not have been

successful at interview if you had employed that kind of language or displayed that kind of attitude.

BOND: Aye, well, I'm sixty-eight and it turns out I wasn't so successful anyway, so fuck you.

EDGAR (*shimmering*): I will leave if you do not restrain your abusive tongue.

BOND (*reaching for the bottle*): All right, all right. Don't go. This is getting good. Macmillan resigns, Home takes over, renounces his peerage so he can sit in the Commons. Conveniently the Member for Kinross and West Perthshire has just died and the by-election hasn't been held, the Unionist candidate George Younger steps aside and Home becomes MP for the safest Tory seat in Scotland, and Prime Minister of the United Kingdom.

EDGAR: That all seems straightforward enough. Your grasp of the facts is impressive, considering . . . (*he waves a semi-transparent arm at the High Commissioner*)

BOND (*ignoring him*): But his premiership is a holding exercise. The next General Election has to happen by October 1964. The Tories lose, and Harold Wilson is in with a majority of four seats.

EDGAR: I am interested in your interpretation of these events, political and otherwise. Those in the public domain and those . . . not, as yet.

BOND: You can't do much with a four-seat majority. So Wilson goes to the polls again in 1966, taking on Edward Heath, who has succeeded Home as Conservative leader, and wins a huge majority.

EDGAR: And what happened next?

Next? Everything went to pigs and whistles. 1966, the year the *Daily Worker* was relaunched as the *Morning Star*, the summer of 'Sunny Afternoon', 'Paint It Black', 'Yellow Submarine'. Mostly bright, occasional showers. But clouds were gathering in the economy: a growing balance-of-payments deficit, rising prices, rising unemployment. Peter was getting used to the London climate.

Peter! Canterbury said as he walked in. No, don't get up, he said, as usual, and plonked himself in the chair on the other side of the desk.

Peter was instantly wary. Canterbury had never called him anything but Bond before.

How are things at home?

By *home* Canterbury meant Slaemill, where Peter had been a month before, shouldering his father's coffin to its grave.

All right, he said, thinking, *why would you give a damn?*

How's your mother coping since your father . . .?

The kindly way Canterbury didn't finish the question was intensely irritating. It sounded like he'd taken a course – unwillingly – in how to be sympathetic.

She's fine, thank you. My sisters are near by. They look after her.

Nevertheless, Canterbury sighed, it must be difficult. He wasn't very old, was he?

Fifty-three, sir.

Canterbury shook his head. Terrible. It was his heart, I think you said?

Yes, sir. *Jesus, what the fuck is this?*

Well, it's been a great shock to you all. Your mother especially. She'd appreciate it if you were nearer, I imagine.

He was imagining rather too much for Peter's liking. How the hell did he know who'd been shocked and how much? And why was he professing to care? When Peter had taken a week's leave around the funeral there'd been none of this. And that word *nearer*. Peter grew more uneasy.

I have some difficult news, Peter. (That was twice. Something was definitely up.) As you know, the present, er, government is facing something of an economic crisis. It has been decreed that savings must be made in public expenditure. Sacrifices are required, right across the board. One would think, of course, that the security of the nation would be protected from the effects of departmental cuts and bureaucratic penny-pinching, but one would be wrong.

Peter worked it out just before Canterbury coughed and said, I'm afraid your time with us here is at an end.

I'm being sacked?

Made redundant, I believe the correct term is. I'm sorry, but there's nothing I can do about it. I am, in this instance, only the messenger.

Is anybody else being . . . made redundant?

I can't answer that question. Operational reasons. Now don't despair. We'll do what we can to soften the blow. Indeed, we can help you to relocate, find new employment and so forth, but there it is, in a nutshell. In the circumstances, however, I mean your personal circumstances, well, perhaps it would be best for you and your family if you were back in Scotland. Yes?

Peter had stood up without intending to. His legs had demanded action if they weren't going to kick the desk in anguish and frustration. Kick fucking Canterbury with his *indeed, we can help*. Pompous fucking arsehole. He walked to the wall with the high window in it and looked up. The London sky was blue. Six years of writing and filing reports had earned him a glimpse of blue sky. Now this. He turned.

You're sending me back to Scotland?

We're not sending you anywhere. But in the circumstances . . .

But I don't want to go, sir. There's no need. My mother is perfectly fine.

I understand, Canterbury said. Look, he said, this is going to happen, whether you like it or not. Whether *we* like it or not. You will no longer be employed by the Service. But we value you, Peter. We've invested in you. We don't want to cut you adrift.

That's decent of you, Peter said. If Canterbury heard the irony, he chose not to acknowledge it.

We do what we can. But you can do something for us too, *if* you go back to Scotland.

What do you mean?

Let's say this would be about redefining our relationship. You know the lie of the land up there. Your particular strengths have been underutilised here. In Scotland, you would be of *immense* use to us.

I've disappointed you in some way, Peter said. You're getting rid of me.

Not at all. Don't see this as a step back. The world is changing. London is no longer the centre of everything. Scotland . . .

Scotland what? Peter said. He could have wept. They were going to send him back. Like faulty goods.

Things are happening in Scotland, Canterbury said.

What the fuck was he talking about? At the General Election Labour had wiped the floor with the other parties in Scotland, gaining two-thirds of the available seats. The Nationalists had managed to contest just twenty-three seats and lost their deposits in ten of them. *Nothing* was happening in Scotland.

But we have people there already, sir, he said, aware that he sounded pleading.

That's true. We have the political parties covered, the trade unions, CND. But what are we missing, hmm? What are we missing? He lapsed into silence once more. Then: Unfortunately, as far as you're concerned, we have a problem.

We do? Peter said.

You've been inside. Once somebody's been inside, that's it, strictly speaking. Agents are agents and the Service is the Service and never the twain shall meet. Well, obviously the two *do* meet, but you understand my meaning. In your case, however . . .

Peter waited.

We need to be flexible, Canterbury continued. *You* need to be flexible. We have a role for you, if you want it.

Peter said nothing.

It would be, shall we say, freelance. Floating. You'd be an agent. We'd give you an officer contact.

Someone who'd run me, Peter said. I'd be outside.

More useful outside. There'd be a period of no contact whatsoever. Then, when we were ready, we'd get in touch. We'd want you to identify what's bubbling under rather than what's already on the surface.

Now Peter knew he was being both screwed and shunted. Because, whatever Canterbury pretended, London *was* still the centre of everything.

Nothing is definitely decided, Canterbury said, but I didn't want you being left in the cold while plans that will affect you are being formulated.

Nothing is definitely decided except that everything's already been decided, Peter said. And I'm out of a job.

Canterbury sighed. Well, yes, there is that. But flexibility, that's the name of the game, Peter. I assure you, we *will* be in touch. And now – he sighed again, and slowly, respectfully, like a hospital visitor beside the bed of a dying patient, got to his feet – now you need to go and see Personnel.

Peter looked blankly at him.

About relocation, job options, severance pay, that kind of thing. He waved his hand vaguely, indicating that such matters were not really his concern, then added, We look after our people, you know, when this happens.

When Peter didn't move, a kind of mild horror spread over Canterbury's features.

Obviously, this is with immediate effect. You understand that, don't you? You can't stay on here now. Not since I've told you all this. Security, you know. You do see that, don't you?

He could only nod at his own stupidity. Obviously he would be escorted off the premises. Obviously that would happen at once. Obviously it wasn't even a question of clearing his desk. Someone else would do that.

There were two things in Scotland that the Service cared about. One was the presence of nuclear weapons in the Firth of Clyde: American submarines armed with the Polaris missile system were based in the Holy Loch and it was important to keep the Americans sweet since they had agreed to supply Polaris to a new fleet of four British submarines, in the process of being constructed, that would also be based on the Clyde, at Faslane. It was vital to keep the anti-nuclear lobby under surveillance, limiting its ability to exert any serious influence on either public opinion or Labour in government.

The other thing, on the other side of the country, was as yet not even a ripple on the surface of people's political consciousness. It might not come to anything, but if it did it had the potential to be huge. *Great Britain has lost an Empire and not yet found oil*, as Mr Acheson might have put it. The government had started issuing licences for oil and gas exploration in the North Sea. Hardly anybody except the licensees were paying attention, and even if they found anything the technical challenges of extraction would be enormous. So far any hopeful signs were in the English sector, but there was an awful lot of sea around Scotland. What nobody wanted was a technical, industrial challenge that turned into a political one.

*

Your role would be, shall we say, freelance. Floating. He can still hear Canterbury's voice, its smug smoothness, the calculation behind the apologies. What he was really saying: you're not one of us, we're sending you back, but actually because we've brought you this far you can't go back, not completely, so now you occupy this special place we have for people like you, on the outside of the inside. No man's land. Ghost territory. You can be useful there. You can be utilised. Naturally we don't mean that in quite the way we say it. Confused? Good, that's how we like you.

Maybe they thought he was a closet Nat. Maybe he was. They were shipping him out in any case, bringing in other people. Correction: they were probably already in place, in another part of the building, or in another building altogether. Sizing up the Scottish problem. He was being forced out and it was up to him if he left London, but if he didn't, if he didn't go back across the Border then they would do just what Canterbury had said they didn't want to do, cut him adrift. Peter couldn't afford for that to happen. The murky half-world he inhabited meant more to him than a so-called normal life in the sunlight. So all right then. He'd show the bastards. He'd make himself indispensable to them. They'd have to come north or summon him south so often for his angle on things that eventually it would be easier to take him back. He would be the oracle that pronounced on the Scottish Question.

He played, in other words, right into their hands. And that was even before he was introduced to Croick.

Peggy said, Have you done something wrong?
No, he said. I've been made redundant.
I don't know what that means, she said.
My job no longer exists so I can't do it any more.
You've been sacked, she said.
No, it's not the same. There are staff cuts right across government. It's to save money.
It seems to me, she said, that they wouldn't sack you without a reason. Not the government.
He tried again. The reason is they're economising, he said. Some people were lucky, I wasn't. That's all there is to it.
He'd arrived back off the train, having phoned to say he was

coming home for a break. She'd had a phone put in since Hugh
died. She'd have guessed something was up from his voice. She
hadn't laid on a feast. But she still stood with her back to the
bunker, arms folded, watching him steadily.

So why didn't you tell me when you telephoned? You said you
were just coming for a few days. How long are you going to be
here?

I didn't want to worry you. I thought it would be easier if I told
you face to face. And I don't know how long. Not long, I hope. Just
till I get my own place. I've got an interview for a job in Glasgow.

In Glasgow? Once she might have thought that a good move, a
step up in the world, but not now. What are you going to do in
Glasgow?

It's a job in a bookshop. I'm in with a good chance. They've
given me a reference.

She shook her head at him.

I don't have any choice, he said.

Your father would be so disappointed, she said. He was that
proud of you when you went to London. We both were.

I know, he said, but it can't be helped. And I'll get out from
under your feet as quick as I can.

You'll not be under my feet, she said. He noticed she didn't call
him anything. It had been the same at the funeral. She'd finally
accepted that he didn't answer to James or Jimmy, but she couldn't
get used to him being Peter. Especially now.

They said you had a great future ahead of you, she said.

Who said?

The men that came to talk to us about you, when you were
away doing your National Service.

What men?

You'd done all these tests and you'd passed with flying colours,
they said. And you were just the kind of young man they were
looking for. You had a great future, they said.

Somebody came to see you?

Of course they did. We had to sign the Official Secrets Act
because of the line of work you were going to do. I don't
understand it. Why would they go to all that trouble and then sack
you, unless you'd done something wrong?

A dimness came over his eyes, like a veil. He couldn't be bothered disputing the word *sack* again. He felt a desperate need for a drink. They came and interviewed you? he said. And you had to sign the Act? Why on earth didn't you tell me?

Because we said we wouldn't, she said. It was a secret, an Official Secret. Your father said enough to let you know we knew, that was all. We kept *our* side of the bargain.

What bargain? he said. There was no bargain.

Oh yes there was, she said. We thought so, anyway.

Och, Mum, he said. He didn't know whether to laugh or greet.

Are you finished? She started taking things off the table, cleared his plate and cutlery away. The next thing her back was to him and she was in at the sink.

I think I'll go for a bit of fresh air, he said.

Nearly six years down there and he'd still managed to fit his life into two suitcases. He wasn't going to stay in Slaemill a day longer than he had to. He thought of Drumkirk being the nearest town and it killed him. He thought of the dark, unfriendly Toll Tavern and that that was about the only thing to recommend the place. His bedroom was a box of childhood memories he thought he'd left behind. He took a quarter-bottle to bed with him every night and disposed of it in the morning. It was no way to live.

He was in Glasgow at the start of 1967, installed in a room and kitchen in Partick. His work was half an hour's walk away. The bookshop, narrow and deep, more academic than general trade, was at the west end of Sauchiehall Street. The job was four and a half days a week, in the mail-order department, processing requests from account customers and occasional buyers in far-flung parts of the country and overseas. There were a lot of orders from schools and other institutions. He worked in a dingy room of dark wood at the very back of the shop. He picked the books from stock or sent away to publishers for them. A man could scrabble away in a job like this for years without anyone noticing, slip out for an hour or two without anyone *really* noticing. The position was kind of pushed in his direction, or he was pushed towards it, and although it was never articulated there was an 'understanding' with or on the part of the proprietor. He knew where Peter had come from and the understanding was that there might be occasions when he would need to take a day or two off at short notice and that would be all right. Peter settled into a life of invoices and string and brown paper and prepared for death by a thousand small boredoms while he waited for the contact that might never happen.

And then suddenly things looked better, as though events might have conspired to drop him in the right place at the right time. Something, he realised, *was* stirring in the undergrowth. In March there was a by-election in the safe Labour seat of Glasgow Pollok: the SNP candidate got 22 per cent of the vote, allowing the Tory to slip through and win. In May the Nationalists won a raft of seats at the county and burgh elections and registered twice as many votes as they'd scored in the General Election the year before. The Secretary of State for Scotland, Willie Ross, was scathing, dubbing the Nats 'tartan Tories' in his best no-nonsense manner, but what was happening?

At the end of May Jock Stein's Celtic won the European Cup in Lisbon, and on 1 June the Beatles released *Sergeant Pepper*, but Peter didn't give a toss about either. What caught his attention was the appearance of a new, radical nationalist organisation, the 1320 Club, a 'research group' loosely connected, mainly through dual membership, to the SNP. Its president was Hugh MacDiarmid, now in his mid-seventies but apparently as keen to stir things up as he'd ever been. At last there was some meat for Peter to get his teeth into.

In September, the Queen came to Clydebank to launch the new Cunard liner, the *QE2*. Thousands of people lined the streets, cheering and waving at the royal party, cheering and waving as the massive ship slid into the water. There was bunting, there were banners and flags, happy smiling people, a sense of achievement and celebration even though the yard that had built the liner, John Brown's, was losing its name and being absorbed into the new Upper Clyde Shipbuilders consortium. It was a launch, a beginning, but also it was a conclusion. Peter saw a woman turn her head away from the spectacle as if there were something else catching her attention; he saw in a man's eyes a deeper assessment of what was going on. But what *was* going on?

There was a mood Peter couldn't quite measure. Was he imagining things?

And then, in November, came the Hamilton by-election, and the summons.

Canterbury said, How the *hell* did it happen?

The room swayed, tipped. Peter righted it by shifting slightly in his seat. He wanted a window open or the door but there wasn't a window and you didn't have meetings like this with the door open and anyway clearly the other two weren't finding the atmosphere as oppressive as he was. Then, they hadn't endured a seven-hour bevvy session on the overnight train from Glasgow. All in the call of duty, he might have joked, but he was afraid to open his mouth in case he wasn't able to speak properly.

He was by now a paid-up member of the SNP, and had been in Hamilton often during the by-election, leafleting, canvassing, watching, listening. The contest had been caused by the resignation of the sitting MP, Tom Fraser, who'd gone off to become chairman of the North of Scotland Hydro-Electric Board. The Labour Party could be forgiven for a certain level of complacency – Fraser had won 70 per cent of the vote at the General Election – but the man chosen to succeed Fraser, an ex-miner and local councillor called Alex Wilson, failed to convince people that they weren't being taken for granted. The contrast with the SNP candidate, a vivacious solicitor called Winnie Ewing, was marked. Hamilton wasn't the most prepossessing place in the world, but Ewing was paying it serious attention. In return, the local people started paying attention to her, and to the wider cause of her party: some gut feeling grew that it was time to *do* something about who they were and what they wanted, even if it was just putting an X next to the word *Scottish*. Polling day arrived and at the end of it Ewing had beaten Wilson with two thousand votes to spare.

After the victory, the triumph. An entire train, dubbed the Tartan Express, was ordered to carry Ewing south to take her seat in the House of Commons, and Peter had to move fast for a ticket to be on it. An opportunity, he thought, to gauge the mood and report in style the next day. A couple of Hillman Imps, symbols of sturdy wee Scotland, were used to bring Ewing and her family to the train. Central Station was crowded, awash with lions rampant and saltires. The train was crammed, everybody desperate to be part of the occasion. The singing started before the train pulled out. At Hamilton the platform was lined with cheering supporters, and more folk piled in. At Edinburgh it was the same, even at Newcastle. Then it was non-stop to London. Winnie did a kind of processional through the carriages then retired to the only sleeper carriage so she could be fresh for her induction the next day. For everybody else it was an all-night party. Just when you thought things were winding down another piper would start to blow or a fiddler scrape out another set of tunes and somebody, from somewhere, would produce another bottle of whisky. *Sleep no more. Johnnie Walker hath murdered sleep.* Peter had managed, finally, an hour of semi-consciousness with another man's elbow in his ribs before stumbling off the train in search of a café. Then he'd made his way, as instructed, to an alley off a side street a few minutes from King's Cross. There was an unmarked door at the back of an anonymous building, and a bell. He rang it. After a while a woman opened it, regarded him as if he were a vagrant but let him in anyway, and escorted him along featureless corridors to a featureless room, to meet Henry Canterbury and the man who would be his contact from then on, John Croick.

A fellow Scot, Canterbury said, doing the introductions, and Peter, peering at Croick through his hangover, thought he looked vaguely familiar but was pretty sure he'd not previously come across him. No surprise there. In the game of circles you didn't meet people who mattered until they had a reason to meet you. Peter knew at once that Croick mattered.

Well? Canterbury said accusingly, as if it were Peter's fault. How does a political party – any political party – come from nowhere, absolutely nowhere, and win eighteen thousand votes and a seat in the Commons? Tell me that.

Peter had a foul-tasting mouth and a sore head. They couldn't not be smelling the alcohol on his breath. Canterbury probably thought he'd reverted to type, the drunken Scot decanted on to London's streets. What a contrast with the thin-lipped, cool, dry-as-dust Croick. Yet in spite of everything, maybe because of everything, Peter didn't care. Perversely he felt, for once, that he was in charge. Wrong again.

Not quite from nowhere, he said, savouring the absence of 'sir' at the end of his sentences: after what they'd done to him, fucked if he was going to call Canterbury anything that hinted at respect.

The SNP didn't put up a candidate in Hamilton at the General Election last year. Or the one before that. That's nowhere, isn't it?

There have been signs of growth, Peter said. He made a real effort and carried on. They've been building quite an impressive network of branches over the last few years. Fund-raising like mad. They poured their people into Hamilton because they sensed the voters might be ready for a change. The Labour man wasn't going to give them that. Mrs Ewing, on the other hand, was a very good candidate. Young, articulate, sparky, female. It was Hamilton but it might have happened anywhere.

Wonderful candidate, Canterbury said drily. Good luck to her. But what next? Is this an isolated incident, or can we expect to see seats starting to fall like ninepins?

STOP THE WORLD, SCOTLAND WANTS TO GET ON, Croick intoned, repeating Ewing's campaign slogan. He spoke English like a learned foreigner, faultlessly and without passion. There was a strong accent hidden away in the recesses. Peter tried to pinpoint it: Aberdeen, Buchan, somewhere up there perhaps? He thought, have I met this guy before?

It could be seen as a warning shot, Peter said. Start paying us attention.

How much bloody attention? Canterbury snapped. You've been given a steelworks, car plants, a bridge across the Forth, hydro schemes, new universities, motorways, better housing. It's not as if things haven't got better. What more do you want from us?

Not *us*, Croick said gently. This isn't a you-and-us situation.

Of course not. I meant, what more does Scotland want? The Scots. He threw an angry glance at Peter.

If it were, Croick said, you'd be alone and outnumbered. Eh, Peter?

Peter grinned, warmed by the slight menace in Croick's voice.

From what Peter's been saying, Croick went on, and from a wider political analysis, we can assess that Hamilton is not, necessarily, an isolated incident. The important question is, how do we make it one? How do we ensure it doesn't happen again?

There was a suitable pause while they all considered that, or it seemed to Peter that that was what they were doing. He said:

That's not really our job, is it?

Canterbury said, What isn't?

Fixing elections.

Croick shook his head sadly, implying that of course we wouldn't stoop so low.

Canterbury said, Why not? but not as if he was disputing the issue, more like a teacher coaching a promising pupil, or a quizmaster on TV: *Come on, ten points if you get this right.*

Well, it's democracy, isn't it? The SNP is a legitimate political party. You can't stop people voting for that, not in this country.

No, Croick said, in a careful, perhaps regretful tone. But you could say that about the CP too. That doesn't mean we don't watch what they're up to.

What if people don't really know what they're voting for? Canterbury said. They think they're voting for a fairer, more equal society, or they're asserting a bit of local pride, but then one morning they wake up and find they're living in Albania only with worse weather. Surely we shouldn't allow that to happen?

Do they get good weather in Albania? Croick said.

Are we talking about Communists or Nationalists now? Peter said.

What's the difference? Canterbury said. They'd both change the country irrevocably if they could. There's a balance to be struck between people's aspirations and what, realistically, is in their best interests. You know that as well as I do, Bond. We don't interfere in the political process, but we monitor it.

When necessary, we manage it, Croick said. Peter's right. It goes without saying that we have to respect the democratic will. We *do* respect it. You're both right. But people should be aware of the dangers, the unintended consequences, of indulging their emotions. They need to be *made* aware of them. We can help there.

Yes, we can, Canterbury said.

That's why we have men like you on the ground, Croick said to Peter. This isn't just about Scotland, this is about the whole country. There are groups and individuals all over this island who, well intentioned or otherwise, want to undermine its stability, overthrow its institutions, and impose their own views on everybody else. We guard against that. We secure the premises. That's what we do.

Any state has to protect itself, Canterbury said. If somebody sets out to destroy the state, we take steps to prevent them. It's a legitimate response.

I take it we're all agreed on that, Croick said.

Peter nodded. He was having a relapse. He was also having difficulty remembering that he wasn't inside any more. The way they were talking, the three of them, it was as if he'd been granted special privileges, an old boy who could still remember the school rules. But he hadn't been to that kind of school. He wanted to get out his handkerchief and wipe from his face the clamminess that was threatening to turn into a full-on sweat, but he didn't do it. He thought, there's a double act going on here and I'm not one half of it.

This 1320 Club, Croick said.

Why 1320 again? Canterbury asked. Probably he already knew, but maybe not.

Declaration of Arbroath, Peter said. A letter sent to the Pope by the barons of Scotland six years after Bannockburn, asserting Scotland's independence.

For so long as one hundred of us remain alive, we will never give in to the English, or words to that effect, Croick said helpfully. Anyway, this club. Sounds like it's all over the place ideologically, and half-in, half-out as far as membership of the SNP is concerned. We like that.

The party leadership don't like it, Peter said. It makes them nervous. Anything involving Hugh MacDiarmid makes them nervous.

You said we could ignore him, Canterbury said.

We can, Peter said.

We want you as close as you can get to this club, Croick said. Join if they'll let you. And tell us what they're up to.

I already know what they're up to, Peter said. They're not very discreet. They think they're a think tank. They're busy setting up committees of themselves to develop policies for an independent Scotland – foreign affairs, defence, natural resources. They think independence is coming soon but England won't allow it to happen so there'll need to be a violent struggle. A provisional army directed by a provisional government. Some of them think about this kind of thing so much they're convinced it's going to happen. They *are* the provisional government-in-waiting.

Comic-book stuff, Croick said, and winked at Peter. Have you come across a man called Derek Boothby?

Indirectly, yes, Peter said. In person, no. He produces a monthly paper called *Sgian Dubh*. I'm a subscriber. That's nothing to do with the 1320 Club, but he's also the club's Organiser. That's what he calls himself.

By all accounts he couldn't organise a piss-up in a brewery, Croick said. (Years later, Peter remembers that one. *By all accounts?*) We think he's someone to watch, possibly someone to cultivate. Army background, good connections, very self-assured.

Peter nodded. Things slid inside his head like unsecured cargo on a listing ship. He pictured the densely packed, marginless foolscap sheets of *Sgian Dubh*, saw in the uneven print the passion with which Boothby bashed out prejudices and proposals on his typewriter.

He drops a lot of hints about military training and units scattered about the country, he said. Ninety per cent of it's what you said, comic-book stuff. Maybe all of it.

Nevertheless, he could be useful, Croick said. Get him on his own. Groom him. Take your time.

They talked it through. Frederick or Derek Boothby was in his late fifties, the son of a naval officer and a daughter of the Earl of Limerick. He'd gone to an English public school, done some ranching in South America and then joined the army. In the war he'd served in a tank regiment in North Africa. He still called himself Major, even though he'd been out of the army for fifteen years on a disability pension. Since then he'd flitted from job to job – estate manager, labourer, caravan salesman – in different parts of England. A top-heavy butterfly, Croick said. He'd disappeared for a while, then re-emerged in Edinburgh, a convert

to nationalism and working for the SNP. He and the party didn't
see eye to eye though and he'd moved on, into wilder political
terrain. He was currently living with his third wife in a cottage in
Lanarkshire, from which every month he sent out duplicated
copies of *Sgian Dubh* to subscribers. Boothby's politics, when you
scratched the surface, were about as far to the right as
MacDiarmid's were to the left, and yet the two men seemed to get
on pretty well. They lived about twelve miles apart.

Croick said, If you go round the back of the moon there's a
good chance you'll meet another lunatic coming the other way.

It bothered Peter that they seemed to want him to go chasing
after clumsy butterflies. It wasn't as if Boothby was unique, with
his dreams of being hunted across the moors by helicopters and
tracker dogs. There were plenty of oddballs like him knocking
about on the SNP sidelines: Gaelic revivalists with cut-glass
accents; former Chindits who stood at the foot of the Mound in
Edinburgh on Sunday afternoons berating London rule; men
who'd been Desert Rats, or liaison officers with the Yugoslavian
partisans, who reckoned it was time for a bit of guerrilla action in
the Highlands. The SNP squeamishly tried to keep them all at a
distance, but how could it? Its cause was their cause: they thought
of themselves as the soul and conscience of the party, even if
they'd left it or been thrown out.

Boothby was just another of these, surely? Or was he? Croick
didn't seem to think so. He seemed to take Boothby seriously.
With Croick, there was another dimension.

Can I ask you a question? Peter said, when they'd finished and
he was about to leave.

Go ahead.

Where are you from? I can't place your accent.

Good, Croick said, with a brief grey smile.

EDGAR: What do you mean when you say there was another
dimension with Croick?

BOND (*swilling the whisky in his glass*): Another agenda. Couldn't
work out what it was but it was there. Like he was an independent
operator.

EDGAR: Perhaps he was.

BOND: Then what was he doing there with Canterbury?

EDGAR: Briefing you, by the sound of things. Look, it's in the nature of a state Security Service to have its rogue elements. If you're in the business of defending the realm you're already *thinking* the unthinkable. Sometimes the unthinkable may actually have to be done. What's the golden rule in that eventuality?

BOND: Don't get caught.

EDGAR: Precisely. Rogues are useful. They can do things the Service can't, not directly. They're prepared to get their hands dirty, allowing the Service to keep its own clean. So far so good. But the trouble with rogues is that often they don't know when to stop. They forget where their loyalties ought to lie. Then *they* have to be dealt with. Damage has to be limited, bad apples disposed of.

BOND: Why are you telling me this?

EDGAR: I thought you were telling me. But you appear (*casting an eye round the debris*) to be having a little difficulty sorting it out on your own. Perhaps I can help.

December 1967: the 1320 Club held a press conference in Edinburgh to launch their new magazine, *Catalyst for the Scottish Viewpoint*. Peter attended. If anybody asked he was a freelance reporter. Nobody asked. The event was at Lucky MacLeuchar's, a pub in Newington. MacDiarmid, Boothby and company were behind a row of tables along one wall, the journalists lined up opposite and fired questions. The atmosphere was pipe smoke, kilts and beards. Peter kept well back.

When the meeting ended, he followed Boothby outside and caught up with him striding down the street, taking enormous, noisy breaths of the cold, fresh air. Could he spare a minute or two? He was an admirer, just starting out in journalism, and intended to write a piece about *Catalyst* and its aims. Now that it was up and running, did Boothby mean to keep producing *Sgian Dubh*? Peter sincerely hoped so. He was a subscriber, by the way.

Boothby stopped his steam-engine impressions and gave him an assessing look.

Your name?

Peter Bond.

Ah yes. And what it is you like about *Sgian Dubh*?

He was a big man, the Major, a solid presence in his kilt and black jacket, with bristling knees and eyebrows and a pugnacious jut to his chin. He had large, gnarled hands, a grey beard clipped like a hedge and a great bald expanse of forehead. A genial face but the eyes were intimidating. Peter started to talk. *Sgian Dubh* was practical, hard-hitting, realistic. It not only accepted the likelihood of violence but also planned for it. He liked the frank discussion of military strategy, the appeals for equipment and uniforms, the advice given on guerrilla tactics. He liked the statements printed on behalf of the Scottish Liberation Army. This was courageous, honest stuff. It showed that there were Nationalists who, unlike the pathetically supine, shilly-shallying SNP, meant business. He only hoped that by being so forthright the editor wasn't handing valuable information to the enemy.

Boothby inclined his head. Meaning?

The British state, Peter said.

That imperious stare again. Young man, for whom did you say you work?

I didn't. I work in a bookshop, but I'm also a journalist. Freelance.

And where has your work been published?

Well, I'm just starting out.

Boothby frowned. Peter hung his head, a nice touch.

Nowhere, as yet.

Boothby looked disdainful.

That's why I wanted to speak to you, Peter said. I want to be useful.

The most useful thing you can do, Boothby said, is not waste my time. Do you think I don't already know that every word I publish is read, pored over, by the authorities? I am deliberately taunting them, challenging them. Do you imagine that I don't dupe them into drawing conclusions about my plans that are *entirely misleading*? I have years of experience, young man, which you clearly do not. So please do not suggest to me that I am unwittingly handing information to the enemy.

Peter backed off. He didn't wish to imply . . . He had no doubt Major Boothby knew exactly what he was doing. What he really wanted to say was . . . perhaps in the future, if he could think of a way to put him to work for the cause . . . he'd be more than willing. He only wanted to help. Grovellingly apologetic, he turned to walk away.

The effect was immediate. Boothby came hurrying after him, put a big clutching hand on his arm. Wait. Don't rush off like that. I can tell you're passionate. We'll think of something for you to do. The cause needs new blood, enthusiasm, keen young minds. But you must learn from older and wiser heads. You must learn from me.

It sounded like a command, it was a command, but it was also a plea. Boothby wanted a disciple.

Others from the meeting were catching up. Now wasn't the time. Write to me, Boothby said. You have the address from *Sgian Dubh*? Excellent. And remind me, where are you yourself? In Glasgow? Good, very good. Glasgow is crucial. Now, I must be getting along. What was your name again?

Bond, Peter said. Peter Bond.

He said it just the way Connery did in the films. Boothby was oblivious.

Peter had a lot to learn about Glasgow. There were codes and signs in that city more complex than anything the Service could devise. Sectarian undercurrents bubbling away in wee towns further east were as nothing compared with what he found in Glasgow. It was the friendliest place on earth but it could turn vicious in seconds if you misread those signs, broke those codes. He overheard two affable, middle-aged businessmen in a West End bar discussing how you could always spot the Fenians. You don't have to know their names, said one. Tone of voice, turn of phrase, that's enough. Ach, who needs to hear them speak? the other retorted. Skin type, colour of hair, curliness of hair. Nine times out of ten I can tell by looking. They were laughing, they didn't really mean it, but actually they did. The disturbing thing wasn't the casual nature of their bigotry but the truth it contained: how the tics and signals became ingrained in people's everyday behaviour, till they hardly noticed them themselves, yet reacted to them subconsciously. Force of habit. Peter stood on Argyle Street or in Central Station as the crowds flowed past, picking out Catholics, picking out Protestants. He knew he was getting it right. He understood that he would have been a master interpreter had he grown up in Glasgow. He did have, after all, the right kind of brain for spotting the enemy, whoever they were.

Except, of course, that he didn't. He sees that now. An innocent walking in the valley of the shadow of faith, that's what he was.

One Saturday, his first summer in Glasgow, he was on Union Street when a huge Orange march swaggered down towards the Clyde. Police and stewards brought the traffic to a halt and crowds of shoppers found themselves stranded at junctions while the parade went past, a train of bright blue-and-red uniforms, orange sashes, bowler hats, banners and flags, ranting flutes and battering drums, followed by a phalanx of white-gloved, high-heeled, steely-eyed women with jaws like flat irons. Behind the lines of waiting pedestrians, some of whom were clapping and cheering while others stood silent and disdainful, a constant stream of drunk, belligerent men kept pace with the procession. When a young woman made an attempt to cut across the street between two marching bands she was flung back furiously by a red-faced steward, and one of the drunks yelled and spat at her. The air was thick with loathing.

All through June and July, whenever Peter heard the flutes and drums of another march, the idea of a Scotland united in rebellion against the British state dissolved into the atmosphere. There seemed to him an infinitely greater chance of folk tearing each other to pieces over religion.

He went to a couple of Old Firm games, one at Ibrox and one at Parkhead, to check the hate levels. He stood with the home support on each occasion, and learned that it was impossible to be a neutral: he had to join in the abuse, the deep, blind passion of tribal belonging, in order to walk away safely at the end of the game. He put on a reasonable display, yet there was a wall between him and the men standing around him, a barrier he could not cross. He was not of their kind and he realised he never would be.

For the mad Nats, as Croick called Boothby and his associates, a new convert meant a new listener. They loved the idea that because they were plotting to break up the British state they must therefore be under its constant surveillance. This meant there were traitors in their midst. Whenever Boothby expressed doubts about X or Y, Peter agreed with him; whenever he was with X or Y, he withheld his opinion until the other party revealed his mistrust or loathing of Boothby, at which point Peter would concur. Boothby changed his mind about individuals on a weekly, sometimes daily, basis: only if they surrendered entirely to his point of view were they 'sound'. Peter never doubted that he came in for criticism when he was absent, but it didn't matter. The least bit of flattery at their next meeting would win him Boothby's confidence again. The others were the same. They all accepted that their networks were riddled with police informers and agents. This was fine: better to be monitored than ignored. They were capable of deep cynicism when it came to each other's motives and activities; but in the wider scheme, most of them were utter innocents.

It takes one, of course, to know one.

From the pages of *Sgian Dubh*, some sound advice from Major Boothby: *The name Scottish Liberation Army is not patented. Any old gang can call themselves that. So be careful what, and who, you get involved with. Be careful who you speak to. Freedom fighters are better without girlfriends – and outside pubs.*

Peter didn't have girlfriends, he'd even given up on going with prostitutes, but he wasn't so good at staying out of pubs. Then again, he wasn't a freedom fighter, was he?

Boothby couldn't bear the idea that anybody else was more monitored than he was. This was a verifiable conceit. Peter left work early one day, caught the train to Lanark and met Boothby at the back of a teashop on the High Street. Peter said he was pretty sure his mail was being intercepted. Boothby glanced round before answering, even though they were alone apart from the waitress and two elderly women who it was impossible to believe were informers.

You think so, do you? Well, I can't tell you how many Nationalists I've met who have told me the very same thing.

Convinced that their every move is being watched by the police. It isn't. Even since Hamilton, I estimate there are no more than half a dozen people in all Scotland in whom the police have an interest because of their Nationalist activities. And that goes for MI5 too.

He paused, looked sternly at Peter. He had on a spiky tweed suit with a thick jumper underneath it, and a shirt collar and tie poked out from beneath that. The suit had an earthy scent about it, the shirt collar was worn. He could have been a farmer, or the headmaster of a prep school on his afternoon off.

If somebody is occasionally steaming open a letter of yours now and then, he said, or doing a bit of eavesdropping on your telephone line, it will be entirely because of your association with me. Nothing will come of it. The government's policy is to contain Nationalism, not to persecute it.

The shimmering Edgar is still there. So is the deputy High Commissioner. His superior has almost expired. One thing about Edgar, he seems to know what Peter's been thinking.

EDGAR: Interesting that Boothby used the same terminology as Canterbury.

BOND: Aye. He sounded like him too. Apart from the beard he even looked quite like him.

EDGAR: But was there any irony in the way Boothby said it? Did he narrow his eyes at you and nod reassuringly? (*perfectly imitating Boothby*) Don't you worry, I know *exactly* what I'm doing.

BOND (*after reflection*): No. Boothby didn't do irony. He was too anxious to tell me about what he intended to do next.

EDGAR: And what was that?

BOND: The SNP's National Council had voted to expel any party members who were also in the 1320 Club. Boothby was furious, not just with the SNP but with individuals in the club. They had compromised its radicalism already. *Catalyst* had been taken over by the literati. There was an upstart with a degree from Cambridge he was particularly incensed with. The club had lost its sense of purpose, the Scottish Liberation Army was all washed up, he himself could only do so much. And yet there was still the possibility of a genuine resistance. What was needed was a fresh start, the establishment of a new military force. He wanted me to help that become a reality.

EDGAR: What did you do?

BOND: I massaged his ego, paid homage to his efforts, and in return he gave me the identities of men who might be enlisted into this new army. Some I knew, some I didn't. We discussed them in detail, their backgrounds, their skills, which of them might be willing to carry out operations.

EDGAR: I want to ask you about Hugh MacDiarmid. Boothby was quite close to him. His wife was a painter and did portraits of both the Grieves. Why didn't you make contact with him?

BOND: He was too well known. Plus he was in his late seventies by then. MacDiarmid might inspire the kind of people we wanted but he wasn't going to give them to us. So I stayed away.

EDGAR: That was your only reason?

BOND (*after a pause*): No. (*another, longer pause*) I stayed away from him because even then I knew I was tainted, corrupted. I didn't want to go anywhere near him.

EDGAR: You felt you'd defile the great man?

BOND: I felt he would see through me. Expose my shame.

EDGAR: Because meanwhile you were giving these names to Croick.

BOND: Yes. And he was giving me names to give to Boothby.

EDGAR: Tell me more about Croick.

BOND: Don't you know about him? You seem to know everything.

EDGAR: You tell me about him. This is your version of events.

Croick came to see him that summer. In Glasgow Croick adopted a kind of demob style, corduroys and an open-necked shirt, as if he could afford to let go a bit. He let his language go a bit too, which he didn't do in Canterbury's presence, but Peter still couldn't place the accent.

They arranged to meet at Central Station. There was no luggage or anything else to indicate that Croick had just arrived off a train. It was a Saturday: the bookshop closed on Saturday afternoons. Croick wanted to go for a walk. They went along Argyle Street, up Buchanan Street past all the expensive shops, then the length of Sauchiehall Street, past the bookshop, on to the museum and through Kelvingrove Park to the university, then down to Byres Road. Some of the more salubrious, prosperous bits of the city, and yet Croick kept repeating, more to himself than to Peter, What a shithole this is.

They're going to put a motorway through here, Peter said at one point, at Charing Cross. They're going to pull a lot of this bit down.

Good on them, Croick said. Nobody'll miss it.

He was more complimentary about Peter's continuing relationship with Boothby. It was important to keep the Major active, even if he was now working completely outside the SNP, because the SNP surge didn't seem to be tailing off. In May they'd picked up another raft of council seats and got more than a third of the votes cast in both Glasgow and Edinburgh. Opinion polls suggested if there were a General Election they'd be the most popular party in Scotland. Home Rule enthusiasts in other parties, the Liberals for example, were using the SNP threat to boost their arguments. There was a group of young, sparky, spiky Conservatives, the Thistle Group, who thought it was the only way to make the Tories popular again in Scotland. And at the party conference in Perth that spring, Ted Heath had seemed to agree, declaring himself in favour of change and that he was setting up a constitutional committee headed by that old reliable, Sir Alec Douglas-Home. Similar opinions were beginning to be voiced in the Labour Party, despite Willie Ross's best efforts to shut them up, and in the wider Labour movement there was further pressure. At the Scottish Trades Union Congress in Aberdeen the miners' leader, the Communist Mick McGahey, managed to persuade the Congress to support, in the broadest terms, some kind of legislation to satisfy some kind of desire from the Scottish people for some kind of Scottish parliament. Willie Ross didn't like such loose talk – who knew where it might lead? He warned the unions not to take refuge in the quicksands of nationalism, but that was exactly where Harold Wilson thought Labour had to put at least one of its feet, and Wilson was Prime Minister.

Nearly half of Wilson's majority at Westminster was made up of Labour's forty-five Scottish seats, and he didn't want to lose any more of them to the SNP. Also, he didn't want to be upstaged by Heath. So he set up a Royal Commission to investigate the matter. This was a lot more important-sounding than a few bigwigs sitting round having tea with Sir Alec. The Royal Commission had the added advantage that it would take years to come to any conclusion and any conclusion it came to would probably be inconclusive.

Still, Croick said, all this official and semi-official activity, and the fact that sections of the press are banging the drum for devolution – all this is reason enough for keeping extremism simmering away in the semi-background. *A spectre is haunting the SNP*, he droned, *the spectre of terrorism*. Then, weirdly unloosed for a moment, he made eerie ooh-ing noises at Peter, and laughed.

He had some names to suggest as possible recruits for the Major's new outfit, the Army of the Provisional Government of Scotland, and as they walked he reeled them off: a few naive patriots, some petty criminals and a smattering of sad, under-educated obsessives. He didn't seem to care about being overheard, and wanted Peter's opinion of his little list. Peter knew some of the names: inadequate, lonely, damaged men with big personal problems. More to be pitied than feared, most of them, he said.

What kind of problems? Croick asked.

Psychological, emotional, financial.

Drinkers?

Some of them.

Good, Croick said. The more fucked up, the better. Don't feel sorry for them. Just feed them to Boothby. Take your time. Boothby's already thinking along the same lines, he just needs a wee nudge. You're very good at that, Peter. The wee nudge. It's your trademark. You probably don't even know you're doing it.

What do you want back? Peter asked.

There are bigger fish, Croick said. The SNP claims it's severed all links with the mad Nats but we don't think they're as clean as they think they are. Nobody's that clean. We think there are quite senior people in the party who are still connected. If Boothby swims out on a long-enough line, maybe he'll bring them in to us.

Croick impressed Peter in a way that Canterbury never had.

Canterbury had seemed always to be worrying about things he hoped wouldn't happen. Croick intended to stop things *before* they happened. Or start them. But who did he have in mind? It simply wasn't credible that the accountants and lawyers in charge of the SNP were in any way mixed up with the mostly mythical Army of the Provisional Government. And nobody in the SNP was that big a name anyway, except maybe Winnie Ewing.

Peter said, I don't think those links exist. He wanted to call him something, but not 'sir', definitely not 'John'. He only ever thought of him as 'Croick'.

Croick said, You can't be sure.

They'd arrived back at Peter's Partick flat. He made a pot of tea and opened a packet of digestives and they sat at the table. It was absurdly domestic, one man making tea for another man, two men drinking tea together but not in a canteen or on a building site or in a café. It occurred to him that they should really be knocking back whisky in mean wee glasses in a bar in Govan.

As if he'd read his thoughts, Croick said, We could be a couple of queens, eh? Tea and biscuits and a shovel up the coal-hole.

No chance, Peter said. Nail that one firmly to the wall, he thought, just in case.

Still get locked up for it here, though, wouldn't we? Croick said. Not like the degenerate south. Just shows you, Scotland still has its head screwed on right about some things. Good old Willie Ross. The Henry Dundas of our times. Do you know about Henry Dundas, Peter?

Peter shook his head.

The uncrowned king of Scotland in seventeen something or other. Delivered the nation on a plate to Pitt the Elder, or Pitt the Younger, I can't remember which. If Dundas said 'Jump!' all the Scottish MPs said 'How high?' Mind you, it was easier then, only a couple of thousand people had the vote.

Peter tried to get back on track. These links, he said. But Croick was on a roll.

We've a long tradition of uncrowned kings, he said. Tom Johnston was one during the war. The Duke of Lauderdale was another back in the days when they were slaughtering Covenanters in peatbogs. I suppose Willie Ross is to Harold Wilson as

Lauderdale was to Charles II. Can't see Willie in a long curly wig and lace though, can you? Not his style at all.

There was no stopping him. Do you think it makes our job more or less difficult, the legalisation of shirt-lifting? he said. I mean, on the one hand it's always been useful to know if someone's queer, and for them to know they can get the jail for it. Good bargaining chip, at the very least. On the other hand your own team can get compromised. The bloke you always thought was meat and two veg and no garnish turns out to be a poof. Believe me, it happens a lot. It's a weakness, somebody's bound to exploit it, you or the other side. So now the ground rules have changed. Now it's okay between consenting adults in private, in England anyway, so maybe we need to move on too. Find other things wrong with people.

He looked at Peter but not as if he were really expecting an answer. Not here of course, he said. Here in the land of Willie Ross we can still send the queer boys to Barlinnie.

Peter thought, is he propositioning me? Aye, maybe. In a repressed wee backwater where you get the jail for sodomy that's just the way a manipulative bastard like Croick would go about it.

These supposed links, Peter said, trying again, and thought he saw Croick roll his eyes, drag himself back to the day's business, you can make them between the APG and other groups, but that's about it. There are still overlaps with what's left of the SLA. There's a bunch called the Scottish Republican Army, there's another called the Scottish Citizens' Army of the Republic. Basically, take a handful of letters, including an S, an R and an L, maybe a W if you really need to emphasise your left-wing credentials, fling them up in the air and when they come down you've got a new movement. Same individuals, different organisation. We're talking about memberships that don't reach double figures. They have a shotgun and a couple of air rifles, if they're lucky an ex-REME guy who knows how to wire up a bomb. But do these people have anything to do with the mainstream Scottish National Party? No, they despise the SNP.

He was aware he'd been speaking fast, to stop Croick

interrupting. It was as if he'd involuntarily gone into competition with him, trying to sound more authoritative.

Croick laughed. Is that the best you can do? Come on, man, what do you think we pay you for? (Because they did, a bundle of notes every time they met, not much but enough to finance Peter's ever-more intimate relationship with the bottle.) We're not exactly overworking you.

Peter had been thinking that for a while himself. He filtered the information Croick fed him, he reported back, but otherwise they left him alone. Canterbury had said if he came back to Scotland he'd be useful to them but how was this useful? It didn't make sense.

I can't dig up more than there is buried.

Why not?

What do you want me to do, invent stuff?

As soon as he said it he realised that was exactly what Croick wanted. But Croick didn't acknowledge it. He stood up and went over to the window, which looked out over a shared washing green. Keeping his back to Peter he said, genially enough, Give me some names.

Peter was off guard. He began to answer, Well, I suppose I could try – but Croick cut in, his voice suddenly hard and loud.

Come on, give me some fucking names.

Jesus, Peter thought, what's this, an interrogation? Kenny McAree, he said.

Electrician, Oban, Croick said. SNP member. Learning Gaelic. Knows how to make bombs. Give me another.

John MacHarg.

Labourer, Alloa. Used to be in the CP, now SNP. Did time for housebreaking. Inclined to violence. Can't handle the drink. Next.

Dennis Hogg.

Miner, Borlanslogie. No political affiliation. Attracted by any scheme, legal or illegal, for making cash. Acquaintance of MacHarg. Next.

William Teague. What's the point of this?

Builders' merchant, Lochgilphead. 1320 Club. Next.

William Nairn.

Works in a butcher's, Inverness. Ex-SNP. Mentally unstable.

Keep him away from the cleavers. The point, Croick said, coming back to his seat, is that we know these people already. Have I invented anything about them?

Peter shook his head.

The insignificant bastards are waiting for something to happen. They want a cause, a war with England, martyrdom. Okay, let them have it. Give them to Boothby. He'll make soldiers out of them.

He already knows Teague.

So he knows Teague. Give him the others. If he knows them it confirms to him that you know what you're talking about. If he doesn't, he'll check them out and get the same result. You won't be his only source anyway. Just nudge him.

And what you're telling me is, if I give Boothby a bit more than is really there, it won't do any harm?

See? You've worked it out for yourself. You can wind Boothby up as tight as you like and the spring won't burst.

Croick drained the rest of his mug, stood up. I need to get going, he said. Somewhere else I should be. You all right with everything?

Aye, I think so, Peter said, also standing.

And you're fine in yourself?

Aye.

We don't ask a lot of you, do we? Easy money. Like taking lambs to the slaughter.

I suppose so.

Croick turned at the door. Don't feel sorry for these cunts. Nobody forced them into this.

Aye, right enough.

You're not going soft are you, Peter? Now you're back among your ain folk? There was contempt in those last three words.

Of course I'm not.

That's good. Canterbury worries about you sometimes. About whether we did the right thing when you left the firm. It's completely against the rules, you know, keeping you on like this. But what were rules made for, eh, if not to be . . . disregarded?

Peter said nothing.

Anyway, I know you better than that big English bastard, don't I? You're all right.

I'm fine.

Of course you are. Right, I'm away. Have you worked out where I'm from yet?

Up north somewhere.

That's a bit vague. Think I'm a teuchter, do you? Maybe I am. I tell you one thing, it's a long time since I went home. Sometimes I forget where I'm from myself.

You won't be his only source. Completely against the rules. Jesus, Peter, how many fucking clues did you want?

Groom him. Another one. Croick's words. That has a whole other connotation these days. Croick told him he was doing well, and Peter, more or less, believed him. He was uneasy about the free rein they gave him but on the other hand he wasn't going to complain. He was doing what they wanted him to do, and it got results.

Boothby laid plans for some kind of military stunt in the West Highlands. These days they'd call it a 'spectacular'. Back then the Scottish version of spectacular was to march around Ullapool in balaclavas for twenty-four hours, for fuck's sake. Probably the good folk of Ullapool wouldn't have noticed they'd been occupied, let alone anyone else. So anyway there were a couple of fund-raising trips. One group went to Liverpool to hold up a bank there. Teague, the guy from Lochgilphead, MacHarg from Alloa and Dennis Hogg from Borlanslogie, all three of them now enlisted in the APG, teamed up and went to Newcastle. They drove down the A68 with a couple of sawn-off shotguns in the car boot, and were tailed all the way. They checked in to a guesthouse in Whitley Bay the day before the raid. In the middle of the night the police surrounded the guesthouse and arrested them all. It was 1 April. Knock knock. Who's there? Room service. Room service who? Bang. April Fool, it's the law. It was a similar sequence of events in Liverpool. By the end of June the trials were over. All involved found guilty of varying degrees of conspiracy, possession of firearms, criminal intent, et cetera. Teague got five years, MacHarg four and Hogg three.

By coincidence (if you trust the phrase – Peter has examined it long and hard over the years, and abandoned all faith in it) this sorry tale of cocked-up conspiracies hit the news right at the start of the 1970 General Election campaign. The SNP didn't do badly in this election but they failed to live up to expectations. They gained the Western Isles but Winnie Ewing was beaten in Hamilton and the party lost most of its deposits in the seats it contested. Maybe they'd peaked. Labour were dominant in Scotland but unexpectedly lost the election in England. The Tories were back in power. Earlier in the year Douglas-Home's constitutional committee had made its report, suggesting a kind of watery Scottish Convention with no real powers at all, and the Tories had stuck this recommendation in their election manifesto. But now Ted Heath was in Downing Street, he made a few noises about waiting to hear what the Royal Commission had to say on devolution, then forgot about it.

Croick, on the phone: Nice work, Peter. And when Peter said, What did I do? Croick said, Nothing. Clean hands, pure heart, that's what we like.

It was nicer still that Major Boothby was untouched, still twitching, fulminating, active, useful. Live bait. There was a trail that went right back to him but strangely the police didn't follow it that far. Meanwhile, the search warrants around the trial turned up a mass of 'new' information about nationalist extremism. Some was produced as evidence and thus found its way into the public domain, and some – how clearly Peter can see this now – was kept back for later.

Future exploitation, Croick called it. That Denny Hogg, he's not a bad lad. Quite bright too, for a fucking eejit. Might exploit him some time.

That was all he said. Peter didn't know Hogg, but later he did notice that he didn't serve even a year of his sentence.

Peter went to London for an overnighter and Croick and Canterbury met him in that same windowless room and they seemed almost to want him back; they talked and talked and while they didn't quite hand over files for him to peruse at his leisure they told him what some of them contained. He recognised things: things he'd written in reports and things he'd told Croick,

308

things that were true and things he'd invented. There was this
blurring of boundaries. He asked them what were they going to
do about it.

About what? Canterbury said.

These files, Peter said. Some of what's in them is genuine and
some is what we originated ourselves. You know which is which,
so would I if I saw them, but somebody coming in fresh wouldn't.

And? Canterbury said.

Well, they're contaminated.

Genuine? Croick said. Contaminated? Peter, it's all contaminated.
We're talking guns and bombs here. We're watching what's
happening in Northern Ireland and trying to make sure it doesn't
happen in Scotland.

You know what I mean, Peter said. There are things I made up
that are being used to put people away.

Shouldn't they have been put away? Canterbury asked. They
were about to rob a bank at gunpoint.

I'm not saying that. It just makes me feel uneasy, this mixing
of . . . He stopped, struggling for the words for what he meant.

Fact and fiction? Croick said, supplying exactly the phrase he'd
been avoiding. Feeling uneasy is what this is all about, Peter.
Listen, I'm not a good sleeper. Six nights out of seven I wake up in
the wee hours worrying. You know what, it's the night I sleep right
through that bothers me. The others I find reassuring. I like the
fact that I can't get back to sleep again, that I have to get up and
think. You know why I like it? It means I'm doing my job. I'm even
doing it in my sleep. I worry when I'm not worried. So should you.

Peter thought, does he sleep alone, does he share his bed with a
wife, a girlfriend, another man? I know nothing about this bastard.
Peter felt a need to defend himself, but what would he be
defending? His innocence? Maybe his guilt, his complicity. And
simultaneously he felt a desire to walk out. And there was
something else: what would he be walking out of? Why did he get
the sense that only the three of them knew this meeting was
taking place? Why did he have the feeling that it was even more off
the record than usual? But before he could say or do anything
Croick, holding up a finger, carried on.

You talk about contamination. This is a process, not a one-off event. We can't muddy the water and then flush it clean again. The whole point of what we do – what you do – is that it stirs up the scum. We know these people and what they might be capable of. We know what they're going to do before they know what they're going to do. You're doing a good job, a necessary job, a vital job. I've told you before, don't start feeling guilty about it.

And Boothby? Peter said. Is he doing a good job?

What do you mean?

Is he one of yours? He wanted to say *one of ours* but he couldn't.

He belongs to us, Croick said. As you know, that's not the same thing.

After the 1970 General Election the SNP momentum seemed to slow slightly, but it was only a temporary lull. They had a long black, slick campaign card up their sleeve and it was called North Sea Oil. They'd had a couple of brains in a back room doing the economics of oil long before anybody in the other parties thought it mattered, long before most voters had even woken up to the energy, employment and revenue implications, let alone the political ones. And even though they consistently underestimated the amount of oil under the sea, and even though the quantities being piped ashore remained tiny until the middle of the decade, people began to pick up on what they were saying. Their slogans had punch. They made an impact. IT'S SCOTLAND'S OIL. That wasn't a comfortable message. It was saying, haud on a minute, that's oors and some other cunt's taking it. RICH SCOTS OR POOR BRITONS? That wasn't very nice. It sounded greedy, grabby. It *was* greedy. But by Christ it made people sit up and take notice.

Peter remembers the way Tory, Labour and Liberal politicians started protesting: I am not a Nationalist. Not with a big N. I am a small-n nationalist. I am as Scottish as the next man. But I am not a big-N Nationalist, oh no, heaven forfend. I stand up for Scotland with a big S but I am not one of those bigoted, narrow-minded, small-s scottish, big-N Nationalists. I am both Scottish and British. I glory in my duality. It is what gives me my entry pass to the House of Commons and my ticket away from the ghastly hellhole from whence I came, the inhabitants of which I have been elected

to keep in servitude. Sorry, to serve. Thank you. Your humble
servant. Here endeth the lesson.

And here's an interesting statistic. No, not a statistic, a graph.
There are two lines on this graph. One represents the electoral
performance of the SNP in the 1970s. The other represents the
number and intensity of 'tartan terror' events in the same period:
pipeline explosions, pylons blown up, caches of guns and
explosives found, letter-bombs sent to public figures or
organisations, trials of suspected terrorists, conviction and
imprisonment of same. Peter has plotted these two lines. He has
plotted them so many times he can do it as a doodle. There you
go. Horizontal axis: the years, and the months of the years.
Vertical axis: votes cast for the big-N Nats; bombs set off by the
nasty nats. Surprisingly – no, not surprisingly – no, not fucking
surprisingly enough – the two lines rise and dip and rise like a flock
of those wee birds you see at the seaside sometimes. Total unison
and you don't know how they do it, twisting and turning and
wheeling together so you'd think they must be joined at the hip.
But wee shoreline birds don't have hips. And we're only talking
two lines on a graph here, not a flock of birds. And actually one
line is slightly ahead of the other, just nudging out in front with
the other one coming along behind, then, whoops, it's as if the
front line gets a fleg from the one at its back and drops off a bit,
then it picks up, then, whoops, there's that pesky second line
again, the one with the bombs and balaclavas, almost as if the
graph is saying vote for Scotland's oil and you get bombed
pipelines, vote for independence and you get bad guys in
balaclavas. Weird, eh, how that repeats? A repetitive pattern.
Spooky even. Like something is happening and you don't know
what it is, do you, Mr Jock, but maybe you'll just stick with the
devil you know for another five years, eh? And another five, and
another, until the oil's all been sooked out of the sea and after that,
well, after that you paranoid schizo sheepfuckers can do whatever
the fuck you like.

Peter sinks another glassful. Can't call it a dram, about six drams in
it. He'd fucking known what was happening, just hadn't been able
to admit it. I don't think those links exist. He mimics himself. *I*

don't think those links exist. Pathetic. Croick and Canterbury made them exist, they put him in the chain and kept him there, adding more links. *You won't be his only source.* A great tangle of chain, with Peter right in among the other poor sods. Linked. Intimately bound.

In heaps around the flat are dozens of different periodicals, newsletters and pamphlets from that period: most of them badly printed or roneoed, some hand-stapled, some not bound at all, the occasional grainy photo or blurry line-drawing breaking up unforgivingly dense text. Spilled religion. People, some people, really wanted to change the world in the 1970s. They thought it was possible, and they thought it could be done from small beginnings, three guys round a table in a public-house snug, with a new take on Mao or Trotsky or Bakunin. It could even be done from Scotland. You couldn't move for revolutionary groups, and every group seemed to produce at least one publication for distribution to the members, or to potential supporters, or just to anyone who might give a damn. Nobody read more of this literature, or read it more avidly, than Peter Bond. He bought it in radical bookshops in Edinburgh and Glasgow, or from rival vendors flogging their variant ideologies round the pubs, or from fugitive stalls, crowded with samizdat-style news-sheets and manifestos, which appeared for an hour on street corners or in university basements. He grabbed it all, ten pence here, fifteen there, and pored over it restlessly, noting down and cross-referencing names, venues, forthcoming meetings and their speakers. He went to the meetings. When he had to give his name he gave it, Peter Bond. If somebody was going to get suspicious then they would get suspicious, regardless of what name he used. Anyway, he worked in the bookshop. Occasionally a familiar face showed up there and clocked his. Occasionally he posted a book to someone whose name he recognised, whose address he then made a note of. Scotland was a small country. It was why he'd wanted to get out of it.

Glasgow was interesting in other ways. A year after gaining power, and having made a big noise about not using public money to support industrial lame ducks, Heath's government nationalised Rolls-Royce to stop it going under. When it refused a subsidy to Upper Clyde Shipbuilders, effectively sanctioning the consortium's demise, thousands of the workers responded by occupying the UCS yards. The unions organised it – not a strike but a disciplined, determined work-in ('No hooliganism, no vandalism, no bevvying') – and it caught the imagination of people across the world. The two most prominent shop stewards, Jimmy Airlie and Jimmy Reid, were Communists but that didn't stop support flooding in from church leaders, rock stars and other celebrities, the Labour Party, the SNP, the Liberals – even some Tories. Workers' control in action. Months went by and it became clear that the government couldn't indefinitely bear the political damage the dispute was causing. After eight months Heath caved in, agreeing to inject a huge amount of cash into UCS.

There was a girl Peter used to talk to around that time. She'd been drawn to Glasgow by the work-in and the heady political fumes the city was giving off. A poor wee rich girl called Lucy, eighteen or nineteen. There were a few of them about, unhappy children who'd rejected privilege and thrown in their lot with the proletariat. She was trying out different ideologies like hats. She wore hats too, a Che-style beret mostly. Peter saw her at some of the same meetings he attended. At first she was with a guy, then she was on her own. He talked to her over cups of tea, or later in bars. Despite his best efforts she wouldn't give anything away about her background, and although he could have found out he didn't. She was edgy and surly and he liked that. Bonnie too, dark-haired and with cool eyes and a sulky mouth. After a few encounters, just when he thought she might be interested in him, she stopped appearing. It was odd: he hardly knew her, but he missed her.

In the autumn of 1973 Lord Kilbrandon's Royal Commission on the Constitution finally published its findings. *A fudge* was how Croick, on another of his visits, assessed it. In the circumstances, he said, it's better than we could have hoped for. That phrase *in the circumstances*, that presumptive *we*, Peter was beginning to find them somewhat irksome. The main report called for a major transfer of power to Edinburgh: a Scottish Prime Minister, a Scottish Cabinet, a 100-strong parliament with responsibility for most Scottish domestic issues, elected by proportional representation (They must be joking, Croick scoffed); in exchange there'd be a reduction of Scottish MPs at Westminster and no Secretary of State. (They *are* joking. What would we do without Willie Ross?) Then there was a minority report: it wanted something toothless, more along the lines proposed by the Tories' constitutional committee. Finally there was a 'memorandum of dissent', which dismissed both of these plans and opted for federalism: Scottish and Welsh assemblies and five English regional ones too.

Croick called his visits *jaunts*. His jauntiness was purposeful and dark, like that of a Wee Free elder slipping out of the service early to kick fuck out of a malingerer smoking in the kirkyard. There was a system for setting up meetings via orders sent to the bookshop marked for Peter's attention, but Croick didn't always use it. His preference was to appear without notice at Peter's door, or come into the shop as a browsing customer and arrange to meet later. Peter presumed this was to keep him on his toes. He wondered how often Croick turned up and didn't find him. Not often, he reckoned. So they knew his movements. No surprise there.

They were in a bar on Mitchell Street, a haunt of journalists from the *Glasgow Herald* and *Evening Times*. It was early evening.

Makes you proud to be British, doesn't it? Croick said, referring to Kilbrandon. Kick a ball into the long grass and when somebody finally goes to retrieve it they come back with three. Great if you're a juggler. Looks like we'll be sticking with what we've got, for the time being, constitution-wise. He Americanised the word *constitution* disdainfully, making Peter think of Bob Dylan.

What does Canterbury think of it? Peter asked. He had a whisky and a beer in front of him. Croick was on gin and tonic. The room was full of noise and smoke. You felt you could say anything and nobody else would hear it.

He hates it, Croick said. It's tinkering with his country. More than tinkering, it'll break it into pieces if it's implemented. Mind you, he thinks the country's going to the dogs anyway, without the assistance of Royal Commissions. He paused, maybe to see if Peter had a view on this, then said, So do I, as a matter of fact.

Croick talked about the war in the Middle East, the price of oil going through the roof, the teetering economy, the threat of strike action by the miners, the ineffectiveness of Ted Heath, the sense of imminent collapse. We all have different ideas about how we stop it happening, he said, leaning in closer. Canterbury would dispense with democracy altogether if he could. Thinks it brings out the worst in people. I know what he means, but as a solution it's not practical any more. You know what his motto is?

Peter shook his head. He wanted more whisky.

The law is there to be upheld, Croick said. *And if I have to break it to make sure it is, so help me God, I will*. I'm pulling your leg.

Peter didn't think he was. He wondered if Canterbury had put him up to it: let's test the oik. Again, he felt he was watching a double act, only this time one half was offstage.

He said, And what's your motto?

Mine? Well now. Croick stared into the drift of smoke above his head. The old grey smile appeared on his face. *A law unto himself*, he said. However, this isn't about me. We were talking about the failings of the democratic system. But the problem isn't democracy, it's how you manage it.

You said that before, Peter said. That's what you do.

Exactly, Croick said. Fundamentally, it's a management problem. Same again?

Nine days later democracy brought out the worst in people again, when the SNP candidate, Margo MacDonald, stormed to victory in a by-election in Govan.

Croick said, See what I mean? Still plenty of work left for you and me.

It must have been around then that Peter first landed up at Jean Barbour's. He was spending more and more time in Edinburgh, and thinking he might try to engineer a flit through to the east. He arrived at her place one night having got in tow with a handful of members of something called the Clan Alba Society. The name had echoes of Clann Albainn, a secret organisation MacDiarmid had supposedly been involved with in the 1930s, and Peter had thought it worth checking out. The Clan Alba Society was indeed a front, but not for insurgency: it was a group of whisky enthusiasts who'd cobbled together a constitution, and nominated a secretary and a treasurer in order to claim funds from the Student Association, which they then spent on expensive malts. Too bloody expensive for Peter's taste or pocket. Still, they had their uses, such as gaining him access to Jean Barbour's flat. For a year or so he came and went, watching and listening. He wore a fawn duffelcoat, a kind of homage to those students on the bus who'd sung about Sky-High Joe, all those years ago. There were other private residences into which he got himself admitted, but hers was the one he liked best. There was a kind of comfort in being there. He used to tell himself he was still working when he was at Jean's, the way Croick claimed he worked in his sleep, but deep down Peter knew it wasn't true. He didn't gather Intelligence there, he didn't learn anything that wasn't already obvious. Aye, all right, leave aside the dram-tasters of Clan Alba, some genuinely dodgy customers appeared from time to time: boys with tenuous links to the Workers' Party of Scotland or Boothby's Army of the Provisional Government, plus a few freelance fantasists. Maybe he was one himself. But the main thing about the gatherings in the Barbour flat was their sociability. He enjoyed being there. He liked the kind of people that turned up, the Catrionas and Helens of young Scotland, even if they didn't much like him. Duffelcoat Dick they called him, behind his back. Once somebody who didn't know it was a nickname called him Dick to his face and barely stifled giggles followed. He didn't care, he didn't blame them for not liking him, he still liked them. He liked the songs. He liked the stories, the long rambling ones told by Jean, the one-liners and jokes that flew around the room all the time. He would sit there with a glass of somebody else's wine or a filched bottle of beer and think how normal it all was, and then a pang of jealousy would come as he saw that once again he was in a state of limbo, inside and yet still an outsider. He was part of it and yet alienated. Was it because of who he was or because of what he was? What was he? A nobody, no wife, no kids, no friends, nothing. The Highland girls were lovely, but they weren't interested in him. He thought of his mother, whom he never saw, and the way she'd believed he was bound for glory. He thought of his father, *ye shouldna joke aboot these things, son*, dead. He thought of Canterbury and Croick, the

weird non-twins of his other world. He knew nothing about their
other lives, their family lives, if they had them. The contents of his
mind slid again into that dark, sloshing corner where there were
no coincidences, only obscure designs and unfathomable plots,
off-off-official secrets like there were off-off-Broadway shows. The
deeper you went into the shadows and side streets, the greasier the
greasepaint. If it was legitimate to infiltrate illegitimate
organisations attempting to undermine the state, was it illegitimate
to infiltrate legitimate social gatherings? It couldn't be. There
were, after all, a few individuals he recognised at Jean Barbour's
who crossed and recrossed the line. They were compromised, and
so they compromised everybody with whom they came in contact.
He himself was compromised. And he realised that, for someone
like Croick, maybe Canterbury too, there was no line. *Everything*
was legitimate, or illegitimate, these words were meaningless.
Nothing was off-limits. They secured the premises, Croick had
said. It was who they were. It was what they did.

But Peter himself. He recognised that there was a line. He just
didn't know where it was, or at any given moment which side of it
he was on. He thought he was so much more clued-up than these
happy folk. But they had good reasons for laughing at him.

And then the Demon Barbour confronted him.

EDGAR (*as* JEAN BARBOUR): What is it you're looking for?
BOND: A corkscrew.
BARBOUR: You know what I mean. (*She shuts the kitchen door and
stands with her back to it. A wee sharp-faced woman, no longer beautiful
but he can see she once was.*) You sneak into my home and sit in the
shadows with your lugs waggling like antennae and you think I
don't know who you are? Don't worry, I'm not going to blow your
cover, but what's so special about us?
(BOND *tips the last of the bottle into the glass. The bottle is thick and
heavy in his hand. A portly chap, the High Commissioner, even when
vacant. He can hear her voice, a husky, sexy voice, and his own voice, dull
and calculating, and underneath both of them his breathing, which
sounds like the breathing of another man, the hand clutching the glass is
the hand of another man, the man slipping down on the settee, staring up
at the abandoned webs round the light fitting, is another man. The haar*

is back. He peers through it, looking for EDGAR. *He sees a figure in the other chair, dimly shimmering.*)

BOND: You still here?

EDGAR: I'm still here.

BOND: With Jean Barbour there never was any point in pretending. *(To* BARBOUR*)* There's nothing special about you. Do you think this is the only place I go?

BARBOUR: I don't care where else you go or who else you like eavesdropping on, but I'm interested to know what you're doing *here.*

BOND: The same as I'm doing everywhere. I'm trying to gauge whether we've reached point critical.

BARBOUR: Meaning what?

BOND: The point of no return. The point where you can't stop it even if you want to.

BARBOUR: And have we?

BOND: No.

BARBOUR: And can you?

BOND: Can I what?

BARBOUR: Stop it if you want to?

BOND: No.

BARBOUR: Do you want to?

BOND: No.

BARBOUR: You don't want to?

BOND *(louder, so she gets the fucking message)*: No. Even if I could I don't want to.

BARBOUR: Well, then, I'll not need to come here any more.

(And in spite of everything he doesn't want her to go but she goes anyway and he is incapable of stopping her, he is incapable, she steps over a collapsed pile of newspapers and into the passage and over to the front door and he hears the door open and the swishing sound of it pushing junk mail back and the door closing and she's gone.)

BOND *(looking around for* EDGAR, *panicking a little)*: Don't go. Please don't you go too.

EDGAR *(homing back into view)*: I'm still here. For the time being.

BOND: I just . . . I just like to talk.

EDGAR: I like to listen. Where were we?

BOND: 1974. Every time there was a council by-election the SNP seemed to win it. Their opinion-poll rating was consistently good, especially among young people. They were on a roll and the roll looked unstoppable. Everybody else was getting very nervous. When I think about it now . . .

EDGAR: Yes?

BOND: When I think about it now it's clear enough. Those months between the two General Elections that year, that was when the whole direction of Scottish politics for the next three decades was laid down. The SNP won seven Westminster seats in the February poll and came second to Labour in thirty-four more. Bound to loosen the bowels a bit, eh, if you were a Labour MP? So the party machine clanked into reaction. Wilson told the Scottish leadership they were going to have to go down the devolution road, like it or not, in order to shunt the Nats into the ditch. Result? Five years of bluster and barter, a failed referendum, eighteen years of Tory rape and pillage, ten years of Labour-led devolution and, at the end-up, a Nationalist government in Edinburgh.

EDGAR: Some might call that a waste of effort.

BOND: Aye, but think of all the oil and gas extracted from the North Sea over those years. Some might call that a good return.

EDGAR: That's a very cynical view.

BOND: Cynical? I'll tell you a story about cynical. Everybody was lining up to say devolution was the way forward. The STUC was for it, even the CBI wasn't totally against it. Wilson was making public noises about the virtues of bringing power closer to the people, but privately telling his Cabinet it was the only way to dish the separatists. But a lot of folk in Scottish Labour didn't agree with his analysis, thought it was playing straight into the SNP's hands. There was a meeting of the party's Scottish Executive. A list of five devolution options, drawn up by Wilson's advisers in London, was on the table for discussion but the general principle of devolution wasn't. Or at least it wasn't supposed to be. It was a Saturday, late June. The World Cup finals were on in Germany and a Scotland team had reached them for the first time since the 1950s. They were playing Yugoslavia that afternoon. They'd already beaten Zaire and drawn with Brazil. Drawn with Brazil! Fuck's sake, there was a real possibility they might progress to the next round! Even Willie Ross was in Frankfurt for the game. Scotland versus Yugoslavia or block grant versus tax-raising powers? Nae contest! The patriotic tendency on the Executive chose the game and who could blame them? Eighteen out of twenty-nine members didn't turn up to the meeting. The anti-devo faction found itself with a majority of one and rejected every Home Rule option on the agenda. No extra time for constitutional tinkering, they decided. Probably about the same time Scotland drew 1–1 with Yugoslavia and went out of the competition on goal difference.

EDGAR: I have never had the slightest interest in soccer.

BOND: That's obvious. So Wilson had to bring the lads to order. Force them to swallow Home Rule and if it made them choke, well, it was for their own good. He wanted to turn his minority administration into one with an overall majority as soon as possible, but he could do this only if he turned the Nat tide. No point in beating the Tories in England if honourable members were being huckled out the back doors of Scotland and Wales by the SNP and Plaid Cymru. The Jocks and the Taffies might be awkward buggers but between them they'd delivered more than sixty seats to Labour, and it was essential to keep all those and if possible add a few more. It was a tricky fix, but Harold would find a way: fixing was what he was best at.

First, he ordered the Scottish party to convene at a special conference. There was to be just one item on the agenda, devolution, and Wilson made it clear there was to be just one outcome, a reversal of the Executive's position in June. Next, he got the union leaders who were in favour of devolution to deliver their block votes and persuade their doubting comrades that this was what was needed to keep Labour in power. There was support from the constituencies too. Even Willie Ross gritted his teeth and agreed that there didn't seem to be any other way of stopping the Nats. The conference was held in August, at the Co-operative Hall in Dalintober Street, Glasgow. It was a dirty business, a grinding, clinical performance – Yugoslavian, you might call it – but it swung Scottish Labour behind Home Rule, committed it to a directly elected legislative assembly and freed Wilson to go to the country in October, when Labour won an extra seat in Scotland and an overall UK majority of . . .

EDGAR: Three. Again, one might ask whether all the effort was worth it.

BOND: It was enough to be going on with. The SNP gained another four seats, but all from the Tories. The Labour vote held up pretty well. Everybody in the party breathed a sigh of relief, then started tearing lumps out of each other. The devolvers talked about how the Scottish Assembly would be a 'powerhouse', an engine for change and renewal, and this set alarm bells ringing all over the place. MPs from the north of England thought Scotland would have an unfair advantage over their areas, which faced the same problems of industrial decay, bad housing and unemployment. Left-wingers like Robin Cook in Edinburgh and Neil Kinnock in South Wales believed in British working-class solidarity and that any constitutional concessions to Scotland or Wales would be a betrayal of that solidarity. Even the Cabinet was full of sceptics who thought devolution was a slippery slope and a diversion from more pressing issues. Meanwhile the Tories dumped Ted Heath and replaced him with Margaret Thatcher, who started undoing the party's dalliance with devolution. Apart from the SNP's eleven, some Liberals and a handful of renegades from the two big parties, there wasn't much enthusiasm at Westminster for the idea of siphoning political power off to the provinces. When the government presented its devolution White Paper at the end of 1975 it was torn to shreds – too weak for the devolvers, too strong for the centralists – and had to be withdrawn for major revisions.

EDGAR: As I've already had occasion to comment, your powers of recall are remarkable. But why such attention to party politics? That wasn't your area of interest, surely?

BOND: It was all connected.

EDGAR: What was?

BOND: Everything. Everything was connected.

Twin track. The lines on that graph do their jerking, swooping tango across the paper, across Peter's mind. 1975 was the year the Intelligence community decided it had had enough of Major Boothby. That was the year they gave him enough rope to hang himself, so to speak. If he'd ever really 'belonged' to them, as Croick had claimed, by 1975 he was no longer considered a valued possession. Maybe he'd outlived his usefulness. Maybe he'd become a liability. Maybe he was about to blow his cover. Or maybe none of those things. Peter still doesn't know. Sometimes he wakes in the middle of a night, in the middle of a day, in a chair, on a floor, and in the brief flicker between coma and consciousness it bears in upon him that Major Frederick Boothby wasn't a spy or a stooge or an agent provocateur; he was just a man with delusions of adventure who really believed all the crap he printed and spouted.

Whatever the truth, the APG trial was a total gift to the opponents of the SNP.

Croick said, as if he wanted Peter's opinion, Have we made progress, do you think?

Well, Peter said, they're all inside. I'd say the Army of the Provisional Government has carried out its last campaign. (Its only campaign, he could have added.)

But is that progress? Croick said. He sounded genuinely unsure. They didn't bring the big fish in for us, after all. We just netted a bunch of sprats. Maybe we should have left them out there longer.

Wouldn't have made any difference, Peter said. You were hoping for links to the SNP, and there aren't any.

Was that what I was hoping for?

That's what you said.

And is that what you think? There are no links?

Aye.

So we've been wasting our time?

Well, like you said before, these people are prepared to use guns and bombs, rob banks.

They're not really important, though, are they? *These* people.

Peter had never known Croick ask so many questions, look so doubtful. He said, So why *have* we been wasting our time on them?

A misguided sense of duty, Croick said. Then he brightened. We'll just need to try harder. Take better aim.

Everything had finally gone belly up for the Army of the
Provisional Government. The previous year one of the Merseyside
bank robbers had been released after serving three years of his
five-year sentence. Before long he was back in touch with Boothby,
or Boothby with him. Others too: a boy recruited in Perth Prison;
a couple of hardmen from Aberdeen and Glasgow; some guys
who played in a band together. And there was somebody else. A
guy Croick had moved in, Peter reckoned, but what the fuck did
he know? Because Croick was shutting him out, closing him down,
that's what it felt like. He had to work it out for himself, and there
was always the nagging, growing fear that he was working things
out wrong.

The APG needed funds. The hardmen had weapons and had
identified a couple of possible sources, more banks in Glasgow. In
January the boys in the band hired a van and drove it through to
Glasgow and everybody piled in and cruised the streets till they
found a bank that was actually open. In they went with a shotgun
and out they came with eight thousand pounds, much of it in
specially marked notes kept in the bank for just such an
eventuality. The gang split. The money went in several directions
too. By the end of the month all the men involved had been
picked up, a couple of them after a prolonged drinking spree in
London. Then the police, acting on information received, maybe
from Croick's plant if there was one, dropped in on Major
Boothby's cottage and took away a few pieces of possibly
incriminating evidence. That was in February. At the end of
March they came back for Boothby himself. In May eight
members of the APG went on trial and were put away for various
crimes, for periods ranging between one and twelve years.
Hugh MacDiarmid appeared as a character witness for Boothby,
which may or may not have helped the Major's case. He got three
years.

What about Boothby? Peter said. Did you want him in the net
or wasn't there any choice? He wasn't involved in the bank raid.
But then he wasn't involved in the other ones, was he?

Croick didn't rise to it. All roads led to Boothby, he said. He'll be
all right. He's a tough old bugger.

He's sixty-five. He's not keeping well.

Your concern is touching, but unnecessary. I've told you before not to waste your sympathy. He'll be out in no time.

He seemed very sure of this.

History, he said. Things move on.

And after a pause he said, in a contemplative tone, As one cell-door slams shut, another opens. I wonder who'll be pushed through it.

Peter sprawls about on the floor, working his way over to a bookcase next to the gas fire. The room smells of many things, all of them bad, and often it smells of gas. Peter doesn't think, I should tell Mr Fodrek, there may be a leak. He doesn't think, sniffing the gas and observing the sliding hills of paper everywhere, thank fuck I don't smoke or this place would go up like a grouse moor in a heatwave. He doesn't think that because he doesn't give a fuck, remember? He's after something, a book stuck behind a jumble of other books on the bottom shelf. He pulls it out, riffles through the pages: a single sheet of notepaper falls out. Yes! Somehow, even lying on his back amid the chaos, he can still home in on what he's looking for. By Christ he can still do it. There.

He is aware of Edgar, hovering near by. Probably mildly amused at the spectacle Peter presents. Fuck him. Peter scrambles back into a sitting position, hauls himself on to the settee, clutching the book and the letter.

> *Brownsbank,*
> *Biggar,*
> *Lanarkshire*
> *15 June 1977*

Dear Mr Bond,
Thank you for your letter asking if it would be all right to pay me a visit.
I apologise for the delay in replying but I have not been well and find it
increasingly difficult to keep up with my voluminous correspondence.
Owing to my poor health I do not generally encourage visits from admirers
however enthusiastic but you make some astute and interesting comments
about the effect of my poetry and polemics on the political thought, such
as it is, of the nation, and I would be glad to see you if you can make your

way here. It would be best to 'phone first (the number is Skirling 255) in
case I am going to be away. I look forward to meeting you.
Yours sincerely,
Christopher Grieve

EDGAR: So you did contact MacDiarmid?

BOND: Aye, but not till much later, as the date shows. It wasn't much to do with Croick and Boothby by then. I had my own reasons for going to see him.

EDGAR: Previously, you'd had your own reasons for *not* going to see him.

BOND: I was afraid he'd see through me.

EDGAR: And now you didn't think he would?

BOND: No, now I *knew* he would. That was what I wanted.

(*The book is MacDiarmid's* Collected Poems *of 1962, and on the title-page is a dedication, 'To Peter Bond, with all good wishes', and the poet's autograph. The handwriting is shaky, and slopes downwards across the page, but the signature is strong, and finished with a line under it that has pierced the paper. Peter remembers the way* GRIEVE, *having signed the book, held on to it for a moment before speaking.*)

EDGAR (*as* GRIEVE): Only a fraction of my life's work is contained in here, but it was very welcome when it was published. A real breakthrough, that year.

BOND: 1962.

GRIEVE: Yes. You've had it since then?

BOND: I was in London at the time. I got it in Foyles.

GRIEVE: There is quite a lot wrong with it. There is quite a lot wrong with me too. But the book will be superseded! My complete poems are being prepared for publication, in two volumes, but it's a long-drawn-out process.

BOND: I hope I'll be able to get you to sign my copy.

GRIEVE (*chuckling*): I hope I'll still be alive to sign it.

Peter had come down from Edinburgh, an hour and a half by bus. When he'd walked up the farm track to the tiny cottage and chapped the door there'd been a squall of barking, and then a solidly built woman with bright orange hair, holding a wild-looking terrier of some kind by the scruff, had appeared from round the side of the building. She was wearing red trousers and a multicoloured shirt but the hair was the most striking thing about her. That, and the scowl on her face and the way she asked bluntly who he was and what he wanted.

Peter wasn't too good around dogs, especially slavering ones that seemed to think of him as dinner.

I've an appointment to see Dr Grieve.

Oh have you? The dog lunged and she hauled it back. What's in the bag?

One of his books. And a bottle of whisky.

Just what he doesn't need. What kind of whisky?

Bell's.

I'll take charge of that. She held out her free hand and he passed over the bottle.

Now I'm going to let the dog go, she said.

I'd rather you didn't, he said.

She let the dog go. It launched itself at him and he retreated before its snarling teeth until he was backed up against the garden gate.

Don't try to pet him, the woman said, or he'll bite you. He might bite you anyway. After that he'll settle down.

The dog grabbed the cuff of his trouser-leg and worried it, then gave up and left him alone.

You must be Mrs Grieve, Peter said.

I am, she said. But you can call me Valda.

He was taken aback at her surrender.

Thank you, he said. Valda.

Don't try to fucking butter me up, she said. She folded her arms, still clutching the bottle, and stuck her jaw out, defiantly pleased that he'd fallen into her trap.

I wasn't trying to butter you up, he said.

Just as well, she said. He's inside. What's your name?

Peter Bond, he said.

You know he's very unwell, I suppose?

He said something about it in his letter.

Come away in then.

She led him in through the front door and half-opened another door on the left.

Christopher, you have a visitor. He says he made an appointment. Peter Bond.

Peter heard a quiet, slightly protesting voice: Who?

He says his name is Peter Bond.

I wrote to you, Peter said over her shoulder.

Yes, yes. Come in, Mr Bond. Valda likes to think of herself as a kind of warder, keeping my visitors at bay.

It's as well for you that I do, Valda said, or you'd have been trampled to death long ago.

Although it was a summer afternoon, the room was dark, smoky and not particularly warm. The breeze blowing through the open window was dry and hot, but inside the air felt dampish, heavy with residual smells – tobacco, old books, dogs, food, coal. There were shelves stacked with books all round the room, and on the walls between the shelves and the low wooden ceiling numerous paintings and photographs of Hugh MacDiarmid striking combative bardic poses, often in a kilt. The man in the room was the same man in the pictures, but different too. It was Grieve, not MacDiarmid, who rose from a brown leather armchair, laying a book on top of a pile of others on the bed that was pushed up against one wall, and held out his right hand. The bowl of a lit pipe rested in the palm of his left. He was wearing a tweed suit, a checked shirt and plain tie. Slippers on his feet. The unmistakable forehead rose to a thick crop of white hair. Peter had seen him often, in photographs and in the flesh, but never this close. The man's head seemed huge, but the body frail, the suit too big for it.

Peter shook the outstretched hand.

Please, Grieve said, sit down. He indicated a chair on the far side of the unlit fireplace. The shelves next to it were full of green and orange Penguin paperbacks. Peter glimpsed names like Erle Stanley Gardner, Rex Stout, P. G. Wodehouse. He thought, why am I surprised?

Valda said, I'll make some tea.

Tea would be good, Grieve said, but what's that I see under your oxter? We'll have some of that to be going on with.

You'll not have much, Valda said, but something changed in the atmosphere. Suddenly she was kind and solicitous, fetching glasses and water for the whisky, then going back out to her weeding in the garden, taking the dog with her. Later she would reappear from the kitchen with tea and a huge pile of sandwiches on a tray. But before that, before that . . .

Peter sat in the chair opposite the old man's and they began to talk. Peter found himself leaning forward all the time because Grieve was not only quite deaf but also surprisingly soft-spoken. He had an engaging way of cupping his right ear with his hand to catch what Peter was saying. He also had a mischievous smile and his eyes were full of laughter, although he was also obviously in some physical pain. He was happy to talk about anything – the bus journey from Edinburgh, Ezra Pound, whom he'd met in Venice five years before, his childhood in Langholm. Peter was amazed at how gentle and easy Grieve was, nothing like his fiery performances at public events or in print. Even when Peter steered the conversation round to the matter of Major Boothby and whether there was any truth in the rumour that he had been an informer, Grieve refused to get excitable.

You know him, you say? Why don't you ask him? He's out of prison again.

I'm interested in what *you* think.

Well, what if he was an informer? He has paid for it now.

If he was, Peter said, he was very close to people like yourself. He could have done a lot of damage. Perhaps he has done a lot of damage.

What does it matter? Grieve said. He did some good work over the years. He kept the pot boiling and we should be grateful for that.

Even if he is a traitor?

At least he has not been an automaton, slavishly, mindlessly serving the establishment. And in any case, if he is a traitor what has he betrayed? There is not, I think you'll agree, any imminent likelihood of revolution in Scotland.

You seem very sanguine about it all.

I have to take the long view. One grows impatient, of course, but I never doubted but that it would take many years to stimulate the Scottish population into action. That has been my task since I came back from the war – the First World War. To aggravate and stimulate. I am a troublemaker, and I recognised the same thing in Boothby as soon as he came on the scene. We need people who are prepared to make trouble. We need that kind of person more than anything. What we don't need is another conformist, another lickspittle of the English ascendancy. Whatever else he is, I don't believe Boothby has ever been that.

Peter nodded. He remembered those discussions he'd had with Canterbury about MacDiarmid, ten, fifteen years before, and he felt ashamed, and maybe it showed in his face because Grieve said suddenly, And what about yourself? For the first time since his arrival Peter detected a sharpening of tone, a slight hint of violence in the voice.

What, do I believe Boothby has been a conformist? he said. But he knew perfectly well that wasn't what Grieve meant.

No. You, yourself. What have you done? Have you, consciously or unconsciously, maintained the status quo? Or have you, as I have, worked all your life against it?

Nobody has worked as you have, Peter said.

That is an evasive answer, Grieve said. There was a pause, which to Peter seemed about to stretch across an unbridgeable chasm, and then the old man spoke again.

You have come to see me, to quiz me about Boothby, yet you know him yourself. Do you think I am entirely naive?

No. Quite the reverse.

Grieve coughed and took more whisky.

Listen to me, he said. I am in permanent opposition. It is my nature. I'll be a Bolshevik until the revolution comes, but after it, when Communism rules the roost, I'll be something else. And I won't have shifted *my* position an inch. Does that make sense to you?

Yes it does, Peter said. I understand that completely.

But not everybody can be like that. Someone like myself, a poet, an intellectual, can. I've always been a loner, and I have never had anything to lose. But if everybody were in opposition there would be nothing to oppose. And most of them wouldn't know why they were in opposition any more than they know now why they accept the status quo. He shook his great head. Complacency is the worst enemy, he said. If you grow complacent, you cease to think. And if you cease to think, you cease to live. You, I can tell, have not ceased to think. It's one of the reasons you came to see me. But you are troubled, and I know why you are troubled. Grieve pointed an accusing yet somehow not unfriendly finger at him. You have been on the wrong side. Actively on the wrong side. I don't wish to know what you have done, but I can see it. *You* can see it. The question is, what are you going to do about it?

I'll need to think about that, Peter said.

The only thing you need to do, Grieve said, is to be yourself.

In January 1976 a portion of the Labour Party in Scotland, fed up with the endless prevaricating and stalling over devolution, staged a breakaway and formed a new organisation, the Scottish Labour Party. The leading figure was Jim Sillars, a charismatic MP from Ayrshire, who could once have challenged Willie Ross for the title 'Hammer of the Nats'. In the wake of the Hamilton by-election of 1967 he'd issued a pamphlet laying into the SNP and any form of devolution: *Don't Butcher Scotland's Future* it was called, but now he'd lost patience with Labour's failure to get to grips with the Scottish question. The Scottish Labour Party was committed to both socialism *and* a Scottish parliament. For a few months the SLP was buoyed up by good opinion-poll ratings and sympathetic coverage from various parts of the Scottish media. Briefly, it looked as though Canterbury's nightmare scenario, an alliance of socialism and nationalism, had arrived.

Peter expected to be told to divert his energies towards this new threat to the stability of the British state. But Croick told him on no account to join or get involved with the SLP. Instead, in the wake of the APG's disintegration, Croick had him chasing other clumps of letters: the SRA, the SCAR, the ASP, the SRSL. It was like stirring alphabet soup, but every time you brought the spoon to your mouth there was fuck-all in it. Meanwhile it looked like the real action was out in the open, being covered by the mainstream media. It made him mad with frustration.

It's all in hand, Croick said. You sit tight. This will take care of itself, you'll see.

Sitting tight was all he got to do these days. He broke sweat sitting tight. The weather didn't help. That summer it didn't rain from the start of June to the end of August. Peter, who turned prawn-pink if exposed to the sun for more than half an hour, kept in the shadows, breathless and longing for thunder. Snow would have been heaven. Every day the temperature seemed to hit a new high. Roads melted. Marching bands ran out of spittle and their drumskins split. If a child dropped his ice cream it was milk the second it hit the pavement. The TV news showed footage of Highland farms, even a small village, drowned in the 1950s by hydro schemes, re-emerging, monuments to their own deaths. But Croick, sitting in Peter's kitchen with a mug of hot tea in his hands and a jacket on over his white shirt, seemed not to have noticed that he was living through the hottest summer on record. Not a bead of sweat on him.

Think of a tree with two limbs, he said. One of those political-cartoon trees from the nineteenth century. One limb says SOCIALISM, the other says NATIONALISM. And nestling right in the cleft of the tree is this big fat honeycomb labelled THE SCOTTISH LABOUR PARTY. And every flying or creeping shit-eating, sugar-sucking creature for miles around is homing in on this dripping feast. How can they resist? The party forgot to make any rules about who could be members. Anyone can be a member. The International Marxists are in there. The Scottish Workers Republican Party's in there along with anybody else who thinks they're the true descendants of John Maclean. Everybody's in there, Peter, which is why you don't need to be. You're doing fine sucking shit and sugar out of all the other wee bushes everybody else has forgotten about. There are even some poor honest folk who genuinely believe the SLP stands for what *they* stand for. Socialism with a Scottish accent. Nationalism with a social conscience. Ach well. More. Fool. Them.

He couldn't keep the derision out of his voice.

By the end of the year, Croick was even happier. He sat on the same chair wearing the same clothes, drinking tea again, and declared himself satisfied with the SLP's state of impending collapse. It was almost as if he'd never been away.

At its first congress in Stirling, in October, the SLP leadership had tried to clear up the mess it had got into over dual membership. The idea had been to keep the door open to sympathisers in the Labour Party, but it was the Trotskyites, masters of entryism, who'd swamped some of the branches. By the time of Stirling the SLP had nine hundred members in forty-two branches, some of which were acting more or less independently. A furious battle over resolutions and procedures ensued and the International Marxists were expelled. They marched out of the hotel where the congress was taking place and into another, where they reformed as the 'Scottish Labour Party (Democratic Wing)'. The official SLP limped on but their membership had just collapsed and the air was poisonous with recrimination and suspicion. Even the sympathetic journalists who'd come to write of hope and idealism could see that there was nothing but bad news to report.

There was even a bit of blood on the tiles in the Gents, Croick said. These people take their schisms and expulsions seriously.

You were *there*?

I dropped in for a bit. Tell you what, you missed yourself.

Peter lost his temper then, half-rose to his feet, banged his fist on the table between them. But you told me to keep out of it, for fuck's sake!

Croick was unperturbed. Right enough, he said. He smiled. We didn't need your input, that's all.

Input? What input? I don't do bloody anything!

Calm down, Peter, calm down.

Peter wanted to hit him. That smile, that word *input*. It was like he was being tested. That was what it was always like. Testing his loyalty, his discipline, his fucking commitment. To what? And had he just failed, with his outburst, or passed? He didn't know, he never knew. So he calmed down, and Croick said, You do enough, Peter, I assure you. Do you know what you achieve, by doing what you're told, by playing the subtle game you play? You matter, believe me.

Why should I believe anything you tell me?

What's that Greek thing? Croick said. Euripides, is it? Whom the gods wish to destroy, they first make mad. That's what you've helped to do over these last few years. This desire for Scottish . . . whatever you want to call it, Home Rule, self-government, independence . . . you help to make it what it is, a form of madness. As soon as there's a possibility of it happening, well . . . blood on the lavvy walls, as I said.

But what have I done?

It's not what *you've* done, it's what *we've* done. You're in a team but you don't know any of the other players. That's okay, you don't have to. It's better if you don't. It's necessary that you don't.

I don't even know what the game is.

Croick raised an eyebrow. Aye you do. I'll tell you anyway, in a minute, but you do. The game is up and running, and to be honest we don't even have to get involved much these days. The civil servants are doing everything they can to *not* deliver devolution, but just in case they have to they're also busy redrawing maps of the North Sea and changing the way oil and gas revenues are assigned. You have to admire the way they kill ambition. Nothing saps the energy like a Whitehall mandarin dragging his heels. And now that the politicians have finally got their act together everything is ticking along nicely.

What do you mean? The politicians are all over the place. They don't know what they want.

Precisely. I take my hat off to Wilson – a genius when it comes to creating plenty of smoke with very little fire. His party might not like floundering around in the bog of devolution but what his tactics ensured was that the SNP would get sucked in too. They did and now there's a full-blown argument going on in *their* ranks between the fundamentalists and the gradualists, the ones who want independence and nothing less and the ones who think an assembly is better than nothing. You know what devolution is? It's the longest way to make sure nothing happens. And now Wilson's away and Callaghan's in charge, and do you think anything much is going to change?

But what about the other parties?

Croick laughed. What about them? The Tories are on our side. Even if a few of them make weird hyooching noises every once in a while, they don't mean anything more than if they were doing an eightsome reel. The Liberals are useful pissers in the swamp of gradualism but who really gives a damn what the Liberals think? In another couple of years people will be sick and tired of devolution and all its works. What on earth were we thinking of? they'll say. We must have been insane. Yes, truly insane. And it'll fade away back to wherever it came from and we can get on with our lives. And you'll have contributed to that.

Peter felt like a wee boy being praised, stroked almost, by a stern but friendly teacher. He could hardly look at the other man.

Croick put his mug on the table. We'll go and get a drink somewhere, eh? I could do with a drink. So could you. But let me tell you something first. My father was a proud Scotsman. Really he was. But he was a proud Briton too. And he knew his history. He used to say to me, the Scots were never any good at running their own affairs. Whenever they were left to their own devices, they started fighting. They murdered their kings and each other, they were treacherous, violent, fanatical, incompetent, poor, hungry and cold. And when the chance of union with England came along the smart ones couldn't believe their luck, they took the bribes and signed the deal and grabbed it with both hands, while the stupid ones, the idiot tendency, sulked and drowned their sorrows and eventually followed that Polack-Italian buffoon Bonnie Prince Charlie to Culloden. And that, my old man said, was Scottish history, and the lesson was, some of us knew which way our bread was buttered and some didn't, but so long as the ones that did had the upper hand we need never be afraid of making a mess of things again.

Is that supposed to make me feel better? Peter asked.

No. None of this is about you, or me. I keep telling you, keep your emotions out of it. But you should know that everything we do is designed to ensure that the present state of affairs continues. It's not heroic or glamorous, but it is the right thing. And you're a part of that.

EDGAR: A part of that. Were you a part of . . . whatever he was talking about?

BOND: Oh aye. I was. (*His head lurches and the cargo slides once more.*) Well, no, I wasn't.

EDGAR: What was he talking about anyway?

BOND: You should know. There were plenty of people in Intelligence who thought Wilson's Labour government was beyond the pale, virtually handing the country over to the trade unions. Some of them even thought Wilson was a Russian mole, for God's sake.

EDGAR: Croick?

BOND: No. He wasn't that stupid. But the general thesis – that there had to be back-up, a contingency plan – he subscribed to that. It wasn't primarily about Scotland. Scotland was an adjunct, but it was his patch, his particular responsibility. That's what he was telling me: once this is sorted we can get on with our lives. I was part of his plan to keep Scotland British.

EDGAR: But *you* knew that. You'd been working at it for years.

BOND: Well, I'd had enough. I tried to get out, a year or so later. This time I used the system to set up a meeting with Croick. I had a good excuse. I was about to be unemployed. The bookshop was going out of business and I thought I'd take the chance. And you know what? I thought Croick would just shrug and let me go. Good riddance. How naive can you get? So we arranged to meet, in this pub on the Southside, in Shawlands.

EDGAR (*as* CROICK): I heard about the shop. A shame, but hardly a surprise. Neither is this, Peter. I can see you're tired.

BOND: I'm not tired. I'm finished, done. It's over.

CROICK: So you want a wee rest? Why not? Recharge your batteries.

BOND: I don't want to recharge my fucking batteries. I want out.

CROICK: Oh, I don't think so. Not after all this time. Let's not lose touch now. We *can't* lose touch.

BOND: What's that, a threat?

CROICK: A statement of fact. We're connected. But what am I saying? Things are under control, so, aye, go off and do your own thing for a while. No reason why you have to stay in Glasgow either. Edinburgh would be good. Get yourself a job in Edinburgh. Go into business. Any idea what you might do?

BOND: You're not taking this seriously, are you?

CROICK: I take everything seriously. Even jokes. I hate it when a joke isn't funny, don't you? Here's one. Why won't Scotland ever be independent? Because whenever the Scots get offered the chance of a free Scotland they know there must be a catch. A bargain-basement Scotland? Sounds interesting. A cheapish one?

Aye, maybe . . . But a free one? No thanks. Think we came up the Clyde in a wheelbarrow? Now, you tell me, is that funny? Think about it. (*He stands up, goes to the bar and orders another round. While he's waiting he goes over to the jukebox and puts in a coin, punches in a selection. He collects the drinks and brings them back to the table.*) Now. Where were we? Oh aye, that joke.

BOND: Forget the joke. What about me?

CROICK (*laughing*): What about you? Your future career? All right. Know what I think, Peter? I think you should go private. You'd be good at it. You've had plenty of training.

BOND: What the fuck are you talking about?

CROICK: Set up on your own. Private detection. Divorces, surveillance, missing persons, dodgy insurance claims. There's a market. Plus you'd keep your skills honed, should we ever need them again.

BOND: I'm telling you, I'm finished.

CROICK: I can put you to sleep for a while, Peter. Maybe for years. But I can't let you go. Not completely. You're an investment. Maybe you'll never hear from me. But you need to know that you might. I'd be lying if I told you anything different.

BOND: Future exploitation.

CROICK: That's it.

BOND: What about Denny Hogg. Did you ever exploit him?

CROICK: Who?

BOND: You know. The lucky bank robber. Don't tell me he got out early for good behaviour. Is he an investment?

CROICK: Let's say he's got an account at the Cooperative Bank.

BOND: And what if he won't cooperate?

CROICK: He will. You will too. I can make it worth your while, one way or the other. I know what you like.

BOND: Maybe I'll change.

CROICK: Maybe you will. I'm not betting on it, but if I can't buy you I can always sell you. Damaged goods. Going cheap.

BOND: You think you've got me for ever, then?

CROICK: Aye, or as long as I need you. You're not stupid, Peter. You're just a little slow. I always reckoned that about you, right from that very first interview.

BOND: What interview? In London?

CROICK: No, before that. (*as* EDGAR) You will learn things about the world, and about yourself, that you would never otherwise know. (*as* CROICK) How true, how true.

BOND (*looking at him suddenly and closely*): Wait a minute. You just said . . . That was the other guy. Edgar. When I was a kid doing my National Service. *He* said that.

CROICK: Said what?

BOND: What you just said. Word for word. But there was another man in the room. Wait a minute.

(*There is a long silence. It might be a minute, it might be an hour. That's the way time is now.* BOND *is sunk in thought. Eventually he looks up.* EDGAR *is still there, sitting across from him.*)

BOND: He said what *you* said. He was there. He was the one in the corner, with the glasses. It was Croick, wasn't it?

EDGAR :

BOND: He picked me. He chose me right at the beginning.

EDGAR :

BOND: You bastards. Did he choose me?

EDGAR :

BOND: I should have walked out then.

EDGAR: You were just a boy.

BOND: And I should have walked out of that pub in Shawlands.

EDGAR: By which time you were a man. Getting on a bit. But you still didn't.

BOND: He bought another round, and then another. I didn't put my hand in my pocket all night. That was the only satisfaction he gave me. I should have walked out but I knew it wouldn't make any odds and I wanted him to go on paying for the drinks. And then, when I was too pissed to stop him, it was him that got up to go. But before that, before he left, his selection came up on the jukebox. You know what it was? The Eagles. 'Hotel California'. It was being played everywhere that year. And he leaned in to me when the chorus started and joined in but he changed the words, he was singing, Welcome to the Hotel Caledonia. And we sat and listened to that fucking song, the guitar solos, the choruses, and those lines at the end, the whole fucking thing. I couldn't speak I was so drunk. And then he got up and left me there. And I knew I was doomed.

EDGAR (*singing softly*): You can check out any time you like, but you can never leave.
BOND: Aye, that's the one.

You kind of step out of yourself, watch yourself. When you're a kid, real life is a game of imagination you play at one remove. Not so different when you grow up. You watched Bob and Bill concocting stories for the *Drumkirk Gazette* and pictured yourself in their shoes, doing it better. In London, when you rented hookers, that's what you did, stepped out and spectated. When Canterbury came to your grey room by the Thames, you floated up to the ceiling and observed his stupidities from a height. When you first saw you were drinking too much you were only a few feet away but you made no effort to reach out and check the hand that tipped the bottle. You didn't argue with the decision, if it was a decision, not to stop. Story of your life: the constant spy. And so it continued after Croick let you go but didn't let you go. You watched yourself barrelling down the highway – brakes on or brakes off it didn't matter, you were heading for a crash anyway and you saw the whole thing and somehow there was nothing you could do to avoid it.

He was determined to cut himself loose from Croick's influence, but it was Croick's suggestion about setting up on his own that lodged in his mind. Sole trader. No dependants, no dependency. Sink, probably, or swim. But not in Glasgow, a city he now just wanted to get out of. He made a couple of reconnoitring trips to Edinburgh, looking for office space that could double as accommodation. The second time he found what he wanted, in a dismal quarter of Leith. A grim wee hole with one window on to the street, a window so filthy you couldn't see in or out, and a crusted venetian blind behind it just to make sure. Behind this room another with a stained stainless-steel sink and a two-ring hob, and squeezed in at the back a toilet with a cracked seat and a shower with several tiles lying in the tray.

The landlord was as welcoming as the premises. When Peter told him he was setting up as a private investigator he said,

Investigate folk round here, pal, and ye'll wind up in the docks.
Dobie, his name was. He wanted three months' rent up front
in return for which Peter got a set of keys. Anything else was
'found'. What do you mean? I mean, if ye want anything else,
find it yersel. There were marks and holes in the walls where
once must have been fixed shelving. There was a phone sitting
on the floor in one corner of the main room. Peter picked up the
receiver. The line was dead. The Eagles' tune went through his
head again.

What was this place before? he asked.

Before what?

Before now.

Dobie threw him a look that suggested he should mind his own
business.

Windae-cleaning, he said.

A windae-cleaner needs an office?

A business needs an office, pal. You need an office, don't ye?

Aye, but windae-cleaning?

Windae-cleaning, roof repairs, building work, plumbing.
Emergency call-oots. That enough for ye?

I just thought in case any of your old customers drop by, Peter
said.

They'll no, Dobie said. We just stored stuff here, he said. Any
mair questions?

Peter shook his head and, as if that meant he'd tried to end the
discussion and it wasn't his prerogative to do that, Dobie went on
speaking.

Ye've got tae keep moving, he said. Keep ahead of the game.
There's money in windae-cleaning but it's territorial, ken. I went
part-shares wi another guy that already had a patch. We were
daein the other work tae but there's only so much ye can dae in
one area. We wanted tae expand on tae somebody else's patch but
somebody else didna want us tae. So . . . He gestured with one
hand at the space they were in. It's better this way, he said.

What about your partner? Peter said.

He moved on, Dobie said. An amicable split, he said.

There wasn't a trace of amicability anywhere on his face.

★

The bookshop closed, but long before it did Peter was away. His possessions from the Partick flat went into two or three cardboard boxes, plus half a dozen more for books and pamphlets, and that was him, out of Glasgow. A guy in his close who had a car ran him and the boxes through to Leith, wouldn't take anything for it, especially not when he saw what Peter was going to. Jesus, he said, you've got to be kidding. I always knew Edinburgh was a dump, but this . . . Peter said, If anybody comes asking, you've no idea where I went. He said it without conviction, knowing that if Croick wanted to he'd track him down in a matter of hours.

He despised himself for taking Croick's advice but he'd have despised himself more if he'd had to go back to Slaemill. He'd thought of London, wondered if he could disappear down there, but he'd had a good look at himself and what he saw was not a man ready to tackle London again. He hated Canterbury and Croick but he'd colluded with them, he was as responsible for what he was as they were. More so.

He felt so low it was liberating. It gave him a burst of something like energy. He had the phone reconnected – it only took three weeks and another deposit – and scoured the thrift shops on Leith Walk and Great Junction Street, picking up a mattress, pillows, a couple of chairs, a desk. He ate fish suppers and Chinese carry-outs and managed to restrict his drinking to cans of beer. He got a Post Office Box Number because he didn't want folk turning up unannounced at the door and finding the office was also his bedroom. No name on the door, no indication of what was behind it. The front room smelled less damp than the back and had an electric fire hanging off one wall, so that was where he slept. In the morning he moved the mattress through to the back. He had about a hundred quid left in the world.

He took out an ad in the *Evening News* and the *Scotsman*, three days a week for two weeks:

PRIVATE INVESTIGATIONS UNDERTAKEN.
Marital, insurance, missing persons, etc. All work considered.
20 years experience with Govt agencies. Discretion assured.

Then the box number and phone number. Everything, with some latitude, was contained in those lines. All the money he had left was in his back pocket. He thought, sink or swim, Mr Bond, sink or swim, and wondered if that was a line some villain had once said to Sean Connery or Roger Moore or whoever the fuck was playing 007 these days. If it wasn't, he thought, it should be.

To his amazement, the ad worked. After two days he'd had four phone calls and a couple of written inquiries. The good folk of Edinburgh had plenty they wanted to find out about their spouses, relatives, friends, rivals, work associates. Mostly it was: who are they sleeping with, who are they talking to, who are they paying, where do they go, where have they gone? There were worried parents, vengeful wives, controlling husbands, men who knew their business partners were ripping them off and needed proof. They wanted to know but they didn't always want to see. I'm your man, said Peter, I'm your eyes. When the two weeks were up he renewed the ad in the papers. He came up with a name, JB Investigations, because he wanted to keep his own name out of it: if the thing died and he had to do something else, he didn't want his history stalking him, not any more than it already was. Later he put an entry in the Yellow Pages, which had only been going a few years. For a while JB Investigations was the only listing under Detective Agencies. People liked going through the Yellow Pages just to see what was in it, and when they saw Detective Agencies they desperately tried to think of reasons why they might need one. Some days the phone never stopped ringing. Aye it did. He thought about hiring a secretary. No he fucking didn't.

He didn't drive and that was a handicap, but the city was small enough for it not to make his work impossible. There were only so many hotels, so many bars, so many saunas doubling as brothels, and usually no shortage of taxis. Sometimes he arranged to meet potential clients on neutral territory, sometimes they insisted on coming to his place of business. He discovered something: they weren't put off by the location, nor by the run-down look of the place or him. Nor by the absence of paperwork, the emptiness of his desk, the fact that he hardly ever took notes. Nor even by the smell of booze that still came off him some mornings. On the contrary, these things seemed to reassure them.

For a while, even though he was keeping his fees low, he was making a profit. That felt good. He bought a seemingly unused Minox spy camera in a pawnshop and found he could take pictures of people virtually in front of their faces without them noticing. Across a street, in a doorway or upstairs window, he was as good as invisible. The original Mr Bond again, almost. He snapped parting kisses, close embraces, married men entering strip bars or gay clubs, or public toilets miles from where they had any reason to be. The work was seedy and tedious but he didn't mind, it was who he was now, and the best thing was it wasn't what he'd been doing before. He'd left one clandestine world behind and entered another where the secrets were dirtier but somehow the dirt didn't cling so much. He forgot about Canterbury. He almost forgot about Croick.

And, he couldn't help himself, the gatherer in him accumulated information about the city and its inhabitants. The filing system inside him kicked into action. Edinburgh didn't make a show of its wealth but the place was awash with it, old money and new swirling around among an assortment of lawyers, bankers, property developers and ethically challenged politicians. And there were the women – wives and mistresses influential and ambitious in old-fashioned ways, but some of them infused with a contemporary determination no longer to be exploited by their men. There were plenty of shady transactions out there, and there was plenty of sex, even if only furtively expressed. If you had an instinct for sniffing out secrets, Edinburgh was rich territory.

Something else: if you gather information you can move it on. Not the secret stuff his clients paid him for, not that, but there was always by-product. He dusted off his old journalism skills, renewed his union membership. He sold a story or two to the *Evening News*. He thought, detective agency, news agency, what's the fucking difference?

He felt like he had his drinking under control. His other expenses were minimal. He put a lot of money away. He wasn't so stupid as to believe there weren't rainy days ahead.

EDGAR: And what was going on politically at this time? For you, I mean.

BOND: Nothing. I didn't care about politics any more. There was the Winter of Discontent, then the devolution referendum, then Thatcher winning power. I didn't give a damn about any of it. Croick wasn't on my back. That was all that mattered to me.

EDGAR: *You* didn't care about politics? About devolution? Oh, come on!

BOND (*sniffing*): I was done with it. But there were other people who weren't prepared to let the devolution thing drop. I was interested in them.

EDGAR: I see. You didn't care but you were interested. And who were they, these interesting people?

BOND: Nobody much. A few activists from Labour, the Nats, the Liberals – MPs, councillors, a trade unionist or two. And just some ordinary people.

EDGAR: Ordinary?

BOND: Sometimes they were in some group or other, but they were fundamentally ordinary, decent people with a cause.

EDGAR: Decent?

BOND: Aye, they were. All sorts. They said the Scotland Act had failed because it had been cobbled together at Westminster out of political expediency. It didn't come from the people and when the people saw it they didn't think much of it. So *their* campaign – the Campaign for a Scottish Assembly – was going to have to do it differently, build from the ground up. It was a hopeless cause, but they believed in it. Most of the media weren't interested. The new Tory government wasn't interested. I went to one of their meetings just out of curiosity. I recognised plenty of faces but there was nobody keeping an eye on things. Nobody *securing the premises*, as Croick would have said.

EDGAR: Except you.

BOND: That's not why I went. I was a free man. I just went for myself.

EDGAR: And no Croick.

BOND: No Croick.

EDGAR: Not a sign of him?

BOND: Not a trace. It was like he'd ceased to exist.

BANG!

He's broken something, saying those words. Did he say them?

He's broken a spell. One second Edgar was there, shimmering in the armchair, the next he isn't. Like *he's* ceased to exist.

Peter struggles off the settee. Everything is a struggle by this stage. The deputy High Commissioner is running the show now. Peter reaches the chair, grapples the empty space where Edgar was. No Edgar. Gone. Not even a sticky drop of that stuff you get, the sauce left when someone spontaneously combusts. Not a trace, just like Croick. Fuck. He was enjoying their wee heart-to-heart. But that's how it happens. Whenever he has company he likes, he ends up alone.

Not quite alone. There's always the deputy, if he can only pin the bastard down. He turns from the empty chair, sways, points and says, I want a word with you. Then his legs give way.

When he woke it was 1985. March. A cold wind was blowing through Leith from the north, rattling an empty beer can up and down the street. And someone was knocking at his door. He rolled off the mattress, finding himself still fully clothed. Whoever it was wasn't giving up. Not hammering, not aggressive, just persistent. Like they really needed him to answer.

He found his watch. It was eight o'clock, presumably morning. He made it to the door, unlocked it.

Hello, Peter. Long time no see.

He had neither the strength nor any reason to stop him coming in. In he came, and took charge. Jesus, Peter, what a tip! He went through to the back room and filled the kettle, filled the sink with hot water and started washing up mugs and plates, the accumulated crap Peter hadn't been dealing with. He restored a bit of order. When he went out again it occurred to Peter that he could lock the door, or go out himself and not come back till Croick had given up on him, but he did neither. Instead he changed out of his four-day-old clothes, washed himself. And when Croick came back he let him in at once.

You've almost made yourself presentable, Croick said. He'd bought the makings of breakfast and got to work at the hob. Peter hadn't realised how hungry he was. He gulped starchy, greasy chunks of bacon roll and washed them down with scalding tea. Croick ate more gently, like a doting mother.

How's business? he asked.

Good, Peter said. Because it wasn't so bad. The volume of cases rose and fell, more or less according to whether he was off or on the booze. The same with the number of stories he sold. There were some weeks he never touched a drop, other weeks he didn't even see go by. Somehow he kept resurfacing. Croick seemed to understand this. He seemed to understand everything.

I can help you out, he said. He took out his wallet, stuck a couple of twenties on the table between them.

I don't want your help. We're through, remember?

Peter, Croick said. He'd finished eating. He put his mug of tea down and looked straight at him. Don't take offence. I hear what you're saying. Actually, it's the other way round. I need your help.

Fuck off, Peter said.

You don't mean that, Croick said. He made a slight gesture to indicate that things were as they had been before, the two of them sharing food and drink in Peter's abode. Look, we didn't treat you so well. As it happens, I'm not the favourite son at the moment either. Take the money. It's theirs, not mine.

Forty quid was forty quid. Peter reached for it. A line was crossed.

Fact is, Croick said, I need a place to crash.

There are hotels, aren't there? Peter said. And safe houses?

If they're safe. Sometimes I need somewhere I don't have to check in and out. Do me this one favour, will you? I'll make it worth your while.

The room they were in, the one at the back, would do. He needed to be able to come and go. Was there a spare key? No matter, he'd get one cut. He wouldn't be in the road, Peter would hardly know he was there. Mostly he wouldn't be. He said, I heard a good one the other day. Somebody on the radio, talking about the '60s, he said, if you can remember them you weren't there. That'll be the story here, eh? You've been places, you've seen things. You don't remember any of it. Do you?

God knows what he was up to. The miners' strike had just

ended. Scargill and the NUM had been designated 'the enemy within' by Margaret Thatcher and you didn't have to be an ex-spook to understand that people like Croick had been crawling all over the strike. Now it was over. The miners had marched back to the pits behind their brass bands, heads held high and all that but there was no doubting who'd won. So maybe Croick had been busy and now he was freed up, but Peter didn't think that was what it was. The strike wasn't Croick's territory. There was something else.

He stayed a couple of nights that first time. Peter gave him the key and he got a copy made. Maybe he had a car parked somewhere because when he reappeared he was carrying a sleeping bag and a small holdall. He made a kind of nest in one corner of the room and it instantly became his space and Peter avoided it. This okay? Croick asked. Peter shrugged. Croick came and went, just as he said he would, and Peter let him. What was he going to do, throw him out?

He decided not to drink because Croick, booze and himself didn't mix. Then Croick went away, and Peter took a drink out of relief, and he took another because, aye, go on, admit it, because he missed the company. Fuck's sake. A couple of days later he stopped, did some work for a week, and it was okay, as if he'd finally shaken it off. But it couldn't last. Croick turned up again, smiling that mocking, unjovial smile, and he brought with him some lager, a bottle of gin and a litre of tonic and that was them. Mixed.

Croick talked and seemed not to care that Peter said nothing. Things have changed, he said. This country's finding its feet again. Say what you like about Maggie, she's got balls. First she stands up to the Russians, and the lesbians at Greenham Common. Then she sees off the Argentines. Didn't flinch when Bobby Sands and his pals starved themselves to death. Came out of the Brighton bombing like a fucking Amazon. I tell you, it's heady stuff. Makes you think there's nothing that can't be done.

You'd think this was a speech of elation, a champagne toast, the future belongs to us. But Croick's voice was flat and his smile was humourless. He looked like a condemned man staring at the gallows.

There's some unfinished business up here, he said. But some people have lost their nerve.

He filled their glasses again.

See if I ever called you, Peter. Short notice. Get yourself here, now. Would you come?

Peter said nothing. A wee tic of excitement was going inside him that he was desperate for Croick not to see. He gulped some gin, wished it was whisky, nodded at Croick to continue.

I can use you. Canterbury and those other cunts, they're too far away. They don't understand what it's like here. They don't trust me any more. Think I'm a bad apple. Do you trust me?

No, Peter said.

Good answer. But if I call you, you'll come, won't you? I know you will. This isn't about the money any more. Of course there *is* money, but it's not about that. Is it?

Peter didn't know what he was talking about. He didn't care. All that mattered was that Croick was letting him – asking him – back in.

Remember you used to wonder where I came from? Croick said. Did you ever figure it out?

Peter shook his head.

Kenya. My father was a police inspector in the Colonial Service. I've told you about him before. He was from Aberdeenshire but he went out in the '20s and never came back. I was born there. My dad had an accent you could have ploughed fields with. Some of it rubbed off on me. When I was eleven he sent me back to an aunt in Aberdeen, and I went to school there because he thought a Scottish education was the best you could get. And then the war broke out, so I didn't go back to Kenya till '45, and then a couple of years later I was in London. So no wonder you were confused. No wonder I was, eh? He paused just long enough for Peter to begin to say something, then went on. I'm joking. *I* was never confused. Neither was my dad. He had a very straightforward view of the world. Good and evil. Right and wrong. Black and white. For him, there wasn't much that wasn't a certainty. He knew how to run the show, how to keep the natives docile. It all went to hell after the war, of course. The Mau Mau and that. He did what he could but he always said the place would go to pieces after independence and it's heading that way. Just taking longer than he expected. Luckily he's not around to see it.

And so on and so on. Peter's attention wavered. The gin helped

him to float in and out. He just wanted Croick to tell him what
he had to do, but Croick seemed intent on reminiscing. He had
stories about how his father sorted trouble before it even was
trouble. Nipped it in the bud with a systematic beating or two
down by the river. It was rough justice but it worked.

Some people really don't know when to back off, Croick
was saying. There's a guy, a lawyer, old enough to know better,
can't stop trying to dig stuff up. Thinks he's got everybody else on
the run. A loudmouth. Thinks he's a big shot. You know who I
mean.

Somehow they were back in Scotland. Peter tried to
concentrate. This lawyer was trying to scupper plans for dumping
nuclear waste. The Atomic Energy Authority had been wanting to
test-drill in the Ayrshire hills and he'd been involved in the
campaign to stop that. The AEA had moved on and so had the
lawyer. Dounreay was a possible site. Glen Etive was another. He
drove around the country waving papers at public inquiries and
asking awkward questions. He was, in Croick's opinion, a pain in
the arse.

He's been warned off, Croick said, but he won't listen. His office
gets burgled, his home gets done over. He thinks he's immune.
Nuclear waste's an accident waiting to happen, he says. He should
know. *He's* an accident waiting to happen. He's not as smart as he
thinks he is. Likes a drink. Doesn't stop him driving. Smokes too
much. No exercise. Gets stressed. Classic candidate for a sudden
exit. Croick paused for a significant second. Heart attack. Typical
fucking Jock really, eh?

Remember all those dodgy pals you had a few years ago, Peter?
All those mad Nats? They were all the bloody same. Drank too
much, smoked too much, kept the wrong sort of company. You
don't smoke, good for you. Stupid habit. I could never ally myself
with stupid people. I always said you weren't stupid, just slow.
Emotion's like cigarette smoke. I hate it when emotion clouds
people's judgement. Right or left, doesn't matter, but all through
history the right's been smarter, more resilient, more sussed, than
the left. Lefties think they're cleverer but even when they are
they're not wiser, and sooner or later they lose their cool and start
ranting and raving and generally being an embarrassment. Nats

are the same. The Scottish Irrationalists. I could never be on the same side as people like that.

I've done the research, I think it's a racial problem. A big proportion, say one in ten of us, are wired up wrong. I've seen it everywhere. London, Kenya, Aberdeen, Hong Kong, Australia. Anywhere there are Scotsmen, which let's face it is everywhere, you'll find the one in ten. You'd think we'd know by now. Just leave it alone, eh? But a lot of folk can't help themselves. Just can't fucking help themselves. Can't keep their fingers off the self-destruct button. They know it's there. They've been told often enough. Like Adam and Eve and the apple. Big temptation. Want to push themselves over the edge, see what it feels like. Bang.

Next day he was gone, with all his gear. Two hundred quid on the table. Like he was trying to offload it. Bang. Peter heard the echo of that last word for a week. The worst thing about it was the absence of exclamation. Croick said it like it was just something that happened. Nothing unusual. Just – bang. End of story.

Of course he knew who Croick meant. The lawyer was called Willie McRae, a member of the SNP since the 1930s, a bit of a maverick who'd held senior positions in the party in the past. Had stood for Parliament three times and come within a whisker of winning the Ross and Cromarty seat in 1974. He was a Glasgow solicitor, with a holiday cottage up there, at Dornie. He had a good conceit of himself. Peter remembered him because, unlike most of the SNP top brass, McRae was one of the ones who crossed lines. Never quite separated mainstream party politics from the nutters on the fringes. McRae kind of sympathised with their madness, Peter thought. He wasn't mad himself but he knew what made them mad. There was a group called Siol nan Gaidheal that emerged in the late 1970s. They liked to strut around in black shirts and wave flags at the Bannockburn rallies. They believed in direct action. Early in the 1980s, about the time they dealt similarly with the socialist '79 Group, the SNP banned anybody in the party from belonging to Siol nan Gaidheal. Willie McRae wasn't in Siol nan Gaidheal but maybe he understood where they were coming from.

He was, as Croick said, a pain in the arse of officialdom,

especially around the nuclear-waste issue. Peter remembers all this about him. And he remembers the news, the facts and the speculation, that started filtering through in April 1985. The kind of stuff he's chewed and chewed at over the months, the years, the decades . . .

Willie McRae had been in a crash. Willie McRae's Volvo had left the road between Fort William and Dornie, careered down a steep bank, and ended up in a burn. Willie McRae was still alive when found. It was a Saturday morning, the day before Easter. Willie McRae had left Glasgow the previous evening. Willie McRae was taken to hospital in Inverness, then transferred to Aberdeen. Willie McRae never regained consciousness. Willie McRae was dead. Willie McRae didn't die from injuries sustained in the crash. Willie McRae had a bullet in his brain. Willie McRae had shot himself. Willie McRae had no reason to shoot himself. Willie McRae had been depressed. Willie McRae had been in exuberant, optimistic mood when he left Glasgow. Willie McRae's appointments diary was full. Willie McRae was writing a book. Willie McRae had been drinking. Willie McRae had a half-bottle of whisky in the Volvo's glove compartment. There was no trace of alcohol in Willie McRae's blood. Willie McRae had left Glasgow with a briefcase stuffed full of documents to work on over the weekend. No briefcase, no documents, were found at the scene of the accident. No briefcase, no documents, were ever found. The police checked the scene of the accident meticulously. The police were unbelievably careless. The police, the first witnesses on the spot, the vehicle-recovery men, were all over the ground and destroyed any potential evidence before anyone knew about the bullet in Willie McRae's brain. The scene of the accident was at this location. The scene of the accident was at another location. The police said it was here. The first witnesses on the spot said it was there. The bullet in Willie McRae's brain was from a .22 revolver. Willie McRae had a .22 revolver. A .22 revolver was found at the scene. The gun was Willie McRae's gun. It had Willie McRae's fingerprints on it. The gun was in the burn under the Volvo. The gun was nowhere near the Volvo. The gun was twenty feet away from the Volvo. The gun was sixty feet away from the Volvo. The gun had been fired twice. Willie McRae had fired it once to test it,

350

then had shot himself. He had thrown the gun from the car. He could not have thrown the gun from the car. A dead man, a dying man, could not have thrown it that far. The driver's door was wedged against the bank of the burn. The driver's window was wound down. Why would Willie McRae, alive, have got out of the car, torn up some papers including a credit-card bill, left them neatly in a pile along with his watch twenty feet from the car, got back in the car from the passenger side, squeezed himself back behind the wheel and shot himself? How could Willie McRae, dead or dying, have done these things? Somebody else was involved. Nobody else was involved. Willie McRae had committed suicide. If Willie McRae had committed suicide, did he decide to do it after crashing his car, on the spur of the moment? If Willie McRae had committed suicide, why were there no burn marks around the bullet wound? If Willie McRae had held the gun to his head and pulled the trigger, how could there not be burn marks? The bullet that lodged in his brain must have been fired from some distance away. The bullet that lodged in his brain could not have been fired from some distance away and hit him where it did because of the angle at which the car lay. The back window of the car was shattered. Another gun had fired the bullet that lodged in Willie McRae's brain. Somebody had been tailing him. Nobody had been tailing him. No other car was involved in the incident. Another car had been following McRae for months. The registration number of the other car was this. The registration number of the other car was that. Information on that registration number was blocked. This meant it was operated by the security services. This meant nothing of the sort. Willie McRae was under surveillance. Willie McRae was not under surveillance. Willie McRae was a troublemaker. Maybe Willie McRae was an alcoholic. Maybe Willie McRae was tired. Maybe Willie McRae wasn't concentrating. Maybe Willie McRae knew the road too well. Maybe Willie McRae's mind was on other things. Maybe Willie McRae was homosexual. Maybe Willie McRae had vital information. Maybe Willie McRae had secrets. Maybe Willie McRae didn't know anything. Willie McRae was a pain in the arse. Willie McRae thought he was immune. Willie McRae was dead. Willie McRae, Willie McRae, Willie McRae.

Croick didn't show and didn't show and Peter thought, what the fuck have you done, have you done something, did you do it, if you did it why did you do it, why did you do it to *him*, why now, why not before, why at all? And if you needed me why haven't you called, and if you needed this place why aren't you here, and if you needed a key to come and go why don't you come and go? Where are you, you bastard, where are you? He felt a responsibility. Somehow it was all his fault.

Weeks went by. Peter was desperate to talk. He trailed round bars in Leith and fell in with other solitary bastards, just so he could steer the conversation round to Willie McRae, tell them what his take was and ask them what they thought. Mostly they didn't think anything and if they did it was uninformed rubbish. He was in these dens of hard, hard drinking and he drank pints of cola, it fizzed around his teeth and he felt superior to the men he was with because they were drunk and ignorant and he was sober and informed. The downside was he was only temporarily sober and not informed enough. There was only one person whose opinion he wanted to hear, and that person wasn't there.

And then the call came. It summoned him out of sleep and he crawled across the floor and reached the phone around the time he remembered he still hadn't had a drink in a fortnight.

Croick spoke in a kind of sickroom whisper, as if he had the flu.

It's me.

Where are you?

Glasgow. Can you come over?

Aye. When?

Now.

It's three in the morning.

There are all-night buses, aren't there?

Not sure.

How come you can't drive a fucking car?

There was something slurring his speech. Maybe drink, maybe something else.

Are you all right?

Just get over here. He named a hotel near Central Station. Room 431, he said. If they stop you on the night desk, say you're a friend of Mr Brown in 431. That's all you need to say.

Anything you want?

Just yourself. I need to show you something.

Right.

Good man. Knew I could rely on you. Listen.

What?

I might not be here.

Croick's voice was fading in and out.

What? Peter repeated.

What I mean is. No, forget it. I'll be here. Need to show you. Don't worry.

Should I be worried?

No. What happens . . .

What happens when?

No, no, don't mean that. The voice slurred off again.

I can't hear you, Peter said.

There was silence at the other end of the line. Then, as if from a great distance, Peter heard Croick's voice: I'm sorry.

It didn't sound like an apology for not speaking clearly.

Sorry for what? Peter said.

But Croick had hung up.

At the bus station there were a few buses sitting in darkness, some cleaning staff, and a guy in a black waterproof jacket that might have been a uniform. He stuck his tongue in his cheek and shook his head. Nae all-night bus here, mate. It's Wednesday. That's just at the weekend.

He had to wait till five for a Glasgow bus. He got the hotel number from directory inquiries and tried calling from a phone box but nobody picked up. When the bus pulled into the stance a queue formed out of nowhere, men in working clothes, men in business suits, men with purpose. Most of them went to sleep for the duration of the journey. Peter sat awake, asking himself questions, asking Croick questions. What does Croick have to be sorry about? What is it he wants me for? Where were you at Easter? Were you in the Highlands? What happened? What have you done, Croick, what have you done?

At a quarter to seven he was walking through a Glasgow city centre already busy with taxis, delivery vans and buses. The hotel didn't exactly advertise its presence. Its name was in black letters in a flickering light box over a glass door, and if you blinked you missed the entrance. Once inside, though, Peter was surprised at how the space opened up. There was nobody on reception. He walked on a sticky carpet through the lobby and round the corner to where the lift was. He smelled stale smoke and old beer. Somewhere not far away he heard the clash of dishes and cutlery, someone singing: breakfast in preparation.

He got into the lift and pulled the cage shut. The fourth floor was the top floor. There was probably some operations procedure about always taking the stairs but he couldn't remember ever learning it. The lift ascended creakily. When it stopped he eased forward to peer left and right before stepping out. He felt like he was acting in a film, playing the spy he never really had been. He was in a deserted corridor, doors evenly spaced all the way along it. Worn red carpet, featureless walls. He made his way to 431 and listened outside. He thought he could just make out voices on a radio or television. He knocked. After a few moments he knocked again. Are you there? he said. He didn't want to say either of their names out loud. He knocked again. Croick, he said under his breath. Then, louder: Croick!

The Spy Who Never Was, he thought. Good title for a Bond movie.

He looked up and down the corridor again. He began to have a bad feeling. What the fuck was he doing here? He should walk away.

He could have walked away. Same as it ever was. He sees that now. Instead he inspected the door more closely. It had a traditional mortise lock with a push-down handle. He reached for the handle and tried it. The door was not locked. He eased it open, and stepped inside.

There was a bedside lamp throwing a low light across the room. The covers of the bed, a double, were still on but rumpled where somebody had been lying on top. Pillows, three of them, had been pushed up against the headboard. The headboard was joined to wee tables, one on either side of the bed, and it was on one of these that the lamp stood. There was a telephone on the other one. The headboard also had a built-in radio-and-alarm system with speakers. It must have been stylish for about a year in the 1970s. The voices Peter had heard were coming from the speakers, a news programme, slightly off-station and turned so low he couldn't make out what was being said.

A copy of *The Times* lay discarded on the bed. Beside the lamp was a glass, an empty half-bottle of gin and an empty bottle of tonic water. Croick's tipple. A key with a tag on it that said 431. A pair of shoes was placed neatly under a chair by the window. On the chair was the familiar holdall. The curtains were closed. Peter went over and carefully pulled the edge of one curtain to one side in order to see out. He was looking at the back of another building. No windows, no watchers, no witnesses. He let the curtain fall back into place.

The radio voices continued to chat. They had nothing to do with whatever was going on in the room. Nothing was going on in the room. He went over to the bed and switched the voices off.

The door to the bathroom was ajar. The light was on, buzzing like a bluebottle. He forced himself to go in.

Croick was lying in the dry bath, fully clothed apart from his shoes. His head, resting on the fourth pillow, lolled to one side. The fluorescent light drained all the colour out of him. There wasn't much to drain. A long splatter of blood and tissue arced up the wall. More blood coiled round his neck and trailed down the white surface of the bath. The pillow was dark with blood. At the other end of the bath the shower curtain had been looped up out of the way, and the shower head was dripping fat drops of water on to Croick's socks.

Peter backed out, breathing fast, and waited till his gorge had subsided. When he looked back in he saw that the tiled floor appeared to be completely clean. Nevertheless he slipped off his own shoes, reached for a towel hanging over a rail on the back of the door, and draped it across the floor. Then he stepped on to the towel and over to the bath. He'd never had a view down on to Croick's head before. There was a patch of baldness under the dark curly hair. The bullet hole in the right temple was a narrow black tunnel full of congealed blood. Croick's right arm was slumped across his chest and there was a gun in the hand. Peter couldn't see the make without moving the hand and he wasn't touching anything, but he could see it was compact, lightweight, almost certainly .22 calibre. Not that that proved anything. The fact that it was in Croick's hand didn't prove anything. The only thing that Peter knew for sure was that Croick was dead.

Either somebody had killed him or he'd done it himself.

Peter started to make calculations. He was a contestant in a game show and the clock was counting down and he had to get everything in the right sequence or else he was out. Croick had phoned him at three. Not from the phone beside the bed, Peter hoped. Four hours later Croick was dead. He knew Peter was on his way, so either he wanted him to find him like this or he didn't. But why would he bring Peter all the way to Glasgow just to see him dead? Why did he say sorry on the phone? Why was his death so like that of Willie McRae?

Does a man get in the bath to shoot himself? Does a man, under orders from another man, knowing he is going to be shot, walk into the bathroom and get in the bath without a struggle? Maybe. If he's ready to go. If he's had enough. If he *wants* to go.

Had the pillow deadened the sound of the shot? No one had come. But the hotel didn't seem like the kind of place where people would interfere if they didn't have to.

The game-show clock was almost out and Peter didn't have the answers let alone the sequence. He looked at the corpse. He was getting used to it now. The eyes were shut, which made it easier.

Croick, the game-show host, said, You're too late, Peter.

No he didn't. Couldn't. Because he was dead.

Croick said, You're just in time, Peter.

No he didn't.

Get a grip, Peter thought. Once you go out, that's it. You'll never see him again. He stood watching, just in case there was anything more Croick would like to say. To see if, lying there in his own blood in the bath, he could answer any of the questions pounding in Peter's head.

Just in time for what? Peter said. No he didn't. That was later. He didn't say a word. He kind of nodded goodbye. Reached for the towel and hung it back on its rail. Pushed the bathroom door back to where it had been. Had he touched the handle? No, only the door itself. He took out his handkerchief and wiped the area he'd touched. He put his shoes back on. He went over to the chair and, using the handkerchief, pulled the zip of the holdall open.

Carefully he sifted through the contents. Pair of socks, pair of pants, shirt. That was it. He zipped the bag back up.

There was a built-in wardrobe. Again using the handkerchief, he opened it. One jacket on a coat hanger. He felt the pockets. Empty. He closed the wardrobe and went over to the bed. The bedside table on which the bottles were sitting had a wee drawer. He opened it. A Gideon Bible and a wallet so fat it was distorted. He lifted the wallet with the handkerchief. Without opening it he could see the edges of the notes. He heard Croick's voice. No he didn't. Aye he did. *Take it. It's theirs, not mine.* He thought, why the fuck not?

Unless of course he was being set up. Who would be setting him up? Croick? But Croick was dead. Somebody else? Canterbury? Didn't make sense. Still, Croick had told him to come and by the time he'd arrived Croick was in the state he was. What did Croick have to be sorry for? Letting him down? Or setting him up?

Need to show you.

Maybe he had phoned from this room, and maybe he wasn't on his own when he did. Peter tried to remember the exact tone of Croick's voice. What tone of voice signified someone was pointing a gun at your head?

What happens.

None of it made sense.

I need to show you what happens.

He heard it clear for the first time. That was what Croick had been trying to say on the phone. Was it?

Time to go. He put the wallet back, complete with the cash. One small victory over himself that maybe he'd always regret, because there could have been five hundred quid there, maybe more. Fuck it. He took the wallet out again, holding it in the handkerchief, flicked it open, made a pincer of his thumb and forefinger and slid the notes free. Much more. Twenties, fifties, there was even the rich red of a hundred or two at the back. He stuck the lot in his pocket and put the wallet away again. Definitely time to go. Had he touched anything else with his hands? No, only the money, which was now his. The radio. He turned it back on again, low, and wiped the switch. The curtains? Didn't matter. He retreated to the door and gently opened it. The corridor was still empty, but a trolley loaded with a linen basket and cleaning equipment was now parked halfway along. No sign of a cleaner or chambermaid. He hadn't heard anybody working either. This disturbed him. He glanced at his watch. He'd been inside the room fully half an hour. Too long. He stepped out, closed the door and quickly wiped the handle. As he walked towards the lift he heard its clunking mechanism in operation. Somebody coming up. He thought, here's my James Bond moment. I dive in the laundry basket or maybe just bend down behind it, shuffling mops and looking servile, and the hard bastards getting out of the lift heading for 431 don't even notice me, and I coolly walk to the lift and take it to the ground floor. Aye, that'll be fucking right. He turned and ran in the opposite direction, past the green fire-exit signs, and bolted down the stairs. Never moved so fast before or since. A minute later he was out in the beautiful damp air of a grey Glasgow morning.

It was eight o'clock. He made his way to Central Station and with one of his new twenty-pound notes bought a ticket to Edinburgh, and soon after that he was slowing his heart on the slow train, the one that went through the wastelands of de-industrialised Scotland, a tour of devastation calling at Uddingston, Bellshill, Cleland, Shotts, Fauldhouse, Breich, West Calder, all those places nobody outside Scotland thinks of as Scottish, the Scotland so real it defies the imagination, the train of half-empty carriages and people who got on for a couple of stops and off again, the train he felt safe on because who in his right mind would use it as a getaway vehicle? And turning his still-shuddering body to the window he drew out the wad of notes and counted one thousand four hundred and forty pounds of dead man's money and wondered if he'd just got lucky or unlucky. He stuck it back in his pocket and stared at nothing until the train rolled through the tunnel into Waverley, and nobody was there to arrest him or follow him or mug him or murder him, no matter how many times he checked over his shoulder as he scuttled down side streets, no matter how many doorways he ducked into, nobody was there, and he walked and waited and walked and waited till he could get into an off-licence for a bottle of something comforting, and then it was on to the sanctuary of JB Investigations to consult with the bottle and to begin the conversations in his head that would go on and on for ever and ever till doomsday.

There was a paragraph in the *Glasgow Herald* the next day: *Body Found in City Centre Hotel*. A spokesman for Strathclyde Police said they were treating it as probable suicide. No more details would be given till the deceased had been identified and relatives informed. That was it. No more details ever were given. Peter scoured the papers expecting not to find anything else about it and he never did. Croick had been wiped. All traces removed.

Periodically an item would appear regarding the death of Willie McRae. The procurator fiscal in Inverness had examined the case. Conclusion: no suspicious circumstances. Disbelief voiced from many quarters. Repeat: no suspicious circumstances. The Crown Office reviewed the case and was satisfied as to the circumstances of Willie McRae's death. Satisfied! No evidence of anybody else being involved. Willie McRae's family wished the matter closed. No further information to be released to the public.

Peter waited. Nobody came. Nobody seemed to be watching him. His phone wasn't being tapped. He'd got away with something, but what? Sometimes he thought he must have dreamed it all. Croick was still alive, out there somewhere in shadowland, and Peter had never had that call, never got on the bus to Glasgow, never gone up in the lift, never pushed open the door and found him lying in the bath with the tunnel in the side of his head.

The money went soon enough. He had no other evidence that Croick had ever existed. So maybe he *had* dreamed it. Maybe he dreamed everything he thought was real, and all he knew of reality were the scraps he remembered from his dreams. Maybe that was how it was. How would you know?

He'd not seen Peggy for years. Slaemill was a place he never wanted to go near again. He phoned every so often and they had stilted, unsatisfactory conversations about her health and his 'career', by which was meant his sporadic journalistic activity. He'd tried to tell her once about the detective agency but she didn't want to hear. She thought it a despicable way to earn a living. He said, It's not so different from what I did before, and you were okay about that, and she said, Don't treat me like an idiot.

Once it was one of his sisters, Etta he thinks, who picked up the phone. She didn't hold back from telling him what she thought of him. He said, Could I speak to our mother, please, if you're finished? No, she said, and hung up on him.

This time he phoned, Peggy said, I'm buying the house. I'd be daft not to. They're giving me a discount.

A discount on what?

On the market price, she said.

It's a council house, he said. It doesn't have a market price.

Yes it does, she said. Everything's got a price. I've the right to buy it, and they've valued it, and because we've stayed here all this time, your father and me, and paid rent all this time, we get a discount. Sixty per cent off.

How much do you have to pay?

Ten thousand pounds, she said. Elspeth and Etta say I'd be daft not to do it.

Why are they telling you to spend that kind of money at your age?

I'm only seventy, she said fiercely. And they're not telling me. It's what I want. Your father had a couple of life policies so I've the money saved. I'll not have to get a mortgage or anything.

You'll need to do your own repairs and maintenance, he said. Did Elspeth and Etta talk to you about that?

Of course they did. At least it'll get done if it's needed.

So you've money put by if the roof falls in?

The roof's not going to fall in. The house is solid as anything. They built good houses back then. It'll see me out, and yes, I've money put by, but Elspeth and Etta'll not see me starve. They'll help me if I need help. Or I could get a loan against the house. Your sisters say the value of a good house like this, in a good neighbourhood, it's only ever going to go up.

I'm sure they've thought it all through, he said. You pay for it, they'll get it eventually.

They look after me, she said. They've been looking out for me ever since your father died. So don't snipe at them. When was the last time you even saw them?

They don't like me, he said.

They don't like what you've become, she said.

He wasn't going to argue about that.

There'll be something for you too, Peggy said. In spite of everything.

Is that why you're doing it? To leave us something?

He thought of her in her three-bedroom, semi-detached house, the stretch of grass between it and the road, the bit of garden with the shed at the back. He remembered when they'd first moved in there, a couple of years after the war. He'd been seven. A bathroom. Paradise.

Partly, Peggy said. But mostly I'm doing it for myself. We could hardly dare imagine we might live in a house like this, your father and me. And then we did. But we never dreamed we could own it. And now I can.

Is that it? he said. Is this going to be your dream come true?

Against his will a sneer crept into the way he said it.

Dinna knock it, son, she said, and the way she switched, just then, for a moment, into the language she'd always tried to correct in him, shocked him. It *was* like a dream, she went on. A total fantasy. We'd go to the pictures to see Errol Flynn and Katharine Hepburn and the like, swanning about in mansions and hotels in their beautiful clothes, and you felt you could just about reach out and touch them, even if you couldn't really. But owning your *ain hoose*? That was beyond the realm of possibility. So don't knock it just because it's not what you want.

Sorry, he said.

I've no idea, Peggy said, what it is *you* want.

JB Investigations was dying on its feet. There were other agencies in the city now, more efficient, more mobile, less prone to losing days or weeks. He needed something else. Around this time there were long and bitter disputes in the newspaper industry. The papers were adapting to new technology and the printworkers and journalists were being squeezed between old practices and privileges and the way the world was going. Often they were being set against one another in a competition for survival. The newspaper owners wanted change, and their managements delivered it, usually without much tact or diplomacy. A sub-editor Peter had worked with suggested he get in touch about a position on a city paper. The interview lasted five minutes. New terms and conditions. Not a great job, not a job with prospects, but a job.

He knew he was being used but that was nothing new. The question of solidarity with his fellow workers occurred to him. He could live with the answer. 'Scab' was a word used less freely, as people came to doubt their own possible future solidarity. Plus it was a chance to wind up the agency and sever connections with the address in Leith. He looked around for the next-cheapest landlord he could find. He found Mr Fodrek, a Slovak who, by some mysterious, never-discussed route Peter suspected might not be unrelated to the kind of underground life he himself had lived, had washed up in Edinburgh several years *before* the Berlin Wall came down. Few questions asked, no info volunteered. Peter warmed to Mr Fodrek almost immediately, if it was possible to warm to a man who never smiled and never wasted his breath on words that weren't about business transactions. Fine. One day Peter posted a final rent cheque to the address in West Lothian, stuck the key through the letter box, and left. No forwarding address. The next day he was Peter Bond, journalist.

BOND: Did you phone from your hotel room or from a call box?
BOND (*as* CROICK): Does it matter?
BOND: Of course it fucking matters.
CROICK: Well, if it makes you happier, let's say I used another phone.
BOND: What happened to your key?
CROICK: Eh?
BOND: The key to my place you had cut. What happened to it?
CROICK: Did you not find it? Should have been in my pocket.
BOND: Didn't like to intrude.
CROICK: It was just a key. Nobody could ever trace it.
BOND: It bothers me, a thing like that. A key. Brings me out in a sweat in the night.

CROICK: Still? After all this time? Why's that?

BOND: Like it's a key to some other door. You know what's behind it but you don't. You have the key but you don't want it. Like Bluebeard's wife. Why did you apologise?

CROICK: I never apologise.

BOND: You did. Just before you hung up. Either you were sorry for something you'd done in the past or for something that was going to happen. Which was it?

CROICK: Neither. I was just, I was just going to tell you what had happened. I thought I owed you that at least. I knew I was finished, one way or the other. I thought I'd like someone to know. Someone outside. You were the only one I could tell. I thought we could have had one of our talks, like old times. But you were too late.

BOND: So what did happen? You can tell me now.

CROICK: No, I can't. I'm dead, remember?

BOND: You killed Willie McRae, didn't you?

CROICK: Ah now, Peter, you're jumping to conclusions there.

BOND: You near as damn it admitted that was what would happen to him.

CROICK: We'd never admit to a thing like that.

BOND: You killed McRae but it wasn't officially sanctioned. Or maybe you didn't kill him but you called someone else in to do it. One of your investments. Was it Denny Hogg, was that who it was? But maybe whoever it was blew it, like they'd blown stuff before. McRae was supposed to die in a car crash but he didn't die so someone had to use a gun. And maybe then they got nervous that you'd sell them or neutralise them now they'd done your dirty work for you. So they decided to move on you before you moved on them. Maybe that's how it was.

CROICK: That's a fuck of a lot of maybes, Peter.

BOND: You were out of line. And you wanted to confess to me but before I got there you blew your brains out or somebody else did it for you. And you knew it was going to happen. You said you needed to show me what happens. Isn't that it?

CROICK: Well, which one are you plumping for? It's show time, Peter. Take the money or open the box. Take the money or open the box.

BOND: Just tell me the fucking truth.
CROICK: Oh, bad contestant! You took the money, Peter. The box stays closed.

He went on taking the money, between bouts of spending it, or was it the other way round? You think back over your life and you hardly believe you existed, that you did the things you did or knew the people you knew. Life was the kind of out-of-control story you'd have been belted for in school. *And then I woke up. It had all been a dream.*

He was sober for a couple of years. He had a good work rate, could turn out a shitload of words in a few hours. He even managed to keep putting money in the bank. Days were trawling for news, writing the stories up, minimum contact with other hacks, subs and editors. Not easy to be a hermit in that kind of environment but he had a good stab at it. Evenings were walking the streets, wandering the aisles of late-night bookshops, then going home and ploughing through every newspaper he'd managed to lay his hands on during the day. Nights were sorting through the bing of books, magazines and pamphlets piling up in the flat, trying to make sense of the years of information. Sleep, if it came, was a twitching, start-stop frustration that gave no rest. Only alcohol would cure the insomnia and he fought its insidious whispers all through the long hours of darkness. At work one day somebody told him he looked like a ghost. He stored that one away. *It had all been a dream and then I didn't wake up.*

He stayed off the booze and on the paper right through till the 1987 General Election, when the Tories lost more seats in Scotland than they did in the rest of the UK put together. There'd been a lot of talk beforehand about a 'Doomsday Scenario'. This was supposed to signify constitutional meltdown: with the Tories lacking a mandate to govern north of the Border, there would be some kind of crisis. He couldn't exactly see Donald Dewar, Labour's leader in Scotland, at the head of a riot, but *something* was supposed to happen. After a lot of noise, nothing much changed. Not true. Nothing *appeared* to change. But it was a turning point. On the one hand, the government reached the conclusion that, no matter what it did, the Scots weren't going to vote Conservative. The argument ran: they buy their council houses and shares in British Telecom, they might take advantage of the new economic liberalism, but they're never going to show their gratitude at the ballot box. So, between ourselves, to hell with them. Clearly Tory majorities in Westminster are and will continue to be utterly non-dependent on Scottish seats. Let's not waste any more time on this. If the Jocks don't like their medicine they can vote for separatism. It'll take decades, on current showing, for them to do that in sufficient numbers to cause any real constitutional crisis. Meanwhile North Sea oil, the cash cow of the Thatcherite revolution, keeps flowing.

It was a realistic assessment based on past experience. But on the other hand . . . On the other hand, Peter detected a new mood shift: the natives finally going native. He thought of Jean Barbour confronting him all those years ago, and the assessment he'd made then, that the people weren't ready. It felt different now.

He felt different in himself too, ready for something. He just didn't know what.

Time ticked on. He tried not to pay attention to the worthy work of the Campaign for a Scottish Assembly and their production of plans for the future better governance of the country. He tried not to be impressed by the Claim of Right when it was published, nor by the broad consensus of political opinion that converged around it. That phase of his life was over, remember? He was, when it came to politics, as dead as Croick.

I need to show you what happens.

He missed Croick. Hated him but missed him. This is how it often is.

He was still dicing with sobriety when Lockerbie happened. The world's media descended on the south-west of Scotland but Peter Bond wasn't among them. Not his area of expertise, he was only a two-bit reporter of muggings and traffic accidents. If only they'd known! He had a free weekend and went down there and found spooks crawling all over the place. Americans, Brits, he clocked them and if they'd been paying him any attention they'd have clocked him back. But their minds were on greater things. All the stuff he'd been involved in, all of Croick's obsessions, seemed inconsequential. What were the deaths of one maverick political activist and one maverick Intelligence officer when global politics had crashed on Scotland? He came back to Edinburgh and started amassing information for no other reason than that was what he was programmed to do, and gradually Lockerbie became another bit of a vast jigsaw with no shape, no edges. He read and read and read. There were so many lies, so many versions of the truth. He thought, is there anything in life that isn't a conspiracy if you scrape down low enough?

Some time in the 1990s he fell off the tumbrel again. No, he didn't exactly fall. For a while he was clinging on as the thing bumped and jolted its way across the moon or whatever desolate scape it was in. He was dragged over the jaggy ground and collected a few cuts and bruises, metaphorically speaking. Literally too. Often the pavement rose up to meet him on his way home. He knew he was on thin ice at work and that the old tolerance for alcoholic hacks was waning. He anchored himself to his desk, typed copy that was just about good enough for the subs to reshape, and didn't care how much longer it was going to last. And when it didn't, when some management face he didn't even recognise told him they were dispensing with his services as a staffer though they'd always be willing to consider freelance submissions – ach, fuck it, he didn't give a toss.

A white knight came riding from the horizon. Peggy's ghost. Peggy died and left her house to him and his sisters, equal shares, so Mrs Thatcher had done them all a wee favour, him in particular. The sisters couldn't stop him getting his share, they would have if they could. After the funeral and the payout it was clear that they would never be in communication with him again.

Fine by me, Peter thought. I just need to make Peggy's pennies last a while.

There was a pub near Haymarket where anybody could drink themselves to death so long as they didn't fight, soil themselves or sleep on the premises in the process. He learned to pace himself there. There was a nice halfway stage between stone-cold and blitzed that he could stay in for hours. In this condition he could read the paper, speak more or less coherently to passers-by or sit in silence rearranging the box files on the shelves of his mind. Late one afternoon a woman sat next to him. He recognised her. She could have been thirty but then he looked at her greying hair and grey teeth and the lines around her eyes and added ten years at least. The hair was long and frizzy, hippyish, the clothes post-punk. When she spoke it was with a posh drawl that she couldn't really disguise by poor articulation and swearing. A kindred spirit, perhaps? What the fuck did he know about it or her or whether they had anything in common? But she sat next to him drinking gin and tonic and this reminded him of Croick and endeared her to him even before he worked out where he knew her from.

She worked in a second-hand bookshop, one of a wee cluster in among the strip bars west of the Grassmarket, the city's so-called Pubic Triangle. No, *worked* was too strong a word. She minded the shop when the owner wasn't there, sitting in a shady corner behind a desk, always reading, hardly bothering to glance up when somebody came through the door. Shoplifters' paradise. When you bought a book she begrudged the time it took to write the title and price in a big ledger and give you your change. Her stock response to any inquiry about a particular title was, If it's not there we don't have it. If anybody was persistent enough to oblige her to leave her chair, her resentment was palpable. Peter admired the complete absence of customer care. And now, on her way home, she was sitting next to him drinking gin and tonic.

He said, I used to know someone else who drank that stuff.

It's not a crime, she said.

No, he said, you're right enough.

She said, I know you.

He said, I know you too. From that bookshop.

Yeah, she said. But also from before that.

When?

Glasgow, she said. Twenty, twenty-five years ago?

I never forget a face, he said, panicking a little because he'd forgotten hers. And he looked at her, trying to take those years off her, and then he remembered. The days of the UCS work-in and the tartan terror trials. She was the poor wee rich girl in the

Che Guevara beret. He'd had a wee fancy for her then but not a lot of sympathy. Now the fancy was diminished but the sympathy was bigger. Like him she was a fugitive from the far reaches of politics, although she'd never been involved with the mad Nats because nationalism was bourgeois and reactionary.

You're Lucy, he said. I never knew your second name.

Smith, she said. You're Peter, aren't you? You were a journalist or something.

Bond, he said. Aye, I was. Freelance, with a special interest in the revolution, but if you want the truth I'm kind of through with all that.

But are you still a journalist? she asked, and there was a strange quickness to the question.

Oh aye, he lied. Got to keep the wolf from the door.

Good, she said.

Where did you go? he asked. Back in Glasgow. One minute you were there, the next . . .

. . . I wasn't, she said. So what fucking business is it of yours?

She gave him a smile, the first time there'd been one just for him for a while. She had a dulled, charmless kind of charm. Soured innocence. Maybe that was what struck a chord. They kept pace with each other when it came to the drinks too.

The third time she showed up he suspected she must have designs on him. He was astonished that any woman might have the slightest interest in the wreckage that was Peter Bond, but more astonished that he might have reciprocal designs on her. When she invited him home he couldn't think of a reason not to go.

She shared a flat on Dalry Road with a Frenchwoman, Claudine, who worked evenings as a waitress. They had the place to themselves. Lucy's bedroom was a cowp but this didn't cause Peter any distress, it was pristine compared with his. The bed was a lumpy mattress on a collapsed futon frame and it was hard to tell what were bedclothes and what were discarded day clothes. They had sweaty, grungy sex and it seemed to satisfy Lucy but when he started to say something afterwards she turned away from him and went to sleep. He thought of the wasteland of all his other nights and couldn't remember the last time he'd lain down next to another person. Then he too fell asleep. When he woke Lucy had run a bath. She went and soaked in it and when she came back he went and sat in her warm water, rubbing at the stale parts of himself with a big bar of soap. The bathroom was pretty clean and he thought he could get used to it.

He went out for a bottle of wine before the shops shut and they drank that in bed and did sex again, not so well this time. Lucy couldn't look at him for more than about five seconds at a time. He wondered if she was bored already.

About midnight they heard Claudine come home. He said, I better go.

You can stay if you want.

I'd rather go.

Whatever.

He started to get dressed. It was too soon to stay all night. It probably always would be. Despite the drink and the sex he could feel the nocturnal restlessness kicking in and wanted to be back in his own hovel.

See you again then? she asked.

You know where to find me, he said.

You know where I live, she said. Where do you live?

Not far away.

So what's the big secret?

It's not that big, he said. I'm just quite a private person, same as you.

What do you mean?

I noticed one of the names on the door is Eddelstane. I'm guessing it isn't Claudine's.

Silence. He finished tying his shoelaces. There's an MP called Eddelstane, he said.

He's my brother, she said. Mr Sherlock fucking Holmes.

So what's that about, guilt by association?

Yeah, sort of.

I don't use my given name either, he said. I'm really James Bond.

She laughed. Seriously?

Aye. Same reasoning too, guilt by association. I used to be a spy.

He saw the double take in her eyes.

I'm kidding, he said. I'm only a journalist. I like my privacy, that's all.

Well fuck off back to it then.

But he could see she didn't want him to go. She said, I hate my fucking Tory brother.

He doesn't seem like the worst of them, Peter said.

He's worse than the worst of them. At least Forsyth and Portillo don't disguise what they are. My brother thinks you can be a nice Tory.

Like you can be a nice Marxist? he said. To her credit, she laughed.

If I got you a story on my brother would you run it?

I don't work for a paper any more, he said. I'm a freelance, remember? And not much of one.

Yeah, but if I got you a good story, a really good story, you could use it, right? You could sell it to the *Scotsman* or the *Guardian* or someone?

Or the *Sun* or the *News of the World*, he said. I'd need to see the story, but aye, maybe I could.

The tabloids can't get enough, she said. They're like mad dogs turning on their masters.

John Major's government was disintegrating under the multiple pressures of mismanagement of the economy, internal policy splits and a persistent trickle of sleaze. Major had tried to clean up the Conservatives' act by announcing a policy of 'Back to Basics' but all that had done was give the press a ruler to beat them over the knuckles with. Some MPs were taking wads of banknotes in return for asking parliamentary questions. Others were exposed for having affairs and neglecting the bastard progeny thereof while castigating teenage single mothers on benefit. Supposedly happily married MPs were caught in bed or outdoor clinches with underage boys, escorts, researchers, secretaries . . . So far the Scottish Tories seemed to have escaped the worst of the sleaze effect but maybe that was because there were so few of them.

Is there a story about your brother? Peter asked.

Yes, she said. I don't know what it is, but there is one.

He stood up to go. She lay there, blotchy and grey and middle-aged, but she looked a million dollars compared with him. He smiled down at her.

I'll see myself out.

She said, I'll get that story for you.

And she did, eventually. The story of the last gasp. It wasn't much of a story but Lucy brought it to him. But first she made him wait for it.

Some winters were hard. More than once you thought your time had come, and then were startled at the ferocity with which you fought against time. You weren't ready to die, you were a survivor. There were days, though, when conditions were too severe even for you, and forced you into a town or city to beg a few coins, enough to get you shelter in a hostel till the weather eased. You hated that, the begging, the sense of defeat. The hostels were for the desperate and destitute and you were not of them, you resented sharing space with such men because in their faces too often you saw faces from that other life, blank with pain and despair and with the mark of death on them. Spring came like a release, a promise fulfilled. You came out of winters like an animal coming out of half-sleep, stretching, easing yourself back into life, and you headed back into the countryside eagerly, anxious to be alone again.

But more than once you tried too soon to be free of winter, of the men without hope. Early in the year it was, this one time, far too early, but there'd been day after day of warm sunshine and so you struck off from Dundee, up through Angus, heading deep into the glens and up and over, aiming for Deeside. Snow covered the higher peaks but the sun was beating down on your back the first couple of days, encouraging you to press on, you felt years dropping off you even though you were no longer a young man. You were alive, and that was enough.

Mid-morning. You were in among a circle of pines, gently brushing the upper inches of the thick needle blanket into a deep, dry bed. You were weary and it seemed a good place to rest for an hour. Your fingers brushed something softer than the needles, nestling between two tree roots, and you uncovered it and it was a squirrel. Cold and dead but whole and un-decayed. You looked at it for a while, the beauty of it, and you thought of all the millions of deaths of animals and birds and how seldom they were revealed, even to you who lived so much in their domain. You might find the skull of a pigeon, the bones of a rabbit, but a still-whole, not-yet-decomposing corpse was a rarity. A sparrow, perhaps, lying as if it had simply gone to sleep, so fine and alive-looking it was hard to believe it was really dead. So it was with the squirrel. If there had been violence in its death you could see no sign of it. Had it gone there to die? Had it known it was dying? Why there and not above, in the tree itself? It was perfect and so had not been dead long. You touched the tiny claws, felt for the wiry toughness of its frame beneath the ample russet coat. The heart that had stopped beating. There was a comfort in that, one final beat and then rest, and you thought that you would want to die that way too, secretly and alone and not, perhaps, knowing that you were dying. You covered the squirrel's body over again and lay down on the pine-needle bed and closed your eyes. Did you sniff the air before you fell asleep? Did you smell the change that was coming? All you remember thinking of was the nearness of your live body to the animal's dead one.

The animals would still be around long after humans were gone. Long after humans had extinguished themselves. Birds would still be around. Insects, fish, seals. Trees, rain, mud, snow, grass. The land would still be here, the sea still eating it away. Only all human endeavour and struggle and stupidity and brilliance and pain and joy and love and hatred would be over. Everything else would be as it was before.

When you woke you had been there long enough for a white sheet to have drifted down over you. You stood and shook yourself. The daylight was a dirty yellow behind the snow that filled the sky. You set off again, stamping to get some heat into your feet, and soon you were on a track across a moor, climbing into the dimming light. The wind rose and the snow came on more densely, piling up with astonishing speed. In a while you realised you'd made a mistake by leaving the shelter of the trees. You trudged on another hundred yards, stopped, looked round for a sign that the weather might lift, walked on again. It was much later than you'd thought. The last of the day drained from the sky. You turned back. How far to the trees? Two, three miles? But now the track had all but disappeared under the whiteness, and the whiteness was losing all definition as the dark came on. You were numb with cold. You stumbled, lost the track, went knee-deep in heather. All the tiredness of years welled up in you. You could lie down but you would not, you weren't ready. You thought of the dead squirrel. Had it been ready? And just as you sought blindly for the answer something loomed before you, black and welcoming. The treeline. You got beyond it and in among the pines. Back down to the glen you went, another hour or so in the thick white darkness, on to a road that was deep and unblemished but a road nevertheless. You were looking for somewhere to dig in for the night, but you'd come down too far, the air was colder, and you didn't have the energy to climb back up again.

Things fall into place. Out of the night came the scent of woodsmoke. A huddle of low buildings appeared at the side of the road. One was a cottage. Light leaked at the edges of its window shutters. You shuffled round looking for an entrance to one of the outbuildings. Inside the cottage a dog barked. A door opened and the light spilled into the yard where you were standing helplessly. Who's there? a man's voice said. Then the dog came, growling and barking. You reached down to clap the dog and it sniffed you and was easy. I need some shelter, you said. The storm caught me out in the hills.

Good God, the man said. What were you doing up there? Come in and get some heat into you. And he called to somebody inside the house to stoke up the fire.

They were a forester and his wife, and they were well used to isolation. They did not ask questions of you, but brought you to the fire and then retreated, giving you a semblance of privacy as you thawed out and took off your wet clothes in silence. The man fetched you trousers and a jersey of his own and took your clothes to hang them for drying. All right now? he said, and you nodded and thanked him. The dog settled itself on a rug in the kitchen. The woman gave you some food, and the man pressed a dram into your hand and insisted you drink it. The whisky burned your throat and made you light-headed. The fire glowed red. The woman was knitting and the man had a two-days-old paper folded on the arm of his chair. The room was full of his pipe smoke. Do you want to look at the paper? he asked. You did not. The room was panelled with dark wood and there were blue-and-white plates on the walls. They talked to you and they talked to each other and if you didn't want to join in, which mostly you didn't, they didn't appear to mind. But occasionally you would see them exchange glances, or one or the other would peer at you with curiosity, as if wondering what kind of man you were. They didn't seem afraid of you, nor was there any reason for them to be.

You fell into a doze. Through your warmed weariness you heard the forester say, I think he was looking for a place to sleep outby, and the woman said, Well, we're not putting him out, so he can sleep where he is, or I'll make him a shakedown on the floor. And the knitting needles clicked on into the night and the newspaper rustled as the man turned its pages.

In the morning when you woke the man was outside, hammering away at something, and the woman was busy in the kitchen. Your clothes were dry and folded on the chair where the man had sat. You raised yourself from the floor in front of the cold fire. There was the newspaper on the chair's arm, at eye level. The headline ambushed you: JAPANESE SOL-DIER WHO THOUGHT THE WAR WASN'T OVER. You pulled yourself on to your knees and started to read.

A soldier of the imperial army had come out of the jungle on an island in the Pacific, clutching a rusted-up rifle and wearing clothes made of tree bark. He didn't know about the atom bombs. He didn't know about the Cold War. He didn't know about anything beyond 1945. A photograph showed a bewildered-looking man about the same age as you. For a sicken-ing moment it was as if you were reading about yourself.

You read the story again. It panicked you a little less. At first you'd thought the whole thing was an invention. Now you saw that it wasn't. The report said something about time having stood still for the Japanese soldier, but this was untrue. Time had gone on for him – by the hour, by the day, by the year, just as it had for you, for everybody. The difference was he had continued to live in a world that no longer existed.

You were not him, you couldn't be. You'd come out of the jungle, beating him and the rest of his kind against all the odds. But weren't you the same after all? He'd never surrendered, never given up. Now he'd come out of the jungle all these years later, and found himself famous, but where were you? You were somewhere else, on another journey that had nothing to do with him, nothing to do with anybody.

You could smell porridge cooking. Suddenly you were alert. You were grateful for the kindness of the forester and his wife, but it was a trap. It was pointless trying to explain this to them. You yourself didn't fully understand, but you knew you had to escape. Quietly you put on your clothes, found your boots and haversack. The kitchen was down a short passage leading to the back door, and the woman could not see you. The dog was nowhere in sight. You went to the front door, taking your coat from a hook beside it, and stepped outside. The sun was shining and the road was a shallow river of slush. You closed the door gently and slipped away from the sound of the man hammering and whistling and from the smell of porridge. You had to go then or you might never have gone.

You left two stones on the hearth, so that they would know you had not been a dream.

Then, like the snow, you melted into the landscape.

PART FOUR

Scenes from Olden Days

Borlanslogie in the 1950s: a small, suffering town always on the verge of getting to its feet, always just about to be cowped over again. Most of the men were miners, or worked in coal-related jobs of one kind or another; the rest, a scattering, were shopkeepers, labourers, bus drivers, postmen, railwaymen, a couple of publicans. A very few worked on farms in the surrounding district. Once long ago there'd been only a village and the entire population had been colliers, a race apart from the rest of the world. Then came roads and railways and the village grew to a town. Then came war and peace and war again. Some of the social divisions frayed, but not many. The mine managers, surveyors and engineers still lived, along with the doctor and the schoolteachers, in the better houses on the out-skirts of the town, away from the worst of the dirt, while the colliers and their families inhabited rows of cottages that seemed to hunch together against the weather, accident and adversity without much expectation of avoiding any of them. These rows had no names, only numbers – 1st Street, 2nd Street, 3rd Street – and only in recent years had the cottages themselves acquired numbers.

The women of Borlanslogie cooked meals for their hungry men, meals as vast as they could make them given the strictures of money, coupons and rations. They washed clothes and cleaned their houses and minded the bairns. During the war some of the women, in addition to all this, had worked in the Logie Coal Company's engin-eering workshop, a huge shed where the bogies and engines and other equipment used in the pits were made and repaired. But with the war over they weren't wanted there any more: some were as capable of working a steam hammer as any man but the men didn't like that fact, and they pushed the women out of the workshop and back into their cottages.

Other parts of the great, grimy old palace of King Coal, however, had long been considered suitable for women to work in: the tra-cing room, for instance. This was where Mary Murray worked.

She'd started during the war and nobody, if she had anything to do with it, was going to force her from a job that paid a steady wage and enabled her to look to the future with some degree of hope.

She was the third of four sisters. The older two, Meg and Alice, were married to miners and were breeding the next generation, three boys and a lass for Meg and twin boys for Alice. The youngest sister, Dot, had been conscripted for munitions work in Birmingham in 1942 and had settled there. Mary's tracing work wasn't physically hard, but she had to concentrate. There were huge sheets showing all the underground workings, the tunnels and roads and the seams of coal, and the type of rock or clay that the coal ran through at different depths and in different sectors. Like an underground city it was, and the surveyors and architects were always adding on new levels and districts, and it was the tracers' responsibility to update the charts and maps on to the big sheets. They had to climb up on to the tables sometimes to do the job properly, carefully copying in the new information, tracing particular sections that then needed to be enlarged on the huge photostat machine, or making copies for the engineers on the even more cumbersome copying machine. Their eyes would be streaming from the ammonia that was needed to fix the images. The amount of detail on the maps was amazing: Mary felt she knew all the workings even though she'd never been in them, she could picture the men moving around down there, ghostly, glistening with sweat. The system the miners used was called 'stoup and room': as they cut the coal they left pillars of it in place to hold up the roof, so she thought of the mine as a kind of Greek temple in black, rows and rows of black columns stretching away in the beam of the men's lamps. As they worked out a particular area they'd put props in and cut out the stoups if it was safe to do so, so as not to waste any of the coal. Mary diligently marked all the stoups on the plans and diligently removed them when they were cut away. Once she suggested to her supervisor, Mr Cochrane, that he should arrange for the tracers to go down in the cage to see the pit for themselves, it would give them a better idea of what it was they were mapping. Cochrane was appalled. 'Mary, there's been nae women doon a Scottish pit in a hundred years. It's no a place for a woman.' 'I'm no wanting tae howk the coal,' she said, 'I'm just wanting tae see what it looks like.' But

Cochrane was dead set against the idea, and so were the other tracers, except for her best pal, Ina, who was game for just about anything.

Maybe Cochrane had a wee fancy for Mary, she thought he must because he was always speaking to her, distracting her from her work. It was disgusting really, he was three times her age at least, but Ina told her to play along with it and she'd get favours without having to give anything in return. Cochrane was married to an ugly old witch she saw in the town occasionally, who always looked like she'd just broken wind and didn't like her own smell, Ina said, so the poor man was probably keen for a bit of civilised female company. And right enough, one day not long after the war was over he took the two of them aside and asked if they fancied a change of scene the next day. He and a surveyor called MacDonald were taking a company car over to Aberfoyle, where they were to survey a portion of forest that the Logie Coal Company had bought for pit props. They were to measure the area that was being bought, count the trees and mark the ones that were ready to be cut down. Aberfoyle was away to the west in an area called the Trossachs, very beautiful by all accounts, and it would mean a full day out of the office, so they both said yes at once and Cochrane's face lit up like a wee pink pig's at sight of a bucket of swill. And the next day a black car with leather seats and polished wood fittings took them, Cochrane, MacDonald, Ina and Mary, across the country to the wet green woods of Aberfoyle, where it poured with rain and the girls shivered and sloshed about in rubber overshoes while the men measured the forest with chains, and had Ina holding one end of a long cloth tape in a leather case while Mary wrote down the numbers they shouted out, and MacDonald daubed the letters LCC in white paint on the trunks of certain trees, and Ina swore every time the mud went over her ankles, and Mary nearly fell over giggling, and Cochrane winked at her whenever he thought nobody else was looking. And at dinner time they repaired to the Bailie Nicol Jarvie Hotel, a splendid, rich-looking place the like of which Ina and Mary had never been in before, and they all sat round a table in the lounge bar and had bowls of cock-a-leekie soup and a glass of whisky each – 'Just tae warm ye up,' Cochrane said, 'and the Company can pay for it too, I think, eh, MacDonald?' And MacDonald looked doubtful but it didn't stop him having a dram, and in fact the men had a second but Mary and Ina were tipsy just with the one, it being the first time either of them had ever tasted whisky. And all the way back to Borlanslogie they rolled into each other on the leather seat, and Cochrane, who was in the back with them, told them slightly risqué stories till they were in fits, more at him than at the stories, because he was a sad wee grey man and the stories were tame compared with the stories Ina could have told. But there was something kind and good about Cochrane too, Mary thought, even in his sadness, and he never laid a finger on either of them. Mac-Donald the surveyor was altogether grimmer and more menacing, and had maybe thought there was to be more to the day than there was, a bit of fun away from the wives; at any rate he glowered at them occasionally from the front-passenger seat, and conversed in low tones with the driver, and maybe it was because he was thwarted that he stirred up the other surveyors next day to complain about the lassies going on the expedition, saying that they had no competence or training and were trespassing on their area of expertise, and the outcome was that such a trip was never suggested again. Mary and Ina stored it up as a precious memory, though, one of the best days of their working lives.

Her wage was small but Mary saved what she could from what she didn't hand over to her mother every week. She didn't know what she was saving for except the future, and then she started going with Jock Imlach and she knew, and she realised too how important it was to keep her job: because Jock's life and Jock's earnings were erratic, and if they should stay together and get married her own wage would give her some stability. He was bold and different, Jock, which was why she fell for him in the first place, even though she was warned by her mother and all her aunts and sisters that he wasn't steady and she'd pay for that in the long run. What she liked about him was that he'd made up his own mind what he did and didn't want to do. He'd worked three years down the pit, aged fifteen to eighteen, during the war: it was a reserved occupation, he'd had no option, but once the war was done he chucked it in and refused to go back. It was the winter of '45–'46: you went down in the dark, you laboured all day in the dark, you came up in the dark and you went home in the dark. 'I'm no a bloody mole,' Jock said. He and Mary were sitting having their Sunday tea with his parents before stepping out for a walk and a cuddle, and Jock said he'd had enough. He didn't want to die young, crushed or drowned or gassed underground, or still alive but coughing his guts up, ancient at fifty. 'What makes ye think ye're special?' his father had demanded. 'Ye're just feart o hard work.' 'I'm no,' Jock had said, and it was the truth, because he wasn't afraid of it, he just didn't like it. 'I'm no special. I'm just sane.' He looked at his father, and Mary could see he was thinking, I don't want to turn into you. And after that he took whatever job came along, he'd work for farmers or builders or the council roads department, short-term labouring work with no security, rain, snow or sun it didn't matter so long as he was up on the surface, better to be there even if he didn't earn what he could below ground. What was the point of good money if the getting of it killed you? 'The miner that walked in darkness has seen a great light,' he said. 'Dinna blaspheme,' his mother said. 'I'm no blaspheming,' he said. 'The blasphemy's in the life the rest o them lead.' And he quoted Joe Corrie, the Bowhill poet, who'd written some fierce stuff back in 1926, the year of the Great Strike –

> Me, made after the image o God –
> Jings! but it's laughable, tae.

And Jock gave a bitter, ironic laugh himself, and threw in a look that made Mary like him all the more although she saw trouble in it too.

They wooed and they wed, and ordinarily that would have meant the end of her job as a tracer, but she had a nagging mistrust that Jock wouldn't always provide, so she went to see Mr Cochrane. Now Cochrane knew she was a good worker, one of his best, competent and reliable, and he liked having her around of course, and he said, 'Aye, Mary, we must move wi the times, I'll no pit ye oot o a job just on account o ye being a mairrit woman.' So she stayed on, right through till January 1947 when the coal industry was nationalised and she became an employee of the National Coal Board, and on Vesting Day there was a bonus for all the workers in the industry. Which was fine, except that Jock, who was well out of it by then, but cynical as ever, said, 'Aye, but look how much they're giein the

Logie Coal Company in compensation. Your wee bonus would slip through a hole in their breeks and they'd never ken it was awa.'

Well, he'd given her a Christmas bonus himself by then, and all through January, February and March of that cold, cold winter, when the best thing you could do to keep warm was go to your bed from dusk till dawn, she grew the new life in her beneath the blankets, and all through the spring she kept going to her work, saying nothing about it until it was too obvious to be denied. Then Cochrane called her in and said, 'Aye, Mary, we'll be letting ye go soon, I see.' She said, 'Aye, but I'll want tae come back. Will ye keep a place for me?' Cochrane gaped at her. 'But ye'll hae a bairn tae look efter.' 'The bairn'll be looked efter,' she said, though she'd no idea how, 'but I'd like tae come back tae my job.' Cochrane huffed and puffed, and said it was unthinkable, but he'd think about it, the main thing was she was to go away and have the bairn and they'd talk about it after.

So she went away and Ellen was born, a hard birth it was but it didn't change Mary's mind, it made her more determined than ever to go back, because she knew by then she'd have to fend for herself and the lassie, she couldn't depend on Jock, he was good for a joke and a story but not for providing life's essentials. Jock seemed to measure freedom by the number of miles he could put between himself and the pits; he went further and further afield for work, anything that promised good pay and plenty of overtime, although more often than not the reality didn't live up to his expectations. He had no staying power, and was always on the lookout for something better. It was the age of the hydro schemes in the Highlands, and Jock worked on one after another of them. Postal orders came home with reasonable regularity, and sometimes they were big, but more often they looked like they represented the scrapings from his wallet on a Monday morning. He spent plenty on drink and gambling, Mary knew it. He'd always been one for the horses. It was one of the reasons he kept taking work at a distance – so she couldn't take his wage packet off him unopened as happened in most other households. If she challenged him about it on one of his brief returns home he got angry and defensive: wasn't a man away from his family and friends to have a few wee pleasures from time to time, and what business was it of hers how much he was earning? 'I'm your wife,' she said, 'and this is your daughter.' 'Aye,' he said, 'I ken who ye are. I'll no see either of ye starve.' 'No, because ye'll be away in Inverness or somewhere,' she said. Then he slammed out of the house on his way to the pub. He was back later with a wee drink in him, daft for her then, and he charmed her in spite of herself, but she knew very well to put no faith in his charm.

So she spoke to Cochrane again, and asked if he'd keep her in mind for getting her job back in a year or so. She had the notion that her mother would take the bairn through the week – somebody would have to, Ellen was that inquisitive and demanding she required full-time attention – but a year seemed an age away, and she could see Cochrane calculating that she'd change her mind or fall pregnant again before she was back at his door, and he said, 'Aye, fine, Mary, in a year,' thinking that would be the last of it. But no, every time he saw her she'd say, 'I'll be back in nae time, Mr Cochrane,' and the months went by fast enough, and in the summer she was at him again, 'Now, Mr Cochrane, Ellen's nearly one and my mither's tae take her frae noo on, so I'll just come in tae start next week, will I?' And he hadn't the heart or the courage to stop her, she was a good worker and he missed her spirit in the office, and another tracer was leaving anyway, they were all away to get married and have bairns, it was like a national epidemic. 'Mary,' he said, 'if ye can dae the work I'll be glad tae have ye.'

§

Ellen came home one day, during her first term at school, to find her twin cousins, Adam and Gavin, in the kitchen, drinking milk as if it were about to be abolished. Her mother was there and didn't seem to care how much of it they drank. They had the bottle on the table between them and were filling up glasses, knocking it back, filling them up again, and when the bottle was finished her mother fetched another from the pantry and let them set about that too. Adam and Gavin were eight, three years older than Ellen, and every gulp of milk they took seemed to make them swell up so she thought there soon wouldn't be space in the house for them all.

Which was upsetting, because it seemed they weren't just passing by on their way to their own house, they would be staying the night. In fact, her mother explained, they'd be staying a few nights, till Auntie Alice was better.

'Is she no weel again?' she said. Auntie Alice was always catching her breath and coughing, and complaining of a sore chest and faintness. She wasn't a strong woman like her own mother.

'Aye, she's very poorly,' Mary said.

Adam, whom she liked the better of the twins, said, 'She fell doon when she was daein the washin and noo she's in the hospital.'

'How can they no stay wi Auntie Meg?' Ellen asked, because they'd done that the last time Alice was in the hospital.

'Because Auntie Meg's got her hands full,' Mary said. 'It's oor turn tae help.'

'Is Auntie Alice gonnae die?' Ellen said, because it had happened before. Uncle Harry, whom she hardly remembered, had died in a terrible accident at the pit.

'No, she's no,' Mary said.

'Aye, she is,' Gavin said.

'No, Gavin,' Mary began, but he pushed away from the table and ran from the house. 'She is!' he shouted. He didn't want them to see him greeting, that was what that was, Ellen thought. And she knew who was telling the truth.

Adam finished the milk in his glass, wiped his milk moustache on his sleeve and without a word went after his brother. If Ellen had used her sleeve as a clout or left the table like that she'd have been shouted back, but Mary let the boys go, following them with a look that was almost tender.

Ellen said, 'Is that them away then?'

'No,' Mary said. 'They'll be back. And ye've tae be kind tae them, Ellen, till your auntie's back on her feet again.'

But Auntie Alice didn't get back on her feet. She had bad lungs and the broon katies but in the end it was the pneumonia that did for her, about a week later. It could have been worse, it might have been TB, there were folk in the city slums dying like flies of TB, and if you coughed you gave it to everybody else and you had to go to a faraway place in the hills where they wheeled your bed out in the snow and left you to freeze all day and night and sometimes it cured you although usually you died. If you had TB nobody wanted to be near you. When Auntie Alice coughed people looked fearful in case that was what was wrong with her. It wasn't but she died anyway and then they all came to her funeral and the boys were in black suits and their hair was stuck down with water and Ellen heard someone say that they were cursed, first their father now their mother, what next?

Uncle Harry had died in an accident in the pit along with six other men. They were still down there. They'd had a funeral for him but Ellen was too wee, she wasn't at it and neither was he, he was buried already, miles underground. They didn't put Auntie Alice deep enough to meet him but he was already away, they'd meet in heaven, that was what the minister said. When the boys left the church they held hands. They were brave. Gavin said he didn't think there was such a place as heaven and Auntie Meg said there was, but Ellen was pretty sure Gavin was telling the truth again.

People still spoke about Uncle Harry, he was a kind of hero and he couldn't help being in the accident, but soon people didn't speak about Auntie Alice, it was as if she'd done something wrong by being weak and not coping. Ellen felt sorry for her but also she resented the fact that her aunt had left her own mother no option but to take Gavin and Adam in. Because her Nana and Dey couldn't take them and Auntie Meg's house was full and one thing was for certain, they weren't being taken away to an orphanage. 'Over my dead body,' Mary said. So they stayed, allied in their orphaned state against the world, and became to Ellen like two older brothers. They all got on well enough. Ellen tolerated the new arrangements partly in the belief that if she behaved herself the boys would eventually leave and things would be as they'd been before, just her and her mother and from time to time her father. It took a while – a year or so – before she finally twigged that they were there for good. By that time there was even a fondness between the twins and Ellen. The boys were big but subdued and Ellen was wee but bumptious, yet somehow it worked, maybe that was *why* it worked, and just as well, Mary said, there wasn't room in the house for fighting. Adam and Gavin slept in the back bedroom that had been Jock and Mary's, and Mary and Ellen slept in the box-bed in the front room, and if Jock was home Ellen got a shakedown in front of the fire, or she went round to her Dey and Nana's on 7th Street and slept there, which was better for everybody and especially for her. In fact, she spent more and more time there, so much that it began to feel as if that was her home, and 2nd Street was a place she visited occasionally for a change of clothes or the weekly bath in front of the fire.

For Mary there'd been no choice in the matter. With Jock seldom home she was the one with the space, and the boys were family. It would have been a betrayal of Alice if she hadn't stopped them from being put in a home. Jock was irresponsible but not cold-hearted and he agreed with her. He grumbled at the extra costs and complained that there wasn't room for him in his own house, but the new situation gave him all the excuses he needed to stay away more or less permanently. He needed to earn more, he said – not that much more appeared on the postal orders. He liked Gavin and Adam, but not enough to make him settle.

Mary didn't have time to argue about the situation. She wanted to do right by her dead sister and by her two nephews. She rushed home at dinner time to feed the three bairns, packed them off to school again, and told them to go to their granny's afterwards till she was home from work. After a few months of this the twins decided to skip the interludes at Nana's. They learned to manage without Mary, to make pieces for themselves and Ellen during the day, and to prepare the tea when they came in from school. They were a unit, almost inseparable, and knew not to expect to have things done for them – not to expect anything much in the way of special attention. Mary was as fair and kind as she could be, and appreciative of their willingness to help around the house, even though she hardly showed it. She persuaded herself that what she was giving them was the best thing they would ever possess – the ability to survive. As their mother never had done, they were coping.

With Ellen it was different. She needed to engage with adults. For years Mary relied on her parents to keep Ellen out of harm's way. Long after she started at the school, she still spent most of her evenings and weekends at her grandparents. Often she slept the night and went to school from there in the morning. This made her feel special and independent. It made her feel like herself.

Nana and Dey were getting old and worn, and so was everything they possessed. Their street was somehow poorer than the others, a begrimed, crouching, sorry-looking row of cottages made sorrier by the bright, bold marigolds Nana grew in the thin beds beneath her windows every summer. The cottage was impregnated with the accumulated odours of years, a mixture of old soup and smoke and sweat and earth, powerful and cloying. Whenever Ellen went in, the smell hit her. It took a minute to get used to it again, then it was cosy and friendly like the house itself, a secret, safe den of a place. Nana was always bustling, never still. She made toast and spread raspberry jam on it for Ellen, and poured her tea from the same pot her Dey had his from, thick and swirling with bits of black twig floating in it. Strangers, Nana called them. She showed Ellen how to pick them out and thump them between her fists to see what day they were coming to visit. Sometimes the tea was that full of strangers her Dey would look around the room in horror and exclaim, 'Guid-sakes, whaur are we gaun tae pit them aw?' He had his tea black with sugar, but Ellen had hers topped up with milk, for it was that strong it would turn your insides to leather and she was too young for that, her Dey said. He had leather insides himself, but that was because he was sixty years old, you didn't want to get them too young or you'd start creaking. 'Listen!' he'd say and right enough she could hear him creaking away like the seats on buses, his lungs wheezing like air brakes. She always listened when her Dey or Nana said she should. If her Dey said, 'Sharpen your lugs, lass, and I'll tell ye something ye dinna ken,' he nearly always did. Or when thunder rolled around the sky on a clammy August evening, and her Nana said, 'Aye, there's God getting his coals in for the winter,' she could hear the din of him doing it.

Coal, coal, coal, everything was coal: her Dey's coal-black spits hissing as they hit the red coals shuffling in the grate; the scuttle full of coal waiting to be thrown on; the layer of dust on windows and shelves. And Nana's jam was coal-dark and thick and luminous with seeds. 'The jam ye get at the shops'll never taste like that,' she said. 'It's no real, the bought jam. They pit woodchips in it tae look like seeds, sae ye think it's the real thing, but it's no.' Her Dey nodded solemnly over the rim of his mug. 'She's telling the truth, lass, and it's no just the jam. The capitalists keep the best o everything for themsels, and the rest o us get crumbs.' 'If we were their dogs they would treat us better,' her Nana said.

Her Dey had worked for years down the Borlanslogie pit, which had been sunk when Queen Victoria was a lassie, he said, and would likely go on giving coal till this new queen, Elizabeth, was in her grave. A long while, in other words, barring accidents or revolution. Even the accident that killed Uncle Harry and closed off one of the main galleries hadn't stopped production, though it had caused a lot of problems quite apart from the loss of seven lives. But her Dey's back and lungs couldn't take being underground any more, they'd brought him up on to the surface, where they paid him less to work on the tables, sorting the coal as it came up. That was where he'd worked as a boy, fourteen years old. 'Ye start on the tables and ye finish there,' he said, spitting black spits as if his insides were not only made of leather but lined with coal like the sides of the tunnels he used to crawl through. When she started school, she finished half an hour before her Dey was lowsed and she'd go up to the end of 7th Street and wait for him there. He'd come down the road from the colliery with some of the other older men, the ones with injuries or illnesses or who were just worn out and worked above ground like him, and although he wasn't as black as he used to be his clothes were still full of dust, and he'd to go through the house to the back and stand there in all weathers, take off his overalls and beat them, just standing in his drawers whacking the stour out of his clothes and hawking and spitting tar on the ground. He wasn't always in the mood to chat to her, he was sometimes tired and crabbit. But a few months later he started to come home cleaner and more cheerful, for they'd finally built a bathhouse for the men up at the pit. Of all the dozen collieries in the area, Borlanslogie was the last to get its baths after nationalisation. 'Noo washed by the National Coal Board on behalf o the people,' her Dey said, pulling his breeks up to display his pure white shins. Some days he didn't need a bath, as if he'd not been at his work at all. But they paid him for the hours he was there, even if there was little to do. That was a change since the coming of the Coal Board. In the old days the Logie Coal Company would never have paid him to be half-idle.

So things were better than they had been. Before the war, there had been weeks, months sometimes, when there'd been no work. The olden days, her Dey called them. He'd go from pithead to pithead, he'd walk for miles looking for any kind of labour, and always where he walked there were other men walking beside him, or returning along the road he was going. The empty-handed days. 'I used tae come hame tae your Nana,' he told Ellen, 'Janet, I'd say, there's naething again. Ye'll need tae tighten oor belts. That was your Nana's job, tae tighten the belts on baith o us sae your mither and your aunties could eat. Ye live in blessed times, lass, compared wi then, but it's nae thanks tae the capitalists that ye dae.' And she looked around at how little they had, the very negation of plenty, and wondered how they could have had less, but in that dark crouched cottage somehow things never seemed to get a lot worse, just as they never got much better.

Next door on the right were the MacLeays. They had three sons who had all emigrated, gone to Australia on £10 tickets. The MacLeays looked permanently sad to Ellen, especially the old woman, whose eyes filled with tears whenever she spoke of her sons on the other side of the world. They had a dog, a fat, waddling thing, a cross between a Jack Russell and a pig, that Mr MacLeay was forever walking round and round the streets. If he stopped walking he would have to sit down and then he would die, that was what Ellen thought.

On the left were the Hoggs, a cluttered household that seemed to change its personnel week by week, though there were usually four or five men – a father, some sons or cousins – going to or from the pit in a dirty, loud crush along the street. Mrs Hogg was a fixture, sweating and clattering around her kitchen preparing meals for this army of Hoggs, and so too was her mother-in-law, Auld Mrs Hogg, an ancient moustached crone with yellowish, wolf-like eyes, long yellow teeth, yellow skin and long grey hair tied back from her ears with a greasy bit of string. Most days she lay in a narrow bed in the front room, talking to herself or anybody who came in and delivering loud, poisonous and frequent farts, so that the room stank of rotten cabbage. Occasionally, if the weather was fair, Mrs Hogg would haul her out on to the street and sit her in a wee armchair while she turned out the bed, washed the sheets and aired the room. And then there was Denny, who was ages with Ellen and – according to Nana – had come along years after the other Hogg bairns because Mrs Hogg forgot herself one night, although how you could forget yourself was something Ellen didn't understand. Denny was unpredictable: he could be funny and friendly one day and the next he'd take the first opportunity to pinch or bite you. He himself seemed to have no sense at all that his moods varied. The only thing you could be sure of about Denny was that he smelled of pee and had a permanent dreep on his nose. Periodically he removed this with an upward sweep of his forearm, naked or sleeved it made no difference, in a snottery salute to the sky. Ellen was both repulsed and fascinated by the Hoggs. She imagined they might be distant relatives of Sawney Bean the cannibal and his extended family, who had lived in Scotland in the olden days and turned passing travellers into stews and pies. She took good care not to get too close to Mrs Hogg when she was cooking, or to Auld Mrs Hogg's claw-like hands, and although she quite enjoyed Denny's company she guarded herself well when she thought a biting mood was on him.

Her Dey had his own chair that he alone sat in and nobody else. Nana had her own chair too but she was seldom in it and other people could use it when she wasn't. There was a table beside Dey's chair for his library books and papers and tea. For all that they were hard up they always had newspapers in the house: in the morning it was the *Scottish Daily Express* and in the evening it was the *Daily Worker*, delivered by Polish Patrick who liked to sit and dissect the day's stories with her Dey over yet another mug of tea. Sometimes Nana used to join in too. She was as sharp as any man when it came to politics. When she was wee Ellen couldn't understand how human beings could spend so long looking at all the tiny print in the papers without exploding with the amount of information they took in. For a long time the only bit she liked to read was the Rupert Bear strip in the *Express*. But her grandparents' habits laid down a pattern for her. In later years she recognised that it was from them, at least in part, that she had inherited her voracious appetite for facts and explanations. From them, too, her ability not to let a political principle obstruct her appreciation of the wider world: so long as capitalism lasted, her Dey would say, there was no harm in the pleasures afforded by Beaverbrook's *Express*; you just had to understand it was all propaganda, even Rupert Bear.

By the time she was eight she never went anywhere without a

pencil and notebook, in which she recorded anything of interest or importance. She had several pages devoted to Polish Patrick, who had fought the Nazis when they invaded Poland in 1939, escaped to Denmark, then, when Denmark was occupied, slipped away to Norway where he'd rejoined the Polish forces fighting alongside the Norwegians. Eventually, when the Allies withdrew from Norway, he'd come to Aberdeen on a listing ship packed with angry, dismayed Poles, Danes and Norwegians, and had spent the next two years building coastal defences and preparing to fight the Nazis when they invaded Scotland. And all this, Ellen learned over many hours in Patrick's company, he had done with no expectation of success or reward, but simply as a small detail in the great saga of human history. With Patrick's help she drew a map of his adventures, and a picture of him, improbably Herculean, straddling a cluster of concrete tank traps on a beach in Fife. He worked for the roads department now, in a depot full of great mounds of gravel and sand, a neat, sombre, sober man with a shiny bald head. He had a voice that came from deep in his chest, that was both purer and yet more guttural than the way everybody else spoke in Borlanslogie, and he said very little but what he did say seemed always to be of grave import. There was never the leg-pulling, the deadly earnest that turned out to be a joke at your expense, the daftness or downright deceit that other grown-ups dealt out: Patrick was kindly and attentive and he took Ellen as seriously as she took herself. Patrick had married a Scots girl but she had died soon after the war and he had not married again. Of his family in Poland, if he still had one, he never spoke. He appeared to have no close friends and yet everybody liked him. At social gatherings he would sit quietly on the edge of things, making the odd dry comment, and in the corner of his mouth would be a cigarette, which occasionally he'd light and take two or three short puffs from, then pinch out till the urge came on him again. He could make three cigarettes last a whole evening like that. He was unfailingly polite and well turned out, the smoking his one concession to self-indulgence. Yet the control he exercised over his appearance and manners seemed not to come from within himself but from somewhere else, as if he polished his shoes and shaved his chin and stood up in the presence of women because he could not help it. He lived his life as if it were in the hand of some great invisible force that he, as an individual, could neither influence nor escape. And maybe this was true, and maybe this was how he'd ended up a Communist, delivering the *Daily Worker* to the proletariat of Borlanslogie.

Stuffed away on a shelf under her Dey's table was a tartan travelling rug. 'I dinna ken why it's cried a travelling rug,' he said, 'it never gangs onywhaur.' Ellen was an Imlach and he was a Murray; the rug was a Murray tartan, which was red with dark bits, it was hard to tell in the poor light what colours they were. He'd unfold it in the cold winter and wrap it round his knees, which ached with the rheumatics, or he'd let Ellen hap herself up in it till just her nose was poking out, being tickled by the fat woollen tassels of the rug's fringe. 'Ye look like a spaewife,' he said. 'Will ye tell me my fortune?' She said one day he would find a pot of gold under a tree and be richer and happier than a king, and he said that would be fine, he could do with the gold but he was already better off than any king could ever be, because he didn't have the blood of working people on his hands. She loved chatting away to him and listening to his stories, and scribbling down things that he said. 'Ellen Imlach, Ace Reporter', her Dey called her, and she liked that and wrote it on the inside cover of her notebook while he told her of John Reed, an American journalist who had written *Ten Days That Shook the World* about the Russian Revolution. Maybe one day, he suggested, she would write a book like that herself. She blew at the tassels and said she probably would. That travelling rug may not have gone anywhere, but *she* did when she was happed up in it.

Pinned to the wall behind her Dey's chair was a bright yellow tea towel on which a fierce red lion stood on its hind legs with its paws up like a boxer, only there was nobody for it to box. 'That's the flag o Scotland,' he told her, 'it's cried a lion rampant,' and she thought a 'rampant' must be a special kind of flag till he explained that that was the proper word for the way the lion was standing. She wrote LION RAMPANT down in her notebook. 'But is the Scottish flag no blue,' she said, 'wi a white cross on it?' 'That's the *ither* Scottish flag,' he said. 'It's cried a saltire. We've twa because we're a special country. We should be independent but the English made us join in wi them and slaughtered us if we objected, so we hae twa flags tae mind us no tae forget we're Scottish.' The blue flag had come about in the olden days when the Scottish tribes were at war with the tribes from England, and just before one particular battle the clouds in the blue sky had come together in the shape of the cross of Saint Andrew, and the Scots had taken this as a sign that they were going to win a great victory, which they did. And ever after Saint Andrew was the patron saint of Scotland, which was fine because he was also the patron saint of Russia, which was the only decent, free and fair country in the world for poor folk. And Ellen wrote down SALTIRE and SAINT ANDREW and RUSSIA very carefully in her notebook, with her Dey spelling the letters out for her in his big, broad voice.

At school the next day she put her hand up and asked her teacher if she could tell the class something interesting and important. Miss Pearson was suspicious of volunteers since they usually had ideas above their station, but she also knew Ellen to be her most precocious pupil and that it was better to lift the lid off her occasionally than have her bouncing like a steamy pudding at her desk, so she granted Ellen her request, and Ellen stood up and repeated the story of the miracle in the sky. When she'd finished, Miss Pearson said Ellen had told the story well, and gave them another, about when the Vikings came to conquer Scotland in their longboats. They came ashore one night very quietly and took off their shoes and crept up on the Scots in order to massacre them where they slept. And they would have done it too, only one of them stood on a jaggy purple thistle. He let out a scream and the Scots woke up and drove the Vikings back into the sea, and ever since then the thistle had been the emblem of Scotland.

Ellen asked about the lion rampant and wasn't *it* the emblem of Scotland? Yes, it was another one, Miss Pearson said, you saw it on flags in places like Edinburgh Castle. It was a *royal* emblem, though, it belonged to the Queen and you could only fly the lion rampant if you had permission from a very important person called the Lord Lyon, who was spelled with a Y not an I. The Lord Lyon, Ellen imagined, was a grand old man who stayed in a castle, not Edinburgh but one out in the country surrounded by a huge forest full of deer and squirrels. He had a tawny beard like a big ruff around his face and neck, and long flowing hair, and yellow checked trousers and a red jumper like Rupert Bear on the cover of the annual, the same colours as the flag, and he was usually quite kindly but he could also be fierce, especially if he found out you had a lion rampant when you shouldn't.

Back to her Dey she went, to ask if he had permission to have the lion rampant on his wall. He was breaking the law if he didn't, she explained, and the Lord Lyon would come and arrest him.

'Haivers. Wha tellt ye that, lass?'

'Miss Pearson. She's my teacher.'

'Aye weel,' he said, and seemed about to say something derogatory about Miss Pearson but restrained himself. 'I doot we'll no fash aboot the Lord Lyon. His heid's ower big for him tae come doon here and arrest me. If ye ask me, the Lord Lyon maks things up in his heid as he's riding alang on his muckle horse. I'll gie ye some advice, Ellen, that'll mebbe stand ye in good stead when ye're aulder. Never trust onybody whase name has a "Lord" in front o it. Beaverbrook, Lyon, Nelson, it disna maitter. He micht hae a voice like silk and a bonnie wee wife and a parcel o deeds and documents in ablow his oxter but he'll steal the shirt frae your back if ye tak your een aff him for a second. Oh, and while I'm aboot it, that applies tae *the* Lord tae. Aw ye need tae ken aboot kirks is that the folks that gang intae them are aye gaun aboot crying their god *the* Lord. As if we owe him rent.' And he spat blackly into the hearth.

Never trust The Lord, she wrote in her notebook. *He will steal your shirt.* Her Dey had a worn old book called *Our Scots Noble Families*. It had been written fifty years before by Tom Johnston, the Secretary of State for Scotland during the war and now the man in charge of building hydroelectric power stations in the Highlands to bring heat and light to the poor folk of the glens. That was what her father was doing, her Dey said, she should be proud of him being involved in such a great work. Her Dey said Tom Johnston was a good man but he moved in higher social circles than he had when he wrote that book and was probably a bit embarrassed about the things he'd put in it. Back then he'd been one of the Red Clydesiders and had run their weekly newspaper, and hadn't been afraid to tell the truth about the bloodsuckers, tax-gatherers and pickpockets who made up the Scottish aristocracy. The history books made out that these people's ancestors were heroes but they weren't, they were thieves, bandits and murderers. The real heroes in Scottish history came from the working class, men like the socialists of Clydeside, and none more heroic than the schoolteacher John Maclean, who'd been sacked for his politics and imprisoned for his opposition to the First World War, and whose health had been broken by the way the authorities had treated him. He'd died a young man still fighting for justice, he was made Soviet Consul in Great Britain by Lenin but that didn't stop him criticising the failings of the Russian Revolution and it didn't stop him breaking away from the Communist Party and calling for a Scottish Socialist Republic. And then Ellen's Nana chipped in from the other side of the fire saying Maclean might have been a saint but he had the faults of a saint too, he believed he was always right. 'Awbody's oot o step but oor John,' her Nana said, and her Dey said that wasn't true, it was just he was the only clear-sighted one among them, and that was the reason he didn't get on a train to go and be a Member of the imperial Parliament in London along with Jimmy Maxton and Davie Kirkwood and Manny Shinwell and John Wheatley and the rest. 'Weel, that's why he didna achieve onything,' her Nana cried, 'the ithers were realists. Whaur was his sense of solidarity?' 'His solidarity was wi the people,' her Dey shouted, 'and that meant no compromise wi the system he wanted tae destroy.' 'No compromise?' her Nana shouted back. 'That's easy. The truth is ye just love John Maclean because he's deid. Ye'd hae found plenty wrang wi him if he'd lived. Like ye find wi Wullie Gallacher.' 'Wullie Gallacher?' her Dey snarled. 'Lenin's gramophone, that's what Maclean called Gallacher.' 'Ach, ye're like a gramophone yersel, ye daft auld bugger,' she said, and she poured him more tea and told Ellen not to pay him any heed, and Ellen knew that for all they argued they did it because they loved and respected each other. They enjoyed arguing, and Ellen enjoyed seeing them at it. If politics was something they could get so angry and passionate about, it must be important.

§

One day when she arrived at her Nana's the Hoggs' house was quiet for once and Nana told her Auld Mrs Hogg had passed on in the night. Ellen sat and read her book for a while, *Heidi*, about a lassie from the Swiss mountains who was happy till she had to go to the city where she was sad, and Heidi in the coloured picture at the front of the book looked like Ellen only she had curls and a red dress. But when Nana was busy making something to eat Ellen slipped out on to the street to see what, if anything, was happening next door. And Denny stuck his head out at the same moment, as if he'd been expecting her, and gestured her over. They were both eight or nine, no more. Denny's mother was at the undertaker's, seeing about a coffin, and all the men were at work, and Denny had been instructed to stay put and make sure his granny wasn't left alone. Which Ellen thought odd, because Nana had said she'd passed on, so surely she wasn't there any more? Denny said it was just her soul that was away, the rest of her was still there and his mam would go daft at him if he didn't keep his granny company. That was odd too, Ellen thought, because Auld Mrs Hogg had often been abandoned by everybody while she was alive, so why would she care now she was dead? But Denny's mother was fierce when roused, so she could understand why Denny was doing as he'd been told.

'Come in and I'll show ye something,' Denny said. 'It's a beezer. Ye'll no believe it.' They went inside and he opened the door to the front room. Auld Mrs Hogg was lying like an oversized doll, propped up on pillows in the narrow bed from which she hadn't stirred for weeks. The curtains were drawn but with the door ajar a little light came in from the passage and fell on the old woman's face. Denny and Ellen stood and watched her. If you held your own breath you could almost imagine she was still breathing, that she wasn't empty and hollow. The room smelled damp, but then it always did. Was Auld Mrs Hogg damper dead than she'd been alive? And how quickly did a dead body start to go off? Ellen had no idea. She'd never been in the presence of one before.

'Dae ye want tae touch her?' Denny whispered. She shook her head. 'Watch this then,' he said, and he crept across the room and put a finger to his granny's cheek, as if performing a dare. Then, placing both hands on the blankets above her middle, he pushed down with sudden violence. He hurried back to the door. 'Listen,' he said, and she held her breath again and suddenly there it was, unmistakable, a long, whining pump from the bed, like a squeaky door hinge. The two of them went into kinks.

'She's been deid three oors and she's farting away the same as ever,' Denny said.

Suddenly Ellen stopped laughing and had an intense need to get out into the open. Denny came with her to the door but he wouldn't leave the house. Ellen felt as if she'd grown taller just by stepping into the light. It was like going from a story into real life, or maybe the other way round, because a strange, unreal figure was coming down the street towards her, a man. She knew everybody in these streets but not this one. He was thin, oh so thin, in a long heavy coat done up to the neck and with a bag slung over his shoulder, if he'd had a stick and a spotted bundle in a handkerchief hanging from it she wouldn't have been surprised, and his face was made of the same material as Auld Mrs Hogg when she was alive and more so now she was dead, leathery-looking, brown and hard. She imagined her Dey's insides looked much the same. And the stranger came towards her and he fixed her with piercing yet distant eyes. She might have been frightened but she wasn't, there was something sad about the man as if he were searching for something; he looked at her to see if she was it but she can't have been, for on he walked, right past her, straight and silent. And then he stopped, in the middle of the street, and turned round. He beckoned to her and although she knew she mustn't go she went, but not all the way to him. He reached into his pocket and took something out and bent and laid it on the ground, and gave her that strange stare again. Then he turned and was gone. And Denny was away back inside and hadn't seen him. Nobody else was in the street. Nobody saw him but herself. She could almost believe he hadn't been there at all, except he had. She went to the spot where he'd bent to the ground and saw it, a smooth white pebble like a huge peppermint. She picked it up and held it, and it was the proof that he had been there. She took it home and kept it, but she didn't say anything to anyone because there was nothing to say, and she didn't write it down in her notebook because it was a secret thing that she could not explain even to herself.

§

And soon after this there was Harold Macmillan telling the British people they didn't know they were born, or words to that effect. 'Indeed let us be frank about it – most of our people have never had it so good,' the Prime Minister said in a speech to the Tory faithful at Bedford. 'Go around the country, go to the industrial towns, go to the farms and you will see a state of prosperity such as we have never had in my lifetime – nor indeed in the history of this country.' Well, maybe there was some truth in what he said but you would never have got the miners of Borlanslogie to admit it. '*Maist* o oor people,' her Dey stressed. 'He's saying *maist* o oor people. He's no including us, then. He canna be. He disna ken onything aboot *us*.' 'We're no haein it as bad as we usually dae, that's aboot the best ye can say,' was her Nana's opinion. If there were Kremlin-watchers in Whitehall, there were Whitehall-watchers in Borlanslogie, analysing what the capitalists said, dissecting and rubbishing the fat lies every night over their tea, with or without the assistance of the *Daily Worker*.

But there were difficulties over the *Worker*. The stories of atrocities and then the stream of refugees coming out of Hungary after the Soviet invasion the year before had led to more arguments in the cottage in 7th Street. Her Nana was inclined to keep faith with Khrushchev: if he didn't take a strong stance the anti-revolution movement, urged on by the capitalists, would infect not just Hungary but every other Communist country, and the great hope of the working classes in the West would be destroyed for ever. Her Dey wasn't so sure. 'We kept faith wi Stalin till Khrushchev denounced him,' he said. 'And if it taks tanks and bullets and mass arrests tae convince the people what's good for them, can it be aw that good for them?' He was especially vexed that the *Daily Worker*'s cartoonist, Gabriel, a Glaswegian called Jimmy Friell, had parted company with the paper after it rejected one of his cartoons. Friell had been ruthless for decades in his depiction of fascists and capitalists alike, but when he produced a picture comparing what the Russians were doing in Budapest with what the British and French had tried to do in Egypt during the Suez crisis, the *Daily Worker* refused to print it. He'd resigned, along with a number of others – a sign, if any were needed, that Dey and Nana's lifelong dream was fading. Polish Patrick still came round with the paper every night, and Dey still bought it off him, but there was something suspect about the transaction now, as if Patrick knew he was selling shoddy goods and Dey knew he was buying them, but force of habit and faith prevented either of them admitting it.

The dream was of a land of equality and peace and plenty. Ellen read a long, glowing description of life in the Soviet Union in Volume 9 of Arthur Mee's *Children's Encylopedia*. When her Dey dreamed she thought that was probably what he dreamed of, in the way other people dreamed of heaven; and she decided that both places sounded far too good to be possible. She was ten and spending more time back in her own home, not just because it was the summer holidays, but because of Arthur Mee. Adam and Gavin, at thirteen, were supposed to keep an eye on her and make sure she didn't burn the house down, but really she was just as responsible as they were so they often left her on her own. And she was happy to be left – happiest of all when she had the place to herself – and the reason was the recently arrived *Children's Encylopedia*. It sat on a shelf in the front room, in ten hefty volumes, and Ellen felt that the world – the whole universe in fact – had somehow entered their house and that her life would never be the same again.

Mary had ordered the *Encyclopedia* from a door-to-door salesman and had signed up to pay for it on a two-year plan. It was costly, but she'd calculated she could meet the payments even without any of the money that periodically arrived from Jock. The books were rich and splendid in their burgundy covers with the lettering picked out in gold. Mary made a rule: you could take down only one at a time, or one plus the last volume, which contained the index. Ellen was determined to read the lot from cover to cover.

They were for her and her cousins, Mary's compensation for not being around as much as she felt she should be, and an investment in all three children's futures, but to Ellen they felt like hers alone because Gavin and Adam didn't have her staying power. They flicked through the pages looking for the colour plates of 'Fishes swimming in foreign seas', and butterflies and moths, and tried to learn tricks such as 'The Inexhaustible Matchbox' and 'The Wizard's Handkerchief', but they were intimidated by the densely packed pages of print, diagrams, maps and photographs. For Ellen, these were the *Children's Encylopedia*'s chief attraction. Knowledge, layer upon layer of it, seven hundred and fifty pages per volume. She could be engrossed for hours with a photographic sequence on 'What Happens in an Ironworks', an explanation of 'The Willow-Pattern Plate', seven pages on 'The Birth, Life and Death of a Flower', 'Music – the Meaning of Dots', and seventeen pages on

'Napoleon and His Conquerors'. She read without judgement or preference, equally entranced by Bible stories, basic lessons in French, nursery rhymes and 'The Right Way to Cook Vegetables'. Although she knew it could not really be the case – and later discovered that he'd in fact died years before, during the war – she half-believed that Arthur Mee had written every word and chosen every image in the books. She was flattered by his easy, avuncular style, the way he explained things as if nothing could be beyond either her intelligence or her imagination. She thought of him as a family friend, old-fashioned but not dull, and she wanted to know everything that he knew. When she read about primates, 'The Animals Most Like Men', and that gorillas were 'peaceful giants, only roused to wrath if their homes are invaded', she immediately liked gorillas and felt that Arthur Mee must have been among them and liked them too. And when he told her that they were entirely confined to 'the dim forests of the western half of Equatorial Africa' and that 'when civilisation reaches there the gorilla will vanish from the Book of Life', she was almost reduced to tears, and felt that when that day came the page she had just read would also, by some fateful mechanism, be removed from the *Children's Encyclopedia*.

Later, Adam came round to it. Ellen found him one afternoon with three or four volumes spread out on the floor, and was about to nag him for breaking the rule, but he was so intent, and when he looked up gave her such a smile, that she just said nothing but sat down next to him and they spent an hour reading articles out to each other. 'Where's Gavin?' she asked. 'Dinna ken,' Adam said. 'He wanted tae dae something ootside but I didna want tae, sae I didna.' They must have had a fight, she thought, but said nothing. A space had opened up between the twins, and a new bridge lay between Adam and herself. After that Adam's thirst for information grew rapidly, till it was almost as great as her own. She liked that, but she still liked it better when she had the *Encyclopedia* to herself.

She came across a sequence of photographs about water power, including images from the Highlands, where her father worked. Water poured over a dam at Loch Ericht: the caption read, 'Tunnels through the solid rock lead the water to the turbines in the powerhouse below.' Jock was home for a fortnight that summer – between jobs, he said – and she showed him the pictures. 'Aye, lass, that's what I build, dams like yon.' She wanted to know exactly what he did and it appeared he did everything: putting up or taking down scaffolding, laying pipes, shifting machinery from one place to another, digging roads, blowing up rocks, pouring concrete. He worked in all weathers too, in waist-deep snow, week-long downpours, Arctic gales that would knock cows over, and in summer, sweltering, tropical, midge-swarming heat, the midges were the size of wasps and if you hung your socks out of the window at night there'd just be a heel left on the ground in the morning, the hard matted bit even they couldn't chew through. There was one time he was working up in Ross-shire, mixing concrete day after day to make huge sections of a dam on some scheme or other, it was winter and nobody had any gloves so first thing in the morning your hands would stick to anything iron and some lads left their fingertips and had to go back for them at dinner time when the sun was up and you could gently ease them off, but the cold preserved them and if you stuck them back on in just the right place they joined up again. And icicles would grow in your beard, all different lengths so you could play a tune on them like it was a xylophone, 'The Campdown Races' maybe or 'I'll Take You Home, Kathleen', whatever you fancied. And you were tipping sack after sack of cement, and it was raining and you were sweating so you got concreted yourself, you were like a harled wall by the end of the shift and had to walk back to your digs like a robot, it was all you could do to eat a meal and then you just wanted to sleep so you didn't bother to wash, you fell on to your bed in a straight stiff line and when you woke in the morning you had to crack your breeks in order to bend your legs and you were dropping grit and concrete lumps off you for the first hour of the day. You were always busy, you never stood still, och you didn't dare, there was a big man from Aberdeen called Archie, the Marble Arch they nicknamed him, and he stood still once, just thinking about something or other, and a boy in a crane thought he was a concrete buttress and picked him up by the collar and if they hadn't all waved and roared Archie would be part of the Cluanie Dam now. On and on with his stories, ones she knew were pure nonsense and ones which were half or maybe even three-quarters true, and funny and heroic and exciting though it all sounded something wasn't right, and it was this: Ellen knew that most men did one job, all the time, and here was her dad doing half a dozen. She didn't know him at all, her own father. She wanted to: she liked him, and he seemed to like her, filling her head with story after story about the folk he worked alongside: daft, roaring Irishmen, quiet Poles and Lithuanians, a German or two left over from the war, even the odd Englishman. The men he spoke about were so real and lifelike, the stories so bold and monumental, yet there was something shifting and insubstantial about himself. Even though he was so much bigger than her she felt she was the more solid.

More serious, certainly: when she showed him the pictures in the Arthur Mee books she turned the pages with confidence and read the text studiously, while he only glanced, his gaze sliding away, his mind always flitting off somewhere. She wanted to find out, whereas he had the look of a man about to *be* found out. He could never settle to anything for more than ten minutes. When Mary came in from her work and they were all having their tea together he'd be constantly glancing at his watch, not listening to her attempts at conversation, scraping back his chair and off out the door even as he forked the last bit of food from his plate into his mouth. There was beer on his breath, more often than not, and he smoked Woodbines ferociously, right down to the nip, and his thumb and forefinger were yellow and hard where the tobacco burned them.

She overheard Mr Hogg in the street one day, speaking to her Dey: 'I see your Mary's Jock was hame again. Is that him awa?' 'Aye.' 'Aye dodging awa up in the glens, is he? What is it he's up tae noo?' And her Dey said, 'Ach, ye ken Jock, he does a wee bit o everything.' 'A wee bit o everything and no a lot o onything, eh?' Mr Hogg said in a joking tone but there was an edge to it. And her Dey came back, 'Weel, he's working onywey. Aye sending his wage hame.' The way he said it, half-heartedly, she knew there was something in what Mr Hogg said. She wanted to go out and shout at him, kick him, defend her dad's name, but she knew she couldn't. *Dodging awa.* He was a dodger, which was one step from being a waster. And if he was doing all those different jobs, how come there was never any spare money in the house, and her mother was always scrimping and saving? Adam and Gavin cost a bit, no doubt, but only in food, and she herself hardly cost anything at all. The

Children's Encyclopedia was the one luxury they had – although to Ellen it wasn't a luxury, it was a necessity. She didn't know at first what it was for, but it was definitely for something. Later, she found out what. If you were going to go out into the world, it was necessary first to understand it.

§

The world was – always had been – intense to David Eddelstane. It pressed itself upon him in the stuffy, airy, hot, cold, bright, gloomy rooms and passages of Ochiltree House, dripped from the towering cedars of its garden, pointed lewd, sticky rhododendron buds at him, pricked him with the stems of huge, pink, scent-laden roses. Life wrapped around him and he pushed through it as if through dense drapes: the blue or grey linen of the day sky, the star-spattered, blue-black velvet of the night. Hedges were heavy tapestries he brushed against, daisies and long grass and tulips were made of lace and cotton and silk. It was like being in a Fuzzy Felt world, but with an infinite variety of fabrics.

His mother, Lady Patricia Eddelstane, when she had nothing better to do, sometimes deigned to read him a bedtime story. Winnie-the-Pooh wanted a balloon so he could float up in the air and reach the bees' honey, but should it be a blue balloon to merge with the sky or a green one to merge with the tree? Pooh couldn't decide. David, at five, felt the intensity of that dilemma. His mother dashed through the pages – she'd come to his bedside equipped with a cigarette and a gin and tonic and both were soon over – and grew frustrated when he insisted on her going back to the bit about the balloon colours. 'Oh *come* on, darling, it's only a *story*.' And so it was, a funny one, but he took it very seriously.

He took everything seriously then, including the rows between his mother and his father, which, no matter how often they occurred, always felt like the opening salvos of a full-scale war. He never witnessed actual physical blows, but a lot of missiles flew through the air: spoons, shoes, books, the occasional plate. Once at Sunday lunch Lady Patricia shied an orange at Sir Malcolm's head. He had just announced a three-month freeze on the Jenners account. 'Miser!' she screamed as she let fly. Sir Malcolm ducked and the orange smashed through the French window behind him. 'Missed, you bitch!' he bawled, glanced over his shoulder at the broken glass then carried on with his meal. It was January: a cold wind blew in through the window. David and Lucy quaked in their chairs. They were eight and five. Even if they had understood that their mother had no intention of observing the Jenners embargo and their father none of enforcing it, the exchange was too loud, too aggressive for comfort. Lucy started to wail. 'Stop that,' her father ordered. She did. David's bottom lip came out, quivering. 'Don't you start,' his mother warned. He didn't. Only Freddy, three years old and perturbed by nothing, not even the plummeting room temperature, appeared not to care.

It never occurred to Sir Malcolm and Lady Patricia that such behaviour might be detrimental to the healthy development of young children. It was part of the rough-and-tumble of daily life and if the children didn't like it they would just have to get used to it, just as they would have to get used to being present and correct whenever there were guests, which was often. On these occasions – dinner parties, cocktail parties, shooting parties – David, Lucy and Freddy were expected to play their well-mannered parts in a family display of love, sweetness and light. David, for the first seven years of his life, lived a double life, privately absorbing the sounds and sights of his parents' spiteful, ramshackle relationship with each other or conspiring in their smooth, charming public relationship with the rest of the world. Sometimes they heaped on him so much praise and jollity in front of visitors that he was almost persuaded they loved him. At other times, when everybody else had gone, he'd catch them, individually or as a pair, giving him baleful stares as if they couldn't quite believe he was theirs. But he was, and would continue to play the dutiful eldest child into adolescence and eventually adulthood. All he wanted from them in return was that they sometimes leave him in peace.

But peace was a rare commodity at Ochiltree House. Unless guests were imminent, the whole place was in permanent turmoil, a kind of playground littered with discarded books, newspapers, cups, glasses, cigarette stubs, shoes, boots, carpet slippers, fishing tackle, shotguns, cartridges, hats, coats, underwear, dog hair, dog bowls, handkerchiefs, socks and unfinished snacks, as Sir Malcolm and Lady Patricia roared and rambled through their day. Outside were gun dogs barking in kennels, hens, a family of ferocious geese, and bad-tempered McLeish, the gardener. All of these, apart from McLeish, periodically gained entry to the house as well. The Eddelstane grown-ups were huge, unruly, selfish children, bullies who had no idea they were bullies. The Eddelstane young were their victims, and two of them, at any rate, knew it only too well. Not Freddy, who took no notice of anything, whether it was his mother shouting or himself trailing hen shit round the house; but Lucy stored her victimhood up for a great explosion years later; and David cycled or ran to escape, hid up trees or in his bedroom or in the attic, or followed behind Mrs Thomson, the housekeeper, as she went from room to room tidying, collecting, rearranging, repairing, dusting, wiping and sweeping. Mrs Thomson and he didn't have a lot to say to each other but at least what she said was delivered in a consistently reasonable tone. He might even have come to think of her with unsuitable fondness – unsuitable, because, for all her understanding of the need to make the Eddelstane household look respectable when the outside world came to call, she was only a woman 'from the village' – had he not been relocated to boarding school at the age of seven. Mrs Thomson, his mother and Lucy – and Freddy, except for one year when they overlapped at prep school – became people with whom he shared only a third of each year.

He saw even less of his father, who was away much of the time, having been elected to the House of Commons as the Member for Glenallan and West Mills in the year of David's birth. He had a flat in London – the word 'flat' sounded unbelievably modern, not at all the kind of place an Eddelstane would stay in – and travelled there by sleeper when Parliament was sitting. Occasionally, under protest, he took his wife with him. For fourteen years he did his political bit, a sozzled, soup-stained, alternately angry and accommodating backbencher offering more or less loyal support to four successive Tory Prime Ministers – Churchill, Eden, Macmillan and Home. In 1960, somewhat prematurely, he had received his reward, a knighthood.

During the 1950s Glenallan and West Mills was solidly Unionist – full of farms, respectable wee villages and half-forgotten clusters of cottages, and, at its eastern extremity, a run of industrial villages, the Mills, still reliant on textiles and papermaking for their survival.

As a Tory MP one could expect support not only from the rural, more affluent parts of the constituency, but also from that sizeable chunk of the working-class population which still defined itself politically through its adherence to Protestantism. This was the Unionism of Scottish politics then – born not from loyalty to the Union between Scotland and England (for who in their right minds was against *that*?) but from opposition to Irish Home Rule and Roman Catholicism. Privately Sir Malcolm didn't give a damn whether God was pink, blue or yellow as long as He kept His distance, but he was brusquely grateful for the Orange vote. He himself wasn't interested in that kind of tribalism. The English, in his opinion, had it about right when it came to religion: bend the knee, pay due homage, then get on with life. But this wasn't England, and he wouldn't look a gift-horse in the mouth. If people wanted to vote for him because they thought he would keep the papists at bay, who was he to argue?

But by the early 1960s Sir Malcolm was beginning to worry. It wasn't just that the Conservative government was running out of steam and its financial ineptitude was making Labour look economically competent. Nor was it simply the disrespect he detected in so many young faces. Something else was going on: hard to say what, but it felt threatening. An undercurrent. He didn't like it.

Was it sex? Perhaps it was. He'd sown a few wild oats in his time, still did when he got the chance, so there was nothing wrong with him in that department. He hadn't married till he was forty, and Lady Patricia was only ten years behind him, but her production of three children in the space of five years proved everything was in working order. Suddenly, though, everybody was *talking* about sex. Why? Sir Malcolm knew: *that* book, and *that* trial. Let sleeping dogs lie, was his view. By stirring things up the Puritans just drew attention to the fact that people, perfectly respectable people, *extremely* respectable people, had secondary lives. Friendships that were nobody's business but their own. Understandings. Everybody knew it went on but why did they all suddenly want to *talk* about it? Why couldn't they just shut up and let things carry on as normal?

Home for the Christmas holidays in 1960, David came across it, *that* book, submerged in a pile of other books and magazines in the morning room, his mother's territory. He found it before

Mrs Thomson did, and took it off to his bedroom to investigate: *Lady Chatterley's Lover*, a Penguin paperback. He sniffed at it: definitely his mother's perfume. At his prep school a copy of the *Scotsman* was left in the reading room every day for the boys, so he knew all about the trial that had taken place two months before. He knew that various writers and critics had appeared to defend the book against the charge of obscenity, and he remembered that a lawyer with a double-barrelled name, who'd been trying to get it banned, had been mocked in the press for asking the men on the jury if it was a book they would want their wives or servants to read. That had made him think of his father, and whether he would want Mrs Thomson or McLeish to read it. David had thought at the time that he wouldn't, but that they probably wouldn't care to read it anyway. David couldn't imagine them reading a book at all. But what about his mother? She might. It looked like he'd been right.

It was bright orange, with a drawing of a bird on a bonfire on the front. *Complete and unexpurgated*, it said, for three shillings and sixpence. David was ten. He didn't know what 'unexpurgated' meant but it didn't take him long to find out. The book fell open at various places where his mother had folded the page corners down. He was a good reader and he was looking for something in the text, though he'd no idea what it was. He read about Lady C. and the gamekeeper, Mellors, and what passed between them. He thought of his mother, Lady E., and the gardener, McLeish, and then he put that out of his mind because the only things that passed between his mother and McLeish were orders and McLeish's wages. Instead, he concentrated on the intoxicating shapes the words made in his mind. 'She felt his penis risen against her with silent, amazing force.' He felt something akin to this stirring in him, not physical but the precursor of something physical. 'Oh, and far down inside her the deeps parted and rolled asunder, in long far-reaching billows.' He didn't fully understand that, but it connected with something he himself felt. The sentences imprinted themselves on his brain and stayed there. He skipped back and forth through the chapters, ignoring the plot, ordering the sequence of sex scenes. He was too young but he understood he had discovered something, a secret. It wasn't in the book, it was in himself, something that only he knew, even if he didn't fully know it. After a couple of days he dropped the book back into the morning room. It wasn't what he wanted. It wasn't *exactly* what he wanted.

§

The film already had notoriety, a magnetism that drew people in. The trailers and other publicity had done their business and when Don and Liz Lennie, with Bill and Joan Drummond, arrived at the Regal in Drumkirk they had to queue on the street for half an hour for tickets. While they waited Don felt a growing distaste at the mass curiosity, and about himself being caught up in it. They were all being manipulated. SOMETHING NEW AND AL-TOGETHER DIFFERENT IN SCREEN EXCITEMENT, the posters proclaimed beside the cinema steps. And everybody was talking excitedly, half-anxious, half-eager, shuffling along like cattle to market. As if Mr Hitchcock himself were herding them in against their better judgement, mockingly corrupting them. *Come on, come on, you know you want to. And you there, complaining about the price, I'll wipe the moan off your face.*

It had been Bulldog's idea to go. 'It's supposed to be a wee bit . . . ye ken?' he'd said to Don, at the Blackthorn the previous Saturday. 'See if ye can persuade Liz. Get the wives oot the hoose for a change, eh?' 'It's no a sex film, is it?' Don asked. The title, *Psycho*, seemed alien and unpleasant, he wasn't sure what it might represent. 'She'll no go if she thinks it'll be dirty.' 'No, no, it's a Alfred Hitchcock,' Bill said. 'A thriller, real edge-of-the-seat stuff. Just right for Halloween. But we canna take the kids, it's X-rated. Joan's game for it. We dinna go tae the pictures enough these days, no since we got the television. We'll get the neighbours tae mind oor bairns, and if you can sort oot something for yours we can all go, gie oorsels a bit o a scare, maybe go for a fish supper efter.' And when Don seemed doubtful he said, 'Och, come on, everybody loves a Hitchcock flick.'

But this was nothing like other Hitchcocks they'd seen. *To Catch a Thief* or *North by Northwest* had been thrilling but they were roman-tic and full of humour too, and Liz and Joan were daft for Cary Grant. There wasn't anything romantic about *Psycho*: it was seedy and malevolent and any humour in it seemed cruel, disturbing. All through the film the Regal resounded to collective gasps, cries and screams. Some people forgot to smoke, others couldn't stop. Quite a few left during or immediately after the shower scene. The rest, Don reckoned, couldn't have got out of their seats even if they'd wanted to. His upper arm ached where Liz gripped on for most of the film. At crucial moments she turned her face into his shoulder.

Afterwards Bill lingered on the steps, ogling the poster of Janet Leigh in her white brassiere, nudging Don with his elbow, but the women hurried them away, past a stern-faced Alfred Hitchcock pointing at his watch and warning NO ONE ... BUT NO ONE ... WILL BE ADMITTED TO THE THEATRE AFTER THE START OF EACH PERFORMANCE. A new queue was waiting to go in for the next showing, and Don found himself looking away in case he caught the eye of someone he knew, someone from his work perhaps. He didn't want them to know what they were letting themselves in for. Is that what you were meant to do? Were you meant to come away feeling sullied, like you'd participated in something wicked? And what if you were a woman? How different would you feel then?

It was a thick, damp night, the pavements were slimy and the fog seemed to swallow them. When Bulldog slipped ahead and then jumped out of a close with a sinister laugh, Liz and Joan both screamed, and even Don's heart quickened. 'That's enough, Bill, eh?' he said, and Bill looked sheepish for all of ten seconds.

Rinaldi's was bustling and noisy, cigarette smoke hanging in the air, the windows steamed up, diners packed in at the wee tables and a queue for carry-outs at the far end of the long counter. The smell of chips and the café clatter were reassuring, familiar. Faith in human nature was restored, almost. But Liz was still white-faced. 'I hope the boys are all right,' she said, as if somehow the awful things that had happened on screen could happen in real life, just up the road in their own village of Wharryburn. She stared at Don and he remembered Janet Leigh's dead eye staring at them from the shower stall. He remembered the water running with blood, the heaviness of the rain Janet Leigh drove through after she stole the money, the brittle shriek of the music, the frenzied attacks in the shower, on the stairs, the chair swinging round in the fruit cellar with the corpse of the mother in it. None of it made sense, and then you saw the crazed figure in the dress and wig wielding the knife, coming to get the sister, and it kind of did. Liz looked like she'd never be able to get the film out of her head.

'They'll be fine,' Don said. 'Betty'll be looking efter them.' The boys had gone next door for their tea, and would be happily watching Betty's television, an item the Lennie household hadn't yet acquired, till they got home. Billy was thirteen, quiet, selfless, responsible. Charlie was a different case but Don trusted even him to behave himself at Betty's, because he knew if he didn't he'd not be allowed back to watch TV.

'We'll get hame just as soon as we've had oor supper,' Joan said. 'Bill will bring the car tae the door here, won't ye, Bill?'

'Aye, door-tae-door service, that's me,' Bill said. 'Eh, what aboot that car sinking in the swamp, though? Wi aw that money in the boot. What a waste, eh?'

'I thought it wasna gonnae go doon,' Don said. 'It stuck for a minute. I thought he'd had it then.'

'It wasna just the money in the boot,' Joan said. '*She* was in the boot, poor thing.'

'Ach, she shouldna have stolen the money,' Bill said. 'That's what ye get if ye're dishonest.'

'She didna deserve *that*,' Joan said.

'I didna say she *deserved* it,' Bill said. 'But it was like that's what happened tae her *because* she was on the run, because she checked in at *that* motel . . .'

'She would hae taen the money back,' Don said. 'Ye could tell that was what she'd decided tae dae. But it was ower late.'

'I'll tell ye one thing,' Liz said, and because she'd been so quiet they all shut up and turned to her expectantly, 'as long as I live I will never go in one of thae things.'

'What, a car?' Bill said. 'Ye'll need tae if ye're coming hame wi us.'

'No, a shower,' Liz said. 'I could never get in a shower and pull the curtain shut. I'd be thinking somebody was gonnae come at me wi a knife every second.'

The waitress arrived with two platefuls of fish and chips and peas, a scliff of lemon on the side of each plate. She went away and returned with the other two plates, for the men, and Bill picked up his knife and made repeat stabs in the air above his fish while imitating the screeching violins from the soundtrack. There was a bottle of tomato sauce on the table and he shook it and splattered a quantity on his chips. 'Blood, blood!' he squawked. 'Oh God, blood!'

'It's not funny, Bill,' Joan said. But she was trying not to smile and then she couldn't stop herself, she did laugh, and Don knew she'd enjoyed the whole experience, including having the wits frightened out of her. She was different from Liz. He wished . . .

In a couple of days it would be Halloween. The boys would go out guising, in black cloaks and hats, and ghoulish flour on their faces and trickles of red sauce strategically placed. Billy was really too old for it now. This would be his last year. He'd go because Don would tell him to, to keep an eye on his brother. Not that Billy had any control over Charlie, it was usually the other way round. When Billy sang songs or recited poems or told jokes he did it with anxious, imperfect effort but folk applauded and handed over sweeties, sometimes even a few pennies. Charlie wanted a reward just for chapping the door. He knew a couple of poems and he delivered them without fault, machine-like, but there was a kind of edge to the way he did it, a threat. *You'd better pay up when I'm finished*. Don had seen it when he'd gone with them two years back, standing in the background as they performed. Even then he'd been worried about Charlie. Now he worried even more. Some kids got into trouble on Halloween, used it as an excuse for a bit of mayhem. That was why Don wanted Billy out with his brother, this year at least, as a witness. Charlie didn't like witnesses.

He wished the English nurse could have been cuddled into him in the dark cinema. Ten years on, yet she still came into his mind. He'd never seen her again.

There was comfort in the good, hot food. The four of them ate, saying little. And then Don voiced the other thing that had been bothering him. 'I ken it's no right,' he said, 'but I felt sorry for him.'

'Who?'

'For the son. For Norman. I feel sorry for him.'

'You're as sick as him then,' Bulldog said.

'Can we talk aboot something else?' Liz said.

'His mother sent him round the bend,' Joan said. 'I didna feel sorry for him, but he was mad, so I suppose it wasna his fault.'

Bulldog speared a long, thin chip and held it up. 'They should've sent him tae the chair. Fried him like this chip. But I suppose he'll spend the rest of his days in the loony bin. The doctors say he's no right in the heid so he gets away wi it.'

'I don't think,' Don said, 'he got away wi onything much. He was a tortured soul, a misfit. He didna fit in at all.'

'Don aye feels sorry for tortured souls,' Liz said. 'Like Jack Gordon. He felt sorry for him tae.'

There was a brief silence round the table, as everybody considered Jack.

'Dae ye ever hear frae Sarah?' Joan asked Liz. 'That'll be, what, two, three year since she left?'

'Aye, aboot that. She sent us a caird the first Christmas, but that was it.'

'The lassie, she'll be half-grown up noo,' Bulldog said.

'Barbara,' Don said.

'Same age as oor Billy,' Liz said.

'And what aboot Jack?' Bulldog said. 'Never a trace of him, Don, eh?'

'Never a trace,' Don said.

He shook his head, and as he did so he saw a look on Liz's face that he didn't understand, but it was the briefest of moments and then she glanced away and the talk shifted to some other subject.

It was only later, back home, with the boys away to their beds and Liz making a last cup of tea while he had all the shoes out on a newspaper and was polishing them up, that she suddenly said, 'I saw him, ye ken.'

'Saw who?' he said, hardly looking up.

'Jack Gordon. I saw him.'

He stopped his brushing and stared at her. 'When?'

'Aboot four year syne. Maybe five.'

'Five years? But Liz, that was . . . that was afore Sarah got the court ruling. How did ye no say onything?'

'I didna ken if it was really him,' she said. 'I was gaun intae Drumkirk, and the bus had stopped at the lights and I looked oot and there he was, gaun in the other direction.'

'What, walking?'

'Aye, walking.'

'What did he look like?'

'Just the same, only thinner if that's possible, and kind o scruffier. He had a lang coat on, that's all I really noticed. But I saw his face, and it was him.'

'But how did ye no say? If he was there in Drumkirk, and ye never said onything?'

'I thought it couldna be him,' she said. 'He'd been missing for years by then. It was just a glimpse I got, and then the bus moved on again. I thought it couldna be.'

'So, what are ye saying, it was or it wasna?'

'It was,' she said.

'But did ye no think tae get aff at the next stop? Did ye no think, Liz? Did ye no think aboot Sarah, wondering if he was alive or deid?'

'Aye,' she said, 'I did think. I thought aboot aw that in the space o a minute and I stayed where I was. It was just a glimpse, he was like a tramp, it probably wasna him at aw, that's what I thought. And then I thought, even if it was him, she's better no kennin. She's better wi him deid.'

'Och, Liz,' he said. The empty shoes and the brushes and the tins of polish lay without purpose on the paper. 'How could ye?'

'I thought,' she said, 'if it was him, it was his ghost.'

This was so far removed from the practical, hard-headed, no-nonsense Liz he was married to that he almost lost his temper at her. And then he thought of his own false sightings, the way Jack haunted him, and he calmed down. He said, 'But why are ye telling me noo?'

She said, 'This is gonnae sound ridiculous, but see at the end o that film, the body in the cellar – there was something aboot it that made me think o Jack that time I saw him. If I saw him. He was aye that thin, but when I saw him that day he was like a skeleton, his cheeks had fallen in and his eyes were like caves. That corpse in the film minded me o him. Otherwise I wouldna hae said onything. Maybe I shouldna hae. Ye're mad at me, aren't ye? I can tell ye're mad at me.'

'I just think, when ye saw him back then, ye should hae said something.'

'I *thought* I saw him,' she said. 'And if I'd said something, what would hae happened?'

'Maybe I could hae tracked him doon.'

'What for, Don? What would hae been the point o that?'

He looked at the shoes needing polishing. 'I dinna ken,' he said. 'But if he's alive . . .'

'He walked oot,' she said. 'If he's alive he disna want tae be here, or wi Sarah. If he's deid he's deid. But if he's alive he might as well be deid as far as she's concerned, so dinna be stirring it aw up again, Don. It's ower late noo.'

'He was my friend,' Don said.

'He walked oot on you and aw,' Liz said.

He bent to pick up the black-on brush. 'I wish ye'd tellt me,' he said. Back then, he meant.

'I wish I hadna,' she said. Just now, she meant.

They looked at each other across a void.

'Here's your tea,' she said. 'Dae the shoes efter.'

'Aye,' he said. He felt suddenly exhausted. She was right. Or she wasn't right, but he wouldn't fight her about it. He watched her as she steadily, purposefully poured the tea. He was forty, she three years younger. He wished he still loved her the way he once had.

§

More and more, as the boys grew up, Don found himself gnawing away at a question, or the question gnawing away at him. Was it all settled – your character, the kind of life you'd lead – by the time you were five? Before you even went to the school? Maybe earlier, when you were two or three, before you were speaking properly? He didn't believe it, he didn't want to believe it. He believed in nurture because what else was socialism but nurture, improving people's lives and improving the people as you did that? And yet whenever he looked at the better lives he and Liz were giving their two sons – better by far than the childhood he had had – he wondered if, in the end, it made any difference. If, in fact, you were happy or sad, good or bad, despite, not because of, your circumstances. A voice nagged in his head: *See your nurture, your socialism? – I'll bloody show ye.* Was that the voice of fate? He didn't believe in fate, but he watched Billy and Charlie turning from boys into teenagers, from teenagers into young men, and he thought, I could have mapped out their paths, their characters years ago, virtually while they were still in nappies. And he knew – and this was worse because it felt like betrayal when in fact it was only truth – he knew that all the way back there'd been one he liked and one he didn't; one he trusted to grow to be decent – feckless maybe, but decent – and one who'd be out for himself and

God help anybody who got in his road. And he hated the idea and hated himself for having it.

Decent was a word he valued.

And *like* was not the same as *love* between a father and a son. *Like* was about mutual respect, give and take. So you didn't like your own son? That was sore enough but how could you not *love* your son? You couldn't *not* love him, however much you might not like him. And that was what really hurt with Charlie. The love that he felt for him even as he saw him turn bad. The love that couldn't stop it happening. The love that raged at him and that seeped out, a little less each time, whenever he had to yell at him, threaten him, take his hand or his belt to him. Till eventually the love would be gone, and all he'd have left would be the empty space it once filled.

Sometimes he thought about being in the hospital with the English nurse, and if she could have made a mistake. If she'd picked up the wrong bairn to show him, or the bairns had got mixed up some time before, or later, and Charlie wasn't his at all, because how could he be so different from Billy? They didn't even look alike. But then as they grew it became obvious that Billy favoured his father while Charlie favoured Liz, so they did both belong, but in different ways. He asked Liz once, did Charlie feel more like hers than Billy did, because of the looks? She said of course not, what kind of question was that to ask, and gave him a hard, accusatory stare. But Charlie still didn't feel like *his* son, he just didn't, and Don wondered in weak moments if – the daftness that had come on him that night, the daft emotion he'd felt towards the English nurse – if fate, in which he didn't believe, had reached down and punished him for it even though he'd done nothing, they'd done nothing, there had just been the kiss, but fate had seen something pass between them and said, *I'll bloody show ye.*

He deplored violence. He'd intended never to have to raise his voice or his hand against his own children. But with Charlie, sometimes, he had no option.

The English nurse. As if he couldn't remember her name. As if it wasn't in him like an old lover's carved into a tree. Marjory Taylor.

§

Charlie lifted a bike from where it was leaning outside the post office, rode it halfway to Drumkirk, crashed it into a dyke and buckled the front wheel, then abandoned it. It only emerged later that he was the culprit because Bill Drummond, driving in the other direction, had spotted him freewheeling downhill.

Charlie used a neighbour's greenhouse for target practice with a slingshot.

Charlie put a cricket ball through the window of a moving bus.

This was *Beano* stuff, the kind of thing most kids do, or miss doing by luck as much as choice, or narrowly get away with. What Charlie didn't get away with, he got leathered for by Don. But every year he got away with more. What was scary was the stuff he wasn't caught for, the stuff for which there was no proof. It didn't matter whether it was Liz, Don, a teacher or a policeman doing the interrogating, Charlie never cracked. It wasn't Charlie who fired the hayricks at Hackston's, it wasn't Charlie who vandalised the school or tortured three cats to death. And even when one of the small gang of followers he'd gathered around him confessed to some misdemeanour or other, he never shopped Charlie. He had a power over them, partly physical and partly psychological, and they feared or admired or envied that and the way they showed it was through silence.

§

The grandparents were dying. First Liz's mother went with cancer, just shrank away to nothing in a matter of weeks, it was in her stomach, her spine, bones, everywhere; then her father, who'd never had a day's illness all his working life, caught the flu and before a fortnight was out was dead from pneumonia. Liz felt the loss greatly. Both of them gone in eighteen months, and neither of them seventy. She felt, too, the final loss of her childhood: without them there, Hackston's Farm wasn't her territory any more. Every weekend she had walked the two miles and back to see them. Now, with no reason to go, she stopped going.

Don had sometimes gone with her. He liked walking for the sake of walking, whether it was out to the farm or up in the woods. There didn't always have to be a destination, an objective. You could just *be*, out in the fresh air, the countryside, the moody weather. Couldn't you?

Liz said, 'What's the point?'

In Drumkirk, the council finally knocked down the tenement where Don had grown up, and built a new scheme on fields out at Granthill. Don's parents, Will and Molly, moved there, into one of the four-storey blocks dotted like Lego across the open spaces. Their two-bedroom flat had windows looking north to the hills and west into the prevailing wind and rain; the living room was big and bright; the kitchen and bathroom full of shiny new appliances. Their own bathroom! At first they loved it, despite the few shops and the infrequent buses into town. But after the first winter the problems started: the condensation, the ill-fitting window frames, the thin walls and the neighbours' bairns with nowhere to play. Then the old man suffered a heart attack, clung greyly on to life for a few months, and died. Now only Molly remained, a captive of the radio, television and her weakening legs. Don visited every week, taking the messages that were too heavy for her to carry. He did what repairs he could to keep the decay and wild kids at bay, complained with little success to the housing department, and feared for what would happen next. Granthill lost its shine in just a couple of years. People in Drumkirk started to use the name as shorthand for everything that was going wrong with society.

Molly said it wasn't too bad but then she didn't go out much, she didn't see the deterioration. Her mind wasn't what it was. Perhaps she'd have to come and bide with them. But how could she? They didn't have room for her. She had a couple of neighbours who kept an eye out for her, but they could only do so much and Don didn't blame them. They were not to blame. Nobody was to blame.

§

Billy, as a teenager, got into folk music and Ban the Bomb marches. Don approved, even went with him to a rally in George Square in Glasgow. He didn't believe unilateral disarmament was sensible, or feasible, and they had long discussions about that, but he respected and admired Billy's convictions. They *were* convictions, though curiously unimpassioned. It was good that his son had a cause, and that it was a left-wing cause.

He remembered talking with Jack about how Jack wouldn't have been there if they hadn't dropped the Bomb. But Jack *wasn't* there. Were the rest of them still there because of the Bomb or in spite of it?

Then Billy went to the Holy Loch to protest against Polaris, and away down south in the school holidays to march from Aldermaston to London. Liz grew nervous. What else was he getting up to, tagging along with a bunch of strangers? Kids with wild ideas and grown-ups leading them God knows where. What if he was arrested? Or abducted? Don told her to relax. Billy could look after himself. Liz raised her brows at him. 'Ye think so?'

Meanwhile, Charlie curled his lip and mocked his big brother for singing 'baby songs':

> Oh ye canna spend a dollar when ye're deid.
> No, ye canna spend a dollar when ye're deid.
> Singing Ding Dong Dollar, everybody holler,
> Ye canna spend a dollar when ye're deid.

He did a devastating imitation of Billy being both earnestly adolescent and pathetically childlike. Don disliked it intensely, because it was so accurate. Such cynicism in a twelve-year-old was disconcerting. Liz excused him: he was too clever for his age and easily bored. She was proud of him, as Don was proud of Billy.

Two brothers. You expected them to fight. You expected the older one to bully the younger, but it was Charlie who intimidated Billy. At two, five, seven, Charlie knew how to work his brother, trigger his sense of fairness or guilt or fear or generosity to get the toy, the food, the attention he wanted. At first it was amusing, intriguing, like watching monkeys socialising at the zoo. By the time it stopped being entertainment it was an established routine. Charlie's key weapon was his willingness to resort to violence, not something that exploded berserker-like out of tantrums, but a sustained, deliberate, controlled violence. Billy had to try to manage being exploited. Fighting back didn't work because Charlie had an appetite for a fight, whereas Billy thought the best form of attack was defence. The fact that they had to share a room didn't help. They had territories with invisible but very real boundaries – their own beds, their own drawers for clothes, their own shelves, their own routes to and from the bedroom door. These had been worked out over time but because they were invisible they weren't fixed, and Charlie was skilled at extracting further concessions in return for staying off Billy's ground.

Don was aware of all of this. Sometimes he tried to sort it out, but it was exhausting. He vaguely resented that Liz didn't manage it better. She argued that Billy had to stand up for himself. He was three years older than Charlie, even if he was slighter and softer. She couldn't fight his battles for him, and neither should Don.

§

One day Billy came home from a demo in Dunoon and said, coyly, 'Guess who else was there? Barbara.' For a moment Don didn't know who he meant, then he did. Jack's daughter. 'Barbara Gordon?' he said. 'Aye,' Billy said, 'she was on the march tae.' 'Is that right?' Don said. 'Young Barbara. And how has she turned oot?' He glanced at Liz and found her looking at him as if it was his fault. A chill went through him, remembering the quiet, strange, intense wee girl of years before.

Billy said, 'She's in CND tae, she's a youth organiser in Fife, she's much mair involved than I am. I'm gaun across there some time. It's no just CND, she's in aw kinds o things.'

In fact he went the following Saturday, and the one after that, off on the bus early and not home till late. Then came the request, at tea one evening, to stay away overnight, for a dance at a youth club in Glenrothes. 'Barbara's mother said I could.'

'Barbara's mother said I could,' Charlie mimicked.

'Cut it oot, Charlie,' Don said. His big hand landed palm down on the table. Charlie shut up. Don had to look away. The expression on the boy's face made him want to thump him, the churn in his belly made him not want to. He'd done it often enough, though not recently. But Charlie was growing fast. In a few years he'd be able to fight back.

Liz regarded Billy steadily. 'She did, did she?'

'Aye,' Billy said.

'And when's that supposed tae happen?'

'Next Saturday.'

'How is she?' Don asked.

'Her mother? She's all right. She made me my tea. She says I've tae call her Sarah. So can I stay there?'

'I don't see why no,' Don said, and Liz fixed that look on him again. 'If ye're sure Sarah – Mrs Gordon – disna mind.'

'She disna,' Billy said.

'She must really like ye,' Charlie said, 'if she made your tea.' From anybody else this might have been an innocent-enough remark, but the cold, snake-like way it was said was designed to wind somebody up, Billy or his father. Don turned on Charlie and snapped, 'Oot. Now.' Charlie went, with contempt for his father and brother in his eyes.

'Well?' Billy said.

'Don't *well* me,' Liz said.

For all his anti-war activism Billy hated confrontation at an individual level, but Don could see him steeling himself, determined not to be overruled, and decided to intervene.

'There's nae harm in it, surely?' he said, just as Billy said, 'Look, ye can telephone her if ye don't believe me. I've got the number.'

'Oh, they've a telephone, have they?' Liz said.

'Aye, it's because of Mrs Gordon's job in the post office, I think.'

'It's no that we dinna believe ye, son,' Don said. 'It's just . . .' But he couldn't think what it was. Because it was nothing.

'It's difficult,' Liz said.

'What's difficult aboot it?' Billy demanded. He took his diary from his pocket, opened it near the back and was about to hand it over when he changed his mind. He turned some more pages, found a blank one and carefully tore part of it out. He slid the wee pencil from the spine of the diary and copied the number down. 'There ye are. Would one of you telephone her, please?'

Liz lifted the piece of paper. 'I don't like tae,' she said. 'I'd be better writing.'

'It's for Saturday,' Billy said. 'Could ye no just phone her?'

'I could dae it, I suppose,' Don said, 'if your mother really disna want tae.'

'If onybody's tae telephone her, it'll be me,' Liz said.

'Well, could ye dae it soon?' Billy said. 'So I ken.' Don had never heard him so impatient.

Billy left them alone. Even with his emotions roused he didn't slam the door. A few minutes later they heard him slipping out of the house.

'I'm no wanting him seeing that Barbara,' Liz said. 'Ye could have supported me, Don.'

'Supported ye? What did ye want me tae say? He's been tae Alder-maston and the Holy Loch. We canna stop him gaun tae Glenrothes tae see a lassie.'

'I don't mind him seeing lassies. I just dinna want him seeing *that* lassie.'

'He's fifteen,' Don said. 'Nearly sixteen. What were we daein at his age? I'd started my apprenticeship and you were working on the farm. Just because he hasna left the school yet disna mean he's no growing up.'

'There's ony number o lassies here he could be gaun wi. His friends' sisters. Lassies at the school. Why does he have tae pick her?'

'It's how things happen, Liz.'

'It's no just her. It's her faither and everything.'

A space lay between them. Billy would be sitting the new 'Ordin-ary' level certificate exams in a few months. Decisions about what would happen after that would have to be made soon.

Liz said, 'He should be studying mair at weekends onywey.'

'He studies plenty,' Don said. 'Every night here at the kitchen table. Look, we canna stop him making choices. Making mistakes if need be. It's the only way ony o us ever learn.'

'God help him if he makes a mistake wi Barbara Gordon.'

'Barbara Gordon' sounded to Don like the title of an old ballad with a tragic ending.

'It'll be all right,' he said. 'They'll go marching and dancing the-gither for a while, then they'll go their ain ways. But if we try tae stop it, it'll make them mair determined tae see each other. Is that what ye want?'

'I dinna want it at aw.'

'Would ye rather I spoke tae Sarah?'

'No! I'll dae it.'

'Well, ye'd better wait till Billy comes back or he'll see ye in the queue, and get embarrassed.'

'What d'ye mean?'

'That's where he'll be away tae, the phone box. He'll be doon there speaking tae Barbara. Why dae ye think he's got the number?'

Neither of them thought of a telephone as anything other than an instrument for communicating necessary information or for use in an emergency. The idea that you might phone somebody just to talk to them seemed absurd, extravagant.

'It's serious, isn't it?' Liz said.

'Naw,' Don said. 'Not at all.' But he was thinking of Billy's determination. Maybe it was serious. And could Billy really look after himself?

They sat in silence. Gunshots sounded from the front room. Charlie was in there with the newly acquired rented television. Slouching, no doubt. Charlie watched the TV in a slouch that said he was neither awed nor puzzled by it, as everybody else was. It was as if there'd never been a time when he didn't watch television. Don thought of Billy with his anxious permission-seeking, his diary, the neatly torn page, his clap-along songs. Charlie despised his brother for these things, and Liz was disappointed by them, that was what Don thought. For all that she wanted to control Billy, for all that he was more controllable, she'd have preferred him to be more like Charlie, to walk a little closer to the edge.

§

Sir Malcolm Eddelstane, after a prolonged argument with Lady Patricia, succumbed to her advice and stood down prior to the 1964 General Election. The Profumo affair, the general disarray of Macmillan's government and a wider change of mood in the country, she said, signalled not only that the Conservatives were due for a spell in opposition but also that a more modern type of candidate would increasingly be required to counter the appeal of Labour. Sir Malcolm was only fifty-five, but looked much older, and was definitely on the traditional wing of the party. 'Choose the time and manner of your departure,' Lady Patricia said. 'Don't be the victim of a plot.' 'I'm not a coward,' Sir Malcolm said. 'I'm not going to cut and run.' 'Make a dignified exit,' she replied. 'That's a better way of putting it.' He blustered and sulked for a few weeks, but saw what she meant. Then, fortuitously, he had some heart trouble. Nothing too serious, a touch of angina, but it gave him an excuse, enabled him to announce that he wanted to spend more time at home, in the bosom of his devoted family. Of course he'd be damned if he was going to give up London entirely, and Lady Patricia didn't insist on this. She did, however, require the sale of the flat, which she suspected as the scene of infidelities, in order to release some capital. Now whenever he left Ochiltree House for London he put up at his club.

Roderick Braco, QC, an Edinburgh lawyer with a house in Glenallan, stepped into his political shoes. Sir Malcolm, not wishing to seem entirely washed up, eased himself into the chairmanship of the constituency association. He was loath to admit it, but Lady Patricia's assessment of the way things were going politically was pretty astute. It was time to get himself out of the direct line of fire.

As it turned out, Glenallan and West Mills stayed Unionist at the election but the margin of victory was much reduced. You could blame the times, or you could blame Braco for not having put in enough effort, or you could say his face wasn't yet well known enough but everything would be all right next time round. You could argue, as Sir Malcolm did loudly and repeatedly, that there had been a substantial personal vote for himself, and that Roderick Braco would have to work hard in the future to earn the equivalent. But after you'd said all that, nobody could afford to be complacent, not even Sir Malcolm. Something would have to be done.

Perhaps the Boundary Commission could be persuaded to redraw the electoral map, someone suggested, at an association meeting called to inspect the damage. The constituency could do with a bit more Glenallan and a bit less West Mills. Somebody else thought that would be tantamount to gerrymandering, and a third person said that it *was* gerrymandering, an observation that was greeted with wounded looks. Sir Malcolm said he'd see if he could have a word with somebody. It was perfectly obvious that the constituency was an odd shape, an unnatural shape, with the two parts having little in common with one another. One could rely on farmers, he said, apart from the Liberal ones. And professional people, the middle class, by and large, one could be sure of them too. But the traditional working-class Unionist vote, where was that these days? And he eyed the room and didn't find any of it present.

He did have a word, but whether or not it was with the right somebody the Boundary Commission took no notice. The constituency shape remained unnatural, and two years later Sir Malcolm had to revise his analysis. It seemed one couldn't be sure of the middle class either. People who ought to have known better were switching in droves to other parties. In the mid-1950s the Unionists had managed to win half of the Scottish vote and thirty-six seats. In 1966 they were down to twenty seats and it was Labour who polled nearly 50 per cent of the Scottish vote. Roderick Braco survived, but what on earth was going on? There was an undercurrent of growing support for the Scottish National Party, but that – surely – was just a temporary protest, an annoying but understandable reaction to the government's obsession with central planning. (At a performance of *The Mikado* put on by the Glenallan Amateur Operatic Society, how the audience had hooted at the inclusion, on the Lord High Executioner's little list, of both a Red-Hot Socialist and a Scottish Nationalist!) Sir Malcolm found himself lamenting the prominence given to the word 'Conservative' in the new formulation Scottish Conservative and Unionist Party. The Conservatives were an *English* party. What the hell was wrong with the old terminology? Three horrible thoughts occurred to him almost simultaneously: one, that he was becoming a bit of a Scot Nat himself; two, that perhaps religion didn't matter much to the working class any more; and three, that even the middle class might be thinking they were better served by socialists than by men with names like Sir Malcolm Eddelstane, Roderick Braco, QC, and, in the next-door constituency, Sir Alec Douglas-Home.

The Glenallan Eddelstanes were at the upper end of the social scale but financially they had peaked a generation before. Somewhat thin and frayed bloodlines connected them to the heroic military Eddelstanes, the renowned engineering Eddelstanes, the revered theological Eddelstanes and the brilliant mathematical Eddelstanes; but, lacking the inventiveness and dynamism of these kinsfolk, Sir Malcolm's forebears had invested money in other people's enterprises rather than establish their own. Over the decades they had done very well. But they were money-made, these lesser Eddelstanes, not land-made, and so they stood slightly apart from, and rather less firmly rooted than, the lairds and aristocrats at the core of Scottish Toryism. They were not law-made either, that other, Edinburgh-centred strand of which Roderick Braco was a fine representative. And now the Eddelstane money was draining away fast. Sir Malcolm's father had lost vast amounts of it in 1929, and Sir Malcolm himself kept buying shares in ventures that promptly bellied: an oil-exploration company in Burma (collapsed when oil production was nationalised by the bloody Burmese socialist government in 1963); the Fairfield Shipbuilding and Engineering Company on the Clyde (filed for bankruptcy in 1965, bailed out by the bloody British socialist government but too late for Sir Malcolm's cash). Ochiltree House might be a substantial pile in the Scotch Baronial style, with a vast garden, including tennis court, maintained by the full-time if ageing McLeish; Sir Malcolm and Lady Patricia might be able to employ Mrs Thomson five days a week to cook, clean and generally keep them functioning somewhere in the second half of the twentieth century; they might be able to bring in catering companies to manage their various parties; they might be able to dispatch their sons to semi-respectable boarding schools, and they might have the wherewithal to send their daughter away too, in order to knock some sense into her airy little skull; but despite all this, there were cracks in the Ochiltree House walls and a certain desperation in the amount Sir Malcolm and Lady Patricia drank and the way they endlessly socialised and the volume at which they raged and railed at each other and their offspring. And their oldest child, David, from his bedroom window at home, or from the distant perspective of his boarding school, could see that by the time he inherited whatever assets his mother and father had left, they would not amount to very much at all.

Boarding school was Kilsmeddum Castle, where Sir Malcolm himself had been in another age, acquiring the grace and dignity of his later years. It was the kind of place, in other words, that might – and did – destroy many a more sensitive soul. David was sensitive but he was saved by sport. A modest performer in the classroom, he excelled at rugby, cricket, running, jumping, swimming and skiing, and this made him reasonably popular with other boys who, if they'd thought about it, would have been hard-pressed to identify any particular thing about him they liked. That was the point, he was one of the crowd, he didn't threaten and he didn't invite attack. He was safe.

The unsafest thing he did was skiing. You had to be a little bit mad to ski in Scotland in the 1960s: you had to climb to the top of a mountain with your skis on your back and then ski down again, no pistes, no fences to keep you away from hidden precipices, just you and snow, ice and rock. Or you went to Glen Shee for weekends – a long, slow, twisting journey from Kilsmeddum – you and a bunch of other slightly mad boys and a partially crazed master or two, to indulge in the steamy camaraderie of wet boots, porridge and sleeping bags. There were only a few tows in Glen Shee then, and such intrusions seemed dwarfed by nature, mere blemishes, not the scars that development would later bring. David loved the different textures of the winter glen, the glide and rasp of ski over snow, over ice, the wind and the sun, the fog and occasionally the blizzards. You were in a group, but you were also apart, yourself. You could *be* yourself. Everything was rough and unpredictable, including the weather, but this, so the masters claimed, would stand you in good stead for whatever the future might fling at you. As if life were a Highland hillside. And maybe it was. You pointed your skis and off you went.

§

Liz wanted a job. The boys didn't need so much looking after. She was bored. The extra money wouldn't hurt either. But what kind of work? She had no qualifications and felt it was too late to get any. Maybe she could be a cleaner. The folk in the big houses at the top end of the village were always wanting cleaners. Betty, her neighbour, had done two mornings a week in one of those houses for years. Liz had never fancied clearing up other people's mess just because they could afford not to have to do it themselves, it went against the grain somehow, and Don, she was sure, would object. Betty told her not to be so daft. It was no worse than any other kind of work. Better than slaving away in a factory with some gaffer cracking the whip. The woman she worked for was dead posh but nice, wouldn't dream of criticising Betty's standards (which were higher than her own) and was so embarrassed by dirt that she usually tidied up before Betty arrived anyway. There was another house up there that had changed hands a few weeks before, a surgeon at the infirmary had bought it, he had a wife and they had three kids, all away at boarding school, and Betty had been asked if she knew anyone reliable who might clean for them. Why didn't Liz apply?

She did. The surgeon's wife, Mrs Cotter, was English and glamorous and wore tartan trousers and a cashmere jumper, neither of which had come out of a jumble sale, and spoke like a film star as she showed Liz around the house, from top to bottom. This took about twenty minutes without dawdling. The bedrooms, six of them, were enormous. There were three bathrooms: one for the Cotters, an en-suite in the main guest room, and one for the children when they were back from their schools. Plus a downstairs cloakroom and a lavvy, beside the laundry room, which Mrs Cotter very diplomatically indicated was the one Liz should use if she had to. There was a 'small' sitting room bigger than any room in the Lennies' house, and what Mrs Cotter referred to as the 'drawing room' contained, among other things, a baby grand piano, two three-seater sofas, two massive armchairs and a fireplace you could have roasted a sheep in. The dining room gleamed with an array of silver candlesticks, wine coasters, napkin rings and cutlery, which Mrs Cotter would like cleaned once a fortnight. As they went through each room she pointed out the things she particularly wanted to be washed or dusted or polished on a regular basis. They finished in the ultra-modern kitchen where Mrs Cotter made coffee and offered Liz a biscuit.

It seemed they'd hit it off. Liz was just what Mrs Cotter was look-ing for, and the fact that she was from the village, a friend of her neighbour's cleaner – well, it couldn't be better. Would she take the same hourly rate? Liz said yes, having established from Betty that the rate was four shillings an hour. How many hours a week, Liz asked, did Mrs Cotter want her to come in? Mrs Cotter looked at the ceiling as if calculating the rooms in a column above her head: she thought three hours on Mondays, Wednesdays and Fridays would seem about right. Could Liz manage that? Liz did her own calcula-tion. That was nearly two pounds a week and even with the size of the place and the amount of silver and ornaments and polishing the brass door handles and scrubbing the baths till they dazzled and beating rugs and vacuuming the acres of carpet she couldn't imagine how she was going to fill the nine hours. Aye, she said. Yes, that would be fine. And Mrs Cotter said that was settled then, with a beautiful smile, and explained that she'd always be there at nine o'clock to let Liz in but would she mind sometimes being left on her own, and locking up when she'd finished, because she herself intended to play golf every Wednesday, went shopping most

Fridays and often had other commitments on a Monday? Liz said she'd not mind.

And Don, to her surprise, didn't mind either. She'd assumed he would resist the idea but the only thing he couldn't get his head round was that the Cotters had five different places to go for a shit. He thought the job would do her good, and it was handy, so why not?

She started the following week. Before long she felt she'd been working there for years. Mrs Cotter continued to be charming and on the rare occasions she was still there when Liz's three hours were up she sat and drank coffee with her. She expressed her extreme happiness with the quality of Liz's work. Mr Cotter was hardly ever home. When he was, he smiled and said, 'How are you?' as if she might be one of his patients. She suspected he spoke to his children in the same tone. The children were so polite and so careful not to get in her way during the school holidays that she sometimes forgot they were there. It was all more than tolerable, but what Liz loved most was when she was alone in the house. Then the three hours went fast enough. They filled her with a weird kind of delight. She'd pause beside the piano and touch a key and hear the note absorbed by the room and wonder at the tranquillity of the rest of the house, the gentle creak of old floorboards, the quiet tick of the grandfather clock in the hall, the light that flooded in through the bay windows, and outside the sweep of the front lawn and the grandeur of the lovely trees. She'd stand at an upstairs window and the view was so spectacular she had to tell herself, out loud, to get on with her work. Mrs Cotter had said she was welcome to have the radio on but why would she, when what she valued was the silence, the emptiness of the house, the fact that for those hours she alone held it in trust? In short, she loved her job.

And then there was the money, which Mrs Cotter left on the kitchen table for her every Friday, the pound note and the ten-shilling note and the two half-crowns and the shilling, always the same every week. She put them in her purse and was tempted to skip down the road. But the road led her past the Gordons' old house, occupied now by people she didn't know, and she walked by and couldn't help thinking of Don and his lost friend Jack, and Billy and his rediscovery of Barbara Gordon, and then she'd think of Charlie and was fearful for them all. What had happened to her and Don?

What would happen to the boys? By the time she reached home something of the peace she got from cleaning Mrs Cotter's house had dissipated, but enough would be left to carry her through the weekend, towards the precious hours she would have to herself the following week, in the big empty house on the hill.

§

Billy's History teacher at Drumkirk Academy, Mr Blyth, was convinced Billy was clever and hard-working enough to justify him staying on to sit his Highers. He was capable, in other words, of going to university. He sent Billy home with a letter to this effect, and asked the Lennies to come in after school to discuss it.

It was a big enough deal that Billy had passed the qualifying exam for Drumkirk Academy, the only senior secondary school in the area. The prospect offered by Mr Blyth was so much more serious that on the appointed day Don hurried home early to wash and put on his suit, while Liz got out the outfit she wore to funerals. Then it was back on the bus to Drumkirk.

Mr Blyth, who seemed about half their age, was in a tweed jacket with leather elbow patches. He had sideburns like hedges and square, black-framed spectacles, and spoke as if he had a large pan-drop in his mouth but was pretending he hadn't. He was, however, kind and patient as he talked them through the process. He had no doubt that Billy could achieve the grades necessary to gain him a university place. He understood that nobody from the family had ever been to university, and that therefore the prospect might be worrying or mysterious. An Honours degree in History, Billy's best subject, or perhaps in Politics or Economics or a combination of them, would take four years – a big commitment for everybody. Nevertheless Mr Blyth couldn't overemphasise what an opportunity it would be for Billy. He hoped the Lennies agreed.

'What would he dae wi a History degree?' Don asked. It was a genuine question, not a sceptical one. He wanted to know.

'The obvious answer is he could do what I do – teach. I think he'd make a very good teacher. But let's not narrow his options too soon. The thing about university, Mr Lennie, is that it opens the door to all kinds of possibilities. It's not education for a particular job, it's education for life. I know History doesn't sound very practical, but

I believe it is one of the best subjects for broadening the mind and preparing you for a whole range of careers. I happen to be a teacher, but others in my year went into accountancy, business management, journalism, broadcasting, publishing. With a degree under his belt, Billy could do anything.'

A glow of anticipation spread under Don's suit. That *his* son could do anything! That Billy's options should not be narrowed too soon! It wasn't that he particularly wanted Billy to be an accountant or a teacher. What he wanted was for him to have the choice.

Liz said, 'How much will it cost?'

Mr Blyth explained. The government would pay the fees, so there was no need to worry about them. As for living expenses, students were entitled to a maintenance grant, but it was means-tested according to one's circumstances. It depended on the income of one or both parents.

'It's only me that's earning a wage,' Don said. (They'd discussed this on the bus, both suddenly nervous that they didn't declare Liz's earnings to the taxman.)

'I can't tell you how much of a grant he'd receive,' Mr Blyth said, 'but I'm sure he would get something. Depending on where he went to study, he could continue to live at home, or he could stay away during term-time. Undoubtedly there would have to be sacrifices, though.' He blushed and cleared his throat. 'I imagine your income is . . .'

'It's no bad,' Don said. It sounded more defensive than he'd intended. 'But that's no the point. We'll dae whatever it takes. Won't we, Liz?'

Liz nodded, frowning. 'It's a thought,' she said.

'It is indeed,' Mr Blyth said, 'which is why it's necessary to start planning now. If it's what you want, of course. I know it's what Billy wants.'

'We want the best for baith oor boys,' Liz said. 'But what if he . . .' – she was struggling for the right words – 'what if it disna work? If he disna finish?'

Mr Blyth smiled. 'You don't have to worry on that score, Mrs Lennie. Billy may not stand out in a crowd, but he's a sticker. If he gets this chance, he'll not fail you. I guarantee it.'

He was telling them things about their own son that they already knew. That Don knew, at any rate. It felt good, secure. He glanced at Liz and she gave him a smile that was at once encouraging and uncertain. She looked for a moment the way she used to when they were courting. It was one of those increasingly rare moments of understanding between them. The uncertainty was not on account of Billy. They were both thinking about Charlie.

On the bus home, they talked it through. If it really was what Billy wanted, they wouldn't stand in his way. If he did the work and passed the exams and was offered a place, they'd support him. How could they not? Liz said it might give him a new focus. Away from Barbara Gordon, she meant. If Billy went off to university, that might be the end of *that*.

'Dae ye think he'll end up speaking like yon Mr Blyth?' she said.

'Maybe he will,' Don said. 'Maybe looking like him tae.'

'My God!' Liz said, and she laughed. He took her hand. They sat on the bus, laughing together.

§

When things got difficult between Don and Charlie, or between Charlie and the village, Charlie took off for Drumkirk and stayed with his granny. This was a relief for everybody. He seemed genuinely fond of her, and she of him. He went for her messages. He kept her company. Maybe her vulnerability would be the thing that turned him around.

But being in Drumkirk, and especially Granthill, brought him into contact with a harder, more dangerous crowd. His granny might like having him around, but that didn't mean she was in control of where he went or who he was with.

§

At the end of the war there had been four shops in Wharryburn. Forbye the post office there had been a butcher's, a draper's, an ironmonger and Reid's, the general store. One by one they'd closed till only the post office and general store were left. Then Reid's was put up for sale and for a while there was no interest and everybody feared it too would go, but at last it was taken on by people called Khan. Some folk breathed a sigh of relief, because what would the village be without a village shop? Others weren't so sure. They'd been hoping for the Co-operative, or just another family business like Reid's, but the Khans, although they were a family, were not like the Reids at all. The Khans moved into the flat upstairs, it hadn't been lived in for years but used for storage, and for a long time there was debris and chaos around the building as Mr Khan and various male relatives, who came and went in beaten-up old cars and vans, worked on making the flat habitable. Or rather, *more* habitable, because the family stayed there while all the repairs were going on. There were complaints about the mess and the noise but eventually the work was finished. Then the Khans started on the shop. People said, why do they need to rip everything out? Could they not just leave things the way they were when it was Reid's? But that was the trouble, it wasn't Reid's any more, and there were mutterings about what it had become. Still, after another few weeks the refit was complete, and right enough it seemed bigger, had more stock, opened earlier and didn't shut till eight, so surely that was all right? Did anybody still have a problem? 'Aye, the wife hardly speaks ony English.' 'Mine neither,' Don said when he heard that one in the Blackthorn. 'Ye're no sae hot at it yersel.' 'Aye, but if ye ask her ony-thing complicated she has tae get her man, and if he's no there, then what are ye supposed tae dae?' 'Come back later?' Don suggested. 'Aye, weel, but that's no the point, is it?' What was the point, exactly? The point was the pigment of the Khans' skin. The well-meaning people called them 'coloured'. Most folk called them Pakis, darkies. The shop had always been 'the shop' or 'the store' or 'Reid's'. Now it was 'the Paki's'.

The Khans had a son and a daughter, eight and six. They went to the village school. They were bright, diligent pupils who did better in class than many of their peers. This did not endear them to some of the other parents, nor even to one or two of the teachers.

Sometimes the fruit and veg in the Khans' shop was, there was no disguising it, tired. Sometimes, especially on wet days, the floor of the shop was dirty. Sometimes the wrappers of chocolate bars and other sweets sold by the Khans were found littering the street. These things had also been true of Reid's, but folk didn't remember it that way. They made faces and tutting noises. 'It shows ye.' 'What does it show ye?' 'It just shows ye.'

Don bought his paper out of Mr Khan's every day, on his walk to the bus stop. On Wednesdays there was the *Drumkirk Observer* too, full of nothing but Don bought it anyway, out of loyalty to the area, to Mr Khan and to Bill Drummond, who'd scrambled into a desk job at the *Observer* when the *Gazette* died in '63. In the evening, if there was anything Liz was needing, Don or one of the boys, usually Billy, would go for it. Eggs, a slab of cheese, a tin of beans. At the weekend Don bought milk and rolls from Mr Khan. He almost wished he smoked so he could buy tobacco from him. Sellotape, shoelaces, shoe polish. They chatted away over the counter. Mr Khan was a round, bald man who looked like he should really have been a college lecturer, or maybe a doctor. There was something old-fashioned about him. He was quiet-spoken, but this was not to say he had no opinions. He had plenty and that was another thing some people didn't like. He had views on football, Vietnam, the pill, the Russians, the Rolling Stones – not all of them what you might expect from a middle-aged Muslim businessman. He was always busy and often seemed weary but he made the time to talk, as if glad of an excuse to stop being a shopkeeper for a while. He'd been in Glasgow, before that Manchester, before that London. He'd come from Karachi with his father and mother and three brothers after Partition, when he was twenty. Before Karachi they had been in Delhi and were part of the mass movement of people between India and Pakistan, because they were Muslims and hadn't felt safe in Delhi. So he had been a migrant all of his adult life and now he had settled in Wharryburn, where he spoke English with deliberate care and accuracy, with some of the intonations white people found it amusing to imitate. If there was a Manchester accent in there it had been overlaid with a Glaswegian one. If there was Glaswegian it was mixed with the strange vowels of England. This was another thing Don enjoyed about Mr Khan: the rich, rolling gutturals of his speech, and the way it moved across frontiers and continents.

Mr Lennie said, 'Please call me Don.'

Mr Khan said, 'Please call me Saleem.'

§

Like his brother, Charlie had passed the qualifying exam for Drumkirk Academy. Now he'd been there three years. The last two of these had been extremely difficult. The school said he didn't apply himself. Furthermore, there was the question of his 'attitude'.

Liz and Don were summoned again, this time by the rector, an altogether more imposing, less friendly character than Mr Blyth. Charlie was a disappointment, the rector reported, a grave disappointment. It was not as if he were not capable: he would not be at the Academy had that been the case. He did not work, and when he was urged by his teachers to do so he responded with the bare minimum. The cause was not laziness but deliberate refusal verging on outright insolence. Worse, he had been playing truant. The rector spread three notes on the desk in front of Liz. 'These were written by his grandmother, I believe. Is this her handwriting?' 'Aye, it is,' Don said. The rector said, 'He has been seen in the town on at least one occasion when he was supposed to be sick. Perhaps you should speak to her about these notes.' 'Aye, we will,' Don said, shamefaced, but he could feel Liz beginning to bridle beside him. 'That in itself is serious enough,' the rector said, 'but when he does attend he is disruptive.' 'Disruptive?' Liz said. 'How?' 'His attitude infects the other pupils, some of the boys especially.' 'What's that supposed tae mean?' Liz demanded. 'Ye make it sound like he's got a disease.' 'I simply mean he affects the more impressionable boys, Mrs Lennie.' 'Ye said "infects".' The rector shrugged. 'Infects, affects. The fact of the matter is, he is disruptive.' 'If he's disruptive does he get the belt?' 'Not any more,' the rector said. 'How no?' The rector flinched. 'It had no effect. On the contrary, the fact that he took the belt with indifference had an effect opposite to that which was intended.' Don saw that Liz was growing more annoyed at the man's superiority, the convolutions of his grammar. 'It made his malign influence even greater.' Even Don bridled at the word 'malign'. 'We're talking aboot a boy here, no a demon,' he said. The rector pushed the objection aside. 'The fact of the matter is, here we regard physical chastisement as a last resort. Frankly, your son's behaviour is what I might expect from a boy enrolled at *another* school.'

Don remembered getting the belt for everything. Not at Drumkirk Academy, which in the 1930s charged fees unless you were clever enough to win a scholarship, and so might as well have been on the moon for all the chance he had of getting there. His school education was over the minute he turned fourteen. The belt was a physical extension of almost every teacher, carried like a sleeping ferret over the shoulder. All the boys in his class were in regular contact with it: for every third spelling mistake in tests; for not enough correct sums; for cheek, which often meant inappropriate use of words like 'dinna' and 'aye'. Sometimes he thought they were belted simply because they hadn't been belted recently, to discourage complacency. But that had been then. Things had moved on. Nowadays, according to this pompous man, the belt was a weapon of last resort. *The fact of the matter*. Well, the fact of the matter was it hadn't worked with Charlie. Thinking of the looks of defiance Charlie gave *him*, all the time now, Don could see why. The boy had absorbed every bit of physical punishment he'd been given, and it seemed only to have made him tougher. Part of Don admired that, but a bigger part was troubled by it. What made Charlie the way he was? Why did he set himself against the world?

He was brought back to the present by Liz's voice, raised now against the voice of authority. 'So what are ye saying? Do ye want him at this school or don't ye?'

'Mrs Lennie,' the rector said, 'my job is to educate the young people in my charge. If a boy does not wish to be educated, then we have a problem. It is my responsibility to bring this to your attention. Either Charlie smartens up his ideas, or he'd be better off transferring to the Junior Secondary. Although, at this stage . . .'

He didn't have to finish the sentence. They knew what he meant: at this stage, it was too late.

Liz said, 'Ye might hae done something aboot this sooner.'

The rector said, 'We've done our best.' There was a faint, snide emphasis on the first word. 'Perhaps somebody else might have more success with him.'

'Like who?' Liz said.

'Well, regrettably National Service is no longer available. But that kind of discipline might suit him.'

'What, the army?' Liz said.

'Or one of the other services, perhaps,' the rector said.

'Is that the best ye can come up wi? "We canna educate him so we recommend him for cannon fodder"? Noo I've bloody well heard it aw.'

Don got her out of there before she started lashing out.

They talked to Charlie again, in the kitchen, the scene of so many confrontations. One last effort. 'What's gaun on at the school? They're gonnae suspend ye, throw ye oot.' Liz talked to him. Don talked to him. Together and separately they cajoled, encouraged, threatened. They pleaded with him, appealed to his conscience and his self-interest. He didn't appear to care. 'And what's this aboot plunking off?' Don said. 'Making your granny write notes for ye, for God's sake. Are ye a complete idiot? Where d'ye go? Who d'ye go wi?' Charlie looked at Don as if he were a caveman. 'Plunking off? It's called dogging it.' Don lost his temper. 'What does it matter what ye call it? Ye're aboot tae mess up the best chance in life ye'll get, ye bloody wee fool!' Liz said shouting at him like that didn't help. She said maybe it was the school that was failing Charlie. Don said it hadn't failed Billy. Look at Billy, away to the university in Glasgow in the autumn. It was Charlie that was failing Charlie. Back and forth, round and round they went, and all the time Charlie watched them as if they were talking about someone else. He stood up to leave them to it.

'I'm no finished!' Don roared. 'Don't you dare walk oot till I'm finished.'

'*I'm* finished,' Charlie said. He headed for the door. Don made as if to stop him, but what was he going to do, wrestle him to the floor?

The door slammed in his face. Liz said, 'Let him go. There's nae talking tae him noo.'

She said, 'He's no a fool, ye ken. Ye shouldna call him a fool. He's as clever as Billy.'

She said, 'And bringing Billy intae it disna help.'

'Jesus Christ!' Don shouted. He cursed more these days. It annoyed him how readily the name of somebody he'd no faith in came to his lips. More quietly he said, 'I just want him tae knuckle doon and dae some work. Behave himsel. Or he's gonnae end up in trouble.'

'I ken,' Liz said. 'But ye just set each other aff. I'll speak tae him on my ain.'

But she'd tried that before. They both knew what it was: Charlie was doing what they were doing, what Drumkirk Academy was doing – ticking off the days till he turned fifteen, and the rector could do his Pontius Pilate imitation. God only knew what Charlie would do after that but it wouldn't involve education. How was he going to earn money? How was he going to survive? These were questions of unbearable weight in the night. The only person who didn't seem bothered by them was Charlie.

§

Don said, 'We're no keeping ye. We canna afford it. If ye want tae stay under this roof ye'll need tae get a job.'

Charlie said, 'Ye don't have tae keep me. I'll go where I'm wanted.'

Liz said, 'We want ye here, son.'

'No according tae that cunt.'

For a moment all the chains came loose. Don lunged at Charlie and Liz clattered her arm into Don to stop him and she was yelling at Charlie who swung a punch at his father's face but Don pulled back and the punch landed on Liz's chest and she fell against the kitchen table and Don caught her as things crashed to the floor. Charlie was ready to come at him again but Don shouted, 'Back off!' and covered Liz with his body and Liz screamed, 'Stop it, baith o ye!' and everything slid to a halt as suddenly as it had started. Charlie was heaving like a bull. 'Dinna come near me, all right, dinna fucking come near me,' the boy roared. Don helped Liz on to a chair. 'Just fuck off,' he said over his shoulder. Liz was grimacing, catching her breath, her right hand up over her chest where the blow had landed, but she smacked Don over the head for swearing.

'That really hurt, Charlie,' she said.

'If he hadna had a fucking go at me, it wouldna hae happened.'

'Stop using that language,' she said. 'Ye never learned tae speak like that in this hoose. Ye should be ashamed o yersel.' And to Don, 'And so should you. He's your son.'

'Aye, and yours too, and he's just hit ye.'

'Forget that,' she said. 'He didna mean tae.'

'No, I meant tae hit him,' Charlie said.

'Ye'd hae done it the once,' Don said.

'That's *enough*,' Liz said. 'Charlie, pack a bag and away tae your granny's. Ye're better there till we decide what tae dae wi ye.'

'Ye don't need tae decide onything,' Charlie said. 'I can fend for masel.'

'Get used tae it,' Don said.

'Not another word, Don,' Liz snapped. 'I mean it. If ye say one mair word I'll walk oot wi him. The two of ye are better off apart.'

There was no arguing with that. Charlie went upstairs. 'Make us some tea,' Liz said. Don filled the kettle. 'I'm sorry,' he said. 'Ower late tae be sorry,' she said.

She went out of the room, and he heard her talking in low tones with Charlie. He knew she was giving him money. The money she earned up the hill. She gave some of it to Charlie regularly. Nothing to Billy as far as he was aware. He heard the front door open and close.

When she came back she put her hand to her collarbone. 'That's sair,' she said. 'I hope I havena broken onything.'

'Liz, if he's hurt ye –'

But she cut him off. 'Aye, he's hurt me.' She touched her collarbone again. 'This'll mend, but.'

He could see she wouldn't stand for it if he started ranting against Charlie. He pushed her tea towards her. She reached for it, gasped with pain. 'Dae ye want the doctor?' he said. 'Ye must be kidding,' she said. 'If it's still bad in the morning I'll go roond tae the surgery, say I tripped on the stair or something.'

They heard the front door open and close again. Different footsteps. Billy put his head round the door.

'I just saw Charlie at the bus stop,' he said. He saw the look on Liz's face, felt the tension in the atmosphere. 'What's happened?'

'He's away tae your granny's again,' Liz said. 'Come in and get a cup of tea, son. Tell me how your day's been.'

§

One morning Saleem practically thrust the paper into Don's hand.

'Look at that!'

Winnie Ewing's by-election win at Hamilton was all over the front page.

'Does that not make you proud to be a Scot?' Saleem said.

Don handed over the money. He shrugged.

'Oh come on, man!' Saleem said, in his best Wharryburn accent, a big grin splitting his face. 'I tell you, it makes me proud to be a Scot and I'm no even a Scot. They've taken us for granted too long, that's what I say.'

'Aye, weel, I wouldna deny that, Saleem. I just wouldna hae had ye doon for a Nationalist.'

'I'm no a Nationalist. But Scotland is a nation, is it no?'

'Aye.'

'Well then. The world is full of nations. It's only natural, isn't it, to want to join the club?'

Down the years Don heard an echo of Jack Gordon. Apart from the beaming smile Saleem even momentarily looked like Jack Gordon. He said, 'You remind me of someone. A man that stayed in the village a long time ago. Before your time.'

'How long ago?'

'Sixteen, seventeen years.' He'd never talked to Saleem about Jack. Jack wasn't mentioned by anybody any more.

'That was about when we came to England. Note my careful use of the word "England". It's not so long.'

'It seems it. He was a friend o mine. He used tae come oot wi aw that Nationalist stuff.'

'Well, and if he was your friend why did you not listen to him?'

'Oh, I did, I did.' Don smiled. 'Naebody else did.'

'So he was a lone voice, was he? A lone piper piping in the misty morning?'

'Something like that.'

'And you don't like the sound of the bagpipes?'

'I've nothing against the bagpipes. I just didna like the tune he was playing.'

'Down with the British!'

'Mair or less, aye.'

'Don, let me tell you what I think. My father was a government clerk when we lived in Delhi. He was an educated man. You could say we did not do badly under British rule. Please note my careful choice of word again. And then you could say that after independence everything went to rat shit for us. Yes, you could say that. We had to move and then we had to move again and it is only in the last few years, here in Wharryburn, that I have stopped moving. I don't want to go anywhere else. But what am I? I am a shopkeeper. What did my father, an educated man, become when he came to England? A bloody shopkeeper. I don't want to be a bloody shopkeeper any more than he did, but it is how he survived, it is how I survive. It is not the desired life, it is not the perfect life but it is a life. It could be worse. We could all have had our throats cut on a train. And yet, in all the troubles my father had, I never once heard him say, "Thank God for the British!" He didn't say "Down with the British!" either but he knew that it was pointless being nostalgic about the past. I think you are too nostalgic about the past, Don. Does it offend you to hear me say this?'

Don laughed. 'Nothing you say could offend me, Saleem.'

'Don't bet on it. Let me tell you one more thing. I think you had better hurry up here in Scotland or you will be the last ones out of the British Empire and if that is the case, well . . .'

'Well what?'

'Well, you will look pretty bloody stupid.'

§

If Barbara Gordon was like a name from a Scottish ballad, Marjory Taylor was the kind of name he heard on the radio sometimes, in English pop songs. Jennifer Eccles. Angela Jones. Marjory Taylor. But why on earth was she still in his head?

§

Liz and he had a new midweek occupation: watching a BBC sitcom about the Home Guard. They both loved it. There was something comforting about the bank manager, the butcher, the spiv and the stupid boy banding together against a common foe. It was intensely satisfying that the undertaker was a tight-fisted, wild-eyed Scottish doom-merchant called Frazer. *Dad's Army* was a weekly event that pulled Liz and Don back together when things were strained. It was a half-hour refuge from change. Yet whenever he watched it, or when it was over, Don remembered what Saleem had said, and felt a little guilty.

§

At first, Billy and Barbara were on a journey together. Gradually they would discover that they were on two separate journeys. This is what happens. People are fellow travellers for a while, for years, perhaps for decades. Later they marvel at the roads they have been on, the people they once were, the distance they went with people whose faces they have almost forgotten.

Billy loved Barbara for her sulky mouth and her cool eyes. He loved her neutral voice, English after her mother's but Scottish enough so it didn't stand out. He loved her long, straight black hair, her long legs, her slim waist, her delicate, bulb-like breasts. But more than her body he loved her mind. No one else he knew had her clarity of thought. He who was so uncertain even as he acknowledged the absolute rightness of yet another cause – anti-apartheid, anti-vivisection, pro-abortion – adored her conviction, her ability to get to the point.

She liked his open mind, his willingness to change, his, if she was honest, malleability. They explored and learned together, but always she was one step ahead.

They would always be honest. This was the promise they'd made to one another when they were fifteen, and which they reaffirmed after every crisis, after every blow to their relationship that honesty delivered. All you needed was not love, but honesty. This was what they believed. No more hypocrisy. Nothing must be not revealed.

§

The big window of Saleem's shop was boarded up.

Don said, 'What happened?'

Saleem shook his head. 'It is nothing.'

'Saleem, somebody's pit your windae in. That's no nothing.'

Saleem shrugged. 'Boys. It was in the night. By the time I got down to the street they were gone.'

'Did you see them?'

'No.' He looked very unhappy.

'Did ye call the polis?'

'They were here an hour ago. It's necessary for the insurance. They wrote down what I told them but I don't expect any arrests. What use are the police? They have to come from Drumkirk. They will never catch anyone red-handed out here.'

Don considered doing what most others would have done at this point – lamenting the loss of the village bobby – but didn't bother.

The last village bobby had been a fat lump who couldn't have caught a cold.

He had a bad feeling. He said, 'If it was village lads it shouldna be too difficult tae find oot who.'

'They are not from the village. I heard a car.'

Don glanced at his watch, mindful of the bus coming.

'A car?'

'Yes, I think they are from Drumkirk.'

'What makes ye think that?'

'Somebody came before. They offered me, you know, protection.'

'Somebody came intae the shop and threatened ye? Would ye recognise them?'

The door opened and another customer entered. It was clear from Saleem's look that he didn't want to continue the conversation.

'I'm really sorry aboot it,' Don said. He felt responsible and ashamed. 'I'll need tae go. I'll see ye later.'

'Thank you, Don.'

Something bothered Don all the way to Drumkirk on the bus, all day at work. The way Saleem hadn't answered his last question, 'Would ye recognise them?' Was it just because of the other customer coming in?

Charlie came and went to his own timetable. He'd had a few jobs, short term, no training, no prospects. Some of them weren't even jobs, they were just things he did and got cash in hand for. He was signing on. He told them less and less, spent more and more time at his grandmother's. Don didn't object to that, it was easier, but he knew a crisis was coming. And now this. Maybe this was the crisis.

He heard things. Charlie was hanging around with a couple of lads his own age who had bad reputations. Also, he was in with their big brothers and cousins. There were gangs in Drumkirk, as there were in most towns of any size, and folk were afraid of the culture. Charlie wasn't afraid of it. He was big and strong and he could scrap if he had to. Mostly he didn't have to. This was what Don heard.

That evening, after work, he went out to Granthill. Ostensibly he went to see his mother, but really he was looking for Charlie. How had it come to this, that he had to go looking for his own son?

Charlie wasn't in, but he'd been sleeping there. His clothes and a

446

few other possessions were in one bedroom. This was some kind of good sign. The flat was untidy and dirty. Don spent an hour clearing up in the kitchen and bathroom. Molly sat watching the TV, smoking. She was hooked on *Crossroads* and thirty Embassy Regal a day. He watched her from the kitchen door. She looked drawn, sucked dry, like the fag end in her mouth.

He opened the fridge. 'What are ye having for your tea?' he called. 'I'll get something later,' she said. 'But there's hardly a thing here.' 'Aye there is.' 'Show me.' Grumbling, she got out of her chair and came through. 'See in that cupboard.' He opened it. A sliced loaf in a wrapper and a dozen tins of baked beans. 'I'll have that.' 'What, beans on toast?' 'I like that.' 'Ye need tae eat better than that.' 'I'm no that hungry these days, son.'

He didn't push it. Actually she was lasting better than he could have hoped. Maybe she just needed to be left alone.

'Charlie looking efter ye?'

'Aye, he's fine, Charlie.'

'But is he looking efter ye?'

'Aye. He's a good laddie, Don.'

He let that one go. 'Dae ye ken where he is?'

'He'll be oot wi his freens. Dinna fash aboot Charlie. He's a good laddie.'

He made her a cup of tea and she settled back down in her chair. He kissed her on the forehead. 'I'll be back at the weekend.' 'Aye, son.' Her hair stank of smoke. She stared past him at the screen. She might even have been taking some of it in.

He caught a bus into the town centre and walked for five minutes, keeping an eye out for Charlie all the way. He arrived at the stop opposite Rinaldi's. What could he do but go home? He was standing there waiting on the next Wharryburn bus when the door of Rinaldi's opened and a bunch of what the papers called 'youths' spilled out, five of them, loud and aggressive. Maybe old Joe had thrown them out, or maybe he was just happy to see the back of them. A moment later – a significant, deliberate space later – Charlie emerged. He stood in the doorway, looking up and down the street as if he owned it. He was wearing blue jeans and a black leather jacket Don had never seen before and he looked much older than eighteen. The others, twenty yards away, turned for him. 'Come on,

Charlie!' Charlie waited, making a point. He wasn't hurrying for anybody. Then he started to move. So did Don.

He cut across the road and came up behind Charlie. He was going to shout his name but instead he landed a slap on the shoulder of the leather jacket. He knew he was going to provoke a reaction, he wanted to see what it was. Charlie spun round flinging Don's hand off and his fists were up and he was good and ready for it. When he saw who it was he eased off but there was no smile of welcome or relief. He said, 'Ye shouldna dae that.'

'Dae what?'

'Come up behind me like that. Ye might get hurt.'

'Maybe,' Don said. 'If ye sent for reinforcements.' He nodded at the gang now ambling back to see what was going on.

'Whae's this auld cunt?' one of them said. They were all skinny, pale, dangerous-looking.

'This auld cunt,' Don said, 'is that wee cunt's faither. And you, son, had better beat it because we're haein a private conversation.'

'Don't tell me tae fucking beat it,' the kid said. He had a white scar down one cheek that ran into a puckered repair job on his upper lip. 'This is a public street.'

Charlie said, 'Fuck off, Kenny. I'll catch ye later. See yese later, boys, eh?'

Don was amazed at how they melted back under Charlie's gaze, deferring to his assurance, his greater intelligence perhaps. Even he, the father and begetter that had once wiped the bairn's arse, was impressed.

The gang sloped off and Charlie fixed Don with a sneer.

'Well?'

'Come wi me,' Don said, and his big hand gripped Charlie's upper arm through the black leather. 'I want tae show ye something.'

'Take your haund aff my jaiket.'

'If it was yours I might think aboot it,' Don said. He was guiding them down a side street, saw what he was looking for up ahead, a close with an open door. He didn't want to do this but he needed to try one last thing. Before Charlie could resist he hauled him in and down the dark passage till they were out of sight of the street. Then he pushed him up against the wall and pinned him there with a hand against each shoulder, arm's length just in case he tried to stick the heid on him.

448

'Now listen tae me,' Don said, keeping his voice as low and controlled and firm as he could. 'I dinna ken where ye're getting aw the gear, son,' he said, 'but I ken it's no aff a wage. So are ye stealing it, or taking a slice aff your granny's pension, or are ye getting it some other way? Eh? Because ye're no earning it. So how come ye dinna hae tae work when everybody else does, Charlie?'

Charlie waited, as if he were picking the question he preferred to answer. 'My gran and me are fine,' he said. 'Aye, she gies me money sometimes. Ye ken why? Because she likes me. She likes me being there. I look efter her. She looks efter me. Any problem wi that?'

'That's no enough. Where dae ye get the rest of your money?'

'In my haund. I dae jobs for folk that dinna bother wi paperwork. That's aw you need tae ken.'

'Have you or ony of your wee bastard friends been up at Wharry-burn threatening the Khans?'

'What?'

'Ye heard me.' Don's arms were beginning to shake with the pressure he was exerting. 'Have ye been threatening Saleem Khan?'

'The village Paki?' Charlie turned his head and spat on to the stone slabs. 'What would I fucking dae that for?'

'For protection.' Don could feel himself beginning to tire. Any second now the arms were going to go into spasm.

'Protection fae what? Mexican fucking bandits? Think we're the Magnificent Seven? They're nothing. Fucking peasants. They're just like everybody else up there only the colour of shite. I wouldna waste my time.'

'If you ever set foot in that shop again I'll come and find ye and break your fucking legs.'

By rights Charlie should have been terrified. He was eighteen, a boy. He should have been pissing his breeks but he wasn't. To show how relaxed he was, he yawned.

'Is that you finished then? Can I go?'

Don saw a slow, wet smile slide across his son's lips. As if they'd both been acting all along, as if Charlie had been biding his time and only now was this thing, whatever it was, really going to start.

'Jesus Christ, Charlie! Is that aw ye've got tae say? "Can I go?" This is me, your faither, speaking tae ye. But who the fuck are you, Charlie? Who the fuck are you?'

He heard himself. He who'd always prided himself on not using curse words was surrendering his tongue to them, even as the last of the strength in his arms ebbed away. He suddenly felt insecure, as if he'd stepped into a dark room and didn't know who or what else was in there.

'Who the fuck am I?' Charlie said. 'Is that really what ye want tae ken?'

He didn't wait for an answer. With one quick shift of his body he threw Don back, smacking him against the opposite wall so that all the breath flew out of him. Before he could refill his lungs Charlie's forearm was pressing hard against his throat, choking him. Charlie levered the arm, forcing him up on the toes of his boots. Don heard the wheeze of the last bit of air leaving his windpipe.

'So this is who I am, *faither*,' Charlie said. The derision in the last word was palpable. 'The difference between you and me is thirty years and the fact that you play at being hard but really ye're saft as fucking butter. Ye dinna like this stuff, dae ye? The violence. Ye're only daein this because ye think ye have tae. Save the poor darkies. Save Chairlie fae himsel. Me, I fucking love violence. I could get the chib oot noo and carve my initials in your face and I'd get a fucking hard-on daein it. Dae ye hear me? I like hurting people. See that wee cunt Kenny. I gied him that scar. He loves me for it. He'd fucking die for me. And that's me being nice. But what am I gonnae dae wi you?'

He lifted the arm slightly and Don's lungs worked like bellows for a few seconds before the air was clamped off again. Charlie had it thought through like a professional torturer. He said, 'Tell ye what I'm gonnae dae, I'm gonnae be *extra* nice tae you, *faither*. No because it's your first offence because it isna, is it? But I'm gonnae let ye go anyway, and ye ken why? Because o my mither. But ye asked me a question so I'm telling ye the answer noo so ye never have tae ask it again. Who's Charlie? This is Charlie. He'll stay oot o your poxy wee village if you stay oot o his toon. Ken what, I'll make it easy for ye. Ye can come intae Drumkirk, ye can even go and see my granny, but no when I'm there, or see that thing ye said aboot breaking my legs, I'll break *your* fucking legs and I'll dae it so ye'll never walk again and I'll fucking enjoy daein it. And see if ye ever see me on the street again, stay oot o my fucking road. Don't fucking come near me. Because if ye ever pit your haund on my shooder again I'll turn roond and I'll fucking cut ye.'

He stepped back. Don collapsed, gasping for air. He thought his head was going to burst all over the floor. He heard Charlie's heels as he walked casually away. He lay retching, but nothing came up. After a while he forgot he was lying in the close.

It had still been light outside when they'd come in but it was dark by the time he started to push himself upright. Gradually the lungs eased off, the pounding in his ears faded. He got to his unsteady feet, staggered a few paces. If anybody stayed in this close they were all stone deaf or too terrified to come out. He felt like an old man. He wasn't even fifty. He felt like an old man whose son had just died.

§

When he got home, much later, Liz wanted to know where he'd been, then she saw the colour of him. What had happened? He couldn't bring himself to confess the humiliation he'd been through. He lied. He'd met Charlie, they'd had another argument, a bit of a fight. He refused to go into more detail.

He couldn't articulate what he felt: the fear, the horror, the despair. He wanted to shut it all out and never think of it again.

Charlie was not to be spoken of in his presence. He never wanted to see him or hear him mentioned again. Liz could work out her own arrangements. He'd not stand in her way but Charlie had made his choices and Don would have nothing to do with him.

Liz said, 'Ye canna dae this tae your ain son.'

'He's done it tae himsel, Liz.'

'I'll speak tae him,' she said.

'Dae what ye like,' he said, 'but I've had enough.'

§

If Sir Malcolm and Lady Patricia Eddelstane could not provide their son with money, they could provide him with contacts. After school, with three mediocre A Levels under his belt, David headed for Edinburgh, where he worked for a few months in an antiques shop owned by a cousin of his mother. He liked the city, although he was astonished at the run-down condition of much of the centre, including the street near Canonmills where he was lodging. He might have stayed, but the cousin was selling up the business, and London, the centre of the known universe, beckoned. Armed with an address book and a couple of offers of work, he headed south.

The two job possibilities were these: an old MP associate of Sir Malcolm thought he might need a 'research assistant', a newish term for an MP's drudge; and the husband of a friend of Lady Patricia had an opening in his property business. It turned out that the MP wasn't intending to pay David anything, so he put politics on hold and took the job with John Harris Associates. He was the office boy but the understanding was that this would lead to greater things. 'We were all the office boy once,' John Harris assured him. 'Isn't that right, Q?' 'Quite right, Mr Harris.'

Harris was a fat, sprawling man who sweated heavily into the collars of his checked Viyella shirts, considered himself a maverick, and let everybody know by never lowering his voice. 'Bugger the rules, that's our motto, isn't it, Q?' he shouted. 'Absolutely, Mr Harris,' said Q.

Q was Quentin Williams, born and bred in Chiswick, never set foot outside London and saw no earthly reason for doing so. He was charged with showing David the ropes.

'Where are you from?' Q demanded. 'Glen where? Never heard of it. You don't sound Scotch. All right, this is what we do. We take bets on the property market. The unlikelier the property, the more we like betting on it. We pay people to take eyesores, wasteland, condemned buildings and empty offices off their hands. Then what do we do?'

'Build something new?' David suggested.

Q snorted with delighted scorn. 'Nah! Too much trouble, too much expense. We get planning permission to build, but we don't order a single brick. We pick sites in areas that are about to come up in the world and we sit tight. If we've done our homework right we don't have to wait too long. Six months, a year, two years if we have to. Mr Harris says it's like gestation. Six months is a monkey, twelve's a zebra, two years is an elephant. Elephants are usually the best but sometimes three monkeys are worth more than one elephant, you with me? We pick our moment and *then* we sell. And the more we do it, the better we get at it. Very few of our investments go bad on us these days. He knows what he's doing, Mr Harris, and so do I. You watch us and learn, you'll be fine.'

Q was five years older than David. He intended to be a millionaire before he was forty. He was affable, self-contained, supremely self-confident. He explained things to David with barely concealed impatience, as if it was adding a year on to his target but couldn't be helped because this was what John Harris had asked him to do. Q didn't drink and he didn't smoke and he thought drugs were as ridiculous as the hippies who took them. He passed through Swinging London every day on his way to and from the office or on site visits, and was untainted by it. He despised them all, the louche pop stars, the self-obsessed artists, the flower people, the junkies, the dropouts, the lefties, not because of how they looked or spoke or what they said but because they were deluding themselves. We all live in a yellow fucking submarine? Not Q. They were so busy agonising and protesting, navel-gazing and peace-signing, tuning in and chilling out that they were missing the main action. Well, it was their loss.

David made a half-baked attempt to excuse them. 'Maybe they just need to let off some steam,' he said. 'Maybe we've all been repressed for twenty years. Ever since the war.'

Q gave him a look: do I look repressed? David backtracked. 'Or probably it's just me. I'm too square. I can't help it but I am.'

'Don't feel bad about it,' Q said, 'don't feel ashamed. You'll still be here in ten years' time. Half of those idiots will be dead, and the others will be trying to catch up with you but they won't because their brains will have turned to fucking mush.'

'I can't even swear the way you do,' David said.

'Listen,' Q said, 'what is it everybody needs? Forget your free love and flower power and your Hare fucking Krishna. People need houses. They need jobs and places where they can do them. They need medicine when they get sick. They need their dinner. A drink to wash it down with. Not me, but I'm not everybody. They need protection, security. They need fuel for their cars, electricity for their washing machines. They need washing machines. They need weapons. You can gamble on everything else and get lucky, but those are the certainties. We do property and that's fine but I'm investing the money I earn in other things too. Have you got any money? Don't spend it on beads and pot. Stick it in the certainties. Spread it around.'

'I don't have any money,' David said.

He didn't, not right then, but there was some coming.

§

It was around this time that Lucy showed the first public signs of . . . what? Mental imbalance? Emotional starvation? Or an intense desire for self-preservation manifesting as self-destruction? Until she was eleven she'd floated around like a timid, idle fairy, easily provoked to tears, underperforming at the village school and generally behaving as if she didn't belong there or anywhere else on the planet. Then she went to a boarding school in Fife. After four years there she shed her fairy wings and emerged as a revolutionary socialist. It was 1969, the summer of unlove. In her last school year she wrote to the embassy of the People's Republic of China requesting two dozen copies of Mao's *Little Red Book*, which she distributed among her classmates. She also smuggled in a small quantity of hashish and was caught smoking it, for which she was expelled. Returning to Ochiltree House, she gathered a few personal belongings and then was off again, pausing only to explain to Sir Malcolm and Lady Patricia that she hated them, their house and everything they stood for, that she was severing all links with them and going to live in a squat in London.

Freddy, home from school for the weekend, was present on this occasion, and reported it later to David. 'I asked her if she hated me too, and she gave me a look that would have turned a lesser being to stone and said I was an obnoxious, bloodsucking letch. Or was it leech? So then I asked her if she hated you, and she said no, she just felt sorry for you because you don't have any guts. I bet that makes you feel good.'

David had already been in London two years. What did Lucy expect him to do, denounce their parents as she did while developing his career in property speculation and beginning to dabble in Conservative Party politics? He might not be courageous but he wasn't a total hypocrite. She, on the other hand, wasn't even consistent. Not long after arriving in London she dropped Maoism and became a vegetarian anarchist.

He tried to look after her, arranging meetings with her once a month in a grubby little café off the Portobello Road that served a lot of beans and a lot of flapjacks, and sometimes bean flapjacks. Against a backdrop of notices fringed with tear-off phone numbers advertising alternative medicine, guitar lessons and rooms to let, he would hand over some cash and buy her something that passed for a nutritional meal. She wouldn't accept the money unless he pretended it was a donation to whatever insane cause she was currently espousing. The cause changed every few months, but the money was always taken with the same total lack of grace or gratitude. At one meeting she berated him for his shallow moral values, his failure to understand his own guilt by association with the evil that was world capitalism; at the next she informed him that she had discarded useless concepts like guilt and morality – the condition of contemporary society could be understood only through analysing and exposing the façade of advanced capitalism, and then creating new situations in which human desires could be fulfilled rather than degraded. She was a situationist. Some weeks later she denied this: anti-situationists had sabotaged the idea by taking it literally instead of recognising the inherently theoretical nature of any situationist situation. 'Say that again,' David said. 'No,' she said, 'if you don't get it you don't get it.' 'I don't get it,' he said. 'That's because you're so acquiescent,' she said. 'No, you're complicit. You voluntarily accept the so-called reality of the present moment. I refuse to do that.' 'Why?' 'Because reality is *obviously* always an artificial construct.' 'How can reality be artificial?' he asked, kind of wishing he hadn't. 'Oh, David,' she said, exasperated. 'The people with economic and political power determine the way the rest of the population perceive the world at any given moment, so it's only real because they say it is.' 'Is this real?' he asked. 'What?' she said. 'Us, here, eating this ghastly food at this present moment?' Suddenly she looked as though she was going to burst into tears. 'Sorry,' he said. He found arguing with her pointless and exhausting, and did it less and less, absorbing her disdain, much as he had absorbed that of his parents, because it was less painful than exposing her vulnerability. If that made him a coward, he liked to think it was kindness that made him one.

He gathered that she moved regularly from one squalid accommodation to another, and that each change of address usually came with a change of boyfriend. From what she told him, every one of these seemed as arrogant, whining or deluded as she was. Sometimes all at once. He wanted to ask her why she fell with a kind of deliberate carelessness into one bad relationship after another, but didn't for fear that she would ask what kind of relationships he had. He felt sorry for her but dared not show his sympathy. Like criticism, like comfort, it was something she couldn't tolerate.

He would come away from their encounters feeling dirty and sad, and grateful that he was returning to the relative sanity of the world he inhabited. When he'd first arrived in London, he had felt himself on the edge of something different and hedonistic. It was almost – but not quite – infectious. You couldn't ignore it – the girls in miniskirts with psychedelic carrier bags on their arms, the purple Mini Minors and pink VW Campers, the music of Jefferson Airplane and Pink Floyd pouring out of boutiques and first-floor windows. He'd let his hair grow over his collar, bought a pair of jeans for weekends and a loudish tie for work, but his heart wasn't really in it. Sometimes he wished he were over thirty and one of the people he wasn't supposed to trust. It will be over soon, he thought. Order will reassert itself.

In June 1970 the Conservatives, led by Edward Heath, won a General Election. Then, in the autumn of that year, the money happened. His maternal grandmother, who'd lived in Northumberland and whom he'd hardly known, died, leaving him £20,000 after death duties, a huge amount for a lesser Eddelstane. He would have to wait till he was twenty-one to access it, but that was only months away. A similar amount went into a trust fund for Freddy, not to be touched till *he* was twenty-one. A third of the legacy should have gone to Lucy but the old woman, egged on by Lady Patricia, had cut her from her will. David felt bad about this, and upped the fraternal donations for a few months; but he didn't tell his sister what had happened. She didn't even care that her grandmother was dead. Neither did he – he'd only met her half a dozen times – but that wasn't the point. Was it? Applying Lucy's own logic, he stopped feeling guilty. What would Q have said if he'd known about Lucy? 'To hell with her,' probably. Anyway, David assured himself, she'd only have rejected the money or sunk it in some new political idiocy. He could almost persuade himself he was keeping it in trust for her. If she ever came to her senses, he could help her out. Maybe.

When the cash was finally his he used some of it to buy a two-bedroom flat in Islington, and took Q's advice regarding the rest. He spread the money around, into banks, insurance, pharmaceuticals, construction, oil, brewing. He shifted it regularly, kept it working, ahead of inflation and then a bit more. He went back to Q and said, 'What was that you said once, about weapons?' Q looked at him quizzically. 'You told me people need weapons,' he said, 'like they need washing machines.' 'Well, they do,' Q said. 'Do you think war stopped in 1945? Do the sums. There's been Korea, Malaya, Algeria, Aden. Now there's Vietnam, Cambodia, Angola, Mozambique. I don't even know where these fucking countries are but they've got a war or they're about to have one. Use your loaf, invest in it.' David must have gone a bit pale. Q saw it. 'Look, it's a hard world out there. Call it defence, if it makes you feel better. The Ministry of Defence used to be called the Ministry of War. If they can change the wallpaper so can you. People have to defend themselves and sometimes that means attacking the other bastard first. Either way they need weapons and there isn't a country in the world, believe me, that won't pay for weapons before it pays for anything else.'

David ditched his guilt again. Each time it was easier. He had a knack for backing good runners which his father entirely lacked. (What on earth could have induced the old fool to put money into Clydeside shipbuilding when it was obvious the glory days were over, and all that was left was crumbs for workers and management to bicker over?) He found that the investments he made in companies with defence interests did better than any of the others. Anyway, it wasn't as if that was all they did. Ferranti, for example: they made power transformers, electricity meters, computers, semi-conductors (whatever they were), all kinds of components and instruments, only some of which were for military use. You couldn't separate civil and military technology, that was the bottom line. Same knowledge, different applications. Q was right: the two went hand in hand and better by far that the advances were being made by British companies, or American ones, than by anybody else.

But as David's confidence grew, so did his frustration. For one thing, he was still working for John Harris, buying and selling properties, and while Harris was now paying him a good salary and healthy bonuses David knew he could do better for himself *by* himself. For another, the more he learned about the market, the more he saw what was out there with the potential to give a good return, yet so much of it was badly managed, and government red tape choked the rest. Even worse, huge chunks of the economy were nationalised. Not just munitions – heat and light, water, telephones, communications, airports, railways. Even holidays – Thomas Cook was a nationalised company. How on earth had *that* happened? Q felt it too. 'You'd think this was Russia,' he said. 'I know things are better than they were under Labour but I should be making ten times more than I am. In America I'd be loaded by now. It's not a free market, it's a constrained one, and that's even before you hand over a great fucking wodge to the taxman. Something's got to change, I'm telling you.'

In his own, less brash, way David was as good as Q at playing the game. Maybe better, because for all that he talked about being super-rich, Q never looked like he was going to strike off on his own. According to Q, John Harris always knew best. David didn't think so. John Harris didn't think far enough ahead. What was two, even three, years? It was nothing. If you had enough capital to keep on buying cheap, you should aim to hold on to properties for longer and longer periods. Ten, fifteen, twenty years. If you held your nerve, you'd trigger a huge payout eventually. You couldn't help winning, the money would make more money. He thought about his father and how much he'd lost over the years. It was because he hadn't kept his eye on the ball. David was extremely focused.

There was a sort of mini-boom going on, but it didn't feel right. He diversified again, into bricks and mortar. He mortgaged the Islington flat (he'd bought it outright originally), and bought another, cheaper, and rented it out. Property prices were sluggish, but the buildings weren't going anywhere and people, as Q had pointed out, would always need somewhere to live. No point in selling anyway, the tax would kill him. The income he got as a landlord easily covered the mortgage repayments. He looked around for more property, amazed at his own boldness and at what you could pick up for an absolute song. Thank you, Gran, whoever you were. He kept thinking of Edinburgh too, recalling the semi-derelict state of many of the buildings in the Old Town above ground-floor level, the shabby potential of certain streets on the fringes of the New Town. Edinburgh was a shadow of what it could be. His next moves were going to be up there.

How grateful he was not to have gone to work as an MP's assistant! Through a combination of business dealings and family connections he'd been introduced to some high-rankers in the party anyway, and they gave him a lot more respect than they'd have given a penniless researcher. He let it be known that the idea of a political career interested him, and they let it be known that he interested them: he had the family history, which was good, but he was more biddable than Sir Malcolm had ever been, which was better. More modern too. He had the sort of image the party needed: longish but neat hair, good dress sense, clean, quiet – not braying and giving off that tweeds-and-heather smell his father had. David Eddelstane had prospects. Nobody knew what lay beneath the surface. He hardly knew himself. It was pretty much the only thing he still felt guilty about, but provided it stayed hidden, what was there to worry about?

§

It was only a year since the election but things were tough politically. Ted Heath was fighting an exhausting campaign with the unions over pay restraint, and there were rumblings in Tory circles about what to do when he lost. No doubt he was doing his best but his best wasn't good enough. Northern Ireland was looking ever grimmer, prices and unemployment were on the rise, there were new strikes every other day and a lot of older industries were on their knees. Furthermore, a growing number in the party were dismayed by the country's approaching membership of the European Common Market. Many on the right weren't convinced of the vaunted economic benefits, but more profound was their fear that Heath was throwing away a thousand years of heritage, and selling the best bits of the Commonwealth, the white bits, down the river in order to gain entry to a club dominated by the French and the Germans. Something precious and irretrievable, they felt, would be lost when the day came. In the same way, even though it had been planned for years, the arrival in February of a new decimal currency, in place of lovable, weighty old pounds, shillings and pence, had been like a slap in the face of Britannia. Bit by bit the country people loved was being taken from them.

David had until then thought Heath an appropriate man to lead the modern Conservative Party, but increasingly at Tory gatherings he found himself in a minority. It was not in his nature to enjoy being in a minority. He shuffled rightwards until he felt more comfortable, nodding agreement with men and women twice his age who believed that Heath was not equipped to prevent a general slide towards chaos. A new direction was urgently required, within the party itself and beyond it. David picked up hints: phrases like 'contingency plans', 'fallback positions'.

At the party conference at Brighton in October his attention was caught one evening by a poster that read IN SEARCH OF FREEDOM? – THIS WAY. He followed a series of signs that brought him to the back of a packed meeting just as the speakers were being introduced: a former SAS man and an American economist with the clean-cut look of a Mormon about him. It was familiar stuff – the creep of socialism, the suffocating hand of government, the erosion of choice – but there was an urgency, a seriousness about the way the men spoke that couldn't be ignored. People listened intently, as if at last someone was telling them what they'd both longed and dreaded to hear. When the questions started it seemed as if half the audience was composed of men who'd once been in the army or police: the other half were angry businessmen who couldn't move for red tape, some of their wives, a few MPs and councillors, and David. When somebody talked about setting up a 'resistance network' if the social and political order collapsed there was an eruption of applause. It was all, at first, as alien to him as the King's Road on a Saturday afternoon. Then rapidly it became less so. These people spoke the same language as his parents, but they were harder, more clinical in their analysis, and they seemed to believe passionately in what they said they believed in.

Back in London he discovered that he too could create a grave, nodding, attentive silence among the very people he had formerly deferred to, by giving his own 'first-hand' account of the nation's decline. He was indebted, for the details that gave his stories the feel of authenticity, to the SAS man, and to Lucy. A group called the Angry Brigade had been planting bombs in boutiques and car showrooms and at the homes of a couple of Cabinet ministers, causing damage and inconvenience but – so far – no deaths and no serious injuries. It was a campaign which Lucy not only approved of but about which she also seemed to have quite detailed knowledge. Omitting any mention of his sister, David gave a good impression of a sensible but streetwise young man who understood what was going on out there and wanted to do something to stop it. There didn't seem to be any downside to developing this role – in fact it was enjoyable racking up the sense of impending doom – so long as he kept Lucy out of the picture. His biggest fear was that she might actually be involved with the Angry Brigade, and would be arrested and charged, tainting him by association. He was much relieved, therefore, when at the end of the year she converted to Trotskyism, attached herself to the International Marxist Group and headed for Glasgow to support the Upper Clyde Shipbuilders work-in.

§

There was somebody from back when he was very small, some woman: not his mother, not the housekeeper, Mrs Thomson, not either of his grandmothers; a woman he found both attractive and frightening. A teacher maybe – there were a couple of female teachers at his prep school, but he could remember them and neither seemed to fit – so probably it was before school; someone associated with his parents. He thought she must have been tall, this woman, yes, that would have been best, but even if she hadn't been he'd only have come up to her thighs. Her shoes, her stockinged legs, her knees, the hem of her skirt. The world from his height then – when he was what, three, four? – was a world of passing legs and feet, mostly women's. He kind of resented the fact that women and men were so obviously different in what they wore when he was that age. Maybe that was the trigger. Resented it yet loved it. The silky feel of that woman's leg, the shine of her black leather shoe, the secret, warm odour he could breathe in when she sat cross-legged and let the shoe hang from her toe, the high heel ticking back and forth beside his head. He sat next to her chair on the floor and didn't say a word. His mother smiled a warning at him but she didn't need to: there was something about the other woman that kept him quiet. Did *she* know?

Smell, touch, look, hear, taste. He kept thinking back, trying to pinpoint moments of change. For as long as he could recall, his senses had picked up on everything from the soft, rich, shiny deadness of pheasants hanging in the pantry to the way the pile of a hearthrug felt when you stroked it, this way, that way. Those senses had been teased by words in books, by the deep-rolling sensuousness of *Lady Chatterley*. Then, as he approached puberty, he began to focus on something more urgent, more desperate: that thing which was already in him but had not yet revealed itself. That sinking, sickly, giddy sensation began to acquire an explanation.

Childhood lobbed strange memories at him. What had been his favourite fairy tale? 'Cinderella'. Not because of the rags-to-riches romance or the pumpkin carriage, not even because of the glass slipper itself, but because of what it meant. In his book there'd been an illustration of the prince trying to force the slipper on to the foot of one of the ugly sisters while the other looked on, towering meanly over him. The prince was bent low, hot with the effort, crouched in obeisance to the foot. It was just a picture in a children's book, a cartoon almost, but it had stirred something at his quick, made him want to turn the page swiftly, but then – always – turn back again.

He remembered other times when he'd tottered around in his mother's shoes, feet crammed down into the toes. She'd laughed at him or flung something at his head – another shoe, a hairbrush, anything to hand – as she sat at her dressing table getting ready for going out, or staying in, whichever it was. Once he'd taken the shoes off and sniffed one and made a *phew* noise and she'd laughed again and turned her back on him and as soon as she had he stuck his nose right in, God Almighty, he wanted to inhale the whole shoe. Yes, he'd do it when her back was turned or she wasn't in the room at all but had swept out in a haze of perfume, shoes and clothes left lying around – the bedroom was always chaotic, his father would trip over the wreckage and stand at the head of the staircase and yell at her why the hell couldn't she pick her bloody things off the bloody floor – and David would wait till they were both downstairs or out and then he'd go in, alone, so yes even then, even that early, he knew it was wrong, or a secret, something that could trip him up and get him into trouble but something that was his, his own, and even then, at three or four, he knew deep down that what he really desired was to suck in the smell and taste and texture of the *other* woman's shoe. The woman who scared him, it was her shoe he wanted.

Shoes, legs, stockings, they were connected but then everything kind of stopped. On the surface he could communicate very well with people but he didn't *connect* with them. Men or women, they were puzzles he had to deal with and he did that as well as he could, he put on a good show but what he needed was something else, the comfort and safety and danger of a strange woman's shoes and nylon-clad legs. And that had been his childhood, and then just as he was becoming conscious, dimly aware of what it was he liked, what he wanted, the 1960s happened. Disaster. Women in trousers, women in shorts, girls in socks, or in miniskirts without nylons at all. Jesus. The years went by. Shoe shops: the intense leather-and-feet smell of them; some of the sales assistants gave him suspicious looks, as if they knew what was going on inside his eleven-, twelve-year-old head, even though he didn't know himself. Then he was at Kilsmeddum. Everybody wanked, as if it were a compulsory extra, like country dancing or the Combined Cadet Force. Sometimes you wanked someone else and he wanked you, in the presence of others, and that was to prove you weren't a poof, but mostly you wanked yourself, by yourself. You were supposed to think about doing sex but when David wanked or was wanked it was shoes and feet and legs he thought of, innocent advertisements he'd torn out of the Sunday colour supplements or memorised from his mother's fashion magazines.

One holiday a strange item from a world that was not the Eddelstanes' world found its way into Ochiltree House: a home-shopping catalogue. Mrs Thomson had brought it in. David had a vague notion that she wanted to show his mother something in it, ask her advice or opinion, and it sat in the kitchen for a week or so. Mrs Thomson called it a 'club book'. Other boys from other backgrounds would have known exactly what to do with a club book. You'd take it to the toilet and salivate over the pages of models in bras and knickers, but he, as if pulled in by a magnet sucking at a lump of metal lodged deep in his belly, went to the pages of women's shoes. He could hardly see for dizziness, nearly fell off the stool at the kitchen table. Erection on him like a cricket stump. It was a relief when Mrs Thomson took the catalogue away and he couldn't look any more.

Fashions came and went, good years (stilettos and three-inch-heeled slingbacks) and bad years (clumpy square heels, no heels, clogs for God's sake). He wandered past the windows of Baird the Bootmaker, Saxone, Clarks and Lotus in a daze, thinking it was like having the flu, eventually it would pass, but already he knew it wouldn't pass, not ever, he had it for ever. Mannequins were good; mannequins that were just legs, better. Tights: you could imagine they weren't tights, you could pretend they were still stockings, but more and more you knew that they weren't, it wasn't the same. He lay awake at night with thoughts of shoes and feet and stockinged legs tormenting him and sometimes he cried because of what he was stuck with, knowing he would have to go through life disguising it, feeding it, disguising it, feeding it, and that it would always contain the possibility of exposing him to disaster: the fact that he didn't want to make love to women, he wanted to make love to their shoes.

§

His father invited him to lunch at his club. Sir Malcolm was down in London for a few days, talking to friends and advisers in the City – not David – about how to shore up his investments. It was spring 1972. Economically, things looked grim. The mini-boom had flattened out, imploded. The trade balance was dreadful, inflation over 8 per cent, unemployment touching a million. Northern Ireland was in meltdown following the shooting by the army of thirteen civil rights marchers in Londonderry in January – the sort of incident Sir Malcolm would once have raged about, blaming the demonstrators of course. Yet David found him curiously unmoved, as if all this were only what he had come to expect and, now he was not an MP, it was no longer required of him to be incensed.

One of the rules of the club was that neither business nor politics could be discussed in the dining room. Amazingly – for surely the waiters weren't going to eavesdrop and report you – the rule was observed. This didn't leave father and son with much to talk about. They muttered inanities at each other over a bottle of claret and schoolish cottage pie and apple crumble, then retired to a corner of the lounge where conversation and smoking were permitted. The place was a caricature of a London club: there were two or three old men asleep in armchairs, a couple more with their noses in *The Times*. Sir Malcolm looked perfectly at home.

'How old are you now?' he asked, lighting up a cigar. As if he didn't know. Maybe he didn't.

'Twenty-two,' David said. A waiter brought them white coffees in Denby cups a couple of shades lighter than the green leather upholstery.

'I could put you up for this place, if you like. Would you like?'

'That would be kind.'

'Wouldn't do it out of kindness. Practical. People who matter are members here. I'd have to find someone else to second you. Shouldn't be impossible.'

'Thank you.'

'I'm not paying for you,' Sir Malcolm warned, sounding slightly panicky. 'I hear you're doing all right. Are you doing all right?'

'Not too bad.'

'Making a bloody fortune, your mother says. Maybe you should be paying for me.'

He gave a sort of laugh but it didn't sound like a joke. David sort of laughed back. 'I think she's exaggerating a little.'

'That money you got from your grandmother was a boost, eh?'

'It's helped a great deal,' David said. 'It was very generous of her.'

'Very,' Sir Malcolm said. 'She wasn't famed for her generosity. Better known for her spite. Didn't like me much anyway. Not a bean,' he muttered obscurely.

'Sorry?'

Sir Malcolm turned the volume up. 'She didn't leave me a bean,' he said, with vehemence.

'Really?' David said. 'But she left mother something, surely?'

His father glared at him. 'What if she did? Doesn't help me, does it? Bitch. Not dignified, having to ask for pocket money at my age. Anyway, I assume you've invested it wisely. Cleverly.' A sarcastic edge came into his voice. He held the cigar in one hand, picked at a mole on his neck with the other. David could hear the horny click of his nails.

'I think so.'

'Stashed it away neatly. Tidily. For a rainy day.'

'That's what I've done.'

Sir Malcolm cleared his throat noisily, as if to get the sarcasm out of his system, and fitted a request in at the end of the prolonged rasping. 'Wouldn't like to invest in your old man, I don't suppose?'

This was what it was all about, then: lunch, the club membership, the barely concealed contempt for his success. Mother held the purse strings and father wanted to tap him for a loan. Possibly even an outright gift. Or maybe the two of them were in it together. David wondered how Q would have reacted. Not with the civilised restraint he himself was showing, anyway. But then, Q wouldn't have got through the door.

'It's all tied up,' David said. 'Couldn't even if I wanted to.' Which was, they both understood, a lie. Sir Malcolm understood it so perfectly that he feigned deafness, pretended he'd never asked in the first place. He picked at his neck more furiously.

'Bugger,' he said. 'Made myself bleed.'

He reached into his trouser pocket for a handkerchief and held it to his neck. 'Hear you're making a name for yourself in the party. Kensington, isn't it?'

'That's right.'

'The Kensington people are stuck up their own arses. Always were, probably always will be. Important people to know, some of them, but they have everything stitched up. You'll wait years for a chance at a seat down here. Presume you want a seat?'

'I wasn't thinking along those lines just yet.'

'No point being in politics if you don't. You should get yourself nominated for an unwinnable. North of England. Scotland, even better. Glasgow. Darkest Lanarkshire. Put up a good fight, show you're willing, next time they'll give you something marginal or better.'

'Something safe would be good,' David said.

'There's still a few left in Scotland. An Edinburgh seat, or Perthshire, or the north-east. Get yourself one of those, they even give you a bloody pension these days.' Another illustration of his father's financial ineptitude: he'd stood down the year before a pension scheme for MPs was first set up. 'Should never have resigned. Your mother insisted. Bloody doctors. Eight years ago. Look at me, fit as a fiddle.'

He looked as if his boiler could burst at any moment.

David said, 'Perhaps I should try for Glenallan.'

'Hmph. Don't think Braco's ready to step aside for some time yet. You know I'm no longer constituency chairman, don't you?'

'No, I didn't.'

'Some stickler for the rules said I couldn't have a third term. By the way, his daughter's in town, do you know her?'

'No, not really.' David remembered a girl, his own age or perhaps a year older, at a Conservative ball. He must have been about fifteen. She'd held no interest for him whatsoever.

'Turned into a peach. Don't know what she's doing down here. Not much, I shouldn't think. Why should she? Braco's as rich as Croesus. Now there's a thing.'

This was Plan B, David thought. Somehow his father had to stay attached to the possibility of sources of wealth other than Lady Patricia. Himself, Braco, it didn't matter. If he could maintain contact some of it might trickle his way eventually. It was pathetic.

David saw Roderick Braco from time to time at party functions. He said he would make a point of asking after his daughter.

'I should. Could do a lot worse. Wouldn't mention that you're thinking of standing for Parliament though. To him or her. Might put the wind up him. Might make him think you had, you know . . .'

'I've forgotten her name,' David said.

'Melissa,' Sir Malcolm said without hesitation. 'Ulterior motives. Nice name. When are you coming home next? Your mother misses you.'

'I was only there at Christmas,' David said. Four days of the usual drinking, eating and shouting. The notion that Lady Patricia missed him already, or at all, was as laughable as his father's attempts at matchmaking.

'How's Freddy?' he asked.

Sir Malcolm frowned. 'Freddy? Fine, as far as I know. Why?'

'Just wondered.'

'He wants to live in America. Can't say I blame him. Friend of ours down in Dorset keeps his garage full of jerrycans of petrol and his motorboat stocked with Scotch. When the Reds take over he's ready to zip across to Guernsey. Good thinking. Plan ahead.'

'I don't think things are quite that bad,' David said.

'Things are bloody awful,' Sir Malcolm said.

After a suitable pause, David said, 'I don't suppose my sister's been in touch, has she?'

'No,' Sir Malcolm said.

'You don't know how she is?'

'Haven't a clue. Your mother won't have her spoken of.'

David had an address for Lucy in Glasgow, but had failed to see her at Christmas. Hadn't tried in fact. From what little he knew of Glasgow, he imagined a grimy tenement near the grimy Clyde, full of wire-haired old women and aggressive little men with impenetrable accents. Broken glass everywhere, for some reason. The idea of standing as a Tory candidate in such a place made him shudder.

'Of course, your mother's plan backfired when it came to that money,' Sir Malcolm said. 'She thought if that girl didn't get any there'd be more coming to her. What she forgot was that her mother was as much of a bitch as she is. Which is why you and Freddy got second helpings.'

David said, 'You might at least call her by her name.'

'So might you,' his father said, and then muttered, as if trying to put a face to the name, 'Lucy.'

'You know she's in Glasgow?' David said.

'What on earth's she doing there?'

'Supporting the shipyard workers.'

'Oh for God's sake,' Sir Malcolm said. He lapsed into silence, puffing angrily at his cigar and periodically inspecting the bright red spots on his handkerchief.

David drank his coffee. In both social and business situations he was party to a lot of worried talk about the coming revolution, couched in the same language he'd heard at the presentation at Brighton. He picked up hints of connections between SAS operations in Northern Ireland and something called the Resistance and Psychological Operations Committee. There were mentions of 'volunteer forces' and 'retained counter-insurgency units'. Words like 'safety' and 'action' and 'freedom' stood out from the shadowy mass of such talk. *Constant vigilance.* 'Have you read that thriller by Douglas Hurd? *Scotch on the Rocks*? Bit of fun, but, believe me, it could happen. If not the Nats then the Reds. More likely the Reds.' To the people who talked in this way it was a game, David thought, but a serious one nonetheless. He played along, nodding and saying very little. Couldn't do any harm. Anyway, there were some truly dangerous people in the unions. And in Labour. If it came to it, he knew which side he'd be on.

§

The chief beauty of the Islington flat was that he lived there on his own. He could afford to. It was a little out of the way, beyond the Circle Line – the outer limit of London as far as most of his political connections were concerned – but it suited him well to be somewhat apart. It was a sanctuary, the place he could retreat to when, as it did every month or so, the need to indulge himself became intolerable.

After work sometimes, if he had a free evening, he would go up to Soho and, heart pounding, dart into this or that shop. He had an instinct for finding places that didn't luridly advertise themselves on the street, but that had the kind of material he was looking for. Things, he imagined, had moved on a lot since the *Lady Chatterley* trial: these places were full of magazines whose existence he couldn't even have dreamed of twelve, thirteen years before. *Shoe Worship*, *Stiletto*, *Heel Boy*. They might have been made especially for him but apparently there were hundreds, thousands, of other men out there with similar desires twisting in their stomachs. He sifted through the magazines, trying to second-guess the contents beneath the sealed cellophane wrappers. Sometimes he got it right, and a whole weekend of frantic but ultimately unsatisfying masturbation ensued; sometimes he got it wrong, and found that these productions were not made especially for him at all. Actually, this was how it was most of the time. That was the thing about porn, it never quite hit the mark. It always disappointed, always promised more than it could deliver, always failed to match the fantasy he thought he had in his head; always, sooner or later, sent him back to the shops for more.

He had a collection of shoes too. A man buying shoes for his wife or his girlfriend wasn't that rare, the shop assistants didn't usually blink, even when he went for heels that were cartoonishly high, shoes you could commit murder with. It wasn't as if he were asking for outlandish sizes such as a man might wear, but still his heart went into overdrive whenever he summoned up the courage to acquire a new pair. Like the magazines, though, they were dissatisfying even though he longed to be satisfied by them. In the end they were useless without the woman they were meant to go with. There had to be a woman. It didn't matter who she was, so long as she was right. But there was no such woman. She existed, incompletely, only in his imagination.

Every so often he'd drain himself so thoroughly of his strange desire that he'd think he really had got it out of his system. He was cleansed, healthy, normal. He'd take the shoes out two or three pairs at a time and dump them in litter bins; the same with the porn, thrown triumphantly away on an evening stroll. He strolled, he strode out. He was free. And then a few weeks later, for no reason that he could discern, the thing would be stirring in him again.

He was a young man with prospects and a flat of his own. Girls found him attractive for all the wrong reasons. He was careful to keep at bay the ones who knew other people he knew, the Kensington and Chelsea set. He let himself be chatted up by secretaries, office girls he met in the pub after work. There was a bad experience when he took one back to the flat. They'd kissed a bit on the street, something he felt he had to do, to get to the next stage. He bought a bottle of wine on the way home, to make it easier. They drank a glass or two, then they were in a clinch on the sofa, then on the floor, then he asked her to sit on the sofa again. She indulged him for a while – 'You're a legs man, are you?' – but then he became too much of a legs man, a shoes-and-feet man. 'Stop it, David.' He stopped it. 'You're weird,' she said, and hurriedly put herself back together again, looking round the walls of the flat as if they were closing in on her. She left without finishing her wine. He was appalled that he'd frightened her. He meant her no harm. He wasn't a rapist or a murderer. He was just an ordinary young man with prospects. And a twist.

He met Melissa Braco again, and immediately liked her. Liked her for herself. She was, as his father had put it, a peach. She was also gentle, generous and trusting, and she seemed to enjoy David's company as much as he enjoyed hers. She was innocent, and experienced London with the open-minded optimism of an innocent, and yet she was not entirely naive. When he talked about his difficult relationship with his parents, she understood. (Hers with her

470

own parents – she was an only child – was seemingly perfect, a mutual exchange of respect and love.) She sympathised when he talked about Lucy. She tried to relate to people less fortunate than herself. She was the beautiful only daughter of rich people and David realised that he would never meet anybody more likely to make him a better wife. They got on so well, in fact, that he would have spilled out his heart to her, confessing his deviation (he thought of it as such now, a kind of sexual wrong-turning, kinder-sounding than 'perversion') and asking her to help him overcome it, except for one astonishing thing: for three, six, nine months, for the whole first year of their relationship, it was not there. It had vanished utterly, was never in his thoughts unless he thought about its absence; it simply wasn't an issue at all. It was all her doing, he con-cluded. He had met the girl who put all that sad obsession into per-spective and made it worthless. They had fumbling, cosy, slightly apologetic sex, and, both being virgins, thought their pleasure and performance adequate and the start of something deep and lasting that would only get better. They were in love. Yes, David decided, that was what it must be. For the first time in his life, he felt content.

Even the two sets of parents, who despite their shared political allegiance had always viewed each other with suspicion, seemed pleased. On a Saturday in late September 1973, between the mili-tary coup in Chile and the outbreak of the Yom Kippur War in the Middle East, at Glenallan Parish Kirk and afterwards at the Monk-barns House Hotel, David, son of Sir Malcolm and Lady Patricia Eddelstane, and Melissa, daughter of Roderick and Julia Braco, were married.

§

Billy and Barbara had been an item for nearly ten years. They'd been to university together, then to teacher-training college. He was a historian, she was a mathematician, both teaching in Glasgow schools. They made the occasional trip to Wharryburn, and Don was always welcoming but Barbara knew she wasn't liked by Liz. Mostly they stayed away.

They lived a couple of streets apart, near Victoria Park, but spent nearly all their time at Barbara's. When her flatmate moved out it made financial and practical sense for Billy to move in with her. For a while they said nothing to anyone about this new arrangement. Eventually, however, it could no longer be disguised. Barbara's mother didn't object, but there was a row with Liz, especially when it became clear that they had no intention of getting married. Barbara said she didn't believe in marriage as an institution, and Billy agreed with her. They didn't come back to Wharryburn for a while after that.

Living together. Don felt uncomfortable about it at first, but was amazed at how rapidly he got used to the idea, and how little he cared. He had another son who was likely to end up behind bars, so did it matter at all? No, except for the rift it opened up between Liz and himself. 'So much for them gaun their ain ways,' she said pointedly. 'Why cast that up tae me?' he said. 'They've proved their commitment so why no accept it?' 'It's their commitment I dinna like,' Liz said. 'Well, as lang as they're no mairrit they can aye split up easy enough, is that what ye want?' Don said. 'What kind o basis for a relationship is that?' Liz demanded, and Don threw his arms up in surrender. The basis of *their* relationship was that they'd made their bed years ago and they'd lie in it till doomsday. Fine, he just wished for a wee bit more when they were there. From himself as much as from her. Not that long back he'd overheard a woman on the bus say in too loud a whisper to her friend: 'My man's good tae me noo. He kens no tae bother me.' And he imagined Liz saying something similar to Joan Drummond or Betty Mair and curled up inside at the thought.

He saw plenty of himself in Billy – the same desire for fairness and equality, the same respect for other people – but there was something new with this generation: they'd ditched an older morality and they were quick to protest against what they didn't like but they'd no fixed ideas about what they valued. That, Billy would tell him, was the point. Theory and analysis told you more about human behaviour, about how people *really* worked, than any priest or judge or politician ever could. You learn, you adapt. And this made sense to Don, it wasn't so far removed from the way he'd always thought, and he only had to think about how he felt about Billy and Barbara living together to see the truth of it. And yet he worried. If you ditched the old morality, what would be left? If Billy and Barbara were good people, decent people, what about the bad? What about Charlie? He felt himself torn between envy and suspicion. For everybody's sake, he didn't want it to go any more wrong than it already had.

§

In the mottled days of Bloody Sunday, Idi Amin, *The Godfather* and Jane Fonda in Hanoi, Billy and Barbara stripped sex back to their primal urges, then built it up again. This happened as Barbara was entering the zone of what Billy later thought of as deep feminism. Trembling a little, he followed her in. For a while there were two manuals by their bed: *The Joy of Sex* and *The Second Sex*. Billy was more turned on by the De Beauvoir but he didn't put it like that, it wouldn't have gone down well. They had promised as teenagers that nothing between them would be concealed, but he found he was keeping small, insignificant matters to himself, and was sure that she too had her secrets.

But meanwhile they did sex. They did it because they loved doing it and then they did it through and beyond loving it till their sexual organs were red-raw and aching, till there was no intimacy, subtlety or spontaneity left in it. They analysed touch till they couldn't feel it any more. He worked and worked at bringing Barbara to the fullness of her sexual being, and he did it in a spirit of generosity and apology, as a drone, tireless in the service of his queen. Beyond the bedroom, they made equal shares of housework, cooking, shopping and anything else that needed to be done. If children came along they'd share those responsibilities too. He didn't have a problem with any of this. How could anyone seriously or coherently argue against women being free from unpaid drudgery, from fear of rape or from actual rape and male violence, from not having control over their own bodies? Sometimes he felt like he was righting the wrongs of untold generations of misogynists, and this was okay, it was the historical moment he inhabited, it was the task given to him and men like him. They could not liberate women because only women could liberate themselves, but they could stop being the jailers.

Here was a difficult one: all men are potential rapists. After lengthy debate and thought he accepted this. He understood that his capacity to rape was a condition of being a man. Barbara assured him this was nothing personal. It was just how it was. Future generations would be different. They read as widely as possible and the argument was convincing. (Years later, he would meet a woman who would be appalled when he revealed that he believed this, and would challenge it, and he would suddenly realise that he didn't believe it after all, not about himself and not about many other men, and that deep down he never had.)

Barbara tasted her menstrual blood. In an act of solidarity, sort of, he tasted his sperm. These were necessary acts of self-discovery.

She stopped shaving her body. Billy grew a beard. Three months later, in the staffroom toilet mirror at his school, he saw the spitting image of the guy in *The Joy of Sex*, and took up the razor again. Barbara said it was different for men, it wasn't a principle thing. He schooled himself not to find the thick down on the backs of her thighs unattractive, nor the black sproutings in her oxters. They were natural, therefore good.

They became vegetarians. They verged on being hippies but it wasn't sustainable, they were newly into responsible teaching jobs and weekend hippydom would be as hypocritical as subscribing to bourgeois codes like marriage and mortgages. Anyway, Barbara said, the Age of Aquarius was self-indulgent astrological bullshit. Women who mixed that stuff with core issues like domestic abuse and equal pay and opportunities were handing ammunition to the enemy. She was a mathematician, with the logical brain of a mathematician. She did not need that kind of delusion in her life.

One of the things she liked about maths was its purity. It worked or it didn't work. There was an extreme school of feminism that said maths was just like everything else from philosophy to flatulence: it had been systematically appropriated by men. A feminist mathematics wouldn't aim so aggressively at proofs, it would be less hard and more fluid, consequently it would have a very different shape. Maths and science, the argument ran, had been deliberately defeminised by men in order to keep women out. Barbara thought – it was one of the reasons Billy admired her, her ability to cut through the crap – this was a cop-out. Women who took this line were out of their depth, they literally couldn't do the maths. This didn't mean there couldn't be a feminist mathematics, but it wouldn't be soft-edged, soft-focused. She needed to do more thinking on this. Billy deferred to her yet again, partly because maths wasn't his area of expertise.

When it came to his subject, on the other hand, everybody was free to wade in. It was open season on *history*, and not just because of the scope its name provided for puns. History was 90 per cent propaganda and even Billy, who'd seen the light, was still a cog in the education machine that delivered it. Where were the women in history? Take out the queens and duchesses and witches and a few missionaries and nurses and you were left with an anonymous, invisible horde. Or hoard. The hoard of herstory. The past needed to be reclaimed as much as the present. Billy agreed, but why did he have to agree so vehemently that he felt he was disagreeing?

He went to work and taught the kids history, always taking opportunities to insert Marxist or feminist viewpoints. He felt that he and Barbara were in the progressive vanguard so how come when he taught history – the French Revolution, 1848, the First World War, Stalin and Hitler – how come he couldn't dispel the depressing feeling that human beings didn't make forward progress, they went round in circles? That you could raise the barricades and oppose hypocrisy and tyranny and repression all you liked, but it had been done before and would have to be done again? He'd always thought of history as linear, heading towards something, but maybe it wasn't, maybe it was just chasing its tail.

§

There were no big secrets between them. But of course there were. At least two subjects were off-limits. The men not in their lives. Her father, Jack Gordon; his brother, Charlie Lennie.

Early on, back in their first summer, he'd asked about her father. He was staying the weekend in Glenrothes, and they went for a big walk, through the old town of Leslie, up the Falkland road and on to the Lomond Hills. A day of sleepy cows, bumblebees droning like military-transport aircraft, crusty peat underfoot and a light westerly breeze to ease the heat. Barbara's bare arms in the sun. Kisses and feels among the scratchy heather. Bliss . . .

They lay on a hill overlooking a reservoir and he asked her. How had she felt when her father disappeared? How did she feel now?

Each question was met with silence. He didn't need to know but he needed to ask.

'What aboot your mum?' In those early days he still forgot, had to correct himself. 'Sarah. She never mentions it.'

'Why would she mention it?' Barbara said. 'He deserted her. He deserted us. I was only three years old.'

'So you don't remember it?'

Sometimes a furious light flamed up in Barbara's eyes. It happened now. 'Oh yes, I remember. I remember him not being there. I remembered it at the time and ever since. That's what I remember about him, him not being there. Not because he died or was killed or because they divorced but because he walked out on us. I can't ever forgive him for that.'

'And Sarah? Has she forgiven him?'

'Yes, she has. That's her choice. One of us has to take a stand.'

'My dad was his pal. I asked him aboot what happened.'

'I wish you wouldn't.'

'He disna like tae talk aboot it.'

'Good.'

'But he did say he thought it was because of the war. Your dad being in a Japanese camp and that.'

'So we can blame the Japanese for him walking out on us?'

'Well, it must have been hell. It must have affected him.'

'Of course it did. But that's still no reason. He wasn't the only one. If he'd committed suicide I could just about accept it but he didn't do that. He just left.'

'Maybe he had tae. Maybe he couldna, I don't know, adjust.'

She had turned slightly away from him. She said, 'Adjust to us? Maybe he just didn't want us. Maybe it was as simple as that. Well, not good enough. He had a duty. He had responsibilities.'

She turned back and he looked for tears in her eyes but there were none. There never were with Barbara. 'I've lived my whole life without him, Billy, so I'd rather not talk about him. And please don't say anything in front of Sarah. It upsets her.'

'Okay,' he said. 'Can I ask one last question, then I'll shut up?'

'What?'

'Do you think he's still alive?'

For a moment he thought she really would cry, but again no tears came. 'That's why I don't like talking about him,' she said. 'If I talk about him, it means he might be alive. I don't want him to be alive. I think he's dead. I really hope he's dead.'

They sat a little longer. A gust rippled the dark water of the reservoir. It looked like a shiver. She jumped to her feet. 'Something's biting me,' she said. 'Let's move.'

Her father was hardly ever mentioned again.

Then there was Charlie. Because she didn't go to the Lennies' house for a long while she didn't meet him. By the time she and Billy were students in Glasgow and only occasional visitors, Charlie was away, staying with his grandmother in Drumkirk. Barbara teased Billy about his phantom brother. She wanted to meet the mysterious Charlie. Maybe she'd fancy him.

Billy said, 'Ye might, he's good-looking, but ye'll no like him. He's bad news.'

'Are you scared of him?'

'Naw. Maybe I was once. Maybe I would be if I had onything tae dae wi him noo. But I dinna. We're completely different.'

'You can't be *that* different.'

'We are. I dinna like him and he disna like me.' There was a silence. Billy was thinking back. He said, 'One time he had me in a headlock for aboot half an oor until I gave in tae what he wanted. I gave in because we were alane in the hoose and I kent he would have kept it up for as lang as it took. Hours, if necessary.'

'What was it he wanted?'

'I canna mind. Nothing important. Disna matter what he wanted. Another time he just kept punching me in the gut every few minutes. He'd punch me, then leave me, then come and find me and punch me again. Like he was on a timer. I shut masel in my room for a couple of hours and when I came oot there he was, waiting tae punch me again.'

'Did you not punch him back?'

'I tried that. It just made him step things up a level. It was hopeless. Whatever ye did, he could aye dae something worse back tae ye. He kind of wanted ye tae react, then he could go tae the next stage. I suppose I just learned tae deal wi it another way. If I tried tae please him, or at least no tae aggravate him, I could stop it ever getting tae that stage.'

'Did your parents not see what was going on?'

'That's no how ye deal wi that stuff, when ye're brothers. Ye're supposed tae sort it oot yersels. Plus I was the big brother. I couldna go greeting tae them every time my wee brither thumped me, could I?'

'I don't know, Billy.'

'I knew I'd get tae an age when I could get away frae him, so I just waited. Noo I dinna hae tae deal wi him at all. And neither dae you.'

'If I do, he'll not scare me.'

'Maybe no. He can be very self-controlled. Ye might think, och, Billy's exaggerating, there's nothing wrang wi Charlie at all, but there is. When he loses his temper, ye dinna want tae be there.'

§

They finally ran into Charlie one drizzly Saturday evening in Drumkirk. They were on their way to the bus station after an afternoon at Wharryburn – their first visit in a year. As they passed the Toll Tavern they had to give way to another couple cutting across the pavement in front of them, aiming for the pub. The man threw a challenging glance at them and then slewed to a halt. The threat on his face changed to a smile and he grabbed Billy's cheek and gave it a hard pinch.

'Well, look who it is. Haud on a minute, Renée, this is my brither, Billy. My *big* brither. Am I hurting ye? See, I don't know my ain strength. How ye daein, Billy? And who's this wi ye? Ye must be Barbara.'

'Aye, it is,' Billy said reluctantly.

'Glad tae meet ye at last, Barbara. Billy's been hiding ye fae us. This is Renée, by the way. Don't walk away, Renée. She hates that song, don't ye, doll? She likes it when it's me telling her, but no the song.'

Renée, a bleached blonde in heavy make-up, smiled tentatively, as if her life depended on watching every move Charlie made and reading it right. But Charlie gave her an affectionate-looking hug as he beamed at Barbara and Billy.

'So,' he said, 'where are ye heading the night, then?'

'We're just gaun for the bus,' Billy said. 'We're away back tae Glasgow.'

'Ye've time for a drink, though. Ye'll let me buy ye a drink?'

'We canna, the bus is at seven,' Billy said.

Charlie consulted an expensive-looking watch. 'There's another bus at eight,' he said. 'Ye can get that.'

'We really need tae go.'

'Ye'll no insult me by refusing a drink,' Charlie said. 'We never see each other. What's an hour? Come on in here oot o the rain, this is a great wee boozer. We come here a lot, don't we, Renée?'

'Aye, we dae. It's a great wee place.'

'We canna,' Billy said.

'Aye ye can,' Charlie said. He'd come round the outside of them and was herding them all in through the door. Short of barging their way out, there was nothing Billy and Barbara could do except enter. The place was crowded, loud and full of smoke and steam. Folk looked round. Some raised their hands or glasses to Charlie. Others, it seemed, turned away.

'Just the one drink,' Billy said, 'then we're definitely heading.'

'Well, I'm no gonnae haud ye against your will. I'm no gonnae bite ye, am I? I'm your brither. What are ye drinking, Babs?'

'My name's Barbara,' she said.

His lip started to curl. 'Pardon me,' he said. Then, 'Naw, ye're right. Stick up for yersel. How else are ye gonnae stay stuck up? That's a joke, by the way. What are ye drinking?'

'I'll have a half-pint of lager.'

'What aboot Billy?'

'You'd better ask him.'

'I thought ye'd ken, ye've been thegither lang enough. Ye're like an auld mairrit couple. Ye're no mairrit though, are ye?'

'No.'

'Good choice. Ye might fancy each other noo, but what aboot five year doon the line? Whae wants tae get lumbered for life wi somebody ye dinna fancy ony mair? Cuts baith ways, that. He might go aff you, but you might go aff him. Then there's aw the other shite. Bairns and bills and fuck knows what. Listen tae me, I'll need tae mind my language.'

In the space of a minute, something in Charlie had changed. Billy saw it. It was Barbara's abruptness: Charlie didn't like it, and so he was trying to cow her by offending her. But Barbara was not cowed. She watched him evenly.

'That's not the point, though, is it?' she said. And she very deliberately shifted her gaze on to Renée. Billy wondered what on earth she was doing. Was she wanting to catch Renée's eye in order to bond with her? If so, she was on a hiding to nothing, he thought.

'Billy, a pint is it?' Charlie said. 'Lager or heavy? Your usual, Renée? What's not the point, *Bar*bara?' There was a wee load on the way he said her name now, stretching it out to demonstrate he'd got the message.

'Not getting married,' Barbara said. 'It's not about not making a commitment. It's about an equal partnership.'

Charlie held his hand up. 'Haud it there while I get these drinks in. Jim, a pint and a half o lager, pint o heavy, voddy and orange. Noo, what's that aboot equal partnership? That's what I was just saying, wasn't it?'

'No,' she said. 'I'm talking about real equality. I'm talking about not deferring to a bourgeois institution which just reinforces the kind of male chauvinistic behaviour you're exhibiting.'

Charlie raised his eyebrows at Billy. 'Jesus Christ,' he said, 'where'd ye learn tae speak like that? Up at the *yooni*?'

'It's not difficult,' she said. She looked at Charlie as if he were dripping swamp all over the floor.

'Wouldna suit me,' he said. 'I dinna want tae sound like I've swallowed a book every time I open my mooth.'

'You have to be able to read before that happens,' she said.

For a second Charlie was speechless. To Billy it was as if Barbara had just poured a pint over his brother, and Charlie couldn't believe it had happened. Then he mastered himself, tried to regain the upper hand.

'Hey, Billy, ye've got a live one here. Did ye hear that? Course ye did, ye must get it aw the time. How d'ye stand it?' Back to Barbara. 'Wee bit o advice, darling. Could get ye intae trouble, that kind o lip. No wi me, I'm faimly. Just wi strangers. Folk that dinna ken how tae take a joke.'

'It wasn't a joke,' Barbara said.

The mask slipped again. 'Fuck's sake. Well, mair fucking fool me. I don't think she likes me, Billy. Renée kens how tae take a joke, don't ye, doll?'

'Aye, Charlie,' Renée said uncertainly.

'That's because ye *are* a fucking joke.'

Triggered, Renée gave a short, mirthless giggle. Barbara stared at her, it wasn't clear to Billy whether with disgust, pity or a mixture of both. Pity was what *he* felt. Because Barbara was scoring points off Charlie, Charlie was having to score some off Renée. Billy knew he'd be next.

The drinks were set up and Charlie broke a five-pound note to pay for them.

'Plenty mair where that came fae, Billy,' he said, passing the glasses out. 'Ye probably have tae watch the pennies, dae ye?'

'We get by,' Billy said.

'Let's grab thae seats,' Charlie said, pointing to an empty table.

'Let's stand,' Barbara said. 'Otherwise we'll be here all night.'

'Suit yersel.' Charlie produced cigarettes, offered them round. Renée took one. So did Billy. Barbara, even though she usually smoked when she was drinking, refused.

'Suit yersel,' Charlie said again, lighting up. 'What were we saying? Oh aye, ye get by. Well, Billy, that's no the game for me. Get by? Fuck that. You sound like the auld man. I suppose ye've been up there?'

'Aye.'

'How's my mither?'

'Fine.'

'Good. How aboot him?'

'He's all right.'

'Shame. Ye see, *Bar*bara, what Billy's maybe no tellt ye is, me and my faither dinna see eye tae eye. Fact is we dinna get on at all. My faither's disappointed wi me. But Billy here, he says he's all right. That's because Billy's the golden boy. He's the one that went tae the *yooni*. He's the one that's bettered himsel. That's how he's ended up wi a smart bird like you, while I'm stuck wi a thick slag like Renée. Nae offence, doll.'

If Renée took any she didn't show it. Billy gulped at his pint. He glanced at the bar, and caught sight of their awkward grouping in the big mirror. The grey, anxious-looking one was himself. *Joy of Sex* man without the beard, the joy or the sex. All he wanted to do was drink up and go.

Barbara leaned over towards Renée. 'You shouldn't let him treat you like that,' she said.

481

Renée sparked up a bit, tossing her lifeless hair. 'Like what?' she said. 'He treats me fine. He's just haein a laugh, aren't ye, Charlie?'

'I treat her like a princess,' Charlie said.

Barbara reached out her free hand and touched Renée's cheekbone, just below her left eye. 'Was he just having a laugh when he did that to you?' she said. 'You've done a good job with the make-up, but not that good.'

Billy suddenly felt very sick. Renée started back as if she'd been given an electric shock. The hand holding her cigarette flew up to her cheek then away again. 'Dinna fucking touch me!' she said, very loudly. Her harsh voice cut through the surrounding noise. 'Whae the fuck dae ye think ye are, touching me? Ya fucking auld boot.'

Barbara said, quite coolly, 'Or maybe you walked into a door?'

The last remnant of a smile vanished from Charlie's face. He stepped away to clunk his glass down on the nearest table and came back and immediately seemed bigger and stronger and more dangerous. He dropped his cigarette on the floor and ground it out with his heel. Renée was still smouldering like a dud firework. And it was as if everybody in the pub had been listening in but pretending not to, and now they could no longer pretend and were shrinking back from the space the four of them occupied, the space where whatever happened next was going to happen.

'What are you saying?' Charlie said. He was leaning, towering in over Barbara. Tall as she was, she was still six inches shorter than him. 'Are you saying I hit my girl? Are you saying I hit Renée? Is that what ye're fucking saying?'

'It's what it looks like,' Barbara said.

'Barbara, come on, ye canna say that,' Billy said.

'Don't tell me what I can't say,' she said. She didn't take her eyes off Charlie.

Billy tried to get between them, but Charlie pushed him back.

'She fucking said it, Billy. She fucking said it and she crossed a fucking line when she did. Ya fucking bitch.'

Billy said, 'That's enough, Charlie,' but Charlie ignored him. If Barbara was frightened she wasn't showing it.

She said, 'What are you going to do about it? Are you going to hit me too?'

Maybe there was a moment when that was possible, even likely, but it was only a moment. Charlie was surrounded by witnesses, not all of them his friends. One of the barmen, a big solid man, had come round the end of the bar but he wasn't interfering, not yet anyway. Charlie turned away from Barbara, shaking his head, shrugging a victim shrug to the spectators. Then he spoke to Billy, loud and clear so everybody could hear how reasonable he was being.

'Ye're lucky ye're my brither, Billy. By rights you and me should be ootside settling this. I wouldna hit a woman – I *dinna* hit women – but I have tae defend my reputation. Everybody heard what she said. I could have her in court for it but like I said, ye're my brother. So let's say I made a mistake inviting ye in here. I buy ye a drink, I try tae be nice tae you and your girlfriend, and then she comes oot wi something like that. Naebody speaks tae me like that. Get her oot o here, and fuck off back tae Glesca, all right?'

'Come on, Barbara,' Billy said. He tried to take Barbara's arm. She flung his hand away. 'I'm coming, Billy. You don't need to drag me out.'

Charlie dropped his voice again. A private word with his older brother. 'Ye fucking should,' he said. 'Ye should take her ootside and show her whae the fucking boss is. But ye'll no, Billy, will ye? Because ye're feart. Ken whit I think? I think she's cut your fucking baws aff.'

'We're going,' Billy said. He started for the door. A path cleared before him.

'You,' Barbara said, 'are a psychopath.'

'You,' Charlie said, 'are a pair of ower-educated cunts.'

'Goodbye, Renée,' Barbara said.

'Fuck you,' Renée said.

From the door, Billy said, 'Barbara, come on.'

She walked down the cleared path. Folk averted their eyes, from her, from Charlie, as if it were a close call as to whom they found more disturbing. But no one followed Barbara on to the street.

Outside a wind had got up. Heads down, they hurried through blasts of rain to the bus station. After the pub the rain might have felt refreshing, but it was Drumkirk rain, greasy and grey.

On the bus they sat dripping, wiping their faces. For a long time they said nothing.

He said, 'You didna hold back, did ye?'

She said, 'Is that a criticism?'

'No,' he said. 'I'm just saying.'

'I clocked the bruise on her face right away,' she said. 'I could have pretended I hadn't but you know me better than that.'

'Aye,' he said. 'I'm no criticising you. You were right.'

'That's not what you said back there. You tried to stop me saying anything.'

'No,' he said.

'You did, Billy. And you tried to get me out before I was ready to go.'

'I was trying tae protect ye.'

'Don't ever do that again, Billy.'

'I'll no.'

They fell back into silence. Billy heard Charlie's words in his head. *Ken whit I think? I think she's cut your fucking baws aff.* He hated Charlie for saying that. He hated the fact that it looked that way.

'Don't think he's like he is because he had a tough childhood or something,' he said. 'We had the same childhood, and it wasna that tough. I made choices, and so did he. He's chosen tae be the way he is.'

A challenge to the way they thought about everything was in his words.

'Is that what you think?'

'Aye,' he said. 'Nothing else explains it.'

§

Roderick Braco, QC, now David's father-in-law, got him alone not long after he and Melissa returned from their honeymoon (two weeks in Spain, tail-end of summer, autumn of the Franco regime). They were at the Braco country retreat in Glenallan for a family weekend get-together before the happy couple settled down to life in London, which was where, for the time being at least, they intended to live. Roderick and Julia had already given them a silver service, a double bed and a promise of help with school fees, as and when required. Now Roderick wanted to offer David something else, something which – as he diplomatically put it – was not in his gift but which he could probably help to push in David's direction.

'Namely, David,' Roderick said, 'this parliamentary seat. If you want it, that is?'

They were sitting in the library, a cosy, leathery room with a log fire, each of them with a malt whisky in a cut-glass tumbler close at hand. The women were in the kitchen, stacking things in the dishwasher, a labour-saving appliance that had yet to make an appearance at Ochiltree House because, as Lady Patricia pointed out, she still had a human one in the form of Mrs Thomson. Although his parents were only a few miles away, they had not been invited to join the party, and David and Melissa would be heading south by train the next morning without calling on them.

'Not, I should say,' Roderick went on, 'that I am planning to relinquish my position just yet. But in a few years – not at the next election but perhaps at the following one – I shall stand down. There's a strong possibility of your being nominated to succeed me. As Conservative candidate, I mean – obviously one can't guarantee election. Nevertheless, this is still a reasonably safe seat. Well, what do you think?'

'It sounds appealing,' David said, 'except that all of my business interests are in London.'

'Well, yes, but if you're an MP you'll be there most of the time anyway. No bad thing, David, to keep a foot in two camps. Here and there, I mean. You never know when you may tire of London. Goodness knows I get pretty fed up with it from time to time.'

'Actually, I've been thinking about making some inroads into the Edinburgh property market.'

'Excellent. Well, there you are. I can help you with that too. You need to know the right people. Otherwise you'll get nowhere. It's that kind of place.'

They talked it through. David, Roderick informed him, was seen as solid, dependable backbench material, and someone with ministerial potential too. The party was changing, and he could be part of that. Roderick approved of what was coming, but he was getting on, he'd have had enough in five or six years.

'What you'll have to do,' Roderick said, 'is cultivate like mad. Cultivate Scotland. Cultivate the party up here. You need to get your face better known in these parts. Obviously you are not *un*known, as your father's son. But your father isn't, if you don't mind me saying so, your greatest asset. He's rubbed a lot of people up the wrong way over the years. Of course now he's no longer

485

constituency chairman he has no influence over the actual procedure. Whereas I . . .'

'Do,' David finished helpfully.

'Quite. Now we need to identify a rock-solid Labour seat. That's where you have to make your mark. It's a bit of a baptism of fire but we've all had to do it. If you can show you've got the guts to fight the blue corner in one of those places where they weigh the Labour vote rather than count it, you'll earn respect. Meanwhile, you and Melissa should come up as often as you can. The Argyll and Sutherland Ball. Fund-raisers, dinner dances and so forth. You know the kind of thing. Then we can arrange a smooth succession.'

'But there's a process, surely?' David said. 'I can't walk in just like that.'

'Certainly not. You have to be a suitable candidate, the *right* candidate. But you are – or you *will* be with a bit of campaigning experience under your belt. I had to run the gauntlet three times, you know, before I was selected for Glenallan. Once in Airdrie and twice in Ayrshire. Have you ever been to Airdrie, David?'

'No.'

'Awful. Have you ever been to Ayrshire? Not Ayr, Ayrshire?'

'No.'

'Ayrshire – the bit I was standing in, anyway, the eastern half – makes Airdrie look positively idyllic. Miles and miles of bog interspersed with miserable cottages and even more miserable towns. I was there for three weeks each time and I don't think it ever stopped raining. There was one particular night at a hustings when I thought I was going to be lynched, just because of how I spoke. The irony was, the natives were completely unintelligible. You'll get your reward in heaven, my agent used to tell me. Actually, I got it in Glenallan. Top us up, will you? Where was I?'

'Selection process,' David said, as he lifted the decanter. Roderick seemed to like having a subservient son-in-law to talk to. At least in this household there was no shouting.

'Yes, well, procedures are more rigorous than they used to be, and there are always plenty of applications for the nomination, but most of the applicants are quite unsuitable. Anyway, strings can be pulled. Like it or not it's the only way to get the correct outcome. Don't you worry about that side of things.'

'I hadn't really thought that far ahead,' David said.

'You don't have to. I'm not budging for at least five years, remember? All you have to think about is the next election. There has to be one in the next two years, and my bet is Ted will go sooner rather than later. So get your skates on and find a rotten constituency to stand in. I can point you to a couple where they're desperate for a good young candidate such as yourself. One thing, though. I shouldn't say anything to your father about all this, not until we've got things settled. Wouldn't want him to think we were doing things behind his back, eh?'

David nodded his agreement. He knew he was thus signalling his engagement in some kind of plot, a form of betrayal, but this did not stop him nodding. He felt that his father was deserving of the betrayal.

§

Melissa was pregnant. Off-limits. They were fine, the two of them, of course they were. But he looked at her swelling belly and the slow, graceful way she adapted to her condition and something went out of him, the passion that had never really been there, and something else came back in. He wanted to explode.

Maybe he was queer. There was no logic to this thought, but it occurred to him nevertheless. Lying beside her as she slept, patient and cowlike, growing the child inside her, he felt slightly revolted by her. At the same time he remembered his schooldays, those brutal manipulations practised on and by other boys, and was excited by the memory. Had he been missing something about himself all along? Had that other thing, the deviation Melissa had killed off with her innocence, been a diversion from something else? He felt an urgent need to find out.

Almost immediately he had the opportunity. They spent August in Glenallan and he left Melissa there for a couple of days and went with Freddy to Edinburgh, where they took in Fringe shows and drank and ate too much, and David wandered around eyeing up shabby buildings in desirable locations. They met one of Freddy's old schoolmates and suddenly David had an opportunity to put his new theory to the test. Michael Pendreich, nice-enough guy and very handsome, but one frolic in the undergrowth was enough to convince David that, whatever else he was, he wasn't *that*. School-boy nonsense. An embarrassment. He came back to Melissa deter-mined to love and appreciate her properly. If she noticed a change, if she suspected anything, she said nothing. He was grateful, but he knew he was in trouble. While she prepared to give birth to their first child, the thing that had lain dormant in him twisted and stirred anew. And now he knew he could not deny it.

§

He went to see his parents. The homestead was crumbling about them. Lady Patricia's face seemed to be caving in at about the same rate. Her lipstick was too red, making her look like a clown or a corpse. One of her eyes was cloudy. Almost the only times she stopped smoking was when she put a glass to her mouth.

'Mother,' he said, 'this is probably a silly question, but did Marga-ret Thatcher –?'

'Who?'

'You know, Margaret Thatcher, the Education Secretary. Did she ever visit us years ago? When I was quite small?'

Lady Patricia stared at him. 'Why would she do that?'

'I don't know. I just have a vague memory . . .'

'But what on earth would she have been doing in Scotland? And why would she have come here?'

'Some party connection? I'm not sure, but perhaps . . .'

'But she's a grocer's daughter or something, isn't she? From Gloucester.'

'Grantham,' he said.

'Well, precisely. Your father rather admires her, but as for coming to visit us, well really . . .'

'Yes,' he said. 'I see. My mistake. Don't know what I was think-ing of.'

§

He'd noticed her, of course – she was a senior member of the gov-ernment after all – but to begin with she didn't stand out. She'd gone the same sort of route to Westminster as David was about to follow, standing twice in a solidly Labour seat in the early 1950s, hunting around for a safe Tory one and finally getting Finchley in

1959. In opposition during the Wilson years she'd spoken in turn on fuel, transport and education. She was in favour of capital punishment and birching, against easier divorce, but voted to legalise abortion and also for the decriminalisation of homosexuality. As Education Secretary she'd had to take responsibility for ending free milk in primary schools, and she'd shown a certain sympathy for comprehensive secondary-school education at the expense of grammar schools. She made robust speeches at conference attacking Communism and its fellow travellers, and the rank and file responded with enthusiasm. But she wasn't hugely loved, it seemed to David. She also appeared to be somewhat isolated in the Cabinet, as if Heath and his closest male ministers didn't take her altogether seriously. He felt – almost – sorry for her.

Or would have done, except that there was a frisson-inducing something about Margaret Thatcher that banished pity, sent it scurrying off into shadowland. She would despise anyone who felt sorry for her, he thought. She had a self-belief, not yet perhaps even fully formed or recognised by herself, that made him both admire her and fear for anyone who stood in her way. He thought about that, standing in her way, and far down inside himself the deeps parted and rolled asunder. At one crowded conference-do he observed other men, from opposing wings of the party, watching her slyly as she passed among them. He was not alone, he saw, in the way he was affected by her: she was not desirable but she was to be desired; she was not touchable but she could be worshipped; *she* was not winnable but she might make *you* hers with a smile. At last his turn came. He was introduced. She took his hand and leaned in towards him to catch his name. The warmth of her smile as they talked, the earnestness with which she listened, the conviction in her eyes as she expressed a view, were almost enough for him. Then as she moved on he cast his own eyes down and saw her legs, her shoes, and his conversion was complete. It was the nearest he would ever get to a religious experience.

§

Liz had an arrangement with Charlie, which at least meant they maintained contact. (She and Don had a phone in the house these days but Charlie never called.) Once a week she went shopping in

Drumkirk and on her way to the bus stop with the messages she would stop in at Rinaldi's for a coffee. Half eleven, every Thursday. If he hadn't turned up by midday he wasn't coming. She never asked what kept him away. That was off-limits. So was any mention of his father. But she was always there and most weeks, looking as if he were not long out of his bed, he joined her. He'd have a coffee himself, and a fag, and they'd talk, but there was little in her life he wanted to hear about and little in his he was willing to discuss. When they'd finished their coffees he walked her over to the bus stop. Once, when she had more bags than usual, he drove her home in his car. He helped carry the bags to the door but wouldn't come in. She saw the disdain on his face: did I really grow up in this dump?

Granthill was a bigger dump but Charlie had made it his own. She'd not been there since the death of Don's mother, three years before. Molly hadn't in the end lost her mind, she'd just entered a kind of dream state in which almost her only requirements were the television, cigarettes and Heinz baked beans. She'd refused Don's offer to come and live in Wharryburn even though she could have had the boys' empty room, and Don, knowing that if she did come the burden of looking after her would fall on Liz, hadn't pushed it. He'd seen her every weekend, timing his visits so that he and Charlie didn't meet, and sometimes Liz had gone with him and between them they'd cleaned the place and reassured themselves that Molly was all right. It appeared that Charlie didn't mistreat her. Molly wouldn't hear a word against him. 'There's naething wrang wi Charlie,' she said, to the end. 'He's a good laddie. I canna see what ye hae against him.' When she said this she included Liz in her accusatory stare, and Liz said, 'It's no me, Molly. It's between Charlie and his faither.' 'What is? It's bloody nonsense, that's what it is.' 'Forget it, Ma,' Don said. 'Aye, that's what Charlie says tae. Bloody nonsense. Ye should grow up, baith o ye.'

She died in her sleep. For the first time ever Charlie phoned Liz, cool as you like, and told her. He'd already had the doctor out and the Co-op were on their way. His grandmother had kept up her funeral plan for decades and given him instructions about what to do. 'Truce,' he said to Liz. 'You can come in here – you and him – and sort oot onything ye want. But one week efter the funeral that's it. This is my hame and I'm staying here and I'm wanting it tae masel.' They managed to get through that week without a fight – without much eye contact or many words spoken between Charlie and Don either – and Molly had been cremated and Charlie took on the tenancy of the flat.

The last time Liz was there was two days after the funeral. Don asked Bulldog to drive them down and they loaded his car with a few boxes of Molly's clothes and possessions – a pitiful collection of cheap jewellery and photographs – nearly all of which, once they'd gone through it back at Wharryburn, they would throw out. Bulldog stood like a nervous sentinel beside his car while they carried the boxes down. The stair stank of urine, stale drink, and cat. Graffiti was everywhere. GRANTHILL TOI. DRUMKIRK CUMBIE RULE. IRA. GERS CUNTS. KILL ALL POOFS. As if all the poison of Scotland had leached into this tiny part of it. It felt like a vicious, hostile place but Charlie seemed at ease amid the squalor, and his Ford Capri sat outside in the rubbish-strewn street without a mark on it. There was something unnerving about that fact. Bulldog felt it too. Driving away he whistled and shook his head and said, 'Jesus Christ. I kent Granthill was bad but I had nae idea. Nae idea.' This from a man whose newspaper was always full of Granthill crime stories – street brawls, domestic assaults, vandalism. But Bulldog, overweight, jowly and short of breath, seldom left the office: he might as well have been editing stories from the dark side of the moon.

At the top of the street Liz looked back and saw Charlie's car and she understood that the people who lived there knew who her son was, and that they were afraid of him.

§

There were strikes and power cuts and elections and a referendum on staying in the EEC. There was Gary Glitter. There was contraception on the NHS. There were the Bay City Rollers. There was a Sex Discrimination Act and an Equal Opportunities Commission to enforce it. There was punk rock. There wasn't devolution. There weren't children.

Billy said, 'Why not?'

Barbara said, 'I'm not ready.'

He said, 'Well, we've been together long enough. When do you think you'll be ready?'

She glared at him. 'What's that supposed to mean?'

'It's no supposed tae mean onything.' On the rare occasions he got passionate his voice shifted out of teacher mode and back into Wharryburn. 'Are we gonnae hae bairns or no?'

Silence.

'Because if we're no, what the hell are we daein wi each other ony mair?'

'Is that what you think this is about? Us having children?'

'Well, what is it aboot, Barbara? I dinna ken ony mair. Dae you?'

She said, 'You sound like your brother.'

'That's ridiculous.' He saw the look in her eyes, which said he'd just confirmed it.

It was about her father. The Lord Lucan of Wharryburn. He knew it was. But her father was forbidden territory. 'I *don't* want to talk about it, Billy.' Whenever they went to Glenrothes he saw the yearning in Sarah's eyes, her desire for a grandchild. At least that's what he thought he saw. But he didn't say anything because he didn't want to upset her.

He was almost beyond whether he upset Barbara or not.

§

Liz had just taken the first frothy sip of coffee when Charlie arrived and she knew at once that something was different. He came in with a fag already going, looking as if he'd been up all night. He kept checking the street through the window.

'What's the maitter, son?'

'Nothing.' A pause. 'I'm making a few changes.'

'Oh?'

'Aye. I hope ye're no wanting a lift hame the day. I've sellt the motor.'

'Ye've sellt it?'

'Aye.'

'What are ye gonnae dae withoot your motor?'

'Join the army,' he said. 'I'll no need it. They'll gie me a tank.'

She laughed and then stopped because she saw he meant it.

'I've signed up. I've been thinking aboot it for a while. Had tae decide noo, ken, because they'll no take ye if ye're too auld. Twenty-six is the cut-aff.'

'You, in the army? Ye're having me on, Charlie.'

'I'm no. I aye fancied it. I'll make a good sodger. I've got the right temperament. That's what they said in the recruiting office.'

'They don't know ye. Ye'll no take the discipline. Getting oot o your bed at God knows when. Obeying orders. Ye'll no take ony o it.'

'I will. There's nothing I canna take. I've had enough of Drum-kirk. Got tae dae something wi my life. They've accepted me, so that's me away next week.'

'I don't believe it,' she said.

He grinned at her. 'Ye'd better.'

There was a long pause while she took it in. She stared at him. His eyes kept flickering to the window. He sucked the life out of the first cigarette and lit a new one. She said, 'What's the real reason, son. Are ye in trouble?'

'No really. No ony mair than usual.'

'Is somebody hunting ye?'

He shook his head. 'Think I'm feart?'

'Aye.'

'Well I'm no. It's just time for a change.'

'How come ye never said onything afore?'

'Didna seem much point. I had tae go for a medical and aw that. Nae sense telling ye if I didna pass.' He grinned again. 'I passed, by the way.'

She asked more questions – where, when, how long? – and he gave her a reasonably full set of answers. But he wouldn't be drawn any further on why.

She said, 'I dinna want this, son.'

'I'm daein it. I've signed on the line.'

'Can ye no get oot o it?'

'Aye, if I want tae, but I dinna want tae.'

Another long pause.

'What'll I say tae your faither?'

'Say what ye like. Maybe he'll be proud o me. He was a sodger once.'

'That was different. There was a war on.'

'There's a war on noo, in Ireland. There'll be plenty mair wars. That's what sodgers are for, tae fight wars.'

'And die in them.'

'Dinna go aw sentimental on me, Ma. I'm twenty-five. I can make my ain decisions. I ken what I'm letting masel in for.'

'Dae ye, son? Or are ye just needing tae get away frae something?'

'I ken what I'm daein. Listen, I'll need tae go. Ye'll manage ower tae the bus, eh?'

'I'll hae tae. Will I see ye next week?'

'Naw, I tellt ye, I'll be away. Are ye greeting?'

'Sorry, son. It's just a shock, that's all.'

'I'll write tae ye.'

'Please.'

'Awright, Ma. Are ye gaun as weel?'

'No, I think I'll hae another coffee.'

'Awright. I better go. I'll see ye.'

He stood and she stood too. He bent to kiss her cheek and she put her arms around him and felt how strong he was. He gave her a last kiss and a smile, her handsome wayward boy, and then he was out of the door, swiftly across the street and out of sight. As if he couldn't get away fast enough. And she wondered what it was he was running from.

§

Billy wasn't that keen on football but a couple of his teacher friends were. Daft for it. Could you be Scottish and male and not daft about football? Christ, he hoped so. What chance was there if not?

Nevertheless he was pissed off enough with Barbara that when his mates invited him on a weekend of debauchery in London, incorporating a return coach trip to alcoholic oblivion and a ticket to the deciding game of the Home International Championship, he accepted. The bus left Glasgow on the Friday night, they had from seven on the Saturday morning till ten at night in London, then it was back on the overnighter to Glasgow. Bed: not required. Change of clothing: not required. Head of steel and digestive system able to accommodate vast quantities of drink and fried food: essential. The back of the bus was so loaded with crates of lager it swayed like a cargo ship on tight bends before it hit the motorway. There were piss stops, a shite stop, a middle-of-the-night-snack stop and a breakfast stop and the same on the way back up. In between came the small matter of a football match at Wembley, which ended in a 2–1 victory for Scotland, delirious drunken happiness, an invasion of the pitch, the destruction of the goalposts and removal of much of the Wembley turf. An uplifting occasion. From what he could recollect, Billy enjoyed himself.

Maybe anything could be pleasurable if you were pissed enough.

Back in the flat on Sunday night, trying not to think about teaching the next morning, he was aware of a frostiness in the atmosphere as he and Barbara watched the news. The mayhem at and after the game was the main story. It had all seemed so good-humoured at the time. Barbara was not amused.

'It's a total embarrassment,' she said. 'Are you not ashamed of it?'

He'd been watching the footage anxiously, half-dreading, half-hoping he might see himself. He'd been pretty close to the goalposts about the time they collapsed. He had a clod of Wembley in his jacket pocket.

'You're right,' he said. 'It's embarrassing. Grown men behaving like that. It'll probably never happen again. Still . . .'

'Still?'

'I'm so fucking glad I was there.'

§

'I need tae tell ye something,' Billy said.

'What, son?'

'I'm moving oot.'

'Eh? Ye've been away for years.'

'No frae here. I'm leaving Barbara. It's mutual in fact. We're splitting up. I'm sorry, I ken it's no what ye want tae hear, but it's no working.'

'What isna?'

'Our relationship.'

Billy had come home alone. They'd had a bowl of soup and a piece in the kitchen and now he and his father had gone for a walk up the hill, the old haunt. Liz had shooed them out. 'I'll dae the dishes.' Billy hadn't argued. The familiar layout and decor of the kitchen oppressed him. Apart from the acquisition of a few new appliances it had hardly changed in thirty years. It had taken the walk in the woods to free him up enough to break this news. The other news – that he'd be head of department from the start of the next academic year – had been easy.

Don and he stood at the edge of the trees, leaning on the dyke and taking in the moorland view, north towards Glenallan and the distant hills. This was better than looking at each other.

'Your relationship?' Don said. 'What's wrang wi it?'

'We don't communicate.'

'So? Your mither and I dinna communicate.' A pause. 'Are ye seeing some other woman?'

'No.'

'Is she seeing some other man?'

'No. It's no that, Dad. We've changed. Baith o us have changed. I've learned a lot aboot masel. I feel trapped. She probably feels trapped, tae.'

'Hmm.'

Billy felt compelled to say something else. 'I feel like I'm on sufferance in my ain hame. Dinna pit your feet up there, when are ye gonnae fix this, clean that up, pit that stuff away, we're no daein that, we're daein this. It's never-ending.'

'I thought ye didna communicate.'

'Ye ken what I mean.'

'Billy, that's what women dae. They organise. They build nests. They want us tae maintain the nest, no lie aboot in it. That's why I spend so much time in the gairden. That's why I hae a shed.'

'I just want my ain space.'

'Exactly.'

Half of what Billy had said wasn't true anyway. Barbara didn't nag much. Her tactic was to look bored, disappointed. Probably because she was. Probably that was how he looked at her. But he'd been trying to explain it in some way he thought his father might understand. Patronising him, in other words. He said, 'I need my freedom back.'

Don laughed.

'I thought it was the women that had got a taste for liberation,' he said. 'Barbara never struck me as much of a nest-builder, right enough. But noo it's you that wants your freedom back. Weel, is it really freedom or is just selfishness? I'm no getting at ye, son, I'm just asking the question.'

Billy shrugged. 'I dinna ken. Maybe it's baith. Maybe it's just part of the process. But I know we have tae separate.'

'Ye've nae sticking power,' Don said. 'That's half the trouble. No just yersel, your haill generation. Look at your mither and me. We dinna see eye tae eye on a lot o things but we've stuck thegither. It's the only way tae get through life.'

'I don't agree. And ye canna say Barbara and me havena gien it a fair shot.'

'Aye, that's true. Weel, at least there's nae bairns involved. I'm sorry, Billy, truly I am. That's a lot o your life ye've wasted wi her.'

'It's no wasted. We did a lot. We've learned a lot. And I've got on fine wi the teaching.'

'Aye, ye've done weel. I'm proud of ye. So's your mither, even if she disna let on.'

'How is she? Is she all right?'

'You've seen her. What d'ye think yersel?'

'She seems tired. A bit flat.'

'She's all right.'

'I ken she's never had ony time for Barbara. That's why I wanted tae tell you this first. Will you tell her?'

'No. You tell her when we get hame. I'll go oot in the gairden. You tell her.'

'She'll be pleased.'

'I dinna think so, son.'

'She'll say, "I tellt ye."'

'No she'll no. She'll be sorry that ye're hurt. Are ye hurt, Billy?'

'No really. No ony mair.'

'That's good.'

They turned to look at the hills again. Billy said, 'How's Charlie?'

'Ye better ask your mither aboot that.'

'Dae ye never hear frae him?'

'Me? No. Dae you?'

'No.'

'Weel then. He's written a couple of times tae your mither. She reads me bits frae the letters.'

'And?'

Don breathed out heavily. 'It sounds like the army suits him.'

'And he suits the army?'

'Seems like it.'

'Dae ye ken where he is?'

'I believe he's in Germany.'

'You believe?'

'Aye. And apparently he's got his first tour in Northern Ireland coming up. Mair than that I dinna ken.'

'Does he ever come hame?'

'If he does I've never seen him.'

'He didna keep the flat on in Granthill, did he?'

'No. I don't think he can go back there. I think he had tae get oot in a hurry.'

'But he must get leave. Where does he go when he's on leave?'

'Billy, I dinna ken where he goes or what he does. Ask your mither.'

'All right. Sorry.'

They were leaning on the old stones not looking at each other. Neither of them was given to displays of emotion or affection, but now there was a slight movement, and Billy felt his father's arm descend on his shoulders, a rough clutch instead of more words. He didn't dare turn his head. He could feel the arm tremble. They stayed like that for maybe half a minute, long enough for the trembling to cease, and then Don gave him a couple of slaps on the back and said, 'Aye, son,' and that was him composed again. So they walked back through the woods, and Billy was thinking, why are we all so fucking closed up? Why can't we tell each other our feelings? But did he say anything? No. No. No.

§

She said, 'Remember that thing about tasting your menstrual blood? Germaine Greer said we had to do it. Not you and me. Us, women. Do you remember that?'

'Aye.'

'Once was enough for me. To be honest I found it all pretty revolting.'

He said, 'Wasn't that the point – to be honest? To overcome your disgust and find your true self.'

'It still tasted foul. How was your sperm?'

'Not so good. A bit salty. How was your blood?'

498

'Metallic. I could have done with a lot more salt actually.'

'Och well. Just put it down to experience, eh?'

'Yes, Billy.'

He thought, how can we be having this absurd conversation and not laughing?

He thought, after today I'm going to laugh. I don't care what happens or if I don't ever meet anybody else, I'm going to laugh. Even if I'm on my own till I die I'll bloody well see the funny side.

He thought of the football weekend in London, the ridiculous camaraderie, the fact that he'd laughed all weekend until he got home. He'd even laughed the next day, on his way to school, as he lobbed the Wembley turf into the Kelvin.

Nevertheless, he was determined not to blame Barbara for the fact that he hadn't laughed enough in his life so far.

§

Ellen Imlach wrote herself down as a story one day, to try to get some perspective. It was 1977. She'd been with Robin for more than a year. That was how she steeled herself to do it: get some perspective, put some distance between you and what's happened to you. Use your journalistic skills. Use the typewriter. This is not about you, this is about somebody else. She set herself a timescale and a word limit. Good training for when she finally went back out into the world to earn a living – something she didn't have to do till she was ready, Robin kept saying, although she knew the money was getting tight, that he'd had to put his own plans on hold and eat into his savings while she mended. And she *was* mending, she was stronger every day. She was going to be so fucking strong after what she'd been through.

She'd submitted some articles to the two Scottish qualities and they'd used a couple, so she knew she could still write. She thanked God, in whom she didn't believe, for Robin, in whom she fervently did. Then she sat at the kitchen table and plugged in the typewriter. Story time. Two thousand words max, two hours to complete. Go.

```
Some girls get into trouble at a very young age.
Others get away from it, only for it to catch
up with them unexpectedly years later. Ellen
Imlach was in the second category.
```

499

As a teenager Ellen was far too smart to fall
for the patter of good-looking boys at the
dancing. If she let a boy walk her home that was
all she would let him do. She was independent and
ambitious. It meant she gained a reputation for
being stand-offish, 'nae fun'; but she could
tolerate that. What she could not have tolerated
was having her independence and ambition crushed
by a marriage of necessity to someone who, by
accident or with intent, had 'bairned' her when
she was not ready for motherhood.

The cottage rows of Borlanslogie, the mining
town she grew up in, contained too many examples
of young women whose lives, in her view, had been
made narrow and miserable by the early arrival
of children and the subsequent slow death of
feeding, clothing and raising them in straitened
circumstances. Ellen was not sure she wanted
motherhood at all, but she certainly did not want
it as the wife of a miner in a tight-knit
community where everybody knew her business and
she knew everybody else's. That was indeed the
limit of some girls' ambition, and Ellen, sixteen
in 1964, looked beyond that. Miners earned good
money compared with many other workers, but who
would want their life, or to be tied to their
life? Her father hadn't. He'd worked away from
home since before she was born, in the Highlands
mostly, out in the light. Ellen hardly knew him,
but she thought she understood that part of him.
The wide world was changing, and she wanted a
different place in it.

Not just wanted, but felt she deserved. If the
world didn't owe her a living, as her mother
repeatedly warned her, it owed her a break. She
had a strong sense that a better, more exciting,
more rewarding life than that which had been the
lot of her parents and grandparents was hers by

right. In this she was guilty of nothing more serious than the arrogance of youth, from which every generation suffers and by which it distinguishes itself from the preceding one. The difference in the early 1960s lay in the sheer number of young people who thought likewise. This was the coming of age of the baby boomers. Since the war, and in many respects as a result of it, society had blown a series of fanfares for the rights and freedoms of all citizens: free health care, free education, freedom from poverty and bad housing, all these were considered, across the political spectrum, to be the marks of a civilised, modern democracy. Other freedoms, albeit more fiercely contested ones, were also gaining ground: freedom from racial and sexual discrimination; freedom of expression in the widest sense. And now the young had arrived to claim their inheritance. Was there ever a song more in tune with the age in which it was written than 'The Times They Are a-Changin''?

She was intelligent, industrious and eager. By *rights*, she should have sat her Higher exams and been a candidate for a place at university. Unfortunately, she attended a school that had no tradition of sending *any* of its pupils to university, let alone the daughters of a place like Borlanslogie. She was, to put it bluntly, from the wrong side of the tracks.

Her English teacher, a Mr Green, recognised her facility with words and her ability to absorb and filter information. He also knew of her interest in journalism. He suggested she write to D. C. Thomson of Dundee, seeking a position that would give her a chance to demonstrate her abilities. The Thomson print empire ranged from comics like the *Beano* and *Dandy*, through a range of weekly publications for women, to the *Sunday Post*, which

sold more than a million copies per week and was
estimated to be read by some 60 per cent of the
Scottish population. As a place of opportunity
for an ambitious young writer, it could not be
bettered. There was a problem, however. The firm
was notoriously conservative, and did not recognise
any trade union representation when it came to
negotiating pay and conditions with its workforce.
Mr Green, being a thoroughgoing socialist, was
obliged to dislike D. C. Thomson on principle,
and knowing Ellen's family background he assumed
that she would feel similarly. He encouraged her
to apply for an interview, but advised her, if
successful, to keep her political opinions to
herself. 'If journalism is really what you want
to do,' he said, 'the training they'll give you
will open doors all over the world.'

Ellen liked the idea of doors opening. She was
also a realist. She did write to D. C. Thomson,
she was called for an interview, and in it she
voiced no opinions of an alarming or incendiary
nature. She had to sit an aptitude test and there
was an information form to complete. One of the
questions asked if she was a Roman Catholic,
another if she belonged to a trade union. She had
an idea what happened to your application if you
said yes to the second of these, but what if you
said yes to the first? It wasn't an issue for her,
but then suddenly it became one. She left a
blank. The man who took the form off her said,
'You've not answered a question.' 'No,' she said,
'I don't think it's anybody else's business. Do
you?' He looked at her. 'Fair enough,' he said.
Two weeks later she was at a desk in Dundee,
shadowing the work of older hands, learning how
to write serials to strict formats, being asked
for her opinion of unsolicited manuscripts and
how she would improve them. After a while she was

composing stories for *My Weekly* as if she'd been
doing it for years.

She worked on this and other titles for eighteen
months, subjecting herself to the discipline of
short sentences and three-sentence paragraphs,
alternating between fiction and factual stories and
sometimes writing a combination of the two. Her
editors liked what she did and did not spurn her
requests for more challenging work. After a series
of small or sideways promotions she found herself
subbing on the daily *Courier and Advertiser*. A few
months later, she managed to persuade her editor
that she needed first-hand experience of reporting.
She was dispatched to parts of Angus, north of
Dundee, that she'd hardly known existed, to chase
local-interest news and write it up, three, four
or five reports in the course of a day. Local they
might have been, interesting they often were not,
but that wasn't the point. She learned more than
how to turn in copy on time: she learned the art
of self-effacement. Her reports carried no byline
and she had to bite her tongue at the kind of
editorial decisions she saw being made, some of
which made no sense to her at all, but she could
see that Mr Green was right: the education in
journalism she got at D. C. Thomson would last her
a lifetime.

It was also at D. C. Thomson that she formed
a firm but firmly platonic friendship with an
illustrator on the *Hotspur* comic, a mild,
unassuming boy from Surrey, recently graduated
from Duncan of Jordanstone College of Art, called
Robin Piggott. That too, though she didn't realise
it at the time, would last her a lifetime.

After Dundee and Fife she had a succession
of more or less satisfying newspaper jobs and
a succession of more or less unsatisfying
boyfriends. The jobs took her to Falkirk,

Manchester, Bristol and Cardiff. By the time she reached Wales she had ceased news-reporting and was writing what were loosely termed 'women's interest' pieces. She went out with a journalist or two, a doctor, a college lecturer, a Welsh MP, a chef and a jazz musician. She had some good times and quite a few arguments. The relationships usually foundered on the rocks of male egotism or her own increasingly vociferous feminism. None of the men she shared a bed with objected to her being on the pill, but most of them found it difficult to accept that in principle she was their intellectual equal, and in practice usually their superior. The journalists drank and smoked too much and eventually tired of the fact that she drank moderately and smoked not at all. She thought she really loved the doctor but they parted because he opposed a woman's right to choose whether or not to terminate a pregnancy. The lecturer thought Enoch Powell was right about immigration; the MP wouldn't leave his wife and kids; the chef was insane; and the musician preferred to go through life permanently stoned. All of these shortcomings took some time to emerge. Ellen longed for a man she could take at face value.

Then a chance conversation led to the offer of a post, on a retained basis, as Scottish correspondent with one of the London heavyweights. It was the mid-1970s, the peak years of the devolution debate, and a weekly column and supplementary dispatches from North Britain, as that portion of the island trudged towards its destiny, was required. She wanted to be away from Wales, and thought she would risk it, building up other freelance work to supplement the weekly retainer. She returned to Scotland, heading for Edinburgh, with some savings as a cushion and

arguing with herself that being alone and
approaching thirty was a mark not of failure but
of feisty success.

She rented a room in a New Town flat and set to
work. She decided to come off the pill for a
while. She'd read that it was advisable to have
a break, and this was a good time since it wasn't
protecting her from unwanted anything. She felt
a little panicked by the speed with which she was
getting through the money she'd put by. The
absence of a regular, full-time wage was not so
liberating. She didn't get on that well with the
woman who owned the flat and didn't see much of
anybody else. She wondered if she'd made a
terrible mistake.

She went to Borlanslogie to see her mother.
They argued and she came away again. She wrote
to her father, who was apparently somewhere
between Peterhead and Aberdeen, laying pipelines.
Over the years she had kept up a sporadic
correspondence with him, interspersed with even
more occasional meetings. This time she did not
hear back from him.

Being alone and approaching thirty began to
bother her.

One day she was standing in the queue in an
Italian deli on Leith Walk when a voice behind
her said, 'Hello, Ellen.' It was Robin Piggott.
She had not seen him since Dundee days. They went
for a coffee. He worked near by, as a graphic
artist for a medical publisher. He'd been there
five years and was thinking of going freelance.
He had a house on the shore out at Joppa, and was
slowly doing it up. He'd just finished creating a
studio space in the attic. 'You should come and
see it,' he said. She said she would like that,
and they exchanged address details.

She wrote a few columns, tedious stuff about

the slow grind of devolutionary politics, and they
duly appeared, but she was dissatisfied with them
and her editor received them with indifference.
'What else is going on up there?' he asked. She
looked about for something more exciting for the
mainly English readership, and wrote a couple of
pieces about the underbelly of the country, the
Scotland that was neither affected nor engaged by
mainstream politics. Then she started to disturb
a story of suitable grit and squalor. The details
of this story are no longer important, indeed she
has wiped most of them from her memory, but it
concerned protection rackets and gangs in Drumkirk
– a place one of her Edinburgh newspaper contacts
derisively referred to as 'Dodge City'. Ellen went
there. It wasn't far from Borlanslogie, but it was
not a place she knew well. The natives weren't
particularly friendly. The people at the *Drumkirk
Observer* resented her intrusion into their
territory and didn't think her story amounted
to much. She asked questions and got very few
answers, was shunted on to somebody who 'might be
able to tell her something'. And then one day she
turned a corner, and there was her past coming
down the street to meet her, in the shape of Denny
Hogg.

It was a surprise, but not really a big one, to
find Denny when she lifted the stone under which
her possible story lay hidden. He was her age,
and had grown up next door to her grandparents in
Borlanslogie. She might have described him to a
third party as a childhood friend, except that
even in childhood she hadn't really trusted him.
She'd always thought it likely he'd fall into bad
company: now, this very thought made her pleased
to see him. That and the fact that he was a
familiar face, and she was on unfamiliar ground.
They talked about Borlanslogie. He still stayed

there. He'd been working down the pit the last
time she saw him, but he'd been out of that for
years. She remembered her mother telling her that
he'd been mixed up with a tartan terrorist plot
a few years before and that he had done some time
for it. He did not mention this. Neither did
she. Instead, she established that he was still
consorting with dangerous people, and that some
of them were probably players in the story
she wanted. Denny was too, but he was on the
periphery. She thought he could be her conduit
to the centre.

She was right, but wrong to think she could
stay in control of the situation. Denny said she
should speak to somebody he knew. This was a
tall, handsome, powerfully built young man called
Charlie Lennie. He was rough but very pleasant,
in fact he was charming. To her horror she found
herself flirting with him. He responded. He said
he could help her.

Of course he could. As it transpired, he knew
everything she needed to know. He just wasn't
going to give her information for nothing. In
fact - although she didn't realise it at the
time - he wasn't going to give it to her at all.

She did a quick estimate: she was way over her target length, but
surely she could find three hundred words to chop. She felt quite
pleased with herself: it hadn't taken that long at all. Then she
slumped: what she'd written seemed pedestrian and false, she'd
nowhere near finished the story and, anyway, knocking that out
shouldn't have been much of a challenge for someone of her experience. So what was it she was trying to achieve?

She hadn't appreciated how exhausted she still was. Feeding
Kirsty, changing Kirsty, bathing Kirsty, playing with Kirsty, just generally being with Kirsty took it out of her. And Kirsty was easy,
according to her own mother, who came to stay for a few days. 'No
like you, Ellen. Ye didna want tae come oot and when ye finally did

ye liked the world ower much. Ye never seemed tae sleep. By, ye were hard work.' Kirsty was, apparently, not hard work. She slept through the night and a good proportion of the day, and when she was awake she was usually happy and placid. Nevertheless, Ellen felt permanently tired.

Her mother had something to say about the bairn's easy nature too: 'She'll just be storing up her badness for later, I doot.' She was only half-joking. Thankfully, Mary was miles away to the north most of the time. Ellen admired her mother, doubtless she even loved her, but you could take only so much doom and gloom. Even if you too were filled with Borlanslogie blood and Borlanslogie brains, Borlanslogie fatalism could wear you down after a while. As it was intended to do. *What's for ye will no go by ye* was a philosophical jibe impossible to disprove.

Mary liked Robin, however, even if his sunny Englishness was quite alien to her. She'd taken to him instantly. People did. Where Mary expected the worst to happen, he had an unshakeable faith that things, sooner or later, somehow, would be all right. Unshakeable, that was Robin. Solid as the Bass Rock. Ellen loved him for that and was constantly surprised at herself. The way things were working out went totally against any script she'd ever imagined for her life story. And yet she felt at ease, more so with every day that passed.

Equally surprising had been her mother's attitude. Mary had been understandably taken aback at how swiftly everything had changed – one minute her daughter was single in Edinburgh, the next she was living in Joppa with a man she hadn't seen for eight years, expecting a bairn. When Mary was told that Robin wasn't the father she'd demanded to know who was, but Ellen had said with all the firmness she could muster that that was not her business. There was a stand-off. Mary came at it all ways but Ellen wouldn't give in. Eventually, Mary gave up and never asked again. She could see that Robin was good for her daughter, was a good man, and maybe that made her decide to keep her own counsel. 'And he's willing tae bring it up as his ain?' was all she asked. 'No,' Ellen said, because she and Robin had talked it through. 'He'll no bring it up as his ain. It's no his. If we have another, that'll be his, ours.' 'But then . . .' Mary began. 'It'll no make any difference,' Ellen said, with conviction.

Mary pursed her lips, drawing deep from the dark well of her scepticism. But when Kirsty arrived, Robin took to her at once and she to him, and he and Ellen shared the responsibilities as far as his time allowed, and at once they were a family. His not being her natural father was not an issue. There was Ellen and Robin, and Ellen and Kirsty, and then there was Kirsty and Robin, thirty years between them but the best of friends right from the start.

Ellen loved Robin for other things too. For the warmth and safety of him in bed. For the gentleness of their lovemaking which, gradually and quietly, they were learning together as Kirsty slept in the cot next door. For the fact that he cooked great vegetarian meals and yet didn't object if she sometimes cooked meat for herself. For the fact that they shared household chores and neither of them was bothered that the house was never immaculate. For his fantastic collection of jazz and blues records. For his dedication to his work. For his eclectic reading and astonishing range of knowledge. The way she felt about him was like a cheesy version of that Elizabeth Barrett Browning sonnet. For his comforting blandness, which defused her anxieties. For the way he treated her, always and without question as an equal. For the way, when he came home that evening after she'd written her story, she was able to show him what she'd done and not have to hide it away. She'd only got as far as meeting Charlie Lennie and she was out of time and space, but it was enough. Robin read it through and said it was fine but there were too many hints of sex, drugs and rock 'n' roll for the *People's Friend*. He didn't think they'd take it. She agreed. 'It gets worse,' she said. 'You don't have to write the rest,' he said. 'No,' she said, 'I don't think I will. Maybe one day.' Then she put away what she'd done and said, 'I need to write something that pays.' Robin said, 'You will,' thereby demonstrating that he had faith in her just as she did in him.

§

'You don't have to write the rest,' Robin said. No, she didn't. It was imprinted in her memory for ever.

Denny wished her luck and said, 'Keep in touch.' Maybe there was a warning in the way he said it but she either didn't pick up on it or ignored it, and he left her with Charlie Lennie, and she was happy to be left. She could look after herself. But now she discovered weaknesses in herself she'd never even suspected. Charlie was the antithesis of the kind of man she *ought* to have found attractive: he was predatory, manipulative, chauvinistic and had more than a hint of violence about him. At D. C. Thomson she'd derided the sub-Heathcliff creations of their various women's magazines, and the readers, the credulous fools, whose fantasies they fed. Now some madness came over her, and with Charlie she abandoned every personal and professional rule she'd ever lived by: she was disarmed by his good looks; she allowed herself to be duped by his lies; and she slept with him when she knew he was the story, or a key player in the story. She took no precautions, not even the obvious ones, and neither did he. She acted, now she was in deep water, as if she carried a charm against drowning. Even as she was trying to dig up information and he was obstructing her while ostensibly trying to help, she knew it was happening. He kept her close when he didn't have business to attend to, and at a distance when he did. She knew that whatever he was involved in wasn't just about fighting with rival gangs. There was money being made, out of protection, resetting stolen goods, drugs. He played with her, letting her see just enough to tantalise, not enough for her to walk away with a complete story. He kept saying, 'Ye're gonnae write aboot us, are ye? I'll show ye some things. You stick wi me.' And like a fool she did.

A woman like her, he said, a woman with strong opinions who wasn't afraid to express them, was exciting, a challenge. She was different from most of the women he'd been with. He got bored quickly but not with her. She was flattered: they challenged each other, and there could be mutual benefit in that. He wasn't like the others, liberal on the surface, flawed underneath. Charlie's flaws were as visible as his tattoos. But she also knew he was lying, she just wasn't sure which bits were lies. All of them, she'd discover eventually. She didn't have the nerve or the wit or the fear to extract herself. Or the desire. If she'd been seventeen she'd have slapped herself and walked away. But she was twenty-nine and old enough to know better, so she stayed.

He had a two-litre Ford Capri – another sign she chose to ignore. He liked to drive her around Drumkirk and out into the surrounding countryside, but despite his promise to show her things she saw very little. She met some other guys but their relationship with him wasn't clear except that they deferred to him. If she questioned him too hard he clammed up. 'Plenty o time for aw that, Ellen. I want ye tae masel first.'

He lived alone in an anonymous flat in an anonymous block in Granthill. Outside was the jungle. Inside was clean but barren. Not much furniture, few comforts. Some locked rooms too, which she never had an opportunity to look into. Bluebeard's palace only without the palatial. Obviously she was not the first woman he'd taken there. She went anyway.

Everything happened on his territory, on his terms. He said he didn't like Edinburgh, it was too stuffy and snobby. She knew this was ignorant prejudice, yet because it connected with some deep-rooted small-town prejudice in herself, and with the way she herself was feeling about the city, she excused it.

Then one winter's evening she found out who she was with, who she was *really* with. She'd been working all day in Edinburgh, and had taken a late-afternoon train to Drumkirk with no journalistic purpose but solely to see Charlie. He'd picked her up at the station and driven her through the dark streets to the flat. They were on the floor in the living room, in front of a too-hot gas fire. She was flushed from the heat and drunk on white wine, and although he seemed to have been keeping pace with her she vaguely came to realise that he was sober; also that she was naked and her clothes scattered around the room yet he still had most of his on. Until this moment she had felt free and relaxed and *in* the moment. Now something jolted as he teased her with his fingers, and suddenly she didn't want him touching her. But it was too late, he'd brought her to the precipice and then as he tipped her almost over she heard the whisper in her ear. 'See this story aboot us? Ye're no gonnae write it, are ye?' She froze, not even sure she'd heard right. He shifted his hand and his weight and undid his trousers and then she felt him going in. 'Ye dinna hae a story but even if ye did ye'll no write it. Will ye?' She gave a gasp, but the pleasure had vanished and now there was only shock and the threat of pain. 'Or ye'll get hurt.' And he drove into her with the violence she'd guessed but never witnessed, and his hands gripped her wrists and pinned her down and he was so strong she couldn't fight, couldn't squirm her way out from under him, and he rammed again and she cried out and he said, 'Shut the fuck up,' and backhanded her across the jaw, the same hand he'd just been using on her, it was like walking into a wall and her whole face seemed to blow up to twice its normal size and she thought of her stupidity and her lack of precautions and her weakness and it was as if – and how she hated even momentarily thinking this – it was as if she had invited him to rape her. She felt theory and philosophy and ideology and rights shatter in the storm of his violence. The script torn up. Everything in her mind rebelled against everything her body had allowed to happen, and everything in her body was ashamed of the idiocy of her mind. He hit her again and she heard herself cry out and knew he had total control, and that he was right, if she got out of it alive she would be so scared and so compromised that she wouldn't write the story, she would just be grateful to have come to her senses. He hit her a third time and then he turned her over and raped her again.

§

Later he sat smoking, fully clothed, while she crawled around, snuffling and snottery, collecting her things and having to dress in front of him. 'Ye've put blood on the carpet,' he said. 'Clean it up.' She went to the kitchen and found a cloth and a bowl which she filled with hot water and she came back and sponged the blood out of the carpet. Maybe there was bleach under the sink or a knife in a drawer and maybe she'd have tried something but she didn't dare look, she had no hope in weapons, only fear of what else he might do. He knew this. He sat and smoked and when she'd finished he said, 'That's better,' like a compliment, and she felt pathetically grateful for that, for the fact that he didn't hit her again. She thought, how can he have reduced me to this, in a matter of minutes? From the woman I am? But it wasn't just minutes, it was days and weeks, he'd stripped her of her defences without her even noticing, but of course she had noticed. He looked at her with total disdain and said, 'Now I'll take ye hame.'

She said she had a train ticket but he sneered and said, 'Look at yersel. D'ye think I'd put ye on a train in that state?' He made her get in his car. It took an hour to drive to Edinburgh, an hour during which he spoke with cold deliberation of what would happen to her, or her mother, or that fucking hillbilly Denny Hogg or anybody else she cared about, if she went to the police or wrote a word or said or did anything about him, or passed the story on to anyone else to pick up because he'd know, he'd fucking know it was her and he'd hunt her and today would be a dolls' tea party compared to how it would be if he had to do that. The rest of the journey took place in silence. If she tried to speak he told her to shut her fucking mouth and she did. She couldn't think of what would happen next, only of what had occurred. She thought she would lie about the street and try to fool him by walking up to the wrong door, but he drove her straight to the flat and parked directly outside it and this terrified her, the fact that he already knew. He left the engine running. He said, 'This is where you and me part company, Ellen. We're no right for each other, and that's the truth. Sad, eh? Better this way, though. You stay oot o my life, right?' She nodded, her throat so dry she thought she would choke. 'Because if ye dinna, I'll be back in yours, right?' She nodded again. 'Say it,' he said. 'Say, "Right, Charlie."' She managed it, a faint whisper. 'Right, Charlie.' 'Now get oot,' he said, and she scrambled at the door handle and he pushed her from the car and the wheels smoked on the cobbles as he took off.

She should have gone straight to the police, bruised, bloody and unwashed, and maybe she would have but there was more to come and then she knew she wouldn't. The woman she rented a room from was waiting for her. She fetched a basin so Ellen could bathe her swollen face, and she fetched her brandy but when Ellen tried to tell her what had happened she stopped her. 'I don't want to know.' Ellen stared at her. The woman looked as terrified as she felt. 'There was a man here earlier.' 'When?' 'This morning. After you went out. In fact, as soon as you went out. Is he your boyfriend?' 'No.' 'He said he was. He said you were moving out.' 'I'm not.' 'Yes you are.' 'I'm not.' 'I want you to.' 'I don't have a boyfriend and I'm not moving out.' 'I want you to.' 'I've been raped.' The woman turned even paler. 'That was him, wasn't it? I don't want him here again.' She sounded on the verge of hysteria. 'He'll no be back,' Ellen said, trying to calm her. 'He said he would be.' 'No, he'll no be.' 'He said he would be if you hadn't gone by the end of the week. I want you to go. I'm sorry.'

Ellen went to the bathroom and was sick. She ran a bath, as hot as she could make it. She took off her clothes. It was like peeling dead skin. She got in the bath, slowly letting herself down into the scalding water. She took her facecloth and the soap and began to scrub herself. Everywhere. She scrubbed herself raw. She knew what she was doing. When she let the water out it was pink. All the evidence drained away.

The landlady's bedroom door was firmly shut. Ellen put all the clothes in the washing machine and set it to the hottest temperature. Then she shuffled to her bed.

This was a Wednesday. Every time she thought of him planning it she came close to vomiting. She spent Thursday in bed, nursing her aching body and trying to make the bruises on her face go down. The next day was rubbish-collection day. She took the crumpled bundle of clothes out of the washing machine, put them all in a black bag and dumped it on the pavement.

On the Friday she had a call from London. It was a coincidence. She knew it was a coincidence but it didn't feel like one. The editor was sorry but he'd changed his mind. Her column wasn't working. He'd give her a kill-fee for the next two weeks but that was all he could do. The arrangement had always been on an ad hoc basis. He said again that he was sorry. It was good of her to take it so calmly, philosophically. Some people would have gone berserk at him.

On the Saturday her landlady was waiting for her when she emerged from her room. 'I meant what I said,' she said, arms across her chest. 'I want you out this weekend.' She didn't seem so frightened any more. 'I've nowhere to go,' Ellen said. 'What about your boyfriend?' the woman said. Ellen stared at her, turned and went into the bathroom, locking herself in. 'I mean it,' she heard through the frosted glass. 'I'll put your stuff on the street.' Eventually the landlady went out. Ellen waited another ten minutes, then went looking for her diary. It was too shaming, too much of a defeat, to speak to her mother. And she was afraid to go to her because of what Charlie had said. She thought of Adam. Maybe Adam. But she was afraid for him too, because he stayed not far from Borlanslogie. She found Robin Piggott's number and dialled it. When he picked up she said, 'Robin, it's Ellen Imlach. I need your help.' Then she started crying. He said, 'Don't go anywhere. I'm on my way.'

He came in a taxi. By the time he arrived she'd managed to get dressed. She saw the shock on his face, the way he resisted asking what had happened. She said, 'I have to get out of here,' and he understood exactly what she meant – not that she had to get out for an hour or two, but permanently. He made the driver wait and they packed a few of her things in a suitcase and he took her back to Joppa. The sun was shining on the sea, she noticed that. 'You're safe now,' he said. He didn't even know what she was safe from. He didn't seem to care what danger or insanity he was bringing into his home. He made up a bed for her and ran her a bath and later she slept for hours between the fresh, clean sheet and the duvet. When she woke up she put on a dressing gown that was laid across the foot of the bed and went through to the kitchen, drawn by the smell of rich cooking. Robin said, 'Here you are.' 'Yes, here I am.' 'Come and see,' he said, and took her to a box room, which miraculously contained the rest of her possessions. 'Me and a mate went and got it all in his car. We'll sort it out later.' She pointed at a rather nice mirror in a tilting mahogany frame with two wee drawers underneath. 'That's not mine.' Robin looked a little horrified, then he laughed. 'It's not going back.' She saw the yellow-and-black bruise on her face in the mirror. She started to cry. Tears poured from her and she could not stop them. She was powerless and when Robin went to put his arms around her she said, 'No, please,' and shrank against the wall away from him. He said, 'It's okay, I'm not going to hurt you.' She knew he was telling the truth but it didn't help much. He didn't touch her.

She couldn't eat the good food he'd cooked. The smell of it made her feel sick. She went back to bed. He left her alone. She managed to get up and make a cup of tea and he came into the kitchen while she was there and she found herself standing as far away from him as possible. She said, 'I'm sorry.' He said, 'You've nothing to be sorry for.' She said, 'I'm sorry. It's not you. It's me.' She started to cry again.

This went on for weeks. She never went out. She hardly ever got dressed. Robin went to his work and when he came back she would still be in bed or she'd be sitting in the dressing gown staring out of the window at the grey sea, the blue sea, the black sea. She grew impatient with herself and tried to stir herself to action, but nothing happened. She grew impatient with Robin's patience. She wanted him to shout, give her an ultimatum, but he put no pressure on her at all. He persuaded her to eat small, easy meals, and that was the extent of his pressure. He said she could stay as long as she needed to. There was nobody else in the house, it was easily big enough for the two of them. 'I'll pay you rent,' she said, after she'd been there a month. 'You don't have to,' he said. 'I'm happy that you're here.' 'But I have to pay you rent,' she said. 'It's just that . . .' He waited, as he always did. 'At the moment I don't have any money.' Tears again. 'What am I going to do?' 'You don't have to do anything.' 'Aye, I do. I'm pregnant.'

She'd missed two periods by then. She reckoned she must be ten weeks gone or more. It wasn't the rape, it was before that. Another thing to face up to. Robin said, 'What do you want to do? Whatever you want, I'll help you through with it.' She said, 'I can't ask you to do that.' He said, 'You're not asking me, I'm just saying.' And then, at last, she was able to tell him what had happened. Everything that had happened. Everything. He listened and watched, and they talked through the possibility of involving the police, and the time that had elapsed, and the absence of witnesses, and the almost nil chances of a successful prosecution. 'Why am I such a coward?' she said. 'We can't leave a man like that out on the loose. Who's he hurting now?' Robin said, 'Let me talk to someone.' 'Who?' she wanted to know. 'I know a guy in the police.' 'No.' 'I promise I won't tell him who you are. Let me ask him about Lennie.' And at that it came to her like the sound of a bell across still water: she knew in that instant, without a flicker of doubt, after what he had done to her, after the collapse of her life, after the way she'd had to throw herself on the mercy of another man, after all of that she knew with an astonishing certainty what she wanted, and it was the last thing, the last thing . . .

'I'm going to keep the baby,' she said.

Robin looked at her. 'You are?'

'Aye. I'm not killing it for that bastard.'

'Okay,' Robin said. 'Then that's what we'll do.'

She almost resented the way he said *we*, as if they were in it together. Then she didn't resent it at all.

'I know it sounds mad,' she said. 'I mean, why would I? I can't explain it.'

'You don't have to,' he said. 'Either way, you don't have to justify yourself.'

She stared at him. She saw him clearly, as if for the first time. Robin Piggott.

'Who are you?' she said. 'Why are you so kind to me?'

He smiled. 'It's not kindness,' he said. 'I can't help it. It's not me, it's you. I'll do anything for you.'

§

'I talked to my policeman friend,' Robin said, a week or so later. 'I told him about something that happened to a woman I know, a month ago. He listened very carefully. He shook his head a lot. He thought the procurator fiscal wouldn't even think it worth preparing a case. So I told him she knew the guy who did it to her was into other bad stuff and maybe they could get him for something else. I gave him Lennie's name. It's another force's area, but he said he'd ask around.'

'And?'

'The police in Drumkirk have Charlie Lennie on their wish-list. They'd love to pin something on him. But he's clever. Clever and scary. There are never any witnesses to anything he does. Or none that are prepared to stand up in court.'

'What about what happened to me?'

'It's what we thought, Ellen. It's too late and even if it got to court you'd only be a witness. Your word against his. "Why did you take so long to report it? Why did you throw out your clothes, any evidence?" The bruises are gone. No jury would convict him.'

'That's it?'

She felt the sense of failure welling up again. But something else too. She was going to have the baby. Lennie didn't even know it existed. She had something of his and she was keeping it. It was his but it wasn't his, it never would be. She was going to be strong again.

'He'll get what's coming to him,' Robin said. 'I know he will, sooner or later.'

'Sooner,' she said, 'would be my preference.'

§

Out of the smoking ruins that were her self-respect, her emotions and her intellect, a strange image began to emerge. She saw herself with Charlie, she saw herself with Robin, she saw herself alone on a dark stage, rehearsing a play, an actress delivering lines. In the stalls a director was shouting at her. She hadn't written the part but she'd learned the lines and now the director wanted to change her way of saying them. The role she was playing was Lady Macbeth. Then it wasn't her in the role, it was another woman. Distance, perspective. Where was Macbeth? What was Lady Macbeth without Macbeth? What was she with him? Amazon, murderess, temptress, manipulator, schemer, victim, bully, coward, demented sleepwalker? A man had written the lines but the character had come alive, moved beyond the playwright's grasp and beyond the lines he'd made for her, and now another man was trying to impose his will on her. On the character, on the actress. Suppose she, Ellen, understood all this, understood the politics of the theatre, of the play, of the interaction between the characters and between the players? Suppose she saw this as clearly as anything, and yet she bowed to the director's will, played Lady Macbeth not by instinct, but in obedience? A strong woman trapped by the play she was in. What would that mean? Who would be to blame? And how many more Lady Macbeths were out there?

She began to sketch out a plan of something, a stage-set for a play she wanted to direct, not perform in.

§

She still woke in the night sometimes, heart racing, and reached out for Robin, and he was always there. 'You're all right,' he'd say. As if he'd been waiting for it. She'd get up to check Kirsty, and when she came back Robin would be asleep again and it would be almost as if nothing had ever happened. But it had. Everything had happened. Kirsty was proof.

§

She thought, there'll come a day when I seek out Denny again. She'd checked with her mother. What was the story about Denny? Mary said he'd been mixed up with some lunatic political group. They'd been trying to get weapons for a nationalist rebellion or something. Guns and raising money would have appealed to Denny, but Ellen couldn't imagine him being interested in politics. Anyway, the scheme had been smashed and the gang members had gone to jail. But Denny was out again in a matter of months. How come? Mary didn't know. Good behaviour? Maybe he'd done a deal. Anyway, he dodged away between Borlanslogie and Drumkirk, and Mary reckoned he was constitutionally incapable of staying out of trouble.

'Why are you so interested in Denny Hogg?'

'I just wondered.'

'Stay awa frae him. He's bad news.'

'Don't worry, I will.'

She didn't want anything to do with Denny, not for a long while. But one day she'd like to clear a few things up with him.

Maybe there'd be a day when she felt ready to clear a few things up with Charlie Lennie, but she doubted it.

§

Robin said, 'If we're going to be honest, with Kirsty I mean, then we'll have to have an answer ready for her one day. *You'll* have to have an answer for her. For when she says, well, if Robin's not my dad, who is?'

'Aye,' she said. 'I will.' On the birth certificate she had left the space for the father's name blank, as she was entitled to do.

'And what will it be?'

'It'll have to be the truth,' she said. 'And when she knows and understands it, she'll have to decide what to do about it.'

After a silence she added, 'That day fills me with dread. To have to tell her whose child she is. But I won't lie to her. Oh fuck, Robin. Did I do wrong, bringing her into the world?'

'No,' he said. 'You didn't, and you know you didn't. Look at her. She's beautiful. Your beautiful daughter. And she'll grow up with us, here, so she'll only ever know love. She'll be all right. She'll do the right thing.'

The way he said it, she just about believed him.

Times came when you almost cracked under the weight of the questions. In the night you'd wake in the ruins of an old kirkyard, among the dead and the ghosts and the crying of hoolets, and there was the ink sky and stars in their hundreds above you and the questions would flood in, bombarding you like tiny meteorites. Who were you and what the hell were you doing and what had you done and why had you done it? And there were no answers so the questions kept piling up, bearing down. You'd get up because you couldn't breathe under them, you'd run stumbling on tree roots, whipped by branches, setting off deer in the shadows. These were desperate hours when you felt utterly alone, and then dawn would slowly diminish the darkness and the blind running panic and again you'd be alone, but now calm and complete. To be apart, to be separate, was to be complete. It was the reason you were how you were. The estranged figures of the past faded in the light.

Times too when you became aware of new people around you as you travelled. You noticed them first on your brief sojourns in the cities. In Edinburgh, bus drivers in turbans. In Glasgow, a group of quiet, brown, wary-looking men drinking tea outside a southside warehouse. Like you they kept themselves apart, or perhaps were kept apart. You passed corner shops, crammed with goods inside and with racks overflowing with fruit and veg outside the door, the women and men who ran them stoically sacrificing their days and nights to the future. Restaurants and takeaways with exotic, unchallenging names – the Taj Mahal, the Great Wall – appeared on the streets of unimpressed small towns. You walked past their steamy windows and inhaled their spicy announcements: here we are. Clusters of black-haired boys and their giggling sisters ran past you to or from schools. You walked on. Things fall into place. Once we were all strangers. Before these folk there were Pakistani pedlars speaking Gaelic to their island customers. Before them were Poles and Italians, before them Irish, before them Jews, before them English, French, Danes, Scots. The swart wreckage of Spanish warships floated in the blood of Lewis, the salt-sprayed vision of Vikings was in the eyes of Angus farmers. 'My ladye with the mekle lippis, that landet furth of the last schippis.' Once were Irish and Picts and Egyptians and Britons and slaves and cave-dwellers and hunters of mammoths and gatherers of clams and berries and once they were not here and once they will not be here again. Only the land will remain. People dug it and cut it and burned it and built on it but the land remained. 'It is we who must reconcile ourselves to the stones, not the stones to us.' You picked up the stones and carried them for a while, then you released them. You yourself were released. You were a skeleton walking out of the jungle, you were a man, you were alive, you were dead, you were bones crumbling into the earth. You were a shadow on the land, someone else's glimpse, their fading memory, then nothing.

§

There was a moment of clarity. You couldn't remember when or where but you remembered the moment. A man said, What's your name? A man who was giving you work, or shoes, or a mug of tea. Of course folk asked for your name. Of course you gave it. Jack. That was all they needed. That was all you gave them. But this time the man said, That's my name too. Jack what?

And it came out of you. MacLaren. Jack MacLaren. You did not say it. It came out of you.

It was a miracle. MacLaren was not dead. He was home, here, now.

It crushed down on you, that miracle. It was a burden. Then it wasn't. You saw that you could save him. You couldn't save the others, they were dead. But you could save Jack MacLaren. That was his name. You were both Jack, like the man who asked the question.

He was home. That was all. You never had to say his name again.

Jack said, Fancy a stroll to India? It was a joke. You all laughed, to show it was a joke. But when you stopped laughing you fancied it. He saw that and together you made your plans. Together you and he went, out into the jungle night. You had a week. Then Jack got sick. He said to leave him but you couldn't leave him. You took him to a village. That was where they found you. They brought you both back but only one of you was still alive.

Jack was too weak. He shouldn't have gone. He was never going to make it.

You were going to die. That was why they brought you back. Jack was already dead but they brought you back to kill you. To make an example of you. All the other men on parade, three sides of a square. You and Jack in

522

the middle, in the blaze of the midday sun. You were kneeling, hands bound behind your back, blindfolded, head bowed, neck to the sun. Jack lay beside you, face down. You could just about touch him if you dared. You did not dare. He was dead. You were going to die.

Hours, you lost count of them, hours passed. The sun was a weight on your neck. Your mind was black with pain and fear. You were going to die.

The officer screamed at you. He screamed at the men all around you. This is what happens if you try to escape. You will be brought back. This is what will happen.

You heard the sword leave the scabbard. You felt the blade rest on the back of your neck. You felt blood trickle from where it rested. Then the sword lifted. You were about to die. Your head. You heard the sword in the air. You screamed. You heard the blade take off your head. Then you heard nothing.

You were in a bamboo cage. There was no room to turn, no room to stretch. You could just about crouch, just about curl. They must have folded you smaller than yourself to get you in. There was no room to be a man.

You were in there a long time. You never knew how long. When you came out you weren't who you had been. You weren't Jack Gordon. Jack Gordon was away. You were someone else. You didn't tell them. You didn't tell anyone.

The sword cut off dead Jack's head but you thought it was yours it severed. They put the head on a stake for all to see. It was a way of saying what would happen next time. They would do it to you next time. They would do it to anyone.

The fact that you were away. You kept it to yourself.

Now – ever since the man said Jack what? – you knew. Now you understood why you left. You left because you could save Jack. You could do nothing for the others, but you could save Jack.

You told 'Tam o' Shanter' to the hoolets. It was all you could do for Geordie. There was nothing you could do for Sim.

You were never going back. You were free. You were never going back in the cage.

There was no room to be a man.

You told 'Tam o' Shanter' to the hoolets, and they cried back. You knew the meaning of their cries.

You knew the meaning of dogs barking.
You knew the meaning of rain, of wind.
You knew the meaning of stones.
You knew.
You knew.
You knew.

PART FIVE

Questions of Loyalties

Fate said, *I'll bloody show ye*. But no, Don didn't believe in fate, God or any of that. He believed in humanity, and that humans had the power and the will to change themselves and the world, but not necessarily for the good, and that was where socialism came in, the only way forward was socialism and democracy, and in Britain that meant Labour, the only party committed to those ideals but rooted and realistic enough to be able to deliver them, or some measure of them. Everything else was a diversion, every other political party either reactionary and anti-progressive, or oppressive and destructive. The far left was insane and out of touch, the right was an offence to ordinary people's dignity. But the Labour Party was in trouble, it had run out of steam, exhausted itself trying to manage an ailing economy in an unforgiving world. Suddenly it looked old: Jim Callaghan looked old, Michael Foot looked old, even Denis Healey – who was only three years older than Don and with whom he'd always felt an affinity because of their shared war experience in North Africa and Italy – looked jaded. They were put out to pasture and the younger, leaner, bolder Tories under Margaret Thatcher moved in. The old compromises were crumbling. Soon they would be gone altogether. Nothing must stand against the new religion of the market. Public spending must be slashed, wages screwed down, the money supply ruthlessly controlled, inflation battered into submission. If the poor, the sick and the weak suffered in the bygoing, this was regrettable, but it was the poor, sick, weak British economy that needed emergency treatment and without it the future would be grim for everyone. If businesses closed and unemployment rose, it showed that the medicine was working. Don, who had once despised what they called one-nation Toryism, a kind of gentlemanly appreciation that it was counter-productive to squeeze the workers *too* hard, now found himself nostalgic for it. Compared with some of the slavering fanatics barking around the Prime Minister's heels – compared with Thatcher herself – it almost rated as *decent.* He detested what he saw on the news every night, the undoing of society. He was appalled by summer riots in Liverpool, London and Bristol, the kind of violence he associated with America, not with England. Labour was breaking up on the rocks, torn apart by ideological warfare. Was he losing touch with his country, or was it losing touch with him? And which country? He remembered Jack Gordon. Scottish Nationalism lay wrecked along with so much else, its proponents arguing amongst themselves. And he thought of Charlie, patrolling the streets of Derry or wherever the hell he was, ready to shoot or be shot at on behalf of Her Britannic Majesty's government. Forty years since the war and still the fighting continued. And for what, for what?

He spent his weekends and many of his evenings out in the garden, putting his back into something he could still be proud of.

§

Byres Brothers had been laying off workers for two years. Most of the drivers were no longer employees: the firm made them redundant, then later hired new men, self-employed men, as subcontractors. Some of the old drivers set up on their own, buying their own cabs, hiring themselves out to the highest bidder. Even in the repair shop, when a man retired he was replaced – if he was replaced at all – by someone on a short-term contract. And Don's union was powerless to stop all this happening. The trade unions generally were disunited: they were competing for members and different unions adopted different methods of dealing with changing employment practices. More than half the men at Byres Brothers were no longer in a union, and those that were were split between two. And Byres Brothers wasn't big enough to get the full attention of senior union officials, who had enough on their plates elsewhere, trying to stop huge job cuts in manufacturing, resisting closures or, more often than not, negotiating thousands of redundancies as plants and businesses all over the country closed their doors.

There was talk of standing up to the management – especially over a wage offer which didn't come anywhere near matching inflation, running at nearly 20 per cent – but it remained just that, talk. Nobody wanted to lose a day's pay when there was no real prospect of the offer being improved, and with the fear of unemployment lurking in the background. When it came to a choice between retaining a skilled job or idleness, there *was* no choice.

Don was the shop steward for his union. Byres Brothers had never directly negotiated with the unions over wages, but in some respects the presence of the unions had made discussions around pay and conditions easier for the business: if the union reps were satisfied that grievances were taken seriously and disputes settled by negotiation then there was a much-reduced likelihood of walkouts, slowdowns or other disruption. Auld Tam Byres had always thought he was giving too much away, but he was shrewd enough to see that open confrontation would cost him more. But Tam was dead. Wullie Byres was in charge now, and times had changed. The latest wage offer was very poor. Don, feeling both that he had to do something and that there wasn't much to be done, went to see Wullie in his office at the back of the depot.

Wullie was friendly enough – he'd known Don for forty years – but he wasn't in the mood for negotiation. 'Ye'll just need tae grit your teeth and let your politics stick in your thrapple,' he said. 'That's what we had tae dae for years. It's your turn noo.'

'The boot's on the other foot, ye mean?'

'Aye, ye could say that.'

'I dinna think the workforce has ever had that much clout, Wullie.'

'Aye weel. I dae.'

'The offer's totally unacceptable,' Don said. 'Wi inflation the way it is, ye're asking us tae take a cut. A big cut.'

'Christ, Don, ye sound like yin o thae buggers on *News at Ten*. Ye'll be banging your fist on the table next. If the offer's unacceptable, dinna accept it. But ye'll no get a better yin. Then what'll ye dae?'

'We could come oot.'

Wullie shrugged. 'Dae what ye like. I've nae mair money for ye. Times are tight. If ye dinna want tae work there's plenty men oot there that does.'

'Ye ken I'm a grafter,' Don said. 'And the others.'

'Some o them,' Wullie growled.

'This is aboot a fair wage for a fair day's work.'

'I'd agree wi ye on that. It is a fair wage.'

Don tried to imagine what was going on inside Wullie's head.

He'd been almost apoplectic in the last months of the Labour government, ranting about uncollected rubbish and unburied bodies as
if he had to step over them on his way to work every morning, and
now he was an enthusiastic supporter of Margaret Thatcher, Geoffrey Howe and the rest of them. He might laugh at their terribly
English voices but he was in awe of them too. 'The lady's not for
turning.' 'There is no alternative.' Maybe you needed a voice like
that to get things sorted. And by God Wullie thought they needed
sorting. Mrs Thatcher was on his side against the barbarians –
Communists, punk rockers, hordes of idle black bastards setting
fires in the streets. If it was down to him he'd shoot the bloody lot
of them – but maybe he didn't have to, because Margaret Thatcher
seemed to have the gumption to pull the country back from the
brink. 'She's mair o a man than maist o her Cabinet,' he'd said to
Don a few weeks before. 'Nae sex tae her, but ye dinna elect a Prime
Minister tae be sexy, dae ye?'

'Listen, Don,' Wullie said now, 'I could walk away frae this the
morn's morn if I wanted tae. I could sell the business and never hae
tae lift a finger for the rest o my days. So ye dinna intimidate me
coming in here and saying ye might come oot on strike. I've no
done a heid count o your members recently but I'm no feart. The
thing is, I'm no ready tae retire yet. I'm like you, I'm a grafter. I'm
sixty-three. My faither was in here till the week afore he died, as ye
ken. What age was he? Seventy-five. I'm no gaun onywhaur for a
while, and there's nae need for you tae go onywhaur either. But ye
may as weel get used tae it. We're in a new era. Either ye fecht it and
lose, or ye work wi it. It's your choice.'

'We'll see,' Don said. He liked Wullie better than he should.
Always had done. And he wouldn't admit it, but he was pretty sure
that Wullie was right.

'Aye,' Wullie said with a wink, 'we will.'

§

A conference was held in Glasgow, in the theatre behind the Mitchell Library. A Saturday in July 1983. Three weeks earlier Margaret
Thatcher had won her second General Election, routing the Labour
Party under Michael Foot's leadership. The conference organisers
had a big question for those attending: 'Which way now for the

Scottish Left?' 'We have to go to this, we have to go,' Adam Shaw said. So they went, he and Mike Pendreich and three hundred or so other disparate souls who might have been described as belonging to the 'Scottish Left'. But on the day some were even unhappy about that designation. They felt that the adjective somehow betrayed the spirit of the noun it described. Someone was selling copies of a poster that said in big letters SCOTTISH WRITERS AGAINST THE BOMB. On it were the names of dozens of writers opposed to nuclear weapons on the Clyde. An argument started. 'Oh, you can't say that.' 'Can't say what?' 'If you say "Scottish writers" you're excluding other writers who are also against the Bomb. That's parochial, that is.' 'Who are you calling parochial? We're just saying we don't want nuclear missiles here.' 'You're pandering to nationalism.' *'We're* pandering to nationalism?' A fight almost broke out.

Those who hadn't come to trade ideological insults had come to lick their wounds after the election, and to see what, if anything, could be done next. Until about a year before, it had still been possible to hope that the Conservatives might only last one term. There was so much unemployment, such general misery and despair, that many on the left didn't think ordinary people could stand any more of it. Even the extravaganza of Prince Charles's marriage to Diana Spencer in 1981 had surely been only a temporary diversion. The opinion polls said there had never been such an unpopular Prime Minister or such an out-of-touch government. But then a fascist dictator in Argentina took it upon himself to invade the Falkland Islands, thereby saving the Thatcher regime and destroying his own. The steel-haired Britannia dispatched a task force to win the Falklands back. Some predicted, or longed for, disaster – Mrs Thatcher's Suez. The predictions were wrong. If it was her Suez she turned out to be Nasser, not Anthony Eden. Suddenly, for millions, Mrs Thatcher was a heroine, the woman who'd put the 'great' back into Great Britain. Boosted by the 'Falklands factor', she won the 1983 election with a huge majority. Labour haemorrhaged support to the Liberals and Social Democrats, and in terms of the number of votes gained were nearly beaten into third place.

A deep depression hung over the Glasgow conference. It was hardly surprising that people bickered over the wording of a poster. There wasn't much else to shout about.

Various pompous, contrite, humble and not-so-humble MPs, councillors and union leaders – almost all male – came to the microphone. Often they took the opportunity to attack the views of previous speakers. The main arguments focused on the question of 'the Scottish card'. What was it, and how could or should it be played? Did the Thatcher government, rejected by three-quarters of the Scottish electorate, even have a mandate to govern Scotland? The Labour speakers could not entertain that proposition. To accept it would undermine the Union, playing into the hands of the SNP. And what if, at a future election, Labour won a Westminster majority that depended on their Scottish and Welsh seats? Where would be their mandate to govern England? The Communist Party representatives, who did not have to worry about the possibility of being in government, said that the Scottish Left had to come to terms with the concept of Scottishness. The SNP left-wingers present enthusiastically agreed, but they were badly out of favour with their own party, which had performed terribly in the election but was nevertheless sticking with the traditional independence-and-nothing-less stance it had reverted to after the 1979 referendum. Left-wingers had little influence within the SNP, and 'soft' nationalists had none in Labour. There was a tension in the air: identity politics versus class consciousness. The one policy that offered some prospect of common ground, devolution, was once again being squeezed from all sides. Nobody loved it, and nobody had much of a good word to say for it. Only the representatives of the Campaign for the Scottish Assembly, the cross-party, non-party organisation that had been doggedly reconstructing the case for devolution since the failed referendum of 1979, seemed genuine in their enthusiasm.

Adam's chin sank on his chest as he listened. Mike thought about taking a break and going to find a cup of tea. Then the next speaker stalked up to the microphone and he decided to wait. It was Robin Cook, his own MP, he who had been so fierce against the very idea of an assembly only a few years before.

'I have not,' Cook said, his red beard jutting out defiantly, 'I have not been an extravagant supporter of the Scottish dimension.' Where previous speakers had droned, Cook yapped, and everybody sat up. 'But I've changed my mind. I don't give a bugger if Thatcher

has a mandate or not – I will simply do whatever I can to stop her.'
There was a stunned silence, then a smattering of applause. Cook
carried on, but whatever else he said didn't really matter. The rigid
anti-devolutionist had moved – out of expediency, no doubt, but it
was a brutal, honest kind of expediency. Adam nudged Mike. 'If he
can shift his position, anybody can.'

Adam's brother, Gavin, the Politics lecturer, was also at the conference. Mike had met him once or twice before, and had found him
very distant. He didn't think Gavin took him or his opinions
seriously. But they went for a drink afterwards, analysing the day
and concluding that in a mostly bleak landscape the Cook movement had supplied the brightest glimmer of hope, and Gavin was
different: friendlier, and as willing to listen as to talk. When they
parted he grasped Mike's right hand in his at the same time as his
left arm went round Adam's shoulder in a brotherly hug. It felt, a
little, like being welcomed into a family.

§

It was the era of postcards selling sex. They filled the interiors of
phone boxes from Euston to Charing Cross. When you went into
some of them around Leicester Square you could hardly see out
through the glass for postcards. That was good, as it meant no one
could see in as you pretended to make a call to your wife or bank
manager while you read the invitations. Every sexual service, every
deviant desire you could imagine, was stuck up there, with phone
numbers and photos, or with old-fashioned line drawings that
David Eddelstane found more subtly enticing. And sure enough,
when he looked, there were cards for what he thought he wanted.
He picked them off and stuffed them in his coat pocket. His hand
trembled as if at any moment the door would be forced open and
the world would be outside pointing and jeering at him. Get a grip,
he told himself, nobody cares. It isn't anybody's business but yours.
But it was, because he was an elected representative of the people.
It would be everybody's business if they ever found out. In the
Islington flat – which he'd held on to all through the 1970s and
was now very pleased he had, as the street had become extremely
desirable and the place was worth six times what he'd paid for it – he
shuffled the cards in wonder and fear. There was one that kept coming

to the top of the pile. It was inevitable that he would eventually dial the number.

'I know what you want, love,' the woman at the other end of the line said. 'You come and see me and I'll make you happy.' He asked a question or two, and she supplied the right answers. She gave him the address and a time, and he went. Walked up and down past the door, round the corner, was he going to do this, was he really going to do it? If there was a newshound on his trail he'd be better off the street than hanging about like an idiot, so back he went, terrified, and rang the bell.

Terrified was what she expected. She was older than he'd assumed from her voice, but that was okay; in fact it was reassuring. Somehow he persuaded himself he could trust her because she was older. He felt the years falling away even as she invited him to sit down and tell her again what he wanted. Then she instructed him to undress. He was a little boy again. 'You're here and you don't even know why,' she said, 'but I do. I know what you want before you ask for it.' He thought he was going to swoon. 'Relax,' she said. 'Deep breaths. This can take as long as you like. You and I are going on a journey together.'

§

Here is a situation: a country that is not fully a country, a nation that does not quite believe itself to be a nation, exists within, and as a small and distant part of, a greater state. The greater state was once a very great state, with its own empire. It is no longer great, but its leaders and many of its people like to believe it is. For the people of the less-than country, the not-quite nation, there are competing, conflicting loyalties. They are confused. For generations a kind of balance has been maintained. There has been give and take, and, yes, there have been arguments about how much give and how much take, but now something has changed. There is a sense of injustice, of neglect, of vague or real oppression. Nobody is being shot, there are no political prisoners, there is very little censorship, but still that sense persists: *this is wrong*. It grows. It demands to be addressed. The situation needs to be fixed.

So there are gatherings and debates. There are long arguments in pubs and round kitchen tables. People write discussion papers, and meet to discuss them. There are music sessions, poetry readings, lectures and political seminars. There are statements of principle, voices of dissent, angry walkouts. There are lines people will not cross, but which, on reflection, they will. There are conversations and compromises. People learn how to talk to each other and how to listen, because the alternative is endless defeat. Gradually it becomes possible for a kind of socialism and a kind of nationalism to exist in the same person, in the same room, in the same political party. And these locations, private and public, no longer have to be battle zones.

There were magazines recording and encouraging this process of self-exploration. They were small-scale, low-budget, sporadic affairs, and their sales were tiny – a few hundred, a very few thousand – but the people running them weren't doing it for the sales. They were doing it to address that pervasive sense of wrongness. And the people who read them – culturally aware, politically active people – were hungry for what they provided. More than anything, perhaps, the magazines said: *you are not alone.*

Mike knew this because it was how he felt. He read the magazines from cover to cover. They filled the gaps of what he didn't learn from Adam or from his wider reading. They gave him the sense that he belonged to a political community that was not being dictated to or managed by the mainstream parties. There was an undercurrent of desire for change, and these publications and anyone involved with them, even if only as a reader, were part of it.

Gavin Shaw was on the editorial board of one. *Root & Branch*, it was called. At the time of the Glasgow conference it had produced only a couple of issues. He came round to the Tollcross flat one evening, on the off chance, so he said, of catching Mike in. Mike made coffee and they sat in the kitchen turning the pages of the first two issues. 'We're trying to build bridges, open dialogues,' Gavin explained. 'What will this country look like in ten or twenty years? We take the view that any viable future for Scotland has to include a strong measure of self-government – let's not be more specific than that – but otherwise we don't have a fixed agenda. We'll publish contributions from anybody if they have something interesting or innovative to say.'

Everybody involved with the magazine, he said, wanted to

improve the general design and layout, and to make the covers more striking without increasing the costs too much. Also, they badly needed photographs – other than those they borrowed or stole from elsewhere, which tended to be of poor quality – to illustrate some of the articles with.

'Adam's talked to me a bit about this,' Mike said. 'He thought –'

'He thought you might lend a hand,' Gavin said. 'He helps out a bit, but he's too busy with other things. And you've got some of the skills we need. There's no money in it, of course. You'd be like the rest of us – doing it for the cause.'

'For the cause?'

'Totally.'

'A lot of the work I do is like that.'

'I know. That's why I'm asking you.'

'I can't really afford the time.'

'I know. None of us can.'

'On the other hand . . .'

'Yes?'

'. . . can I afford not to?'

'That's how we all feel.'

'Okay. Count me in.'

'Brilliant. There's an editorial meeting tomorrow evening. Are you free?'

'What's tomorrow, Wednesday? Yes, I can do that. I can't do Thursdays or Fridays, I work in a restaurant those nights. That's just for future reference.'

Gavin held out his hand. 'We'll bear it in mind.'

§

Mike has a complete set of *Root & Branch* on his shelves at Cnoc nan Gobhar. Because it was run on a shoestring budget, the magazine relied on income from sales of one issue to pay the printers for the next, and its appearance was therefore irregular. It also depended on the willingness of its contributors to write for nothing. To have produced twenty-five issues under these conditions seems now not far short of miraculous. Once every two or three months, armed with scalpels, steel rules and Tipp-Ex, the entire editorial team gathered for a weekend, and spent it cutting up the bromide sheets of typeset text, spray-mounting them and sticking them down by hand, page by page, before delivering the whole thing to the printer. Then, when the printed copies came back, another evening was devoted to sending them off to subscribers, and packing orders to bookshops, art galleries, health-food shops and other outlets. A meeting to plan the next issue followed hard on that, and the routine of commissioning, writing and image-gathering would begin again. Even then it was a process being superseded by new technological advances. Two decades on, it seems antique to Mike, belonging to another age altogether.

Sometimes he'll pull an issue down and glance through it, and is still surprised by the range of people who wrote for the magazine: ecologists, feminists, anarchists, churchmen, poets, playwrights, filmmakers, historians, social scientists, retired diplomats, civil servants, and politicians and party workers of every hue – even some renegade pro-devolution Tories. Some of those contributors are dead, some retired, but others are senior members of governments in either Edinburgh or London, and many of the non-politicians have become prominent in their own fields. The rebels became professors, the barbarians walked through the palace gates and took over. And not a shot was fired.

Mike remembers clearly the night Gavin asked him to be involved. He had no hesitation in saying yes. He attended the meeting the next evening and from then on, for five years, supplied photographs, designed covers, worked on the layout, and rediscovered his schoolboy talent for cartooning. Others, led by Gavin, later joined by his cousin Ellen Imlach, drove the magazine editorially. Mike was happy in his back-room role. There were other, more visible, magazines with similar agendas that achieved much more in political terms, but Mike still feels a touch of pride when he looks at a copy of *Root & Branch*. And yet the argument that was conducted in its pages, as it was in the pages of those other journals, should not have been necessary. What was it again? It was, in the end, so convincingly won that it is hard to reconstruct it. Did the professors, when they were rebels, have a clearer sense of direction than he did? It seemed at the time that they did, but perhaps that wasn't the case. Sometimes, he thinks, the surest thing you do is a confused scuffle with fate. You push forward into the dark, not with certainty but with determination. If you keep going forward, you may eventually come out of the dark and into a place you recognise.

It wasn't until the years of *Root & Branch* that Mike really got to know Ellen, even though when he was first with Adam she was already living in Joppa with Robin Piggott and their daughter, Kirsty. Only Kirsty wasn't their daughter, not Robin's anyway. They behaved as if she was, but there was a story there Mike did not know, and that even Gavin and Adam seemed in the dark about. Whatever had happened in the past, Mike decided, it was none of his business. Robin was working for himself. Kirsty was in primary school. Ellen seemed happy. She'd published her first, slim, sparky book, *The Other Lady Macbeth*, a few years before and was at work on a second. The first had been attacked not only by some male reviewers but also, with greater ferocity, by both radical and conservative women. 'I must have got something right,' Ellen said. Her journalistic skills and freely donated opinion pieces were major assets for the magazine.

Robin didn't like to stray far from his nest, so he usually took care of Kirsty after school. Occasionally, following an editorial meeting or some other evening event, Ellen would go with Mike and Adam to Jean Barbour's for an hour or two. From what Mike remembers, Ellen seemed to enjoy the atmosphere and the conversations, but then would come those moments when everybody had to hush for a song or a story. The fact was, she and Jean didn't get on. Ellen disliked or was jealous of Jean for having never had to work for a living – and for being, as she saw it, self-indulgent. She baulked at the sight of grown-up people sitting on the floor like schoolchildren before their teacher. On the one hand she thought 'tradition' was another word for 'conformity'; on the other she used to get annoyed at Jean's penchant for twisting postmodernist knots into the tales she told. If that was what she was doing. 'Either tell them straight,' Ellen complained, 'or don't tell them at all.' Eventually she stopped coming, after being asked once too often to keep her voice down.

For her part, Jean disliked the self-righteous streak in Ellen and thought her opinions insubstantial. It was true, Ellen's book wasn't remarkable for its footnotes or extensive bibliography, but that wasn't the point: the point was she wrote cracking polemic. She was also almost as critical of female behaviour – the ambitions, deceits and treacheries of her various Lady Macbeths – as she was of men, and this was what drew the feminist as well as the chauvinist guns on her. Ellen didn't care. Mike remembers going out to Joppa one day: Robin answered the door and said, 'Welcome to Dunsinane,' and there was Ellen behind him, roaring with laughter. As if the whole thing, the serious import of her book, were nothing but an enormous joke. 'Don't believe a word you read,' she told Mike. 'Not just in my book. Any book.' She had in her, she said, in more or less equal quantities, a thirst for the truth and a conviction that there was no such thing. 'All stories are lies, Mike. The secret is to work out how big the lie is. That's why we keep believing in a thing called truth. It doesn't exist but we can't help looking for it. It's one of the most endearing of human failings.'

§

Liz stood in the bay window of the drawing room, looking down on the world, and it was green and alive and unbearably beautiful. For weeks now, months, something had been wrong and she could no longer deny it. Even this view didn't stop the sick feeling she had about herself. It wasn't that she was in any particular pain, although there *were* pains, sudden and sharp and insidious, it was more the constant exhaustion that told her she was in trouble. Her energy was gone by mid-morning. Lately she'd been stopping twenty minutes early and having a coffee to recover, before walking slowly home down the hill. Then she would sleep for an hour, sometimes longer. She didn't tell Don about this. But Don would be retired soon and then she wouldn't be able to hide it from him.

She could hardly believe it but she'd been working for Mrs Cotter twenty years. They'd agreed a few years back – about the same time Mrs Cotter finally said, 'Liz, this is ridiculous, please call me Elaine' – to cut her hours to two days a week, but even at that there was very little to do. Maybe she should retire herself, she was old enough, she was already drawing her pension. But if she quit she wouldn't ever have the house to herself again. And if she couldn't come to the house then whatever was wrong wouldn't go away even for those few hours. But the reality was that it didn't go away. She was going to have to do something.

The worst thing was being sure what it was. She felt things. There was a lump in one breast, there was something else that didn't feel right under her arm. Why had she not done anything before? The answer was simple: fear. She'd seen it take her own mother, quick as anything, and that ought to have made her act but it had had the opposite effect, it made her incapable of action. Maybe if she and Don had been talking more she'd have had more courage. Maybe if she told him, even now, it could still be all right.

Mrs Cotter – Elaine – had turned grey in an elegant, sophisticated kind of way. But when Liz looked at herself the greyness was anything but sophisticated. It was the grey of sickness. Sometimes Elaine said, 'Are you all right, Liz?' And she always replied that she was fine, just a little tired.

And Mr Cotter was a surgeon. His job was cutting into bodies like hers. She couldn't bear the thought of it.

She left the window and sat on the piano stool. It was a quarter to twelve. An hour to go. All she wanted to do was sleep. She pressed the white keys, one, two, one, two, three, and heard the start of a tune. By accident, because she didn't know how to play, she'd struck the first few notes of a song. What was it? She tried to think of the words. Then she tried to play the notes again but they were gone, she couldn't get them in the right order.

Oh my love, my darling, I've hungered for your touch . . .

She hadn't had a letter from Charlie for months.

She just wanted to put her head down and sleep.

§

Adam and Mike lay awake at night, talking. They would have sex then talk, or they would talk then have sex. They talked about everything. They were the best times they had, some of the best hours of Mike's life. The intimacy of shared bodies, shared thoughts. They played word games to induce sleep, but the words would stimulate more words and they'd stay awake. They talked about survival – which one of them would survive out in the desert or lost in the hills, which one would have survived in a concentration camp. Adam was physically tougher but he thought Mike was more stoical, therefore more resilient. 'You survived in that school,' he said. 'You survived being gay in a mining town in the 1950s,' Mike said.

'Up on the bings.' And they would wrap themselves around one another, and maybe one or both of them would be thinking of those distant times.

They both learned about survival afresh in the 1980s. Something began to seep into their lives around the middle of the decade. They heard rumours, then more detailed stories, then definite news, emanating from California, from New York, from London. They weren't in any kind of scene. They knew where in Edinburgh to go if they wanted it, but they didn't want it. Mike didn't anyway. They kept themselves, mostly, to themselves. But even so they couldn't avoid it when people started talking about 'the plague'. It was supposed to be about gay men, so they couldn't ignore it – but to begin with in Edinburgh it wasn't about gay men at all. It was about a different scene altogether, involving people they hardly saw, hardly knew existed, out in the peripheral schemes, heroin users sharing needles. That was where HIV flourished in Edinburgh at first, but eventually it touched everybody.

If Mike liked someone enough to want to have sex, then he probably wanted more than sex with him. That was how he felt. It's how he still feels. It had been his objection to Sam, the biker. It wasn't the sex that put him off, it was Sam. When he was with Adam, he didn't want sex with anyone else but him. He believed Adam felt the same.

They ran into Sam now and then, on rare occasions when they were out on the town, and each meeting reinforced for Mike the way he felt. Sam reminded him of what he didn't want. There was even something reassuring about Sam's strutting, peacock personality. Mike had grown to like him, in spite of his reservations. And – the worst kind of complacency – he felt sorry for him. It seemed to him that Sam had aged rapidly since their first encounter in Sandy Bell's. He worked out a lot, but he looked haggard, not healthy. He still tried to get off with Mike, and when he saw that he was with Adam he tried to get off with them both. To avoid difficulties they made a joke of it, until finally, one night in the Marquis, Sam conceded defeat. 'You can only take no for an answer so often,' he said, 'before your ego starts to protest. I was made for sex. It's what I'm here for. I'm not sure what you're here for, but you're missing out, darlings. I mean, if you want to play mummies and daddies, why come here?' 'It's an education,' Adam said coolly. 'No offence,' Sam said, 'but I've been trying to educate this one for years. He has to learn to separate this' – he tapped Mike's chest above his heart – 'from this.' He reached forward and briefly cradled his crotch in his hand. 'Don't you think?'

Adam looked for a moment as if he wanted to punch him and then he smiled at Mike. 'Aye, maybe,' he said. 'But no the night.'

It was just what Mike *didn't* want to do, separate love and sex. He wanted a relationship, deep and abiding, and he thought that was what he had. Adam's smile was kind but it was patronising too. Mike should have paid more attention to it.

Sam was restless, relentless. He went on crazy sex-filled holidays to Spanish islands, he went to London, he went to Amsterdam. And he got greyer and gaunter. And then they didn't see him any more. Months went by without a sight of him. Mike didn't think about it much. It wasn't as if he missed him. And then one day he did. He hadn't been in the Marquis for months, and he went in and asked someone about Sam. 'Oh, you've not heard?' And so he discovered that Sam was gone, wiped out, killed by devotion to his own desire. It was shocking and upsetting. He was the first AIDS victim Mike knew personally. He remembered him in the shadows at Greyfriars, telling him what he wanted, what *Mike* wanted, and he felt a terrible emptiness because Sam wasn't there, would never be there again.

§

There were other issues to contend with. Every month, sometimes it seemed almost every week, there was another rally or march or demo in opposition to something. Nuclear weapons, nuclear power, factory closures, privatisations – the Thatcher government had opened up so many fronts that it ran the opposition, official or otherwise, ragged. Once, Mike remembers, they marched in support of unemployment benefit, because claimants were being penalised if they didn't sign up for some useless training scheme or other. How mad that seems now, that they were cornered into defending the right not to work. But it didn't seem mad at the time. It felt necessary to resist, like M. Lucas, at all levels and every opportunity.

Whenever Mike began to flag, Adam would urge him on again. In his own way Adam was as relentless as Sam. Mike struggled to keep up. He can't now remember all the places where bold pledges were made to keep factories open, but he can remember this: every one of those struggles ended in failure. British Leyland, British Steel, British Aluminium, Carron, Caterpillar, Singer – the names became a jumbled heap of rusting iron, broken concrete and junked machinery, and it seemed as if the corpses of thousands of workers lay crushed and trapped under it all. Bathgate, Linwood, Methil, Uddingston, Dundee, Falkirk, Clydebank – even when he checks the many photos he took of men gathered round braziers, of ragged marches snaking along grey streets, of chained-up gates and derelict sites, the details of who made what where don't always come back. It was another country, and it is no more. And, for all the passion that was poured into defending it, he doesn't miss it much. All that devastation is reduced now to the chorus of a pop song by the Proclaimers – a song that, even at the time, always sounded more sorrowful than angry.

§

Then came the miners' strike. It was an explosion that had been waiting to detonate for years: the right wanted revenge for 1974, the left wanted to stop Thatcherism in its tracks. A confrontation between Margaret Thatcher and Arthur Scargill was probably always inevitable. Class warriors, dogmatists, idealogues – they could have swapped roles and people would hardly have noticed. They even had similar hairstyles.

The miners' strike kicked off in Scotland, a fact sometimes forgotten. The Coal Board wanted to close Polmaise Colliery as 'uneconomic' and the Scottish miners came out against it, and at the same time the Yorkshire miners came out over proposed closures in their area, and it spread from these two locations. There was never any question whose side Adam and Mike were on. You were either for the miners or for the Tories and that was it. And if you were for the miners then you believed in the rightness of the struggle, and that victory was possible. And if you couldn't wholly subscribe to those articles of faith, as Mike couldn't, you tried your best not to let it show. He always doubted that the miners could win, not because he doubted the miners, but because of their leader. Arthur Scargill made mistake after mistake with startling conviction. He refused to hold a national ballot, which would have legitimised the strike in the eyes of the world, he alienated not just public opinion, which was largely sympathetic to the miners, but even union opinion, and his egomania was such that he doomed the miners to defeat. The contrast with the leaders of the Scottish NUM, Mick McGahey in particular, was stark. McGahey might have been Scargill's loyal deputy throughout the strike, he might have talked dismissively of 'ballotitis' and said that the issue was not the holding of ballots but the justice of the cause, but somehow when he said these things he sounded like a man of principle, whereas when Scargill said them he sounded like a bully. McGahey was an honourable, straightforward, card-carrying Communist. He had dignity, nobility even, and he stood head and shoulders above Scargill even when he stood in his shadow. Mike would have gone on strike for Mick McGahey.

For many that kind of thinking was tantamount to betrayal. You had to take the whole package, including Scargill, and not deviate one inch from the true path. If you deviated you were suspect. Mike was suspect, and when he voiced his doubts Adam made no attempt to disguise his disappointment. 'I don't expect ye tae understand,' he said, 'but it's like following your team. Ye stick wi them through the bad times as well as the good. That's what it means, tae be a supporter.' 'Sorry,' Mike said. 'I'm not into football.' 'Even if ye were,' Adam said, 'maybe this just isna your team.' There was a cruelty in the way he said it. It hurt Mike deeply: it opened up a space between them that, naively perhaps, until then he hadn't realised existed.

There's a photograph, taken near the end of the strike not by Mike but by Angus, that was widely used at the time. The NUM leaders have emerged from some meeting or other and are standing on an open bit of ground. Scargill is as defiant as ever: he is looking at the camera and his hand is making that characteristic chopping motion to emphasise whatever he is saying. But the figure your eye is drawn to is that of Mick McGahey. He is next to Scargill yet a little apart. His stance shows how weary he is of the strike, and there is a look in his eye, which Angus has captured though it must have been there only for a moment, that seems also to show how weary he is of his president's voice. That's what the photo says to Mike. Solidarity and despair combined. An old warrior staring defeat in the face. It is a tragic image.

It is also, Mike sees, yet another example of how Angus made better pictures than he ever could.

Meanwhile, in spite of their differences and along with thousands of others, Adam and Mike marched and chanted and sang and collected for the miners. Mostly Adam was involved on his own patch, at Borlanslogie. Things were peaceful there, because the strike was solid from first to last. Not a single miner crossed the picket line during the twelve months the strike lasted, though some must have been sorely tempted to do so. But, because of that very solidarity, there was much to be done in terms of fund-raising and supporting the Borlanslogie miners and their families. The difficulty for Mike was that Adam didn't want him there. He went once but that space between them opened up immediately. Maybe, Mike wondered, Adam was worried in case they met one of his old lovers, but it wasn't about that at all. It was simply that Mike didn't fit. He embarrassed Adam. So after that one time he stayed away.

They went elsewhere together though. They went to the Ravenscraig steelworks at Motherwell to try to stop the lorries taking the coal in, and got caught up in a clash with mounted police. Adam was nearly trampled and Mike only just saved his camera from getting smashed. They heard of folk, heading to Hunterston to picket the coal depot there, being stopped at roadblocks, hauled out of their vehicles for questioning and prevented from travelling on, as if they were football casuals or drug smugglers. If you were a miner arrested on the picket line that was it, you never got your job back. Men were arrested for a gesture or a spit. And in the faces of some of the police you saw how much they hated what they were doing, how much it frightened or disturbed or dismayed them, and in the faces of others, as they slapped their truncheons into their gloved palms, you saw how much they were enjoying it. It was a violent, fearful time, and it ended in defeat and, a few years down the line, not a single deep pit left in the whole of Scotland.

§

The steelmen needed the miners needed the railwaymen. The steelmen needed the miners to supply coal to keep Ravenscraig operating. If the furnaces shut down, even temporarily, British Steel would have the excuse they wanted to close the whole plant. If

Ravenscraig closed then heavy industry in the west of Scotland would effectively be dead. The miners needed the railwaymen to carry the coal to Ravenscraig. The railwaymen needed the steelmen to keep Ravenscraig working or their jobs would go too. And the miners needed the steelmen because Ravenscraig was the sole customer for at least one of the few remaining Scottish pits.

Arthur Scargill wanted to bring Ravenscraig to a halt in order to win the strike, but the steelmen refused to be sacrificed on the altar of Arthur Scargill. So a deal was reached, brokered by the STUC, between the Scottish miners' leader Mick McGahey, the steelmen and the railwaymen. Two trainloads of coal a day from the coal depot at Hunterston to Ravenscraig – theoretically enough to keep the ovens ticking over and the fabric of the plant intact, but in practice enough to go on making steel. Okay. But British Steel weren't satisfied with the production rate, nor did they feel beholden to Scargill, McGahey or anybody else. They started adding trucks to the trains. Soon the trains had doubled in length and required two engines to pull them. The miners were furious and the railwaymen couldn't pretend they hadn't noticed. The deal was renegotiated: one train a day. Not enough, said British Steel. They switched to road haulage. They put the word out to haulage firms and non-union lorry drivers: £50 a trip for taking coal into Ravenscraig. Suddenly there were convoys of lorries laden with coal racing through Ayrshire and Lanarkshire from the coal depots to Motherwell. And there were mass pickets at the steel plant's gates, trying to stop them getting in.

Don only had two months left till he turned sixty-five and he knew the miners' strike would be won or lost regardless of his intervention but nevertheless he went back to Wullie Byres.

'What's gaun on, Wullie?'

'What dae ye mean?'

'Ye ken fine. Ye've pulled half your lorries aff the usual jobs and they're aw cairrying coal intae Ravenscraig.'

'So ye ken fine yersel. What are ye asking me for?'

'Ye're making money hand over fist and ye're helping tae break the strike.'

'What dae I care aboot the strike? It's a job.'

'What I care aboot is it's scab work.'

Wullie raised himself off his chair and leaned on his knuckles across the desk.

'Dinna you fling that socialist shite at me, Don Lennie. The miners' strike is nane o my concern. If they want tae die in the trenches for that arsehole Scargill that's their business. My business is tae take a contract when it's offered and deliver on it. Dae ye think I'm gaun tae leave it tae Yuill and Dodds tae make a killing? The money's too good no tae take. And, by the way, it's keeping the likes o yersel in a job. So dinna gie me ony mair shite aboot scabs.'

'Ye're paying the drivers bonuses for gaun in there.'

'Aye, and what for no? It's dangerous work. Ye seen it on the telly? If that mob gets a haud o them they'll be torn limb frae limb.'

'The lorries are getting damaged. These extra guys ye're hiring think they're Starsky and Hutch. They don't gie a damn aboot onything forbye the cash they get in their pockets.'

'Och, Don, come doon aff your soapbox. Was there ever onything else *worth* giein a damn aboot? Oh, and by the way, I can see where this is heading. Ye'll no service ony vehicles that are being used tae cairry coal, is that it? Ye'll no repair a lorry that's been driven by a scab? Ach, well, it's your choice. Ye've been here a lang time, Don, ye're weeks awa frae your pension and I wouldna like tae see the back o ye afore ye're ready tae go, but listen hard tae me. If ye start ony o that secondary action nonsense ye'll be oot, and sae will onybody else that joins in wi it. That's no an idle threat and this time I'd hae the law on my side and you wouldna hae a leg tae stand on.' He paused for a moment, breathing fiercely, and then his big ugly face split into a grin. 'Or even a soapbox. Noo fuck off, will ye. I dinna like playing the heidmaister tae a man o your years.'

Don had always thought a principle was a solid rock standing against the tides of compromise and storms of greed. To his dismay, he found principle crumbling like sand, and that half the men in the shop didn't give a toss about it. 'Aye, it's aw very weel saying support the miners, but what aboot supporting the steelworkers?' And even the ones that were sympathetic sighed and said, 'What can ye dae?' And what about himself? The best he could do without the support of the other men was to go slow on the tools, take longer to fit a new part or sign off a job, but it wasn't heroic, it wasn't noble, and it went against another principle – his belief in doing a sound job.

Basically, he was pissing in the wind. He felt old, ashamed. God knows what he was going to do when he retired – there was only so much gardening a man *could* do – but as the day loomed, for the first time he began to look forward to it.

He'd always had a fancy to read the classics. Dickens and such-like. Maybe he'd read his way through Charles Dickens.

§

David Eddelstane woke in the dark and the low rumble was there at once. He lay still and listened, trying to identify its source. Refrigerator, dishwasher, plumbing? No. Digestive system at work? No. Melissa's snoring? No. Melissa didn't snore, she breathed like a princess. Gossamer breaths. She slept deep and dreamed sweet dreams. So did the children. Not like him. When had he last had a decent night's sleep? And he remembered about the rumble, how there wasn't any point in trying to locate it. It was a noise that woke him most nights but it wasn't really a noise at all.

Very gently he slid out of bed, found his slippers and put on his dressing gown. At the door he paused. There was a night-light on the landing and in its dim glow he looked back to see Melissa's curled shape beneath the covers. If she'd heard him get up she wasn't acknowledging it. He felt an urgent need to protect her from everything. He creaked softly along the passage and checked in each of the children's bedrooms. Both out for the count, as sound as their mother. Jessica, nearly twelve, about to leave childhood behind, lay with one arm flung out as if she were hailing a taxi. Daniel, approaching nine but small for his years, had his hands crossed on his chest, a mouse at prayer. Another surge of love went through David. He went downstairs to the kitchen, boiled the kettle, made himself a mug of weak tea. The oven clock said 03:15. He padded along to the study and sat at his desk, switched on the green-shaded lamp and turned it away so it shed only a little, calming light on the desk. There was a box of Kleenex. There was also a small pile of correspondence from constituents, a much larger one of briefing papers and policy documents from party HQ and God knows what else but he hadn't come here to deal with any of that. He actually enjoyed the paperwork; he liked being an MP; he felt a real pride in the role. But he was here now because it was the middle of the night and he could be alone and, relatively speaking, at peace.

He'd read somewhere that lots of people heard background noise – a rumble or a distant whine – and that there were many weird and wonderful theories about what it was they were hearing. All bollocks, as far as he was concerned. If he sat here long enough the rumble would diminish and, if he did what he needed to do, it would stop altogether. He knew what *his* background noise was. It wasn't external at all. It was inside his head and it was the sound of existential panic. Some had black dogs, some had nightmares; David Eddelstane MP had a low, constant rumble.

The nearest real sound he could liken it to was the drone his father, Sir Malcolm Eddelstane, made for two days on his deathbed, slipping in and out of consciousness. As if he were trying to laugh, or trying not to, as what was left of his brain blundered off into the dark after seventy-three years of self-indulgence, most of them drink-sodden.

If Lady Patricia made a noise when she followed her husband into the great unknown two years later, nobody knew what it was. She died at the breakfast table not long after the first slice of toast and the second cup of coffee. Massive stroke. Only sixty-five. Mrs Thomson's daughter, who'd 'inherited' the job of cleaning Ochiltree House from her mother, found her. David imagined his mother might have said, 'Oh, hell's bells!' or 'Not now, for God's sake!' before putting down her cup and heading off with whoever'd come to get her. He wondered if it had been his father.

The low sound of panic. He heard it fading a little. The silence that grew to replace it was wonderful.

Freddy, now living in New York, where he worked, if that was the word, in publishing, had come home for both funerals, naturally. Lucy hadn't, naturally. But even Freddy had seemed supremely indifferent to the passing of his parents. For himself, David had been surprised – and still was, at unexpected moments – at how upset he was to lose them. They had been such big, spoiled children. He just wished he could have understood them better, not been so intimidated by their rosy-cheeked loudness. Too late now, though. His father would tell him to stop snivelling. His mother wouldn't be far behind.

He suffered from the panicky sense of always being trapped, pulled between opposing desires, contrary forces. The desire to please others, the desire to please himself. The forces of moderation and restraint, the forces of radical action. Politically this division manifested itself simultaneously in, on the one hand, appreciation and awe for the dynamic, deadwood-slashing verve of Mrs Thatcher and her most devoted disciples, such as the Member for Stirling, Michael Forsyth; and, on the other hand, a strong preference for the company of Tories of the old school, the lawyers and landed gentry he understood. Men like his father-in-law, Roderick Braco, from whom he'd 'inherited' Glenallan and West Mills at the '79 election. They were all, without question, wherever they were on the dry–wet spectrum, immensely grateful to their leader; they admired her to a man for her conviction, and perhaps not only in David's case there was the added frisson of sexual fear and desire; and to the question that she now no longer needed to articulate – 'Is he one of us?' – they all responded, self-referentially, with enthusiastic affirmatives. But sometimes, in a secluded corner, one or other of the old school would, tentatively, advance the view that yes, well, that might be the case, but . . . 'She's not really one of *us*, is she?'

Of course David agreed with the dismantling of the excesses of the Welfare State. Of course he wanted to see an end to the dependency culture, especially in Scotland where it was so deep-rooted. He favoured the reining in of the trade unions, the control of irresponsible local authorities, the outsourcing of services to private contractors, the privatising of the utilities, the reduction of income tax, the sale of council houses, the renewal of the independent nuclear deterrent. Of course he supported these policies, and voted for and defended them whenever and wherever he was called upon to do so. As you unfettered capital, and made it easier and more profitable for people to do business, capital would grow and businesses flourish. This was obvious and he himself was proof of it. He had extensive property portfolios in London and Edinburgh, and shares in various companies collecting refuse, repairing roads, supplying electricity and providing care for the elderly. These were only the start. He was a rich man. He had already been rich when he and Melissa moved into her parents' Glenallan home and the Bracos retired to one of David's finest properties in the heart of Edinburgh's

New Town. He had been made richer by the sale, after Lady Patricia's demise, of Ochiltree House. With its idyllic setting and its two acres of ground (complete with planning permission for a sixteen-house 'executive-style' development with the main house to be renovated and divided into four 'luxury apartments') it had been very desirable indeed, and had realised a handsome sum – just as well, as there had been precious little hard cash in the parental coffers. Freddy had received half the proceeds and David the other half, Lucy still being a non-person, or non-Eddelstane at least, when it came to legacies. They had talked about a 'goodwill gesture' towards their sister but Freddy hadn't seen any reason for one, and when David had said he'd helped her out in the past and would do so again if required, Freddy had said that was his choice, but nothing to do with him. 'You won't get any goodwill back,' he'd warned, but David already knew that.

On paper and in property, if not in actual cash, David had long since made that first million Q, his old mentor when he'd first gone to London in the 1960s, had dreamed of. Neither he nor his family were ever going to starve. And in time jobs and enterprise and prosperity would trickle down to the bottommost layers of society. Yet despite all this – the rolling back of socialism at home, the crumbling of Soviet power abroad, his own personal success – he had qualms. He had, and not just in the middle of the night, panics.

He wondered what they had unleashed. He had thought it would be beautiful but sometimes it wasn't, it was ugly. He disliked the appearance of Qs everywhere, brash and callous and uncaring of anyone beyond their own circle. Was this snobbery on his part? Certainly. The Qs were the human expression of precisely the trickle-down effect he wanted to see happen. So what was his objection? Perhaps it was a deep-seated mistrust of the excess, the flaunting of wealth, the fact that more and more people seemed to be able to make vast amounts of money out of nothing. He was a part of it but nervous of what might flow from it. Where did it all come from? Yes, of course, at one level he knew the answer, he knew how he himself had made his fortune. But while all this was going on the country appeared to have given up making *things*, real, hard *things*. And the communities that had made things had been flattened. Had it really been necessary to lay Teesside and South Wales and Lanarkshire so utterly to waste? Was it necessary to humiliate and destroy the miners quite so completely? Wouldn't that all be visited upon the nation somewhere down the line? What if it all went hideously wrong? What if Great Britain plc collapsed?

He wished somehow – impossible, he knew, but still he wished – things could be as they had been. Settled rural communities. Cities and industrial areas doing their bit, and places like Glenallan able to go on quietly being themselves. But the Thatcherite revolution – and he applauded it, he really did – had ended the idea of quiet continuity.

He thought of the oil pumping ashore north of Aberdeen. Astonishing feats of engineering had been performed to extract oil and gas from the depths of the sea. Amazing ingenuity combined with hard sweat and great braveness had achieved a daily production of two and a half million barrels of North Sea oil. Without that the public finances would be a disaster. Nobody mentioned this fact. The SNP whined about how prosperous an independent, oil-rich Scotland could be, and the other parties rubbished their claims, partly because they didn't dare admit that without the oil revenues the whole of the UK would be bankrupt. *Don't mention the oil!* It was the great unspeakable of the age.

In 1983 his vote had gone up slightly on the previous election. Given the landslide victory nationwide, he should have won by ten thousand. In fact his majority was barely half that. On such a showing his fellow Conservative MPs in England would be looking around for a safer seat. But Glenallan and West Mills was about as safe as it got in Scotland. Not safe at all.

His left hand clutched the mug of tea. His right hand clutched his penis through his pyjamas. Like a nervous wee boy. This was the thing, then: he didn't feel safe any more.

There was no *reason* for his panic. There'd be another election in a year or eighteen months and there was absolutely no *reason* to suppose Maggie wouldn't romp home again. Maybe there would be some casualties. Maybe he'd be one of them but he didn't think so. Glenallan couldn't go any other colour than blue, surely, and West Mills was getting nicely divvied up between the socialists and the Nats so he should be all right. Throw in a scattering of Liberal supporters and all he needed was about 35 per cent of the vote. He remembered his father worrying about this kind of thing, and thinking Roderick would come a cropper. Well, that was more than twenty years ago and here *he* still was. There was no reason to panic.

Nevertheless, he did.

What Sir Malcolm used to refer to as 'the staff of life' was making a menacing tent of his pyjamas. He closed his eyes. He knew where this was leading.

The other great unspeakable. What he did, imaginatively, when he was alone. What he did for real in London when he had the opportunity. Not Edinburgh. There were places in Edinburgh, he knew there were, but it was too risky. It was a village. Too easy to be recognised. London was big enough to be, relatively speaking, safe. But how safe was safe?

Nothing was safe. That was part of the excitement. The risk. The absolute fucking insanity of going to see her. She Who Must Be Obeyed.

In Edinburgh it would be even more insane. Perhaps even more exciting?

He closed his eyes. His prick was hot in his hand. He leaned forward, grabbed at the box of tissues. He had to do this or he wouldn't sleep again. He had to do this or he'd go back *there* again. He had to do this or he'd betray Melissa, the kids. Jesus Christ. Damned if he betrayed them, damned if he didn't. He loved them, he loved them, so why did he have this bastard thing lurking inside him, wanting to destroy him, destroy them? Why?

He'd go back anyway.

He imagined her hand, somebody's hand, making him wait, making him get down on his knees, making him wait, making him, letting him, making him letting him kiss

her

cruel

high

heeled

SHOES!

It came spurting out of him like a confession extracted by torture. He captured and sealed it in a wodge of tissues. In the aftermath he became aware of the sudden grunt merging into a long loud groan that he made as he came. He listened for a few seconds, but there was no movement upstairs. There never was.

He pushed back in the leather chair, stretched his legs, allowed his pulse to slow. Yes! Rumblelessness. Pure, blissful silence. Over and out. For the time being.

§

She'd never quite conquered her aversion to showers, especially ones with curtains rather than doors. Seeing *Psycho* all those years ago really had made an impression on her. There was no shower at home, although Don sometimes muttered about putting one in over the bath. In the Cotters' house there were three, all with doors, which she had to step inside to clean. Somehow this was fine with her clothes on, or without the room getting steamed up. There was the other important difference that the Cotters' house was bright and happy, completely devoid of the brooding menace of the Bates Motel.

In fact, the Cotters' own bathroom was so luxurious and comfortable, and the shower in it – a spacious chrome-and-glass rectangular cabinet – so much part of the luxury, that sometimes when she cleaned it she imagined standing naked in it, the flow of hot water cleansing her body. In the same way, she often imagined being Mrs Elaine Cotter, speaking like her, dressing like her, having her grace and confidence. She didn't want to *be* her, but she did wonder what it would be *like*.

The Cotters were on holiday in France for a fortnight. It was July, and Elaine had given her a key and asked her to pop in once a week to water the house plants and also the tubs outside if it was dry. Liz had been coming in every second day. Don, now retired, said, 'What are ye needing tae go up there so often for? There canna be that much tae dae.' In fact there was nothing. One reason was to get away from Don, whom she wasn't yet used to having around the house all day. Another was because she didn't think she'd be there much longer, and she wanted to make the most of it.

Don was reading *Great Expectations*. She'd read it years ago, when she was a lassie, and when he said, 'Dae ye mind this bit, Liz?', and then read a passage to her, as excited as a boy, she remembered, and her heart seemed to fill her chest. She would listen and smile, and he would smile back, and she would quickly have to go out of the room for something, before the tears came.

In the Cotters' drawing room she sat at the piano and pressed keys and wished she could play. She stretched out on the three-seater sofa and dozed for half an hour, then woke, refreshed but guilty, and spent an hour needlessly dusting immaculate surfaces. She listened to the silence. She crunched round the house on the gravel paths and watered the plants. The weight of the watering can tired her again. As she watched the light catching the threads of water arcing from the rose, she thought of the shower inside, upstairs. Why not? No one would ever know.

From the linen cupboard she selected one of the enormous white fluffy towels that she'd always wanted to wrap herself in. She went into the bathroom and turned on the shower, adjusting the temperature so it was hot enough. It was a warm day but she wanted a hot shower. Then she went back to the Cotters' bedroom and undressed, calm in the utter silence, folding her clothes and placing them on the upholstered chair where Elaine sometimes left her own clothes. She walked over to the wardrobe with the full-length mirror and looked at herself: the veins on her legs, the slight sag of her backside, the doughy greyness of her skin. She lifted her arms and felt in the hollows, looked with suspicion at her breasts and felt for the lump in the right one. A ripple of nausea went through her. No more putting it off. Then she turned and caught herself at another angle and in spite of everything she wasn't look-ing bad for sixty-two. Elaine, though only a few years younger, no doubt still looked wonderful in the nude. But this wasn't about Elaine Cotter, it was about Liz Lennie, about to conquer her fear of showers.

She had a sudden, brief vision of Janet Leigh, the knife stabbing into her flesh. She dismissed it – history, ancient history – and went barefoot, as if on grass, across the carpet and into the bathroom. She laid the towel on the edge of the bath. The tiled floor was cool. She slid open the shower doors. Nothing could be as fearful as what she would have to deal with later. She stepped in and pulled the door to behind her. The gushing water welcomed her. She went in under, all of her, hair and everything, and gasped at the hot force of it. And then she let it, let it, let it run all over her.

Later she would sit on the cork seat of the stool, wrapped in the white softness of the towel, like a child waiting to be rubbed dry. Later she would find a hairbrush and dryer and sit at Elaine's dressing table and blow her hair dry. Later she would dress again, go downstairs and put the towel in the washing machine. Later she would go home and talk to Don, and no doubt she would cry, and maybe he would too.

But for now she was safe in the shower, letting the water run all over her for ever.

§

From the kitchen window, as she dried the coffee mugs, she watched Don down on his hunkers, pulling a few weeds. He was looking great, tanned and fit and handsome. Retirement wasn't doing him any harm. He read the paper a lot, had finished *Great Expectations* and returned it to the library and now was deep in *David Copperfield*. He kept reading out what Mr Micawber had to say about things. The perpetual optimist. And there was always the garden. Twice he'd even cooked the tea. He hadn't made a bad job of it either. She'd not been hungry but she'd eaten what she could, so as not to disappoint him.

He looked up and gave her a wave. She waved back. He'd only gone out twenty minutes ago. They were shyly, slowly, getting to know each other again. But how much time would they have? And was this why she still hadn't managed to tell him that she was ill? Because she didn't want to have the answer to that question?

He came back in. 'It's a braw day. Dae ye fancy gaun for a wee walk?'

She could actually have done with a sleep but she thought, again, that she didn't want to disappoint him, and he was right, it was a beautiful day. 'Aye, all right. Where will we go?'

'I thought we could go tae the ferm,' he said. 'We've no been oot there for years.'

So they set off for Hackston's Farm, the old familiar route, and as they went they reminisced, talking of Liz's parents and what it had been like when they were first married and staying out there with them. The road out of the village had a few new houses on it now, built in the 1970s, they weren't bonnie but they had wonderful views over the open countryside.

Liz said, 'Probably one day there'll be hooses aw the way tae the ferm.'

'That'd be a shame,' Don said.

'D'ye think we should buy oor hoose?' she said.

'If ye'd asked me that five years ago I'd have said no,' he said, 'but noo I'm no sae sure. Maybe we should look intae it.'

'Aye,' Liz said, 'maybe we should.'

Because everything was changing. He hated the great sell-offs of publicly owned companies and utilities that the Tories were pushing through. BP, British Aerospace, Cable & Wireless, the National Freight Corporation (he remembered how he'd half-hoped Byres Brothers could have been included in it when, as British Road Services, it had been created as a nationalised business after the war), Jaguar, British Telecom. The list stretched out into the future. The Gas Board, British Airways and British Steel would be next. For several years now people like themselves had had the right to buy their council houses. Selling off public housing went against all his principles but where were principles nowadays? They'd been shredded. He and Liz had built up some savings and it wasn't so much a question of could they afford to buy the house as could they afford not to? With a deposit and the discount it wouldn't cost them any more than paying the rent.

They'd gone about a mile. The road narrowed to a single lane between scrappy hawthorn hedges. Wee birds darted in and out of the hedges with unconscious urgency, and in the fields on either side fat, silky cows grazed. They paused at a gate to watch them, and Liz recalled helping her father bring the herd in for milking, but these weren't dairy cows, these were stirks being fattened up for slaughter. They hadn't milked cows at Hackston's for twenty years.

'Will we go on?' Don asked, and she said, 'Aye,' and then as she stood away from leaning on the gate an excruciating pain shot up her spine and she cried out with the suddenness of it. She clutched at Don and he was there, his arm was there, strong as anything but there was horror in his face.

'Liz, Liz, what is it?'

She felt the sweat on her face and the tears starting from her eyes and she knew all the colour must have gone from her.

'I dinna ken,' she said. 'I'll be aw right in a minute.'

'Take your time,' he said, and she did, shallow-breathing till the pain began to ebb away. It did but it left her exhausted.

'Can ye walk?' he said.

'Aye, but no yet. I think I'll need tae go hame. You go on if ye want tae.'

'Tae hell wi that. Just take it easy. We'll get ye hame.'

They walked with infinite slowness back to the village, pausing when she felt the tear-inducing pain coming on again. And she knew that this was it, the beginning of a new phase. She saw him at these moments, his face full of kindness and concern where for so long she'd looked and not found anything, or not even looked, and she felt his anxious, muscular support and this too made her want to cry. She thought what a bloody mess, what a bloody stupid mess we make of things, and then she determined not to think like that, and at last they reached the street and then their house. She lay down on the sofa and he took off her shoes for her and arranged the cushions and she dozed for a few minutes, hearing his voice distant on the phone. Then he was beside her, bringing her a cup of tea. He sat on the floor against the sofa and took her hand.

'I've called the surgery,' he said. 'I've made an appointment for this efternoon. Half-five.'

'God, Don, how did ye manage that?'

'I tellt her if she didna find a space for ye I'd bring ye onywey and the deputy editor of the *Drumkirk Observer* would be wi us tae. For a useless bugger Bulldog still has his uses sometimes.'

She smiled briefly. 'Thanks,' she said. Then: 'I'm sorry.'

'What hae you tae be sorry for?'

'I'm no weel. I should hae tellt ye months ago.'

'That disna maitter,' he said. 'The main thing is tae find oot whit it is and get it sorted.'

'Aye,' she said. 'I'm no sure that it can be.'

'Dinna say that,' he said, a new fear in his voice. 'For God's sake, Liz.'

She sipped the tea but it was too hot and he took it from her. She closed her eyes again and drifted off and when she woke a few minutes later he was gone.

'Don?'

A bulky haze moved towards her, frightening her for a moment till it came into focus and she saw it was Don.

'I'm here,' he said. 'I was just in the kitchen. What is it?'

'Dae I look terrible?'

'Ye dinna look great.'

'I'm feart.'

'I'm feart tae.'

'I'm gonnae hae a sleep.'

'Go ahead. I'll be here.'

'If ye've things tae dae ootside . . .'

'I'll be here,' he said. 'I've my book tae read. You go tae sleep. I'll be here when ye wake up. Then we'll get a taxi tae the doctor's.'

§

The papers, billboards, the television were full of sleazy, side-of-the-mouth advertisements in the run-up to privatising the Gas Board: IF YOU SEE SID, TELL HIM. Building a shareholding democracy, they were calling it. Don called it theft on an epic scale. Sid was anonymous, a punter about to miss one of the bargains of the century. *Pssst! Spread the word.* To Don, Sid was some English wide boy into dodgy wheeling and dealing. He refused even to contemplate buying shares in privatised utilities. They belonged to him already. Why would he pay to own a bit of what was already his? He'd baulked at getting the house on the cheap too. There was a principle which he could not betray. Thrawn and stupid it was, no doubt, but he couldn't help himself. Besides, he had other things on his mind. His wife of forty years was dying.

The gas sale went ahead without him. British Gas plc was born. Don read *Barnaby Rudge, A Tale of Two Cities, Oliver Twist* and *Bleak House*. He read during the day when Liz was sleeping, he read aloud to her in the evening, he read through the night when sleep would not come to him. He silently thanked Dickens for the size and number of books he had written.

Liz said, 'Don, we need tae talk.'

'I ken.'

'We need tae say aw the things we've no said for years.'

He nodded. Something like an ocean was welling up inside him.

'And I need tae see Charlie.'

'Right,' he said.

§

The angst grew even worse in the run-up to the '87 General Election. The electorate, egged on by pro-devolution pressure groups and mischievous elements in the media, had become frighteningly sophisticated at tactical voting. The four main parties fielded candidates in every Scottish seat, and in most Conservative seats it was fairly easy to identify the opposition party with the best chance of beating the incumbent. In Glenallan and West Mills it was Labour. In the months before the General Election various voices, local and national, called for Nationalist and Liberal voters to switch to Labour in order to eject him, David Eddelstane MP, from Westminster. The three parties declined to endorse tactical voting, at least in public, but despite that, and the fact that the same thing was happening to his colleagues, David felt as if he were being personally picked on.

In the final week of campaigning things looked extremely grim. Canvassing returns showed that West Mills was solidly Labour and, worse, that the rural vote was soft, likely to switch at the last moment or not come out at all. It was as if people were ashamed of voting Tory, as if they'd rather keep their grubby little habit in the closet. David knew how they felt, though obviously he couldn't explain why. He, Melissa, his agent and numerous party workers spent much of election day organising lifts to and from the polling places, wheeling the aged, the sick and the demented in to make their mark. They weren't quite holding the pencils for the old dears but they would have done if it had been permitted. By midnight it was clear that while Margaret was heading for another stunning victory UK-wide, the Scottish situation was far from healthy. MPs in once-watertight constituencies from Aberdeen to Bearsden were being dumped by the voters. As news of their defeats trickled in, David didn't know whether he should envy or console them. There would be safety, wouldn't there, in losing? But then he remembered how much he liked Westminster, being part of the great tradition. And having reasons to be in London often, on his own. Did he really want to lose all that?

Eventually his own declaration was made at half past three, after fears that there might have to be a recount. He had squeaked in by 497 votes. Big hugs from Melissa and everybody in the team. Immense relief, which melted almost at once. He was one of only a handful of Conservative MPs left in Scotland. There had been twenty-one the day before. Now, with some results not yet declared, it was not even certain they would make double figures. Four government ministers were out. The media had been touting this as the 'Doomsday Scenario' – a massive Tory win south of the Border, a massive defeat north of it, with consequential constitutional crisis – and even as he made a brief acceptance speech a gang of angry Nats at the back of the hall started a chant: 'No mandate! No poll tax! No mandate! No poll tax!' He found himself stuttering and mumbling, trying not to antagonise them. He wasn't cut out for this game. He probably never had been. So what on earth was he doing in it?

In the ensuing months the threatened constitutional crisis didn't occur, although things began to get very unpleasant as the community charge – a policy David happened to believe was right in principle, even if it was being applied rather insensitively – was rolled out. Everywhere he went he encountered protest and hatred. He blocked the panic out, but it came back in the dark hours of night worse than ever, its rumble sounding now like the engine of a docking ferry, and his own despairing masturbation was less and less successful in making it disappear. He was permanently tired, permanently unable to get a good sleep. Melissa said she was worried about him. *She* was worried about him? 'We haven't made love for months, darling.' 'I know, I know. I'm sorry.' Actually it was getting on for a year. They were apart so much, and when he was home they often went to bed at different times. Even when they went together he couldn't summon up the energy for sex, regardless of whether he'd expended it by himself the night before. He apologised. He blamed stress, too much to drink, mind on next week's debates – anything, really. The fact was, he loved her but was completely uninterested in her sexually. If he'd thought it would make a difference he'd have asked her to spice things up. Would she mind doing this, letting him do that?

But there was no point. It wasn't her he wanted. It was someone else, someone anonymous and all-knowing.

§

Saleem said, 'I'm very sorry to hear that your wife has passed away, Don. Very sorry indeed.'

'Thanks, Saleem,' Don said.

He was in for milk and his paper, same as always except that he'd missed a day. This was Tuesday. Liz had died on Sunday. And the word was out. Betty Mair would have told Saleem and it would have been round the whole village in minutes. Not that it was unexpected, with Liz having been so ill.

Milk and a paper. The wee things didn't stop. In fact they were what kept you going.

Saleem asked, 'When is the funeral?'

'Next week. Monday morning at the crem in Drumkirk.'

'And what time?'

'Eleven o'clock.'

'I don't know if I can be there.'

'Ye'd be very welcome.'

'It depends if I can get Nasreen to look after the shop.'

'I understand,' Don said. He was standing with his paper under his arm, a finger hooked through the handle of the plastic milk carton. 'I hardly ever see her these days,' he said.

'I am an abandoned man.' Saleem smiled. 'First my children leave me, then my wife. She prefers being a granny,' he said. 'You know our daughter has a wee lassie herself?'

'Aye, ye told me that.'

'Nasreen can't stay away. She's always going to Glasgow to be a babysitter. She goes for two days and stays for a week. She says this is so our daughter can go to work. She's back part-time, you know. She's a biochemist.'

'Aye, I ken,' Don said. Saleem was extremely proud of his daughter and her achievements – almost more so than he was of his son, who was an accountant.

'But actually, I know this is not the real reason why Nasreen goes,' Saleem said. 'The real reason is, she's tired of being a bloody shop-keeper. So she goes babysitting instead.'

'And you're left here.'

'That's right. Abandoned. The last of the Khan bloody shopkeep-ers. Somebody has to do it, though.'

Don couldn't think of a time when he'd heard Saleem say 'shop-keeper' without sticking 'bloody' in front of it.

'Ach, weel,' he said, 'I'd better get up the road.'

'Right then, Don,' Saleem said. 'You know what?' he added.

'What?'

'If Nasreen isn't here, I'll close the bloody shop. I would like to pay my respects to you, to your wife. Liz. I liked her very much.'

'Me tae,' Don said, and laughed, and Saleem smiled. 'We had oor ups and doons, but we came through them maistly. We were fine at the end.'

'That is important,' Saleem said. 'After someone has gone, you cannot say sorry.'

'We said sorry,' Don said.

§

On a clear, cold January morning David met Lucy, for the first time in over a year. They'd had very little contact since he was first elected. This was hardly surprising: she had been in Glasgow for most of those years, and she'd also made it clear that his parlia-mentary career had pretty much wiped out any residual sisterly affection she might harbour for him. But she still accepted cash donations from him. In fact, she took cheques these days, which meant she'd compromised with capitalism enough to open a bank account.

He'd lost track of which movement, party or pressure group she was in. Frankly, he didn't care any more, and when she got in touch, in a note sent to his parliamentary office saying she required an urgent meeting about something important, he was irritated. Typ-ical Lucy. It would doubtless turn out to be supremely unimport-ant. One thing he detested about the left in general was its self-righteous arrogance. The farther left, the more bloody arro-gant. It was a fact of life, he had come to recognise, that people who went on and on about humanity and democracy and rights for all and how putridly evil and nasty the establishment was, tended to be the most vicious, dictatorial, backbiting, cynical, self-seeking, prejudiced, petty bastards around; whereas your average old-school Tory – the kind of person supposedly intent on grinding the faces of the poor – was generally polite, generous, warm-hearted, affable and kind. Of course, the lefties would say that your average old-school Tory was well-heeled enough to be able to afford the luxuries of affability and kindness, so was still scum. You couldn't win.

He wasn't, therefore, in the best of moods when he met Lucy, for old times' sake, in the café off the Portobello Road. Only it wasn't the same café, it had been replaced by a cheerful Mediterranean-coloured tapas-coffee-wine bar, which lightened David's heart a little, especially when he saw how much Lucy hated it. She kept sniffing and looking around nervously as if she were transgressing some rule of comradely misery just by being there. She was wearing a long black woollen coat, not cheap by the look of it, and a black beret pushed back on her head. He noticed grey flecks in her hair, deep tracks between her eyebrows. For the first time he was struck by how much she resembled their mother.

It was half past ten. They were almost the only customers. She didn't know what she wanted to eat or drink, so he ordered himself a cappuccino and pecan pastry, and she said, 'Oh, I'll just have the same, then.'

'How are you?' he asked.

'All right, I suppose.'

There was a silence. He thought, is she refusing to ask how *I* am or does it just not occur to her?

He tried again. 'So, where are you these days?'

'What do you mean?'

'It's a simple enough question, isn't it? Where are you? Physically, not ideologically. Glasgow? Here? Somewhere else?'

'Here,' she said. 'And Edinburgh sometimes.'

'Really?' He was quite often in Edinburgh. He'd rather it was a Lucy-free zone.

'I've got a friend there I can crash with. I think I may move in with her.'

'Oh. So you've left Glasgow?'

'Glasgow's finished. You shits have destroyed it.'

'I don't think so,' he said. 'There's to be a garden festival there this year. That's millions of pounds' worth of public and private investment. Then it'll be European City of Culture in 1990. Glasgow's being reborn.'

'You've got to be kidding,' she said. 'Flower beds instead of shipyards? Fucking opera? City of unemployment and poverty more like.'

'You're not a philistine, Lucy,' he said, flashing her a patronising smile because he felt like winding her up, 'however much you try to be one. The only thing that'll destroy Glasgow will be if it tries to live in the past. Anyway, if that's how you feel, shouldn't you be showing some solidarity? How come you've left the sinking ship? If it is sinking, which I don't accept.'

'I'm not even going to debate it with you, asshole,' she said. He noted the Americanism, in amongst her unconvincing effort to sound working class, and was tempted to mock her for it, but did not. He thought, so maybe I'm screwed up, and probably Freddy is in some way I don't know about, but surely neither of us are even a tenth as screwed up as Lucy.

She'd eaten half of her pastry and pushed the plate with the other half away, a kind of feeble protest. She seemed very deflated and in the past this would have aroused his sympathy, but now he wondered, without much hope or patience, if she could finally be coming to her senses.

'So what do you want to talk about?'

She threw him an accusatory glance. '*I* don't know.'

'For God's sake, Lucy. You said you had something important to discuss. You wrote me a letter to that effect.'

'Okay, okay. But I'm your sister too, aren't I? Can't I just want to see you?'

'Yes, but you never do. Just want to *see* me. You only get in touch when you want something. What is it this time? Money, I presume.'

'I think I'm due a bit, don't you?'

'What's it for? I'm not giving to any more lousy causes.'

'You don't have to. It's for me. I've decided to buy somewhere to live.'

'I thought you said you were moving in with a friend in Edinburgh?'

'I said I'm thinking about it. I've got to have a roof over my head, haven't I? But if I'm going to buy a place I need a deposit, and then enough to pay the mortgage.'

This was amazing. She really seemed serious.

'That's quite a change,' he said. 'I thought you were against private property.'

'Are you going to chuck everything back in my face today, is that it?'

'No, Lucy. I'm pleased, very pleased. How much do you want?'

She rolled her head, looked at the ceiling, then back at him. 'A hundred thousand.'

'What?'

'A hundred thousand pounds.'

'You're kidding.'

But she wasn't, any more than he had been about Glasgow's renaissance. She said, 'It's not as if you don't have it. You and Freddy cleaned up between you when the dinosaurs died. Don't think I don't know how much you sold Ochiltree House for. And there was our grandmother's money before that. I've never seen a penny of any of it. I mean, actually, if you divide it by the number of years since I left home I'm hardly asking for anything. Five thousand a year or something. I just want it in a lump sum, that's all.'

'You walked out. You wanted nothing to do with our parents. You never spoke to either of them again. I've been giving you money for nearly twenty years – not much, I know, especially to begin with, but not chicken feed either, if you add it all up. Which I don't do, by the way. I don't keep a tally. And now you want me to write you a cheque for a hundred thousand quid just because you've woken up to the fact that the world isn't ever going to be a communist veggy-paradise or whatever the hell it is you believe in these days. Well, sorry, Lucy, I may be a mug but I'm not that bloody stupid.'

He was quite pleased at how rapidly his anger had boiled over. After all these years of indulging her – because that's what it was, pure bloody indulgence – he'd finally had enough.

'You owe me it,' she said.

'I owe you nothing. Let me underline that, Lucy. I owe you nothing. The world owes you nothing.' He dropped his voice, because a woman sitting a couple of tables away had glanced up from her glossy magazine, but speaking quietly only seemed to add intensity to his words. 'For years now you've sponged off me, and I've let you because I felt sorry for you.'

'Listen, don't think –'

'No, *you* listen. You've come to me with this cause or that cause in your pocket, and despised me for my politics while expecting me to subsidise yours in whatever pathetic form they take. You know why I've done it? Because I care about you.'

'You don't care about me.'

'Yes, I do. Why else would I have gone on handing you cash? I did it so you could feed yourself and pay your debts, and if that meant you carried on in some disastrous relationship with whoever happened to be your ideological flavour of the month, Sharky the beagle liberator or Leon the black brother or whoever, well, that was too bad. My God, I even paid you through your lesbian phase.'

'Those aren't real names,' she said, like a child catching another child out.

'I know that, Lucy. That's the point I'm making. Have you ever picked a partner because you actually liked them and not just their politics? As a real person?'

For a moment she looked so hurt he felt guilty. Then she came back at him.

'So what are you saying? That's what you did, is it? Melissa fucking Braco wasn't the perfect political choice for you?'

The woman two tables away cleared her throat disapprovingly.

'I expect that's how it looks from where you are. But Melissa and I happen to love each other.'

'Well, lucky you. How convenient. She ticks all your boxes, you tick hers. That's all your kind of love is.'

'And what's your kind of love?'

'It's precisely the opposite. It's about difficult choices. It's about commitment.'

He felt completely in control. 'We'll have been married fifteen years this September. That's commitment. We have two children we would do anything for. That's commitment. They have an aunt they've never met, but that's another story. Fifteen years, Lucy. Most of your relationships are in trouble after fifteen days.'

'That's not true. Anyway, the only reason you're so smug is

because you've never had to struggle. You don't know what the word means.'

He'd had enough. He drained the cold last inch of his cappuccino. '*You* never had to struggle, Lucy. You never *had* to struggle. You *decided* to struggle. But that doesn't make it heroic or admirable. I can admire single mothers in sink estates trying to bring their children up to be decent human beings. I find people scraping a living from rubbish tips in Mexico City heroic. But I just find your kind of struggling infantile and useless.'

'Plus,' she said, as if she hadn't heard any of that, 'you're so hypocritical. Playing happily families with Melissa and your brats, as if everything's bloody perfect. You're all the same. You're all cheats and liars. Cecil Parkinson set the standard, smiling that smarmy smile while he was busy shagging his secretary. So who are you shagging, I wonder? Or maybe you're into something a bit more interesting. A bit more Cynthia Payne, perhaps?'

For a moment his sense of control wobbled. Payne was a celebrated madam whose customers had needs not entirely dissimilar to his own. Did Lucy know something? How could she know something? She hardly knew *him*. She couldn't know anything.

'If that's the level we've descended to, I've nothing more to say.'

'So you're not going to give me my money?'

'No, Lucy. It's not yours. You made choices a long time ago about that. I'll write you out a cheque for five hundred pounds right now. No, let's make it a thousand, so you won't starve and can pay your rent this month. But this is the last. You're going to have to stand on your own feet from now on. I realise, especially listening to the spiteful things you've just come out with, that me helping you out over the years hasn't done you the slightest bit of good. Time for a bit of tough love, perhaps.'

It was a phrase he'd heard quite a bit lately, in relation to curbing youth crime or drug addiction. Don't indulge, kill the dependency, foster self-reliance and responsibility. It made the kind of American sense he liked, whereas 'asshole' he just found lazy and second-rate.

'Fuck off,' Lucy said. She pushed her chair back noisily and stormed out. But he knew her too well. She strode up and down outside, fuming, pretending not to look through the window while he got out his chequebook. Tough love. He imagined himself using it in an intervention in the Commons as he bent over the tiny table and wrote out the cheque. Then he stood up to leave.

'Sorry,' he mouthed to the woman with the magazine, who gave him an imperious stare, as if she had no idea who he was, which was probably the case. A little thrill of desire went through him. He paid the bill and stepped out into the cold sunshine.

'Here,' he said, and Lucy grabbed the cheque and stuffed it into her pocket.

'Goodbye, Lucy,' he said.

'I hate you,' she said. Then she turned and marched off.

'I know,' he said to her retreating figure. She hated him. What he didn't yet understand was how much.

§

Jock came home to die. Mary phoned Ellen and said, 'If ye want tae see him ye'd better no leave it ower lang.' The next weekend, a hot, dusty Saturday in July, Ellen left Robin and Kirsty in Joppa and drove north to Borlanslogie. The town's High Street was almost deserted, half the shopfronts shuttered or boarded up. When she turned off the engine and got out she felt the air heavy with despair. Three years since the miners' strike, two since the pit closed, and the place was dying. She walked to the end of the street and turned left, then second left, the route home. It all looked familiar but felt alien. Did I really come from here? she thought.

Mary had set Jock up in their old bedroom. She'd made a bed up for herself in the front room. 'Come ben for a cup of tea first, afore ye go in,' she said, ushering Ellen through to the kitchen. And while she made the tea she said, 'He's no looking good, Ellen. Ye'll be shocked at the change in him.'

'Why did you take him back after all this time?' Ellen asked. 'He never supported us. Why are you supporting him now?'

'Because we're man and wife,' Mary said. 'I ken he's no been the best but he hasna been the worst. We're aye mairrit, efter aw.'

'But he never –'

Mary cut her off. 'What was I tae dae, turn him frae his ain door? He's my husband. And your faither.' She paused. 'But I dinna blame ye for no liking him. He wasna there much for ye.'

'It's not a question of liking him. I liked him well enough when I saw him. I just feel I hardly know him.'

'Ye hardly dae,' Mary said.

She had made the double bed up with extra pillows and a white duvet. Jock, lying in the middle of it, looked like a bird in a patch of snow. He seemed to have shrunk to half his real size. He was dozing when Mary pushed her in – 'Here's somebody special tae see ye, Jock' – but he woke up soon enough and Ellen could have wept at the smile he gave her. 'It's yersel, lass,' he croaked, and then he had a coughing fit and between them the women helped him sit up against the pillows and take a drink of water till his chest calmed down again. The doctors said it was silicosis he had, and maybe that was true, because God knows what was in him from the years of working on the dams; he'd have inhaled clouds of concrete dust in the damp Highland air and maybe there was asbestos in there too, but anyway his lungs were choked and on top of that he'd smoked all his life so one lung was cancerous and they'd taken it out, and now the other didn't have much more than a month of breath left in it. This was what Mary had told her in the kitchen. 'I'll no be able tae keep him here,' she said, 'no when the pain gets really bad. I dinna hae the facilities.' She shook her head as if this were a failing on her part. 'He'll hae tae gang tae the hospital at the hinner end.'

She left them to it then, Ellen and Jock, and Ellen sat on a chair beside the bed and talked about Kirsty, whom he'd seen once, when she was about three, and now she was at the big school and thriving, and Robin, whom he'd never met, was fine, and life was fine and she was getting plenty of work, so much that she was turning some down, she had articles every week in the papers and was working on another book so, aye, everything was fine. Jock listened and she held his hand and sometimes she could tell his mind went away for a moment to cope with the pain.

'Is it sair, Dad?' she said.

'Aye, but it's better than working.' As if even dying was a bit of a skive.

She said, 'Dae ye mind all those stories ye used tae tell me?'

'What stories?'

'From the hydro schemes. A guy called the Marble Arch, and enormous midges and everything.'

'Oh aye, them.'

'I used tae think they were true,' she said.

He hauled himself an inch off the pillow. 'What dae ye mean? They *were* true.' And she laughed but he wouldn't give way. 'It was hard, hard labour, lass, in hard, hard weather. Oh aye. But I stuck it oot. Sent the wages hame every week. I did it aw for you, d'ye ken that? And look at ye, ye're thriving. But I'll tell ye something, Ellen.' He had another bout of coughing and needed more water before he could continue. 'I'll tell ye something. I'm glad I never went oot *there*.'

With a bony finger he pointed at the window.

'Where?' she said.

'Oot *there*. The rigs. I ken there was big money tae be made but ye'd never catch me sitting on a Meccano set in the middle o the bloody North Sea. Nae chance. Maks me seasick just thinking aboot it. And onywey, forbye the danger there wouldna hae been enough places tae hide frae the gaffer. And noo this Piper Alpha thing. Horrible, horrible. Jump or burn, that's what I heard. It was jump or burn. Jesus, I canna imagine it.'

But clearly he could. He fell silent imagining it and then he said, 'Aw the things I've seen and done in my working life, I never saw onything like that. And I'm grateful for it, I'll tell ye.'

He was quiet again, but only for a minute. 'I did it aw for you, lass,' he said, as if he'd got stuck in a kind of loop. 'But I never would hae gane oot there.' He closed his eyes, and she moved from the chair to the edge of the bed and said, 'Dad?' but he was asleep. And she watched him, a wee fledgling, skeletal, with a soft, downy growth of beard on his sunken, papery cheeks and his hand on the duvet so fragile and fleshless she was afraid to take it in case it broke. But she did take it, and she held it as his breath rasped in and out, ten long minutes watching her father ebbing away, and then she let go and went through to the kitchen where Mary was waiting for her.

When Ellen repeated what Jock had said, about doing it all for her and sending his wages home, Mary gave a short, bitter laugh. 'Believe that and ye'll believe in fairies,' she said. She sounded hard and she looked hard but there was something else, a softness seldom revealed but Ellen had known it was there as long as she could remember.

'I don't know where you get your strength from,' Ellen said.
Mary looked at her. 'Aye ye dae,' she said. 'Ye ken fine.'

§

After the miners' strike many Conservatives thought they were invincible. Nothing could stand in their way. This was an illusion, of course, but an intoxicating one. It took the poll tax to shatter it.

The poll tax – or community charge, as it was officially known – was born of the Scottish rates revaluation of the early 1980s. When property owners saw what their new bills were likely to be, they howled, and the Scottish Tories, anxious to appease their own natural supporters, badgered the government to come up with something – anything – with which to replace the rates. It happened that a group of radical right-wing intellectuals, who had first coalesced around the University of St Andrews and later developed their ideas in think-tanks named after luminaries of the Scottish Enlightenment, had a solution. They had dreamed up a scheme whereby almost every adult, regardless of circumstances, would pay the same amount for local services: a levy per head of population, or poll tax. This was an offering of such pure simplicity that nobody bothered to consider whether it would actually work. It was seized upon as the answer to the Scottish rates crisis. Margaret Thatcher and others in her government enthusiastically endorsed it, and decided it could be implemented in England and Wales too.

Because the problem and the panacea both emanated from Scotland, it made sense, if you accepted the logic of the tax, to introduce it there a year ahead of everywhere else. But what if you thought the whole idea unjust and unworkable, the tax regressive and grossly unfair? What if you didn't believe the Conservatives had a mandate to govern Scotland anyway? And what if, after an election in which the proposed tax had been a key issue and the Tories had lost half their Scottish seats, the government nevertheless insisted on imposing it? You might, as Mike did, think that your country was being used as a guinea pig for a massively unpopular tax. You might, as Mike did, recall M. Lucas's call for resistance. The question was, how to resist?

As with devolution ten years before, there were two opposition camps: there was a non-payment camp, inhabited by the hard left, anarchists, Nationalists and many others of no particular political affiliation; and there was a camp that held that non-payment would be counter-productive, resulting in reduced income for local government. This second camp was dominated by Labour politicians in the tricky position of having to administer both the poll tax and the services it paid for. They believed they had to behave 'responsibly'. The first camp thought that the second camp would be doing the Conservatives' dirty work for them by administering and collecting the tax. The second camp thought that the first camp would be doing the Conservatives' dirty work by forcing cuts in local services. Together, the two camps might have stopped the poll tax in its tracks. Apart, and fragmented even within themselves, they could only disrupt its implementation.

In the end, the political resistance at council level, the non-compliance with registration, the letters of objection, the refusals to pay, the poindings and fights between protestors and sheriff officers – all these things, so long as they were happening only in Scotland, damaged and delayed but did not destroy the poll tax. What destroyed it was when it came into force in England, and the Conservatives there saw how hated it was.

§

Root & Branch came to an end, but the movement it was part of continued to grow. The Campaign for a Scottish Assembly, which had struggled to survive at the start of the 1980s, was now paid increasing attention. Despite the CSA's own name, people were talking less about an assembly and more about a parliament. Folk whose names and faces meant nothing to the general public worked heroically in what Gavin Shaw had called 'the cause' – spending countless hours in meetings, brokering discussions between politicians who deeply mistrusted each other, steering negotiations around treacherous constitutional reefs, arguing tactical details and strategic principles, and drafting and redrafting documents so that as many key figures as possible could be persuaded to sign up to them. They built alliances across parties, local authorities, churches, trade unions, small businesses and cultural organisations – across that very society that Mrs Thatcher had declared did not exist. Out of the CSA came a committee, out of the committee came a document, the *Claim of Right*, out of the document came the Constitutional Convention, and out of the Convention came the blueprint for a Scottish parliament. There were still many hurdles to leap – not least the refusal of the government to countenance any form of devolution – and plenty of doubters, especially in the Labour Party. But at the end of 1988 the SNP dropped a timely bombshell in the form of another astonishing by-election win in Govan. The victor was Labour's old-time Nat-basher-in-chief, Jim Sillars, who had transformed himself into an extremely effective Unionist-basher, and who wiped out a huge Labour majority in the time-honoured fashion established by Winnie Ewing and Margo MacDonald (who by now was Sillars's wife). This concentrated minds in the Labour Party and it decided it had better participate in the Convention. Three months after Govan the SNP, in yet another fit of independence-and-nothing-less fever, decided that the Convention was 'rigged' and that they'd have nothing to do with it. Like the Tories, and in spite of dissent from the pragmatists in their ranks, including the new MP for Banff and Buchan, a certain Alex Salmond, the SNP were left carping and sniping from the wings. Labour couldn't believe its luck. It took another year before the SNP pragmatists won back control of the party, with Salmond easily beating Margaret Ewing, daughter-in-law of the redoubtable Winnie, in a two-way contest for the leadership. But by that time the Convention was at work, and Labour was irrevocably committed to establishing a Scottish parliament if it ever won power again at Westminster.

§

When it came to the poll tax, Mike was firmly in the non-payment camp. Apart from the principle of the thing, he couldn't afford to pay. Eric Hodge had married Moira and moved out of the Tollcross flat years before. He was a GP now, in a practice in Fife. A succession of temporary flatmates, mainly overseas students, occupied Eric's old room. This created all kinds of problems for community charge registration, especially as Mike was designated the 'responsible person' – the member of each household required to provide information to the registration officer about everybody who stayed there. He was off the dole by then, but earning a precarious and intermittent income, and was constantly arguing with Lothian

Regional Council about who lived in the flat, what he was due to pay and how much of a rebate he could claim. Every couple of weeks a new demand notice arrived and he wrote back disputing its accuracy. He enjoyed these exchanges: whether he was dealing with a human being or with a computer they seemed incapable of supplying accurate or even consistent information. He suspected that some of the staff were being deliberately incompetent and bloody-minded. This was heartening: when the administrators of any system start to sabotage it, then the system is doomed. At one point he was in receipt of three notices, issued on the same date, demanding significantly different amounts of money. It seemed quite possible, so long as the argument continued, that he would never pay any poll tax at all.

Meanwhile, he had an idea for a photographic project: he would make a pictorial record of the progress of the tax, and its effect on individual lives. He envisaged a series of images that would movingly and eloquently portray the despair and anger and financial pain it caused. On good days he fantasised about a book, or an exhibition, or an exhibition with accompanying book, and rave reviews in the *Guardian* and the recently launched *Scotland on Sunday*. He got some distance into this project before it ran out of steam. With help from a friend employed by the Regional Council he slipped into one of its buildings and photographed staff surrounded by mountains of registration forms; he photographed friends in shared flats arguing about who was going to be the 'responsible person'; he photographed the chaos at a sheriff officers' premises in Glasgow, where payers on their final warning went and, under the intimidating gaze of brawny men in black nylon jackets, chucked notes and coins into a plastic bucket and were given receipts in exchange; he photographed Tommy Sheridan and his Anti-Poll Tax Federation comrades mobbing other sheriff officers at a poinding until it was abandoned. This was the year of revolutions across Eastern Europe: the Berlin Wall came down, despotic regimes were overthrown by mass protests, the Ceauşecus were deposed and executed. Was Mike recording a tiny, marginal part of that bigger story? Perhaps. And he was still gathering images – under what he thought was a nicely ironic working title, 'Responsible Persons' – when the Trafalgar Square riots of 31 March 1990 happened.

He had gone to Glasgow that day, to photograph an anti-poll tax demo due to take place there. It passed off peacefully enough, and he failed to take any satisfying pictures. It wasn't till he got home and switched on the TV that he saw what had been going on in London. Just a few shots from those riots would have neatly concluded the narrative he had already built up. He found himself wishing there had been similar violence in Glasgow.

Adam had some other commitment that day. He came over in the evening. Things were strained between them. Like Mike he favoured mass non-payment of the poll tax as the best way of stopping it. But he was a councillor, and said he couldn't in all conscience tell the people who'd elected him in Borlanslogie to get themselves into deeper financial trouble than they were already in. When coal-mining had ended, three years before, the town still hadn't recovered from the effects of the strike. Half of Borlanslogie's men were unemployed. The week before, Mike had made a stupid remark: if they were unemployed they'd get a full rebate, so what did they have to lose? Adam had looked at him with undisguised contempt. 'Aye, ye're right, they've lost everything, absolutely everything. Dae ye hae ony idea what that feels like? But if they refuse tae register, or if they're assessed as haein tae pay some o the poll tax and they dinna, or canna, they'll hae their furniture taen aff them by the sheriff fucking officers. Am I supposed tae encourage them tae get intae that kind o mess? I canna dae it, Mike. They're my ain people. But I don't expect you tae understand that.' So that night they sat and watched the news with mixed feelings, together yet separate, and avoided any discussion that might end up in an argument. They'd been doing that a lot of late.

The next day they were up early. Adam made some breakfast while Mike went for the papers. He was hardly back through the door when Adam announced that he would have to be getting away. He had a pile of work to do at home. Mike said that was a pity, and could he not have brought his work with him? Adam said no, and that it wasn't a pity, because they probably both needed a bit of space, some time apart. Mike said he didn't need that, but obviously Adam did. Adam said Mike made too many emotional demands on him. Mike said that was nonsense. Things became heated. Adam said he had to go. He went.

The current flatmate was away for the weekend: Mike was left with the place to himself. It felt very empty. Had their relationship just come to an end, or was it a temporary misunderstanding? He didn't know, and what surprised him was his lack of anxiety about what the answer might be. Maybe Adam was right, and some time and space to himself would do no harm.

He slumped down on the sofa and started on the papers. The *Observer* had a big, wild picture of the riots on the front page. Inside was a further spread of photographs, but these had a different tone. Thoughtful, understated, offbeat, they focused on quiet, elderly demonstrators on the fringe, not window-smashing guys in balaclavas; they used humour instead of anger – a dog wearing a CAN'T PAY WON'T PAY coat, a beaming man in a REVOLTING PEASANT T-shirt spattered with red-ink gore; and in one the camera homed in not on confrontation but on conciliation, as a female goth bent to shield an injured policeman lying on the pavement. In their own peculiar way, they said things that were being lost in the general din. They were, of course, Angus's work, and Mike's first reaction was to deride him: he'd gone soft, sold out, missed the point. But the more he looked at the pictures, the more he was forced to admire them. Once again Angus had found his own angle. Once again he had beaten Mike at what was, quite obviously, nobody's game but his own.

§

Lothian Regional Council and Mike reached an impasse in negotiations over his community charge liabilities. He was overdue a full year's tax plus 10 per cent as a penalty for non-payment. Driven by a combination of principle and opportunism, he'd held out for as long as he could, but was about to be served with a summary warrant to recover the money. Because he wasn't on benefit and wasn't officially employed they couldn't arrest his income through either of those channels. If he didn't settle he could expect a visit from the sheriff officers. His photographic equipment would be the first items they would seize and sell, to make up what he owed. He decided to settle, and the council's clerks and he, very amicably, agreed a programme of weekly instalments. But he had virtually no money. He still did a few hours at the restaurant but the paid photography work was infrequent. It wasn't enough.

There was a camera shop in Rose Street with the imaginative name of Rose Street Cameras. It was run by Jeremy Tait, a Yorkshireman who liked Mike's pictures and with whom he'd often had long conversations on technical matters. The next time Mike was in he asked Jeremy if he needed a part-time shop assistant. No, Jeremy said, as a matter of fact he needed a full-time one. He was about to open another shop in Perth and one of his staff was moving up there to manage it. Half an hour later Mike had accepted Jeremy's offer of work, five days a week, every fourth Saturday off, starting the following Monday.

He wandered home feeling elated but also rather shocked. The pay wasn't great but it would mean a regular income, his immediate requirement. He told himself he didn't have to do it for ever. But he'd had to act. He was in his mid-thirties, and was about to have what Eric Hodge would have called a 'proper job' for the first time in his life.

§

Maggie was gone! The lady who was not for turning had been turned out! Her refusal to backtrack on the poll tax, her hostility to Europe, the steady gaze that to some observers looked increasingly like the glint of insanity – suddenly she was an electoral liability, not an asset. A succession of friends and traitors, men of principle and men of self-preservation, queued up to give her their tuppence-worth. The rank and file of the party still adored her, but they couldn't stop the assassination. David Eddelstane watched the whole thing unfold – her failure to win a large enough majority over Michael Heseltine in the first ballot of MPs, her decision not to stand in the second ballot, her tearful departure from Downing Street – with a mixture of anguish and dumb acceptance. Must she go? She had to go. Could they live without her? They must learn to do so. At least the arch-rival Heseltine's ambitions were derailed. The bland John Major, a safe pair of hands apparently, took over. The party entered a strange period of celebratory mourning. Without her, they might just cling on to power.

Three months later David was invited to a reception arranged by a small but influential, if you believed its own publicity, Edinburgh-based think-tank. Normally he wouldn't have bothered with such an event, but this time he could fit it in on his Friday-afternoon journey from London to Glenallan. He also had another reason for detouring into Edinburgh before catching a train north.

On the flight from Heathrow, he asked for a Bloody Mary, a drink he only ever had on aeroplanes. He liked the clunk of ice in the plastic glass, the thickness of the tomato juice, the smear of Worcestershire sauce as you stirred it in. He liked the textures more than the taste, in other words. He sipped at it, reflecting on his meeting that morning at Dover House, the London office of the Secretary of State for Scotland. He'd been summoned for an 'informal chat' about a junior brief in the Scottish Office. The Secretary of State had been all charm and efficiency. Nothing was decided but, what with the reshuffle and the need to resolve the poll tax issue and the fact that the existing team was already stretched – too few ministers juggling rather too many responsibilities – well, David could see, couldn't he, why the Secretary of State wanted to sound him out? Given the unfortunate shortage of Scottish Tory MPs, only the seriously unhinged or the intellectually challenged – 'You know who we're talking about, David' – could continue to enjoy the luxury of backbench life. 'Any questions? No? Well, we'll keep you updated.'

A few rows in front of him on the plane he spotted the familiar head of one of those other backbenchers. He hoped he could avoid him when they landed, but not a chance – the Honourable Member was keen to talk. 'Didn't see you in Departures, David. Much on this weekend? A surgery this evening and that's my lot. Mind you, might not get too much more free time. Keep it under your hat, but . . .' He too, it transpired, had had an informal chat at Dover House, the day before. 'May come to nothing of course but it's all hands on deck if we're to secure a fourth election victory, so I'll await the call.' David nodded and made the appropriate noises, but said nothing of his own interview. They parted at the taxi rank and David headed into town. Previously anxious at the prospect of ministerial office, he was now despondent. If they were sounding *everybody* out, then who did they *really* consider to be 'unhinged'? The idea of being thought of as 'intellectually challenged' was even worse. At least 'unhinged' was interesting. But he was neither. A self-made, more or less, man, that's what he was. What was their bloody problem?

The Dundas Research Institute was housed in a nondescript basement flat in a crescent in the West End. The entrance was gloomy, but at the far end of a long corridor was a surprisingly bright and spacious room looking out on to a garden. Twenty or thirty people, some of them known to him, were standing around in conversation when he arrived. From time to time trays of sandwiches and fresh bottles of wine were brought in from another room. Displayed on a table were copies of an austere-looking pamphlet, the reason for the event. *What's Left for the Right?* it asked in sky-blue letters on a cloud-grey background.

After a few minutes a man chinked a glass with a knife, welcomed everybody in a soft American accent to the Dundas Research Institute, of which he was a director, and craved their attention while he said a few words about the contents of the newly published pamphlet. It took David a minute to recognise the speaker as the same Mormon-resembling economist he'd heard all those years ago in Brighton. He had a stoop and was silvery now, but was no less passionate. So much had been achieved, he said. Here in the United Kingdom and throughout the West, the insidious creep of socialism had been stopped in its tracks and rolled back. Further afield, the Berlin Wall had fallen and the Iron Curtain raised. Gone were the regimes that had imprisoned their peoples behind it. A revolution had taken place but, unlike most left-wing revolutions, it had been almost entirely bloodless. People, given the freedom to choose, had chosen to be consumers not recipients, owners not slaves. He quoted Sir William Harcourt, a Liberal Chancellor of the Exchequer in the 1890s, who had introduced death duties and excused himself by saying, 'We are all socialists now.' No longer, the economist declared. 'We are all customers now. Lenin predicted that in a truly communist society the state would wither away. How wrong he was! Only in a truly capitalist society can the state wither away. And so we are at the start of a new era: unlimited freedom, unrestricted movement of capital and labour. But nothing is guaranteed. What can we do, as pragmatists who believe in the essentially liberating power of the market, to ensure that there is no return to the dead hand of statism, to ensure that the dependency culture is banished for ever?'

The silvery Mormon outlined a few proposals for doing this.

They were, he said, gone into in more detai ~~~~ ~~~~
lost interest, or track. Maybe it was all too fam~~~~
knocked back too many glasses of wine. Maybe the bur~~~~
isterial responsibility, though it wasn't actually on his shoulder~~~~
and perhaps never would be, was weighing too heavily. Or maybe
he was thinking that, like the collapsed regimes of Eastern Europe,
the order of which he was a part would not last, would be under-
mined by events and the shifting tolerances of the people. And
maybe that was what the economist was saying too: we won't be
around for ever, so we'd better make sure we build in some security
for when we're gone.

The speech ended and there was applause, followed by a rush to
refill glasses. David exchanged a few words with another backbencher who had turned up but who, if he too had been to see the
Secretary of State, was saying nothing about it. (Probably the man
for the job, then, David decided.) There were a couple of Edinburgh
councillors present too, and a woman from the party office round
the corner. He had a few words with each of them in turn, or was
it they who had a few words with him? He was never quite sure, on
these occasions, who was patronising whom.

Then he should have been on his way, but he lingered. He should
have been catching a train at Haymarket, phoning Melissa to ask her
to pick him up. It would just be the two of them at the weekend.
Jessica was seventeen and at the same boarding school Lucy had
attended – though Jessica, an academic achiever and rather brilliant
pianist, was making a much better fist of it than her aunt ever had.
Daniel was fourteen and in his second year at Kilsmeddum Castle.
He wasn't as clever as his sister but he'd survive. Possibly he'd flourish. As David had survived, and possibly flourished. Melissa, though
herself a product of and believer in private education, had refused
to send either of the children away before their teens, and was
doubtful of Kilsmeddum, but David had overruled her. 'It didn't do
me any harm,' he said, consciously echoing his father's opinion and
almost believing it. Tradition trumps reform. It was one reason why
he liked Westminster so much, and opposed devolution.

So he lingered. Why did he linger? Was it because he couldn't
face the thought of forty-eight hours alone with Melissa? No,
because they wouldn't be alone all that time, there was a surgery in

.. morning and a dinner party on Saturday night and no doubt some other function he'd forgotten about which he or they would have to attend. Anyway, he was fond of Melissa. He loved her. It wasn't her fault. Then what was it?

Whatever he was lacking it wasn't to be found at home. He didn't want to go home. He wanted to be out, unrecognised, without responsibility. He wanted to be anonymous.

Other people were leaving. Soon there was just a handful of them left. He had another glass of wine. The economist, whose name he kept forgetting, who earlier had been so eloquent and looked so competent, just as he had in Brighton, now looked as misplaced as David felt. It was as if, now that his pamphlet of ideas was launched, he had no reason to be there.

'Hi,' he said. 'Thank you for coming along tonight.' He appeared not to have a clue who David was, for which David was grateful.

'Not at all. Fascinating stuff,' he lied.

'Thanks. Be sure to take a copy with you. Take half a dozen if you know anyone who might be interested.'

'I must pay you for them. After all, we're all customers now.'

The economist laughed. 'We printed seven hundred. We can spare a few. We're not expecting it to make us rich. That's not what this is about.'

'I remember hearing you speak many years ago,' David said. 'Conservative Party conference in Brighton. You were talking along the same lines even then.'

'Was I?'

'Yes. I remember being impressed by your arguments.'

'Impressed? What about inspired?'

'I suppose I must have been. Otherwise I wouldn't be an MP now, would I?'

'I guess not.' The economist didn't seem to care that he was an MP.

'It must be gratifying,' David said, 'to see how far we've come since then.'

'It is. But you know what's more gratifying? The fact that we're getting our message across to the other side. Not directly. You won't catch Neil Kinnock or John Smith darkening our door. They wouldn't want to be seen hobnobbing with the likes of us, oh no. But the younger ones in Labour, they're different. They may not pick up a pamphlet called *What's Left for the Right?* but they're thinking the same thoughts.'

'They are?'

'You bet they are. If we published this with a different cover – and maybe we should, let's call it *What's Right for the Left?* – they'd sign up for just about everything that's in it. They can see the old politics are all washed up. This isn't just about cutting themselves off from Arthur Scargill or rooting out the Militant Tendency – everybody with a brain knows they've had to do those things. But the younger ones, they want to go further. They don't *want* to go back to old-fashioned Labour values, they want to tear that all up and embrace the market. Yes, they do. The Conservative Party has done all the dirty work, but Labour want to be there to reap the benefits. And sooner or later they will. Sooner or later Labour will be back in government. But it won't really be Labour any more. So whatever happens at the next election, or the one after that, doesn't really matter, not at a fundamental level.' He paused. 'That's not to say it won't matter to you, at a personal level. You might be a casualty, being subject to the whims of the electorate, but in a war there are always casualties.'

'Yes, there are,' David said, and the economist smiled sadly at him, shook his hand and moved on. David was thinking of the fighting in the Gulf, where Saddam Hussein's forces had just been ejected from Kuwait. There had been relatively few casualties on the Coalition side. It couldn't hurt any less, he thought, if your son or your husband was one of the dead, to know that he was one of only a few. Maybe it hurt more. There had been several incidents of 'friendly fire' too. That, he thought, must make your loss intolerable.

He collected a single pamphlet from the table and left. There was a train in five minutes and another in an hour. He called Melissa from a phone box and told her he'd be on the second one. Then he went for a walk.

He knew, though not precisely, where he was going. This was his purpose, to reconnoitre. It was a dark, damp night, and, although it was Friday, as soon as he'd put two streets between Haymarket and himself he was alone. He strolled through the sedate crescents and terraces, unremarked. If he did enter the government, or if he lost

583

his seat at the next election, either way he was likely to be spending more time in Scotland, in Edinburgh. He needed to check an address, its discreetness, even though he'd already been reassured about this in a preliminary discussion on the phone. He'd called from London, dialling a number in a contact magazine dealing in specialities. The woman had been very understanding. She catered for a variety of tastes and she could accommodate his. No names, no pack drill, of course. (She hadn't put it quite like that.) His only concern was the location. But already, as he entered the crescent, with its black railings, its heavy, evergreen foliage, its stony gravity and its firmly shut front doors, he knew it was going to be all right. He had a sudden flashback to that time in the undergrowth with the photographer's son. That had been somewhere around this area. He'd got away with that and he'd get away with this. Sure he would.

The address was a basement flat, like the Dundas Research Institute's only with no brass plate on the iron gate at the top of the stone steps. There was a number on the door, an illuminated electric doorbell, and that was all. While you waited for the door to open you would be almost completely out of sight from the pavement. A passer-by could easily think that nothing went on behind that door at all.

Satisfied, for now anyway, he walked to the end of the crescent, found an even subtler route back to the main streets, then headed for the station.

§

It happened again, at the usual ungodly hour somewhere between Saturday night and Sunday morning. He woke to the sound of the rumble and he groaned because he was so tired yet knew he couldn't lie there, he'd have to get up, have to go downstairs, make himself tea, the prelude to relief. Melissa stirred. 'What?' 'It's all right, darling, go back to sleep.' And she did. And he slipped away.

In the study, in the secrecy of that hour, he conjured up images of what would happen in the basement flat in Edinburgh. It would be the same as what happened in London, the same but different. This was good. There was comfort in habit, there was excitement in change. He didn't keep porn or anything else in the house in Glenallan. He might be mad – unhinged? – enough to visit prostitutes (not that he, or they, liked to use that word) but he wasn't a complete idiot. So here he had to depend on memory and imagination, sex in the head, as he lay back and thought of her, whoever she was, and her feet, her shoes, her heels, her shoes, and his hand was on his prick and here it comes here it comes here it comes and . . . aaaahhhh!

'David?'

Jesus! He jerked forward, still spouting semen into the clump of tissue. His eyes couldn't focus, he was still coming for God's sake, and she was there, she was bloody well there, silhouetted in the glow of the passage light she'd put on, in her angelic white night-gown, the mother of his children, looking wide-eyed and horrified as she said again, 'David? What on earth is going on?' And the rumble was suddenly a roar, like a jumbo jet taking off, or like the sound Jericho might have made when its walls came tumbling down.

§

It became a tradition in the 1980s to gather at Jean's place on General Election night. Jean frequently and loudly expressed her loathing of television, but she was a hypocrite, for she had a set in her bedroom and on election nights would trundle it down to the front room and plug it into an aerial socket beside one of the windows, and after the polls closed the others would arrive – the left-leaning nationalists, the nationalist-inclined socialists – to watch the results. They came, usually, more in fear than in hope. Mike doesn't recall it happening in 1979, but maybe that was because in 1979 everybody knew what was coming: the blessed Margaret, quoting Saint Francis. But he remembers the communal despair in 1983, when she wiped the floor with the opposition; likewise the briefly raised expectations of 1987, the so-called 'Doomsday Scenario' election, which was supposed to demonstrate that the Tories had no mandate to govern in Scotland – and it did, and they carried on regardless. There was 1992, when the gathering really believed the long, dark winter was about to end, and it didn't; and 1997, when finally it was over, and things, for a moment, could only get better. Off on, off on, like a light, like a relationship. Like the relationship he had with Adam.

Over the years, Mike took a special but silent interest in the fate of one particular MP, David Eddelstane. He'd never said anything to Adam about their brief liaison. It was too embarrassing, politically and personally, and so long ago. Adam knew that Eddelstane had been at the same school as Mike, albeit some years earlier, but that was all he knew. At each election Mike would wait for the Glenallan and West Mills result, expecting David to be ousted, and each time he would survive on a diminished majority. The others in the room would shout or groan with disappointment, not because of any personal animosity towards Eddelstane but because he was a Scottish Tory MP who supported every government policy that they objected to, and this was reason enough to wish him to lose. And Mike would shout or groan with them, and it wasn't personal for him either. And yet, though he could not say so in such company, of course it was.

Of all those election nights, 1992 was by far the most depressing. On Jean's big table that night bottles of wine and beer, and sandwiches and crisps, were all laid out, in preparation for celebrating the long-looked-for rout of the Scottish Conservatives. After Thatcherism, the poll tax, the Constitutional Convention, the closure of Ravenscraig, whatever happened south of the Border the Tories could surely only suffer further electoral disaster in Scotland. But two hours after the polls closed most of the bottles remained unopened, the sandwiches were curling up on their trays, a song had not issued from Walter Fleming's lips and even those who weren't smokers had ash in their mouths, because not only was John Major heading for victory, but the Tories had also made a small recovery in Scotland and gained a seat.

Why the surprise? There'd been a kind of silliness in the air throughout the campaign. Major had stood on his soapbox and been taken seriously; the SNP had unfurled a ludicrous slogan, FREE BY '93, as if independence were just a step away; and, on April Fools' Day, Adam and Mike had watched, in horror, the TV coverage of a huge Labour rally in Sheffield, with Neil Kinnock, helicoptered in, running on to the stage and punching the air, arms flailing as he leaped about shouting, 'We're aaall riight!' like a bad imitation of Mick Jagger. Mike had imagined votes for Labour shelving off in their thousands, like ice crashing into the sea in Antarctica, as someone announced, with unintended irony, 'Here is your next Prime Minister.' So even then, before the vote itself, the signs that it could all go wrong were visible. Even after thirteen bloody years of misery there could still be some horrible convulsion, some idiocy from Labour, some puerility from the SNP, some last venomous gasp of life in the Tories, enough to give them another five years. Five years! Was it conceivable? What further damage would they do? What would be left in another five years? By midnight on that election night, those were the questions Mike and Adam and all their friends were facing. The hangover arrived before they'd even taken a second drink.

Predictable morning-after-the-night-before things ensued. Labour and the SNP continued to tear lumps out of each other. Jim Sillars, who had lost his Govan seat back to Labour, turned his scorn on the Scottish people and accused them of being chest-puffing, ninety-minute patriots. John Major said he would 'take stock' of the Scottish situation but basically made no concessions on the question of devolution. New cross-party, non-party, pro-devolution, anti-Tory groups, with names like Scotland United, Common Cause and Democracy for Scotland, sprang into existence, full of good intentions. Rallies and marches were organised, but nobody broke open the Home Rule vintage champagne that had been lying in the cellar for a century. Nobody broke open the case of Kalashnikovs in the attic either. Nothing much, in other words, changed.

§

Ellen came into Rose Street Cameras one day and hung around till Mike had finished serving a customer. It was a while since they'd seen each other.

'I've been meaning to get in touch,' she said. 'Do you want some work?'

'I have work,' Mike said.

'No, real work.' As if working in a shop wasn't real. 'I've got a commission and they've asked me if I have a photographer in mind and I have you in mind. Interested?'

'What's the job?'

'A mining town, twelve years on,' Ellen said. 'I'm going back to my roots. I'm going to write about Borlanslogie, what it was like when I was wee, what it's like now, since the strike, since the pit closed. And I thought you could take the pictures.'

'Sounds good. Who are you writing it for?'

'The *Observer*.'

'Are you sure you've got the right Pendreich?'

'Why, is that forbidden territory?'

'No, but it is occupied territory. Or at least it was.' But Angus was seventy-two now. He wasn't doing much work any more, and hadn't had anything in the *Observer* for a while.

'I like your father's stuff,' she said, 'but it's not him I'm asking.'

'I'd love to do it,' Mike said. 'I'm flattered.'

'Don't be,' she said. 'You've never been to Borlanslogie, have you?'

'Aye, once, during the strike. With Adam. What does he think about this?'

'I don't know. I haven't mentioned it.'

'Aren't you going to interview him? Ask him about then and now?'

'Why do I need to ask him about anything?'

'I just thought, with him having been a councillor . . .'

'He's not a councillor any longer,' she said. (Adam had stood down in the run-up to council reform, which would abolish the two-tiered regional and district system of local government, and was back full-time as a clerical officer in the Health Service.) 'Let's leave Adam out of this. It isn't about him, it's about *my* home town.'

For a moment Mike's old loyalty to Adam asserted itself. Then he remembered the way Adam had excluded him from Borlanslogie during the strike. He didn't need his approval or engagement any more than Ellen did.

'Aye, let's leave him out,' he said, and it sounded too quick, almost eager.

Ellen looked at him sharply. 'Are you two all right?'

'Aye, sure.'

'The last time I spoke to him he wasn't very forthcoming about you.'

'He's tired, Ellen. He's up to his eyes in stuff at the hospital. They're reorganising everything again.'

'I've not seen you together for ages.'

'Well, we are. Together. Just not as much as we were. I'm in here three Saturdays out of four on top of everything else.'

She shrugged. 'I'll mind my own business. Are you working this coming Saturday?'

'No, as a matter of fact it's my weekend off.'

'Doing anything with Adam?'

'Nothing planned.'

'Then I'm booking you, okay?'

'Okay.'

Saturday came. Ellen picked him up and they drove to Borlanslogie. For an hour or so they scouted for possible images. They went up to the pithead and walked round the perimeter fence, peering through the wire at the rusting winding-gear, the red-brick and concrete buildings with their moss-thick corrugated roofs and smashed windows, a litter of bottles and cans where kids had got in over the years. It was all supposed to be landscaped eventually, Ellen said, but the only landscaping that had taken place so far was the invasion of grass and weeds. Mike took some photographs but of course there were no people. Ellen seemed to read his thoughts. 'We need some *human* dereliction,' she said. They headed back into the town.

The sky was grey, threatening rain. Perversely the light was quite good but Mike didn't know how long it would last. He could sense Ellen's impatience. 'Why don't I wander around on my own for a bit?' he suggested.

'Okay,' she said. 'I need to go and see a couple of folk. How long do you need?'

'An hour or so?'

She looked at her watch. 'Fine. It's half past one now. Let's meet at my mother's at three. She's only five minutes' walk away. Wait for me if you're there before I am. If you don't turn up I'll organise a search party.' She gave him directions, which seemed straightforward enough. 'She's dying to meet you,' she said. 'She'll not let on that she is, but she is.'

She drove off, and Mike started walking. He was disturbed by Ellen's remark about human dereliction. It seemed to him that that was precisely *not* what they should be seeking out, was not what would be remarkable. Human dignity or survival maybe, but not wreckage.

In a bedraggled park he came across a trio of young lads, fifteen or sixteen at most, slowly spinning the afternoon away on an ancient roundabout. For a while they didn't notice him. Each of them was sprawled in one of the machine's six divisions, and every so often as

589

it slowed one of them would extend a foot to the ground to keep it moving. Their conversation was utterly banal and it seemed likely they could keep it up for hours. They'd been smoking or sniffing something, judging by their disjointed ramblings, but they seemed at the same time secure and united in their companionship. One of them saw Mike at last and for a while they were happy to include him in their chat. Then he asked if they'd mind if he took some photographs of them. This provoked some remarks about pervs and poofs, and half-serious demands for payment for their trouble, but they didn't sit up, let alone pose, just kept the roundabout turning as he clicked away. It was no trouble to them at all. When he said goodbye they seemed almost sorry to see him go.

He went into the Co-op and talked to the women at the tills and some of the customers, and again was met with polite, easy indifference. 'Aye, on ye go, son, take your photies.' It was as if they had nothing to do with the process. They fully understood, however, that having got what he'd come for he would disappear again and that neither good nor ill, fame nor fortune, would come of the encounter.

It was the same in the pub across the street, although here he was questioned more aggressively before he was allowed to take anybody's picture. The half-dozen men drinking and smoking were less resigned and more desperate than the women in the Co-op. They had all worked underground, and knew they would never work again. There was, Mike thought, nothing left for them but to get out of the house and kill time. They told him that their community had been murdered by the government, the Coal Board and capitalism. But they said it almost triumphantly, because they were still standing, still defiant in the face of what had happened to them. He listened, and wondered about the men of Borlanslogie who were not in the pub on a Saturday afternoon, and what they were doing. Whatever the 'community' now was, it was surely more than this.

He made his way to Ellen's mother's. He knew he had some good images, and that they reflected, at least in part, the slow death the town was undergoing. But he knew too that whatever it was he had captured in the faces of the men and women, it wasn't dereliction. Even the careless resilience of the three kids was impressive.

He was ahead of Ellen. Her mother, Mary, was another survivor. She'd worked, first as a tracer, then in a variety of clerical posts, in the coal industry for thirty-seven years, retiring the year before the strike. She had a hard, narrow-eyed gaze but was friendly enough. By the second cup of tea they were discussing Adam. Clearly she had no problem with either his sexuality or his relationship, irregular though it now was, with Mike. Mike found himself trying to highlight Adam's good qualities, which Mary grudgingly acknowledged only in order to point out faults. But for all that she criticised, it was obvious that she respected and cared deeply about him.

Then she started asking what Mike thought of Ellen. Again, she wanted his opinion only as a cue to giving hers. She disparaged Ellen in order to praise her, praised her in order to disparage. She'd read Ellen's books and thought they were too clever – but then again, they made you think. Ellen could write well and she'd plenty of ideas but she would have, wouldn't she, she'd had her nose in books since she was a bairn. Mary wouldn't have brought Kirsty up the way Ellen had, but times changed and Robin was a fine man, Ellen was lucky to have him, and Kirsty was nineteen now and seemed to be turning into a fine young woman.

'It's no as if they had an easy start,' she said. 'Ye ken Robin's no Kirsty's faither?'

'I do,' Mike said. 'But I've never really known what the story is there.'

'It's no for me tae tell ye, if Ellen hasna. Mind, she hasna tellt me either, but ye work things oot, don't ye? Weel, I dae.' She laughed and watched him through those narrow eyes. 'She was raped. Kirsty's the bairn o the man that raped her. Ellen tellt me a few years efter Kirsty was born. That's aw I ken. She wouldna say who the faither was but I hae my ain ideas aboot that.'

Mike said nothing, waiting for her to say more.

'Oh aye,' Mary said. 'She's cairried that aroond wi her lang enough. We're different, Ellen and me, but we're the same tae. We're baith tough.'

'Does Kirsty know?'

'Aye, Ellen's no hidden it frae her. I dinna ken hoo much she kens, but she kens the worst. She'll be aw right. She's aye had Robin. He's been a great faither tae her. Ellen never really kent her ain faither because he was aye away working on the hydro schemes and that. And then Adam and Gavin came tae bide wi us, so that was hard for her. Twa big brothers just appearing like that. It was hard for us aw back then.'

'Her father's dead, isn't he?' Mike asked.

'Jock? Aye, he died a few years syne. His lungs gave oot. He came back hame for the last weeks and Ellen came ower tae see him a few times. She had mair time wi him then than she'd had for years.'

'I hear he could tell a good story.'

She laughed her short, hard laugh again. 'He could that. Ye'd think he'd built the dams single-handed the way he went on some-times. But the weird thing was, when he died and we had the funeral, aw kinds o characters turned up. I dinna ken how – I didna invite them – but word must hae got aroond and there was a haill mob o them. Irish and Polish and Greek and Italian, it was like the United Nations at the purvey, and hauf o them fou o the same nonsense he used tae come oot wi. And fou wi drink tae. Jock'd hae loved it. Aye, he really missed himsel that day.'

After a minute she added, 'Ellen has that frae her faither. She can tell a story. She disna aye get it richt, mind. This thing she's writing noo that you're taking the pictures for, she'll get that wrang. She's been away ower lang. She disna ken the toun ony mair.' Another pause, a quick smile. 'So dinna even think aboot taking my picture. It's naething tae dae wi me.'

He tried to look surprised but she wasn't fooled. He'd been itch-ing to get the camera out. She had the very survivor's face he thought would be right for Ellen's article. But Mary was having none of it, and he was powerless against the strength of her will.

§

Ellen drove out of town and up the hill towards the Hogg residence. There was a scattering of new houses up there, and Denny's was the biggest, a sprawling, brash, fuck-you announcement surrounded by a Spanish-looking white wall and a set of iron gates bearing a BEWARE OF THE DOG sign. And all, so the story went, built on run-ning a taxi firm in Drumkirk. Aye, right.

She parked outside the gates and peered in, wondering if she should risk it. She didn't know what kind of dog Denny had, but she'd bet it wasn't a chihuahua. As she sat there summoning up courage, the front door opened and a familiar figure stepped on to the porch. She got out of the car and went to the gate.

'Denny!'

He stood a moment longer, then started towards her.

'Remember me?' she said. 'It's Ellen Imlach.'

Squat and muscular, a bit paunchy, Denny didn't alter pace. The cropped head jutted forward as he walked. He was wearing trainers and sports gear and close up she saw that his skin was coarse from too much sun or too many sunbeds. He had a bullish, mean look about him, the look of a man you didn't make eye contact with unless you had something to say.

'Ellen,' he said. 'What are you daein here? I saw the car parked ootside and I didna recognise it. Wasna expecting onybody.'

'Do I need to make an appointment?'

'No you, Ellen. Ye coming in?'

'If it's safe.'

'Ah, the dug's locked up. In ye come. Just leave the motor ootside.'

He took a gadget from his pocket and clicked it at the gates, which unlocked and swung open. She stepped in and he pressed the gadget and the gates closed gently behind her. There was a moment when she thought he was going to kiss her, then it was gone. The smile seemed friendly enough.

'Sure I'm not disturbing you?' she said.

'Aye, nae bother, ye're aw right. There's naebody else here. Marie's oot wi the lassies. Ye've no met Marie, have ye? They'll be back later.'

She followed him across the gravel. There was a wide lawn and a statue of an angel or a wood nymph in the middle of it, hideous, and a pair of concrete lions at the front door. Denny ushered her in. 'First left,' he said, and followed her into a room full of black leather furniture and with a black marble fireplace with a gas fire in it. The house was roasting hot, presumably from the central heating, but Denny had the gas up high anyway. She resisted the urge to hurry to the bay window and let in some fresh air.

'Ye wanting something? A drink or something?'

'No, I'm fine,' she said.

'I'll get ye something. I was just fixing masel a soda and lime. Bit early for alcohol for me but ye can hae onything ye like.'

'Soda and lime would be fine,' she said.

'Back in a minute,' he said.

She took her coat off and laid it on an arm of one of the two sofas. The room was comfortless. The sofas sat on an oatmeal wall-to-wall carpet on either side of a square, low glass-topped table. An armchair with an extendable footrest was on one side of the fire, facing a large television. There were two huge paintings, one over the fireplace and the other on the opposite wall, Highland land-scapes done in a splashy, bright, semi-abstract style that at first glance seemed challenging, at second lazy. Apart from the TV and an enormous sound system and a shelving unit full of CDs and videos, there was nothing to suggest any life went on in the room. Even the heavy curtains tied back with brocade ropes on each side of the bay window looked like they were never drawn. There were no lamps or sidelights, just a candelabra suspended from the middle of the ceiling. No magazines or books lying around, no glasses or coasters, no candles, no ornaments above the fire. A utilitarian space for home entertainment, was how it seemed to Ellen. She hated it.

Denny came back carrying a round metal tray with two tumblers full of fizzy greenish water. He'd put straws in them. He put the tray on the glass table and gestured at her to help herself.

'Take a seat,' he said, and lowered himself on to one of the sofas. She sat down opposite him on the far side of the table. A brief, awk-ward silence followed. Denny picked up his drink and sucked a couple of inches out of it.

'So what are ye daein here?' he asked again.

'I'm writing something,' she said. 'Twelve years on from the strike. Death of a community, that kind of thing.'

'For a paper?'

'Yes.'

'We're no deid yet,' he said. 'So, is this you coming tae interview the local bigwig or what?'

'No, Denny, I'm not here to interview you. I just thought I'd come and see you. It's time.'

'Aye,' he said. 'How long since we've seen each other, then?'

'Twenty years,' she said.

'A lot o water under the bridge since then,' Denny said. 'But ye're looking good, Ellen. We're nane o us getting ony younger, but ye're looking good.'

'Thanks,' she said. 'My mother doesn't think so. She says when a woman gets to my age, she does one of two things. She either widens or she wizens. She told me that and then she looked me up and down and said, "And Ellen, ye're no gonnae wizen."'

Denny stared at her. He didn't get it. 'Right,' he said. 'How is she onywey? I never see her.'

'She's just the same as ever. What about *your* ma? Is she still alive?'

'Christ, aye. Alive and kicking. She spends maist o her time in Spain. She's got an apartment oot there. Loves it. Beats Borlanslogie in the winter, that's for sure.'

'But you're still here.'

'Well, it's different in a hoose like this, eh? And the lassies are aye at the school. Once they're away, maybe Marie and me'll spend mair time oot there tae. It's a good life. Sun, swimming pool, cheap food. And nae hassle. Nae bastards chasing ye for tax or getting jobs done. Aye, I can see us oot there six months o the year.'

'What are your lassies called?'

'Tracy and Shelley. Tracy's sixteen and Shelley's fourteen. Right wee madams they are. Cost me a fortune but that's daughters for ye, eh? What aboot your Kirsty? She must be grown up by noo, is she?'

'How do you know about Kirsty?'

'Word gets aroond, Ellen. Ye can leave a place like this but ye dinna ever really leave it, dae ye? Ye dinna speak the way ye used tae but ye're aye yersel. Folk in Borlanslogie aye ken aboot the folk that left. So she'll be, what, nineteen or thereaboots noo?'

'You're well informed, Denny. She'll be twenty in a few weeks.'

'I've aye kept my ears open for news aboot you, Ellen. We go way back. I was glad tae hear ye were daein aw right. Ye had a book published, didn't ye?'

'Two.'

'Two? Ye must be loaded.'

'It doesn't work that way with books. I'd say, looking at this place, you've done better. Money-wise.'

'Money-wise but no style-wise, ye mean? Ach, ye were ayewis a wee snob, Ellen, in spite of whaur ye grew up. I'm no criticising. I liked that in ye, ye ken. It showed ye were gonnae go places. No like me.'

She glanced round the room. 'You've done fine. Good money in the taxi business, is there?'

'See, there ye go again. Aye, the cabs are okay. Used tae drive one masel. No noo. Get other buggers tae dae aw that. Had tae clean up some drunk bird's puke once ower aften. Plenty o boys oot there that like the hours but no me ony mair. Same in your line o work, is it no? Back shifts, night shifts, double shifts. Ye get tae a bit where ye wonder what the bloody point is, don't ye?'

'I don't work like that any more.'

'That's what I mean. Ye've sorted it.'

They were circling round the subject, the big presence in the room. She thought he looked uneasy, as if he wished she'd drink up and leave, as if he'd keep her at arm's length as long as he had to. But just as she thought that he said, 'So why are ye here, Ellen? Ye want tae tell me aboot Charlie?'

'That was going to be *my* next question,' she said.

'What dae ye want tae ken?'

Her mouth was dry. She picked up the soda and drank from it through the straw. Denny sucked on his, making the ice rattle. They could have been two bairns again.

'He's deid,' he said.

For a few seconds nothing moved anywhere in the world. She put her drink back on the tray.

'Are you sure?'

'Aye. One of my drivers heard aboot it. He was in the army. He was killt in an accident on a training exercise. That's what I was tellt.'

'I heard he joined up,' she said.

'How did ye hear that?'

'Friend of a friend. A policeman. Apparently things got too hot for him in Drumkirk. Is that right?'

'Aye, that would be aboot the score.'

'Were you involved?'

'No me. I steered clear of Charlie back then. I was bad news but he was really bad news. So I steered clear. There was a lot of heavy stuff gaun doon in Drumkirk but I wasna a Drumkirk boy. I was better oot o it. I got in again later. Efter Charlie was awa.'

'But you introduced me to him.'

'Aye, I did. That was before.'

'You must have known what he was like.'

'I had an idea. But I thought you could look efter yersel.'

'So did I.'

He put his empty tumbler back on the tray. 'He battered ye, didn't he?'

'Aye. No just battered, Denny.'

He saw in her face what she meant. 'Fuck,' he said. 'I'm sorry.'

'It wasn't your responsibility. Was it?'

'I heard he was violent wi a couple o other lassies. But I didna hear that till later.'

'You don't have to make excuses. Or apologise.'

'I'm no apologising. It was a lang time ago. Twenty year.'

She nodded.

'And then ye had Kirsty?'

'That's right.'

'And she's his?'

'That's one way of putting it.'

'And did he ever ken aboot her?'

'Not unless you told him.'

'I never seen him again. Some other guys I kent, they'd had enough o him. He didna ken whaur tae stop. There was a big fight and the next thing he was awa. I dinna ken if they forced him oot or he went aff his ain back, but I kind o think he must hae decided tae dae it.' He gave a short laugh. 'Maybe he wanted a bigger challenge. Maybe he thought he'd take the army on and see who'd win.'

'And the army won.'

'Naw, I dinna think so. It was an accident. I think they baith lost. I bet Charlie ended up being a good sodger. He probably . . . found himself.' She could tell he felt embarrassed even saying it. She wondered if Denny had 'found himself', here in this barren room in this soulless house with his womenfolk away out and him on his own waiting for them to come back. She wondered if he was a good father and what that meant, 'a good father'. She wondered if she was a good mother, if she'd 'found herself' with Robin. She thought of Kirsty and how much she loved her and that she would have to tell her that her father was dead.

'You aw right?' he said.

'Aye, I'm fine, thanks. When was he killed, can you mind?'

'Two, three year ago. Nae mair than that. Ye could easy find oot.'

'Aye.' The silence returned. She wanted to know more, she didn't want to know anything. She was happy, she was sad, she was shocked, she was relieved. She didn't know what she was.

'What about you?' she said.

'It's naething tae dae wi me, Ellen. I don't need tae find onything oot. I'm just telling ye because ye asked. Because ye're here.'

'No, I mean, what were you doing all that time?'

He stood up and went to inspect the painting over the fire. 'This is aff the record, right?'

'I'm not here as a journalist, Denny.'

'Ye might hae a wire on ye.'

'Dinna be daft.'

'Are you warm enough?'

'More than.'

'I'm gonnae turn the fire aff then.' He bent down to the switch and when he came back to his seat she saw that he had broken out in a sweat. He drained the melted ice from his glass.

'I done some bad stuff, Ellen. I seen some bad stuff and I heard some bad stuff and I done some o it. Afore the cabs it was drugs, onything really. I'm telling ye, even the cabs are bad these days. It gets so ye're aye looking ower your shooder tae see wha's coming. In the cities the Russians and the Albanians and the Chinese are aw muscling in. It's only a maitter o time afore they reach Drumkirk. I'm wanting oot afore they get here. Quit while ye're ahead, that's something I learned a lang time ago. Ye were right earlier on. Look at this place. I canna complain. I've got away wi stuff. Ye think it'll aye be like that, ye'll aye get away wi it. Then ye think of what ye've got tae lose. Marie and the lassies.' He breathed in and out hard, as if he were pumping himself up for a fight. 'See if onybody tried tae touch them, I'd kill them. I wouldna stop tae think aboot it, I would just kill them and then I'd think aboot it.'

She believed him. If somebody tried to hurt Kirsty, she'd be the same. For the first time since she'd come into the house she felt a kinship with Denny, a line going back to their childhoods. He looked across at her and she saw his brute strength and his brute fear together.

She said, 'Did you ever do that? Kill someone?'

He shook his head. It wasn't a denial.

'Off the record, Denny. I've always wondered about you. How come you got such a light sentence for that political business? How come they let you out so soon?'

'Don't fucking ask,' he said.

'How come you got away with a lot of things after that too? You must have sailed so close to the wind. I know you.'

'Ellen,' he said, 'I was a different man then. I was a fucking eejit. I've got a wife and bairns noo.'

'Is that why you have the electric gates and the dog? Is that why you check out the cars that park outside? You think somebody's coming for you one day?'

'I've made plenty o enemies,' he said.

'What happened, Denny? What happened after they let you out?'

'Some things are better buried.'

'What things?'

'Just leave it alane, aw right?'

'Did somebody buy you?'

'Ye could say that. Ye could say I paid for it onywey. Paid for being an eejit.'

'How?'

'I did a job. Unfinished business. I finished it. That's aw ye need tae ken.'

'What did you do, Denny?'

'Just. Fucking. Leave it.'

Silence again. She thought, there is a world beyond my world that I can hardly imagine any more, let alone touch. I don't want to touch it. Denny doesn't want to touch it, but it touches him. It's in his eyes. He lives with it every minute of the waking day.

She said, 'I didn't mean to upset you.'

'Forget it,' he said. 'Onybody else, I wouldna hae let them start. But I aye liked ye, Ellen. Ye're smart.'

'I was out of line.'

'Ye're closer than ye think.'

They looked at each other. She thought, Charlie Lennie is dead. That's what I came here to find out. I don't need to know anything else.

'I'd better go,' she said.

He jumped to his feet. 'Are ye sure? Ye dinna need tae. Ye could wait for Marie and the lassies. They'll no be lang.'

'I need to go and see my mother.'

'They'll be sorry they missed ye.' But she knew if she was away before they returned he'd wash her glass and not mention her to them.

They walked across the gravel past the angel or the nymph, whatever she was. At the gate he held out his hand and she took it in both of hers and his other hand came up and joined too, a good hard grasp.

'Dae ye mind my granny?' he said.

'Oh aye, I mind her fine,' she said. 'I mind when she died.'

'She was a wicked auld bitch but I'll tell ye, she had a great life and we kept her at hame right tae the very end o it. Nooadays folk stick their auld people in nursing hames as soon as they pee the bed. Fucking barbaric that. Nae fucking respect. I thought my gran was a rotten crabbit auld witch but I fucking respected her tae, and I would never hae let her end her days in one o thae shiteholes. And it'll be the same wi my mither tae. If she canna cope in Spain or doon the road she'll come here. I look efter my ain. That's aw ye can dae, Ellen, eh? Look efter your ain and fuck everybody else. Eh?'

'Maybe,' she said. 'Maybe you're right, Denny. But I hope you're wrong.'

He did the thing with the gadget and the gates swung open and she stepped back on to the road again.

'I hope I'm wrang tae,' he said. 'But I'm no.'

§

Ellen arrived at her mother's house half an hour after Mike. She apologised for having taken so long. Mary poured her some tea. 'Whaur were ye?' she asked.

'I went to see Denny Hogg. A childhood friend,' she explained to Mike.

'Denny Hogg?' Mary cried. 'That gangster!'

'If he's a gangster he's been one since he could walk,' Ellen retorted.

'Of course he's a gangster,' Mary said. 'Hoo else could he hae a hoose like yon? It's a ranch, Michael, up on the hill, wi a big wall for keeping the riff-raff oot even though he's nae better than the rest o us. He thinks he's J. R. Ewing.'

'He runs a taxi firm,' Ellen said.

'That's no aw he runs. What did he hae tae say for himsel?'

'Och, nothing much,' Ellen said. 'We were just catching up.'

Mary snorted. 'He and Ellen used tae play thegither,' she said. 'He's a bad, bad laddie.'

'Tell me how you got on, Mike,' Ellen said, unsubtly changing the subject. 'Did you get any good pictures?'

It wasn't until they had left Borlanslogie and were driving back to Edinburgh that Denny Hogg's name came up again.

'Your ma didn't seem to have much time for the gangster,' he said.

'Denny? No, she doesn't like him.'

'You were away for ages.'

'Denny and I have a long history. He stayed next door to my granny's house, where I spent a lot of my childhood. Most of it, in fact. He went down the pit but chucked it after a while, and then he got into some trouble and ended up in the jail, but he wasn't there for long. He's looked after himself, Denny. He was made for the '80s: every man for himself, that's his motto. My mother doesn't like him because he's a dealer, or at least he used to be, and because she thinks she knows something else about him. But she doesn't.'

'What does she think she knows?'

They were crossing the Forth Bridge and it was gusty but that wasn't why she gripped the wheel hard and kept her eyes fixed on the carriageway ahead.

'She thinks he's Kirsty's father,' she said.

'Ah.'

'But he isn't. Her father was a man called Charlie Lennie. It was Denny that introduced me to him. I used to curse him for that, but not any longer. Charlie Lennie's dead.' She was quiet for a minute, weighing up what more she wanted to say. 'I just learned that today,' she added. 'I'd thought he might be, but I didn't know. Denny told me. So I can draw a line. It was a bad relationship. You knew that, didn't you?'

'That's what I guessed.'

'You guessed right. But that's it. He's dead. It's over.'

'Do you want to tell me about it?'

'Not in any more detail than that.'

'Are you okay?'

'I'm fine,' she said. 'Even if he wasn't dead I'd be fine.'

'Will you tell Kirsty?'

'Aye. I'll tell her at once. That the father she never knew is dead. And then that'll be over too.'

'Did she never meet him?'

'No,' she said. 'And she never wanted to. She has Robin. We both have Robin.'

'He's a good man,' she said.

'Everybody says that,' Ellen said. 'Whenever Robin's name comes up, people say, "He's a good man." And you know something? They're right.'

§

The article appeared in the *Observer* a few weeks later. Ellen subsequently told Mike that she'd had a row with her mother about what she'd written, but that Mary had said she thought his pictures were good. Mike told Ellen that he'd waited in vain for a comment from his father, and that, eventually, when Mike had phoned him, Angus had said he thought it was a fine piece of writing. 'And the pictures?' Mike had asked. (They'd used one of the boys on the roundabout, one of the men in the pub, one of the Co-op women, a shot of the main street and a big spread of the pithead.) 'Aye,' he'd said. 'Not bad.'

'And that,' Mike said, 'was that. Not bad.'

'Old bastards,' Ellen said. And they both laughed. What else could they do?

§

It felt like a long drop from Westminster to Glenallan these days. When David Eddelstane came back for weekends, held surgeries, opened a fête or a new industrial estate, it was sometimes hard to believe that anybody at all had voted for him in 1992. He represented the constituency in the House of Commons but he no longer had a sense of who or what he was representing. Four and a half years on the only friendly faces now belonged to old dears in retirement homes who weren't quite sure if he was the minister or the doctor. Even businessmen and bank managers – the kind of people whose votes the party had once been so sure of it hadn't even bothered to take them for granted – even they looked pissed off at him these days. They weren't going to vote for anybody else but by God, their looks said, you're asking a lot if you expect an X in the box from us, you shower of arrogant bastards. It wasn't so much the corruption they objected to – although they didn't like it – it was the fact that government ministers and MPs kept getting found out. Hardly a week went by without some new scandal being gleefully exposed in the media. The utter futility of John Major's 'Back to Basics' campaign, in the face of wave after oily wave of sleaze washing in, was well beyond a joke. Insider trading, cash for questions, dodgy foreign investments, dodgy foreign arms sales, dodgy everything. And then the sex: multiple adulteries, homosexual affairs, affairs with secretaries, love children with secretaries, toe-sucking mistresses, whipping sessions with rent boys, assignations with prostitutes, death by auto-erotic asphyxiation. (That was the one that always got to him. The tabloids had made their usual saucy meal of it, but it was just tragic, a horrible, lonely tragedy.) There was even talk in some circles that the PM himself wasn't as pure as the driven snow. And he, David Eddelstane, was included in the general denunciation, even though he'd not been found out. Yet. Not been splattered across the tabloids. Yet.

There was a lot of psychobabble in the media every time a prominent public figure was caught in a compromising situation: *he wanted to be found out, he needed to get caught.* Well, perhaps. But David did not want to be found out. Not for the time being, thank you, no. He'd much prefer to lose his seat and disappear into semi-obscurity first. In fact, once you were semi-obscure, nobody gave a damn about your secrets.

Things had never been the same since the poll tax. Internal party splits over Europe hadn't helped. Fifteen per cent mortgage interest rates and the meltdown that followed Black Wednesday had dished the myth that the Conservatives were more financially competent than Labour. Sleaze was the icing on the teetering cake. If David represented anything at all, it wasn't this particular bit of Scotland at Westminster, it was the Tory Party in this bit of Scotland, and frankly, not only was he not making much of an impression, he'd rather have been flogging tickets for a seal cull at a Greenpeace rally.

How glad he was, after all, that he hadn't been made a minister of state. There had been a Cabinet reshuffle a couple of years back, and the Member for Stirling, Michael Forsyth, had become Secretary of State for Scotland. Forsyth was an ardent, unrepentant Thatcherite in what was supposed to be a post-Thatcherite age. The story was that when the civil servants at St Andrew's House heard of his appointment they went around picking windows to leave by. Forsyth had been a hate figure as a junior minister and as Secretary of State he attracted greater unpopularity. He'd just engineered the return of the Stone of Destiny in what looked like a desperate attempt to improve the government's tartan credentials, but even David could see through that one. Here's a lump of sandstone, okay? So now you don't need to bother with this devolution/separation nonsense. David didn't think that was going to make many people change their views, or their vote. The stone came up from London under military escort and when it crossed the Tweed at Coldstream in an army Land Rover Forsyth was there to meet it. 'A momentous occasion,' he was quoted as saying. It was all rather embarrassing, and David was content not to have anything to do with it, and not to be any more closely associated with Mr Forsyth than he already was. Head down, fixed smile, see out the last few months – that was his philosophy now.

The trouble was he was so indecisive. He liked the luxuries and kudos that his life brought him. He liked providing for Melissa and the kids, who were now both students, final year and first year. He'd embraced the wealth and privilege of his own upbringing, and by astute dealings increased the former many times over. Was he to be blamed or brought down for doing what most people in the same circumstances would have done? All right, he could have done a Lucy and rejected the lot, but who'd have gained? Nobody. Not himself, not Melissa, not his children. Certainly not Lucy, wherever she was. He hadn't seen her for years, not since that last awful meeting in London, and he doubted he ever would again. The idea that he should have sacrificed everything out of some misplaced sense of guilt was absurd. And yet, and yet. There were times when he wished he wasn't who he was, times when he wanted to hide away, as he had in childhood from his parents' monstrous behaviour. Oh for the quiet, obscure life! Well, if he'd really wanted that, he should have resigned at the last election, or the one before that. Got out while the going was relatively good. But he hadn't, and why not? Because he hadn't wanted to disturb the tricky balances of his life. And he'd been right not to, because it looked like he was going to make it. The election was less than six months away and it was quite obvious that he was going to lose the seat. He was going to be able to ride out these last months, lose with dignity rather than run like a rat, *then* disappear into the backwoods. He might even end up with a knighthood. Sir David Eddelstane. He wouldn't need to work, wouldn't need to do anything except be. And that could still include being that part of himself that he kept private and guarded. The time bomb was ticking away but it would cease to tick after the election. He would lose, and after that nobody would care. The malevolent gremlin sitting in the depths of him, waiting to pop its grinning features out into the world when it was likely to cause maximum damage, would have missed its chance. He'd been carrying the little bastard around for decades, caressing, feeding, pacifying, indulging it, and it still wasn't tamed, still was both part of him and apart from him, still had the capability to humiliate and destroy him – but not for much longer. A few more months, weeks even – that was all he needed.

And dear Melissa, who knew something, need never know the whole truth. After that time she caught him in the study, she'd demanded to know what it was he was hiding. Was he having an affair? No. Was he gay? No, no. Then what? He'd started to tell her but he couldn't, he didn't want to sully her with the stupid, sordid details and anyway they were *his* details, he wanted them to himself. She'd said, 'David, I love you. I don't know if I can do whatever it is you want, but I love you and I want to help.' 'No,' he'd said, 'you can't help.' 'Do you love me?' she'd asked, tears running down her face. 'Yes, yes, darling, I love you very much.' 'Then don't reject me.' 'I'm not rejecting you, it's just something I have to sort out in my head. On my own.' And he'd given her some baloney about the pressures of the job and the exhaustion and the sleeplessness and how it messed you up. A rejection, however he adorned it. 'So where does that leave us?' she'd said. 'Still here,' he'd said, 'still together.' 'Should I expect anything awful to happen? Exposure, public humiliation, anything like that?' 'No,' he'd said. 'Don't worry. I'm not a fool. Everything will be all right.'

So he'd lied to her. Twice. Once throughout all the years she never suspected, or never asked, and again when she did ask. But it had been worth it. He was still in one piece, still undiscovered. It *would* be worth it, if only he could manage the deceit for just a little longer. Then the rumble would be silenced for ever.

§

He came so close, less than a month to go. And then somehow, somebody found out. One minute he was about to emerge from the escape tunnel, the next there were searchlights blazing, loudspeakers and panic. And that was just in his head. He came home one afternoon from the campaign trail and Melissa was standing in the hall with a note in her hand, ashen-faced, saying that some journalist had phoned and refused to speak to her but had a story about him. 'What is it, David?' He said, 'I don't know,' but he did. 'A letter came too,' she said. 'Marked "Private and confidential". I haven't opened it.' And then he really felt it, he knew from the emptiness in the pit of him that the gremlin had escaped, the rumble was out, and he took the note and he went into the study and closed the door and read the number and the name Peter Bond and wondered what information he had and how he had got it, and there on the desk was an A5 envelope, unopened as Melissa had said, and he opened it and saw the photograph and thanked God it was what it was because it could have been so much worse, but then maybe there *was* much worse, and he broke into a sweat and wondered if there was even a remote chance that he could save himself and Melissa and the kids but there wasn't, and he looked at the calendar above the desk, twenty-three days left, and thought, this is it, I'll stand down, the association will be mad but to hell with them, this isn't about them any more it's about us. And then he lifted the receiver and dialled the number.

§

The story of the last gasp. The original Mr Bond's final case. He beds the girl – not a classic Bond girl, it has to be said – and she leads him to the villain, who turns out not to be a villain but a sad bastard like himself, but nevertheless old Bondy has a job to do. The bad guys have fucked him over once too often – Croick, Canterbury, Thatcher, Major, Forsyth, they're all part of the same team – it's just a shame that the only one in his sights is an inferior specimen of bad guy called David Eddelstane, but that's how it works sometimes and Jimmy Bond has only one throw of the dice, one last stick of dodgy gelignite to detonate, and he goes for it. What the hell has he got to lose? Sorry, pal, this is going to hurt you a lot more than it hurts me. Sky-High Joe's identity revealed at last – and jings! it was Wee Jimmy all along!

Lucy was using Peter and he was using her. No deception there, it was an honest relationship based on mutual exploitation. She went down to London and followed her brother around and then she came back to Edinburgh and did some more snooping. A proper wee detective. He could have given her some tips but he left her to it. Claudine, the waitress flatmate, knew a girl who knew a girl. Lucy talked to her. Then, on the crumb-strewn, wine-splashed, lumpy mattress she talked to Peter. Did he know what 'strictly by appointment' meant in the small ads? Yes he did. And that most of the city's saunas were brothels? Yes. But that there were other places, hidden away, out of the limelight? Yes. This girl worked in one of them, or had done so. Discretion was the watchword of such operations but Lucy had found out what her brother liked. Peter said, Do I want to know this? Lucy said, Of course you do, isn't that what this is about?

It wasn't much. It wasn't anything really. He had a thing about shoes and what he enjoyed was a woman who made him worship her shoes, her feet. There was more, about him lying on the floor and being walked on, cleaning the shoes with his tongue, that kind of stuff. A foot-and-mouth outbreak, Peter said, but this time Lucy didn't laugh. It's pathetic, she snorted. And it was. The point, though, was not that it was pathetic but that it was paid for. In the current climate that was enough.

We need proof, Peter said. But Lucy wouldn't tell him where Eddelstane went to get his kicks. Peter said, I could shadow you shadowing him but let's not get complicated. He gave her his Minox camera. Get me a picture or two. Lucy said, She won't do that. Meaning the shoe goddess. He said, We don't need him in the act of licking. We just need him entering or leaving the premises. That's all.

It was autumn, then it was winter. Everything was brown and dead. For weeks, months, Peter missed Lucy in the pub near Haymarket. He rang the doorbell of her flat and no one answered. He thought, she wants some kind of justice of her own, or maybe she wants money. He lamented the loss of the wee camera.

Then one day she was there again. She sat down without a word. He went to buy her a drink and when he came back the camera was on the table and next to it a slim white envelope.

What kept you? he said.

I had to be patient.

He opened the envelope. There were four photos, all the same: David Eddelstane MP, unmistakable in the light flooding on to his face from behind the door that was being opened to him. There was a legible number on the door, and the person opening it, though obscure, was definitely female. There was also a sheet of paper with Eddelstane's home and office details and phone numbers.

Is it enough? Lucy asked.

We'll see.

I want him destroyed.

The look on her face. Peter didn't like it.

For this?

For everything. They got Al Capone on tax evasion, didn't they?

He laughed, then stopped when she didn't.

Later, back at her place, after they'd done sex, before he got up to go, he tried to reason with her. He didn't want to leave, he said. He'd rather stay. He'd missed her. He said, I'd like us to be together.

What? she said.

We could be together. The two of us on the one life-raft. I think we might just about keep one another alive.

She shook her head. What are you talking about?

He said, Lucy, I really like you.

She said, You must be fucking insane then.

He said, You don't really want to do this, do you? Why do you want to do it?

She said, I got you the fucking photographs. Don't change your mind now.

He said, I never . . .

He said, Lucy.

He said, You're hurt, Lucy. You've been an outsider so long you've forgotten what it's like to have someone care about you. I care about you. Why don't we let it all go?

She said, If you care about me you'll do this one thing.

She was immovable. She turned away from him. She told him to get out. She said, If you don't do it I'll fucking do it and I'll take us all down with him.

He got dressed. He said, I need to think it through.

She said, from under the sheet, Do it for me.

To think it through he had to stay clear of her for a few days. He stayed away from the pub – from all pubs in fact. He came off the booze completely. One last effort. Okay, supposing he did it? What power did the photograph contain? And if there was power, what would it achieve? Maybe if he'd had time he'd have come up with the answers but it was the Croick business all over again, he didn't have time. Time was running out for everybody. Parliament was dissolved in mid-March and a General Election scheduled for 1 May. Six weeks of suicide for the Conservative Party.

He thought, I'll do a test run. He called a news editor he'd done freelance work for in the past. He said he had a story about an MP in compromising circumstances. Who hasn't? the man said. This one's Scottish, are you interested? Aye, maybe, who's the MP and what are the circumstances? Do you think I'm stupid? Peter said, but then he gave him enough to keep him interested. Is the story watertight? Peter said, Yes, but I can't reveal my source. (Because

Lucy had made that a condition.) The man at the paper said, Either we need proof or we need an admission from the MP. Peter said, Leave it with me.

A week later the Scottish Tories went into self-destruct mode, thus at least demonstrating their Caledonian genes. One MP announced he wasn't seeking re-election following revelations about an affair. The party chairman withdrew from being proposed as a candidate when allegations were made about a homosexual relationship. Recriminations and accusations among rival officials and factions followed. Peter thought, what the hell, if I don't move now I'll be trampled in the rush.

He had nothing to lose. Except Lucy. And he didn't want to lose her.

He dialled the Glenallan number.

EDDELSTANE: Why are you doing this, Mr Bond?
BOND: It's my job.
EDDELSTANE: Is that really why you're doing it?
BOND: What other reason would there be?
EDDELSTANE: I can think of many. It takes a special kind of person to do a job like yours.
BOND: I'll take that as a compliment.
EDDELSTANE: I dare say you will. And I dare say, too, that nothing I can say will dissuade you from running your grubby little story?
BOND: It's not me that made it grubby. If it isn't true, you know what to do.
EDDELSTANE: You don't even know me.
BOND: You're the Member of Parliament for Glenallan and West Mills. Do you not agree that the public has a legitimate interest in your behaviour?
EDDELSTANE: You say that almost as if you mean it. This is not yet about the public interest though, is it? It is about you writing a story about me. Actually, Mr Bond, I don't expect you to believe me but I don't care about myself. It's my family that concerns me. You will do my family irreparable damage.
BOND: I think it's you that has done the damage, Mr Eddelstane.
EDDELSTANE: You sound very sure of yourself. I hope you can live with your conscience.

BOND: Can you live with yours?

EDDELSTANE: I shall have to. This isn't going to be about David Eddelstane MP after a day or two. The circus will have moved on. This is going to be about me, my wife and my children. I shall have to hope that they will forgive me. Have you thought of that? I'm asking you to show a little mercy. No, not even that. A little kindness.

BOND: That's not what this is about.

EDDELSTANE: No? Well, if it isn't, what is it about?

But here, as elsewhere, as always, the transcript goes to ratshit. The original Mr Bond murders the High Commissioner and several of his lackeys but one of them manages to wallop him on the head on the way down so he slips into something less comfortable and the walls close in and all the voices and all the one-versations merge and overlap. Croick is dead but long live Croick as Canterbury as Lucy as Edgar as Eddelstane. The shoe-licker. Never met him face to face but by Christ Peter can still hear his voice down the phone line he no longer has. The accuser accused. The accused accusing. Whichever fucking way round it was. Eddelstane sounded dignified. He was the one going down to defeat and he sounded like a bloody martyr. Whereas Peter . . . And for what? He went looking for Lucy and she was gone, vanished, not a trace of her, disappeared as suddenly and permanently as old Uncle Jack. A ghost. The paper ran the story and the cheque fell through the letter box but for what, for what? Betrayal. Endless fucking betrayal. *I need to show you what happens.* Betrayal of others, betrayal of self. *And let the lesson be to be yersel.* Bondy in the lion's den. The voice of the arch-villain, the evil genius with the nuclear bomb, the white cat and the soft-spoken voice of unreason. *What is it all about, Mr Bond? Answer me that. What are we to be if not ourselves? What are we to be if not kind to one another? What else is there to be? To be cruel, to be brutal, to hurt or destroy by hatred – where is the profit in that? Profit isn't even the right word. Where is the humanity in that? We all have it in us to be kind, Mr Bond, because somewhere in us we all desire the same – that someone else be kind to us. Yes, even me, even you. That someone think of us, remember us, consider us. I'm not even talking about love. I'm talking*

about being treated with consideration and care. That's all. Not love, just
care and consideration. Do you understand that, Mr Bond? Mr Bond?
Mr Bond?

§

With less than a month to go before the General Election, the air-
waves were suddenly full of the latest scandal to hit the Conservatives. Out of the blue David Eddelstane announced that he would
not be seeking re-election as MP for Glenallan and West Mills.
There he was on the evening news outside a Glasgow hotel, looking
like he was going to throw up, with his wife beside him looking
equally sick as he read from a prepared statement and said that after
he'd finished reading it he would not be answering questions or giving interviews. Allegations, he intoned, concerning indiscretions in
his private life were about to be made public – allegations which he
had no intention of either disputing or discussing. In the current
climate of fevered interest in any politician's perceived misdemean-
ours he believed it was best for his party, his constituents and most
of all for his family that he step aside immediately and allow another
candidate to fight the seat. He deeply regretted the great distress his
actions had already caused his wife and children, and the embarrassment and difficulties they were likely to cause the Conservative
Party, and asked the media to show some humanity by allowing
him the time and space to attempt to repair the damage he had
done to his friends, colleagues and loved ones. Thank you very
much.

Cue mad media scrum and shouted questions as the Eddelstanes
disappeared back inside the building. Cut to a BBC correspondent
who said that the allegations were 'believed to centre on Mr Eddelstane having paid for sexual services at premises in both London
and Edinburgh'. 'Presumably, Brian,' the newsreader asked, 'this is
something the Conservatives could do without right now?' 'Frankly,
Jackie, it's the last thing they need. I understand that Central Office
is, to put it mildly, absolutely furious.'

There was more in the next day's papers, specifically about
Eddelstane's predilection for ladies' footwear. That evening Adam
turned up at Mike's flat, full of derision regarding Eddelstane's
predicament.

'A shoe fetish? I'd have expected a decent family man like him tae admit tae a boyfriend at least,' he said.

'There might be one out there,' Mike said. 'He has form, after all.'

It was a stupid thing to say, but it could not be unsaid. Adam looked at him sharply. 'How d'ye mean?'

'Forget it.'

'Naw, how d'ye mean? What dae *you* ken aboot his form?'

'It doesn't matter.'

'Aye it does. Tell me.'

Mike shrugged. 'I had a wee fling with him once. I probably wasn't the only one.'

'You what?' Adam's face was dark with anger.

'Like I said, forget it.'

'Ye had sex wi that Tory bastard? When?'

'I didn't say that. I said a fling.'

'Well, I assume we're no talking aboot a Highland dance. Or is "fling" public-school slang for something mair innocent, like a snog behind the bike sheds?'

'He'd left school before I even got there,' Mike said. 'We met by accident later, here in Edinburgh.'

'And?'

'And something happened.'

'What?'

'Nothing.'

'Well, either something happened or nothing happened. Which was it?'

Suddenly Mike was angry too. 'I don't have to justify myself to you.'

'Aye ye dae,' Adam said. 'A fling? What exactly did ye get up tae wi him?'

'Nothing. I shouldn't have mentioned it.'

'Well, ye fucking did, Mike!' Adam shouted. 'So fucking tell me what happened.'

'It was years ago!' Mike shouted back. 'Decades ago. Nothing fucking happened. We had a wee grope and that was it.'

'So why are ye fucking boasting aboot it?'

'I'm not boasting about it. I'm ashamed of it. I just said it because there he is in the news and I remembered.'

'So ye should be fucking ashamed. Was he an MP when ye had your wee fling?'

'No. It was years before that.'

'He was still a Tory. Once a Tory always a fucking Tory.'

'So am I contagious? Am I only allowed sex with card-carrying members of the Labour Party?'

'So ye did have sex wi him.'

'No, I didn't.'

'Ye just admitted it.'

'I didn't admit it and I don't have to admit or deny fucking anything.'

Adam stared at him coldly. Then he turned and walked out of the room.

'Adam!' Mike called.

The front door slammed.

He didn't come back for hours. Eventually Mike went to bed. He thought he wouldn't sleep but sleep came and so did a dream about David Eddelstane – a dream so vivid that when he woke it took a minute before he was sure it *was* a dream. David and Melissa and Mike were on holiday together – some weird location that might have been a Hebridean island but could equally have been a Greek one – and they were talking about Kilsmeddum Castle and David said, 'My son's just finished there.' 'You sent your son to Kilsmeddum? But it's a dump.' 'No it isn't.' 'That time we met in Edinburgh, we discussed it and we agreed it was a dump.' 'Well, it is a dump, but it's still a great place to spend your formative years. Character-building. Didn't do me any harm.' And Melissa said, 'You met in Edinburgh?' And David said, 'Not married yet, Mike?' And Mike said, 'No, I'm gay, remember?' 'Oh, surely not?' 'Yes, like you.' 'I'm not gay. I like women. Well, I like their shoes.' 'No, you're gay. I can prove it.' And Melissa said, 'No you can't.' 'I can.' She said, 'Well, don't. Please. Just don't.'

He woke and the words were clear in his head. And Adam was getting undressed, climbing into bed. 'Where have you been?' 'Walking. Go to sleep.' And they did, and in the morning for a moment it was as if none of it had happened, but it had.

They never really repaired it. They apologised, as they had in the past, but sometimes you know that the wound is deep and the patching-up inadequate. It was as if they realised they only had to keep things going a little longer, and then they could stop pretending.

§

1 May 1997: there was the usual gathering at Jean's on election night: Adam, Mike, Ellen, Robin, Walter, a few others. Everybody came in disguise: after the disappointment of 1992, nobody dared show any optimism for the outcome, whatever the opinion polls were saying. The polls had been wrong last time. But this time they weren't.

It wasn't until past midnight that they realised it was really true, that the eighteen years were over. They cheered and applauded as, one after another, heartily loathed Tory MPs were tumbled from office. Some poor woman, parachuted into Glenallan and West Mills as a last-minute substitute for David Eddelstane, was dispatched without mercy at about half past two, shortly after Michael Forsyth. As the extent of the Conservatives' defeat became clear – their complete extinction in Scotland and Wales – the mood changed to one of wonder and joy. It was a drunken night in that plenty of booze was consumed, but it wasn't especially riotous. More than anything, there was a sense of relief at having completed a long journey. It was, Mike remembers, like coming home after years away and finding everything familiar, and yet also different, because you yourself have changed. Everything is as you thought you left it, but you did, after all, leave it. And so in the sense of regaining there was also a sense of loss.

Around half past three, after John Major had publicly conceded defeat, Ellen cornered Mike. 'What's going on with you and Adam? You've hardly looked at each other all night.' 'Och,' he said, 'we're going through a rough patch.' 'Go and speak to him,' she said. 'He's in the kitchen.'

Mike went. He hadn't noticed, or much cared, that Adam was missing from the front room. He was on his own, leaning out of the wide-open kitchen window.

'Adam.'

He pulled himself in and turned round.

'All right?'

'Aye,' Adam said. 'Just needing some fresh air and contemplation.'

'What are you contemplating? Not jumping, I hope?'

'I'm just thinking aboot tonight,' he said. 'We'll no see the likes o this again, ye realise that? This is history. Efter tonight, naething will ever be the same again.'

'I know,' Mike said.

'In a lifetime ye ainly get something like this once, twice at maist. The last one was 1945, and you weren't alive for that and I was just months old. It's like a door opening. It won't stay open for lang. But ye never forget the view through the open door.'

'I understand.'

'Dae ye?' he asked. 'Take it in, Mike. It's a big moment.'

He was right. The enormity of what had happened politically was worth looking at. But the distance between the two of them was also immense. Of course Mike knew exactly what he was talking about.

'It's over, isn't it?'

'Aye, I think so.'

'Let's not fight any more. Come back and join the others.'

'Aye, okay.'

Suddenly even this felt better. Mike picked up another bottle of wine and took it through, and it might have seemed to Ellen, if she'd been paying attention, that they'd made it through their rough patch. And maybe they had. There was more drink and more laughter, and a song or two, until at last tiredness overcame them all and light began to fill the world outside. Then Adam and Mike walked home and went to bed together for the last time. And it was true that they didn't fight any more, because there was nothing left to fight about.

§

It was the summer after the election. Adam was back near Borlanslogie and Mike was still in Edinburgh. They saw each other occasionally, and got on better than they had for years. They were still high from whatever had been in the air on that night in May. Life seemed hopeful: disillusion had not yet set in, despite the still-to-be-leaped-over hurdle of a two-question referendum, which the new government, headed by Tony Blair, insisted would have to precede the establishment of a Scottish parliament.

One day Jeremy Tait, Mike's boss, told him that the manager of his Perth shop was thinking of leaving. Would Mike consider a move there, to take over? Mike grabbed eagerly at the chance. He was sick of the Tollcross flat, where he'd been for nearly a quarter of a century. A change of scene, better pay, more responsibility – he decided he could handle all of those things.

It turned out that the Perth manager wasn't going till October. The two-question devolution referendum was scheduled for 11 September. For much of August, on days off and evenings, Mike did his bit for the 'Yes, Yes' campaign, stuffing leaflets through doors and handing them out on Princes Street, urging people to vote both for the parliament and for it to have some power to vary the rate of income tax. The spectre of 1979 haunted the campaign. The 'No, No' side was understaffed, poorly funded and demoralised: there was little to fear from it. What was to be feared was public indifference or exhaustion, another vote of little or no confidence. A big turnout was needed, an overwhelming affirmation that, whatever else emerged in this new political era, nobody would later be able to say that the Scots had had their parliament imposed upon them.

On the last day of August came the accident in Paris that killed Princess Diana and Dodi Al-Fayed and suspended all politics – virtually all normal life – for a week. It felt to Mike like a massive distraction, as if some external force had lobbed a meteorite at the democratic process and said, 'Thou shalt not have the undivided attention of the people.'

But, a few days after the princess's funeral, the referendum did finally happen. Mike went out to vote thinking of M. Lucas and his prophecy at Bannockburn, that a time to accept would come, and that when it did the ghosts of history would whisper in people's ears. And so it turned out. Overwhelmingly the people voted to have their parliament back. As the results came in, live on television, Labour's Scottish leader, Donald Dewar, who had the look of a dyspeptic heron according to one commentator, punched the air and it was endearing, not stomach-churning; Alex Salmond of the SNP grinned his widest grin and it didn't look remotely smug. A few weeks after that, Mike Pendreich closed the door for the last time on the Tollcross flat and drove his few possessions in a hired car to a new flat in Perth. He was not sorry to go. It was a good time to be on his own again.

Adam and he did not see each other for a year and a half, but they kept in touch, and eventually arranged to meet. One Friday evening Adam came to Perth by train and they went for a meal. There was an underlying restlessness in Adam, kicking against the new politics. The first Scottish parliamentary elections had just taken place, but he had played no part in the campaign. Mike was surprised: he'd thought it possible Adam might stand as a candidate. No, Adam said. Even if he'd wanted to, the party machine wouldn't have let him. He was Old Labour, not the right flavour these days. Better men and women than he had been vetted and found wanting by the party they'd served for years. Labour had won the election but half of its new MSPs were time-serving nonentities. In every sentence he uttered Mike could hear his disappointment.

'Still,' Mike said, trying to lighten the mood, 'some progress has been made. We're a dark land now, overrun by homosexuals. Apparently.'

The American evangelical preacher Pat Robertson had just described Scotland in these terms. There was outrage because the Bank of Scotland was trying to set up a business deal with Robertson, whose extreme, negative views on gays, feminists and the United Nations were well known. Later the bank dropped the idea.

Adam barely smiled. 'We're a dark land all right,' he said.

'What's wrong with you? You sound so depressed.'

'Maybe I am. Or maybe I'm just Scottish.'

After the meal they went for a drink, and then they walked to the station so that Adam could catch the last train. It started to rain. Adam had an umbrella and they huddled together under it. And as they went he couldn't help himself, he let all the bitterness flood out.

'I'll tell ye the truth, Mike, I've had enough. Aye, the old political certainties are changing, and that's aw for the good. It's what we wanted, and it's happening. Proportional representation means the parties canna assume old loyalties ony mair. They have tae work for their votes. Onybody can vote for onybody noo and if they dinna like the big parties there are greens and socialists and God kens who else tae vote for. Fine. Or they can vote for naebody. But there's something I canna get oot o my heid. It's the thought that just at the point when we've won, when we've got what we worked for aw these years, right at that moment we throw it away because nae-body can be bothered ony mair. Thatcher won after all, in spite of everything. That's what I think.'

'How can you say that?' Mike said. 'Her own party chucked her out. She fought against devolution all the way, and we beat her. And the Tories won't be back in power for years.'

'They don't have to be. Blair and Brown are gonnae dae it aw for them. It's true. The market is king. So what aboot this parliament of oors? It's twenty years ower late. It's like we fought our way tae the bar just in time for the barman tae tell us he's stopped serving.'

'No,' Mike protested. 'I don't feel that. We're at the start of some-thing new and different. It *can't* be like it was before.'

Adam laughed. 'Like it was in the olden days, ye mean?'

'The olden days,' Mike said. 'My mother used to go on about them. The Middle Ages, knights in armour and no plumbing is what she meant.'

'Aye, and ye ken what it means noo? It means no that lang ago. When I was young. It's me that's middle-aged, and you're no that far behind me. We're frae the olden days just the same as Robert the Bruce and Bonnie Prince fucking Charlie.' The rain came on stronger and a gust of wind tried to jerk the umbrella out of Adam's hand. 'I think I'll dae what he did, go into exile,' he said. 'I'm sick of this weather, apart frae onything else.'

In the station they stood on the long, almost empty platform waiting for Adam's train.

'What aboot you?' he said. 'What'll you dae?'

'I'm not going anywhere,' Mike said. 'I'm sticking around to see what happens.'

'I hope it's what ye want, whatever it is,' Adam said.

'Remember what I told you once,' Mike said. 'Everything comes to he who waits.'

'Bollocks! It was bollocks then and it's still bollocks. Look, even this bloody train isna here.'

But a few minutes later it was.

§

Everything from then on is another story. The new parliament, the new country, the personal and the political. From where Mike sits, looking out from Cnoc nan Gobhar at the hills and the loch, every-thing beyond that point happened in another life. Except for one thing: the death of his father.

Angus died at Inverness in September 2005. He went to his GP complaining of chest pains and then had a heart attack in the sur-gery. If you're going to have a heart attack it's as good a place as any to have one, Mike thought later, but the doctor could do no more than stabilise him, then have him moved to Raigmore Infirmary by ambulance. There he had a second attack and died before Mike could get up the road from Perth. He'd seen him only a month before, as he'd spent part of August at Cnoc nan Gobhar. One rea-son for the visit was to encourage Angus to sort out his archive, but he wasn't interested, so Mike did some work on it himself. The rest of the time they went for short walks on the beach, or Mike went off on his own for an hour or two, leaving Angus with the paper and the crossword. In the evening Mike cooked dinner, while his father sat in the sun room and fell asleep over a book. It was all quite easy but vaguely dissatisfying. However, Mike did at least rediscover how much he enjoyed being in the north.

He organised the funeral at the crematorium in Perth. No more than twenty people attended. In his last years Angus had cut himself off geographically and socially, losing touch with most of his old associates. Male friends had never been that plentiful. Despite a couple of obituaries in the papers, the few still alive mostly didn't know he'd died till some time later. As for his women, the only two who turned up were Jean and Isobel.

It was a secular ceremony. Angus had always considered religion to be utter nonsense. An appreciation was given by a distinguished journalist colleague from his London days, now resident in Edin-burgh. For this Mike was very grateful: difficult as he finds such a task even now, it would have been all but impossible then. Or so it seems to him.

Afterwards, Isobel and Mike stood at the chapel exit and received everybody's condolences. Since he'd moved to Perth he and his mother had been more communicative, and he'd told her on the phone that she shouldn't feel under any obligation to attend, let alone do the line-up. She and Angus had been divorced for forty years, after all. He meant it kindly, but she insisted on being there.

'None of the little friends are going to do it, are they?' she said. 'None of the little friends, I imagine, are going to turn up. It's on occasions like this that one needs a widow.'

And on the occasion, Mike had to concede, she did her bit, glamorous in black at seventy-two, shaking everybody's hands as well as freezing out Jean (whom neither Mike nor Isobel categorised as a mere 'little friend'). Mike missed this moment. He was being commiserated with by Bob Syme, who had come with Isobel. Bob still lived along the road and still was not her boyfriend.

Mike had arranged for the usual provision of tea, coffee and alcoholic refreshment at a nearby hotel. There were far too many sandwiches – too much food altogether, including a tray of those greasy, flaky sausage rolls that never fail to appear at funeral teas. Bob Syme took it upon himself to reduce these to a respectable remnant. He also insisted on buying Mike a double whisky, and zealously bought drinks for anybody else who needed one. Isobel was driving so this included himself, several times.

Jean spoke to Mike for a while, then said she had better be going. She had a train to catch, she told him, and ended up sharing a taxi to the station with the distinguished journalist. Not long after that the party was down to three: Isobel, Bob and Mike.

'Thank you, Mum,' Mike said, 'for coming today, and for doing the honours.'

'Somebody had to.' She was silent for a moment, then said, 'I presume your father was not penniless. What will you do now?'

Mike had already had a meeting with Angus's lawyer and knew that everything had been left to him. Angus had obviously lived well and spent well, as 'everything' amounted to surprisingly little. However, with a frugal lifestyle, there might be enough money to stretch over two or three years. Mike would need it. He couldn't count on being a shop manager much longer. Jeremy Tait was getting on, and kept threatening to close the business. He couldn't compete with internet prices any more.

'I don't know,' Mike said. 'I might go to Cnoc nan Gobhar for a while. 'It's mine, apparently.'

Isobel sniffed. 'For what it's worth.'

'It's worth a lot to me. A roof over my head, all paid for. That's a relief.'

'You may find it's a trap as much as a relief,' she said, and he knew she was referring to her own situation, the house in Doom in which she had lived since childhood.

'Well, I like it,' Mike said. 'I'd forgotten how much, until I was there in the summer. I expect that's where I'll go.'

'Really?'

'The shop won't last much longer. I fancy a change. I couldn't afford to go back to Edinburgh. Why not try Sutherland for a while?'

'You'll become like him,' she said. 'A hermit. People will forget you exist.'

'I'll take that chance,' he said. 'What about you?'

'Me?' she said. 'What about me? Nothing will be any different for me. I don't expect anything from him,' she sighed. 'Not after all this time.'

'Are you all right?' Mike asked. 'Financially, I mean.'

'No,' she said. 'But I don't want anything from you. You look after yourself. Anyway, Bob is very kind.'

Bob had had his eyes closed during this exchange. Now he gave a snort and opened them again. Isobel looked at him anxiously. He was flushed and short of breath and slightly slumped in his seat. He'd always been portly: now he was enormous.

'We should be going,' she said. 'Do you want a lift?'

'No thanks. I'll settle up and walk back into town.'

'Isn't it rather far?'

'A couple of miles. I could do with the walk.'

Bob sat up. 'So could I,' he said, 'but let's be realistic.'

'You've had too much whisky, Bob,' Isobel said, in a surprisingly uncensorious tone. Or perhaps, given what she'd just revealed – her dependence on him, which wasn't that much of a revelation – it wasn't surprising at all.

'You're right,' he said. 'Sorry. Where's the Gents in this place, Michael?'

Mike started to give directions, but then Isobel decided she would go to the Ladies, so they all got up and Mike showed Bob the way. They stood next to each other at the urinals, saying nothing. Mike had washed and dried his hands before Bob had finished emptying his bladder, but it seemed somehow impolite to leave him there, so he waited.

Bob said suddenly, 'Do you have a pal?'

'I'm sorry?'

'I thought you might have a pal. Boyfriend. Partner, I suppose, is the correct term.'

He looked very hard at Mike. 'A good thing to have, at a time like this.'

'No,' Mike said. 'I don't have a partner. I did have, but we split up.'

'Sorry to hear it. What was his name?'

'Adam.'

'No chance of a reconciliation?'

'No, Bob. It was a while ago.'

'Oh?'

'Quite a few years.'

'Oh. Sorry. Nobody else on the scene?'

'No.'

'Isobel doesn't tell me anything, you see.'

He shook himself vigorously, did himself up, and came over to the washbasins.

'To be honest,' Mike said, 'I'm amazed she told you I'm gay.'

'She didn't,' Bob said. 'I mean, she didn't exactly volunteer the information. It came out by accident. This would be, I don't know, nine, ten years ago? We were talking about the fact that neither of us have grandchildren – well, obviously *I* don't – and that led on to you and I never even thought, I just said, "So has he not found the right woman or does he prefer men?" and she said, "How did you know?" and I said I didn't, which I didn't. And that's when she told me. She never told me about this Adam, though, or that you'd split up.'

'She didn't know about him,' Mike said. 'She doesn't know anything about my life. She doesn't want to.'

Bob finished washing his hands and grabbed a couple of paper towels.

'I wouldn't be so sure about that,' he said. 'Thank God attitudes have changed,' he went on. 'I mind when I was doing my National Service, there was a lad in our squad, just couldn't help himself, a nancy boy to his fingertips, and some of the others gave him a lot of grief, well, we all did, I suppose, can't say I was blameless, but most of us eased off after a while because the bastard sergeant major really had it in for him, I mean it was relentless, merciless. And then the poor sod, if you'll pardon the word, the poor sod went and hung himself. Terrible. All hushed up, as you'd expect. Shameful.' He shook his big, soft head. 'Nobody was held responsible, nobody was punished. I made a vow to myself after that, which I hope I've kept. I swore I would try never to be deliberately cruel to another human being again.'

They stood facing each other in that washroom. Mike didn't know what to say. Then, thinking of Isobel waiting in the lobby, he said, 'We'd better go,' and Bob said, 'Aye.' Reaching out a podgy hand, he touched Mike briefly on the shoulder.

'Your mother finds it difficult, Michael,' he said. 'I know she shouldn't, but she does. Partly generational, partly who she is. If I had a son, or a daughter, I wouldn't give a stuff what they liked doing so long as it didn't involve hurting anybody else. But that's me, Mr Easy-osy. Your mother's not like that. It doesn't make her a bad person, though. I'm very fond of her.'

'I know that, Bob, and I'm glad.'

'God knows what she sees in me, though, fat, boring, ignorant, baldy bastard that I am. Your dad was a handsome man, wasn't he? I've seen a picture or two.'

'Yes, he was.'

'Ach well.'

Mike held the door open, and Bob started to lumber through, then stopped.

'Do you miss him?' he said. 'Not your dad. Your partner. Adam.'

'Sometimes,' Mike said. 'Usually I don't at all, and then sometimes suddenly I do.'

'I bet you do,' Bob said. 'I miss Iona like that sometimes, even after all these years. Just comes out of nowhere and hits you. But I'm lucky. I've got Isobel.' His fat hand came up and hit Mike's shoulder again. And off he trundled.

'Be with you in a minute,' Mike called. He had to wait in the Gents for a little longer. After all, after everything, it was Bob Syme who made him cry at his father's funeral.

§

I wouldn't call it love at first sight. Not at second sight either – as if we'd harboured it all those years. I certainly didn't. *He* says he always

624

kept a thought of me in his heart. I like the idea of that but if I'm honest I'd pretty much forgotten about him. It was just an incident, something that happened once, a long time ago. *When Don met Marjory*. And nothing happened anyway. It's not as if anything *happened*. I sneaked him a look at his new baby, and that was it. But he says to me, Oh but don't you remember when we waited in the corridor for somebody to go by, and you were pressed against me in the shadows, and you were so clean and lovely? And I say, You remember it so clearly. And he says, Aye, I do. Don't you? And I say, No, not like you do. But maybe I do, a little. And maybe I always did.

But not love at first or second sight, definitely not. Love among the tinned beans? Not us! We just met there, in the supermarket, him pushing his trolley and me pushing mine, and he recognised me and we started talking. If he hadn't, if he'd been looking the other way, we'd have been trolleys that passed in the aisle. But he did. That's how it works sometimes. Actually I think that's how it works all the time. It's *meant*. Don't ask me to explain, but that's what I think.

We were older, of course, than we had been. Years and years older, and the world was older too. The world was crazier but maybe we were wiser. We were both missing something and we'd been missing it a while. It was twelve years since Ray died. Call it love if you like, or companionship, or friendship. Call it trust. We'd both missed that and within minutes we knew we'd found it. Yes, I'd say that was true.

He said, Excuse me, and I thought he wanted to get at the beans. Really I did. I moved my trolley and he said, No, excuse me, but is your name Marjory Taylor? I looked at him. What was I supposed to do, deny it? I said, It *used* to be. He said, Oh. Like he was disappointed. We're talking more than forty years later! He said, I'm sorry, I hardly ever come in here, I don't like it in fact, but I was in the town so I just thought I'd get a few things and then I saw you, I knew it was you right away. I looked at him, this tall, handsome, dignified man, and I said, Do I know you? He said, Aye, but it was a long time ago, you probably don't remember, you were a nurse. I said, I still am, you never stop being a nurse, where do you know me from? And then he told me who he was, and when we'd last met, at the infirmary. The *only* time we'd met. And after we'd gone through all the oohing and aahing and isn't that amazing, I said, You owe me a drink. And he said, So I do, I don't suppose you'd like a cup of tea in the café here? And I said, and it was ridiculous because I felt like a girl again, there was kind of fluttering in my tummy, I said, Yes, all right, but I'd like a proper drink later. So right from the start, within five minutes, I trusted him, and he trusted me. You could say he picked me up in Tesco, but really we were both picking something up from over forty years before.

He was past seventy then, and I was well into my sixties. Neither of us looked our age, though I say it myself. We do now. But what does that mean, 'look your age'? It means nothing. You're the age you are and how you look is how you look. To me he looked a bit like Nelson Mandela, only white and Scottish, if you can imagine that. Anyway, we went to the café and started talking. That's what we did. We started talking and we've never stopped.

I told him my life and he told me his. I told him about Ray and how we'd got together, and Ray's engineering work that took him all over the world, and how hard it was for me bringing up the kids on my own for months at a time. And then how we'd settled in Aberdeen when the oil boom started, and Ray said he'd never need to go abroad for work again, and the children grew up and I went back to nursing part-time, and then the first grandchild came along and then Ray got ill and how ironic was that – that he got cancer when I was the one that smoked, although I packed it in quick after that. And then when he died and the family were all further south, Edinburgh and Glasgow and Liverpool, I decided I'd had enough of Aberdeen and I'd always liked this part of the country so I sold up and came back and here I was, ten years on, cruising the aisles of Tesco in Drumkirk.

I said, What about your boy, it was a boy, wasn't it? And he said, Aye, our second. I said, What was his name? Charlie, he said. And what happened to Charlie? I said. He died, Don said. And I felt such an idiot, I put my hand on his arm and said I was sorry, and he said, Don't be, and the pain on his face was awful to see. Don't be sorry, he said. He didn't die as a boy. He grew up and then he died. He wasn't a great loss to the world. I was shocked to hear him say that about his own son. It must have been a great loss to you, though, I said. Well, he said, it's a long story, but I lost him long before he died. He didn't tell me it all then, because it *was* a long story, but he told me about Liz, his wife, and how *she'd* got cancer, just when he'd retired, and she went down very fast and here he was on his own seven years later, still living in the same house in Wharryburn.

I said, What about your other son? Billy? he said. Billy's all right. He's a teacher in Glasgow, teaches History and Modern Studies. Billy took a while to sort himself out but he's fine now, second time round, he's very happy. He's with a lovely lass, a Gaelic-speaking girl from the Highlands. Do you mind that slogan MAKE LOVE NOT WAR? he said. Billy took that to heart. He met both his bidie-ins on peace marches. He met the first one marching against Polaris and the second one marching against Trident. But for all that he's not given me any grandchildren yet, he said. I said, Is that a disappointment to you? Sometimes, he said, but I believe you have to try to rise above life's disappointments. Anyway, I can always hope. Catriona – that's his partner – Catriona's still just young enough, if they want bairns. But if it doesn't happen I'll not complain.

Neither of us seemed to want to leave, and neither of us had to. It wasn't as if we had to get home for anybody else. He'd come into Drumkirk on the bus – never had a car in his life, he told me, he could service one, repair one, drive one, but he'd never owned one, didn't see the need – so I offered him a lift home. We put our shopping in my car but before we drove off he said, Do you fancy a walk by the old infirmary? So we went down by the river, and parked and went for a walk. The new hospital's out of town, and the old one's been converted into flats and the grounds are all landscaped. It looks very nice but the prices are insane. Anyway we walked by the river, just talking and talking, me telling him about my children and grandchildren and him laughing and saying how lucky I was, and on the way back we wandered in through the old infirmary gates and had a look at the place. Over there's where you asked me for a cigarette, he said. So of course we had to go and admire the trees, even bigger than they had been then, and where the nurses' home used to be there was a brand-new building, another block of flats with cars parked in numbered spaces. There was a woman with a dog, she was picking up its business with a trowel and putting it in a plastic bag and the look of disgust on her face made us both laugh. As if she was thinking, did that really come out of *my* dog? And then a man came over with a disapproving look on *his* face and asked if he could help us. Don said he didn't think so. This is private property, the man said. Well, Don said, we're not doing any harm, my son was born here, and this lady used to work here as a nurse. In fact she helped deliver my son. The man looked a bit fed up, as if this happened all the time. I see, he said, it's just that we get all these kids coming in here, causing havoc. We're not kids, Don said. What do they do, these kids? I asked. They ride their bikes all over the grass and drop litter everywhere, the man said. Don said, Terrible, isn't it? They should reintroduce National Service. Absolutely, the man said. And the birch, Don said. And hanging, the man said. And send all the darkies hame, Don said. And at that point the man realised he was being made a fool of, and he went very crimson and turned on his heel and stalked off and we went back through the gates laughing and then I said, It *is* terrible, though. A lot of people really think like that. I ken, Don said. *He* does, for a start. I loved the way he spoke, I could listen to that voice all day, I thought.

I drove him home and we passed a nice-looking hotel and he said, What about that drink? I could buy you it in there, and I said, Okay, but not today, because I was feeling a little overwhelmed at the pace we were setting. Tomorrow then, he said, and I agreed. He said, They've got a good restaurant, let me take you for a meal, and I agreed to that too. And when we got to Wharryburn he invited me in for a coffee and I didn't even hesitate, in I went. The house was fine, a little austere in the way men on their own often live, but very clean and quite spacious. It was mad but I was doing that thing already, sizing it up, thinking about what I would do with it. We sat in the kitchen looking out on the garden, which was immaculate, full of flowers and shrubs and vegetables. He took me out and showed me up and down the grass paths he'd made, pointing out different things. He said, The garden's been my territory for years. My zone of influence. Liz's zone was indoors, the house. I'm still getting used to that being mine too. I said, You make it sound like the Cold War and he said, Well, at times it was, but we learned to be tolerant. What's that thing called, MAD? Mutually assured destruction. We knew which buttons not to push. But we'd kind of lost each other and then I retired and it was like we woke up, we saw what a poor way of living we'd got into. And we started to make it better and she gave up the cleaning job she'd had but she got ill almost at once. The truth was she'd been ill for a long time but I didn't know. She was in pain, she was sick, and eventually she couldn't deny it any more, *we* couldn't deny it. She had breast cancer and they operated but it was too late, it had spread, what's that called again when it spreads? Metastasis, I said. Aye, he said, that's what had happened. It was in her bones. They gave her six months. She said she'd thought there was something wrong with her for years but she couldn't face it, she put it down to the menopause or working too hard or anything except the truth because she was too frightened. Her mother went the same way. If we hadn't drifted apart maybe I'd have made her do something about it earlier, but I didn't. I'll never forgive myself for that. We had some good times before she went though. In the end she managed eight months. We had wee holidays together, just a few days away here and there. We found each other again. And Billy was a great support, he was brilliant in fact, he was on his own at that time and he helped look after his mother right to the end.

What about Charlie? I asked. Was he still alive when his mother died? Aye he was, Don said. He came to see her a couple of times. He'd have come more often but he was in the army by then, you see. He came these two or three times and while he was seeing her I came out here into the garden. We hardly said a word to one another. When we knew she hadn't long left I got a message to him through his regiment and he came one last time – compassionate leave – and I asked him if he'd come back for the funeral and he said, No, why would I do that? He'd said goodbye to her and he didn't need to say anything to anybody else. And he went back to the army and that was the last time I saw him.

He looked at me and said, Listen to me, I'll be frightening you off spouting all this stuff at you. I said he wouldn't and then it just kind of happened, I took his hand to assure him of that, and we went back into the house holding hands and we didn't let go till he made some more coffee and that was when he told me more about his sons. And our hands met again over the table and that was it really, I knew we were going to be together even though nothing else happened that time, we just held hands.

It was all over with Charlie by then. He'd been dead a year and

Don could talk about it without too much trouble. Charlie had been wild as a young man, he left home and ended up in Granthill, which is about the worst bit of Drumkirk there is, and he got involved in a lot of crime, gang-related stuff, which was when he and Don fell out, they had a big confrontation and Charlie nearly killed his father, and that was the end of their relationship. Well then, years passed and Liz used to see Charlie but Don and he didn't communicate and then something happened. Don never found out what it was he did, but he heard things through a friend of his who worked on the local paper. Charlie could be violent and he did something very bad, he overstepped some boundary and the other gangs gave him an ultimatum, it was either get out or they'd shop him to the police, so he got out, he joined the army. And it saved him. No, that's not true. That's my interpretation and I don't know and anyway it didn't save him, that's a stupid thing to say. But it changed him, or at least it controlled him. Maybe by going into the army he found a way of channelling all his anger or something. Don and I have talked about that and he says maybe I'm right but it's not exactly something you want to think about, is it – young men channelling their anger armed with assault rifles. And the truth is we'll never know and it still didn't bring about a reconciliation between them, not even when Liz died.

He was in the army for seventeen years altogether. He served in Northern Ireland and the Falklands and some fathers would be proud of a record like that but Don said he'd had enough war fifty years before to knock the pride out of him and anyway the Falklands was the stupidest, most pointless war anyone could have fought in. I didn't think so and we discussed that but we didn't fall out over it, we just agreed to differ. And then there was the Gulf War and Charlie was out in it but he came home safely from that too. Don didn't know this at the time because there was no contact between them. He only found out after Charlie died. An officer came to see him to tell him the news, and it was from him that he learned some of the details of where Charlie had been on service. Don talked about the officer visiting, I think it was the next night, when he took me out for our first meal.

This officer turned up at the door one evening. He asked for Mrs Elizabeth Lennie and Don said she was dead and the officer looked a bit awkward and asked who he was and Don said he was her husband. The officer asked if he was the father of Sergeant Charles Lennie, and when Don said yes the officer said he had some bad news. He came straight out with it, he said Charlie had been killed during a training exercise on Salisbury Plain. He'd been in a jeep which collided with an armoured vehicle and overturned, there were three of them in the jeep but the other two were thrown clear, only Charlie was killed. He was driving. It seemed the jeep had been in an area where it wasn't supposed to be and the armoured vehicle came over a hill and pretty much rolled over it. Don said, And how does a thing like that happen? And the officer said, It was an accident, there'll be a coroner's inquiry but it was just a terrible accident. One of those things. And that was the irony. Charlie had been in all these places where the enemy had tried to shoot him or blow him up and in the end he was run over by a British tank.

The officer came back a few days later and talked more about the accident and the inquiry, and he had a whole lot of notes in a briefcase, in case Don needed to ask any questions, but Don said he only had one, and that was whether Charlie had made a good soldier.

The officer looked a bit surprised and shuffled through his papers and said yes, he'd been a good soldier, he'd been in the army for all those years, he'd served his country well, that kind of thing. And Don said he didn't give a damn about any of that, he'd barely spoken to his son in twenty years and maybe he should rephrase the question because what he wanted to know was whether the army had made something of him. And the officer looked through his papers again and said yes, I think we did. It's not uncommon for there to be disciplinary problems with new recruits, Mr Lennie, but Charlie came through them, and after all he did end up a sergeant. Don asked what he meant by disciplinary problems and the officer said he didn't have all the details but it seemed Charlie had taken some time to adjust to the military regime. He said, We sorted him out, Mr Lennie. Often young men join us because there is a lack in their lives, and we supply whatever it is that's missing. A sense of self-worth, duty, comradeship, a sense of family. When your son signed up it was a two-way contract. Perhaps you could say we remoulded him. And then he said that he hoped the answers he'd given were some kind of comfort, and Don said no, not really, but Charlie was dead now and there was nothing more to be said or done about it.

Obviously I'm paraphrasing. I wasn't there but when Don talks about something from the past it's very intense. He didn't describe what the officer looked like or anything, but it was as if he was there at the table beside us, as if Don was seeing him and not me, having that same conversation with him. But after a minute he was back with me. He said, Marjory, I feel like I can tell you almost anything. And I said, That's good, that's the way I feel too. He said, I'd like you to meet Billy some time, I think you'd really like him. And I said, I'd like you to meet my children too. Well, you don't say things like that at our age without realising the significance. We knew what we were saying all right.

And of course I did meet Billy and I do like him, very much. He's quiet and deep but he has a generous spirit, like his father. And Billy's a wonderful father. Another lifetime, or a fair bit of one, seems to have gone by since Don and I got together. Billy and Catriona have their children, growing up bilingual in Glasgow – trilingual, Don says, because he feeds them as much Scots as he can on top of the Gaelic and English – and I have seven grandchildren and there's a serious danger I'll be a great-grandmother before I die, I can hardly believe that. And we lead a life of contentment. I don't know how else to put it. We don't fight, we don't argue, and it's not because we bite our tongues or one of us defers to the other, we just get on. What fortune is that! To live in this beautiful country and be old and healthy and be with someone you love and respect every minute of the day, every day of the week. What fortune is that!

I've asked him once what he meant when he said he always kept a thought of me in his heart. He said, I mean just that, I never forgot you. He said, I think most people go through life a wee bit disappointed in themselves. I think we all keep a memory of a moment when we missed someone or something, when we could have gone down another path, a happier or better or just a different path. Just because they're in the past doesn't mean you can't treasure the possibilities. I said, But there was no possibility, not for us, not then. You had a wife and two young children. We weren't possible then. Aye, he said, you're right of course. So we didn't really miss each other, I said. No, he said, but maybe we put down a marker for another time. And now's the time. Now we can do whatever we want to do.

And that's it, isn't it? We've reached that place, that stage. It's a shame there's not that much time left, but we can do whatever we like with it. And we do. We do.

A time came when you knew the time was coming. Your bones were sore, the vast distances you'd once covered were no longer possible. You had become an old man, aged by seasons and weather and the fierce grace of your journey. You put your crooked hand to your cheek and the hollow hardness of it was satisfying to you. The woman you had married, if she still lived, would not be an old woman, not in the same way. The child you had had, whose name you could not remember, would be a woman of advancing years. They were lost to you, and surely you were lost to them. You did not regret. Regret was somewhere far, far back and it did not touch you.

It was autumn, the merciful season of decay. You had always thought that when you finally surrendered it would be winter. You'd imagined a walk in a night of snow and ice, your senses closing down as the cold closed in around you. So when you felt the time coming and it was autumn, a little well of gratitude bubbled within you, though you did not consider what it was you were thankful for. Slowly, slowly, as the days diminished and the leaves fell and the land lowered itself through red and ochre and yellow and gold and brown into sleep, you travelled north and west, pointing yourself like an arrow to the distant corner, the turning point of the land. You were heading for something you knew but did not know, like a fish, like a bird. Perhaps at last you were heading towards yourself.

You left the last of the houses, the last of the people behind. You followed a track and the track led through great dunes to a bay. The wind had the last warmth of the south in it and drove spume and veils of sand across the beach. The great ocean roared and crashed beside you. Gull feathers and the empty armour of crabs scurried before your steps. You crossed shallow waters rushing like ropework. The sky piled up in the distance. You stopped, looked back. Nobody. You were alone in the vast expanse of land meeting water. You trudged on, your steps heavy now as you counted them down, the last of all the millions you had taken.

You'd not eaten for days. You had no hunger left. No hunger, no cold, no heat, no pain. Memory was draining from you. You were pouring from yourself like the water to the sea. Your time was coming.

You knew the meaning of everything and the meaning of nothing. You were ready to leave. Afterwards, everything would be as if you had never been.

You settled on a bank of sand under a low cliff. The debris of birds and fish and stone and shell was there. Some years perhaps the sea would reach you. The wind wrapped itself around you. Sand shifted and bedded in your folds.

Night came. Morning came. Night came. Morning came. You did not move.

Nobody else was there.

Your fading hand reached into the pocket where the stones were. There were hardly any left. All the others you had gathered and sown were gone. Now it was your turn.

You were going.

The smooth white pebbles sat cool in your mouth. You sucked, creating a moist coat for each one. You swallowed them slowly, one after another.

You were going.

You ate the stones, and the sea faded, and the land faded, and the sand filled your ears and eyes and nose, and you faded into the land, into the sea. You were going, and you were not coming back.

You were gone.

PART SIX

The Gift of the Moment

Applause. A cheer or two, clapping that roars then dies away like the sea over a pebble beach. He nods, smiles, thank you thank you. Clears his throat and – a hint of nerves? – taps the microphone even though they all know it's working.

'Well. Here we are. Thank you, Duncan, for those kind words. I'd like to endorse what you said about Ellen Imlach's introductory essay. She wrote it at very short notice and it's both provocative and reflective and says things about my father and his work that I don't think I could ever have articulated. So, thank you, Ellen. And thank *you* all, for turning up. Actually, thank you for sticking around.' Laughter from the front rank. 'As Duncan's just said, this show has been a long time in the making.'

Here we are. Rows of faces. A semicircle of heads, seven or eight deep. Mike Pendreich can't quite believe how many people have come. Everybody looking up at him at the top of the short flight of steps. He's in that slightly hunched position adopted by people who aren't used to microphones. *The mike stand* – he could take that personally. Duncan Roxburgh off to one side, looking proudly proprietorial, as well he might after the blood and sweat he's expended, most of it not his, to get this place established. People are craning their necks, shuffling sideways for a view. In other circumstances it would be Mike doing the stretching and shifting, trying to get the right line, the right background. Trying to capture the subject. But today, now, they're all looking at him. As if there's a camera inside every head, and every blink is a shutter action. As if all the faces he's ever photographed are busy taking him with their eyes. And it makes him think of something else and he decides to depart from his prepared speech. Only he doesn't because he doesn't have a prepared speech, he was just going to step up to the microphone after Duncan and say a few words people would instantly forget, but suddenly it's important to say something they'll remember. He's never been much good at forward planning. Let the moment dictate what you say, what you do. And now, this is the moment. He feels the density of it, he hefts it like a glass paperweight, or one of those perfectly smooth, tide-rolled stones from a particular bay on the north coast, not far from Cnoc nan Gobhar, where the retreating waves sometimes sound like rounds of applause, and he wants to hold it out to this crowd of people and say, Look at this. This is what we have. Treasure it. Remember it.

'A long time in the making,' he says. He hears himself, the familiar, unfamiliar sound of his own voice amplified. 'I'm thinking of that massive painting that David Octavius Hill, one of the fathers of Scottish photography, did of the Disruption of 1843.' Should he go down this road? Will they get what he's talking about? Too late, he's started. 'You know the one I mean?' A few nods, thank *you*, this is the temple of the camera, the National Gallery of Photography, after all. 'Over a period of years Hill and Robert Adamson made calotype portraits of most of the ministers who walked out of the General Assembly of the Church of Scotland that day to found the Free Church. And then Hill recreated the scene in a painting, using the calotypes as the models for the people in it. And this painting, which hangs in the Free Church buildings on the Mound to this day, it's huge. How big is it, Duncan?'

'Oh, about five feet high by twelve feet long.'

'About five feet by twelve feet. And there are hundreds of people in it, I can't remember exactly how many . . .'

'Four hundred and fifty-seven.'

'You see how useful it is to have an oracle at your side?' Laughter. 'And some of the people in the painting weren't present on the day but were instrumental in setting up the Free Church, and many of those who *were* present were photographed years after the event, looking much older than they were in 1843, so the whole exercise is like a reverse of the process of airbrushing people *out* of history. Hill brushed them *in* to his painting. Yes, the Scots invented everything – including Stalinist methodology long before Stalin was even born.' A few knowing, appropriately grim chuckles. 'So. Not a historically accurate picture, but a representation of a moment, a movement, in history. And it took Hill, with his wife's assistance, twenty-three years to complete it. A long time in the making.'

He pauses. Some eager, attentive expressions, some glazing over, a bit more shuffling. He's trying to say something here, but what? These people have come to celebrate the opening of an exhibition of his father's work and what do they get? A lecture about a Victorian religious schism most of them, even if they've actually heard of it, know nothing about. Make the point, Mike, and move on.

'The Disruption,' he says – and it starts to spill out, it amazes him that he sounds so confident when he feels so unsure, it astounds him that he's accumulated such vast amounts of information and can access it so easily, but what is it for, what is it for? – 'the Disruption is a moment from the past that doesn't seem to have anything to do with us. *What* was it about? Whether a congregation had the right to elect its own minister or was obliged to accept the choice of the local patron? Who gives a damn? It's hard to believe that an issue like that could split a country down the middle, but it did. It was traumatic and it mattered. It made Francis Jeffrey, one of the founders of the *Edinburgh Review*, say he was proud of his country, that there wasn't another on earth where such a thing could have happened. How strange is that, to be proud that people stuck to a principle that created division and disharmony throughout the land? Or is it strange? Maybe it is, maybe it isn't. We could have an argument about that. We could argue that it was the supporters of patronage, the government, the establishment, who caused the division and disharmony. But even at this distance, don't we understand precisely what Francis Jeffrey meant? Because although most of us have rejected organised religion and don't believe in God any more, we absolutely believe that no other bastard, and particularly no other rich bastard, had the right to impose his brand of religion on our ancestors.'

More laughter. Even in this year not of our Lord 2008, some people in gatherings of this kind still get a kick out of the odd mild swearie word relayed through a PA system. Or maybe it's just relief, he's lost them with all this talk of painted ministers and calotypes but they appreciate the tonal value of *bastard*. Or they appreciate the historical referencing, the overlap of different eras. What's that thing William Faulkner's supposed to have said? 'The past is never dead. It's not even past.' Aye, quite. He can use that. Anyway . . .

'Anyway, the point of all this is that such moments from long ago do still continue to have something to do with us. Years after the event, David Octavius Hill knew what the story was he wanted to tell with his great big painting, and he told it. But at the time it happened, who knew what the outcome of the Disruption would be? He didn't. Nobody did. When we're *in* the story, when we're part of it, we can't know the outcome. It's only later that we think we can see what the story was. But do we ever really know? And does anybody else, perhaps coming along a little later, does anybody else really care?

'Certainly, when my father began taking photographs after the war, he didn't set out to sew a narrative thread from one image to the next. He was creating a body of work but each image was supposed to stand alone, to contain its own story. His famous picture of Harry Lauder's funeral – the one you see right at the start of the exhibition – isn't about the grand occasion, it's about the wee boy looking in the other direction. His picture of Elvis at Prestwick Airport – it's as if Elvis is just a convenient excuse to take a picture of the fans on the other side of the fence. And neither of these photographs necessarily had anything to do with the other, or with ones he took earlier or later – they weren't linked in any deliberate, conscious way, except by the method, by his eye. And when he was taking those photos my father had no idea that he'd have a son who'd also be a photographer, and that several years after his death that son would make a selection from his work and mount an exhibition called "The Angus Angle" and try to make a story out of the selected images. But that's what has happened, and so – here we are.'

Here we are. Who, exactly? A few old friends – Walter Fleming, Ellen Imlach, Eric Hodge, Jeremy Tait, Gavin Shaw. Adam? No, despite being invited, Adam hasn't flown in for the occasion. Jean Barbour has declined to make an appearance, citing an abhorrence of crowds as her excuse. Mike is staying two nights with her again and is pleased to see that she no longer appears to be dying at quite the same rate, although she's smoking just as furiously. So, no Adam, no Jean. But his mother has astonished him by turning up, with Bob Syme in tow looking like the next big breath could set off a heart attack. Earlier, when Bob shook his hand and gasped, 'We're awful proud of what you've achieved here, Michael,' Isobel warmly agreed. 'Your father would be proud too,' she said, and gave him a kiss. Somehow, his family, including Angus but not yet Murdo, are reunited in this place, on this occasion. Now he catches Isobel's eye and she gives him a discreet, happy smile.

Bob Syme, worker of miracles.

Who else? Other photographers and artists and scores of folk from Duncan Roxburgh's contact database – patrons, founder-members, Friends and sponsors of the NPG, arts-administration heid-bummers and apparatchiks, media persons, critics, reviewers – the usual suspects, in other words. A handful of high-heid-yins from the world of politics: the Presiding Officer of the Parliament, the Deputy First Minister, the Lord Provost of Edinburgh; a smattering of cooncillors and MSPs. The great and the good and the not so. The worse for wear and the better by far. Scotland's a wee country. When you put a couple of hundred of these folk in a room you're looking at a spider chart of how the place works. They don't need to network much because the web's already there, they were at school together or are cousins or played in a band or were in a folk club or are married to each other or once were or had sex when they were students or last week or grew up in the same street or support the same team or work in the same building. They don't all like each other and some of them are eaten away with hatred and bile but that's not the point. The point is there's always a connection.

'So in doing what I've done, making the selection I have, have I laid a false trail? Or am I simply able, from where I am now, from where *we* are now, to see the route we came, to look back and see the trail clearly marked? If my father were alive we would have an argument about that too. I'd say I can see the lines on the map, and he'd say the map is covered with many lines, you only see the ones you want to see. And we'd both be right.'

There's a guy from the *Telegraph*, name of Crombie, a black-bearded pugilist who turns up for most things, so says Duncan, who ought to know since he turns up for most things too. Crombie's a good writer but types wearing knuckledusters, way over to the right in relation to what passes for mainstream political opinion here, not that that's necessarily a fault, somebody has to challenge the new orthodoxy. He's hated the whole devolution thing from the start but at least he had the balls to stay and be counted, whereas all the Tory politicians he might once have cheered on slithered off to England after the 1997 wipeout and got themselves new constituencies there,

643

or became directors of merchant banks or chairmen of southern water boards. Rats leaving a listing ship, which is now, slowly, righting itself. Exception: David Eddelstane, also present – didn't expect him to turn up but there he is, and looking good, as relaxed in his own skin as David Eddelstane can be in public. He heads up a charity for rehabilitating young offenders through outdoor activities such as mountaineering and skiing, and apparently does it very well. His son, Daniel, works with him. Melissa's here too, a little less lovely than she used to be but standing loyally by, same as ever. All of this Mike has taken in or takes in as he gets through his speech.

Crombie is standing beside a couple of other journos, one from the *Scotsman* and one from the *Sunday Herald*, both of whom disagree with Crombie's opinions but they stick together these guys, a kind of mini-pack of newshounds, and somehow they all look alike, they have the blotched, bag-eyed, paunchy newspaper look that tells of too many evenings hammering out eight hundred words with two fingers in twenty-five minutes, too many pints sunk between putting the morning edition to bed and getting home to their own, too many fags sucked dead on chilly street corners outside offices and pubs. These are the political hacks. On the other side of the room is a cluster of feature writers, women mostly, they do arts and lifestyle and the political guys half-challenge half-patronise them all the time: what you lassies write is all fluff and padding, the real bits of a newspaper are politics, sport and business, not always in that order, ask the editor if you don't believe me, och don't go in the huff, if you canna take the piss-taking get back in the kitchen, dear. And, standing apart from both these groups, in the same trade but less so these days, still writing what she wants for whom she wants, is Ellen. They all know her, she knows them. It's an edgy relationship. She looks at them and sees how thin their loyalties have been stretched by successive regimes at their various papers, how insecure their jobs are as newspaper sales slide and news becomes something people snack on 24/7, bite-size, nothing too hard to digest, thank you, and almost always off a screen. They look at her with a mix of admiration and envy. They wish they were in her shoes, they want to tell her she's a parasite, if it wasn't for them grinding out papers every day where would she place her opinions? Ellen doesn't look that fazed. She has Kirsty with her. Even if he hadn't known she was coming Mike would have recognised Kirsty. The cool, slightly remote teenager he remembers has turned into a replica of her mother a quarter of a century ago. The same determined set of the jaw, the same alertness, the same stance as they listen to him. Jesus. We are all prisoners of our genes.

'Sadly, Angus isn't here to object to how I've arranged his work. Fifty years of Scottish life, 1947–1997. History is written by the survivors, but what is that history? That's the point I was trying to make just now. We don't know what the story is when we're in it, and even after we tell it we're not sure. Because the story doesn't end. As William Faulkner put it, "The past is never dead. It's not even past."'

Got it in! Fine. He catches Walter's eye, is he looking bored or contemplative? Walter, who's always seemed about sixty to Mike since they first met thirty-five years ago, but must in reality only be in his seventies now, is as grudgingly generous as ever. In a minute Mike will invite him to sing. 'Something appropriate for those fifty years,' he said, when he spoke to him about it on the phone a few weeks ago. 'I leave the choice to you.' And Walter said, 'Only fifty years? You're narrowing my options there.' Mike posted him an early copy of the exhibition book so he could get a feel for the range of images, knowing that he would weigh against them what he might or might not sing, and he does not doubt that Walter will come up with the goods.

'I'm going to shut up now . . .' A ragged cheer from Eric, Jeremy and some others. The Polish and Romanian girls and boys in their black aprons are lining up on the outskirts with replenished trays of wine and fizzy water. What happens when you leave a country, when you arrive elsewhere? Do you take your own story with you? Or are you like a new character entering an old story? Those intersecting, overlapping map lines again. You see the ones you want to see.

'I'm going to shut up now, and Walter Fleming's going to step up and sing for us. But before he does . . .' He pauses again. What is it, this precious, ponderous thing that he holds, that he wants to give to these people, that he wants them to take away, back on to the streets, into the bars and restaurants, into their cars and the last trains to Glasgow and Stirling and Dundee, back to their homes and their own private and personal griefs and joys, their family gatherings and their couplings and their solitudes? What is it he has for them? 'Before he does, I want to pass something on, something that was said to me recently by an old and dear friend who can't be here tonight. You have to go away and think about this. It seems very simple but I think it's profound. Trust the story. That's all. Trust the story. Whatever it is these pictures tell you, individually or collectively, trust the story. We're only human after all. Whatever else we put faith in will, in the end, betray us or we will betray it. But the story never betrays. It twists and turns and sometimes it takes you to terrible places and sometimes it gets lost or appears to abandon you, but if you look hard enough it is still there. It goes on. The story is the only thing we can really, truly know.'

A suitable silence. He steps back from the microphone. The clapping starts. He used the word 'profound' and immediately he's beset with self-doubt, wondering if they'll think him the very opposite of profound. Maybe they'll go away empty-handed. *What the hell was that about?* But the applause goes on and he feels its warmth again, as if – even if they don't understand what he's said, even if they don't believe it – they accept his offer, accept that he wants to give them something. And this is doubly strange because he feels remote from their warmth; he's come down from the north and he'll retreat there again in a day or two, and does he really have a connection with them, here in bustling, packed Edinburgh at the start of August? If he does, why does he feel such an overwhelming need to withdraw, to get away from them again?

He has a sudden yearning for Murdo. He wishes he had come. Yet is glad he chose not to.

He moves into the crowd as Walter, passing him with a smile, goes to the microphone.

§

Trust the story. Ellen thinks she knows what Mike means. She's also identified the absent source, though: Jean Barbour. What if you don't trust the storyteller, Mike? But as soon as the question forms she sees how he would answer it: the storyteller may dissemble and deceive, the story can't; the story can only ever be itself.

Aye, weel, mibbe. It's her own comment but the voice in her head is her mother's. Eighty-three when Mary's number was finally called last year. She didn't come out to the fish van and the fish man knew there was something wrong, keeked through the window and saw her lying on the sitting-room floor. He forced a window to get in and she was still alive but cold as one of his fish; she'd been there all night and it was February. The television blethering away in the corner. He phoned for an ambulance and sat with her till it came but she couldn't speak, couldn't move. While he waited he became aware of a burning smell and went through to the kitchen just in time to lift a pan of what had been tomato soup off the ring as it caught fire. 'Burned my bloody fingers daein it,' he told Ellen later, 'but at least the hoose didna go up. She was a good customer tae me, your mither, and she never owed me a penny.' She can hear the fish man, she can hear Mary. *Aye, weel, mibbe.* By the time Ellen got to the hospital Mary was hooked up to everything. 'Dinna let them resuscitate me,' had been her plea to Ellen and the boys. 'See if I ever keel ower and if I come back I'll be a vegetable, dinna let them resuscitate me.' And there she was, hooked up, but she was never coming back. She didn't speak another word before she went. Ellen sat beside her, trying to mind the last time they'd spoken on the phone, what they'd said. Her mother's last words to her. And she couldn't remember even though it had been only a couple of days before. So does that mean they said nothing of any consequence? Surely the thing of consequence was that they'd been speaking. The importance of banalities. 'My mother made it clear,' she told the doctor, 'that in these circumstances she just wants to go. So if there are machines here that are just keeping her going, without which she'd be away, switch them off, please.' The doctor nodded. It wasn't quite that simple. But he got the message. Three hours later Mary was, as she'd wished, away.

Mike has said something else that she wants both to think about and to let pass. It's the kind of thing that worries her in the middle of the night while Robin sleeps untroubled beside her: *does anybody else, coming along a little later, really care?* What gnaws at Ellen is the shrug or vacant look Kirsty sometimes gives her when she's sounding off about this or that political issue; the look that says, why do you get so worked up about this stuff? As if it has nothing to do with her at all. No, scrub the 'as if'. Politics and Kirsty are total strangers. In Ellen's mind it's a kind of moral failing that her daughter doesn't vote. But whose?

Kirsty, next to her, is slim and lovely and seems free of care. She's wearing a green linen dress Ellen doesn't dare imagine the price of. That's another generational thing: society hasn't managed to eradicate poverty but it's done a good job on wiping out thrift.

Stop it stop it stop it, she tells herself. She's your child. Is it her fault that she's grown up not to be you? Don't resent that, be grateful for it.

It's not just Kirsty though, it's the world she inhabits. She works for an independent film and TV production company based in a renovated warehouse in Leith. Ellen can never remember her job title but she seems to do a bit of everything across marketing, acquisitions, rights and human resources. It makes Ellen think of Jock, her father, and how, bizarrely, he might have been ahead of his time the way he dodged and danced through his working life, the difference being he did it as a manual labourer. He had plenty of bullshit but no qualifications in it. Kirsty on the other hand has a degree in Language and Communications Studies and an MSc in Media Management. She works long hours, in fact she never seems to stop and yet Ellen can't help feeling that there's something phoney about what she does. Even phonier than what *she* does. With each generation there is less contact – real, physical touch – with the tools, the materials, even the products of its labour. Jock Imlach started as a miner and, even when he moved on to the hydro schemes, concrete and rock and water were what he had to work with or dodge working with, and dust was what killed him. Ellen's world has gone from roaring, oily printing presses, clattering typewriters and tramping the streets to digital typesetting, research on the internet and articles emailed in from home half an hour before the deadline. It's decades since she physically put a story on an editor's desk. Kirsty's world is a step further along the road, so virtual it's almost invisible. Meetings about meetings about meetings. Pitches, development, pre-production commissions. Apparently you can turn a profit from *not* making programmes. It's the unreality of reality TV, all that crap. Where's the substance? Ellen feels she's losing touch.

§

On a bench under one of the screened-off high windows, some distance from the back of the standing crowd, an elderly couple sit hand in hand while the speechifying goes on. Don Lennie and Marjory Taylor, as was. Later she became Marjory Forrester, and still is, but Don always thinks of her as Marjory Taylor, the English nurse. Don has bought two copies of the Angus Pendreich book, one for them and one for Saleem. Marjory says he should have waited, maybe they'll give him a freebie when they realise who he is, but that's not the way Don operates. Apart from anything else, he feels an obligation to buy, since they're here on false pretences. Billy's Catriona had rushed in excitedly one evening a few weeks back, waving a big postcard under his eyes. 'Look!' she said, and he looked, and there they were, Saleem and him, standing outside Saleem's shop. 'It's an invitation to the opening of an exhibition,' Catriona explained. 'It's come to me because I know the son of the photographer whose work it is. That's the only reason I can think of. Billy and I can't go because we're away on holiday, but you can. You must. You're in it.' He studied the card. 'So it would seem,' he said. 'I mind that time. The fellow just appeared one day when we were ootside talking and asked if he could take oor picture and we said aye and then he wrote doon oor names and drove away, and then it was in one of the Sunday papers, but tae be honest I'd completely forgotten aboot it.' 'Will you go?' Catriona said. 'I'll email Michael, that's the son, and tell him you'll go.' Don hummed and hawed but Marjory sided with Catriona. 'You must,' she said. So he agreed. And here they are.

The next day he saw Saleem and tried to persuade him to join them but he wouldn't. Saleem was delighted with the photograph though. 'We look pretty good, don't we?' he said. 'At least you do. But why aren't we smiling?' 'It was how ye posed for photies in thae days,' Don said. 'I probably tellt ye tae wipe the grin aff your face. Weel, if ye'll no come wi us, I'll bring ye a book back.'

So now he has the two books. He paid in cash, two twenties and a tenner, a rush of extravagance in his eighty-ninth year, and the lassie at the till seemed a wee bit perplexed, as if she didn't often see the real stuff any more, but she took it anyway. Pretty soon, perhaps, shops will start surcharging folk who pay in cash, to cover the cost of taking it to the bank. The way you're already penalised if you don't pay your gas bill by direct debit, or the way they give you a discount if you're rich enough to pay your house insurance in a oner. The world we fought for, Don thinks bitterly, and then, as he always does now, he shrugs it off. Not his problem. Anyway, Catriona's pal, the photographer's son, Michael Pendreich, is going on about this and that and in spite of the PA system Don can't hear very well so he thinks this may be a good time to go and find a lavatory, because his bladder is a bit suspect these days and needs emptying on a regular basis. So he hands the books in their thick but transparent plastic bag to Marjory and heads off, leaving the voice and the low undercurrent of crowd noise behind him.

§

Earlier, Ellen and Kirsty met for a drink in a bar at the top of Leith Walk. Everywhere was filling up – locals on their way home or warming up at the start of a long night, tourists and theatregoers, the city's usual August mix. Ellen grabbed seats while Kirsty shimmied her way to the bar, returning promptly with two enormous glasses of white wine.

'How's Robin?' she asked.

'Same as ever,' Ellen said. 'He sends you his love.'

'No chance of persuading him in from the Far East, I suppose?'

'For tonight? You know Robin. Not his scene. He might come in early one weekday morning, see the exhibition when it's empty. Or he might not. He's already been through the book.'

'Which you've written the intro for?'

'That's the one.'

'As a favour to Mike?'

'Partly.'

'Is he going to pay you for it?'

'He says so. Not a lot, but I'd have done it anyway.'

Kirsty raised an eyebrow.

'What? Is that so awful, doing something for a friend for nothing?'

'No, but you're always telling me there's a going rate for every job, and if women don't hold out for it . . .'

'I know, I know. There are always exceptions. Anyway, I like the photographs. I had things I wanted to say about them. And Mike was in a fix. He'd tried writing it himself but got stuck.'

'Probably he was too close to it,' Kirsty said. 'His dad and everything.'

'Aye, I think that was it.' Ellen touched her daughter's wrist. 'Listen, I hope you've not had to put anything off for this.' It was Friday night after all. As far as she knew there wasn't a man in Kirsty's life right now, but she didn't tell her everything.

'No, I wanted to come. I want to see the new gallery. And it'll be nice to see Mike again. I can't remember when I last did. Definitely not since he and Uncle Adam split up.'

'Well that was a while ago. You were still a student. Your other uncle says he's hoping to come along, by the way.'

'Gavin? Good. Haven't seen him for ages either. But not Adam?'

'I don't think so. He's too settled in Barcelona.'

There was a brief silence. Maybe they were both a little pissed off with Adam, or a little jealous of him. Then Kirsty said, 'I thought I might come out this weekend. Otherwise I'll never see Robin. Would that be okay?'

'Of course it would.'

'Sunday?'

'That would be lovely, if you're not doing anything.'

'That's what I'm doing. A day in Joppa. Ask Robin to cook us something amazing.'

'And we'll go for a walk on the beach.'

'Brilliant.'

The house in Joppa is tall and narrow, on three floors. On the top floor are two long, narrow attic rooms with coomed ceilings and dormer windows looking out on to the firth. Up there you feel like you're miles above the cars and buses, the people exercising their dogs on the beach. One room is Robin's studio, the other is where Ellen works. Between the rooms, at the top of a steep staircase, is an alcove with a sink, a kettle, tea, coffee and mugs. Every so often one of them switches on the kettle and they come together for a twenty-minute break. Interludes of quiet conversation or comfortable silences. There is a window seat in Robin's room and sometimes they just sit there gazing out at the sea and towards Fife, so close on some days, so distant on others. The studio seems to Ellen like the control room of a spaceship floating high above the earth. It throbs with energy: there are light-boxes, drawing boards, a huge expanse of desk, racks stacked with pencils, pens, scalpels, scissors and geometric instruments; there are drawers full of other equipment, shelves crammed with art books and design manuals, the iMac loaded with sophisticated software, a scanner, a laser printer that purrs when it prints; and in one corner is an acoustic guitar that Robin plays for half an hour at the end of each working day. His sign-off music. Everything about him is calm and measured. He seldom goes to the theatre or cinema or to art galleries, in fact he hardly ever leaves Joppa and can usually be found, if he's not at home, walking on the beach. And yet somehow he keeps abreast of the latest news, cultural events, new voices in music and literature. He's the most thoughtful, unflustered, courteous, gentle, well-read person Ellen has ever met and she still can't quite believe that she is now into the fourth decade of living there with him, ever since he rescued her. Does he love her? She never doubts it, even though he doesn't often tell her. Does she love him? Oh yes, oh yes, oh yes. And Kirsty too. They are, as Robin always said they would be, surrounded by love.

Kirsty drained her glass. 'God, that's gone straight to my head. I feel like something exciting's going to happen. That's stupid, isn't it?'

'Probably,' Ellen said, 'but if we have any more nothing at all will happen because we'll not be able to stand up. Come on, let's move.'

So they moved. And now they're here, and Ellen glances at Kirsty again, with her empty wine glass, and wonders if she drinks too much. And if she's going to find a good man, and if they'll have children. And even now, with Kirsty in her thirties, Ellen still looks for traces of Charlie, and is always relieved not to find many. Kirsty is overwhelmingly her mother's daughter. Charlie's long gone, as out of their lives as he'll ever be.

She sees Gavin making his way towards them. She's about to point him out to Kirsty when Walter starts to speak.

'Two songs. Mike asked me tae choose something that would be right for the half-century that these photographs represent. An impossible task. Weel, I thought I'd try tae find something frae the beginning and something frae the end but the trouble wi songs is they'll no stay in their place. They keep moving and they keep resonating in unexpected ways. So in the end I just looked at the pictures in the book and ye can call me perverse but I kept thinking o aw the folk that weren't in them. Men and women, and some men in particular, and that gave me the first song. And the second song, weel, these photographs go aw roond the country and that's what the second song does. That's the best I could dae. Mike, the first yin's ootside your fifty-year period by two or three years and the second yin's oot by a lot mair than that, but that's the way it is.'

Then he switches the mike off and steps away from it, to the side, almost as if he doesn't want to be there, a kind of practised modesty. And he takes a breath and his voice rolls out into the room.

§

Walter sings, and Mike absorbs it, the song and all it contains. Something happens when he is this focused, he slips beyond himself, is present but also apart. He hears the words Walter sings, he sees the past the song describes but also he thinks of the time that's coming. The time of change. The time when Murdo will say, 'No, wait, let's do something different.'

He knows that time is coming because already today, in the late afternoon, Murdo has done something different, something rare and wonderful. He has telephoned. This was so unexpected that when Mike answered, standing alone in the middle of the exhibition space, it took him a second or two to realise who was speaking.

'How is it all going?'

'Murdo?'

'Yes?'

'It's yourself.'

'So it would seem.'

'What's wrong?'

'Nothing that I'm aware of.'

'I thought maybe my house was on fire or something.'

'Why would it be? And if it was I would have put it out. I am right in front of it now and there isn't a trace of smoke.'

'You're at Cnoc nan Gobhar?'

'Aye. There were a couple of things still to fix in the sun lounge. I thought I'd take the opportunity.'

'You got in all right?'

'And out. I know where you keep the key, remember?'

'Of course. Oh well, thank you.'

'That's not why I am phoning you,' Murdo said. 'It's a beautiful day here, but that's not why either. I wanted to wish you luck.'

'With the opening?'

'Yes, what else but that? And to say I'm sorry I am not there.'

'You didn't want to come.'

'No, I didn't. But I am sorry not to be there. With you.'

Mike's heart gave a wee lurch. 'I'm sorry too,' he said. 'But there'll be other times. You can come and see it later.'

'I would like to.'

'Let's do that then. Come to Edinburgh together to see it.'

'Very good.'

'Murdo?'

'Aye?'

'Thank you.'

'You enjoy yourself now. When will you be back?'

'Monday, I think. Sunday or Monday.'

'Let me know and I'll meet you at the station.'

'I will.'

He wanted to say something more but then he didn't. And now he's glad no more was said. It can be said later, before or after or at the same time as Murdo says, 'Let's do something different.'

And whenever that is, it will be between Murdo and him and no one else, past or present, and it will be good. And afterwards they'll sleep, both of them, and the night will pass into morning and they'll wake together. Maybe Murdo will have a mug of tea and a slice of toast before he goes off to whatever work he has on that day. Goes from the house, and returns to the house. And while they're eating and drinking there will be a question in Mike's head and it will be this: 'When will they know?' And another: 'Will it matter when they do?' The questions will be for Murdo not for Mike, because Mike will be happy, happier than he's ever been, and so he won't really care what anyone thinks, but he cares about Murdo and the place where he's lived all his life. He cares so, so much, and hence the questions. And Murdo will know what Mike is thinking. He'll take Mike's unworked hand in his rough, hard one – almost, Mike sees, almost as a father might take a son's – and he'll speak, or he won't speak, but what he'll be saying with the gesture, with the words if there are words, is, 'Don't worry. It will be all right.' And it will be.

§

The Gents is down a corridor off the main lobby. Don is alone. The place has a tiled coolness, a clean hush, that pleases him. He unbuttons and waits. Typical. You feel you need to go and then when you're standing at the ready nothing happens. Patience. This is not a false alarm. The brain has sent the message all right, it's just that the messenger is old and doddery and takes a while to get down to the nether regions where the machinery is a bit decrepit and the operator's deif, but he *is* on his way. Finally, finally, the trickle starts. And Don has that usual moment of anxiety, in case this is a dream and he's actually pissing the bed, but he's not, if he's checked then he's awake, it's when he doesn't check he needs to worry, by which time it'll be too late anyway. Hasn't happened yet, thank God. Marjory, being a nurse, would cope, but he doesn't want her to have to.

He's going strong now, a steady stream, and he thinks of the other occasion that always comes to mind when he's having a pee, every time. It's like the way a piece of music triggers a memory, instant, beyond your control. With him it's peeing, and suddenly he's back there, standing in the trees at Ochtermill, the stars out and Jack Gordon on the road waiting for him, and then there's the older memory *that* triggers: Italy, the bombs falling, the air thick with mud. So he's standing in the Gents in the National Gallery of Photography and Jack's there with him. The other guys are all dead, definitely dead, dead for more than six decades. Jack? Don knows he too must be dead, probably has been for years, but it never quite feels like that, it's as if he's still standing somewhere in the shadows, waiting for Don to finish and go on up the road with him. And tonight, in this building full of these people and these photographs, he feels it stronger than ever.

There's a voice drifting towards him, very faint, a man's voice singing, as he shakes himself and makes himself decent. He steps away from the urinal and the laser flush kicks in, he loves that, it knows better than you do when you're finished. He puts his fingers under the tap and hot water squirts out, then when he takes his hands away it stops. Fantastic. He grew up in a tenement in

655

Drumkirk sharing a toilet with five other families. Hot water frae a tap? Aye, and the King came roond for his tea on Thursdays.

Back out in the corridor the singing voice is stronger, beckoning him, and Don finds himself hurrying across the entrance lobby, back towards the big room where they're all gathered. A solitary, unaccompanied voice. He knows the tune, he knows the tune, and as he pushes through the doors he knows the words. He can't believe somebody is singing this song while he's been in the lavvy. It must be forty years since he last heard it, maybe more. He stands there inside the doors, slightly breathless, and the melody of 'Lili Marlene' comes towards him. The singer is a burly, fine-looking character with snowy-white hair and moustache. He's over there on the steps where the speeches were made, but the words are from another place, they're the words of all the men Don went through Italy with in 1944:

> Naples and Casino, we took them in our stride,
> We didn't go to fight, boys, we just went for the ride.
> Anzio and Sangro, they're just names,
> We only went to look for dames.
> We are the D-Day Dodgers in sunny Italy.

Don tries to join in, humming the tune, but the sound sticks in his throat. So he mouths the words instead, he has them as suddenly and effortlessly as if he sang them only this morning in the shower, but he never had a singing voice like this man's, slow and rich and gentle and glorious:

> Dear Lady Astor, you think you're something hot,
> Standing on a platform and talking tommyrot.
> You're England's sweetheart and her pride.
> We think your mouth's too bloody wide.
> That's from the D-Day Dodgers, in sunny Italy.

Marjory has half-risen from the bench, waiting anxiously for Don. She knows the tune, of course, and she knows *about* the song, because Don has talked about the so-called D-Day Dodgers, having been one himself, and she thinks she must have heard it being sung

back in the 1940s, and here it is again; it's travelled six decades and
thousands of miles straight into the heart of this gallery in twenty-
first-century Edinburgh and probably the one man in the building
for whom it has any direct, personal meaning is missing it, and yet
everybody else is transfixed by the power and pathos of the tune
and the words. She looks frantically towards the exit and then sinks
back down with relief because she can see him at the door, not
missing it after all. He looks frail and yet strong, she wants to go
to him but she waits, afraid to disturb it, him, she's almost afraid to
breathe, and everybody else in the room is standing still, listening
to the song, it's as if they've all been frozen in time for as long as it
lasts.

> Look along the hillside in the mud and rain,
> See the scattered crosses, there's some that have no name.
> Heartbreak and toil and suffering gone,
> The boys beneath them slumber on.
> They are the D-Day Dodgers who stayed in Italy.

Walter's voice is so quiet by now she thinks it might disappear,
but he's singing into total silence and the words fill the room, they
would break your heart if you let them, and Don is standing there,
his hand going up to his eye then down to cover his mouth, and she
knows he cannot speak, that memories he has never shared with her
are brimming up in him. And the people begin to clap, they're
applauding Walter and the song but from where she's standing it's
as if, without knowing it, they're applauding Don. Marjory stands
and walks briskly over to him and he sees her and the hand comes
away from his mouth and she takes it. 'All right?' she asks. He nods.
'Come over here,' she says, leading him back, and he's happy to be
led, to sit down and get his breath back. And Walter starts his second song, and for a moment Marjory finds herself thinking, Christ,
don't make it another tear-jerker or you'll finish my dear old darling
off, but it's all right, it's going at a medium pace, waltz-time, she
recognises the tune again but not the words. It's one of those dust-
laden Scottish songs, of which there seems to be an inexhaustible
supply, that hark back to old, long-abandoned country ways that
people on plastic seats in bars and on sofas in central-heated sitting

rooms still somehow seem to relate to. Sometimes the songs are about battles or feuds or murders, and sometimes, as now, they're about the road, and there are occasions when it all seems horribly sentimental to Marjory but it's also what she loves about the land and its people, the clannishness that stretches and twists back into history, the deep-rootedness of it:

Come aw ye tramps and hawker lads, and gaitherers o blaw,
That tramp the country roond and roond, come listen ane and aw.
I'll tell tae you a rovin tale o sichts that I hae seen
Far up intae the snowy north and sooth by Gretna Green.

A surprising number of people seem to know the words. With each verse, more and more join from all over the room in swirling, joyous affirmation, so that Marjory too finds herself humming the melody. And though Don beside her is silent, it's clear from the way his head is nodding and his lips moving that he too is no stranger to the song:

I'm happy in the summertime beneath the bricht blue sky,
No thinkin in the mornin at nicht whaur I'm tae lie,
In bothy, byre or onywhaur or oot amang the hay
And if the weather treats me weel, I'm happy aw the day.

There is one last verse, which the entire assembly now sets about with a kind of evangelical gusto –

Oh I think I'll gang tae Paddy's land, I'm makin up my mind,
For Scotland's greatly altered noo, I canna raise the wind,
But I will trust in providence, and if providence prove true,
Then I will sing o Erin's isle when I come back tae you.

– and a slowing down on the last line, and then a great round of applause for Walter. Marjory waits for it to die away and turns to Don. 'That's a good song,' she says, but she sees at once that his mind is still set on the first one. He nods, 'Aye, it is.' And then, 'There's something I've no tellt ye. Aboot the war.'
'What?'

'Dae ye mind the name Jack Gordon? Dae ye mind me speaking aboot him, Jack Gordon?'

'Yes, of course,' she says. 'I remember.'

'He's the only yin I ever tellt. There was never onybody else I could tell.'

'You don't have to tell me,' she says.

'Aye,' he says, 'I dae, but later. When we get hame. No here.' He eases himself on to his feet again. 'But since we're here let's dae what we came tae dae. Let's hae a look at these pictures.'

§

Mike passes Duncan Roxburgh, giving him a nod. Duncan momentarily makes his eyes go big, an SOS. He's in some kind of confrontation with a tall, angular man, goatee beard and glasses, could be a professor or possibly the Moderator of the Free Church in mufti because he's saying, 'Four hundred and fifty-eight, I think you'll find.' Mike pauses to hear what's going on, and Duncan replies, 'Well, my memory is . . .' and the prof-cum-cleric, oblivious to Mike's presence, says, 'Where did you get your information from?' in a polite but determined tone that means *I am not going to let you go till we have resolved this.* Duncan says, 'Well, um . . .' and the other man says, 'I know, I know. From MacMillan or some such supposed authority, or perhaps off the internet, yes? That's how mistakes happen, you know, it's how they get perpetuated. But there are four hundred and fifty-eight people in that painting and I know, I've counted them. I downloaded a copy of it and magnified it and printed it on to A3 sheets of paper and marked them all off. Four times, starting from a different corner each time. An X on every face and a number for every X. I could hardly believe it when I discovered the true number. This mistake has been handed down from one generation to another. Dictionaries of quotations are the same, you know. Compilers don't bother to check, they just reproduce. It's how history goes wrong. But there's an even more crucial issue, the mystery I'm trying to clear up, and it's this.' Dramatic pause: the man really believes he's on to something. *'What is the identity of the extra person?'* It is clear that he is far from finished. Mike puts mock horror on his face, displays it to Duncan over the interrogator's back, and moves on swiftly. Seconds later he's face to face with the Eddelstanes.

'Hello, Mike.'

'David. Great to see you. Melissa, we've not met before. Good of you to come.'

'Yes, well, we don't usually do much of this sort of thing,' David says, 'but it was so kind of you to send the invitation, and we happened to be in Edinburgh, so . . .'

'It *is* a wonderful exhibition,' Melissa says, slightly apologetically. Did she come thinking it wouldn't be?

'Thank you.'

'Marvellous,' David says. 'But rather like seeing your life flashing before you.'

Close up he's not looking so good. Perhaps his life has flashed before him a few too many times. The face is very lined, the skin sallow. Mike notices that neither of them is drinking wine. They both look nervous, as if at any moment somebody may spring an unpleasant surprise on them.

'I saw your rehab work mentioned in the news the other day,' Mike says. 'A parliamentary committee report, wasn't it?'

'Yes,' David says. He sounds exhausted. 'Unfortunately there's a question mark over our funding. Some MSPs are suggesting it should be cut because 30 per cent of the kids we take on reoffend within a year. They think we're a cushy number for hardened criminals – the usual stuff, you know. And they say we're not good value for money, but we are. For the kids that actually complete our course, the reoffending rate is only 10 per cent, but quite a few drop out early. And when you compare our record with average reoffending rates, we're streets ahead. It's frustrating, because we know we're doing good work, and you can't do it on the cheap.'

'And it *isn't* cheap,' Melissa says, 'but that's not to say it isn't cost-effective.'

'It's a lot cheaper than having someone spend the rest of their life in and out of prison,' David says. 'That's the thing that matters. Still,' he says, trying to brighten up, 'you don't want to hear about our worries on an occasion like this, do you? Sorry about the lecture.'

'Hopefully sense will prevail,' Mike says, trotting out a platitude because David is right, he doesn't want to hear their worries. Then, immediately guilty and concerned for them both, he adds, 'But all that aside, you're well? You're doing all right, are you?'

'Yes, yes, we're in good spirits,' David says. There is a pause, threatening to become awkward. He adds, 'We just keep our heads down and get on. And you?'

'I'm doing fine,' Mike says, and the exchange stutters to another halt. 'Look, I'd better circulate.'

'Absolutely, catch you later.'

'And thanks again for asking us,' Melissa says.

He moves on, wondering if this is what happens as you age – you even start to feel sorry for fallen Tories.

A space has cleared, a line of vision opened up. Over against the far wall he sees two people moving along the lines of photographs, examining each one with care. They have the Bell Rock lighthouse to their left, Arbroath Abbey to their right. An elderly couple, man and woman. The man is tall but stooped, distinguished-looking. Mike thinks he ought to know who he is. Did he invite them? He'll have to get across and speak to them.

Near them is another figure, solitary, dishevelled, drifting past the 1960s. Second sighting in five months but this time Mike recognises him at once. It's Dick, Duffelcoat – or should that now be Duffelcoatless – Dick, and he suddenly remembers something else about him: that it was *his* name on the story which forced Eddelstane to resign. Yes, of course it was. Peter Bond. What on earth is he doing here? Have he and the Eddelstanes encountered each other yet? But why would they recognise Bond? Most likely they never met and David never knew the face of his nemesis. Peter Bond is somebody else Mike is determined to have a word with, but the throng is closing in again. Will he be able to reach him, or will Dick slip away in the confusion, now you see him now you don't, the way he used to?

Walter bars his way, expansive, relaxed now his job is done, a glass of wine in hand.

'All right, Mike?'

'Great. Walter, thank you, you were superb. Not a dry eye in the house.' Another bloody cliché. 'What are you doing after this?'

'I thought I'd wander up tae Jean's, see how she is. Maybe pick up a fish supper or something on the way.'

'I'm staying with her,' Mike says. 'I tried to persuade her to come, but she wouldn't.'

'Dinna take it personally,' Walter says. 'She's a thrawn besom. If ye'd tellt her she was barred she might have turned up.'

'I'll remember that for next time. Well, I'll see you there then. Or we can head up together. I'm not sure when they'll want us out of here.'

'Maybe we should take a few o the others wi us, turn it intae a ceilidh.'

'Now that's an idea. If she'll not come to the party, the party will have to go to her.'

'Right, I'll pit the word oot. A ceilidh at Jean's.'

'She'll hate us for it.'

'Aye, but she'll love it really. It'll shake her oot o hersel,' Walter says gleefully.

'Mike!' Somebody else is wanting his attention. Indeed, the next twenty minutes are full of exchanged greetings, business cards pressed into his hand, promises to meet for lunch next time he's in town. He thinks, what do I need their business cards for? But maybe it's time to re-engage. He scribbles his signature on the title-page of several copies of the book, spends time with Ellen and Gavin, catches up with Kirsty, reminisces with Eric Hodge about the nightmare landlady of their early student days. And he knows he's doing that thing he hates, glancing over people's shoulders as they're speaking to him, so they believe that he's not interested in them, that he's anxious to move on and network with the important people just over *there*. Whereas what he really wants to do is connect with the *un*important people off in the distance. He keeps seeing them, the three misfits, through or beyond the churning scrum in the centre of the room. In fact, they seem to be almost the only people bothering to look at the pictures. Clearly they don't know how to behave at a launch party. He likes them more for it, wants to join them. Even Duffelcoatless Dick, the sleekit creeping bastard, he warms to him because he's inspecting Angus's photographs so closely. He redoubles his efforts to break away. If he speaks to no one else tonight, he must do this.

§

But by the time he gets through, Dick has disappeared. Briefly Mike wonders if he only imagined seeing him, but he knows he did

see him – not once, fleetingly, but several times. There was no mistaking him. But it seems he has made his exit.

On a night of such celebration, Mike feels unaccountably let down.

He is standing at one end of a long wall of photographs. Halfway
along are the old couple. At least *they've* not escaped. He homes in
on them. They're just leaving M. Lucas and arriving at the family
paddling in Loch Lomond.

'Are you enjoying yourselves?'

The woman turns and gives him a big smile. 'Very much so.'

'I'm Mike,' he says. 'Mike Pendreich.'

'We know *that*,' she says, taking the hand he proffers. 'I'm Marjory and this is Don. We were just admiring Don when he was
younger. Probably when he was about your age actually.'

The old man turns and puts a firm, brown hand into Mike's, and
suddenly Mike understands why he looks familiar – because in the
photograph behind him is himself, thirty years before. DON AND
SALEEM, WHARRYBURN, 1978.

'That's you in front of the shop!' Mike says.

'It is,' Don says.

'You were on all the invitations we sent out.'

'So I was,' Don says.

Mike points at the photograph. 'Wharryburn's near Drumkirk,
isn't it?'

'Just a few miles,' Marjory says.

'I've never been there. Is that where you stay now?'

'Aye,' Don says. 'I've been there sixty year. No much point in flitting noo.'

'And your friend, Saleem, is he . . .' He hesitates for a second,
stops the word 'still' and changes tack. 'Is he here?'

'No,' Don says. 'We tried tae get him tae come but he wouldna.
I've bought a book for him though.'

'Oh, you shouldn't have to pay for a book. Not if you're in it.'

'That's what I said to him,' Marjory says.

'I bought two,' Don says.

'I'll sort something out with the gallery, get you a discount at
least.'

'That's aw right, son.'

Mike looks at the image again, then back at Don. 'This is wonderful.

I thought I recognised you earlier, but I couldn't work it out. Oh, I wish my dad could be here to meet you again.'

'We never really *met* that time,' Don says. 'He was there and then he was away. But I liked that. Nae messing aboot.'

Mike remembers the email from Catriona. 'Wait a minute,' he says. 'You're . . . you're . . .' But the name doesn't come.

'I'm Don Lennie, and this is Marjory Forrester. We're gatecrashers really.'

'No, I remember now. You're Catriona MacKay's partner's father. Is that right? She emailed to say she couldn't come, but you were on the invitation – I mean, really *on* it – so you'd come instead.'

'Aye, that's aboot the strength o it,' Don says. 'Catriona's my son's bidie-in.' A wee light is in his eyes. 'I never got used tae folk haein partners,' he says. 'We prefer the term "bidie-in", don't we?'

Marjory says, 'We do,' and giggles like a teenager.

'Catriona sends her apologies and asks tae be remembered tae ye, by the way.'

'Catriona MacKay from Inverness,' Mike says. ' This is incredible. We were students together.'

'So she tellt us.'

'We were good friends. Close friends. And your son, what's your son's name?'

'Billy.'

Mike becomes aware of Duncan Roxburgh hovering at his side, no doubt wanting to take him off to meet someone else. He tries to ignore him. 'Billy Lennie?' he says. 'I've never met him. But then I've not seen Catriona for years. It's a shame they couldn't come too.'

'They're in France,' Don says. 'They have tae keep tae the school holidays because of the bairns, and because Billy's a teacher.'

Again, Mike is taken aback. Catriona, a mother. But why wouldn't she be? 'How many kids do they have?' he asks.

'Two,' Marjory says. 'A boy and a girl. Fifteen and thirteen.'

'They were late developers,' Don explains. 'The parents, I mean.'

They all laugh and in the break of conversation Duncan Roxburgh makes his move. 'Mike, I'm sorry to interrupt, but there's a queue of folk wanting their books signed, and a photographer from *The Times* who needs us as well. Would you mind?' This last half-question is addressed to all of them.

Mike grasps Don's hand, Marjory's hand. 'Please don't leave just yet. I'd love to talk to you some more. Give me five minutes –'

'Make it ten,' Duncan says.

'I'll be back as soon as I can. Your glasses are empty. I'll find some more wine and come back. Will you be here?'

'Dinna fash, son.' Don says. 'We're in nae rush. We'll just keep looking at the pictures.'

Reluctantly he leaves them to it. As Duncan leads Mike back through the crowd, he glances around for Peter Bond, and again feels that twist of disappointment. Among all those many faces, the one he wants is absent.

§

Don pauses, inspects, leans in to read the caption and date, looks again, moves on. There are so many images. Sometimes he looks for just a few seconds, sometimes for much longer. Mick McGahey; the UCS work-in; a farmer with his prize bull, hard to tell them apart. The photographs are not chronological, at least not consistently so. He thought he was working his way forward in time but now he seems to be going back. The 1960s. Mad Mitch of the Argylls, home from Aden to a hero's welcome; Jock Stein, barely smiling despite having just won the European Cup; a string of men in shorts and singlets with numbers on their backs, heads bent into driving wind and rain with the Wallace Monument in the distance. The caption says STRATHALLAN GAMES, AUGUST 1966, but apart from the running gear the white-legged, mud-streaked, wiry men could be medieval peasants running straight out of history towards the lens. Don loves it.

He thinks of Saleem's nephew, who has the village shop now. A nice-enough fellow, but not as talkative as Saleem. The nephew has a daughter who helps out behind the counter. Almost every day this summer Don has seen her, setting off on a long run in the early evening, tall and lithe and graceful in her immaculate tracksuit, so different from the bauchlie wee men in the photograph yet somehow he can see her in it, following them, overtaking the stragglers. She runs easily, effortlessly, she's sixteen or seventeen he thinks, he sees her from his window, loping down the street, fair weather or foul she's almost always out there. He is familiar with her long, even strides, the way she turns her head to check for traffic, he checks too because he wants to protect her, but she is careful, she is quick, she is safe. He wants her to be safe, he wants her to have a good life. Once in the shop he asked her what she was training for and she smiled her bonnie smile and said she was building up to do a marathon. When he sees her running he wants to be her age again, to be her friend, to run with her like a deer, he wants to have life all over. She fills him with the joy of life just as Marjory does, but in a different way. She fills him with the joy of the future that will not be his.

He tells himself to stop dreaming, shifts along. His legs are tired. The next image is of big sea, land, sky, and the unmistakable golf-ball shape of the nuclear plant at Dounreay. Don has never been there but who wouldn't recognise it? Like you wouldn't recognise the Forth Bridge, Edinburgh Castle, the Falkirk Wheel, Ben Nevis. You don't have to have been there to know them, they are part of your country. The caption says DOUNREAY, 1964. He stares. He stares and he stares.

Marjory is a couple of photos behind him. He calls to her. 'Marjory!' His voice sounds hoarse and urgent, even to himself. 'Marjory!' He turns back to the picture, feeling the clutch of the past at his chest.

§

Peter in the Gents. Still shaky, a bit sweaty. Not surprising. Only what you'd expect after a paranormal experience. But recovering now, thank you. Nice and cool in here. Cool and empty.

Bladder empty too. Head full though. Spotted Eddelstane at a distance, kept it between them. Listened to Pendreich, saw a few other faces from the Demon Barbour days. Then everybody started singing – except Peter. Why not him? He opened his mouth but nothing came out. Strange. Flashback to that other time in the bookshop, shouting the odds during the oratory. Same thing only different. Didn't want a repeat, but the wine gauge was flickering into the red zone and after that anything can happen. Time to go. Time to exercise some self-control. Merely thinking that, let alone acting on it, is a good sign. There have been one or two lately.

He'd have liked to talk to Pendreich, but never mind. Saw the name, the exhibition previews, came along. Didn't realise it was a private function till he was inside. Nobody flung him out. Another good sign. Still, let's not tempt fate, eh?

Stops in front of the big mirror. Guy looks familiar. Hello, Jimmy. Hello, Peter. Shit. One paranormal experience after another. Can a ghost haunt itself?

Peter speaks and Jimmy's lips don't move. Jimmy speaks and Peter's lips don't move. The thing is to get them working in sync. Then you'll be fine.

JIMMY: What paranormal experience?

PETER: Just seen a ghost. The ghost in the camera's eye. Mad Uncle Jack.

JIMMY: Uncle Jack's here?

PETER: Came right off the fucking wall at me. Sorry. Bad news when the effing and blinding creeps in. Indicates I'm about to peak. After that, all downhill.

JIMMY: You don't need to tell me.

PETER: No, I don't, do I? You're James Bond, after all.

JIMMY: The original Slaemill edition. The pre-Connery, pre-Roger Moore, pre-Timothy Dalton, pre-Daniel fucking Craig version. Sorry. That's me at it now.

PETER: My excuse is I've had a few glasses of el vino, Jimmy. What's yours?

JIMMY: Let's blame it on a general aversion to pretendy spies. Real and imagined.

PETER: See that Sean Connery, I used to like him because he seemed so much better than the ones that came after him. He could even act a bit. But age has not mellowed him, no. It has overripened him. The Nats should put as much clear blue water between themselves and him as they can. The man's a joke, a parody of himself.

JIMMY: Shir Sean, shulking till he got his knighthood from the very eshtablishment he shays he wants Shcotland to break away from. Fuck off, that's what I say. What do you say?

Peter grips the edges of the basin. He steels himself not to answer. To say nothing. This is the problem. You're doing fine and then the wine or the whisky kicks in and you get into a ranting match with yourself. So. Deep breaths. Calm yourself. Then head for the street.

And as he breathes, he sees the face in the mirror begin to fade. Slowly at first, breaking up, the nose, the mouth, the eyes becoming hollow sockets, the flesh retreating. Skeletal, then nothing.

You're a ghost, remember? You're on the other side. People see you, then they don't. And this is the easiest, safest way for you to be. To be the thing that once haunted them, and no longer does.

Like Lucy Eddelstane. Gone for good. Gone for a ghost. Not like her brother, the survivor. Peter went looking for Lucy, but he had no luck. Maybe she went ahead, into the other. Maybe if he goes too, goes for good, he'll find her again, a sulky wee spectre of love.

Like Uncle Jack. If you go back to that picture, the one of Dounreay, what's the betting he's not in it? What's the betting there's an empty space where Uncle Jack used to be?

But it's too late. Can't go back. You're away as well. Pendreich saw you, but now there's an empty space where you were. And so it will always be, until the next time.

Take a hike, Peter. Take a train. Take a bus. Take a walk up there where the wood meets the moor. Take a stroll up the hill with Uncle Jack. Take his hand, the pebble that's in it. Take a deep breath, then go.

Next time around, you'll live a better life.

§

Mike, being photographed – alone, with Duncan, with a dignitary or two – Mike signing books, is puzzled by the name Billy Lennie. The words *Billy Lennie's dead* sound from long ago but don't ring true. Because Billy Lennie isn't dead, he's with Catriona, he's the father of her children. So why is that phrase in his head? It troubles him.

And then the last of the books is signed, and he puts down the pen and stands up from the table, and across the way, as the party begins to break up, he sees Ellen with Kirsty. Ellen waves at him, and he hears her voice from years back and the name isn't Billy, it's Charlie. *Charlie Lennie's dead*. Kirsty's father is dead. Charlie Lennie, from Drumkirk, a ten-minute drive from Wharryburn.

'Jesus Christ,' he says. Duncan has been buttonholed again by the counter of ministers. Mike feels diminished and isolated by the enormity of his thoughts, by the fact that he can't quite master them. A kind of indoor mist swirls about him. Then he hears a voice, and a woman is bearing in on him out of the mist. Marjory Forrester.

'Mr Pendreich,' she says, and this time it is she who seizes his hand. 'Please would you come? Don is in a state. He is very anxious to speak to you.'

'I am very anxious to speak to him,' Mike says. He goes with her at once, her old, soft hand clutched in his as if she were someone he has known for years, an aunt, a family friend. 'Please call me Mike,' he says. 'Is he all right?'

'He's quite agitated. He sent me to find you.'

'Wait.' He brings her to a halt. 'I need to ask you something first. Does Don have another son?'

'No,' she says quickly. 'I mean, yes, but he's dead.'

'And his name was Charlie?'

'Yes, that's right. Why? What about him?'

'I don't know,' Mike says. 'I'm confused. I need to think.'

'They were estranged,' Marjory says. 'It was all very bad.'

'Yes.' Mike says. 'I can see that it would be.'

'Did you know him?'

'No, but I knew about him. Don't say anything to Don. Not yet.'

'About what?'

'I don't know. Let's see what it is he wants to tell me first.'

They set off again. Don is still in front of the Dounreay image. He seems mesmerised by it. But when Marjory says, 'Don, here's Mike,' he turns at once and his eyes are piercing with intent. 'Tell me aboot this picture,' he demands.

'Well,' Mike says, 'as you can see, it's Dounreay, not long after it was built. We were on a family holiday and my father took us there.'

'Aye, aye, but this man, what aboot him?' Don stabs so fiercely at the gaunt figure on the road that he almost hits the glass and it's as if his finger is responsible for the explosion of cloud and light in the background. Mike and Marjory both move to stop him pitching forward but he stops himself. He seems angry, he seems exultant, he seems on the brink of something.

'He happened to be there,' Mike says. 'He was walking along the road and my father got him to take a photo of the three of us, my mother, my father and myself, and then Dad took this picture as he was going on his way.'

'But ye dinna ken who he is!' Don says. It's a statement, not a question, and Mike looks again. Did he miss something, then or now? *Should* he know who the man is?

'No. We kind of thought maybe he was a tramp. Or a local man passing by. He hardly said a word. He did make quite an impression on me, though. He gave me something. He was . . . intense.'

'Aye,' Don says. 'He was.'

The way he says it. Mike feels everything suspended. He knows he will remember this moment for ever.

'Don't tell me you know him?'

They are both staring at the man in the picture and the man is staring back at them. He is staring from the past, from the future in the past. Don says, 'Aye, I kent him. What was it he gied ye?'

'Nothing special,' Mike says. 'A stone. It was just a stone out of his pocket.'

'A stone.' Don is silent. Then he does something so unplanned, so unexpected, that it makes Mike catch his breath. He reaches out his hand, the index finger no longer pointing but cupped with the others, and he touches the glass where the man's head is. The hand cradles the head for a moment. 'Jack,' Don says. There is a weight of tenderness that the short, soft syllable seems hardly capable of bearing. Mike glances at Marjory and sees the emotion she feels, and he feels it himself, the knowledge that Don has lost someone, found him and lost him again in the instant, someone behind the glass but he is trapped, he is trapped and also he is gone, and this is the truth of the image, the truth all three of them face about themselves, their brief lives, the constancy of their impermanence.

'Do you know what it meant?' Mike asks. 'The stone?'

Don shakes his head.

'Who was he?'

Don lowers his hand. 'He was a friend,' he says. 'Oh God,' he says. 'He had a wife and a bairn, a lassie. Oh God.'

'It's all right, Don,' Marjory says.

'This isna the time,' Don says. 'I would like tae tell ye aboot him, but this isna the time.'

'Maybe it is,' Mike says. 'We'll go somewhere after this, and we'll talk.'

There are things he needs to say too, to Don, to Ellen, to Kirsty. To Isobel. To Murdo. There are so many things to say, so many people to say them to.

He turns from the image of Dounreay, of the strange, intense man – Jack, Don called him – that he met on the road all those years ago, and looks back across the room, emptying now, to a cluster of people preparing to go to Jean's: Walter and Gavin, Ellen and Kirsty, some others. He thinks, where do you begin? How do you tell a man that he has a granddaughter he never knew existed? How do you introduce someone who never knew her father to her grandfather? How do you make the connections between Don and Marjory and Ellen and Kirsty that must be made, that will be made? He doesn't yet know. But the connections, more of them even than he can know or imagine at this moment – with Catriona and Billy and beyond, with the wife and daughter Jack had – the connections will be made, and he understands that it has fallen to him to make them.

Acknowledgements

'The Summons' by Edwin Morgan is reproduced as the epigraph to this book from his *Collected Poems* (1990 edition), by kind permission of the poet and the publisher, Carcanet Press Limited.

My sincerest thanks for their support and encouragement go to my agent, Natasha Fairweather at A. P. Watt Ltd, to Simon Prosser, Juliette Mitchell, Anna Ridley and all at Hamish Hamilton, and to Sarah Coward.

Thanks also, for technical, cultural and anecdotal information and discussions of various kinds, to Joseph Bonnar, Geoffrey Elborn, Robin Gillanders, Ian Hamilton, Jimmy Hutchison, Brian Lambie, Alan Lawson, Annie Matheson, James Miller, Judy Moir, Dudley Treffry, Rory Watson and many others.

I gratefully acknowledge the receipt of a Creative Scotland Award from the Scottish Arts Council in 2006, for the purposes of researching and writing this book. Without this award the project might never have been begun, and certainly would have been much more difficult to complete.

The details of the pit disaster at Borlanslogie (an imaginary place) bear a close resemblance to real events that took place at Knockshinnoch Colliery in Ayrshire in September 1950, and some of the words of the survivors are adapted from testimony given by miners at Knockshinnoch.

Many books, magazines, journals and other documents – too many to list here – were valuable resources in constructing the political parts of this novel. Particularly helpful were: *The Battle for Scotland* by Andrew Marr; *Poets, Pubs, Polls and Pillar Boxes* by John Herdman; *Britain's Secret War* by Andrew Murray Scott and Iain Macleay; *The*

Road to the Scottish Parliament by Brian Taylor; *'We in Scotland': Thatcherism in a Cold Climate* by David Torrance; and *The Road to Home Rule* by Christopher Harvie and Peter Jones.

My deep appreciation goes to my parents, John and Betty, for all their love and wisdom over the years.

Finally, I cannot adequately express my thanks to Marianne, for the unflinching support and astonishing patience she has shown during the four years of toil that have been spent in the writing of this novel. The last and biggest thank-you is to her.

JAMES ROBERTSON

THE TESTAMENT OF GIDEON MACK

LONGLISTED FOR THE MAN BOOKER PRIZE 2006

SHORTLISTED FOR THE SALTIRE SOCIETY SCOTTISH BOOK OF THE YEAR AWARD 2006

For Gideon Mack, faithless minister, unfaithful husband and troubled soul, the existence of God, let alone the Devil, is no more credible than that of ghosts or fairies. Until the day he falls into a gorge and is rescued by someone who might just be Satan himself.

Mack's testament – a compelling blend of memoir, legend, history and, quite probably, madness – recounts one man's emotional crisis, disappearance, resurrection and death. It also transports you into an utterly mesmerising exploration of the very nature of belief.

'Fascinating, extraordinary, strange, rich' *Sunday Telegraph*

'Overwhelmingly compassionate and thought-provoking. Demands another read' Irvine Welsh, *Guardian*

'Hugely enjoyable, very funny, deeply refreshing . . . its touch of devilry makes it even more of a joy' *Herald*

He just wanted a decent book to read ...

Not too much to ask, is it? It was in 1935 when Allen Lane, Managing Director of Bodley Head Publishers, stood on a platform at Exeter railway station looking for something good to read on his journey back to London. His choice was limited to popular magazines and poor-quality paperbacks – the same choice faced every day by the vast majority of readers, few of whom could afford hardbacks. Lane's disappointment and subsequent anger at the range of books generally available led him to found a company – and change the world.

'We believed in the existence in this country of a vast reading public for intelligent books at a low price, and staked everything on it'
Sir Allen Lane, 1902–1970, founder of Penguin Books

The quality paperback had arrived – and not just in bookshops. Lane was adamant that his Penguins should appear in chain stores and tobacconists, and should cost no more than a packet of cigarettes.

Reading habits (and cigarette prices) have changed since 1935, but Penguin still believes in publishing the best books for everybody to enjoy. We still believe that good design costs no more than bad design, and we still believe that quality books published passionately and responsibly make the world a better place.

So wherever you see the little bird – whether it's on a piece of prize-winning literary fiction or a celebrity autobiography, political tour de force or historical masterpiece, a serial-killer thriller, reference book, world classic or a piece of pure escapism – you can bet that it represents the very best that the genre has to offer.

Whatever you like to read – trust Penguin.